THE STRANGE ENCHANTMENT

With a background of an English seaport, London and Berlin, this is the story of two sisters, Isabel and Sarah Rowland, over the years 1898 to 1936. Isabel is a brilliantly talented pianist for whom a great career seems certain, but things constantly go wrong for her, while for her untalented, charming sister things equally constantly go right. Isabel marries a naval officer who is killed in World War I and later a German business man who takes her back to Berlin, where he uses up her savings in the German post-war inflation. Her career is gradually ruined. Meanwhile Sarah has married a successful chartered accountant and lives in circumstances of increasing comfort and prestige. The sisters remain apart, but Sarah's son David goes to Berlin in 1936 to learn German and to look on at the fabulous Nazi scene. It is through David and a touring ballet company which has arrived in Berlin that Isabel suddenly has another chance. She takes it and is a great success, but the applause has hardly died away before the strange enchantment, which has had such a dominant effect in her life, shows itself again. . . .

GEOFFREY COTTERELL

THE STRANGE ENCHANTMENT

EYRE & SPOTTISWOODE · LONDON

*This book, first published in 1956,
is printed in Great Britain for
Eyre & Spottiswoode (Publishers)
Ltd., 15 Bedford Street, London
W.C.2, by Northumberland Press
Limited, Gateshead on Tyne*

Wie sich Verdienst und Glück verketten
Dass fällt den Toren niemals ein

GOETHE

In golf it's not who you are, what you are,
or what you have that counts. It's "How
badly do you *want* to win?"

BYRON NELSON

PART ONE

CHAPTER ONE

One afternoon in March 1898 Mrs. Charles Rowland, a pale, pretty woman of thirty, sat in her drawing-room writing a note to the local Primrose League. Now and then she glanced out of the window for an anxious survey of the street – it was one of comfortable, moderate-sized houses and led to the sea front. In the distance a gun boomed, a ship's siren hooted. These were usual sounds and so were the closer ones, a scream or two and some banging about, which came from the top of the house. She frowned the insincere frown of one who was eager for interruption. " I shall be delighted to help with the whist drive on the 30th," she had written, and now she considered uncertainly whether " delighted " should not be written " delihgted ". She wrote the two versions down on a separate piece of paper and stared at them. Both looked wrong. But it was her nature to be hopelessly uncertain about small problems. She went through life feeling herself to be an outsider who didn't know all the rules. In her brown, very humorous eyes there was often a look of puzzlement that things turned out as well as they did. She had no idea that this outlook made her an unusually pleasant person.

"Blast their whist drive," thought Mrs. Rowland, whose favourite vice was to swear outrageously to herself. And she looked round with a start, as if she had been overheard, for the door had opened.

" Just seein' if the fire's all right, m'm."

"Oh, Emmy, what a noise the children are making," said Mrs. Rowland in the slightly agitated voice which she always used with servants.

" I'll send Milly up to shut 'em up, m'm. 'Tisn't Master Denny since he's in the kitchen worryin' me life out."

"But he has no business to be downstairs. Why isn't Milly up with them now? "

8

" Well, m'm, she was helpin' me out seeing as I didn't dare durty myself – and now there's the doorbell! "

" Oh, good heavens, whoever's come as early as this? " Mrs. Rowland exclaimed. It was the first Thursday in the month, her At Home day, and up to the last ten minutes there had been a general atmosphere of frantic confusion. Every part of the house which the guests might possibly see had been swept, dusted, or polished for twice as long as perfection required. The tea trays and folding tables with their load of cakes and sandwiches, the burnished kettle on the delicate little spirit stove and the silver tea-pot waited like troops disposed in battle position. It was the moment of dramatic stillness before action. Mrs. Rowland, whose letter-writing had merely been a balm for her nerves, rose hurriedly as she heard voices in the hall deploring the weather. When Emmy opened the door again and announced, without enthusiasm, " Mrs. Mather and Miss Truscott ", she had already taken her seat by the kettle, after a last anxious look round. She rose again as if she had been sitting there all the time. The first two guests came in with a rustling of skirts. They were her cousins.

" Ada – Phyllis – how are you? Has it started to drizzle? What a shame! Come and sit by the fire," she said breathlessly.

" Bessie, you're looking a little tired," was Mrs. Mather's greeting, in an abrupt, damp tone of voice. She was a plump, stately woman with a discontented face. She gave a critical glance everywhere as she took her place on the sofa, while her sister went to a straight-backed chair far away from the fire.

" Am I? " said Mrs. Rowland, already busy with her kettle. " Well, I probably am. Phyllis, surely you can find somewhere more comfortable? "

" Oh, no, Bessie, thank you, I prefer it here, I really do! " Miss Truscott said, flushing. She was a tall, awkward person, six years older than Mrs. Rowland. " You know my back hurts if I'm not perched up – besides I can look out of the window – haven't they new curtains opposite? How nice everything looks, Bessie! Are the children all well? " She always spoke in this animated, good-natured, jerky way, going from one thing to another, or remaining quite silent.

A*

" They sound well," said Mrs. Mather, with the strange little smile that seemed to be fixed to her lips.

" They're behaving like demons," said Mrs. Rowland. " That girl is never where she ought to be, she is supposed to be up in the nursery with them and she is down in the kitchen gossiping with Emmy." She rang the bell at the side of the mantelpiece, then excused herself to her cousins, and went angrily out of the door to meet Emmy in the hall when she came up from the basement. The two ladies in the drawing-room heard her repeat her complaint with great force, heard Emmy's defence, heard Mrs. Rowland, who could not maintain anger for more than a minute, weaken. All the time Mrs. Mather's little smile remained, and she went on with her inspection of the room, which contained a good deal that she admired, the ormolu clock on the overmantel, the pictures of Nelson dying at Trafalgar and of a storm round a lighthouse, the ornamented cabinets full of Goss china knick-knacks, the brown striped wallpaper, the flimsy writing table with a silver inkwell. She noticed the half-finished letter, a piece of typical untidiness, and her gaze reached the piano, on which there were articles she admired much less. These were the family photographs : Mr. and Mrs. Rowland, Mr. and Mrs. Rowland and children, Mrs. Rowland with a baby in arms, Mrs. Rowland's parents. The sight of them never failed to stir Mrs. Mather, for the bearded, frock-coated figure in the furthest silver frame had been her uncle – a drunkard, an unsuccessful commercial traveller, a brawler in public houses and an unendurable trial to Mrs. Mather's parents until they finally outlived him. As for the other photographs, she was irritated by their reminder of a marriage which had changed her hostess's status from a poor to an envied relation. Charles Rowland was now the assistant manager of Rushcombe, Newby & Co., the big local flour milling company. Six hundred a year and three children was something very different to three hundred and seventy-five and five children – Mr. Mather was in a bank, the Southern Counties in Peter Street, and unlike Charles he had clearly gone as far as he would go. Moreover the Rowlands were so much younger. Every time she came to their house Mrs. Mather was deeply conscious of unfairness and injustice.

"And not another sound—" came Mrs. Rowland's voice from outside. Then she appeared again in the room, flushed and rather guilty looking. "I am dreadfully sorry!" she exclaimed, returning to her kettle. "I really had to read the riot act—they take no notice, no notice—Phyllis, are you sure you're not in a draught? Shall I get you a shawl?"

Miss Truscott started at being addressed and hastily assured her that she was all right. She had spent the last few minutes in stiff discomfort, quite certain that she had been the cause of the bother. But she was truthful about not wanting a shawl. Like the other two she wore a dress that extended from the top of her neck to her ankles, and underneath it were layers of wool and flannel and whalebone.

"Well," said Mrs. Rowland brightly, "you're such strangers, tell me all the news—I thought you were going away again, Phyllis—oh, hooray, boiling at last."

"No, Phyllis still has nothing," Mrs. Mather remarked, staring into the fire.

"No, nothing," Miss Truscott agreed humbly, and flushed. "There was a family in Wiltshire—that's what you're thinking of, Bessie, I nearly went—but it turned out I must be perfect in French or I wouldn't do."

"So she didn't do," Mrs. Mather said, with her little smile. "Personally I wasn't at all sorry. Apparently it was a very haughty woman, full of airs and graces—"

"It was a lovely house," put in Miss Truscott.

"And three children, but only the same money for Phyllis. What was it they were?"

"Soap manufacturers," said Miss Truscott with a nervous giggle.

"Yes, soap," Mrs. Mather went on, nodding her head with sudden merriment. "I was very amused. I told Phyllis she was well out of it, and besides she's much more use helping me. Isn't that a new piano stool, Bessie?"

"Only the cover," said Mrs. Rowland, who was thinking how dreadful it was for poor Phyllis to have to be a governess, and also wondering how much the lady in Wiltshire had offered her; she did not like to ask. She passed Mrs. Mather her cup and then rose to take Miss Truscott hers. Meanwhile the sounds of childish play from the top of the house had gone on intermittently and now were added to by the loud hushes and shushing of Milly, as she hurried by with Mrs. Rowland's small son. At this moment the door was pushed open and an old setter made his untroubled, self-centred way towards the fire rug. Gasps of concern came from the cup. "Jerry!" she exclaimed, exasperated. "You know perfectly well you're not allowed in here! Go away, you bad dog, go away at once. Go back to the kitchen and stay there, you hear me." She spoke to the dog as if he were human, and waited imperiously by the door. Jerry turned round reluctantly and went past her. Miss Truscott was amused and begged for him to be allowed to stay, but Mrs. Mather was disapprovingly silent.

"Milly!" Mrs. Rowland called up. "You know quite well that Jerry stays in the kitchen and yet you let him out – I will *not* have him up in the nursery either." She returned once more, smiling. "Poor girl," she said. "That little imp Denny twists her any way he wants to."

"He is the dearest little boy," said Miss Truscott. "Oh, Bessie, these sandwiches are delicious."

"Then you must eat a lot of them. Ada, how is your cup? How is Clarry?" she enquired after Mr. Mather. "And the children?"

"Well," Mrs. Mather said, "no news is good news. They're all well, though Clarry has had a touch of his neuralgia. It comes from leaving the warm bank and going straight into a cold breeze. He never wraps up enough and won't be told."

"My dear, they are all the same. Charles is awful, he won't wear a scarf, he simply won't," Mrs. Rowland smiled. After a moment she added, "Well, *I* have news."

Mrs. Mather glanced at her and understood at once. Her eyes widened with interest.

"Really?" she said. "Well, that's splendid, Bessie. And when?"

"September."

"Yes, it's splendid," Mrs. Mather said again, with a real smile. She insisted on putting down her cup and moving to give Mrs. Rowland a cold kiss on the cheek. Her pleasure was sincere. Child-bearing had ruined her own figure and she would not take it amiss if it were to ruin her cousin's. A fourth child moreover would be at least some more expense for the Rowlands.

" I'm so happy for you, dear," she said. " Isn't it wonderful, Phyllis? "

But the news caused Miss Truscott's bony face to go pink and she evidently found it difficult to express herself. She addressed her congratulations more to her trembling tea cup than to Mrs. Rowland, and looked shy and foolish.

" I was glad you came first so that I could tell you – " Mrs. Rowland began, but then Miss Truscott, looking out of the window, exclaimed: " Oh, here come Mrs. Lane and Wendy! "

The doorbell rang, and then rang again as more guests arrived, and within half an hour there were a dozen ladies in the drawing-room, talking animatedly. Emmy had already been in twice with more water, and Mrs. Rowland, who had quite forgotten her news in the strain of social duties, was beginning to feel that once more things were going off reasonably well. With her bright, nervous smile she looked round all the time, trying to see when cups were empty, and if the cakes and sandwiches were going. " They seem to be enjoying it," she would think now and then, as if she were amazed, and also " Whatever are they all talking about? " She always felt herself to be at a loss for conversation and when someone new arrived, she would be taken unawares with the tea-pot in her hand and greet them confusedly, without a trace of composure. She was certain that her hair was out of place and she often forgot the names of people she knew intimately. " Oh, what a fool you are! " she criticized herself, and did not take any credit – nor was she given any – for the fact that people generally stayed longer and had more to say in her house than in any other of their circle.

CHAPTER TWO

Mrs. Mather had been joined on the sofa by the wife of a wine merchant, Mrs. Abbott, a vivacious little person, who began by discussing a crochet pattern – crochet work was one of their principal activities, and sometimes they all went to crochet parties – and then, dropping her voice, told how only that morning their Rector, to whom she had bowed across the street, had crossed over hurriedly and begun a long conversation with her.

"But just when I was preening myself – almost swooning, my dear – for he's so charming, isn't he, don't you think? I realized that he was simply escaping from Charlotte Weston. I saw her lying in wait in the entrance to Debson's! Wasn't it humiliating?" She laughed at her story, which she had already told twice since she arrived.

"Poor Rector, pursued by old maids – not that he doesn't deserve it – but you should have seen his face when he left me and I said as sweetly as I could, 'Any time I can be of service, Rector!' Men never think you notice anything."

By the window, where they could share a view of the street with Miss Truscott, and still note everything that went on in the room, were two other spinsters, the Misses Younger, daughters of a solicitor, dressed alike in white blouses with mutton-chop sleeves and stiff collars at the neck. They had walked three miles to come and were full of an incident which had occurred on their way. They could hardly talk about it for laughing, and when one Miss Younger collapsed into splutters, she was rescued by the other, until she had to be rescued in turn. A man had been selling chestnuts . . . a gypsy, a seaman from heaven knew where . . . and while he was shouting, a woman had dashed towards him, bawling out like a fishwife . . . it was too funny . . .

Elsewhere in the room crochet patterns were being dis-

14

cussed, or the subscriptions concerts which were just coming to an end, or the day someone had spent in London last week – every Thursday a cheap excursion train crammed full left the town for the trip, there and back for nine-and-six – or what was on at the local theatre. Almost everybody had met each other the day before, at Mrs. Abbott's musical afternoon, but everything they had said there they said again now, sitting erect and tight-waisted, with great hats attached by pins to their brushed-up hair. Before anyone knew it an hour had passed, and nobody showed any signs of going. It was always like this at Mrs. Rowland's At Homes. The hostess poured out tea and passed round cakes, but made so little attempt to impose herself that no one took much notice of her. She began to wonder, as usual, whether they would all be gone, as she hoped, before her husband came home. She could hear the children still making a noise upstairs, in spite of the presence of Milly. "I suppose Isabel is having a tantrum," she thought. The behaviour of her second child, who had an exceedingly bad temper, worried her. A scream rang out, and she glanced round nervously, but her guests, with one exception, were all talking too loudly to hear a thing.

Mrs. Mather was the exception and she at once said, "Bessie, I do hope we're going to see those dear children."

"Well – in a moment, perhaps," said Mrs. Rowland uncomfortably, and a few minutes later she had a hurried conversation with Emmy, full of words like "scrubbed", "brushed", "behaviour" and of general instructions for Milly. Everything had been said before, earlier in the afternoon, but she had no confidence that any of it would be remembered. She felt quite tense after Emmy had gone and envied those people – everyone else, it seemed to her – who were able to have their way without any fuss at all.

One of the guests, Mrs. Waterhouse, a thrusting woman no one liked very much, though at one time or another she had formed a close acquaintance with each of them, came across and touched her sleeve. She was married to a Naval Stores officer and was always full of interesting gossip, but her main aim in life was the promotion of her almost grown-up daughter, whose voice she considered to be of professional standard.

"We've been talking about the song Elsie sang yesterday which everyone liked so much!" she exclaimed, smiling brightly. "I wish you'd ask her to sing it."

A flushing, oversized girl of seventeen stood behind her, obediently waiting to be pushed forward. The request had apparently been formal, for Mrs. Waterhouse hardly waited for an answer before she sent Elsie out for her music, announced the treat ahead, still smiling brightly, and also nominated Miss Truscott to accompany.

Mrs. Rowland could do nothing but nod and smile. She knew that no one else would have put up with it, and that no one else would have had to. Mrs. Waterhouse opened the piano, Miss Truscott took her seat and conferred over the music with the daughter. Then the door opened and the children came in, accompanied by the dog.

"Oh, Jerry!" said Mrs. Rowland furiously. "Emmy! Oh, well, let him go – " The old setter pushed his way through an avenue of rustling skirts and lay down on the hearthrug. And Mrs. Rowland, losing all her annoyance, recognized with considerable pleasure that the entrance of her children was holding up the concert and making Mrs. Waterhouse most impatient. Moreover, the children, to her relief, looked, as usual, like three angels; there was no trace of the high feelings which had been going on, and they were clean and tidy. "Thank God," thought their mother. Denny, a very handsome little boy in a sailor suit, was still young enough to be petted and kissed, which he quite enjoyed. Isabel, a year younger at four and a quarter, with her queer pale face and wide open eyes, refused to mingle, but not impolitely. Sarah, the prettiest and the youngest, ran straight to her mother. They all made a very good impression, spoilt a little when Denny, released from someone's arms, asked loudly for cake, and Isabel, at the same moment, began excitedly jumping up and down with her neck tilted backwards.

"Oh, settle down, both of you, for goodness' sake," Mrs. Rowland said. "Be quiet, Denny! Isabel! Sit still and be quiet and listen. Miss Waterhouse is going to sing." She looked contentedly towards the piano, feeling rather like a schoolgirl who had succeeded in making a minor disturbance in class.

Miss Waterhouse sang, accompanied thumpingly by Miss Truscott. The song was called "Beloved, it is Morn", and the singer was neither better nor worse than average. But halfway through there came whispers and giggling from the Misses Younger in the window, and then there were one or two other whispers in the room. And this was caused by Isabel, who had gone slowly across to the piano and stood there with her head on one side, watching Miss Truscott's hands with a queer, intense, solemn look. "An odd child," thought Mrs. Rowland, sighing to herself. She knew where she was with Denny and Sarah, but Isabel unsettled her.

"Come away, dear," she whispered urgently.

The little girl, however, was too fascinated to hear her. She was such a quaint and comic sight that the attention of the room was on her rather than on Miss Waterhouse, who was conscious of this and faltered once or twice, to her mother's annoyance. When the song was over and duly applauded, one of the Miss Youngers cried from the window, "Mrs. Rowland, that sweet little thing must be musical, it's always a sign when they do that."

"Is it?" Mrs. Rowland said. "Well, I suppose it's possible. I've never seen her do it before, though she does get dreadfully excited when a band goes by."

Miss Younger and her sister laughed gaily. It often happened that Mrs. Rowland said something quite seriously and found herself being taken for a wit. Mrs. Mather wore her set little smile again and was most irritated to see her sister with her arm round Isabel, doing runs with her free hand over the keys, and cooing whimsically at her. Far from being a governess, Mrs. Mather thought, her sister needed one; at the slightest provocation she would behave as if she were still in the nursery.

"Won't Elsie sing again?" she asked Mrs. Waterhouse. "If not, Phyllis and I must be thinking of going."

"Bessie," said Miss Truscott excitedly, turning round on the stool, "do you know I think Miss Younger is right? Isabel has a real pianist's hands, haven't you, dear?" And she bent down to kiss the child, who flinched away. Miss Truscott, who

17

was accustomed to rebuffs, laughed, " Oh, what a little Miss Muffet! "

Mrs. Mather said again that she and Phyllis must be going. But she was relieved to see that Mrs. Rowland had taken little notice of her sister's misplaced enthusiasm; instead, she was exclaiming, " Denny, come away from the dog! All right, children, we've seen enough of you, be off. Away you go, Sarah, my pet – "

When the children had gone Miss Waterhouse sang another song and after that people began to go, all of them on foot, except for three who shared a cab, whistled up from the end of the street. None of the guests was grand enough to have a carriage. They all had to be in their homes before their husbands, but some delayed for the pleasure of discussing those who had gone, what they had been wearing or how they were looking or what fools or how unreliable they were. Mrs. Mather was one of the last to go, so that she missed nothing, and also avoided being an object of discussion herself. When they had finally all departed, Emmy came in to draw the curtains. Outside the street lamps were already distributing their cosy yellow light to the misty evening.

" Well, I thought they'd never go! " said Mrs. Rowland. " Good heavens, the master will be back any minute and just look at the mess. You'd better hurry down to the kitchen. I'll put the things on the table."

" Yes, thank you, m'm," said Emmy, hurrying away.

There had been a great busying about before the At Home and now it was the same after it. Mrs. Rowland and Emmy were like scene shifters at work between acts. The former went round the drawing-room picking up the cups and plates and the special tea-party knives and teaspoons, and she collected all the chocolate biscuits that were left and took them into the dining-room to lock away in a special tin. Then she put the crockery and cutlery in the dumb waiter in the passage, and returned to the drawing-room to push back chairs into place, pat cushions and pick up crumbs.

Meanwhile, in the kitchen beneath, wearing a rough apron over her best uniform, Emmy put three mutton chops to broil on the black shining range, two large ones for the master, one

18

small one for the mistress – who had eaten her principal meal at midday with the children – and then went out to the yard to bring in a pail from which she gingerly extracted twelve oysters. She was a red-faced girl of twenty-five and like Mrs. Rowland she was at the moment full of a faint nervous agitation. She began opening the oysters, flew to the chops, returned to the oysters, ducking each time under the arrangement of bars and pulleys used for hanging up washing.

Mrs. Rowland went upstairs. Her room was on the first floor along with the guest room, a dressing-room used by her husband as a study, and the bathroom, which had been converted from a bedroom the year before; there was a great iron bath with a rather terrifying geyser. On the next floor was the nursery, the children's room and another spare bedroom, and above them the attics – one used for junk, and the other where Emmy and Milly slept.

In the nursery Denny was splashing about noisily, half in and half out of the hip bath in front of the fire-guard, while Milly struggled to dry and powder Isabel, who was very over-excited, and had upset a glass of milk; from the next room Sarah, already in bed, screamed for company.

"Oh, you blessed varmints!" cried Milly. "Sarah, me darlin', you go to sleep this second or I'll throttle you like a little bird, I will." She was a snub-nosed Irish girl who had emigrated in search of high living and security, and considered she had found them both. "Stop that splashin', Master Denny, or you'll catch such a smack as you haven't dreamed of. Now, me little beauty, keep still before you drive me mad – "

But soon they were all in bed. Mrs. Rowland, having splashed her face with cold water and pushed up her hair, came up to kiss them good night, while Milly tidied up the nursery.

Before long a dog-cart came rattling busily along the street and drew up in front of the house. A tall youngish man jumped down from it.

"I shan't want you any more," he said to the driver. "Go and get drunk. Eight o'clock sharp in the morning."

"Thank 'ee, Gov'nor. Good night, Gov'nor."

Charles Rowland was back and, as he expected, his household was waiting for him. Milly, on her way down to the kitchen, helped him off with his overcoat and took his hat, shaking with nervousness.

" Children in bed? " asked the master, genially.

" Yessir! " Milly said.

" You come and take my boots, then." He went past her into the drawing-room, turned up the gas – his wife, for economy's sake, tended to live in semi-darkness – and sat down in an armchair. He stuck out a foot and Milly knelt down to unlace his boots. Her hands were red and raw from hot water and scrubbing. He noticed the smell of boiled linen which emanated from her, not unpleasantly, and wrinkled his nose. While she was still busy the old setter pushed into the room again and gave a cumbersome welcome, pawing at the master's chest.

Mr. Rowland said, " Hullo, you sloppy old devil."

Milly, red-faced, fetched his slippers from a shoe box and then, relieved to escape, took the boots down to the kitchen. A boy called Larriman came every morning at seven o'clock to clean all the boots and shoes, which he did for a shilling a week, as well as the front door brasses.

" Master's back," Milly reported.

" Good or bad temper? " Emmy asked.

" All right."

" Well, that's something."

CHAPTER THREE

Mrs. Rowland came into the drawing-room, sighing humorously.

" What an afternoon! Really, I thought they were all going to stay for the night. Charlie, why is it that I càn never get rid of people? Oh, how you spoil that dog – well, have you had a good day? " She bent down and touched his forehead, not expecting an answer, and then sat on the edge of the sofa. " So it's lucky you're late," she went on, " or you'd have found Ada here, she was the first to come and last

20

to go as usual. Never anyone had so much to say as Ada." She considered the afternoon.

"As it happens," her husband said, after a pause, "I've had quite an interesting day, Bessie."

Mrs. Rowland looked at him in surprise. He sat back, looking thoughtfully upwards. He was a handsome man – another point which irritated Mrs. Mather. His face was finely modelled, eyes deep-set and cheeks hollowed, a nose longish and slightly hooked; his hair and moustache were dark brown. He looked strong, although he was slim. Above all he gave an impression of being relaxed. His hands rested gently on his knees, palms down. But it was the restfulness of an animal, changeable to action in a second.

Before she could ask what had made the day interesting – although he showed no sign of expanding his remark, she was sure there was something out of the ordinary – Emmy knocked and looked in.

"It's all ready, m'm."

"Thank you, Emmy," said Mrs. Rowland, frustrated, for she knew she would get nothing out of him while he was eating.

They went into the dining-room and sat down. He began at once with the oysters, without a word. He did not like talking over his meals. Even when they went out to dinner he was liable to remain perfectly silent, quite indifferent to anyone else's embarrassment. But he seemed to get away with it, for they were invited out more and more – too much, for Mrs. Rowland's taste. She was not made for social life. Her childhood had been too pinched and uncertain for her to go out much, she had grown up without being accustomed to meeting people.

She envied Charles's ability to fit in with any sort of company, which was due, she saw, to his refusal to try to fit. Ever since her marriage she had been conscious of a strain to keep up with him.

She had not realized that this might be so at the time of their engagement. In fact Ada Mather had warned her that she might be marrying beneath her – impossible though this might seem. It was true that no one knew anything about him. He was English, but he had spent his childhood in Belfast. He had worked in flour mills in Plymouth and Swansea. Mrs. Mather was not sure that flour was genteel. They had met because Charles had some business to do for his firm at the bank, had fallen into discussion, while he waited, with Mr. Mather the cashier, and the latter had taken him for a game of billiards at the Conservative Club, then home for some cold meat and cheese; and Bessie Truscott happened to be staying, as she often was, with the Mathers. He had done the incredible thing, he had fallen for her. Mr. Mather had dutifully tried to find out more about him, but Charles was not a man who could be questioned easily. He had a job and she could take him or leave him. She had taken him, and just before the wedding they learned that his salary was already more than Mr. Mather's. She had felt quite guilty about it, and hardly knew how to look at Ada. She had always been puzzled to know what he had seen in her.

After the oysters, the chops, the glass of burgundy. She was sure that he was more than usually thoughtful. She hoped nothing had gone wrong. Nothing ever had gone wrong for him, as far as she knew; his attitude that the world was there to be of service to him led, as such an attitude generally seemed to lead, to the world doing what was expected of it. But Mrs. Rowland, the product of a childhood in which things had always gone wrong, could never get used to things going right. One day, she vaguely felt, the world would turn around and behave in the way that was familiar to her. This fear had crept into her thoughts, surreptitiously, for years. She was ashamed of it, and always tried to dismiss it. She tried to do it now by opening a conversation.

"I wish you could have seen the children this afternoon when they came into the room. They looked really sweet, and behaved beautifully. I had a lot of compliments about them."

"Good," he said, with a nod of indifference, which did not fool her.

"Are the chops all right, dear?"

"Quite all right, yes."

"Mine is delicious, but I was afraid you'd find them a bit overdone." She went on, "But there was quite a curious thing. That wretched Waterhouse woman forced Elsie Water-

22

house on us – practically at pistol point – and poor Phyllis had to accompany. In the middle of the song Isabel did the strangest thing, Charlie. She suddenly went over and stood by the piano, and stared at Phyllis's hands as she was playing."

He seemed to think about it, while he chewed. Then he said, flatly: "Well, what's strange about that?"

"Well, it was the sort of rapt look on her face. She's such a queer child sometimes, so much more withdrawn than the other two. Miss Younger, the plump one, said it must mean that she's musical."

"It sounds a damned silly reason to me. Still, she probably is. You'd better get a teacher on to her, and find out. So long as she's never in the house when I am."

"Oh, Charlie, I didn't mean she should have lessons!" Mrs. Rowland said, shocked. "She's so young still – though of course Denny must start soon – I just meant it would be nice if she *were* musical. And, as a matter of fact, I have noticed her banging things as if she were keeping time with a tune. Can't you see me at Mrs. Waterhouse's demanding that Isabel should play?" She shook with merriment, and ended rather breathlessly, "No, what I meant was I wonder if I oughtn't to try teaching her myself –"

"For God's sake, don't do that. If she's worth teaching, get it started properly."

"All right," Mrs. Rowland said meekly, and thought to herself, "All the same, there's no need to shout at me." She pressed the bell attached to the table leg. She was now quite sure that something had happened during the day, good or bad, and she could hardly contain her curiosity. "There's a woman who comes to the Primrose League and doesn't look as if she's got two ha'pence for a penny," she said. "I'll go and see her. Probably it is better to start early, anyway. I suppose I'd play better if I had. I didn't have a lesson before I was eight, and then there were always gaps when we moved." She shook her head. "Poor Mother," she said irrelevantly, as Emmy came in with an apple pie and a jug of cream.

When the meal was over they did not go back to the other room. The dining-room was the most lived-in part of the house, except for the nursery and the kitchen. There were two leather armchairs in front of the fire, beside one of which Mrs. Rowland kept a work-basket. There were also books and magazines – she was a great reader of novels and serials, and easily moved to tears. The table and the sideboard were mahogany, the curtains brown rep, the wallpaper had a dark pattern, and the walls were hung with samplers, a picture calendar and a barometer. In fact the whole room was a concession to Mrs. Rowland, which enabled her to tolerate the formality of her drawing-room. This, to her, was home. She sat opposite to her husband with the coffee-pot at her side. Sometimes he did become conversational at this stage of the evening, but he was showing no signs of it.

"He isn't going to tell me," thought Mrs. Rowland. She was disappointed but not annoyed. She did not expect to be taken into his confidence on anything but domestic matters; and she was glad it was so, for her mother had been driven to despair by knowing too much of her father's ups and downs.

He leaned forward and began to pat the dog, who had settled on the rug between them.

"Well, you old fool, do you want to come for a walk?" he said. He took Jerry out every evening, and then came back to retire to his study, to read or work. "Go on, then, get your lead," and he added, in the same tone, to Mrs. Rowland, "There's something you'd better know. I'm leaving the firm."

She very nearly upset her coffee. Then she put down her cup and stared at him. She assumed immediately that he meant he had lost his job. Misfortune had struck them, just as she had known all along that it would. All in a second she surveyed various angles of the calamity, from the children with their security knocked away – for such jobs were not easily, might never again, be found – and the ill-luck of a new baby coming, to the house which they must leave, the furniture they must sell, the friends they must lose.

"Oh, Charlie!" she said in a shocked whisper. But her eyes were bright. The fact was that the prospect delighted her. She saw it as an opportunity to prove her worth, for this was a field in which she was a trained expert. He knew about success, but she knew about failure. Behind her was a whole childhood spent in grinning and bearing, in keeping up appearances and morale under strain. She half rose, with the intention of putting her arm round him.

"I think it's the right time to do it," he went on, while he stroked the dog's ears. "Anyhow, a chance has come along and I'm taking it. I'm starting on my own, Bessie."

She sat rigid, not understanding, except that her immediate conclusion had been wrong; and this at once made her feel extremely foolish.

"Well, it's a decision one's got to make some time. I've been perfectly happy at Rushcombe's, they've given me a free hand as far as possible, and they're expanding. They'd look after me if I stayed, but my feeling is that I shall be able to look after myself a good deal better."

"But, Charlie, how can you be on your own?" she asked incredulously.

Charles Rowland smiled, and thumped the dog on his back. He was obviously, she now realized, controlling feelings of some excitement.

"Look here," he said, "you know there's a place about three miles from Peter Street that even the local trains don't stop at?" Peter Street was the town's main railway station.

"Yes, of course, I know," she recited the names of stations as one left the town. "Peter Street – Moon Lane – Cowley Road – Landen's Mill – is that where you mean? Good heavens, is there a mill there?"

"There is, and a siding, and a house, and an orchard, and three acres. We'll use it all in due course. For the moment I've just got the mill, and an option on the rest of it. The house is rented to someone for the next couple of years."

"But, Charlie!" she exclaimed. "I don't understand! You mean you've bought all this? But what with? Where has the money come from?"

"My dear girl, this is a business deal," he said, with some impatience. "It isn't like buying a hat. The banks are supporting me. Between us we're having to find about eleven thousand."

"Eleven thousand pounds!" She was terrified.

25

"As a matter of fact it's the devil of a good bargain. Of course it's all out of date and the goodwill's worth about fourpence. That's why I can get it. The last fellow drank what profits there were. He'd be bankrupt now if he hadn't died. But personally I can see a very good chance for a well-run business. Well, I'll drive you out there one Saturday, Bessie. You can have a look for yourself, not that it'll mean a thing to you. You can glance at the house, though. It's a rambling old place, rather pleasant. It would give us some more room and be very convenient for me. You know, I rather have the feeling that we're growing out of this place." And he looked round the dining-room critically.

"But, Charlie — "

"Well? "

"I don't understand about the money, though it sounds frightening — but it all seems so dangerous — you have such a wonderful position already — " She clutched at a faint hope. "I thought you had a contract — perhaps they won't allow you to go — "

"That's all arranged. They're releasing me at the beginning of June." His voice had become abrupt. He was looking at her now in the way he had looked at the room. "Look here, Bessie, what the devil are you talking about? Here's a great opportunity in a business I know backwards. Do you suppose I haven't weighed it up carefully? Do you suppose I'm suddenly being irresponsible? Dangerous? Well, of course it's dangerous — up to a point. It's only when there's a danger of losing money that you can make money. When you give birth to a child, it's dangerous. Does that stop you from having children? This is good news, not bad news. Don't you want us to get on, to go up in the world? Good God," he said angrily, " what is there to cry about? "

For Mrs. Rowland was in tears. He stared at her in amazement. She sat forward in her chair, holding a hand to her forehead.

"You shouldn't have married me," she whispered.

"What damned nonsense is this? " He got up and stood in front of the mantelpiece. He listened impatiently to her answer, a low murmur of miserable nonsense.

26

"You may be growing out of it, but I'm not. Why should we want to move to a bigger house? Goodness knows this is big enough." She was very agitated. She dropped her hand and looked up at him beseechingly. "You don't know what a strain it is for me, Charlie. To think of going somewhere bigger, and knowing other people, I'll never be able to do it. Just when I'm getting used to things – oh, I know it's wrong for me to talk like this, but when everything's gone so well, surely it's tempting fate to throw it all away – and with the new baby coming, and there'll be the schooling for the others before we know where we are – "

"My dear girl," he briskly interrupted, "I shall be able to provide much better for the children by running a successful business of my own. As for the house, that's not in question at the moment. If you're feeling a strain, why don't you say so? We can get another servant. I don't believe in this never spend a penny where a halfpenny will do attitude. A penny buys more." Suddenly he changed his tone. More gently, he asked, "Look here, are you feeling all right?"

"Oh, yes," she said wearily. "It isn't that. I'm so afraid of being a drag on you. I'm such a dreadful coward about all these things, I haven't your confidence. I don't know whether I'm more afraid of it turning out well or badly – "

He smiled and bent down quickly to kiss her forehead, without bothering to comment. She watched him go out of the room, followed by the dog. A minute or so later the front door closed behind them. Mrs. Rowland, left alone, became angry with herself. The reaction she had shown to his news had been stupid and unworthy. She could not blame him if he were disgusted with her. Applause was just as important in the big moments as sympathy in the bad. And why should she have this ridiculous dread? She should be proud of his ability and enterprise, and she should have told him so. "The truth is, I'm a fool," she thought.

The two servants went past the door on their way up to bed. Mrs. Rowland tried to pull herself together. Perhaps the outburst had been due to her condition, just as – luckily – he had suggested. She must encourage, not discourage. She determined to face everything optimistically. For the moment, however, there was still the cosiness of her dining-room, never more attractive than at the end of the day. Forcing herself into a more cheerful mood, she opened her work-basket, and began to crochet.

When Charles came in, he went straight up to his study, so a speech she had been preparing for several minutes could not be delivered. She relaxed with a sigh. The dog pushed the door open with his nose and lumbered his way back to the fire. He was damp and Mrs. Rowland hastily fetched a towel which was specially kept for the purpose of drying his paws.

" D'you think he's angry with the missis? " she whispered confidentially. She often held one-sided conversations with him.

At a quarter to ten she went upstairs, having packed Jerry off to the kitchen. She heard Charles's pen busily scratching.

" I've gone to bed, dear," she said as she went into the bed-room, and a grunt was all the answer she got, or expected. And ten minutes later, lying between the icy sheets, with her toes now and then painfully jabbing the stone hot water bottle, she again prepared the words which would make good her damping reception of his news. She would tell him that she was very excited and very proud. She would tell him that she knew he would make a success of the new business, and that she would try to be his support.

She lay back on her pillow and the noise of the pen-scratching still came through dimly. Now and then she heard him clear his throat, in his specially brusque way, or the sound of a book being moved. The bed became gradually warmer and a pleasant drowsiness came over her, which she resisted.

Before he went to sleep that night he must be assured that she was worth more than he thought. She made herself think of her At Home – after all, it had not gone badly – perhaps her lack of confidence was foolish. But heaven knew what lay ahead if Charles went on making progress. The sound of that scratching pen overawed her. Where would he stop? Supposing they became rich? Supposing he stood for Parliament? He was capable of anything, for he was afraid of nothing. " Lady Rowland," she thought suddenly – why not? " Sir

Charles and Lady Rowland – how do you do, Lady Rowland? "
she heard the voice of Mrs. Waterhouse, and the whole room
was laughing – she started in dismay and woke up.

The bedroom was in darkness and Charles lay beside her,
breathing steadily.

" Oh, damn, damn, damn," Mrs. Rowland thought.

CHAPTER FOUR

As soon as she had found out the address of the music
teacher whom she had met at the Primrose League
Mrs. Rowland went to see her. It was a fine afternoon,
the sky was almost cloudless and there was a faint, warming
breeze – it was one of those days in March which decide for
a few hours to give a preview of the coming spring. She
walked along briskly. The street was at its best and even the
houses which badly needed painting looked fresh and clean.
From various basements came the last smells of midday meals
just over. She saw the Misses Tritton coming towards her –
they lived with their father, a retired colonel, and sometimes
were friendly, sometimes not – and, full of sudden tension, she
bowed stiffly. The Misses Tritton bowed stiffly back and Mrs.
Rowland went on, wondering if they would have smiled if she
had. As usual the cabs were waiting for work at the end of
the street; the horses looked pleased with the sunshine. There
was a lovely salty tang in the air. Mrs. Rowland turned the
corner, having recovered from the Misses Tritton, and the
Promenade was before her with its great stretch of green grass
and even the sight of a cruiser steaming out to sea in the
distance. There were a few sailors walking about in pairs,
some youths playing football – they would be chased off if a
policeman saw them – a few prams with mothers or nurses.
She decided to walk along the sea front side of the Promenade,
although this added to her walk.

As she went to cross the road a carriage came flying down,
top-hatted coachman and footmen perched up in front,

epaulettes on their shoulders, dutiful grandeur in their faces, and in the back was their mistress, a fat old woman covered in furs.

Mrs. Rowland held up her hand to keep away the dust. And for some reason she changed her mind about going along by the sea and continued down the inland side of the Promenade. Ten minutes later, beyond the public lavatories, which had been opened in the Jubilee year before – and which she pretended, even to herself, not to see – she turned into a series of increasingly less prosperous streets. The street she was looking for turned out to be one of small two-storeyed cottages. It was a superior working-class street. The doorsteps were white-washed and several women were holding door-to-door conversations which were interrupted as Mrs. Rowland went by – at least she thought they were. She felt quite relieved when she stood on the music teacher's step. The only brass plate in the street was on the door. It read : Miss E. Treddye, L.R.A.M. Mrs. Rowland felt a glow of pleasure that she was bringing work and money to her. "Here, but for the grace of God – " she thought, looking up and down the dreary street. The door opened.

"Good afternoon," said Miss Treddye, a plump little woman with a very snub nose. She made a lightning top-to-bottom inspection of her visitor's clothes before looking at her face and recognizing her. "Oh, it's Mrs. – Mrs. – "

"Rowland. I've come to – that is, I hope you – I want to ask you about starting my children at the piano – "

"Come inside, Mrs. Rowland, you're lucky to find me here. I was just on my way to give a lesson at Mrs. Debeyer's," said the teacher, mentioning a name of great distinction, for Mrs. Debeyer was the rich and aristocratic wife of one of the city's M.P.s. "Did you come on foot? " she added, glancing into the road, as if she were astonished not to see a carriage and pair drawn up.

Mrs. Rowland followed her in, thoroughly deflated by her reception, for she had privately been considering herself in the pleasant rôle of a Lady Bountiful.

"Sit you down," said Miss Treddye, and Mrs. Rowland found herself in a tiny parlour smelling of aniseed. Round

30

the walls were samplers with mottoes like "Manners Makyth Man", and there were photographs of the Queen, Lord Beaconsfield, Lord Salisbury and of, presumably, Miss Treddye's family. There was an upright cottage piano. "The poor man was tired out last week, apparently," went on Miss Treddye, nodding to Lord Salisbury's picture, as Mrs. Rowland sat down. "I only hope Mr. Chamberlain isn't worrying him, as everybody says. Still, thirty-eight Dervishes killed – that should buck him up." She shook her head and glanced at Mrs. Rowland sharply. "Well, to work, then – *revenons à nos moutons*. How old are the children?"

"The boy is six and the little girl four and a half."

"Well, that's young enough," commented Miss Treddye, as she wrote it down in a book.

Mrs. Rowland hastily explained the circumstances, which seemed unconvincing, and ended, "Anyway my husband insisted – "

The teacher threw up her hands, in great good humour.

"If our lords and masters say, we must obey, Mrs. Rowland!"

Mrs. Rowland was not too pleased at being treated so casually; she put a sharper edge into her voice for the rest of the interview. Miss Treddye, however, was truculent and deferential in turn. She had a way of standing as if she were constantly about to sit down on her piano stool. She explained her methods and recited a list of successes gained by her pupils. When the arrangement had been made – two lessons a week at two and a half guineas a term for both children – she would not allow Mrs. Rowland to go without letting it be known that she was not used to such confined surroundings, and that she had never expected to have to earn her living and that, furthermore, she had rejected several excellent offers of marriage. "But I'm very happy as I am, thank you!" she asserted, bowing a shattered Mrs. Rowland out with a return of her original spirit.

The following Saturday Charles Rowland took his wife to see the mill he was taking over. They sat together, strapped in the dog-cart with Mr. Rowland's man, Dockray, in a bowler hat and jacket, perched in the rear. It was a drive of about five miles. They raced along the Promenade, skirting the busy centre of the town, all the way past the Imperial Hotel and the Yacht Club and the fashionable terraces to the dockyard gate and the barracks. They had to stop at the sound of approaching music, which made the horse restive. Dockray jumped down to hold his head and they went into a side turning to wait while a military funeral went by. It was always an impressive, though a commonplace sight in the town, the slow marching, the band playing Chopin's "Funeral March", the creaking gun-carriage, the dead man's equipment on the flag-draped coffin, the troops with reversed arms, the subaltern. "The one glorious day in his life," said Charles, repeating the usual local joke. He was in a good mood. They went on through the industrial part behind the dockyard and past Rushcombe, Newby & Co., an impressively large establishment with big granaries and office buildings apart from the mills. Mrs. Rowland again felt a chilling nervousness at the idea of giving up its protection. The road climbed and soon they had a view of the sea, warships at anchor and hundreds of small craft busying about, and the town lying in a huge semicircle. Ahead of them stretched the downs. Charles pointed out that though this was still a comparatively rural district, it was bound to be built up within the next few years. "A little investment in land around here is going to pay big dividends," he said. The road dipped down to a valley, cutting out all the view. It was very dry and they kicked up clouds of dust. They went under a railway bridge and round the bend came three veiled and boatered lady cyclists, who panicked and nearly collided with one another. "Damned women," said Charles, with a grim smile, and the dog-cart speeded up the road. Mrs. Rowland could see the railway station she recognized as Landen's Mill, a small and desolate affair, with a cluster of cottages and a pub close by. A hundred yards farther on was the siding which led into what looked like a tall old house. There were two large iron wheels attached to the side of the building, and a large notice above them read: The Landen Milling Company. It all looked so much less impressive than Rushcombe, Newby & Co. that Mrs. Rowland felt at first quite relieved. When the dog-cart halted, Dockray

32

jumped out to unstrap her and help her down. Two workmen came rushing out from the mill, caps in their hands; it was quite an overwhelming welcome, and she was glad she was wearing her new blue toque.

The mill was not in operation and Charles took her inside for a tour of inspection, explaining the succession of iron rollers and revolving cylinders, all driven by steam, through which the grain was passed, resulting at various stages in bran and middlings and semolina and flour. Mrs. Rowland, who did not understand a word, listened admiringly but only came to life when he showed her the dusty room that was to be his office.

"Oh, Charlie," she said, "I'm so proud of you."

He looked surprised, and also pleased. He could not know that for days she had been planning to say it during this trip. It sounded impulsive and she was delighted to have got it out at a suitable moment. But her main feeling, though she believed what she had said, was more than ever one of anxiety. To run all that machinery cost money, even to clean those offices cost money – she could see nothing but a load of debt and responsibility, and none of it necessary.

Through the window, grimy with railway smoke, the outskirts of the town could be seen a mile away.

"There's nothing to stop suburban development reaching here within ten years," Charles said.

"I hope not, it's so pretty," Mrs. Rowland said, adding to herself, "except just here."

"It'll be pretty enough if we own some of it. Anyhow, if you want something pretty, come along."

He took her out of the mill, across a yard and down a hedged path which ran for fifty or sixty yards to a small white gate. He opened it and Mrs. Rowland passed through.

"Oh, Charlie!" she said at once, very impressed.

"Well, this is the Mill House. We can live here, if we like. There are people in it at the moment, which is just as well, but in two or three years – it's not bad, though, is it? That room at the side is a billiard room, which appeals to me. We could have a tennis court. It's all hidden from the railway, and from the mill as well. There's an entrance to the road on the other side."

"Oh, Charlie, it's very lovely –" Mrs. Rowland was speechless. They were standing beside an oak at the end of a pleasant garden. She saw rhododendron bushes, a not very well kept lawn, and a house which, though of moderate size, nevertheless seemed to her to be frighteningly large. Then she asked nervously, "Aren't we trespassing?"

He smiled. "Yes, but we're rather special trespassers. In a manner of speaking, we're more or less the landlords. Still, we won't go in."

"Oh!" said Mrs. Rowland, almost in despair. "But, Charlie, how could we think of living here? Why, the upkeep – and this garden – we couldn't possibly –"

"We could, and we will, Bessie. Don't be frightened of everything. There are only two or three more rooms than we have now, the rates are the same or less, we just need a man for the garden, and besides it'll be splendid for the children."

"Splendid, yes, as long as it isn't too splendid. Charlie – please – promise me you won't suddenly thrust it at me –"

"Don't you like it?" he said, puzzled.

"Oh, of course, of course I like it!"

He put his arm round her, an unusually demonstrative action, and said quietly, "Now don't get upset, my dear girl. As far as this side of it is concerned, it'll be entirely up to you. I promise you that."

With this easy shift of responsibility Mrs. Rowland knew quite well that the matter was settled. This was where they were to live. She said nothing more. They stood there for several minutes, just inside the gate, and she could not get used to the idea. All the same, when they were home again and she looked round affectionately at her familiar surroundings, which she would never leave if she could help it, there was no doubt that everything had changed, and even her drawing-room had shrunk a little.

Isabel in her straight little Empire frock stood at the piano, doing a five-finger exercise. For Miss Treddye had come that morning to give her first lesson. It had been only partially successful, Denny had hated her at sight, and his sulkiness had resulted in his not going on his trip to the mill. Miss Treddye, in a brief report as she left the house, had said, "Well, he's difficult, like all men – all the men that *I* know, Mrs. Rowland – and I have known many, I assure you. But boys always come round to me. The little girl is quaint – of course, it is a little early, but I think you're right that she's musical." Mrs. Rowland watched her now, repeating the same succession of five sounds with absorbed attention. Her nose was in line with the keys. Mrs. Rowland was about to lift her on to the stool when Charles followed her in and said immediately, "That'll be enough of that. There'll be no piano practising when I'm in the house, any more than lessons. Let's have that an established rule from the beginning."

"Very well, Charlie," said Mrs. Rowland patiently. "Isabel, dear, run along upstairs."

Isabel rushed away, for orders were obeyed when Mr. Rowland was about. But during the next few days she was always having to be chased from the piano. Her mother regarded it as a temporary enthusiasm, and wondered merely when it would die down, but she also realized that the child was not banging about at random for the pleasure of making a noise. She was performing the first simple exercises Miss Treddye had taught her with a precision and a smoothness which seemed rather extraordinary. Mrs. Rowland mentioned it to Charles, but he was unmoved, for he took it for granted that his children should be talented. However, she was not prepared for what Miss Treddye told her at the end of the next week.

The children were having their lesson and Mrs. Rowland was in the dining-room, embroidering a nightdress case and listening inattentively to the piano and the sound of Miss Treddye's voice from the next room. There was a knock on the door and the teacher's plump, shining face appeared.

"Mrs. Rowland? Forgive my interruption. May I have a moment? Oh, how cosy you look!" Miss Treddye bustled in, swaying from side to side as she moved, in quarter-deck style. "I can see at a glance that you're a mistress of stitchery."

" I'm nothing of the sort, I'm afraid, Miss Treddye. It's the colour making the work look more solid than it is. It's just a wide-herring-bone stitch, really."

" Ah, modest, modest! " said Miss Treddye roguishly, glancing round the room. Then she became serious. " Mrs. Rowland, I want to ask you – do you know what sort of pupil you have given me? "

Mrs. Rowland at once looked anxious.

" You mean – Denny? " she asked.

" Denny! " Miss Treddye brushed him aside with a smile. " Denny is the sweetest little boy and we are getting on famously. No, no, my dear Mrs. Rowland, I mean Isabel. Frankly, I am very impressed by her. I was, indeed, at the first lesson, but I said nothing. I wanted to be sure, before I raised any hopes. The fact now is, Mrs. Rowland, that tiny little tot has learnt as much in three or four lessons as I would expect a girl of twice her age to learn in as many months."

Mrs. Rowland was not equal to this. She stared at Miss Treddye wide-eyed.

" What do you mean? You don't say that she's a – oh, what's the word? "

" A prodigy? Too soon to say, but it's possible. She seems to understand things before they're explained, without knowing, as it were, what she's understanding. She has a remarkable sense of pitch, and I wouldn't be surprised if it isn't absolute – and that's something very rare. Of course some people say it can be a disadvantage, and it's possible to have it without being a musician – but in my opinion even the virtuosos who haven't it would be better off if they had. Mind you, my dear Mrs. Rowland, she may not develop – you never, never can tell and especially at that age – and music, believe me, is the land of disappointment. What else would one expect from the food of love? " Miss Treddye said, lapsing into her roguish mood. " But, Mrs. Rowland, I thought it my duty to let you know my opinion. Please see that she has every opportunity possible. Take her to concerts, even the band concerts on the Promenade, the child has a hunger for music – a positive hunger! If you were in my position, you would know how thrilling that is. Of course, if she does develop, there won't be two ways about it. It will be work, work, work! Practice, practice, practice! Year after year!"

"Oh, lord," said Mrs. Rowland, faintly appalled, "do you really think it's worth it?"

"Worth it?" Miss Treddye exclaimed breathlessly. "Worth it? It is a duty!"

She was so carried away that her absurd figure was imbued with nobility. Mrs. Rowland felt herself reproached. She was conscious that she deserved it.

"Of course," she said, with an attempt at apology, "I didn't actually mean – I am quite taken aback, Miss Treddye –"

"Come and listen to her," the teacher said.

Mrs. Rowland put down her nightdress case and followed her obediently into the drawing-room, where Isabel sat perched on two cushions on the piano stool. Denny was also present, gloomily blowing on the window and making lightning drawings with his finger-nail. Isabel played a simple version of "The Bluebells of Scotland" without pausing, without a wrong note, staring at the music and reading it with ease, although she had not begun to learn the alphabet.

"I don't know," said Mrs. Rowland. "I really don't know. Good heavens, in the next room I thought it was you, Miss Treddye. How does she do it? That was very nice, dear, come and give me a kiss –"

"Keep the little wrist upsy upsy," Miss Treddye interrupted. "Watch this, Mrs. Rowland." She put Isabel's thumb on the middle C and said, "Up and down, now, up and down, upsy and downsy." Isabel played the scale quite smoothly, and went on, evidently enjoying herself, until Miss Treddye said, "All right, now close your eyes, dear."

Isabel buried her face in her hands and Miss Treddye played a note.

"Open – which was it?"

Isabel uncovered and pointed at once to the key which had been struck.

"You see?" said Miss Treddye. "What a musical memory! If that isn't a perfect sense of pitch, I'm a Dutchman. All right, dear, now go and give mother her kiss."

Mrs. Rowland was a little put out both by the phrasing of

this order and the reluctance with which Isabel obeyed it. She had a fleeting, absurd thought that Miss Treddye was stealing her child away from her, for the two seemed to have a communion to which she was a stranger. The idea no sooner occurred to her than she was ashamed of it, and she gathered up Isabel in her arms all the more warmly.

"My clever little girl," she whispered.

All the same she felt more comfortable watching Denny, who now sat unwillingly on the piano stool and had forgotten, Miss Treddye said repeatedly over her shoulder, every single thing she had taught him. Wrong notes, sullen silences, tears were all produced by her son, and Mrs. Rowland, as she went on hugging Isabel, was proud of him.

CHAPTER FIVE

Two years and eight months later quite a grand occasion was taking place in the Assembly Room of the Imperial Hotel, a charity concert, in aid of a hospital building fund, at which the guest of honour was a general who, having lost five battles in succession, and scraped through the sixth, had been enjoying a hero's welcome for the past few weeks on his return from South Africa. The gallant general sat in the front row next to Mrs. Eustace Debeyer, who was dressed, so the reporter of the local daily paper had already noted, "in black, with large black chenille flowers raised in relief on the corsage over white chiffon". She also wore "a dog collar of pearls and diamond combs in her hair", but these were not so easily seen since, for the moment, she also had on a shawl to protect her from the draught. Mrs. Debeyer was telling the general, who thought her profoundly witty, that the whole audience would be covered with fleas, because that was always the result of the felt carpeting the Imperial put down to cover the dance floor. On the platform her husband, plump, pink-faced Mr. Debeyer, M.P., was reaching his peroration.

" And so, my luds, leddies 'n gintlem'n, by giving, by giving with good heart, to this noble cause, the care of the sick, the safeguarding of the health, of the national health which is the only true national wealth, we are indeed witnesses to the same cause our most distinguished and gallant patron of the evening has been so brave a witness to – in a word, the safeguarding of our colonies and oversea possessions, which our gallant volunteers – "

" What in the world is he talking about? " whispered Mrs. Debeyer.

" We should be nowhere without them – I repeat, my luds, leddies 'n gintlem'n, nowhere – and yet by these little sacrifices, and by standing together, and pulling together, shoulder to shoulder, we may serve our Queen, God bless her, and may hope to remain what we are now – I say it in the teeth of the cheers which have been given to a certain visitor in Paris – the justest, the happiest, the greatest people on the face of the earth! "

There was tumultuous applause, for the general mood was patriotic and hundreds of Union Jacks decorated the Assembly Room. Long-delayed victory had been in the air in recent months. It was a smart audience – the street outside had been jammed with carriages – and it included the port admiral with, as the reporter noted, " the chatelaine of Admiralty House, wearing black satin, and a white opera cape of lustrous satin, deeply vandyked with pleated white chiffon ". The county was also present in some force, and there were Army officers with Army wives, and Naval officers with Naval wives. All these were in the first few rows. Behind them, in the middle of the audience and in a row of nurses, sat Mrs. Mather and Mrs. Rowland. Mrs. Mather was there in the place of Mr. Rowland, who was working late at the mill, and since she was an expert on the gentry and what was called " the *élite* of the neighbourhood ", her eyes had not been still from the moment they had taken their seats.

" Did you see her? " she asked. " Talking all through the speech? What manners! "

Mrs. Rowland shook her head. She had seen nothing, heard nothing – she knew only that the interval was now coming to an end, that the second half of the concert was about to begin and that the first item on the programme read: "Pianoforte . . . *Blumenlied* . . . (Lange). Miss Isabel Rowland." Pride that her daughter should be appearing before such a distinguished audience alternated with her fear, her certainty that the whole thing was a terrible mistake.

"If she feels like me she won't remember a single note!" she said, panic-stricken.

Mrs. Mather smiled her thinnest smile. She did not go so far as to say that if it were her own daughter, she wouldn't have permitted the risk of such a fiasco, but she implied it. She also implied that there was in any case nothing to get excited about and any other child of the same age might be in Isabel's place.

"Oh, heavens, I ought to be with her, I know," Mrs. Rowland said for the tenth time. "How can she ever face all these people? It's a good job it isn't me, I'm dying with fright, Ada. But Miss Treddye insisted, she insisted I'd do more harm than good – but, Ada, perhaps she was wrong, there are times when a mother – "

"Bessie, who is that sitting at the end of the second row, in blue?" enquired Mrs. Mather. "If I had a neck like that, I think I should cover it." This was an oblique reference to her cousin's dress, new for the occasion, a good deal smarter than her own, and rather low at the neck. It was wasted. Mrs. Rowland was too distraught to notice anything, except that Mr. Debeyer was back on the platform, holding up his hand for silence. His mood was now heavily whimsical.

"My luds, leddies'n gintlem'n – "

"Well, I only hope she isn't going to talk to the general all the time Isabel is playing," Mrs. Mather said.

"We are about to be entertained by Miss Isabel Rowland, and I had better warn you that she is a very old lady. Only last week, so they tell me, she celebrated her seventieth – I beg your pardon, her *seventh* birthday!"

"Great fool," murmured Mrs. Mather indignantly. With a sudden tenderness she pressed Mrs. Rowland's hand, for beneath her jealousy of her better-off cousin she was fond of her.

Mrs. Rowland, staring in agony at the platform, saw a strange little girl appear, whom she hardly recognized. Isabel was a prim, solemn, self-possessed figure in white. There was a burst of clapping and genteel "ooh's" and "ah's". She curtsied and strode to the piano. Mrs. Rowland was feeling a momentary relief when her daughter ruined everything by disclosing all her underwear as she climbed on to the stool. Spontaneous, delighted laughter filled the Assembly Hall. Mrs. Rowland froze and wished to die. She could not look. She had known all the time that something ghastly would happen. She should never have given in to Miss Treddye, she should never have allowed – but Isabel, unaware of the riotous effect she had caused, was already playing. The laughter was swept away, and in its place was a clear, simple melody. The little girl was no more concerned than if she had been prac- tising in the drawing-room at home, and a kind of tenseness settled all around. People had begun by wanting to be kind. They had not expected to be overawed.

At the end of it there was almost a roar of applause and as Isabel ran off Mrs. Debeyer left her seat and hurried on to the platform to gather her in her arms and hold her up in the air. Mrs. Rowland sat with tears in her eyes, foolishly smiling.

Mrs. Mather said, "Just like her to get the applause for herself." But the clapping went on and there were shouts for an encore. Mr. Debeyer appeared and read from a slip of paper that Isabel would play the *Sonatina in C* by Frederick Kuhlan. Mrs. Debeyer led her to the stool and helped her on, to avoid the previous accident, and this gesture, too, went down very well. She then returned to her seat beside the general. Isabel's encore was just as successful. Once her hands were raised above the keys she seemed to cease being a small child; she was just somebody who knew what she was doing. Though the pieces she played were simple, she made music of them, and gave them colour and emotion; that was the mystery which made for the sense of wonder in the audience. Her face remained expressionless and pale. When the applause began again, she took no notice and ran off the platform. This time she was allowed to stay and Mrs. Rowland hurried round to the artistes' room, while the concert continued with a baritone singing two patriotic songs, "Come, Rally Round the Old Flag, Brothers" and "Marching through Pretoria", followed by a soprano singing "A Mother's Cradle Song" and "Alas, that Spring should vanish with the Rose".

She found Isabel coolly sipping a glass of milk and Miss Treddye in a state of exaltation.

"Wasn't she wonderful? Wasn't she marvellous? Oh, the angel! But I shall scold her for taking it too fast, the little imp!" said Miss Treddye. "It is the beginning of a great career, I know it, I feel it! She will do everything I failed to do," went on the teacher, feeling an onrush of that sadness which always accompanies success. She took out a handkerchief and dabbed her eyes. "Excuse me – oh, how silly!"

"You've worked so hard with her –" Mrs. Rowland said hesitantly. Now that the terrible moment was over, and had been such a triumph, she hardly knew what she was feeling. She was no more comfortable than she had ever been about the idea of a great career. She kissed Isabel possessively, and received congratulations from the other performers in the room. But she was annoyed that once they had spoken to her they then went on talking about something else, and the applause that came through from the Assembly Room was almost an irritation – it seemed to her that Isabel was already forgotten by everyone but Miss Treddye. And when she met Mrs. Mather again at the end of the concert, the latter's first words were about the excellence of the violin solo. But by then Mrs. Rowland's irritation had passed, she was seeing things with her usual self-deprecating humour.

"I must say," Mrs. Mather said in the cab that took them home, a special extravagance for the occasion, "I expected you to be at least presented to Mrs. Debeyer, after she had made such an exhibition of the poor child." Mrs. Mather was already speaking as if Isabel's performance had been nothing up to much, and her reason for mentioning Mrs. Debeyer was to emphasize the gulf which existed between people like Mrs. Debeyer and people like the Rowlands. "But still I suppose that *they* don't think that *we* count for anything," went on Mrs. Mather. As usual it was all wasted on her cousin.

Mrs. Rowland was merely thankful that the fuss was over, and as she hugged her sleepy daughter she hoped there would be no more of it.

The next morning, however, there was a notice of the concert in the daily paper which served the town and the county. Mrs. Rowland read it when she was alone in the dining-room after breakfast. Charles had gone off in his usual hurry to the mill – they were to move to the Mill House early in the new year, and she hoped that she would then see more of him – Denny was on his way to school, Isabel and Sarah and their new brother, Nicholas, aged twenty-six months, were upstairs with the nursery governess – Miss Wood, who came for two hours every morning for ten pounds a year. The notice was a long description of all the dresses worn in the front rows. But a sentence at the end ran, "The highlight of the evening was the performance of the seven-year-old pianist Miss Isabel Rowland, daughter of Mr. C. Rowland, of the Landen Milling Company, which made it evident that the town is happy in the possession of a musical prodigy."

"Oh, my God!" said Mrs. Rowland, and read it again. Miss Treddye, then, was right, for what was printed could not be wrong. She put the paper down and stared out of the window.

CHAPTER SIX

The Rowlands continued their steady, pleasantly upward course. The move to the house at Landen's Mill went off smoothly, and within a month Mrs. Rowland hardly remembered that she had lived anywhere else. She had a capacity, of which she was unaware, of bringing things down to her own level. They soon knew half a dozen families in the neighbourhood. Her At Homes were crowded as never before, for not only the new people came, but all the old ones as well – owing to the convenience of the station. Isabel of course played. Perhaps that was part of the reason why the Mill House was popular, for she was already mildly famous in the town. A dozen press cuttings had followed the first. Her name was monotonously at the head of the local results of the Associated Board examinations of the Royal Schools of Music, and she was always getting "honours" over the heads of girls twice her age. This was small stuff, but one of the visiting professors told Miss Treddye: "This child has real talent. I hate prodigies as much as anyone, but she's a musician. That talent must be cherished. She must come to the Academy, it's the only place for her." Miss Treddye told Mrs. Rowland, who told her husband, who wished to know where the Academy was. It was in Tenterden Street, Hanover Square, London, W.1. Charles Rowland said, "Well, I'm not having any damned professor tell me what to do with my daughters. She can grow up properly here."

Mrs. Rowland agreed with him, heartily relieved, for she knew that he was quite capable of having the child sent off. She had no conscious wish to be a cramping influence, she was nowadays full of ambition for her children. This feeling, however, was largely concentrated on the boys, and she could not see further than an ardent desire that they should be professional men. She did not care what profession. It could be anything, so long as it guaranteed a respectable living; anything, in fact, which would save them from being like her father. The business of the mill, which had been successful from the start, she regarded as entirely the province of her husband, a prodigy in himself; and she thought of it as the means whereby the boys could get into something secure. As for Isabel and her sister, it never occurred to Mrs. Rowland that there could be any goal for them but marriage. It was wonderful that Isabel played so well; she could not appreciate that it might be important. Mrs. Rowland had an unalterably "we-they" mind. What "we" might do or think about was one thing and clearly limited. What "they" might be concerned with included fame, achievement, aristocracy and so on. There were subdivisions under these heads: firstly, that Charles Rowland was a law to himself, and secondly, that the "we" field for men was wider than for women. Consequently no newspaper cutting, no visiting professor's second-hand words, no eulogy from Miss Treddye could convince her that Isabel might become a really celebrated pianist. That she should be celebrated locally was quite another matter, and filled her with pride and delight.

Isabel, meanwhile, began to attend another Academy together with her sister. It was in the town, which meant a railway journey every morning, full of porridge, a food in which their mother profoundly believed. It was almost a school train, for dozens of other children were coming in from the country to the big grammar schools and high schools. The school attended by Isabel and Sarah was known in the town as "Murray's", but its full name ran: "Miss Murray's Select Academy for the Daughters of Gentlemen." Miss Murray existed. She had run her school for thirty years and it owed its success, as she always told parents of prospective pupils, to her insistence that "select" meant "select". With her pince-nez, black serge skirt and chatelaine she terrified Mrs. Rowland.

"It is our purpose," said Miss Murray, "to create an atmosphere for the child which will remain of benefit to her in after years. Now one of the most important components of such an atmosphere is the friendships the child will make amongst her schoolfellows. Friendship between children who are unlikely to meet in later life on equal terms or to have similar interests is, in our opinion, undesirable. I hope you agree with me?"

Mrs. Rowland had nodded, convinced that the look in Miss Murray's eyes plainly said, "For example, we couldn't possibly take your children." It was not known in fact whether Miss Murray had ever refused anyone prepared to pay the fees, but the parents had the pleasant feeling that they had been tried and approved. This feeling naturally spread to the pupils, who were thereby helped to have a good opinion of themselves. Though it was the done thing to laugh at Miss Murray's old-fashioned views, the laughter contained a pinch of very agreeable smugness. Not that any excessive illusions were cherished.

The two girls settled into this genteel but realistic academy with great ease, Sarah especially, with her pretty fair hair,

her wide innocent eyes and her constant giggle. She made up
to everybody, teachers and girls alike, with the unsnubbable
persistence of a puppy; she gave so strong an impression of
liking people that she was liked in return. There was almost
a competition to walk beside her in the breaks. But in the
midst of the solemnest conversation she would suddenly burst
into giggles and fly away to some corner and shake there by
herself. The slightest thing would provoke it. Miss Trumper,
who taught mathematics, wore a wig and the knowledge
of this caused Sarah to writhe in agony the moment she
appeared. Or a fly that buzzed around the head of Monsieur
Fromm who came three times a week to teach French. Or
hearing anybody recite in the elocution class. Consequently
she was always getting into trouble. Again and again Sarah
had to leave the room. She wrote hundreds of lines, "I must
not raise my voice, I must not raise my voice, I must not
raise my voice –" She was kept in during the morning break
and had to have her milk by herself. None of it mattered to
her in the least. And the only thing she seemed to be serious
about was her adoration of her sister, who lived firmly in
the clouds and hardly bothered to speak to anybody. When,
as sometimes occurred, Isabel was accused of being stuck up,
Sarah defended her heatedly. "She is *not*!" she cried to
Charlotte Benyon, whose father was an R.N. Commander.
Charlotte was mean and jealous, but her estimate was sound.
Isabel was certainly stuck up, and in fact received a great
deal more credit for modesty than she was entitled to. Everything seemed to come easily to her. At the annual prize-giving
she not only played a Chopin *Étude*, which was applauded
for two minutes, and put everyone else in the shade, but also
came up to receive a good share of the prizes: first in her
form for French, first in algebra, first in composition – all with
her usual solemn, serious expression, as if she hardly knew
where she was. Subjects she was not interested in she ignored.
Nothing would make her work at them, so she was contentedly bottom or near to bottom in needlework, scripture
and geography. But these blemishes enabled her to be popular.
She was very placid and never hurried, even if the bell went
when she was late. She did not like joining in games and ran

46

about very little, but at the sports she suddenly won a race, while Sarah, who ran everywhere all the time and could never keep still, came in last in everything, panting and laughing.

Twice a week in the afternoon Isabel made her way to Miss Treddye's cottage, sometimes accompanied by Sarah, who was no better at the piano than at anything else but, of course, had lessons. These walks through the town were one of the greatest pleasures the little girls had. They investigated everything, chatted with strangers, took it in turns to ask passers-by the time and smiled at clergymen who were left feeling guilty about their bad memory for faces. And all the time they were arrogantly proud of their wide-brimmed straw boaters with the "P.M." initials on the band, which stood for "Philippa Murray", and entitled them, they believed, to the respect of the population. They were, however, always a little nervous in the neighbourhood of Miss Treddye's cottage, where working-class children were apt to call after them. Then both could feel their hearts beating and they walked hurriedly along with their heads in the air and their necks stiff, until they were safe in the aniseedy smell of the music teacher's little parlour.

So life went on pleasantly enough. Isabel's private world of music took on more form and shape. She practised for hours every day, and avoided jobs like dusting and helping in the house which Mrs. Rowland made Sarah do, and going for sharp walks with Miss Wood, who came in the mornings nowadays to look after Nicholas, or going to tea with Mrs. Mather and her family – a terrible bore, for the Mather girls were older and went nowhere as exclusive as Murray's – or, in fact, doing anything she didn't want to do. And she played for her mother's guests, and in half a dozen drawing-rooms of her mother's friends, when they held "musical afternoons". Three things had become passions with her. One was the sound and mysterious meaning of chords; the effect of a musical combination of notes was not merely pleasant to her, but stirred up wild and intoxicating feelings that made her thin, bony little frame quiver. Melodies meant much less. She knew and did not have to be told that this was something private for herself alone. Miss Treddye, perhaps, understood, but certainly no one else. The second passion was simpler, but equally private. She was still the local prodigy, but with every month the exclamations of wonder that greeted her playing naturally grew less. Vaguely conscious of this, she became greedy for applause, flattery, congratulations. It gave her no positive pleasure; but she was angry if she played her piece and the effect was less than usual. Instinctively she began to develop the showman's trick of making the easy things look difficult. She was already showing a remarkable gift for improvising, which Miss Treddye encouraged. But now she was using it to impress – although all the time she remained solemn and poker-faced, as if the effect she was having on her listeners was of no concern to her at all. This, too, became an act that she developed. She would hurry away from the piano and, while everyone in the room was clapping or praising her, she would run to Denny or Sarah and pretend to be absorbed immediately in some quite irrelevant pastime. " I am an ordinary little girl, really I am," she seemed to be saying, and she was delighted if she could hear the guests murmuring how charming it was for so clever a child to be so unspoilt.

When she had a birthday party and a dozen children and their parents came to the house, Miss Treddye was also invited. It was a splendid party, for Mrs. Rowland's powers of disorganization allowed the affair to proceed riotously. Miss Treddye was also a useful and highly efficient accompanist to musical chairs and similar games. There were tears, quarrels hastily patched up, Denny was twice sent up to the nursery in disgrace, and one of the parents had a great success as a conjuror. Isabel blew out the nine candles on her birthday cake, but her moment was as usual when she played. She looked sweet and dainty as her small hands raced over the keys. Children and grown-ups alike were rapturous and made her go on playing, although she cried excitedly that she wanted to have more games.

It was all a great success until she went for her next lesson with Miss Treddye. She rang the bell at the cottage impatiently, for she was looking forward to some words of praise.

The teacher, however, was rather off-hand. She mentioned the party but only to say how much she had enjoyed it, and then started the metronome and the lesson with scales and arpeggios. Isabel worked hard.

"All right," said Miss Treddye, when it was time for a rest. "Now I want a word with you, young lady."

Isabel stared up at her, surprised by her tone. She was already feeling rather resentful.

"What about?"

"If you don't know what it's about, then I'm more ashamed and disappointed than I thought," said Miss Treddye angrily, her hands clasped in front of her.

Isabel shrugged, very much on her dignity. But she was all at once full of uneasiness.

"I don't know."

Miss Treddye moved about the room in an agitated way, patted a cushion, picked up a book and put it down, and finally burst out, "I was shocked when you played at your party! Shocked! It was dreadful, do you hear?"

Isabel turned red. Hard words from anyone else meant nothing to her, although she did not often receive them. But this was something quite different. She could not bear to be criticized for her music – and from Miss Treddye herself, it was shattering. She felt as if she were caught in the middle of an earthquake. Everything she had depended on was suddenly giving way. The worst of it was that, the bubble having been pricked, she was suddenly conscious of the crime. She pretended not to be and tried to look astonished.

"You may be able to fool other people, my child, but you can't fool me," Miss Treddye went on. "No wonder you haven't been making progress lately! You come here and we work hard, I put everything I have into training you because I believe in you, and then I have to hear you play like that! Playing for applause! Don't you know that it was an insult not only to me but to everyone else?" She sat down, breathing hard, her plump cheeks mottled with pink. "Now, you listen to me. When you improvise, you improvise – that's all right. But when you play a piece, you play it as it's written. Or you can find another teacher, you understand? Oh, I know you're arrogant. You have to be arrogant in this world if you're to get anywhere, but arrogance is still dangerous, my dear. It's like making a face when the wind changes – one day you find that you've left yourself where you didn't want to be. You have to be arrogant, yes, or the world will break you, but you have to be humble or you'll break yourself, my little dear. The impudence of you, to think you knew better than Chopin! The impudence! " Miss Treddye uttered a sigh, leaned forward and jumped up energetically. She set the metronome going again. "Now, miss, we'll get on."

But Isabel stood up, too, her face working. She was astonished, furious, betrayed. She had not followed Miss Treddye's words exactly, but their meaning was clear to her.

"I'm going home," she said, in a small, trembling voice.

"Ah!" said Miss Treddye. "Are you, indeed?"

"I'm going home!" Isabel repeated, more fiercely.

"Very well," said the teacher and stopped the metronome. "Hurry up. Get your coat on."

She had all the advantages in a battle of bluff. The enemy indicated recognition of defeat by losing her temper. Isabel stamped her foot, then turned suddenly towards the piano and banged both hands hard on the keys. She kicked the stool. She burst into tears. Miss Treddye, with masterly restraint, said nothing. She was aware that she could dictate the armistice terms. While the storm continued, and having started to cry Isabel showed no sign of stopping, the teacher pretended to busy about the little room, flipping dust, tidying music books, as if unaware that anything out of the way was going on. When the interval beween gulps increased she went out to her kitchen. She returned with some milk and biscuits.

Isabel was looking through the net curtains breathing heavily. The afternoon light was going fast and cottage chimneys opposite were beginning to throw up sparks. Miss Treddye looked round for matches.

"Now, then, you just take a drink of milk," she said. "It does us all good to have a cry now and then. The nonsense that's in us goes out with the tears." She went back to the kitchen and her voice came through the open door. "Where I put those matches I'll never – I'm a scatterbrain – ah, it's temperament with all of us in music, my dear – I wasn't meant to look for matches – out of the way, puss – here they are – and let me tell you," she went on, returning, "it's not the last time you'll be doing it. Not by a long chalk! Yes, I'm all for a few tears when you feel like it." So Miss Treddye, having crushed Isabel, tried to restore her self-respect and to take the edge off her humiliation. She lit the gas nervously and gave a little sigh of relief when no explosion occurred. "There, that's some light on the subject."

Isabel had not moved, and Miss Treddye, who was beginning to be surprised by her own wisdom, sat down at the piano and began to play. Liszt's "Hungarian Rhapsody" seemed suited to the occasion. It had verve and a lot of noise. After a moment she was conscious that milk was being tasted, a biscuit nibbled. She played on with fierce concentration, and not only because her tactics were succeeding. Miss Treddye realized that, though she wanted Isabel's success with all her heart, she had at the same time taken some pleasure in this episode, a pleasure that rose from envy. She knew that she was really playing now as a rival showing what she could do. "Well, I'm as bad as she is," she thought guiltily, and stopped in the middle of a phrase. Then she swung abruptly round on the stool and met Isabel's gaze.

"Within a year you'll do better than that," she said impatiently. "In two years you'll have drained me and be looking for fresh fields. You'll be on the concert platform in the end, not just here, but everywhere – London, Paris, everywhere – if you work, and if you're humble!"

Isabel went on gazing at her, and felt for another biscuit. She had quite recovered her usual pale calm, but she gave no sign whether or not she understood. But the teacher went on as if she were talking to an adult.

"Yes, you can entertain the drawing-room now," she exclaimed with deep feeling. "But you're above drawing-rooms, my dear, and you have to stay above them – and you can only do it by going after perfection all the time. Year in and year out, every day, and even so you'll never reach it! A terrible, lonely, difficult life, my dear – that is to be your privilege. But as for reward and applause, the world will be at your feet, not just a dozen of your mother's friends who aren't even listening—"

She stopped abruptly, conscious that she had gone too far and that she had allowed bitterness to intrude.

"Now come and do some scales," she said.

Silently the little girl replaced her on the stool. The matter was not mentioned between them again. And Isabel lost her taste for drawing-room showmanship for several weeks.

The third passion in her life was Nicholas. Her baby brother, now four, was thin and inclined to be sickly, but full of a beguiling cheerfulness. She adored him, played with him, went for walks with him. Her mother watched this with pleasure, for she had considered Isabel to be slightly lacking in affection. The only trouble was that Isabel did nothing by halves. If he was ill, she wanted to stay up all night with him. If she heard him cough, she would chase round the house to find Mrs. Rowland, and put her in a panic. He played the part of Isabel's favoured courtier. Unlike his sisters and his brother he was not good-looking. But he was very sharp for his age and he constantly wore a smile so engaging that he had the effect of making everyone with him unusually gay. One of his principal pleasures was to hold a conversation with the old dog Jerry. Beneath the kitchen table his voice could be heard in a special dog-talk monologue which he was whispering into Jerry's ear.

"I ses to meself and I ses to meself and I ses to meself I ses. I ses to meself and I ses to meself and that's what I ses to meself."

Whenever she heard this, Isabel ached with laughter, but only because Nicholas did it.

CHAPTER SEVEN

A week of the 1905 summer holidays was gone and Denny Rowland, aged thirteen and a half, a veteran of his first and worst year at a boarding school, waited non-chalantly on the Landen's Mill station platform to meet a friend. He wore a straw hat, a blazer and white flannels. From time to time he removed his hat to use it as a fan, for the afternoon was hot, and also to take the opportunity of noting, in the mirror fixed for the convenience of ladies in the automatic chocolate machine, that his hair was correctly untidy. He was complacent about his appearance, and it was more to admire than to reassure himself that he looked in the glass. But he felt quite nervous and excited when the train came into sight, from the country direction, not the town. A tall slim boy of about his own age jumped out.

"Oh, hullo, pig," Denny greeted him.

"Hullo, piss-pot," replied his guest. "Why are you all dressed-up? You look perfectly frightful." His own attire was rather less formal, a Norfolk jacket and thin tweed trousers which stopped an inch above his ankles. He walked with a confident bouncing motion.

"I told you there'd be some tennis," said Denny. "This way, you ridiculous ass, we go over the bridge."

"Tennis, oh, yes, you did tell me, piss-pot. I forget, I forgot. I nearly forgot to come, to tell the truth."

"Lying king of all the pigs," said Denny.

"So this is the putrid spot where you live? Very suitable, I must say. What a creaky old bridge!"

"If you deign to look to your right you can see our mill. I hope you also see that the station is named after it."

"That ridiculous little barn place? Good heavens," said the guest, bounding ahead over the bridge. But Denny found his attitude very complimentary. His name was Talbot and he lived about six miles away, quite close to Fritham, their school. The Talbots were very well off. His father was the chairman of the Board of Governors, there had been Talbots at the school for three generations, and everywhere you went the name met you – the Talbot Cup for cross-country running, the Talbot Cup for gymnastics. Talbot therefore had a vaguely royal position, though this was not of course acknowledged. Both had been fags, but he had for some reason appointed himself as Denny's protector, which was very fortunate, for Denny, spoilt by Mrs. Rowland and easily prone

53

to tears, had had a bad time. All that was in the distant past of months ago, and there had been the summer term, in which they had both played in the Under 15 XI, though Talbot was by far the more enthusiastic and competent cricketer, and walked together round the ground pulling other members of the team to bits, the sport within a sport which helped to make cricket interesting. One afternoon, when they were free, they had cycled to Talbot's house. Denny had never been so impressed. In the first place it was the biggest house he had ever been inside. There was an enormous drawing-room, where he had tea with Talbot and his mother and nearly had a heart attack when he bent a teaspoon. There were also, he remembered for days, a library with thousands of books and deep armchairs round the table in the billiard room. In addition he admired the fascinating gun-room, the stables and, above all, Talbot's father, not so much for himself – he was an agreeable, round-shouldered man with a hook nose and still held the quarter-mile record at Fritham – as for his monocle. Denny cycled back with his friend to school, saying nothing, but with his mind full of that excitement which comes with every disturbance of a previous outlook on life. He did not feel envy of Talbot, but an even greater respect. This was the return visit.

He was glad that Talbot could see the station's only porter salute him with a respectful touch of his cap, though with a slightly less respectful wink as well. There was at least a touch of the feudal about it. Moreover it lent colour to his own privately cherished idea that this was the Rowland's own station. Talbot gave up his ticket, but instead of leaving by the entrance they went along to the end of the platform and down the slope, and then across the line of the siding. This was one of Denny's trump cards as a host, for it was certainly a privileged exit – no one else, after all, except rail-waymen, ever left stations in so unusual a manner. Talbot was whistling a tune called "Under a Panama". He kept his hands in his pockets and appeared to take everything for granted. His lack of criticism told Denny that the first impressions were favourable. Then there was an unexpected piece of good luck as they passed the entrance of the mill. His father was just driving away in the new 16 h.p. Napier. Denny wondered anxiously whether to introduce Talbot, but a decision was not necessary. Mr. Rowland stared at them as if they were trespassers and started off.

"That's my father," said Denny, relieved. He always made a fool of himself with Mr. Rowland when someone else was present. "My mother's out with my young brere" – brothers were always breres at Fritham – "but there'll be my sisters," he added apologetically.

"I suppose he was going off to deliver a sack of flour," Talbot said. "Not a bad car, though," he went on, as Denny punched him. They reached the garden, wrestling intermittently. Denny's immaculate appearance was rather spoilt, but he was delighted that his guest was behaving informally. For the visit to Talbot's house had been, from this point of view, rather a strain, in spite of his excitement.

As they crossed the lawn Denny was a little less pleased. He had left a scene which he thought would be quite suitable for Talbot to enter. Sarah had been in the hammock, idly swinging, and from the house came the sound of Isabel practising some impressively complicated piece. But there was no Sarah, and no sound of music. As he could not hope that they would have had the decency to disappear for the afternoon, he distrusted both the absence and the silence. He glanced anxiously at Talbot to see how he reacted to the view of the house and garden, but he could see neither approval nor disapproval in his friend's eyes.

"We'll get the balls and rackets," he said. He was anxious to play, for he rather fancied himself at tennis. He led the way through the french windows into the drawing-room, which was empty. He was conscious that Talbot must be thinking it all very small. But the sound of giggling from the hall disturbed him more, especially as they had to go into it. It was quite a large hall, disproportionately so for the size of the house. As they entered it, the two sisters were coming solemnly down the stairs, side by side. At the bottom they both bowed in the direction of the front door and then turned, Sarah to the left into the dining-room, Isabel to the right into the cloakroom. They were unaware of the two spectators and a few seconds later they reappeared and dashed upstairs to the first floor landing.

"Baron Hardup and the Widow Twankey," Isabel was heard to announce.

Once again the descent of stairs, the bows to the front door, and the left and right turn.

"What the deuce are they doing?" whispered Talbot.

Denny sighed, gritting his teeth. It seemed to him that they had purposely connived at doing something as ridiculous as possible – it had been a favourite game all through the year since they had been to the pantomime after Christmas. The game was to imitate the grand finale when the company came down two by two to take their bows and then stood on either side of the stage. He had played it himself on occasion, but was reluctant to explain it to Talbot, who must be rapidly forming a terrible idea of his home life. But they had been seen and heard, and the imaginary company on the stage disintegrated. Sarah flew from the dining-room to the cloakroom. Muffled sounds indicated a state of embarrassment. The cloakroom unfortunately was where the rackets and balls were kept. Hot with indignation Denny followed in, and found the girls clinging to each other hysterically in its cluttered-up darkness.

"What *are* you doing?" he whispered in fury. "I bring in a man from school and –"

"We were only doing Cinderella, we didn't know you were there," spluttered Sarah.

"Do you *have* to be so childish?"

"Childish!" Isabel exclaimed, with a gasp.

"Isabel, stop him! He's p-p-punching me!" Sarah exclaimed in a suffocating voice.

"Be quiet, I haven't touched you. But I jolly well will punch –"

Sarah rushed out again, and stopped dead in front of Talbot, who found her, the sound of the quarrel, and everything else enchanting. He greeted her politely, and Denny, emerging with his face red, rackets and balls clutched in his arms, found to his great relief that dignity had returned. Isabel followed him out, and formal introductions were made. Since no grown-ups were present, they all behaved with great politeness. They sat about on the chairs in the hall and made conversation. Talbot became more suave every minute. When he heard that Mrs. Rowland was at a garden party, he said, "I detest them, don't you? Hoop-la and palmists and chicken mayonnaise." His audience was deeply impressed and Sarah, who did not understand a word, was overwhelmed. After a time Denny suggested tennis again. Talbot invited the girls to join it, much to the host's annoyance, but it was now Isabel's turn to be impressive. She said that she couldn't possibly play because she had to look after her hands.

"Why, what's the matter with them?"

"Well, I'm playing at a concert next month, you see."

"Really, where? Are you an awfully good pianist, then?" And so, to the astonishment of both Isabel and Sarah, it was disclosed that Denny had never mentioned her playing. "Play us something."

"Oh, do let's get some tennis, it'll be *dark* soon," Denny groaned. "If you had to listen all that we have to—"

Talbot agreed to tennis. But he looked as Isabel most respectfully. Denny recognized that his scatter-brained sister had once again come out on top, and he felt rather grateful to her. They went outside at last, accompanied by Sarah, while Isabel sat at the piano and practised. So the scene was more or less as Denny had planned. Talbot was astounded by the sounds which came out of the drawing-room.

"Rowland, how can an ass like you have a sister like that?" he asked. But he was almost equally attracted by Sarah, who acted as his ball-boy. Denny began to feel that his sisters were doing too well, and he felt slightly jealous as well as pleased. He let Talbot get ahead and prolonged rallies on purpose to keep him interested. After they had played two sets he suggested a hundred-up at billiards. Sarah objected. She thought it would be a good idea if they all swung on the hammock. Talbot irritated Denny by agreeing to swing her.

Mrs. Rowland arrived with Nicholas, while Sarah was explaining that the stone beside the hammock marked the burial place of their dog Jerry. She had put on a very pathetic voice for the purpose, and her eyes shone with tears.

"This is Talbot, mother," said Denny, who had been lying sulkily on the ground.

Mrs. Rowland shook hands pleasantly with Talbot and asked his Christian name, which was Edwin. Denny found this amusing. Nicholas, a short, pale little boy, also shook hands, laughed at nothing in particular and hurried off to the house, from which the sound of the piano had never ceased. Sarah announced with a sigh that she wished it were tea-time. The presence of an adult, though well disposed, had reduced them all to children again.

"Well, it certainly isn't tea-time, you silly girl," said Mrs. Rowland. "Oh, how hot it is! I hope they're looking after you, Edwin."

"Excellently, thank you, Mrs. Rowland," said Talbot in his most dignified tone.

Denny was very satisfied with his mother's appearance. The garden party had fortunately caused her to wear her best summer outfit and an enormous hat in the style that was fashionable that year, decorated with a great many artificial roses. He felt that she stood up to Mrs. Talbot very well. Mrs. Rowland, unaware of this kind of scrutiny, sat down heavily in the hammock and announced that she would never get up.

"Let's take the boat out!" Sarah said excitedly.

"Boat?" said Talbot, smiling at her.

"Yes, we've got a rowing boat and it's only a mile to the river and we can swim, too."

"It's much too late," replied her mother.

"Sooner play more tennis, anyhow," said Denny, an indifferent rower.

"Besides your Aunt Ada is coming to tea and perhaps the girls."

"Oh, mother!" cried Denny, horrified, and the afternoon which had seemed on the whole to be running so smoothly was now, out of the blue, ruined. He had never liked Mrs. Mather and he absolutely disliked her children. The boys had been or were still at a large day school in the town, which could hardly be mentioned in the same breath as Fritham, and the girls equally attended somewhere far below the standard of Murray's. He was frankly ashamed of such relations. It was humiliating that Talbot of all people should be confronted with them. As for Aunt Ada herself, she was not even his aunt, and he could never see why his mother should seem to insist that the kin was closer than it was. The attraction of an hour or so on the river suddenly became plainer to him.

Nicholas came running out of the house, followed by Isabel, whom he had persuaded to play bumble puppy with him. A desperately amateurish game of pat-ball tennis ensued. Sarah invited Talbot to join in. Talbot agreed, and was taking off his coat.

"No, let's go and get the boat out," Denny said. It was not for this childish nonsense that he had spent the morning whitening the lines of the court.

His mother interrupted relentlessly. "You cannot possibly go into that dirty old boat in those flannels! Just think what a mess you'll be in. Besides you must wait and say hullo to Aunt Ada. She hasn't seen you since last holidays. To come all this way and find you not here would be such a disappointment."

"But, mother, I didn't know she was coming. We could easily have been on the river all the afternoon."

"Without any tea?" said Mrs. Rowland. "What nonsense! Besides, dearest, you know now."

Denny became sulky and spent the next twenty minutes lying on the grass, while he made up innumerable speeches which he ought to have used in reply to his mother. Shrieks and laughter came from the net. Mrs. Rowland pushed herself up from the hammock and departed to give orders in the kitchen. The game stopped when Nicholas had a fit of coughing – his chest was weak, and this was always happening; he was not supposed to take violent exercise. Isabel was still nursing him when a procession appeared at the end of the garden, Mrs. Mather and Miss Truscott, and three Mather daughters, all dressed up for "going out to tea", chests forward, skirts trailing the grass.

"Here comes Mother Goose and family," said Talbot. It was a brilliant description, and enabled the Rowlands to collapse into undignified hysterics. Mrs. Mather, fatter and more stately than ever, looked at them all with disapproval. The Mathers were always slightly defiant when they came to the Mill House – though not Miss Truscott, who had been consistently downtrodden for so long that she took a vague pride in it. The girls, in their late teens, stood behind while Mrs. Mather kissed Isabel, Sarah, Nicholas and Denny in turn, averting her eyes.

"How lucky you all are to have this lovely garden to play in on a day like this," she said. And the Miss Mathers behind her murmured agreement, not so much that the garden was lovely as that the Rowlands were lucky.

"This is a friend of mine from school," Denny said, introducing Talbot in some confusion. Talbot bowed, looking very superior. Mrs. Mather gave him her thinnest smile.

"I hope you've been working hard," she went on to Denny. "Not every boy has the opportunities that you have, and your dear mother is so proud of you. Where is she, by the way? Ronnie and Jim are at Scout camp, or of course they'd be here. We are very proud of Ronnie just now because he has been accepted by the bank. He is going to start next month."

"Jolly good," said Denny, reddening, and he gave an agonized glance at Talbot.

Mrs. Rowland appeared, interrupting the flow of humiliation, "Ada – Phyllis, how nice to see you – girls, what pretty coats! Denny, Sarah – hurry and get deck chairs. Shall we have tea out here? It's so warm."

"I was just telling the children how lucky they were to have this lovely garden, Bessie," said Mrs. Mather, while Miss Truscott, laughing nervously, disclosed that she was present only because, once again, she was out of a job.

So the tea-party began, and hardly a word was spoken which did not cause Denny to shudder. A year at Fritham – a minor public school, which had so far produced no cabinet ministers – had introduced him to the important theory that this was a world in which the vast majority of people did not "pass" – nor did anywhere that was not coloured red on the map or a fellow, even a Fritham man, who used hair-cream or who openly swotted – and in which it was vital to

60

belong to the minority who did "pass". The Mathers certainly did not "pass". For example, one should not say, as Mrs. Mather relentlessly said, "We passed by the Yacht Club on Friday – all the upper ten were there, to judge by the carriages and cars – " Especially as Talbot's father was a member of the Yacht Club. Nor should one say, "I wonder if I might have a serviette, Bessie." No, there were no compensating factors for the Mathers. Denny was in an unfortunate position. Isabel and Sarah, his juniors, had hardly reached this stage of sensitivity. He alone bore the brunt of it and was terrified every second that some new brick would be dropped. His own mother, moreover, seemed bent on encouraging Mrs. Mather's deadly course. She was busy saying how expensive everything was, and that the children's clothes were driving her to despair. Every new topic seemed to be designed to pull the Rowlands down to the Mather level. Even the mention of tennis led to the disclosure that, though the Mather girls would like to play, the few local clubs were only open to the services and professional classes, and they feared the snub of being refused. This depressing state of affairs seemed to be accepted by the girls themselves. They giggled sadly and nodded, and perspired in their thick skirts and layers of underclothes, and ate sandwiches with enthusiasm. Denny put his hand over his eyes. He was sure that the friendship which meant more than anything to him had been ruined.

"Not another slice of cake, Edwin?"

"No, thanks awfully, Mrs. Rowland."

"Denny, what a bad appetite you've got, too! Most unusual."

"Mother, can't Talbot and I go off now? We've got time for a swim."

"Dearest child, you can't swim directly after tea."

Mrs. Mather, who had been eyeing Talbot stealthily, now said to him, "So you're at school with Denny? And what are you going to be when you grow up?"

"Mother, really – "

"Hush, Denny, can't you hear Aunt Ada speaking to Edwin?"

" The British plenipotentiary at Zagreb, I think," Talbot said.

" The –? " Mrs. Mather was taken aback, unprepared for witticism. Denny spluttered – wilder than ever in his admiration for Talbot, who was always so composed, and would never bend a teaspoon in agitation, as he had done at Talbot's house. If only he himself could achieve such nonchalance! He was almost glad the Mathers had come in order that that splendid answer could be given.

A second later the matter was forgotten, for Charles Rowland came across the lawn, cool and strong-looking in his white stiff collar and dark business suit, and greeted them all indifferently. The Mather girls at once became very flustered. Their mother and Miss Truscott burst into a duet of praise of the garden, the house, the train service, the looks of the children. Mr. Rowland gave the impression of half listening. He nodded grumpily now and then, while sipping tea which he told Mrs. Rowland was not strong enough. Even Talbot looked at him with respect – there was some masculine, dominating quality about him which made it hard not to. It soon became apparent, however, to everyone's relief, that he was feeling cheerful. He flipped Denny, who was scared of him, in the stomach and balanced Nicholas, who was scared of nobody, on his knee for two minutes. When he had finished his tea he said to Talbot, " Well, you look all right. Come and have a swim from our boat." Denny was already running in to get swimming things while Mrs. Rowland raised a series of weak protests.

He returned to hear Miss Truscott asking if Isabel would play. His sister rose mechanically.

So the tea-party broke up, the ladies agreeing that perhaps it would soon start to get cool, while Nicholas and Sarah joined in a fruitless campaign to avoid the concert – they, too, wished to row and swim, but were more firmly under the command of Mrs. Rowland. Sarah was especially pettish, for since the coming of grown-ups the elegant Talbot had ceased to notice her.

" I don't see why I shouldn't – "

" Be quiet, darling – "

"Does Charles intend to swim himself?" enquired Mrs. Mather in a low voice. "Shouldn't he be more careful at his age? Clarry would never think of such a thing."

"He's a very strong swimmer!" said Denny indignantly.

Mrs. Mather was annoyed at having been overheard. She gave him an icy glance.

"Do hurry up, dear, your father's waiting," said his mother anxiously. "And don't dare make any more marks on those flannels."

Mr. Rowland and Talbot were already half-way across the lawn. Denny raced after them with the towels and bathing costumes. They were deep in conversation about the performance of the Napier.

"Are we driving down?" Denny cried. "Oh, hurray!" But, though Talbot gave him great pleasure by slapping his shoulder, neither took any more notice of him. He just tagged along. He was not a technical expert. But Talbot seemed to know a good deal about the internal combustion engine. "They have *two* cars," Denny told his father when he could get a word in. "A Lanchester and what's the other one?"

"Only the little De Dion," Talbot said. "It's for my mother. She's learning to drive."

"Bravo," said Mr. Rowland and smiled at Denny. "Can you see your mother learning to drive, boy?"

Denny exploded with laughter, not so much at the absurdity of the thought but to express his own happiness. He had never known his father to be so affable – except from afar off, when he was entertaining business friends. He could see that Talbot was most favourably impressed and bounced up and down as he walked more than ever. Mr. Rowland was a quick mover. When they reached the yard in front of the mill Denny was further astounded. His father asked Talbot if he would like to see inside.

It was almost as much a visit for himself as for Talbot, for the mill was strictly out of bounds to the family, even to his mother. They spent twenty minutes watching grain being turned into bran and semolina and flour, inspected the steam-operated power plant, watched men stacking sacks and

met plump, white-coated, obsequious Mr. Jenkins, the foreman, who greatly endeared himself to Denny by calling
him "sir". Talbot seemed genuinely interested. "Twelve
thousand meshes to a square inch – I say!"

On the drive to the river, along a narrow winding lane
from which the car kicked clouds of dust that seemed big
enough to travel for miles, they discussed the French fleet – in
honour of whose visit the town was at present decorated:
the Kaiser's yacht, the Russo-Japanese peace. What was so
satisfactory about Mr. Rowland as a conversationalist was
that he made no attempt to come down to a schoolboy level.
He treated Talbot as a public meeting of his contemporaries
and, though this might have been tedious to a contemporary,
it was flattering to Talbot. The car was parked at the entrance
to a farm, and they walked across two fields.

The river was not a river at all, but part of the innermost
stretch of an inlet from the sea. The water was salt, tides
came in and out, farm-land reached to the water's edge, and
faced more farm-land on the other side. One day it would
doubtless all be sold for building or ruined by trippers. In
the meantime there was a five-yard square patch of stony
sand which the Rowlands treated as their private beach.
Everywhere else was mud. By a small financial arrangement
with the farmer they were able to rent a rowing boat which
was kept tied up close by. Here the family came for picnics,
and Denny and Nicholas caught crabs with which to terrify
their sisters. Mr. Rowland himself was fond of the boat – he
had found the place, made the arrangement, and announced
it one morning two years before – and he liked to row out
into the middle of the water and sit there, a solitary bent
figure, apparently lost in thought. But no one knew what he
thought about. The previous summer he had always been
accompanied by the old setter, Jerry, who late in life had
discovered a passion for swimming. It was always hard not
to see his ghost, the loving, desperate eyes, the paws working
like pistons as they trod water. In the autumn paralysis had
affected his back legs and he was put to sleep, and buried
by the hammock on the lawn – saddest day of the family
history.

64

They made three piles of clothing, and put on the knee-length bathing costumes. Then they pushed the boat out, a long push over a stony mudbank, for the tide was low. Mr. Rowland took the oars. A stray little yacht which had escaped from the fashionable regatta five miles away passed busily by. The solitary yachtsman waved to them, and they waved back. Otherwise they had the farm-land, the muddy shore, the setting sun, the peacefully rippling water all to themselves. Mr. Rowland pulled the oars in and dived off. He swam away with a strong breast-stroke across a pattern of silver and red and gold, as if he had had enough of them and now wished to be alone.

"Topping chap your father is," Talbot said, looking after his dark, diminishing head. "Far too good for you, piss-pot."

"Oh, rats," Denny snorted, reddening.

He could have cried, so deep were his feelings of pride and happiness – if life were ever perfect, this might have been the moment. But it was not, of course. Just as he had been mildly jealous when Sarah's pretty babyishness seemed to have made an impression on his friend, so delight that his father had "passed" and had rescued the afternoon from Mrs. Mather was almost at once mixed with a faint envy that he could win Talbot's respect so easily. However, life was nearly perfect. He stood up, frowning a little. Vaguely aware that he was being provocative, he tossed his hair back with a jerk of his head and jumped into the water. Talbot followed after him with a war-like yell.

CHAPTER EIGHT

As Isabel grew up she was mentioned from time to time by the local press. The pieces were cut out, dated and pasted in an album which Mrs. Rowland kept in the drawing-room and showed to visitors.

"Trinity College, London. Local examinations in vocal and

instrumental music. Result of practical examination held at the Town Hall on Tuesday, Wednesday and Thursday, March 15th, 16th and 17th. The candidates are arranged in order of merit. Maximum marks 100; minimum marks for honours 80, for pass 60. No honours can be obtained in the primary division. Senior division : pianoforte, honours, Isabel Rowland 92. The Mill House, Landen's Mill. Miss E. Treddye, L.R.A.M." *25th March, 1904.*

"To encourage local talent is one of the objects that the promoters of the Town Hall Popular Concerts have set before them. And certainly the brilliant pianoforte playing of little Miss Isabel Rowland on Wednesday evening last was an instance of local ability of which the township may feel justly proud. Miss Rowland, who is only twelve, very fresh and charming in a simple cream frock, played a 'Fantasia' by Mendelssohn, an 'Étude' by Heller and Liszt's brilliant study, 'Rustling Woods'. All, as my musical readers will know, present many difficulties, and all were rendered with the ease and smoothness which belongs to an experienced artist." *14th November, 1905.*

"H. F. Corwin's Concert. The programme arranged by Mr. H. F. Corwin (R.G.A.) for his Symphony Concert at the Town Hall, on Tuesday, was very varied and enjoyable. But the outstanding feature of the concert was the Liszt Concerto No. 1 for piano and orchestra, in which Miss Isabel Rowland was the soloist. It came as a surprise to many of the audience that in their midst was a young artiste of such brilliant ability as the exacting nature of the concerto demanded. It displays all Liszt's well-known power of writing for the piano, with a facility of composition, a wealth of melody, and a redundance of ornamentation such as is, possibly, unequalled. The orchestral part of the work is mainly a setting for the soloist, although there are some charming duet passages in the first movement. Miss Rowland, who is not yet fifteen years old, played firmly when required, and was exquisitely delicate in lighter passages. She interpreted all the varied moods of the composer with true musicianly feeling and the audience, waxing unusually enthusiastic for an afternoon concert, insisted on a repetition of the final 'Allegro Marziale Animato'. Miss Rowland's remarkable performance was admirably supplemented by the orchestra, which sustained and accompanied her solo without at any time unduly asserting itself. For the rest Dvorak's 'New World' Symp –" *October 26th, 1908.*

"The annual winter term prize-giving ceremony at Miss Philippa Murray's School in Barbary Road was held on Wednesday, when Canon K. F. Jeffreys, D.D., presented the prizes. In a short but inspiring address Canon Jeffreys spoke of the full life and the right use of leisure. He was so glad that Miss Murray's pupils were encouraged to foster varied interests. The pupils' concert which followed the prize-giving was remarkable for the brilliant performance of Chopin's Mazurka in D flat by Isabel Rowland and for the recitation by –" *November 10th, 1908,*

"The coveted licentiate diploma of the Royal Academy of Music (L.R.A.M.) has been gained by Miss Isabel Rowland, the fifteen-year-old daughter of Mr. Charles Rowland of Landen's Mill. She took the examination in London in January and learned last week that she had passed. This is a remarkable achievement for so young a musician, and the town may well be proud of the event. Miss Rowland, who is at Miss Murray's school in Barbary Road, intends to study at the Academy. A pupil of Miss E. Treddye, L.R.A.M., she was prepared for the examination by Mr. Clement Durrell, the well-known academy professor and Matthay exponent." *February 2nd, 1909.*

"Dr. Preston's concert. The first symphony concert given by Dr. Preston's Orchestral Society, which took place in the Town Hall on Wednesday evening, and which is, by the by, the tenth of the series, was opened, as usual, with some ceremony, the Mayor being received by the National Anthem, played by the orchestra. Mr. Gosford was wearing his chain of office, and was accompanied by the Mayoress, who was in black velvet with a boa of white ostrich feathers. The symphony proper of the programme was Schubert's in D minor, which has not been performed before at these concerts.

It is certainly not the most generally attractive of the great composer's works, but the 'Romanza' was a very charming interlude, and the finale was well worked up. In the second half, the *pièce de résistance* was Saint-Saëns' pianoforte concerto in G minor. In this brilliant and exceedingly difficult work Miss Isabel Rowland (who was looking very dainty and pretty in cream) played the solo part with such ease, power and facility as to fairly rouse the audience to enthusiasm, and she had to repeat part of the last 'Presto' movement. A similar compliment was—" *9th October, 1909.*

Isabel had become a pale, handsome girl. Most of her puppy fat had gone and she stood very erectly with her head thrown back. She had developed a certain charming arrogance like that of a young princess to whom privilege is natural, and in fact she had had something of a royal upbringing. She had been so accustomed to stand out, from the age of four onwards, that when she mixed with girls of her own age at school, it was rather as if it were a purposefully democratic gesture, the extraordinary trying to appear ordinary. She was noted for dreaminess, untidiness, failure to make polite conversation and lateness for meals—all of which tended to be excused, or even admired, on the ground of artistic temperament. And there were practical advantages. Because she played for the curate, Mr. Westerby, at mothers' meetings, it was easy to be excused his Friday night bible classes. She had her own way in almost everything. Of course, she was not happy. Only she knew of her dreadful lack of confidence in dealing with people of her own age, which was disguised by an off-handed or domineering attitude. Only she knew of her occasional burning desire to be treated as an ordinary child. And yet if this did happen—and her mother was occasionally guilty—she was apt to resent it sharply. Then she was the princess who wishes to be treated as a commoner and having her wish granted finds it less attractive than before.

She became very withdrawn and spent much time alone, and developed a perceptiveness which seemed to be denied to others.

She would have hidden the press cuttings book if she could.

She did not understand how her mother failed to see that people were not always keen on having her success rammed down their throats. She had become used to a queer look that was quite common in the eyes of visitors, a look compounded of admiration and yet, somehow, of resistance. "Thank heavens we are normal" or "Thank heavens my children aren't like that" this look seemed to say. And with it often went a bright, polite smile and a speedy change of subject. Not always, of course. Sometimes the admiration was free and unbounded. All the same she wished her mother would not confuse the effect, say, of the French prize, hardly a very notable achievement, with that of her concert performances. And she wished that if her mother insisted on showing the book, she wouldn't find it necessary to support the rest of the family at the same time. This was not because Isabel grudged them praise. But it did not make too much sense to treat her L.R.A.M., for example, on the same basis as Sarah's enthusiastic but uneven Greek dancing at the school concert. Her mother seemed to have no sense of proportion. She was apt to be deeply impressed by things of no account at all. A compliment from old Canon Jeffreys, who was half deaf, weighed more with her than the praise even of Mr. Durrell, the London teacher. (They had been up three times to see him, staying at a Paddington hotel. The third time was also the examination.) And nothing had meant so much to Mrs. Rowland, apparently, as Miss Philippa Murray's controlled reference to "your very talented daughter". All this amazed Isabel, who thought the hush in the hall or the room when she sat down to play, and the sighs and the clapping when she finished, were a good deal more impressive.

Her father, on the other hand, did not think any of it so remarkable as the future he not so much predicted as insisted on for her. At first only mildly interested in Isabel's playing, he had become an enthusiast after her first success at a Town Hall concert, for which people had paid to come in. From then on he considered her worthy of respect, and in her he saw himself adapted to another field. He did not care personally for music. It was an unfamiliar industry in which he was delighted to find that he held some shares. He chatted to Miss Treddye and to Dr. Preston, the cathedral organist who ran the town Orchestral Society. As a result he changed his mind about sending Isabel to the Academy in London, though he remained adamant that her ordinary schooling should be completed first, whether she was or was not a prodigy.

And of course she was becoming less of a prodigy as she grew older. Remarkable at ten, she was less remarkable at fourteen, fifteen, and sixteen, though her accomplishment was greater. She was vaguely conscious of this, and a small fear nestled in her mind that perhaps when she did go to the Academy she would find herself one amongst hundreds of equal or greater ability; and this fear was in conflict with another feeling, that she was too good to waste time being taught in any institution – even Mr. Durrell himself in London had hardly criticized her at all, so that it had seemed scarcely worth while going to him – though his lack of criticism, of course, had given her great confidence. Accordingly she did not show any wild enthusiasm at the idea of going. In any case she would be seventeen before she went, and that was a long way off.

Most days she practised for three or four hours at least. Mr. Rowland preferred not to be in the house when it was going on, but he generally checked to make sure she had done it. Her mother often tried to rescue her from it by suggesting that Isabel came shopping or went somewhere to tea with her – she believed in girls getting about, getting air at least and not being stuffed up indoors. She encouraged Isabel to go on picnics, to go rambling with Sarah and Sarah's friends – Isabel herself had no time to make friends – and generally provoked exasperation.

"Mother, of course I can't! You know I'm working on this new piece, I can't waste the afternoon chatting with lunatics."

"My dearest child, you must not say things like that!" said Mrs. Rowland, genuinely horrified.

"But they *are*. You haven't talked to them, mother. Besides, Sarah and Denny may like dashing around like children, but *I* don't. Besides, if I went blackberry picking I could easily hurt my fingers. If I must go out, I'll take Nicky for a walk."

"No, he's going with me to Mrs. Russington's. Come with

us, if you change your frock. Oh, you don't have to put on a face — "

But her father was very different. He was annoyed if she wasted her time on trivial matters like the others. Moreover, he had become as greedy for the applause and compliments which followed her playing as she was, and was not above leading the clapping himself. He drove her to Dr. Preston's concert at the Town Hall, which had been her biggest occasion so far, rather like the father of the bride — while Mrs. Rowland, Sarah and Nicholas went by train.

Both were silent all the way until they were a hundred yards from the Town Hall when Isabel exclaimed, "I can't remember it! I can't remember a note!"

Mr. Rowland drew the car in to the kerb, removed his goggles and stared at her. There was little to see, for Isabel was heavily clothed and veiled for protection of herself and her frock against the dust of the motor ride.

"What confounded nonsense is this?" he asked.

But she was in despair, overcome by a sudden blind panic she had never known before. She could neither nod nor shake her head. A flush of anger came over Mr. Rowland's face.

"Do you think you're going to make me look like a fool? I'll tell you what you're going to do, my dear girl. You're going to go in there and play the damned thing or you don't touch the piano again in my house!"

This speech, which was delivered loudly enough for passers-by to overhear it, had the effect of making Isabel nearly lose her senses. Her father, however, believed in the theory, one not to be despised, that if one spoke loudly and firmly enough, one's aims could generally be achieved. This turned out to be the case once more. For he started his car again and delivered her at the Town Hall. Isabel spent the next two hours in a state of frenzy, and when she was led on the platform by Dr. Preston, the conductor, she was still convinced that she could not remember a note. But she proceeded to play the concerto brilliantly.

When she was being congratulated afterwards, her father, in white tie and tails, came up and looked at her closely for a second, before giving her a sharp little nod.

CHAPTER NINE

"You must send a postcard immediately, you understand. Immediately, mind. I know what you're like, living in a dream. Sarah, you remind her," said Mrs. Rowland in a voice pitched high with worry. She gazed at her two daughters as if they were off across the Atlantic by raft, instead of to London for a five-day trip. "Oh, I don't like this idea at all – you are to speak to no one, don't forget. I shan't have a minute's peace until you're back."

"We shall be perfectly all right," Isabel said, with the mixture of affection and condescension which her mother often inspired in her. She concealed a sigh. Really, it had been fuss, fuss, fuss for weeks, rising to commotion twenty minutes before when it was found that all the *Ladies Only* compartments were full. Mrs. Rowland had rushed up and down, demanding assistance from porters, and finally when they had settled in at last with an elderly married couple who seemed "safe", had had an urgent talk with the guard, who promised to keep his eye on them.

"We'll write at once!" Sarah promised, for the fifth time, her eyes brimming with tears – she reflected all her mother's moods – as she leant through the window and kissed her.

"See that you have enough blankets. I know these London bedrooms. Be sure and ask Mrs. Slocombe if you haven't. I only hope it turns out all right. See that you go to bed early. Don't talk to strangers on any account – always policemen. Oh, my pets, I know I should be with you, but your father – good-bye! Good-bye!" The train had shuddered. "Oh, heavens, I thought you were off."

"There wasn't a whistle," Isabel said, very coolly – and was at once furious with herself, for the lightning hurt on her mother's face did not escape her. But there was a demon inside her, with which she was now familiar, that forced her to come out very often with small, gritty, impulsive remarks. She tried to recover by kissing her mother warmly.

"Well, I hope you enjoy your lessons, old lady," said Mrs. Rowland, whose eyes were wet. "Now it *is* going, anyway. Good-bye! Write at once!"

"Good-bye! Good-bye, Nicky!"

"Have a good time!" called Nicholas, a thin knicker-bockered figure who made up the farewell party.

"Good-bye!"

"Good-bye!"

Frantic waves, and the two on the platform receded, looking a little pathetic. Advertisements raced by, Lipton's Tea, Try it in your bath Scrubb's Ammonia, My Biscuit is Pat-a-Cake, Return visit The D'Oyly Carte Opera Company, Mazawattee. The girls sank back opposite each other.

"Thank goodness," Isabel said, and was a little annoyed to see that Sarah, who had been almost in tears a minute before, was now seized by a fit of silent giggles. She was taken aback by this rapid change in mood, all the more because she was conscious of a slight lump in her own throat. In spite of herself she had been quite moved by the parting scene, for love, even when, as it seemed to her, poured out unnecessarily, could not be ignored. But her emotional feelings, which were much stronger than Sarah's, were usually concealed. Sarah, who had seemed so much more, was in fact much less affected than she. This was quite as usual, although no one but Isabel was aware of it. Her sister's fit of giggling continued.

"Whatever's the matter?" she asked, in her severe, elder sister voice. But she knew, of course, that the matter was the inability of her sister, and of her brothers as well, to find themselves in the presence of strangers without struggling against a collapse into laughter. Here was an old man with a pink nose and a habit of sniffing, and a big stout woman holding a muff. Clearly nothing could be more amusing. Isabel shared this terrible family habit and felt herself yielding help-lessly, while the lump in her throat quite disappeared. When the old man cleared his throat, she had to hold her handkerchief against her mouth. As for Sarah, her eyes were closed and she was trembling.

A quarter of an hour passed before they could control themselves enough to look calmly out of the window. It was reasonable for them to be excited. This trip was, in effect, a foretaste of freedom, and one which had come about by accident. It had been agreed at the beginning of the year that Isabel should have some more lessons from the London teacher, Clement Durrell. The idea was that, as before, Mrs. Rowland should go up with her. Mr. Durrell had to be booked a good way ahead. It was not until the end of February when Mrs. Rowland contemplated writing to book a room at the hotel where she and Isabel had stayed previously, that Mr. Rowland became aware that he was to be left without her for several days. He pointed out coldly that he had no intention of being left at the mercy of servants; if Mrs. Rowland wished to stay in London, it would be with him, not without him. Mrs. Rowland was at once exasperated.

"It was you who insisted on her having the lessons."

"I still insist on her having the lessons. And I insist on not being deserted here for a week. She's practically grown up. She can go alone. Good God, I was earning my—"

"Don't be so ridiculous, Charles! If she goes, I must go. You'll be perfectly all right, but if you say not, very well. Cancel the lessons. Personally they don't seem all that necessary to me."

The argument continued for several weeks, overheard by Isabel in snatches. She did not think of raising her own voice. Mr. Rowland's children one and all had to take what came to them. But she had been quite confident that if her father wanted her to go, it would happen. Then Nicholas was in bed for three weeks. When he was allowed up again Mrs. Rowland now said firmly that she could not leave him. As a compromise she suggested that Denny, who had spoken with her privately, should take her place. Mr. Rowland became more annoyed than ever at the suggestion. He had always had little respect for his elder son, and he pointed out sharply that the boy had better spend his holiday time studying. Denny was to join a firm of chartered accountants at the end of the next school term, a solution to his future which satisfied his mother's hope that he would become a professional man and his father's candid wish that he should learn something useful before, if ever, he had anything to do with the mill. When deadlock appeared to have been reached solution came from an unexpected quarter. Miss Truscott suggested a Bloomsbury boarding-house for students, with which she was acquainted. She wrote at once to the landlady, Mrs. Slocombe, who had been housekeeper at a place where she had worked as a governess. Miss Truscott enthusiastically claimed that Mrs. Slocombe was both very respectable and very responsible. Mr. Rowland supported her intervention, letters were exchanged with Bloomsbury. And somehow, when all the arrangements had been made, it was found that Sarah was going, too, as a companion for Isabel. She had achieved this by looking extremely pathetic, and making a great show of not being envious. Living side by side with talent, and possessing none herself, Sarah had realized instinctively for some time that it was not necessary, after all, to have any. Her aim in life, so far as she was conscious of one, was simply to be liked. She had found the simplest means of achieving this was to offer praise on all possible occasions to all possible people, and she did this with the greatest sincerity, though instantly forgetting what she had said when the encounter was over. She realized also that praise can be offered by respect and obedience when these are called for. So, with very little trouble, she found herself on the trip to London along with Isabel, for whom it was the result of an outstanding childhood career, and hundreds of hours of work.

At the first junction the train stopped and the old man got out. This caused a further collapse on the part of the Rowlands, who had been under the impression, as had their mother, that they were sharing the compartment with a married couple. Then the stout woman bought a two-and-sixpenny luncheon basket offered from the platform. The extraordinarily funny mistake – for they both found it so – coupled with the prospect of seeing her eat made Sarah choke so much that she had to retire to the corridor. When she returned, red in the face, the sight of the basket's chicken and ham and cheese and preserves was sobering. The sandwiches they had been provided with – doorsteps for growing girls, as Mrs. Rowland put it – were rather less exciting. Here the sisters reacted typically. Isabel looked grimly out of the window at the passing countryside, bathed in April sunshine. Sarah, oblivious of the order about not talking to strangers, asked the stout woman very prettily if she happened to know the time. Almost at once they were deep in conversation.

"That's my sister, you see, and she's having lessons from a famous teacher, she's a wonderful pianist – "

Isabel tried to send some furious glances across, but Sarah was unconscious of them. She was soon sharing the luncheon basket while the stout woman beamed at her lovingly, and told her in great detail – to make it worse she was not especially genteel – about her friend in Lewisham who had such trouble with her gall-bladder and whom she was on her way to visit, after goodness knows how many years. Finally Isabel was drawn in, after a long-drawn-out attempt to preserve dignity and obedience – not that it would ever occur to Mrs. Rowland that she and not Sarah would make such an attempt. She consented to eat some chocolate while Sarah began again to explain her accomplishments, and the woman said admiringly that there was no doubt about it, some people were clever and no mistake, and she only wished she were. She told them about her husband and how there was never a word to be got out of him, and sometimes she thought that life wasn't worth living, because it was all give and no take as far as women were concerned. And suddenly it came to both the sisters that here they were on a train to London, by themselves, conversing with a stranger, who though a very ordinary sort of person – they both had a clear eye for such distinctions, you could not go to Miss Murray's without developing one – all the same was treating them as if they were adults. It came to both of them – and Isabel knew this, for she caught Sarah's eye once, in the way that was enough to set the latter off giggling, and this didn't occur; but instead she understood, in the silent language which can be used by sisters close together in years, that Sarah had decided to leave the schoolgirl kingdom for the moment. All three spoke seriously and happily, and the woman was not a comic grown-up, with her tatty muff, and the little tyres of flesh bulging over her high lace collar, and the unsuitable hat, but merely another human like themselves. As the train approached London Isabel felt strangely – and knew that Sarah also felt – that unknown barriers were being crossed in a hurry, and that this journey in itself was some great stage in their growing up.

London appeared, disappeared and appeared again more strongly. As they came into Paddington the woman said, "Well, what a nice old chat! You've done me good, you really have – do you know, you've made me forget my feet, and it takes a lot to do that." Then the compartment which had become almost as familiar as a home was cold and unfriendly again. They were on the platform, and the two girls watched her hurry painfully away, without even a good-bye. She had been a symbol to them of the outside world. They looked at each other, but neither thought of anything appropriate to say. The plump woman lost herself in the crowd.

"There's someone who looks as if she's looking for someone," Isabel said after a pause.

CHAPTER TEN

M rs. Slocombe came towards them, chest forward, backside back, a patrician figure, tapping the platform firmly with her borzoi-headed umbrella. Her enormous crinoline hat, trimmed with roses and foliage, bobbed up and down with her head. She looked impressive.

The girls were overwhelmed by her.

"You are the Miss Rowlands? I thought so, I was terrified you might not be, you were so exactly – porter! Where are your bags, my dears? Oh, these are all you have? It's all right, porter, we don't need you. Pick your things up then, and come along. You were so exactly, I was saying, as I imagined you would be, so fresh-looking – I'm fond of you both already – I seem to have corresponded for several years about you with your mother, who seems such a very dear person. I picture her as someone quiet and purposeful, with a fund of humour all her own. Am I right?"

"Well, yes, in a way –" replied Isabel, who was hurrying along beside her, trailed by Sarah.

"Well, yes, in a way!" Mrs. Slocombe laughed. "Of course! All mothers are, my dear – that's how I knew. Which one of you is the pianist?"

"Me," Isabel said breathlessly.

"Which one is the pianist? Me! I like that very much. Which one is the pianist? Me!" Mrs. Slocombe said, bubbling with private amusement. She glanced backwards over her shoulder at the other sister. "And you? What about you? What do you think of the station, eh? Isn't it big?"

"It's so enormous!" cried Sarah, who fitted easily into any required mood, and saw that this curious woman wished her to be impressed.

"It's so enormous! Lovely! Lovely!" And Mrs. Slocombe plunged ahead of them through the exit doors, while the girls looked at each other in amazement. Outside they saw their landlady wave her brolly at a taxi. "Come on, my dears, don't lag behind!" she called to them: "We'll have a trip down Oxford Street and you can see the shops."

When they turned into the Edgware Road, Isabel, who had recovered from her fluster and was now rather on her dignity, said, "I'm sorry if it was inconvenient to come to meet us. We could easily have managed by ourselves."

"Bless you, my dear child," said Mrs. Slocombe beside her. She sat tremendously upright with her hands clasped in front of her over the umbrella handle. Sarah was on one of the bucket seats, darting her head from side to side and down and up. "I promised your dearest mother and that was that. She was quite right to ask me and the affront to my convenience matters not at all. One cannot be too careful with you young girls. Town is not the place for you to travel about alone – it is all too easy to be insulted. You know nothing of that, my dears. Look, here is the Marble Arch. There's a good deal of traffic, isn't there? Town, of course, is filling up for the Season." She glanced towards Park Lane, in a way that was quite possessive and proud. "Now tell me," she went on, "how is my dear, gay Phyllis?"

She could only mean Aunt Phyllis, Isabel realized, taken aback by the word "gay".

"Oh, I believe she's very well, thank you."

"Dear Phyllis! Such a character! What a pity she buries herself away!" said Mrs. Slocombe. "Oh, goodness, how she can make one laugh! One is in stitches!"

The taxi continued all the way down Oxford Street, past the Electric Palace, D. H. Evans, the tantalizing glimpse of Regent Street, Peter Robinsons, Warings, golden Frascati's – Sarah was fairly bursting with excitement, and the more she stared and gasped, the more delighted Mrs. Slocombe was. Though she was putting it on, it was true that she never had seen anything to touch the great shops or the traffic, far more motors compared to horses than at home, some of them magnificent affairs with a footman as well as the chauffeur, and such a splendid hurrying bustle of smart-looking people on the pavements. Isabel was less concerned with it all. She had seen it before, of course, but far more than that she could not get over the extraordinary fact that Aunt Phyllis, who was known at home, when mentioned by grown-ups, as "poor Phyllis", a dim, back-row figure if ever there was one, was here in the metropolis a witty person who sent people into stitches. It was strange, and it was also a little exciting. She was very conscious of a process at work that was tearing away veils and showing her life as it was, more puzzling than ever and more interesting, too.

They got out in Bloomsbury, before a tall, narrow house in Woburn Square. Mrs. Slocombe paid the fare, tipped economically and noted the total sum, plus twenty-five per cent, in her little book, while they were still on the pavement. While this was going on Sarah whispered to Isabel that she wished they would hurry inside for she had urgent need of the lavatory. Isabel replied that she should have gone in the train.

"Come on, my dears. Welcome to Woburn Square," said Mrs. Slocombe with a complacent glance upwards, and she led them into the house. The front door was open all the time, she explained, for otherwise the servants were constantly disturbed, whether guests had keys or not. They followed her down a tall, dark passage, and though this was thinly car-

79

peted and there were gloomy pictures on the walls, and great mahogany banisters ascending on one side, there was an institutional feeling in the air, and the landlady's rustling skirts and very feminine smartness seemed highly unsuitable. The girls became rather nervous. It was as if they had had a brief moment in the open, looking at London, and now they were captured again.

They went through a door covered with green baize into a sitting-room full of rather insecure-looking furniture, including an upright piano. The room had a stale scented smell. There was a view of some depressing bricks on the other side of a narrow courtyard, and there seemed no reason for Mrs. Slocombe to look around with a sigh of contentment.

"Well, this is my own special den, and you may use it so long as you're tidy, and remember that everything is valuable. Personally, I find I have to be surrounded by good things if I am to feel rested instead of restive. Through here is your bedroom, I use it really as a dressing room and it's so useful for one's friends when they're passing through Town. Phyllis used it, of course, bless her."

They went through a door on the other side of the sitting-room and Mrs. Slocombe stood by habit with her hands clasped in front of her, in the professional stance of a landlady. There was a single iron bedstead, and another bed had been made up on a divan. It all seemed very uncomfortable and even Sarah was unable to look enthusiastic.

"Well, there you are!" Mrs. Slocombe said brightly. "You can see that your little home is as cosy as can be. Those curtains are new from Shoolbred's only last year and the bedcover cost me thirty-five shillings alone. That's right, put your bags down. I'm going to show you round right away, so that you've got your bearings – but of course you understand that you are not to leave these rooms unaccompanied. This is a houseful of students, you understand."

They understood only vaguely, but followed her out and became conscious for the first time of the presence of lodgers. Somewhere upstairs a young man shouted down a passage to another, "Can't, old boy, I'm going to have a bath to-night." Mrs. Slocombe pursed her lips and glanced at the girls, who were automatically pretending to have heard nothing. They were used to the vulgarity of their brother, of course – but a brother was not quite the same. The meaning of the phrase "a houseful of students" became excitingly clearer.

Mrs. Slocombe opened a door, but put out her hand to prevent the girls from more than peeping inside. It was a large and quite comfortable sitting-room with a grand piano and several leather armchairs, one of which was occupied by a lodger sleeping beneath a newspaper, and another by a ginger-headed young man who jumped to his feet, turned pink and at once tried to look casual.

"Good evening, Mr. Bentham," Mrs. Slocombe said, in a very grand voice. "Do excuse me disturbing you." When they had withdrawn she told them softly, "That was the lounge. Of course you will never go into it, unless I am with you. That Mr. Bentham is a medical student, a very quiet young man, just the type I like to have. I have a number of medical students. I flatter myself that students of the better type find the atmosphere here congenial."

Then they went through a door beneath the staircase and down a flight of stone steps to a basement passage which led to a large kitchen, which was used as the lodgers' dining-room. A long, well-scrubbed table was laid for about thirty. A plump, depressed-looking woman wearing a mob cap gave them an oily grimace and continued to poke the fire of a stone grill. Mrs. Slocombe glanced at an exercise book which hung on the wall beside it.

"How many are you expecting to-night, Cook?"

"Them as comes I do my best to satisfy," replied the cook.

"I thought as much. No wonder so many potatoes were wasted yesterday. How many times must I tell you to make sure that everyone ticks his name in or out at breakfast?"

"If they says they'll come in, they doesn't," said the cook with a furious poke. "Them as comes I do my best to satisfy."

Mrs. Slocombe closed her eyes for an expressive second. Then she turned to the girls and said brightly, "Don't you think it has atmosphere? I always like to feel that there's just a tinge of college hall about it – the bare old table, you know – of course there ought to be an old painting of the founder,

I admit." She laughed gaily. Outside in the passage once again she lowered her voice. "Well, you see what one has to put up with. I pride myself on having a really broad and advanced outlook, just like dear Phyllis – but the lower classes can be very trying. One gets no thanks for giving good treatment. They won't attempt to help. You see, this is cook's room, which she has all to herself," Mrs. Slocombe went on, pointing to a door. Above and to one side of it a rather grubby looking window, above eye level, faced the passage. "We won't look in. I make a point of giving them privacy. I have to pay her twenty pounds a year. That's what things are like in London. Mind you, I believe in high wages as a matter of principle, but one can't help feeling that the old ways were best. They were happier, too. Now, then, through this end door, believe it or not, is our billiard room, such an asset for men! Oh, dear, someone is playing. Well, we'll just take a very quick peep."

"Ask her where it is," Sarah whispered, in despair.

"I can't now!" Isabel whispered back.

Mrs. Slocombe knocked and beckoned the girls to look round her waist. Two young men were at the table, jacketless. One was studying a shot, the other looked at Mrs. Slocombe and waved his hand.

"Holloa, Mrs. S., what have you got there?"

"Excuse me intruding, these are two young friends from the country – "

"Not a gathering of the Slocombe clan, surely?"

"No, Mr. Nash. Excuse us, please." Mrs. Slocombe withdrew full of dignity. As they went back along the passage laughter sounded behind them. "I really must apologize, my dears. But that is just what I was saying. Mr. Nash means well, but he isn't quite quite, if you understand me. Between ourselves, of course. That is why you must strictly obey the rule to stay in your rooms. Now we'll go back and you can settle down."

They returned upstairs, still without hearing where the lavatory was. The sisters did not dare to ask and either Mrs. Slocombe did not think of it or did not care to mention it.

"Why didn't you ask?" Sarah said angrily when they were

alone. "I shall just have to go and find it, that's all. I'll let her get away – I say, are we prisoners, or what? That's perfectly ridiculous."

"I agree. You know I can't imagine mother knew about all these men, can you? I expected a lot of stuffy old people. And I can't understand the way Mrs. Slocombe talks about Aunt Phyllis, can you?"

"Distant cousin Phyllis. No, that's positively amazing! Fancy someone like Mrs. Slocombe – " For the landlady had impressed both of them.

"I know."

"It's funny to think that she slept in here. Of course, I suppose what it really was, poor old Phyllis didn't even know there were students here. As it is we shall lose our virtue." What Sarah meant by this was merely that some young man might speak to her in a familiar way. Just then, somewhere at the front of the house, a gong was struck, and at once doors were slammed and people could be heard coming downstairs and also going along the passage outside the sitting-room. The sisters listened attentively.

Isabel yawned. "They're probably all very boring," she said. "Besides I expect, dear child, they'll think themselves above a mere schoolgirl – "

"They don't have to know *that* – "

"And for my part I shall have too much work to do, which reminds me I haven't played a note to-day. I'll try out this drab old instrument."

"We haven't un*packed* yet, Isabel."

"Bother unpacking."

"And you promised to write a postcard as soon as – "

"Later, later, later," Isabel said, opening the lid of the piano. She ran her fingers over a few notes.

"Well, don't forget I reminded you. Don't you think you ought to ask if you can play – "

"It's in tune, more or less, thank goodness." Isabel sat down on the stool and began to play, ignoring her sister's last question. Over her shoulder she said, "We haven't a stamp yet, anyway. Heavens, my fingers are quite stiff after that journey."

Soon the room trembled with sound, for nowadays Isabel always played as if she were in a concert hall. Sarah went into the bedroom and unpacked. She used the two empty drawers Mrs. Slocombe had indicated, washed her hands at the basin behind the pink screen, inspected the bottles in the toilet cupboard above it, and wondered if she dared to use the almost empty *Ess Viotto*. Then she returned to the sitting-room.

"I'm going to look for it," she said. Isabel nodded without interrupting her playing. Once she was at the piano she did not greatly care what went on.

Sarah went to the door, opened it and gasped. Two young men were leaning against the wall opposite. They came to life and bowed.

"Hope you don't mind our listening—"

"We couldn't help hearing—"

Sarah was convinced that they must guess where she had been going and she was already shutting the door, her face red with embarrassment.

"There are *two* men outside!" she exclaimed in a whisper to the pianist.

"Are they still there?" said Isabel, who was playing a brilliant series of arpeggios. "Peep through the keyhole."

"No thank you!" replied her sister, looking at the door half in excitement and half in alarm.

Isabel suddenly rose from the stool. Sarah held her breath as she watched her hurry across and open the door, and could have died with admiration when she heard her ask with the greatest calm:

"Excuse me, have you a stamp?"

"Certainly. George, produce a stamp immediately for the lady. French, German, Italian, madam?"

"For a postcard."

"How extravagantly dull. *Ein britisches Postwertzeichen.*"

"Yes, a British one, please," said Isabel, who had done a year's German at Miss Murray's. Sarah listened excitedly from just behind her, and thought how wonderful her sister was. It was a fact that Isabel seemed able to run and manage almost any situation.

"Here's a penny one," said the young man whose name was

George, producing it from his wallet. "I wish you'd go on playing. We were really enjoying it, weren't we, Sadler?"

"It even stopped us from going down to supper. It was the most elevating experience we have ever had under the roof of Mrs. Slocombe. May we ask what you are doing here?"

Both were very grown-up young men and she was privately overawed by their impudent calm. She replied gravely, "We are staying here for a few days. It is very kind of you to oblige us with a stamp. Now, if you don't mind, I must go on with my practice."

"Please do. My name's Sadler. This is Haines. Ring for him if you want another stamp. Your playing is wonderful, Miss—"

"Thank you. Our name is Rowland."

"Here's the penny," said Sarah, appearing unexpectedly.

"Oh, that's not necessary, please," protested Mr. Haines.

"Yes, it is," Sarah cried, her voice rising with her colour. "One must always pay for stamps." She gave the penny to Isabel, who was rather annoyed at her interruption and held the coin out between the tips of two fingers.

"Thank you, good-bye," Isabel said, closing the door. They backed away from it, as if anticipating that it might be burst open. There was a murmur on the other side, but nothing more, and they looked at each other excitedly, in a way that said, "Nothing like this has ever happened before."

"I think they've gone," Sarah whispered after a moment, but at once there was a knock on the door and she smothered a gasp.

"Yes?" said Isabel, throwing her head back.

"I've come to set the table, miss." The door opened and it was a maid. Before it was shut they saw that the passage was empty.

"I must write the postcard," Isabel said breathlessly.

The maid busied about getting a table cloth from a drawer of the secretaire—things were kept in odd places in Mrs. Slocombe's room—and then mats and doilies and cutlery from a cupboard by the fireplace. Her uniform rustled and her shoes made a terrible squelching sound as she moved round. Sarah noticed Isabel's lips tremble and it was enough.

85

She collapsed on the sofa and put a handkerchief to her mouth.

"Please, can you tell us where the lavatory is?" Isabel asked; with the lower orders she felt less need of reticence.

"First landing, the door on your right, miss."

Sarah rushed out hysterically. Isabel went into the bedroom to fetch her writing things from her suitcase. She was conscious that the room which had looked so unfriendly when they arrived less than an hour before had now taken on quite a different aspect. From below came the sound of plates and voices, and the feeling she had had in the train, that this was altogether a fresh chapter in her life, came back more strongly. The young men had made it clear that, whatever attitude Mrs. Slocombe might take as their guardian, this stay would not be at all like being in an hotel with her mother – when she had spoken to no one, except Mr. Durrell and the examiners. She found the postcard and her fountain pen and sitting on the bed she hastily wrote, "Dear Mother, We arrived safely. Mrs. Slocombe met us and we came by taxi. Everything very nice. Your affectionate daughter, Isabel." She felt that she ought to show a little more extravagance in her affection, but she did not like being publicly emotional – Sarah could supply that with a postscript; it was her street, not Isabel's.

When she had scribbled the address she lay down on the bed for a moment and stared at the ceiling, listening to the sounds of the basement supper, the squelching of the maid's shoes in the next room – not at all funny, when Sarah wasn't there – and she was conscious, too, of other sounds, dim traffic noises from surrounding London. A smile crossed her lips. Next year she would be here by herself, and suddenly now she realized how marvellous it would be to be young and talented and in this city.

She shivered with exultation at all that lay ahead.

Then she heard Sarah return – breathlessly slamming the door, as usual – and she sat up again in a hurry. When her sister burst in she appeared to be just finishing the postcard.

CHAPTER ELEVEN

ondon looked attractive the next morning. Its men were drab but tidy, but its women, from the middle classes upwards, wore large hats decorated with flowers and richly coloured materials for their dresses, and its houses were freshly painted and decorated by window boxes.

The sisters marched through the Bloomsbury streets on their way to Mr. Durrell's studio, which was in a mews off the Marylebone Road. Isabel's mood of exultation was still with her, and not surprisingly, for the evening before had ended in a triumph. Hardly had they finished their supper with Mrs. Slocombe, an enormously gossipy meal during which the landlady found out almost everything there was to be known about the girls and their family, while they heard some highly-coloured accounts of Mrs. Slocombe's experiences housekeeping for the aristocracy – and the way she bandied eminent names about was tremendously impressive – when there was a knock at the door. Mr. Sadler stood there and was wondering politely if Miss Rowland would care to play in the guests' lounge. This was rather a bombshell, for the passage incident had not been mentioned to Mrs. Slocombe, who was quite flustered; but the landlady was more of a procuress than a chaperone by nature. " You wicked little creatures! " she had told them reprovingly, but also roguishly. " I've a good mind to send you straight home to your mother! " The girls had never been so complimented, and finally they had all three gone into the guest lounge, where Isabel played to an appreciative half-dozen, and then before long to at least twenty young or youngish men. Sarah sat with Mrs. Slocombe on a sofa, pleasantly conscious that some of the listeners found her an agreeable sight and she privately felt that some of the clapping was as much for her face as for Isabel's playing. Isabel, however, was at her concert best and Mrs. Slocombe was clearly enraptured that such talent had come under her roof. At nine-thirty they had returned to the sitting-room and had coffee and cakes. And now it was a sunny morning, they were to go to a matinée in the afternoon and a concert in the evening. Isabel could not help reflecting again and again how splendidly one got on on one's own.

To begin with the lesson was rather dampening. She had prepared a very special, very modern, very fashionable piece of Debussy. She was rather put out to begin with when Mr. Durrell, a jumpy, excitable little old man, seemed barely to remember her. "Well! Well! How are you? " he said, shaking hands with her, and looking away from her eyes. "Let me see, you were here a year ago, wasn't it? " It was not the way she expected to be greeted, and when she sat down at the piano – in the bare room which looked out on to stables – it was with an iron determination to give the professor a lesson rather than to receive one. Then as she began to play she noticed with further annoyance that he had settled down at a small rickety table and chair, the only articles of furniture apart from the piano, to work through a mass of papers.

She played brilliantly, no doubt about that. A mess of a slur, but he hadn't noticed. Also at one moment some bad pedalling – most irritating – but apart from that she had never been more assured. Now a beautiful change of tempo. Now it was flowing. She came serenely to an end. There was a rustle of papers from the table. Then Mr. Durrell had a fit of coughing, which lasted for a minute.

"Excuse me – damned dust – " he said between gasps. "Yes – well – that was very nice, my dear, very – " More coughing, and Isabel gazed at the wall, trying to conceal that slight revulsion which signs of physical decay inspire in the young. "You haven't – oh, damn it – excuse me – ah, that's better – done much work on it, have you? "

She was rather taken aback.

"Well, I don't know – " she began, with faint indignation.

"I mean – look, tell me everything you think went wrong," he interrupted.

"Well," Isabel said again, "there was a slur that was bad, and there was that spread chord where I made a mess of my pedalling, I don't know if you noticed – "

"Otherwise it was a perfect interpretation? " said Mr.

88

Durrell, smiling. "My dear child! My dear child! Isabel, isn't it? Tell me now, what do you think about Debussy?" he asked in great good humour, with emphasis on the "think". "If you want to know what I think, I think he's overrated. But still he exists, an anti-Wagnerite, which can at least be said in his favour, don't you agree? I don't put him in the first class, any more than I put one of your Impressionist painters in Leonardo's company. All the same he's subtle, you know, and the simpler he is the subtler he is. He's precisely the kind of composer who's death to the amateurs, poor dears. He gives them the kind of thing that's easy to learn and, bless them, they miss all the point. Now, in your own case, well, to start with you didn't keep strictly in time, and with a man like Debussy you *must*. When you had groups of two quavers instead of three you hurried them, didn't you? Then that second crescendo – do you know you lost the point of it altogether?"

Isabel was astounded. The enormous confidence she had brought with her had not entirely gone, but it was sagging. Her mouth trembled a little as she gazed at the professor. She hadn't up to now thought of him with any particular respect. When she had had her previous lessons from him, he had seemed excitable but undistinguished – not at all what one expected an eminent London musician to be. He wore a shiny, untidy lounge suit which was not even Bohemian. It was the same suit now, shinier than ever. But now she was remembering that he was a professor, after all, that he had written some dreary book analysing Bach, that Miss Treddye spoke of him with reverence. She was conscious of a dry feeling in her throat.

She found herself unable to speak.

"Now, now, now!" went on Mr. Durrell excitedly. "Don't be depressed about it! What's the use of coming if there's nothing to learn? The great thing is to realize that there is lots to learn. You see, that's why I asked you to prepare a simple piece – an apparently simple piece. You're quite an accomplished technician – but it takes an artist to play a simple piece as it should be played. How can you be an artist at your age? It's impossible. You could be a prodigy, but not an artist.

89

There are barely six people alive who can play that piece properly, as a matter of fact. And you can pay money in a concert hall and hear a performance as bad as yours. You know I'm supposed to advise your father about your future? "

Isabel stared at him.

" How can I give advice? " asked Mr. Durrell, rocking backwards and forwards on his chair. " Come on to a platform on roller skates instead of walking, and you may be made for life. Your father wants you to go to the Academy. It's the best place for you, it's interesting, it's lively, if you stay in music you'll have made friends you'll meet again and again. You'll have to learn another instrument, and that's a fine thing. But if your father wants to know whether you'll be a success, he'd better ask you, not me, my dear child. Are you prepared to practise every day for ever, all through the years? Is it fame and applause and money you're after, or music? I don't know. You probably don't know yourself, do you? "

It wasn't in the least the kind of lesson Isabel had expected. It occurred to her that perhaps he didn't know about her public appearances, although she had been under the impression that Miss Treddye had written about her in detail, and presumably her father had also mentioned it. But he knew that she had obtained the licentiate's diploma, and a " concert standard " was required for that.

" I wish I could go to the Academy now, Mr. Durrell," she said, feeling more at ease. " School seems such a waste of time."

" Well, you could go if your father would let you. You could have gone years ago, if it comes to that. But I don't believe in that sort of thing. It's the student life that's so priceless, and in a year's time you'll be able to make much better use of that. By the way, have you many friends at school? "

" Oh, yes," Isabel said, surprised at the question. But she went on thoughtfully, " At least – no, I haven't, I mean, I get on with – well, I suppose it is that I haven't much in common with – they often seem so silly –" She was even more astonished at herself. She hadn't spoken to anyone, ever, as intimately as this. It was as if this queer old man, sitting inconsequently at the rickety little table, hardly looking at her, allowed her to drop all her defences. But the trouble was that words never quite explained what you meant, even when you were prepared to tell the truth. He encouraged her to go on, not by saying or doing anything, but simply because he appeared to be listening, which was a rare thing for anyone to do. "You see, I don't feel I belong – " she continued earnestly. "It probably sounds very conceited. I think perhaps I'm old for my age. There's my sister now, who's staying up with me" – and was possibly waiting in the mews outside – "she belongs – but then – she's more like the others – she can be interested when they're all talking in a way I find, well, boring. So I think if I were with people who only cared for music – or if I were free to do nothing but music – " She stopped. She realized that she was beginning to say not what she thought so much as what he probably liked to hear. What she was saying was true as far as it went, but it left out her greed for applause, for success and its quickest possible arrival. She stared at Mr. Durrell, who was idly making patterns on the cover of an exercise book, and said, "Why did you say it was no good asking you if I'd be a success?"

"Ah, the most fascinating of all questions, my dear child," he answered, without looking up. "I'm delighted that you don't attempt to conceal your interest. As you've explained, you don't mix with people, so the solution is that you should climb up on a pedestal, and that then people should accept you up on it – then mixing is possible, because you're up there and where you belong and they're down there where they belong. That's a motive for success, all right. *N'est-ce pas?*"

"Possibly – " Isabel admitted, with an unusual flush. She was shocked at hearing some of her thoughts put into words. She was all attention, for the subject of herself was both more embarrassing and more fascinating than any other possible topic.

"Well, suppose that is the motive, suppose it were the main motive – you can see that at some point on your determined climb you might – let's say at the Academy – find yourself in congenial company. Lots of friends, lots of acquaintances, fellow students perhaps, and because you can now mix freely with these new people, who can talk about music just as well as you can, the pedestal isn't so necessary. You follow me. The motive for success has been weakened. An organist from Yorkshire proposes to you and you settle down in Sheffield – a very fine musical town, by the way. You admit the possibility? "

" Yes, I suppose so."

"But it may not be like that. You may be such an outstanding Gold Medallist – by the way I speak as an outstanding Gold Medallist – that you're almost forced into prominence. You are engaged to play a concerto at Queen's Hall. Agents fight to give you engagements. You appear all over the country. Then Paris, Brussels, Amsterdam, Vienna! That, too, can happen. I notice you find the prospect more agreeable, dear child. But which will it be? Supposing it is neither. You spend two years at the Academy, as I warmly recommend, you emerge a first-class *exécutante*, full of sound musicianship – but no one seems to care! You suddenly find yourself one of the great army of talented unemployed. Then, dear child, you can still have all you want – if you have a thick enough skin and if you're as importunate as a puppy. The world is yours if you really want it. The amount of your talent and its quality are only an aspect of the situation. And now, dear, you know all you need to know about success. We don't have to discuss the matter any more. It has been dealt with. Now we'll concentrate on music. Our friend Debussy has made music, and we must admit that only a genius could make passable music from the whole-tone scale – he was here last year, you know, or was it the year before? A man with an enormous head. Now, dear, we've only ten minutes left, so start the whole thing again. Give the notes their proper value and keep your rhythm – "

When she met Sarah again, Isabel had the strange feeling of having finally left her childhood behind her. She was no longer a prodigy, but she had become a student. She was now competing with the world. On that basis she had not impressed Mr. Durrell, but he had not discouraged her from thinking that she would do so. How amazingly different from her last visit to him! Then it had been simply a matter of preparation for an exam, now a whole career was in question. She felt the excitement which comes when a fantasy is suddenly real. In spite of his shiny suit and his cough Mr. Durrell had not merely seen but had met Debussy, knew Busoni, Carreno, everybody – she had learnt all this in the last few minutes and Mr. Durrell had grown at once to the stature of these great names which he could use so familiarly – while she herself had grown for the simple reason of knowing Mr. Durrell.

"You've been ages!" Sarah exclaimed. "We've only just time to go to Shoolbred's. How did you get on? The next pupil was terribly impatient – did you see her?"

"She passed me on the stairs. That's her playing now, I suppose." The notes of the piano came dimly into the mews as they walked away. Isabel had glimpsed a rather florid young woman wearing expensive furs and an exotic perfume. She was impressed to think that this was a fellow pupil.

"She asked me the time because she could see I was waiting, too. She's giving a recital to-morrow afternoon at the Aeolian Hall. I told her all about you –"

"She's giving a recital?"

"Yes, and she's given us tickets!" She triumphantly flourished the two cards, with the word "Complimentary" printed across the name of the pianist – Dorina Conti. "I didn't ask or anything, she just suddenly handed them out. Isn't it terribly exciting? Imagine something like that happening at home."

"It couldn't happen at home," said Isabel delightedly. "Dorina Conti, I thought she looked foreign."

"She isn't foreign at all. She's a Londoner, she said. I asked her. It's her professional name. She comes from a place called Stoke Newington and her father is the organist at the church there. She said if we like we can go to the artist's room afterwards; we tell the attendant and get directed."

"Here, what did you tell her? I hope you haven't been exaggerating –"

"Not at all! What do you take me for?"

They had to walk quickly to get to Tottenham Court Road for window-shopping at Shoolbred's. Sarah was overwhelmed by the size of the store, less because she was actually surprised by it than because she was determined to be overwhelmed by everything on her visit. Her gasps and exclamations drew a good deal of attention, most of it benevolent. Isabel wished her sister would not be quite so exuberant, at least when she was in her company. But her *coup* in getting the tickets was undeniable. Isabel suffered it all patiently.

In the afternoon she practised while Mrs. Slocombe took Sarah for more window-shopping. In the evening all three went to Queen's Hall for a Beethoven concert. Mrs. Slocombe proved an indefatigable conversationalist and only stopped talking with reluctance when the music began. Her topic of the moment was how to make use of stale bread and was inspired by her discovery just before supper of gross wastage in the kitchen. And cook had said impertinently that the guests disliked bread puddings. At supper Mrs. Slocombe began to explain how she had answered cook. Had she never heard of putting crusts into soup stock, thus saving flour or sago? Once given a theme Mrs. Slocombe had a good deal of Beethoven's ability to embroider it, thrust it aside, return to it, give it universal dimensions. Between the movements of the Emperor she described to Sarah how stale bread could be used in making a gooseberry charlotte. She had quite fallen for Sarah, who listened to her with wonderful attention. In the interval, stale bread being finally disposed of, she returned to their afternoon shopping. They had been as far as Kensington and at John Barker's Mrs. Slocombe had seen a cashmere gown with a belt of soft satin which might have been made for her, while Sarah had wondered whether to buy a pair of net cuffs for her mother – she thought of little else but what present she could take home, a fact that endeared her still more to Mrs. Slocombe. Isabel paid little attention to any of it. She was carried away, by the music, by the quality of the orchestra – she felt it would be worth dying to play to such an accompaniment, and the orchestras at home seemed dreadfully pathetic by comparison – by the technique of the pianist, by the marvellous assortment of the audience, the intriguing snatches of conversation between people who gave the impression of being or at least knowing celebrities. In fact she felt herself to be at the centre of things and it was an extension of the pleasure she had felt all the afternoon, working at

Debussy in Mrs. Slocombe's sitting-room, with an absurd sense of pride that she was doing it in London and not at home. This was the place for her, there was no doubt about it. The air was busier and more urgent and full of an intoxicating quality for the ambitious. She heard Mrs. Slocombe's penetrating voice, "What I call a nice costume—" But the sound of it was dim. She was too occupied in dreaming that the posters advertising the Ysaye-Pugno recitals really read Ysaye-Rowland to care what the landlady said. How was she to endure another year at school, when all this beckoned? That year, and then two years at the Academy seemed like an eternity stretching out—though the Academy was itself something to look forward to. She had become quite confident about it. She would learn another instrument, and play in the students' orchestra—invaluable experience, Mr. Durrell had said. Probably most members of this orchestra had been there or at the Royal College—she wondered suddenly if they had all started out with the hope of being soloists. The depression vanished at once. Ysaye-Pugno—it was more attractive to dwell on the world-famous. Ysaye-Rowland.

And then the rest of the concert, and Mrs. Slocombe on the way back suddenly disclosing that she had once spent two years in China.

"Yes, my dears, don't be so surprised! Don't I look like a woman who's seen the world? Oh, what a pity, all the shutters down at Peter's." She referred to Peter Robinson's, the store at Oxford Circus. "We'll have a look there to-morrow, Sarah, dear. Oh, that China—the Celestial Empire, they call it—I had a few other names up my sleeve, I can tell you! No shopping every day there—you had to order your groceries once every six months and think of everything you'd need. And then the meat going off all the time. Still, it's all experience, that's what I always say. Poor Mr. Slocombe died out there. That was from goat's meat. What those Chinamen used to get up to—they'd actually pump water into the goat's carcase to make it look fat and tender. Then, oh dear, when you came to cook, of course it all withered away—and tough! No, give me dear old England." Mrs. Slocombe raised her umbrella in a commanding gesture to a bus that was, in any case, stopping.

They got on, and Mrs. Slocombe was already talking about the forthcoming appearance in the sky of Halley's Comet.

"It travels millions of miles a day and it was last here seventy-five years ago. I'm sure I don't know how they work it out. Mr. Slocombe would have enjoyed it, he was a great one for the stars. He was at sea as a young man, and of course that explained his interest. He'd have me looking up at the sky for hours, telling me which was which."

They left the bus in New Oxford Street and Mrs. Slocombe led them through Bloomsbury. All was quiet, but it was somehow exciting. Even the man clearing up manure from the road in front of the boarding-house seemed to the girls to be invested with a certain metropolitan magic. Then as they entered the house the door of the guests' lounge was open and they saw cards being played, and felt a certain smoky masculine atmosphere – and before they had gone by Mr. Sadler appeared in the doorway, and bowed to them politely.

"No concert for us to-night?" he enquired.

"Mr. Sadler! The very idea!" Mrs. Slocombe said. "Certainly not, it's much too late."

"Good night, then, Mrs. Slocombe. Good night, Miss Rowland. Good night, Miss Rowland."

"Good night, good night," came one or two other voices from the lounge. Mrs. Slocombe appeared to draw in her breath sharply, and hurried the girls on before they could reply. A thermos of cocoa waited for them in the sitting-room and as she poured it out Mrs. Slocombe kept on saying, "Oh, the daring things! The daring things!"

They lay awake for an hour after going to bed.

CHAPTER TWELVE

The next morning Mr. Durrell was pleased with her.

"Altogether different, my dear! Even the composer might faintly recognize it now. Now we can *start* work on it."

This morning there were no digressions. It was an exhilarating lesson. He showed her how infinitely more there was in this simple piece than she had imagined, but in so masterful a way that she felt she herself had thought of it all. Then there was a lecture on interpretation, and he demonstrated how this phrase and that would be tackled by this and that virtuoso – Pachmann, Carreno, Paderewski – and in doing so gave a virtuoso performance himself. Isabel was breathless with admiration and enjoyment. She felt herself being raised to a new level of thought. At the end of the lesson he produced two tickets for his pupil Dorina Conti's recital that afternoon and she stopped herself in time from telling him that she had tickets already; he was clearly bestowing them on her as a mark of approval. She was also rather pleased at no longer being in debt to her sister.

"What shall we do with the other two?" Sarah asked, when she heard. "Mrs. S. can't come." For the landlady had announced her intention of resting that afternoon. "Shall we give them away? There's bound to be someone in the guests' lounge."

"Certainly not," Isabel exclaimed at once.

"But why not?" Sarah's eyes were large with surprise.

"It wouldn't be suitable." Her tone was authoritative, but the fact was she had already thought of Sarah's suggestion herself, and for some reason this made her very annoyed. However, the house seemed to be empty when they returned. They lunched with Mrs. Slocombe, who discussed the theatre – she badly wanted to see Charles Hawtrey's new comedy and if the girls liked they would have an expedition to pit or gallery before the end of the week. Sarah was so excited that she almost fell off her chair. Afterwards there were postcards to be sent home, to Mrs. Rowland and to Nicky, to Miss Treddye and to Aunt Phyllis. They were in a hurry when they left the house, and then Sarah had to go back for a handkerchief. She returned pink-faced and smiling, and Isabel looked at her curiously, but said nothing. They were getting late for the recital and had to walk fast. This was very warm work since, beneath their long skirts and flannel blouses, both

SE – D

wore flannel petticoats and woollen combinations among other layers.

They were breathing hard when they reached the bus stop, and only more or less composed when they finally entered the hall in Bond Street, where the shininess of the doors, the thickness of the carpet, the clothes of the people going in with them, the professional level of the organization all impressed deeply. Isabel showed Mr. Durrell's tickets and they were led to seats in the tenth row. Most of the seats ahead of them were filled and some of those behind; the hall was just more than half full. They felt that they were stared at as they sat down and held themselves perched upright, conscious of being two children amongst a gathering of distinguished adults. It was some minutes before Isabel felt the tenseness leaving her and she could look for Mr. Durrell, whom she at last saw talking to several people in the front row. Having pointed him out to Sarah, she gazed with mounting excitement at the open piano that waited in solitude on the platform against a dark rich velvet background. She began to feel so nervous for the pianist that it might have been her own recital. She could feel her heart thumping. How could Mr. Durrell look so calm? She read the biographical note on the programme – born . . . studied under . . . Conservatoire . . . under Clement Durrell . . . heavens, how much this person had accomplished, how many places she had been! Must she too do all this before her London recital? Isabel was considerably upset at the idea. On the other hand she herself was under Clement Durrell. But – another slightly uncomfortable thought struck her – Mr. Durrell had been so brilliant this morning, so dazzling in his technical demonstrations, why wasn't *he* a world-famous name? However, there was activity on the stage. A man in overalls appeared, opened the piano and adjusted the position of the stool. The house lights dimmed. Then there was a polite burst of clapping as an elderly frock-coated gentleman of immense distinction led on the artist, who was in white and seemed to Isabel to be unbelievably calm and cheerful, as she bowed to the audience. The distinguished gentleman disappeared, his work over, and the pianist sat down and began the recital. Isabel

98

promptly lost all the nervousness she had felt on her behalf and listened very critically. It was a mixed programme, designed to show off the pianist's good points and conceal the bad ones, some inevitable Chopin – it was his centenary year – Debussy – no recital was complete without Debussy – and Schumann. It was all quite well received, and the pianist produced a fine singing tone, but Isabel felt convinced that the standard was no better than her own. She clapped enthusiastically at the end of the first part. Miss Conti returned to take several bows. Then decorous chatting broke out as the lights brightened. Isabel glanced sideways down the length of their row, and at once turned angrily to Sarah.

"What are they doing here?" she whispered.

"Who?"

"You know who. Those two. When you went back to the house you gave them your tickets! I thought you were looking funny."

"Well, they happened just to come down the stairs as I – well, I thought it was mean, since we had too many – and I just said, to give them to anyone – "

"But why didn't you tell me?"

"I knew you'd make a fuss, just like you are at this very moment. Besides, I didn't know they'd come."

Isabel was extremely annoyed, not least because she knew herself to be pleased and excited by the presence of the men. For the second time her sister had brought off something quicker than she had, the tickets and now this. It was slightly disturbing to the dignity owed to her seniority. She did not like to admit that Sarah was better at dealing with people, but it seemed rather obvious – and with it she was so irresponsible. If it were true that she had told them to give the tickets to anyone, heaven knew who might have turned up. She sat smouldering and only just heard Sarah whispering, quite unconcerned, "Do you think Mr. Durrell is looking for you?" Then she noticed the teacher standing up with his face to the audience. She wondered if she ought to bow to him, but he was waving at somebody else. At that slightly humiliating moment Sarah received a slip of paper from the attendant. She uttered a little gasp and passed it to Isabel, who read,

"Will you have tea with us afterwards? Thanks awfully for our seats. J. Sadler. G. Haines."

"Look, they're looking at us!" Sarah whispered excitedly. "It would be all right, wouldn't it? Oh, no, we can't, of course, because we're going round to Miss Conti."

"Well, we can't do that now," Isabel said at once. She did not know what forced her to this decision. She had been looking forward tremendously to the back-stage visit.

"Why not?"

"Because we can't. If you – if you insist on bringing those two here, we're naturally obliged to –"

"But I told you, I didn't even know they'd come!"

"All the same we'll at least have to go back with them."

"Well, perhaps we can do both, they'll wait for certain –"

"No, it's impossible," said Isabel firmly, and having been annoyed with her sister, she was now far more annoyed with herself. She hadn't meant a word she said, and yet she had been impelled to say it. She added, for Sarah was busy shrugging her shoulders expressively towards the end of the row, "Do sit back, for goodness' sake. There go the lights down again."

The second half of the recital was Bach, Dohnanyi and Rubinstein. The sisters sat flushed and irritated through most of it. At the end the applause was quite heavy, Miss Conti was presented with two bouquets and the audience began searching for gloves, programmes and parcels. One had to follow the general progress to the aisles.

"Miss Rowland" – Sadler and Haines were intercepting them, having taken a short cut down the row behind, which had emptied more rapidly. The sisters paused. It was in fact a momentous occasion, for nothing like this had happened before in their lives. Mr. Sadler, of course, was the one who did the talking. "Did you get our note?"

"Yes, thank you."

"Well, and are we to be honoured? It was a jolly good recital but we both thought you'd have been better, didn't we, Haines?"

"Knock spots off her," Mr. Haines agreed.

Isabel was not pleased by these remarks, though she agreed

with them, because she was not sure that they were serious.

"You can walk with us," she began, "but I don't think we can have tea —"

"I think someone wants you," Mr. Haines said.

Over the heads of the crowd Isabel saw Mr. Durrell beckoning to her.

"I don't think he can mean me," she said hesitantly.

"Yes, of course he does! " Sarah exclaimed. "Go on down to him, hurry! " She went on to the young men, "That's her teacher. He's very famous, I expect he wants us to go behind. Actually we were —" Isabel decided to go, hoping that Sarah was right and that she would be forced to do what she had wanted to do all the time.

This was exactly how it worked out. Mr. Durrell greeted her warmly and invited her to go round to meet the artist.

"Oh, thank you very much, Mr. Durrell," said Isabel, already being propelled along by the force of his hand under her elbow. She tried to glance back, but there was no time, Mr. Durrell maintained the pressure of his hand and they hurried together through the door at the side of the stage, along a passage, up three stairs into an ante-room full of people, all of them at first sight very grown up and very impressive and all talking loudly in superlatives. Miss Conti was in the middle of it, looking smaller and less powerful than she had on the platform, with a fixed smile on her mouth. As soon as she saw Mr. Durrell she pushed towards him, still with the fixed smile, but her eyes bright with anxiety. Isabel felt her elbow released and she strained to overhear.

"Oh, how was it, how was it? " Miss Conti murmured desperately.

"My dear, splendid," Mr. Durrell murmured back.

"Do you mean it? Oh, my God. My fingers were like putty. Was it really all right? "

"It was splendid and I'm proud of you." Their voices had been pitched so low that only Isabel heard them and she felt thrilled. It was equally fascinating that Mr. Durrell went on loudly and gaily, as if these were the first words he had spoken, "It was an enchanting afternoon. A real success. A

real musicianly performance," and Miss Conti laughed,
"Dear, dear professor! If you say it was musicianly, I'm
content!" She drew him across the room, talking in an
excited manner, though treating him with great deference.
Isabel was left in a corner by herself, watching and listening.
As her nervousness died down she saw that about twenty
people were present, and that they could be divided between
those who were there professionally or because they were
somehow distinguished, and those who were there because
they knew or were related to Miss Conti. It was like a wedding where one of the partners was going from one world to
another, and for an hour the two worlds mixed uneasily.
Unfortunately she couldn't make out very much of what anyone was saying, but the general effect was wonderful. Well-
known names were dropped in a familiar way that thrilled
and entranced her. She learnt that one spoke of other people
as if one were full of affection for them. One did not
apparently say "Busoni" but "dear Busoni", not "Henry
Wood" but "dear Henry Wood".

Suddenly a plump man, perhaps in his late twenties, with
a grey waistcoat and pearl buttons, was beside her and about
to speak. Her nervousness returned.

"I saw you come in with dear Clement Durrell. Are you
a pupil of his?"

Isabel nodded, overwhelmed by his enormously grand and
affected accent.

"I thought perhaps you were. I think he's wonderful, don't
you? In my opinion he's better than Leschetizsky."

"I've never heard of him, I'm afraid," Isabel said rapidly.
She felt quite out of her depth and could hardly hear herself.
The plump man looked surprised and at once burst out
laughing.

"Bless you for that," he said, as if she had been extremely
witty. "Did you enjoy the afternoon? But of course. Such
tone, such assurance – I felt it most invigorating. Do you
know Dorina?"

Isabel shook her head.

"Such a relief when so many people are setting out to be
virtuosos without a virtuoso technique to hear someone, who,

102

to put it bluntly, knows her job, don't you agree? Not that I consider her well advised to dabble with Chopin. She is not a Chopinspierlerin in my opinion. After all, how can a mere woman understand the feminine approach? There should be a law passed against women – who is that rather enchanting little creature in the doorway?"

Isabel turned her head and saw Sarah looking shyly at the crowd.

"That's my sister," she said briefly.

"But how charming, and is she under the professor as well?"

Before Isabel could reply, Miss Conti noticed Sarah and burst out, "Why, it's my mascot! So you came! How sweet of you!" She hurried across, full of excitement at being the centre of attraction, and took Sarah by the hand. "Did you like it?"

"Oh, it was wonderful!" cried Sarah, with such enthusiasm that at least half a dozen people stopped talking to look at her. She blushed and put her free hand to her mouth. Miss Conti laughed and pulled her to Mr. Durrell.

"This is she I told you about, professor, waiting outside the studio – "

"Oh, I thought it was that one," said Mr. Durrell, with a nod to Isabel, who found Sarah's display mortifying.

"That's my sister," Sarah exclaimed to Miss Conti. "She plays, I don't. I can only listen."

"Dear child – " began Mr. Durrell, but there was at once a competition between him, Miss Conti and one or two others to remark gaily that less players and more listeners were just what was wanted. Then Mr. Durrell beckoned to Isabel. "Here is a player," he said benevolently, and Miss Conti shook her hand, smiling. Isabel tried to think of something well-mannered and complimentary – she had heard the most extravagant praise being thrown about, and realized that it was the thing to do – but she was too nervous to say anything. It did not matter, for Miss Conti was already busy saying good-bye to people and offering gratitude as extravagant as the praise she had received.

"Are they still there?" Isabel whispered to Sarah.

"They're waiting outside. Or they said they would."

"We'd better go, then, if we can." And it was easier to go than she expected. Miss Conti smiled at them vaguely, busy with other people – "I'm going on a tour of eighteen towns," Isabel heard a woman say to her – and Mr. Durrell was talking to an elderly man whom she gathered was a critic. She did not want to leave, but it was better not to outstay one's welcome.

They hurried through the auditorium, empty except for some cleaners, and she was suddenly conscious as they reached the foyer that the plump man who had spoken to her was close behind them. She did not know why, but she felt a sensation of fear. She was very glad that Sarah was with her. She was certain that he was following them, and that he was going to speak. She almost pushed Sarah forward and she was quite limp with relief at seeing Mr. Sadler and Mr. Haines waiting patiently on the pavement outside.

"Well, here we are!" she said breathlessly. "I'm afraid we were a terribly long time –" She could not help turning her head to look as the plump man came out behind. He stared at her, a curious little smile on his lips, and then went straight on down towards Piccadilly. Her heart thumped madly – she *knew* he had been going to speak to her. She heard Mr. Sadler saying it had been a pleasure to wait. She turned back to him gratefully, and the odd thing was that at once she saw that he and Mr. Haines were nothing but two students, amazingly unimportant, and all the more comforting for that. Calming down, she found herself able to smile. "I think we ought to go right back; Mrs. Slocombe will be expecting us and I've got my practice to do."

"After we've waited all this time?"

"We could have a very quick cup somewhere," put in Sarah, who was anxious to miss nothing.

Isabel glanced down towards Piccadilly, but the stick, the velvet-collared coat were out of sight. She at once began to feel regret.

"Well, all right, but we must hurry," she said, and to herself she added, "It would have been different if Sarah weren't with me."

They walked up Bond Street to Oxford Street, the girls leading and the men behind. A stop to look at a shop front – oil-
paintings – changed their positions. Mr. Sadler was now beside
her and Sarah behind with Mr. Haines. Sarah, who had been
oddly silent, was now talking volubly. Mr. Sadler asked if
there had been anyone interesting behind the scenes. He had
clearly been impressed by this incident. He said he supposed
that she would be giving a recital like that. Isabel replied that
she intended to be satisfied that she had a virtuoso technique
before setting up as a virtuoso, and was astounded by her
own brilliance. She asked him about himself. He was a law
student.

He intended in due course to codify English Law, to do
for Great Britain what Napoleon had done for France. Isabel
was astounded to find that he was brilliant, too. His father
was a rector in the Midlands somewhere, which gave him
social status in her eyes. He told her that clergymen's sons
were usually dissolute, which struck her as daring. By the
time they had sat down in the tea-room in New Oxford
Street, which Mr. Sadler had chosen with an eye to economy,
they were discussing Halley's Comet. How small they were,
how big was the universe, was the theme which developed,
while Isabel wondered if a concert pianist could be married
successfully to a lawyer.

Then they returned to the boarding-house, and had a second
tea with Mrs. Slocombe, who had barely recovered from her
afternoon's sleep and was not at all concerned that they were
late.

CHAPTER THIRTEEN

Three more days passed like lightning. They lay in bed
on the Sunday morning, regretfully considering the
journey home. They might have arrived yesterday,
things had gone so quickly. They might have arrived last
year, there seemed so much they had done. Three concerts,

one theatre, four lessons, five museums, a view of a suffra-
gette procession, several trips in the Underground and un-
limited window-shopping from Oxford Street to Kensington.
All this and Mr. Sadler as well. Isabel raised her knees and
stared at the ceiling. She was in love. The meaning of the
stupendous phrase had at last become clear to her. It meant
that when Mr. Sadler said "Miss Rowland", one could almost
faint with pleasure; and it meant that if one had an excuse
to leave the sitting-room when one thought he was in the
guests' lounge—he had twice accompanied her to the post
box in the square, unknown to Mrs. Slocombe—one could
hardly breathe for excitement. And if he were not there, one
felt a disappointment as sharp as toothache. There was that
to think about on the one hand, and what was so marvellous
about it was that he did not let admiration for her playing
prevent him from treating her as a normal being—with him
she seemed to be in the charmed circle where Sarah spent
her life. On the other hand there was Mr. Durrell—but she
now thought of him as "dear Clement Durrell", just as she
was now returning to "dear Eileen Treddye"—who had said
good-bye to her yesterday holding both her hands in a tight
way that slightly embarrassed her. He had told her in his
queer rasping voice, "Well, my dear, see that you don't waste
the time between now and when you come up again. Look
after your talent. Work hard at German, French and maths,
they're all useful. It's really most useful to be educated.
Remember that you cannot be a pianist unless you are also
a musician. Remember that the music you help to make is
more important than you. Remember that you will never be
appreciated in the way that you ought to be appreciated.
Remember that no talent is worth a bean without humility
and practice, practice, practice, whether it's summer or
winter, whether you're happy or miserable. And remember
that it's more difficult to shine at sixty than sixteen, for
no matter how well you begin, everyone else is catching
up with you all the time. Keep your left wrist higher.
Good luck." It occurred to her that Mr. Durrell might have
made this little speech with only slight variations to others,
but she was still inspired by it. Mr. Durrell had been care-

ful with his praise. But he had left no doubt that he thought she could have all the success she dreamed of – although music itself, of course, was the important thing, she reflected hastily. She clasped her knees and sighed. Apart from looking forward quite a little to playing Debussy in an improved way to Nicky, and also, perhaps, to Miss Treddye, she felt no desire to go home. Apparently, to judge from the sighs and murmurs that came from the divan bed alongside the opposite wall, Sarah was also depressed at the idea.

"I suppose we'll have to get up."

"Train doesn't go till eleven," Isabel said, yawning.

"Yes, but we've got to have breakfast and pack everything. School again next week. Isn't it horrible? I almost hope we have an essay on how I spent my holidays. I shall write reams and reams. Oh, isn't it wonderful just lying here! No one dragging us to church. No one calling out to get up – though we must get up, really, Isabel."

"Well, I'm not stopping you."

"I will get up," Sarah said firmly, but without stirring. "There may be people about to say good-bye to. George Haines and everybody. Don't you feel we've been here for months? I think it's agony going home – just think, it was only Tuesday – "

"Thank goodness I shall be coming back fairly soon."

"The only thing is there's no tennis here. I think I should die, really, without tennis, now I come to think of it."

An hour later they had a gloomy breakfast with Mrs. Slocombe, who had decided to reassume her grand manner for the last morning. The landlady had been chatty and down to earth – only yesterday she had given them some fascinating details of life with Mr. Slocombe – but now she seemed rather on edge as if she were worried that she had been too free and the girls might not take back quite the right sort of report to Mrs. Rowland. She sat very upright and made prim conversation, and extended her little finger when she held her coffee cup.

"More bread and butter, Isabel?"

"Thank you, Mrs. Slocombe."

"I expect your dear mother will be looking forward to seeing you."

"Yes."

"You will give her my very best regards."

The sisters kept their eyes down, very conscious of the change in mood. Isabel was almost glad of it, for she was in a state of anxiety. She had not seen Mr. Sadler since the day before at lunch-time – he had gone somewhere to play football, an activity that rather surprised her – and she hoped passionately to see him before leaving.

After breakfast they finished their packing, while Mrs. Slocombe left them to prepare herself for the taxi ride to the station. There was almost no sound from the rest of the house. Some of the guests were away for the day and had gone off early, the rest were evidently still lazing in bed. The sisters' gloom increased. Now and then one or the other made a purposeless journey to the first landing, the one journey they were permitted – there could be no excuse for going to the post box this morning – but there was never anyone about. The two suitcases were locked and placed by the door, looking extremely melancholy.

"Why don't you play?" Sarah suggested hopelessly. She did not add, "Perhaps that will make them come," but she meant it. Isabel understood, and shook her head.

"I don't feel like it," she said, and at once she remembered uncomfortably that Mr. Durrell had said this was a phrase used only by amateurs.

"Why not go in the lounge and use the grand? After all, no one's about and it's the last morning; Mrs. Slocombe can't say anything now. Anyway it doesn't matter if she does."

Isabel was about to get on her dignity and to refuse, but the memory of Mr. Durrell's remark bore on her. She moved towards the sitting-room piano, then reflected that if she were going to play at all she might just as well play in the lounge.

"Well, if you insist," she said.

The lounge was empty. It was also untidy and filled with stale air from the night before. Someone had drawn the curtains, but nothing else had been done. Isabel opened the piano

108

and began to practise trills, then some scales and arpeggios, while Sarah walked restlessly about the room, now and then glancing out into the hall and upstairs. After twenty minutes she played her Debussy piece. The house remained silent. Occasionally there was the echo of a servant's voice from the basement, but that was all. Suddenly they heard the sound of several people rushing downstairs. Isabel's heart thumped. But the feet rushed past the door of the lounge, and no one even looked in. Isabel turned to Chopin. She told herself that the great thing about music – as Miss Treddye had told her first – was that you could forget any sort of suffering by immersing yourself in it. She hardly noticed Sarah leave. She did not see Mr. Sadler come in. She was trying to be pathetic with Chopin, but in fact was rather more conscious of her improving technique – and all at once she became aware of his presence. She glanced over her shoulder. There he was, sitting on the arm of a chair, looking as if he had got up rather hastily, with wet plastered-down hair and a shiny rawness about his skin – as if he had not yet settled into the day. She saw that he was young. She had not noticed it before. She went on playing in a glow of ecstasy. When the sound finally died away into the sad silence, after a second she burst out impulsively, " Did you win at football? "

" No, we lost. We generally do."

" Oh, I'm sorry."

" It doesn't matter."

" Well, we're going this morning," Isabel said. She remained at the piano. Her neck felt suddenly so stiff that she couldn't turn round.

" Miss Rowland – "

" Yes? "

" I hope you have enjoyed your stay here."

" Oh, yes, we have, thank you very much."

" It has been very pleasant to hear you play, Miss Rowland."

" Thank you," Isabel said in a voice that trembled. What had really stirred her more than anything was her discovery that he knew absolutely nothing about music. For some reason he was attracted to her for herself, and she couldn't get over it. "Will he kiss me?" she thought, full of excitement. She could hear Sarah laughing outside, probably with Mr. Haines or just as probably with someone else. The noise her sister made lessened her own tension. She ceased to be paralysed. She began to play a melody with her right hand, and went on playing it as she turned a quarter way round on the stool so that she could face him.

"I wish you were staying longer," he went on gracefully. He was very much at his ease, and she admired him for it. He was no doubt experienced. The thought inspired no pang of jealousy; she was much too pleased that for the moment he was interested in her. "What have you enjoyed most?"

"Talking to you" would have been the most nearly accurate answer, but she tried to look thoughtful and then said, "Oh, I suppose the concerts."

He nodded. Her right hand went on playing. And all at once, for no reason, the thought occurred to her, "This is perfectly idiotic, you must be mad." She saw that he was really very ordinary and that the idea of being thrilled because he spoke to her was quite absurd. What had she ever seen in him? She couldn't imagine.

"I want to ask you," he said, creasing his forehead. "Will you write to me, if I write to you?"

Isabel became tense again. She could not look at him and her hand froze over the keyboard. It was as if she were seized by an enormous bashfulness, when in fact she simply did not know how to say that he was ridiculous. She was furious that Sarah had, of course, handed out their address indiscriminately.

"I'll write, anyway," he said.

"I ought to go," Isabel replied hurriedly. She got up and began awkwardly to close the piano. In a second he was helping her, she felt his fingers brushed against her wrist, his breath against her cheek, a moist, momentary pressure to the side of her mouth. "He's kissed me," she thought in astonishment, which was all the greater because she had found the sensation agreeable. A chorus, like something from the ninth symphony, appeared to be sounding in her ears, mixed with the voice of Mrs. Slocombe who was coming downstairs.

He stood a little away, waiting for her reaction.

"There's still some soap under your ear," she said breathlessly.

Mrs. Slocombe passed by the outside door, talking busily to someone.

"I love you," Mr. Sadler whispered.

"Oh!" Isabel gasped. Her heart thumped wildly. She gave a nervous glance towards the door, and then startled him in his turn by flinging her arms round his neck and kissing him back. It seemed to her, in the circumstances, the right thing to do. The smell of his recently soaped skin was very pleasant. Then she exclaimed, "I simply must go – Mrs. Slocombe –"

"You'll write to me?"

"Yes."

She hurried across the room, leaving him to close the piano, out into the hall and along to the sitting-room. She was so excited that she could hardly see. "So that's what it's like!" she thought, marvelling. A whole new world had been revealed, delightful and insane, and one in which, above all, she had been a brilliant success.

Her absence had not been noticed. Mrs. Slocombe and Sarah were discussing the scarf which had been bought as a present for Mrs. Rowland, from the points of view of colour, material and price – everything had been gone into several times before, and now they went enthusiastically over it again.

"You can always depend on Peter's –"

"If only it's the right shade of violet –"

"Here's Isabel. I've telephoned for a cab, dear. It'll be here any minute. I'm just telling Sarah that your mother is bound to love the scarf –"

"Oh, I do hope it's all right." Sarah sighed.

Isabel went into the bedroom, pretending a last inspection, so that they should not notice her face. She held on to the bed-rail and breathed deeply.

When the cab came the mood of the party at once became sad. Both of them had a slight feeling of let-down, for nobody appeared to help them down with their cases to the cab, and owing to Mrs. Slocombe, and then to the windowless rear seat, they couldn't see if anyone was watching from the house. However, they were kept busy making polite conversation, for Mrs. Slocombe, dressed in regal garden-party style, leaning forward on her borzoi-headed umbrella, said again and again that she hoped they had enjoyed themselves, and the girls went on assuring her that they had and thanking her all the way to Paddington.

Once the train was moving, one might as well be home. It was all over. They stared gloomily out of the window. The train, which had crawled into London, seemed to be leaving it at indecent speed. Factories, warehouses, slums, neat little houses and dreary little gardens, all were touched by the metropolitan wand, as far as Isabel was concerned. She envied everyone she saw walking about.

Two ladies shared the compartment with them and occupied the opposite corner seats, next to the corridor. They chatted energetically.

"So I said to him, 'Thank you, I'm not exactly a busker,' I said to him."

"My dear, it was the same with me in Leeds—"

"He gave me a look that was supposed to be devastating and the next thing was Mr. Ferris came up and apologized."

"I was with *Lady Madcap*—"

"But I wasn't going to be got over with apologies. 'I'm in the quartette or I'm not,' I said. 'Let's have it straight out,' I said."

"I had three lines and I never missed getting a laugh, not even on a Monday, and that was quite enough to annoy—"

Isabel glanced at Sarah, who was already beginning to listen avidly. Soon it was clear that they were travelling with two actresses, and also that the rest of a touring company was spread over the next few compartments. London was forgotten. They both made several journeys to the W.C. in order to have a good look. The women were disappointingly dull, and many were asleep; the men seemed rather fat. Some were playing cards. On one trip along the corridor Sarah spied a label on which was printed "Mr. Everard Jackson's famous production – *The Girl from New Orleans* – Number One Company". She hurried back to get out her autograph book.

"Excuse me, but are you in the *Girl from New Orleans*?" she asked the two in the compartment.

"Yes, we are, my dear."

"Oh, how wonderful! Will you please sign my book?"

"Of course!"

"Are you going to be at the Royal?" asked Isabel, mentioning the town's principal theatre.

"All this week."

"Oh, I hope we can go!" Sarah cried. "Mother and father often go, if there's anything worth – I mean, they often go –"

The two actresses were far from displeased by this enthusiasm, and at once began talking gaily to the girls. They sent them to get all the autographs in the next compartments, and then on a trip to a first-class carriage, where the leading lady was travelling in state. The latter was a well-known musical comedy actress. Their appearance was regarded as a good omen by all. The leading lady gave them a signed autograph each, but not, as Sarah hoped, an offer of free seats. When they returned to the compartment the two actresses wanted to know what the leading lady had said, and then told scandalous stories about her to each other. Next, two of the men came in from next door and there was more theatre gossip. The girls could hardly eat their sandwiches for listening. The dullness they had first noted had entirely disappeared. When these people spoke, there was style, abandon, enormous confidence – they had had triumphs everywhere, apparently. For the moment it seemed to the girls that there could be no more amusing or exciting life than to move about with a musical comedy from town to town. The journey passed at amazing speed. Outside, the country looked lovely, summer was on the way. They were astonished when they passed Landen's Mill.

"Look, that's our home! That's where we live!"

"Is it really, dears?"

"Well, you can't see the house –"

"Who wouldn't live in the country?" said one of the actresses.

"Do you know we didn't even *look* when we were going the other way?" Sarah said to Isabel, then sighed, "Oh, everything looks wonderful, I'm *glad* to be back."

Twenty minutes later at Peter Street, the town station, they looked out excitedly for Mrs. Rowland. There was no immediate sign of her. They had to get out with the company, which was gathering together on the platform from different parts of the train.

The girls said good-bye to everyone they had met.

"Good-bye, dears! Come and see us!"

"We will if we can!"

"Good-bye! Bless you both!"

Then they were by themselves, and there was still no sign of Mrs. Rowland.

"She said she'd be here," Sarah complained, disappointed.

"She said 'at the station' on the postcard. P'r'aps she meant Landen's Mill."

"I wish I could sing, I'd go on the stage," Sarah said.

Isabel nudged her suddenly.

"Look – there's Aunt Ada!"

"And Aunty Phyllis!" her sister exclaimed.

Mrs. Mather and Miss Truscott were coming towards them, an unexpected welcoming party.

CHAPTER FOURTEEN

The sisters greeted them politely rather than warmly. They were quite fond of Aunty Phyllis, but Aunt Ada remained beyond the pale, as far as any impulsive display of affection was concerned. They were kissed, however, more forcefully than usual. Isabel was at once conscious that there was something strained about the two women.

"Where's mother?"

"She's at home, dear," Mrs. Mather said, looking intently

over her head. "She asked us to come to meet you, she's not feeling very well. Have you had a nice time?"

"Simply wonderful," Sarah said. "We've heaps of messages for you, Aunty Phyllis, haven't we, Isabel? And who do you think we came down with—"

Isabel noticed that Miss Truscott was terribly pale. A feeling of uneasiness came over her as Sarah chatted away. Then she realized that things were moving according to a drill arranged beforehand. She found herself going ahead with Miss Truscott with the other two trailing some way behind.

"Aren't we catching the local?"

"Well, we thought you'd like to have a cup of tea at Aunt Ada's first—" Miss Truscott's voice trembled. "But let's sit down here for a moment. I've something to tell you."

Behind, she saw that Sarah and Mrs. Mather were also sitting down. The long platform was already empty except for two or three porters. Evidently what had to be told could not wait. She put down her suitcase and sat, staring at the motionless carriages of the train they had just left. She was frightened.

Miss Truscott sat beside her and took her hand.

"Isabel, dearest, you need all your courage. You must believe that God—"

"Is it Nicky?"

"It's your father," Miss Truscott said.

"Father?"

Miss Truscott's grip became vice-like. Then her halting, reluctant voice went on and on. There had been a dreadful accident, she explained. Isabel listened fairly calmly, for she could not associate the possibility of real disaster with her father. She heard that he and Nicholas had taken the boat out. Her father had decided to have a swim and probably because the water was so cold, he had an attack of cramp. He went under. The tide was going out, which didn't help. Nicholas tried desperately to reach him with the boat, and then went in the water himself, but it was no use. A sailing dinghy had fortunately come along and picked him up or he would have gone, too. As it was he had been taken to hospital suffering from shock and exposure.

115

Miss Truscott came to the end of her appalling news and waited tensely. But when Isabel spoke, it was in a queerly matter-of-fact tone.

"When was it?" she asked. She understood what had happened, but could not connect it.

"This morning, just before lunch."

"While we were on the train?" Isabel said, as if this had importance.

"Yes, I suppose so, dear."

"And Nicky's all right? It was awfully dangerous for him to go in the water."

Miss Truscott was taken aback by her calm. She said almost brusquely, "Yes, he's still at the hospital, but they say he's all right."

Isabel nodded. Suddenly she jerked her head.

"You mean, father's dead?" Her voice rose.

Miss Truscott looked relieved.

"Dearest –"

"Oh, no," Isabel said, and she began to shake all over. "Oh, no!"

Further down the platform Mrs. Mather was trying to comfort an hysterically weeping Sarah.

CHAPTER FIFTEEN

In the next few dreadful days it was Mrs. Mather who saved them, pulled them together, got the wheels turning. Mrs. Mather, triumphant in shiny black, pullulating in every corner of the house, interrupting, interfering, poking her nose in, prying or, as she herself constantly put it, "helping poor Bessie and those poor children". And as she went about this business there was let loose from her usually pursed lips a flood of phrases, such as "It only shows one never knows what will come next" and "They mustn't be allowed to sit about" and "A nice walk will do you good", designed for comfort and effective in stirring up intense

116

exasperation. She slept in the house for the first two nights and then came daily. One morning, just after her arrival, Isabel murmured, "I can hear that disgusting great bosom downstairs." Sarah at once went into a fit of giggles, cut short abruptly as she realized with horror what she was doing. But it was done. A note of gaiety had returned. In their growing detestation of Mrs. Mather the Rowlands found strength for survival.

The funeral took place, and they were amazed at the number of people who came, for the most part quite unknown faces. They were not overcome by the slightly dreaded ceremony. "The mater's taking it very well," Denny said, with some pride; and it was true, for Mrs. Rowland was in full control of herself and immensely dignified, rising to all that was demanded of her. Her children were also inspired by the fact of being the general centre of attraction. Conscious of sympathy all around they were not compelled to demonstrate how they were or should be feeling. Denny, in particular, felt that he was being admired for his manly restraint. Afterwards they stood beside their mother as people came up and murmured awkward words of tribute. There was something odd to Denny and the girls about some of those words. That Charles Rowland had been highly esteemed, respected and so on was not of course remarkable. But that he had had a reputation for cheerfulness, that, above all, there were people who had thought him high-spirited was scarcely credible. It was as if they must be making a mistake and had come to the wrong funeral. "He was always so full of life, he was such good company." "It'll be a duller world without him." "I never knew a man more generous." It had never occurred to them that their father had been a person. Now, at his funeral, he appeared to them for the first time as an ordinary human being, and one moreover whom they could hardly recognize. It helped them to preserve their calm, but added a touch of resentment. If they had only known one aspect of Charles Rowland, how big an aspect had it been? They were jealous of all the people who had known the other aspects, and felt themselves to have been slightly betrayed by their father. At the same time, of course, it was gratifying to know what an impression he had left.

When they were in the carriage on the way back, Denny said quite enthusiastically, "I say, I never thought so many people would come. Quite a compliment for the pater, what? Funny to hear people talking about him." He felt a nudge on his ankle from Sarah and saw her glancing at his mother. What he had said seemed at once horribly out of place and he waited in dread for her to break down.

Instead she spoke in the preoccupied tone she used when making arrangements for a party or a picnic.

"I don't know how those men are going to be paid. I haven't the money and your father would never let me know anything. I only hope Mr. Webber can fix something up. It really worries me; men can't wait for their wages, after all."

They were all slightly surprised, for, although it was a relief not to have a scene in the carriage, there was such a thing as carrying calmness too far. A few dignified tears would not have been amiss.

Denny looked gloomily through a space in the window not covered by blinds. "It's a pity he didn't let me in on things a bit," he murmured. "I needn't have been so useless." He was protesting now at his mother's lack of confidence in him. She had gone straight to Mr. Webber, the solicitor, without a word, had conferred with Aunt Ada behind closed doors. After all, he was the oldest surviving male, and no longer a child – next term would be his last at Fritham and he was a prefect. He felt himself to be the head of the family; but it had not occurred to anyone to treat him as such. He was still merely the charming boy, a state which normally he had found agreeable.

"Well, there it is," Mrs. Rowland said. "I wish I knew how they were all going to get paid."

"That's just what I mean. I mean, if I knew something about it, I could go over to the mill and –" He stared helplessly at Sarah, who was all at once shaking and panting, convulsed with sobs. "Oh, look, old thing, bear up for goodness' sake, or we'll all start –"

"You don't care!" she wept. "None of you care, it's – disgusting – you all just talk –"

118

This was where his mother should take over and she did nothing, but went on sitting there, motionless, apparently lost in her worry about the wages. Isabel was pale and aloof. But, no, he saw a tear trickling down her cheek and felt a lump starting in his throat. "I shall go away," he thought, exasperated. "I can't stand it here. I'll go to Canada or somewhere." He went on staring resolutely out and Sarah's fit of sobbing slowed down to a series of painful gasps. Then there was silence which at once became unendurable.

At home they were surrounded by Aunt Ada and the Mathers. Sarah disappeared and returned, having washed her face. The Rowlands, once again on their dignity, handed round port and lemonade and cake, and whisky for Mr. Mather. The Mather children hardly seemed aware of the nature of the occasion, for whereas in the past they had always been silent and embarrassed when they came to call, now they were chatting confidently, and Mr. Mather himself could not help standing in a proprietary way in front of the mantelpiece. They were no longer the underdogs and it was impossible to hide their satisfaction. Only poor Miss Truscott behaved as if she were a mourner. Denny resented them all furiously. The Mather girls were more awful than ever. Their brothers he found unspeakable. His mother's voice was raised now and then, nervously wondering about the mill's pay-day problem and he wished to goodness she would keep private affairs to herself. He was glad to see that his sisters, at any rate, kept themselves as apart as possible from their relations.

However, when the Mathers were going and Mrs. Rowland had firmly refused Aunt Ada's offer to stay for the rest of the day — "Bessie, you know that if there's *anything* I can do, or any of us —"— the Rowlands found themselves suddenly reluctant to be left alone. After the guests had all trooped off across the lawn towards the short cut to the station, the house became oppressive. Lunch was served by Edith, a fresh, plump, emotional girl who, bumping against Mr. Rowland's empty chair, made a sound in her throat which was either a suppressed sob or a giggle. She spoke, when necessary, in a hurried whisper. The family ate lamb chops and prunes in silence.

After lunch Mrs. Rowlands said she would go into town to visit Nicholas.

"Can't we go, too?"

"I don't think so, Sarah dear. It might upset him if – it's so difficult to know what's best. He's probably asleep anyway, they're making him sleep as much as possible. Then I want to see Mr. Webber again to make sure about the pay."

"I think we ought to go," Isabel said.

"Very well, dear," Mrs. Rowland said, giving up.

Denny said that he had work to do. The others walked to the station and caught a train into town. As they passed by the mill they heard its engine throbbing, and smoke was coming out of the chimney. The garage door was open and they had a glimpse of the car, gleaming as if its owner might possibly appear at any moment.

They found Nicholas awake in his white cubicle. He was pale and his eyes had their curious smouldering look. But he sounded cheerful.

"You're all in black," he noted, when they had settled down alongside. "Will I wear black, too?"

"Oh, no, I don't think so, dear."

"Is Denny in black?"

"Yes, he is," Mrs. Rowland said, delving into her reticule. Her tone was determinedly cheerful. "Look, Nicky dear, here are your crayons you wanted, and *Chums* and the *Boys' Own Paper*. It's the new one."

"Aren't I going home, then?"

"Very soon, dear, but not to-day."

"Oh." Nicholas turned his gaze to the ceiling. "Is father in hell?"

"My dear child!" exclaimed Mrs. Rowland, momentarily shocked into a normal voice. "How can you say such a thing?"

"He was swearing. I heard him. Damn and bloody and other things. When he was in the water." He looked at her suddenly in despair. "I *heard* him."

Mrs. Rowland felt an equal despair.

"My darling, of course he isn't in hell, only bad men –

well, good men like father go to heaven – look, you're making mother cry. Isn't that silly? "

"Is he buried? "

She nodded helplessly. Nicholas turned his face into the pillow. He began to sob.

"You girls go home," Mrs. Rowland whispered hoarsely as she bent over him.

They hurried out, handkerchiefs to their faces, and met the Sister coming furiously towards them.

"Look at you. I shouldn't have allowed – be off with you! "

Outside, Sarah was angry.

"There was no need to speak like that. How would she like it if – "

"Oh, nobody likes it," Isabel said, taking her arm. She felt torn apart by her brother's misery.

"How did he know it was the funeral anyway? He was so calm yesterday, just lying there – and if he was thinking *that* all the time, it's just too terrible, Isabel. Do let's hurry away from here – I *hate* hospitals, they're so cruel and foul – everything that's beastly – "

"It's awful to think he was swearing," Isabel said.

"He may have imagined it."

"No, it made it so real and horrible – "

As they walked towards the Promenade they began slowly to feel better. It was a fine afternoon and the sea air tasted pleasantly, as if insisting, "You see? This hasn't changed." When a funeral passed them they noticed it with a certain expertness.

"Faster than ours."

"One less carriage."

They reached the Promenade. They sat down on a bench and stared sadly out at the sea.

"It's awful that we're alive," Sarah said.

"Yes."

"Look, there's Grace Banks – who's she with? Oh, it's Sybil." Two girls of about their own age approached, laughing and talking twenty to the dozen. They were in Sarah's class at school, and she was wide awake with interest.

"Fancy, I didn't know *they* were friends. What shall we say, Isabel?"

"Oh, say nothing. It's our affair."

But the girls had evidently seen them, for their laughter died and they quickened their pace, and changed direction so that they passed further away, as if without noticing them.

In the distance the sound of laughter rose again, the heads could be seen bobbing once more.

"They saw us all right," Sarah said furiously. "I hate them."

"They probably thought they were being kind," Isabel said, but not with conviction. She was equally put out.

"Not them."

They watched a destroyer for a few minutes, chopping its way out of the harbour. Everything was going on as usual, people were out with children, dogs sniffed at each other, and an attendant was purposefully arranging chairs round the bandstand. The *Marche Militaire* would begin the four o'clock concert given by the Marines.

"Really it's almost warm enough for tennis," Sarah murmured with a sigh, her indignation having faded.

Isabel was stepping on to the platform at her first London recital – a day-dream which was intermittently with her. She broke it off with a feeling of guilt, and nodded.

"Let's go to a church," she said after a moment. It was an impulse caused by her shame.

Two young sailors strolled by, eyeing them, before Sarah could answer. The girls stared haughtily ahead. The sailors paused, considered an approach, decided against it and went on.

"What cheek!" Sarah said, with some colour in her cheeks. "*Sailors*. Church? Do you mean – to pray? Surely this morning –"

"Yes, but it's awful to have all that this morning and nothing else!" Isabel cried impatiently. "There's his soul and we don't know – well, also he may be watching *us*, and how would you like it if –"

The air was full of words she could not say and thoughts she did not know how to think. Also the tiny incident of the sailors had brought the face of Mr. Sadler to her mind – he had not yet written – and her shame increased.

Sarah agreed reluctantly, not wanting to seem less eager. They got up and began walking again.

"Which one shall we go to?"

"It doesn't matter."

The first one they came to, however, was a Catholic Church. It was a large ugly building with a presbytery.

"We can't go in *there*," Sarah said with Protestant nervousness as Isabel pulled at her elbow.

"Why not? It's – it's consecrated." She marched determinedly towards the entrance, conscious that if this impulse were not obeyed as quickly as possible they might not go to a church at all. Also she had a vague idea that it might be helpful to her father to be supported from an unusual quarter.

Rather to their surprise, several people were kneeling in the pews or merely sitting. Fascinated and a little scared, they watched a woman who came in just after them touch the holy water and cross herself, then bow and cross herself as she came opposite the altar. The girls followed her hesitantly, but when Sarah was about to cross herself Isabel stopped her with a glance.

"Better not," she whispered.

Sarah shugged her shoulders. They found a pew and knelt. Isabel felt tears stinging her eyes and was glad that they came so easily. But the deliberate thought of her father was too agonizing, and the lump in her throat rose dreadfully. After a few moments the emotion died down and she began to find the atmosphere oppressive. She touched Sarah, who nodded.

Then as they hurried out, pretending not to hurry, they saw the same woman who had come in after them put money in a box and light a candle.

"Let's do that," Isabel whispered.

"All right," Sarah nodded. "How much have you got?"

Isabel looked in her purse, although this was not necessary.

"One and four," she answered truthfully. It was with a slight effort, for the sum was unusually large.

"I've only got sixpence."

Isabel said after a moment, "Well, we'll have a shilling

one." It was quite a considerable sacrifice, but as she put the coin in the box she reproached herself bitterly for the hesitation which preceded it. They lit their candle and watched it. She was conscious of a lifting of her heart. The oppressive feeling vanished. She pressed Sarah's hand. Something practical had been done. Sarah smiled at her.

Outside it was warmer than ever. They walked along briskly.

"You must have my sixpence," Sarah said.

"No, then you won't have anything." Having made the sacrifice, Isabel did not want it to be whittled down. However, she waited a little for Sarah to insist. But her sister was content to leave the matter as it was. Isabel was rather surprised, but she felt a glow of self-righteousness. She went on, "We'd better not say we went in there. Mother would have a fit, and as for Mr. Forbes—"

Mr. Forbes was their Rector. He had read the service that morning.

"Think if he'd happened to see us coming out!" Sarah exclaimed. She found the idea very amusing. "He'd have grown another double chin on the spot. Whatever would we have said? And he's so Low Church too—it's why mother likes him."

"We oughtn't to laugh," said Isabel, who also was laughing. "It's a pity in a way; I might not have had to play at his beastly concert party. Which reminds me, did you hear about Mr. Durrell's letter? I haven't liked to mention it, but he sent father a wonderful letter—isn't it awful he never saw it, that's the most awful thing, I think; I mean anything good that happens he won't see—unless—well, Mr. Durrell said he was tremendously impressed, I was already an accomplished artist—an accomplished artist."

"Well, we know that already."

Sarah, intending a compliment, had said the wrong thing. Isabel looked annoyed.

"That's what mother said, of course. I expect it from her, she just doesn't understand—good heavens, it's one thing to be accomplished round here—" She pronounced the "here" with deep contempt. "But when someone like Mr. *Durrell*

124

says it — don't you understand? It's different. It's London. What I wonder is, whether I oughtn't to go to the Academy right away, I mean the sooner I start earning money the better now. Perhaps the Academy is a waste of time, though Mr. Durrell is keen about it — but the quicker I give my first London recital — "

" You mean like the one we saw? "

"Of course, of course," Isabel went on in her irritated voice. But this was really to disguise her excitement. "There's no real reason why I shouldn't be doing it now. Why, some people have been performing all over the world at my age."

"You'll be famous," Sarah said, entering into the mood. " I know you will! How wonderful! "

"I shall be," Isabel nodded. " I *must* be. For father's sake."

"You'll be rich, too. I shall sit in a box with my husband and applaud like mad." Sarah gave her a sideways look. "Incidentally, have you heard from — ? "

"No." Isabel sounded indifferent. With so much sorrow about, the fact that Mr. Sadler had not written, as promised, was a very small thing. All the same, she was distinctly conscious of it.

"Nor have I," Sarah said, unnecessarily, for both knew that neither had had a letter from London. Under ordinary circumstances the matter would have been discussed daily. This was, however, the first time it had been mentioned. Their trip to London had seemed to have taken place years ago. Now, once again, it was only a matter of days.

"As a matter of fact, I wouldn't reply if he did," Isabel said. She couldn't get over the fact that Mr. Sadler had asked permission to write and had not done so. "Besides, I shall have no time for that sort of thing."

"You mean you won't ever marry? "

"The point is, music has to come first. No, marriage is unthinkable, unless it's someone like Schumann. That would be ideal. Do you know he injured his hands permanently by trying to make their spread bigger? Isn't that wonderful? "

Sarah nodded doubtfully, but Isabel was seeing herself fully in the part. She went on, "There's no reason why I shouldn't be a Clara Schumann. And if I could have a husband who could write a concerto that I would make famous, just as she did – but you see, he may not exist."

"It's a lovely, romantic idea – and I can see what you mean –" Sarah reflected. "Of course, my husband will be quite different. I think I'd like him to be famous, perhaps. Yes, why not? He'll be young – no, it doesn't matter about that – he will be wealthy – not too wealthy, you understand – but with lots of money. We shall give garden parties, and it'll be a tremendous thing to get an invitation. And then of course there'll be my enormously famous sister –"

"Yes, I shall be just back from a tour – in Russia –"

". . . who is just back from playing to the Tsar – and my husband asks me to try to persuade you to play for someone very important – Royalty incognito –"

". . . and I refuse, of course."

"To begin with, of course, but you let yourself be persuaded – you wouldn't be so mean not to – after all, I'm the hostess –"

Their voices had risen and they could be heard from yards away as they walked along.

CHAPTER SIXTEEN

"My dear Mrs. Rowland," Mr. Webber said, "please, I beg of you, don't concern yourself about these things." He was a sharp-faced man and his hearty, consoling voice, designed for the bereaved, had a slight edge to it, for this was the third visit Mrs. Rowland had paid him. If there was one thing Mr. Webber disliked it was to be hurried. "You don't have to worry about the mill at all. It's going on and will go on quite satisfactorily. We've got your bank account going, and as you know, you can draw up to five pounds a week, and that should see you through quite comfortably. Just what your position is going to be, I really can't tell you. These things must move at their own speed and there's nothing we poor lawyers can do to hurry them." If there was another thing Mr. Webber disliked it was the idea of letting go any property he happened to be responsible for. "Of course, I don't have to tell you that you're not going to be as well off as – as in the past. But just take things calmly."

"It's the children," Mrs. Rowland said. "I'm so worried about Denny – you know – my son – whether he'll still be able to do his articles."

"I'm sure he will," Mr. Webber said. "I don't suppose it will be easy, but as I've told you, until we have the full picture of your husband's affairs, we just don't know."

"His father was set on him qualifying as something," Mrs. Rowland said, expressing in fact what was her own ambition.

"Very sensible, too, Mrs. Rowland. There's nothing like having a profession, and you can't do better than accountancy. If I had a boy, that's where I'd put him. The law's dead, quite dead." Mr. Webber became gloomy as he appeared to think for a moment about his own income. "Of course," he went on, "there is one economy you could make – isn't he still at school?"

"Well, he has one more term at Fritham – then again, Mr. Webber, I'm so worried about the younger boy –"

"Yes, Mrs. Rowland, but as to the older boy, it seems to me that if his office were prepared to accept him right away – I take it he's matriculated?"

"Last year, yes, but the vacancy was for the autumn; I know Mr. Teape lunched with my husband –"

"Ensor, Teape and Wilcox, a good firm. I know them very well. Shall I talk to them? You might save a term's school fees, and the boy would be getting to work sooner."

"But the cost; I believe it was four hundred pounds –"

"Well, I expect the estate can just manage it, and no doubt there'll be some sort of arrangement, whereby you have, say, two hundred returned in the form of salary – well, I can talk to Teape about it, Mrs. Rowland, and if you agree, and if Teape is willing, I'll send in the notice to Fritham. Perhaps you'd better have a word with the boy first, but I've no doubt he'll jump at it. School is largely a waste of time. I remember I left it with the greatest pleasure."

"What about the girls? They're still at Miss Murray's."

"Oh, I should leave them there for the time being. It'll keep them out of your way at home," Mr. Webber said.

CHAPTER SEVENTEEN

"How dreary," Talbot said. "Things won't seem at all the same without your pale, pretty face."

Denny was paying his friend a visit which had been arranged at the end of the previous school term. It was a week after the funeral and they sat smoking cigarettes on the terrace behind Talbot's house.

"Dreary for me, too."

"Dreary for you, too," Talbot nodded.

"We seem to have no money," Denny said. "Or almost none. It's rather a bore."

"Consider it a challenge," Talbot said. "Learn how to make some as quickly as possible."

"It'll be four or five years before I get through my finals."

"A moment in the life of man, dear boy. Look here, I'm not wanted around this hole this evening, how about us going into town? We could have a drink at the Rotunda, it's not a bad hole though it's full of snotties – and we might go to the Empire. It'll cheer me up no end. Two prefects out on a spree, or rather one prefect and one ex-prefect. Do you know that my heart is absolutely broken about your not coming back?"

Denny was not at all sure that he should do anything like going to the Empire. But he knew Talbot was trying to cheer him up and it would be ungracious not to fall in. Besides the idea of going to the Rotunda was not unexciting. He had once been taken there to lunch by his father, but he had never been in its well-known bar. It was also unlikely that he would be seen by anyone he knew.

"All right," he said. "Good scheme." He couldn't help reflecting that only two weeks before it would have been right out of the question. He had been fond of his father, but he had been afraid of him. There could be no doubt that he was now a good deal more free than he had ever been.

"Let's have fifty up first. I hope you've brought some pennies."

They left the terrace and went to the billiard room. On the way, they met Mrs. Talbot, who spoke to Denny with embarrassed kindness, fearful of saying the wrong thing. Talbot pushed him on. They played for an hour. There was a table at home and he was quite a competent player. Talbot was brilliant but erratic, and Denny had no difficulty in picking up half a crown which, in view of the possible expenditure to come, was rather welcome. He used the lavatory next door. The towels were thick, the soap and toilet paper of a special quality, items that never failed to impress him greatly. These were the really solid signs of wealth, and helped to create an unpretentious, but enormously expensive atmosphere. As he dried his hands on the thick towel he reflected that if Mr. Talbot were to die it would all still go on, Talbot would still go to Oxford, they'd have as much money as ever. The fact that Talbot was rich had always filled him with admiration rather than anything else. But now, for a moment, he was shot through with envy. He wished he were going back to school so that the old relationship could continue. As it was, he sensed that it was over. Talbot was being polite and kind, bending over backwards to prove that nothing had changed, but in the lavatory Denny began the process of losing illusions. He could no longer think he belonged to that thickness of towel and that quality of toilet paper.

"You've been the hell of a time," Talbot said.

"Why not? It happens to be my favourite bog," Denny answered.

"I've just thought, there's an awfully nice little pub a couple of miles away – let's have a drink there instead of the Rotunda, shall we? Then we can get a train and go straight to the Empire."

"All right."

"I don't know why I suggested the Rotunda at all. All those bloody N.O.s get on my nerves."

Denny was a little disappointed, but a little relieved as

well, for the Empire meant no more than the price of a ticket; and the Rotunda bar might have turned out to be expensive – it would be horrifying if he found himself without enough.

They left the house without seeing either Mrs. or Mr. Talbot. Talbot's parents were always pleasantly remote, living lives of their own. They were not a constant presence on the scene as Mrs. Rowland was at the Mill House, or as Mr. Rowland had been, a shadow looming all the time whatever one was doing. It was something that went with the thick towels, and it was something Denny felt to be extremely attractive. It was an intolerable nuisance not to be wealthy, there was no getting away from it.

They walked cross-country for half an hour and Denny pretended to enjoy it. Talbot was energetic and talkative. When they got to the pub they drank bitter and Talbot was at once deep in conversation with three villagers. Denny pretended again to enjoy it. He admired the way Talbot got on with these sort of people, although he got on well with them himself. But he did it because he used his charm. He liked to be liked. Talbot, on the other hand, was absolutely indifferent to what anyone thought of him. He spoke to men twice his age like a nurse dealing with children. He was friendly and familiar. But Denny was aware that the complete absence of any tendency to put on airs was a sign of wonderful arrogance. It all went to show what a pleasant thing it was to have a couple of breweries behind you.

Another half-hour's walk and they caught a train into town. This was a journey of almost an hour. As the train stopped at Landen's Mill he had a strong feeling that he ought to get out and return to the dutiful gloom at home, but he remembered that he was free now; he wasn't a schoolboy any more, and Talbot was only trying to take his mind off the gloom. At Peter Street Talbot said, " Look here, it's still quite early, let's go and have one at the Rotunda first."

" All right," he said, as casually as he could, while he made a quick calculation. He had just about six shillings on him. In spite of the half-crown he had won at billiards he was not too well off.

Outside the station a newspaper seller called to them hopefully, "Naval appointments, sir?"

"What a damned insult!" Talbot said.

Denny laughed, "They always do that to flatter the townees." But he was flattered himself at being considered to look mature.

The gilt and plush Rotunda had two entrances. You went through one for the grill room and a downstairs bar to which ladies were not admitted and through the other for the long bar, which was well known for the fact that ladies were admitted. Talbot led the way first to the downstairs bar. It was a square, low-ceilinged room, full of smoke and the conversation of naval officers. The latter were not in uniform but in what they called plain clothes. However, they all wore such similar old jackets and flannels or faded tweeds, and wore them in such a similar way, elaborately untidy, that the plain clothes became another kind of uniform.

Talbot marched in his springy, confident manner to the counter and ordered two pink gins. Denny was not over enthusiastic about the taste, but he was impressed by the idea of drinking gin. Next to him two men greeted each other: "Hulloa, Gilbert, didn't know you were back!" "Hullo to you, my sprig o' fashion. Yes, I'm channel-groping again." "For your sins." "For my sins." Denny was impressed by this as well. He wished he were going to be something more exciting than an accountant.

"Have the other half?" he said, a few minutes later, after Talbot had tried unsuccessfully to talk to the barmaid.

"Yes, old man, but we'll go to the other bar, I think. This is too dreary. Reminiscences of the old *Britannia* on all sides; I can't stand it." Talbot did not lower his voice and the two men next to Denny rewarded him with a quick, extremely critical glance.

They went upstairs and through the grill room where a trio was playing a selection from *Madam Butterfly*. The headwaiter came up and Denny admired Talbot once again as he refused a table. Talbot gave the impression that for two pins he would sit down and order a magnum of champagne. It really was a nuisance to miss this last term with him.

The other bar was beyond the grill room and rather gayer than the one downstairs. All the same it was not very gay. Three or four women were talking to each other in one corner, none of them very attractive except for the faintly dramatic effect of their use of powder and rouge. Denny felt his heart thumping at the sight of them.

"Same again?" he grinned self-consciously at Talbot. He wished he had the latter's dark, faintly leonine look that made him seem so adult.

"Yes, all right – oh, good lord, there's someone I know!"

A young man who stood by himself at the bar had turned to inspect them. He wore an untidy old pepper and salt jacket and creaseless grey flannels, but he wore them with an air of great elegance.

"What the deuce is a little boy like you doing here?" he greeted Talbot. His manner was very friendly.

"Same as you, fighting boredom. Are you going to buy us a drink?"

"Not on your life. I shouldn't be able to look your dear mama in the face ever afterwards. Don't you know that you're in a haunt of vice?"

"This is Rowland, great friend of mine. Rowland, old son, this is George Nunn. He's in the Navy."

"Yus, the blooming hold Nye-vy," Mr. Nunn murmured, turning a smile of enormous charm on to Denny, who blushed.

"How do you do, sir," he said.

The lieutenant looked surprised and shook hands with him.

"Your friend has better manners than you, Edwin," he said to Talbot. "You know, I told your mother you ought to have been put in the Navy. You'd have been thrashed into decency by now. Lord, I'd like to have had you under me in the gun-room."

Talbot winked at Denny.

"There's been lots of interesting research work done about people with ideas like yours," he said.

"Damned impudent cub," said Mr. Nunn, smiling once more at Denny. His teeth were white and beautifully even. "Are you as idle as this abandoned wretch?"

132

"Not half!" Denny grinned, with all his own brand of charm.

"Actually, he's a very hard worker," Talbot said. "He's an accountant."

"Not yet!" Denny exclaimed, and at once felt extremely foolish and less charming.

"Well, he's going to be one. So far he has had the inestimable benefit of being educated with me."

"Poor chap," said Mr. Nunn.

"And he could beat you at snooker, George. Or at tennis."

"Oh, could he?" said Mr. Nunn, looking at Denny with full approval.

Denny blushed again and laughed, once more secure on his pedestal. He wondered if he ought to ask Mr. Nunn to have a drink, but he was too shy to ask. When the other two were busy talking he gave the order for two pink gins surreptitiously. Mr. Nunn had one already, anyway. The next moment he was quite shocked to hear Talbot tell the lieutenant casually – perhaps to explain his black armband – that he had lost his father. Mr. Nunn said to Denny just as casually, "Oh, hard luck," as if it were a regrettable but minor incident, and went on with a conversation about somebody lending him a rod. Denny was not at all indignant. He felt that if it were not his but Talbot's father who had died, or Mr. Nunn's, they would have mentioned it in just the same way. It was the way they talked at Talbot's house, and it was the difference between Talbot's house and his own.

Mr. Nunn looked at the clock above the bar. It was a quarter to nine.

"I have a compelling appointment with a pair of perfectly wonderful brown eyes," he said. "So I wish you a very good evening, gentlemen. Where the deuce did I put my lid? Oh, here it is."

He found an extremely battered trilby, nodded to them both, winked at the barmaid, who blew him a kiss, and disappeared.

"Went off without buying us one," Talbot said. "Typical N.O. for you, Rowland, old boy."

"Is he a friend of your family?" asked Denny, who had been distinctly impressed, both by Talbot for being on equal terms with a fully grown-up naval officer, and by Mr. Nunn for being clearly an intimate of the Talbot family.

"Oh, I suppose so." Talbot never said very much about his home affairs, although he wanted to know all about Denny's.

"Rather a nice chap."

"He's all right. He's one of these people who has no friends but only creditors."

"Brilliant," Denny laughed. "Sounds like a portrait of my future."

He regretted saying that, for it seemed to him that Talbot looked for a moment slightly embarrassed.

"Let's knock these back and go on down to the Empire," Talbot said.

"All right."

When they were outside, Talbot said, "I didn't fancy any of those women, did you?"

"No," Denny agreed emphatically, and he couldn't help reflecting again that had his father been alive he simply wouldn't have dared do this sort of thing.

They jumped in a tram, which was full of soldiers, marines and sailors. It was one of the advantages of living in a dock-yard town that there was always plenty of life after dark, but up to now of course he had not been able to think of taking part in it. The family's rare visits to the theatre – always the Royal, the repertory theatre which the touring companies used – had been rigorously conducted. His father had worn evening dress, and they always sat in the same seats in the third row of the left-hand side of the dress circle. Denny hoped that Talbot would not realize that he had only once before been to the Empire, and that had been to a Christmas pantomime.

The tram halted in front of a tattooist's. Denny had a fascinated glimpse inside of two sailors waiting their turn. Other sailors considered possible patterns on display in the window. An Italian hoky-poky man had his barrel by the kerb, another sign of the coming summer. Next door to

134

the tattooist's a barber was open. Then there was a pub and ahead was the old variety theatre, with its strings of yellow lights and the steps crowded with people. Talbot pushed ahead, slim, confident and loping in his usual way. Denny followed hurriedly, again trusting that no one would recognize him. But it was hardly likely at the Empire.

"We'll get a couple of promenaders," Talbot said. "And I declare, look who's in front!"

Mr. Nunn was at the ticket office, hanging on to a red-haired girl whose scent came all the way down the queue. Denny heard the lieutenant pleasantly but somewhat arrogantly saying "Box", as if he had no intention of wasting words.

Talbot bought the promenaders, which entitled them to stand at the back of the stalls or the circle and to go to the bar behind.

The show had reached turn number five. They listened briefly from the back of the circle to a Lancashire comedian in the middle of a monologue. It was a full house, mainly of men. A notice in the programme read: "Members of the audience are asked to refrain from whistles and catcalls during the turns, as this is both unfair to the artists and inconvenient to the majority of patrons."

"Come on," Talbot said. "Let's give them the once over."

Denny was reluctant, for he was enjoying the atmosphere of the crowded house, but Talbot always got what he wanted.

Behind the circle was the long, high-ceilinged bar. In spite of the show going on it was noisy with people talking. A tango was being danced by a few couples at one end. The music came from a gramophone with a big horn, and it was rather a mystery how all this did not penetrate into the theatre itself. They went to the counter and Denny ordered two pink gins – since Talbot had paid for the promenaders – and the barmaid called him "dear". He began to be a little worried about his money, but he was too excited and feeling too doggish to care much. They stood with their backs to the bar, looking round.

Quite close to them two girls sat at one of the small bamboo tables, occupied with serious conversation, which now and then they interrupted to stare at somebody. One of these stares was directed at Denny, who at once felt everything inside him begin to thump.

"We've clicked, old boy," Talbot said. "What do you think of them?"

"The one on the left has jolly nice eyes," Denny murmured.

"Leave it to me, old boy," Talbot said, and to Denny's amazement and admiration he went over to their table. "We're just back from China," Denny heard him begin. "Will you honour us by having a drink?"

The conversationalists stared at each other, then at Talbot and then again at Denny, who felt terribly self-conscious but very excited.

"Does your mother know you're out?" asked one of the girls frigidly. Both of them seemed to Denny alarmingly mature, and well-dressed. They were also, he thought, extremely common.

"No, does yours?" said Talbot, beckoning Denny to come alongside.

"Well, we're expecting friends in a minute."

"My name's Talbot and this is Mr. Rowland," Talbot said, alarming Denny by his lack of discretion. "What can we get you?"

There was another conversation between the girls, conducted entirely by eyebrows and shoulders, and then one of them said, "Well, if you insist, two port and lemons, but we're expecting friends, as I said."

"I'll get them," Denny said. He was anxious to spend as much as or more than Talbot. As he put the money down on the counter he felt as if his youth were now behind him. With this gesture he had passed into the adult world.

A few minutes later they were dancing to the one-step which had followed the tango.

"I could tell you were in the Navy," Denny's partner said. "You're ever so young, though, aren't you, you don't mind my saying?"

"I'm older than I look, you see."

"Why are you wearing that black band?"

" My – somebody died."

" Oh. Not close, I hope? We've all got to go, that's what I say. Have your fun while you can or you may never have it. I say, your friend is a nut, isn't he? He told my friend he was sure he had met her in Newcastle, did you hear him? She's never been there and I bet he hasn't either. Don't hold me so close, dear. It's not respectable."

Denny laughed. He was enjoying himself. The drinks he had had made him feel pleasantly light-headed. He noticed that Talbot was also doing well, which was, of course, to be expected. All the same it was surprising that all those discussions in the prefects' room at Fritham should turn out not to have been hot air, after all. Here they were at the Empire with a couple of tarts, and it couldn't be denied. It was a pity he was not returning to Fritham to enjoy the added status the episode would grant them.

They went back to the bamboo table just as the interval began and people started to crowd into the bar. Talbot joined him at the counter, where he was about to spend the last of his money on some more port and lemon.

" No, old son, this is my shout. How's she treating you? "

" I think she's rather nice. How's yours? "

" Wonderful. She has the most soft, luxurious lips – why, hullo, George! "

" Good lord," said the lieutenant, who had appeared beside them. " You *are* having a night out, young Edwin."

" Two pink gins and two ports and lemons," Talbot said airily over the counter, putting down a sovereign.

" Two nice port and lemons, ducks," the lieutenant said. " What have you got hold of? I'm glad to see the accountant's still with you, at any rate. Two Kümmels, please, Freda," he called to the barmaid, over Denny's shoulder. He went on to Denny, " At this particular moment of the evening it is the *only* drink."

" What have you got hold of, George, if it comes to that," Talbot said. " Quite a corker, I must admit, but we can't have these goings-on, you know. I shall have mother write to the Admiral to-morrow. Come and join our party, we're at that table – "

He broke off and Denny, looking towards the girls, saw that they had been joined by two men whom they appeared to know.

"They said they had friends coming," he began, but he saw that Talbot's face was pale and enraged. "You remember, they said—"

For his part he didn't care, for it was already late and he must be getting home fairly soon.

"Poor old Edwin, you've been given the bird, I see," the lieutenant said, sympathetically. "That'll teach you, son. I'm afraid solid citizens of the town rate more than we do any day."

"We'll see about that," Talbot said, and Denny realized with surprise that he had lost control of himself and was about to behave ridiculously.

"Let them go, old son, let them go," the lieutenant said. He received and paid for his two Kümmels, and at once held the two small glasses hidden one in each pocket of his trousers so that he could take them round to his box. "Be good now." He nodded to them and walked away carefully.

"Better cancel the port and lemons," Denny said.

"I'm damned if I will. I don't know what you think, Rowland, but I'm damned if I'm going to stand for this." Talbot picked up the drinks he had ordered and went over to the table, where he was overwhelmed with explanations from the girls.

"So you see, dear, we're really with these two gentlemen—"

"My friend and I are with these two ladies," Talbot said rudely and loudly to the men, both of whom were quite large and at least thirty. They were not gentlemen, Denny saw. They stared at Talbot in astonishment, but his manner was so excessively absurd and pompous that they at once became annoyed.

"Who the blazes do you think you are?" said one gruffly.

"Cheeky young blighter, aren't you?" said the other.

"Don't be so damned impertinent," Talbot exclaimed, in a voice high-pitched and loaded with contempt.

Immediately Denny found things becoming confused. He

thought Talbot had overstepped the mark, but he was full of admiration as well as concern. He looked round for the lieutenant, but Mr. Nunn had disappeared towards his box. Meanwhile there was a babble of angry voices round Talbot's head and the latter kept saying loudly, "Damned impertinence." There was a good deal of noise in the bar anyhow, since it was now very crowded, but Talbot's voice rose above it.

"Come here, Rowland, old boy. Come and sit down."

Denny was beginning to feel rather ill in his stomach, but he tried to obey. Talbot, the girls and the two men were all shouting at each other. He went forward, and a large arm barred his way. The next moment he found himself walking in the opposite direction and a large man in commissionaire's uniform was whispering with a sort of gentle hate, "That's all, sonny, outside for you, and don't come back, get it?" He was held by the elbow, in an invincible grip. Talbot, on the other side of the commissionaire, choked furiously. The commissionaire had his fist doubled round the back of shirt collar and jacket. Denny had a confused glimpse of amused faces looking at him, but it was all over in a moment. They were down the grand staircase and out on the steps, and the commissionaire was repeating, "Get along, see? Don't come back, see? Get out."

Talbot, released, made as if to attack him, but thought better of it.

"Come on," Denny implored him, and to his relief Talbot came along. They were shouted at by some sailors who were just going into the pub opposite. They took no notice, and Denny kept thinking with great satisfaction, "I've been thrown out of the Empire!" It was no small achievement.

"Let's get another drink," Talbot said, panting, when they felt that the commissionaire's interest in them had faded.

"Well, I ought to be getting home. There's a train in half an hour."

"Perfectly right, perfectly right. We'll get a growler." Talbot stood still and shouted as hard as he could down the almost empty, gas-lit street. "Cab! Cab! Cab!" He began to retie his tie and straighten out his jacket. "That damned

139

fellow tore a button off – Cab! Cab! Why don't these damned cab-men listen?"

"Do shut up, old boy!" Denny was doubled up with laughter. He found Talbot wonderfully amusing.

"I'm tight, Rowland," Talbot said. "I'm furious about those damned women, though, aren't you? I told them something, though. I tell you what, let's go to your house and have a game of billiards. Look, here comes a growler."

They caught the cab, after Talbot had complained to the cabby that it was not a car. Half-way to the station they had to stop so that Talbot could be quietly sick into the road underneath it. He managed it with dignity. Denny himself still felt ill but it seemed that he was not going to be sick, so he felt rather superior. At the station Talbot gave the cabby half a sovereign. He was fond of making lordly gestures.

"I feel rather like an eighteenth-century rake, don't you?" he said.

In the train he dozed. Denny was relieved that there was no further mention of billiards at home – he could not imagine what sort of reception they would have at this hour, and it might have been difficult to dissuade Talbot from coming if he had stayed in his party mood. When the train started Denny felt the motion uncomfortably, and he had to struggle to prevent himself from vomiting. He had never had so much to drink before. It had certainly been a night out. But he could not help thinking of the sovereign and half sovereign that Talbot had produced so carelessly. Even if his father had lived that disparity would have gone on. Outside the school world in which money was of little importance it became of great importance and he could not see how he could go on knowing Talbot. It was the same feeling all over again of the soap and the towels in the lavatory at Talbot's house. Talbot didn't have to think about money and he did. He had one and sevenpence left in his pocket, and Talbot could never understand how he felt about that one and sevenpence.

At Landen's Mill he tapped Talbot on the shoulder.

"Cheerio. Here's my station."

"Oh." Talbot looked at him in a vaguely startled manner.

"Are you going? Well, cheerio. Jolly good evening, wasn't it?"

"Yes." Denny stepped on to the platform. "Have a good time next term."

"Cheerio, then. We'll get together again in the hols."

But Denny, watching the train pull out, felt it probable that he would not see Talbot again. He was extremely depressed. He went over the bridge and out of the station, past the mill and down the path to the house. He found it terribly unjust that he was not as well off as Talbot. What was the use of being young if you could not enjoy your youth? He realized that his attitude was probably contemptible, but he did not care. On the way across the lawn, however, the scenes of the evening began to pass across his mind and he could not help feeling complacent. He saw his part in the row at the Empire in a more heroic light. It was certainly true that he had got on very well with his girl, or rather, woman. He had danced quite efficiently. He wondered what the lieutenant was doing now.

Before entering the house he remembered to wipe his face with a handkerchief and to smooth down his jacket. He hoped he looked presentable and as if he had merely spent a quiet day in the country. He also hoped that no one would be about to see him.

His mother's voice, however, called out to him at once from the drawing-room, "Is that you, Denny?"

"Yes, mother," he answered, sighing – once more back to depression. Had she waited up for him? There would be no question of Mrs. Talbot waiting up for Talbot.

"What a long day you've had!" His mother was busy with some knitting. "Did you have a good time?"

"Oh, fairly good."

"Do you want anything to eat? You do look tired."

"No, thanks." He kissed her on the forehead, careful that she did not get his breath.

"Well, Bedfordshire then," his mother said, and he realized suddenly that she was more than tired. She went on, "It's been a worrying day. When I went to the hospital they said that Nicky's lung had been active again. Everything's all right now, but he had a small hæmorrhage. They said I could go back, which was very worrying. So I did, of course, but he was sleeping nicely. I didn't tell the girls – they thought I'd just spent the evening at Aunt Ada's. I only caught the ten o'clock back – oh, dearest, I hope everything will be all right, but I'm afraid – I'm terribly afraid – though to-night they assured me there's nothing to worry about."

He was sick with shame, not least because his main feeling was of horror that she had been so close to seeing him and Talbot. His face went red. He could hardly speak.

"I oughtn't to have gone out."

"Oh, nonsense, dear. I don't want to alarm you – it's just that it's a comfort to me – and you have to know these things – I'm sure I don't know why it must all happen to us –"

When he went upstairs, Sarah called to him softly from her room. She always kept her door open, and Isabel always kept hers shut.

"Hullo, is that you? What a time you've been! How was the county? Did you meet Lady Vere de Vere?"

"I had a jolly good day if you want to know."

He went to the bathroom, and then to bed, to sleep heavily. Mrs. Rowland followed him upstairs soon afterwards. About an hour later, at the hospital six miles away, her younger son had another hæmorrhage and died.

CHAPTER EIGHTEEN

The second blow made it seem to the Rowlands, suddenly reduced in number from six to four, that they were living in a nightmare. It was hard to accept the facts. One looked out of the window and half expected to see Mr. Rowland and Nicky come walking across the lawn. The nights, when one was alone with grief, were terrible. But those mornings were the worst, when one had a dream in which the dead were still alive, and one woke to realize slowly that it had been a dream. Mr. Forbes, the Rector, called dutifully several times, and also one of his curates, Mr. Plessey. They comforted Mrs. Rowland, perhaps, Sarah, perhaps, Isabel, not at all. Isabel wished to die, and believed that Nicky had died because he had had the same wish. Denny, fortunately involved in a new atmosphere, had a good proportion of each day free of terrible reminders. The others were never free. The second disaster had had another effect. Friends and acquaintances who had been quick with sincere sympathy on Mr. Rowland's death simply did not know what to say a second time – the Rowlands had become within a few days people to whom things happened; it was in a way as if they had some sort of disease, were tragically abnormal. It was not that friends and acquaintances did not feel sorry for them, but the words they knew were not adequate; they would try being bright and cheerful, or they would try to avoid all contact, determined to maintain the structure of their own illusory world, to shut the door against an unpleasant draught. Sarah and Isabel occasionally murmured bitterly about the behaviour of this or that person; it was, of course, pointless : they both knew they would have been exactly the same themselves. Supposing it were Mr. Mather, who had died, and one of the Mather children? But the unlovable, dreary Mathers were all smugly alive – they, as a matter of fact, had behaved better than most people about Nicky, since their previous sympathy had been accompanied by a certain vulture-like satisfaction. One knew that somewhere deep down they were slightly pleased, and probably because they were guilty about this, they were able to show more positive sympathy about Nicky's death than those who had not shared their contemptible, though natural, feelings about Mr. Rowland. The Mathers, in fact, let loose a torrent of sorrow at the second funeral which they had manfully concealed at the first. This helped Sarah, Denny and Isabel, for once reacting to something in unison, to maintain an icy self-control. Mrs. Rowland, however, was greatly moved.

Her husband had died. Nicky had died. Day followed day, and the moments of disaster receded. Pain apart, Mrs. Rowland was worried by the normality of everything. She became used to her cheque book. Mr. Webber had now arranged that she could draw up to eight pounds a week for the time being, until things were settled. It astounded her that she was apparently the sole beneficiary of Charles's will. It took time for her to become accustomed to being the head of her own household – and, in fact, she never did entirely – and since some instinct made her avoid being too confidential to Mrs. Mather and it did not occur to her to attach any importance to her children's views, she felt herself relying heavily on Mr. Webber. She made any excuse she could think of to call on him. Her reception remained polite but subtly less cordial every time. Meanwhile Denny appeared to be settling down to his office work. The girls, of course, went off to Miss Murray's. "I suppose I'm managing all right," Mrs. Rowland thought, astonished, and a little uneasy.

One afternoon when she was on her way into town to have tea with Mrs. Mather she decided to see what was happening at the mill. Instead of going on into the station she paused in the road opposite the office entrance and as if impulsively she made for the door. There was nothing impulsive about it, in fact. It was an operation she had been planning for some time. She had every right to do it, it seemed, since Charles had left everything to her. The fact that she was so nervous was due to Charles's rigid rule that the family, herself included, were to have nothing to do with the mill. Only a major crisis would have been an excuse to telephone him. Years ago when they had first come to the Mill House and the Rector – Mr. Forbes's predecessor – had paid a call at tea-time, she had hurriedly rung Charles up. She did not speak to him, but left a message. To her surprise and confusion, Charles did not arrive – in those days Mrs. Rowland had thought that a visit from the Rector was such a high honour that her husband would be bound to drop everything and hurry over – and that evening he was angrier than she had ever seen him.

When she pushed open the door of the front office she half expected Charles's voice to ask her testily what she thought she was doing. Behind the counter a thin, round-shouldered clerk was chatting to a young woman, also some kind of clerk. The man was smoking a cigarette and Mrs. Rowland was sure that this could never have happened when Charles was about. They gazed at her in surprise.

144

"Can I help you, Mrs. Rowland? " the clerk asked, after a pause.

"Well, I found I had a few minutes before the train. I thought I would look in and see if – that is, if there were any problems –"

"Perhaps you'd like to see Mr. Jenkins? " the clerk said.

"Mr. Jenkins – why, yes, certainly – but I don't want to –"

He was already leading her upstairs. It was a long time since Mrs. Rowland had been there and she was remembering the day when Charles had first driven her out to the mill in the dog-cart. It had been dusty then and now it was dusty again. Rather to her surprise the clerk led her to Charles's office. He asked her to wait for a second while he went inside. She heard a hurried conversation and then she was ushered in. Standing beside Charles's desk was Mr. Jenkins, like a mayor waiting to shake the hand of a celebrity about to step off a train. She was filled with uneasiness – so far as she knew he had been nothing much more than a foreman, and surely it was impertinent, an outrage that he should be in this room? She could not be certain. She knew nothing about it. She hoped it was all right.

"So you've come to visit us? " said Mr. Jenkins, in a tone that was at once guarded and jocular. "Very pleased to see you, I'm sure – m'm."

The "m'm" was slightly reassuring.

"Well, I happened to be a few minutes early for my train," Mrs. Rowland began again nervously. "It occurred to me that I ought to come in and make sure – that is – what I mean is, is everything going all right? "

"We're getting along fine, m'm. Right as ninepence."

"Yes – good – I'm sure you are, Mr. Jenkins," said Mrs. Rowland, at a loss, for she had not been asked to sit down.

"Webber's been yere and 'ad a talk with me, and 'e knows I can manage things. Nothing to worry about."

She was so amazed by his fantastic lack of respect for the lawyer that she did not know what to say or think. She glanced uneasily at an ashtray with several butts in it and then out of the window. The irony which had always been waiting to help her when she was taken aback now deserted her completely. Then she had another shock. The car appeared in the yard, with Dockray at the wheel. It was like a ghost – a dirty ghost, for it was not, as usual, gleaming with polish.

"Oh!" she said, "is that being used?"

Mr. Jenkins's effort to be pleasant was over. His face darkened.

"Yes, m'm. Got to get about, you know." He added defiantly: "The Gov'nor was always on the move, and 'e was right. I like to do business man to man. There's some blighters, m'm, would have said nothing and done nothing, with a place left on their 'ands. It's not my way. Ah, that car's useful."

But it was not all right. It was Charles's own car. It was unthinkable that Mr. Jenkins should be using it. He was a workman. She did not believe he could do business with anyone.

"Matter of fact I was just on the point of going out, m'm."

Mrs. Rowland was pale. She had an idea that this was impudence. She stood there irresolutely, wishing she knew what questions to ask, and Mr. Jenkins looked more assured. Then he spoke again and this time there was no doubt about the impudence.

"How're Denny and the girls?"

"Very well, thank you, Mr. Jenkins." She could hardly speak for anger. At the funeral he had unctuously mentioned "Master Denny" and "the young ladies" and she had been worrying about his wages.

She gave a last glance round the room. Mr. Webber had removed all the personal things, but here Charles had worked, leaned against that mantelpiece, looked out of that window, pressed that bell; and yet there was not a trace of him – though in his study at home it was hard to believe that he had not just left it or was not about to come in and sit down. She turned towards the door. "Please don't bother to come downstairs."

She managed to speak coldly enough for him to look surprised. He made no attempt to see her out, in fact he had not moved during the whole interview. But once she had made her escape and was walking quickly to the station she asked herself if she had not been to blame, had not been rude and overbearing. She always felt dreadful afterwards when she

146

spoke haughtily to anyone. He was only a simple man and she might have hurt his feelings. But "Webber", the car, the clerk smoking, "Denny" – no, she was sure things were not right. If Mr. Webber knew, if only Charles could come back even for five minutes, if only Denny were older. Mrs. Rowland felt helpless. What could she tell Mr. Webber that would not seem a reflection on himself? But Mr. Jenkins was more than likely to mention, perhaps even to complain that she had called. So it was absolutely necessary to get in first.

When she got out at Peter Street she went straight to the solicitor's office. She had to wait twenty minutes, which left her shaken, and then was received with slightly weary cordiality by Mr. Webber.

"Ah, Mrs. Rowland, and what's your trouble this afternoon? Do sit down. Nasty misty day, but I think it will clear up."

"Mr. Webber, I – I happened to be passing the mill and – "

"The mill?" interrupted Mr. Webber gently, as if he hardly knew what mill she meant.

"Well, I went in out of – interest – Mr. Webber, are you sure it's all right there? I mean, are they – you see, I saw Mr. Jenkins – " In this incoherent way she had managed to say exactly what she had not intended and Mr. Webber's reaction, she saw, was just exactly what she had feared. His attitude became chilly.

"Now, Mrs. Rowland, there's no need for you to go bothering yourself about these things. As you know, I've been there personally."

"Oh, I know, I don't want you to think – "

"These things always take a little time to be cleared up. Now, if you want more money for special expenditure, you have only to let me know. Leave the worries to me, Mrs. Rowland."

When she reached her cousin's house and explained to Mrs. Mather where she had been – although not why – the latter said at once, "I still think it should be cleared up by now. When father was taken there wasn't all this delay."

"I'm expecting everything to be settled any day now," said Mrs. Rowland. "Everything's perfectly all right. Mr. Webber assured me himself."

"Lawyers! Everything's always all right for them. Besides, in my opinion he's got a shifty face. Bessie, I wish you'd let Cyril have a word – you know a *man* can so often – "

"Oh, no," Mrs. Rowland said hurriedly. "Thank you very much for thinking of it, Ada, but I'm sure he needn't trouble."

"Very well," said Mrs. Mather, staring huffily at the ceiling.

Mrs. Rowland had been glad to take Mr. Webber's advice. There was sufficient money to pay the housekeeping bills and the maids' wages. She was sure that one of the girls should be given notice, but she could not bring herself to the point. In any case, since they were in mourning there was no question of expenditure on the theatre, or any similar excursions, and of course she did no entertaining. The girls were at school for the greater part of the day, and Denny had his work. It seemed to her that she was managing very well, after all. The mill seemed to go on working and though she would never dare to see Mr. Jenkins again or to intrude in any way, she did have the satisfaction of noticing that the car had been locked up, out of use; it might be that Mr. Webber had taken more notice of her than he had indicated.

The only event which stirred them was the sudden news towards the end of July that Miss Treddye, of all people, had received a proposal of marriage from a well-to-do Exeter coal merchant, had accepted and was to go off in a matter of days. The news was brought back by Isabel, who every so often called on the music teacher on her way home from school and played to her for an hour or two.

Miss Treddye had been bursting with it, had kissed her excitedly and knocked more things over than ever as she rushed about her tiny house.

"You mean you're really going? " Isabel had said in a disbelieving voice. Her eyes had filled with tears. This little room was part of her life. It was here and nowhere else that she had really grown up, had worked her hardest. In this room she had come all the way from the Gurlitz tutor to the Saint-Saëns concerto. And Miss Treddye was brimming over with pleasure because it was all over. She did not know what to say.

"Yes, on Thursday, dear. You see, there's so much to do
148

with a marriage and all my relations, besides, are in Exeter. I should never have left it, really. Here's the photo of my fiancé. D'you like it? Don't you think he's good-looking? "

Isabel stared in silence at what seemed to her the likeness of an elderly bargee, wearing a gold albert across his broad chest. She detested the sight of him and was utterly unable to imagine how Miss Treddye could even think of living with him.

"You'll have to come and see us," rattled on the gay teacher, spilling tea into the saucer as she poured Isabel's cup. "Just as soon as we're settled down. My dear, you've no idea how sudden it all was. And we've known each other for years. None so blind – it's the truth. Now, Isabel, you're to write to me if ever I can help you. And I shall watch for news of you, you know – so proudly, my pet! "

Miss Treddye was far too excited to bother whether she played or not. Isabel drank down her cup and left as quickly as possible. At home they were still having tea.

"But she's so old! " exclaimed Sarah.

"Old? " said Mrs. Rowland. "Listen to you, you absurd child. How dare you speak of – Miss Treddye is still quite young. By to-day's standards, anyhow."

"You'd hardly call her a flapper, though," Denny grinned. The cheerfulness of the conversation would not have been possible even a month before.

"I expect she'll come and tell us all about it," Mrs. Rowland said. "Did she say exactly when the wedding will be, Isabel? Oh, dear, it'll mean a present. Of course we couldn't go, that is, unless it's some time off."

"She didn't say when."

Nor did she come to see Mrs. Rowland. A note to Isabel was found in the letter box. It gave an address in Exeter and said : "You can always reach me here. Thank you for being so splendid a pupil. Good luck and give my regards to your mother. E.T." Her house was shut up and empty of furniture. Miss Treddye had gone. Isabel could not believe that such a thing had happened so casually. Miss Treddye had been an institution, a part of the background, like the mill or the Promenade. Isabel had taken it for granted that she and, moreover, the whole family, had equally meant a great deal to Miss Treddye. Evidently it was not so. She kept the feeling to herself, but she felt angry and humiliated. It was so much worse than if there had been a quarrel.

Three weeks later a little packet of wedding cake arrived. And that was that. They never heard from her again.

CHAPTER NINETEEN

There was an evening in October when Isabel came downstairs to find Denny grinning up at her foolishly.

"Hullo. Got kept late. Had to see a man."

"You've been drinking," she said in amazement.

"Don't be ridiculous. Merely had a pleasant hour with a chap at the office. Nice chap. No possible harm."

"You can't go upstairs like that. Mother mustn't see you like that."

"Don't be ridiculous."

Sarah arrived and gave Isabel support. Together they persuaded him to go upstairs. He went protestingly. When he reached his bedroom he was sick. The girls, full of disgust, but also of excitement, ran about clearing it up, bringing him water and burning a cork, to take away the smell. It was the first time either of them had "looked after" a man, and they found it curiously enjoyable. Denny appeared downstairs an hour later, very pale, but composed. Mrs. Rowland accused him of overworking.

"Why don't you take the girls to the theatre to-morrow? I shan't go, of course, but at your age it's no good just moping—"

"You come, too, mother."

"Well, I'll see."

That was the end of the Rowlands' mourning. The Christmas holidays approached and the girls were again beginning to visit houses, and as before Isabel played everywhere. She knew that she had improved considerably, but she missed the enthusiastic voice of Miss Treddye telling her so. Still, she did not feel herself alone. She felt Mr. Durrell all the time in the distance – she was hoping that her mother would let her go up to London on an excursion train just for one lesson, to keep her going – and the Academy was daily drawing nearer. That also meant that she must learn a second instrument, and it was the one aspect of the new life which depressed her a little. Any time not spent at the piano seemed to her slightly wasted.

The return to social life made one fact disagreeably clear to Mrs. Rowland. The children needed clothes. They were growing at an alarming speed. And it was no longer possible to pass on Isabel's things to Sarah. Sarah was almost as tall and was slightly plumper. She had a different colouring, and that was now a matter of importance. She also had a will of her own, in spite of her sweetness. She could be, in Mrs. Rowland's phrase, a proper madam. They went shopping, and a bill was sent to Mr. Webber. Possibly this reminded him of the Rowland estate, but, in any case, two days later he sent a note to Mrs. Rowland asking her to call on him.

She arrived at the office, flustered. The arrangement that had been going on suited her very well, and she did not at all like the idea of being saddled with the responsibility of Charles's money. She was shown in at once and was quick to perceive, as she was sitting down in the visitor's chair, that the solicitor was not quite at ease. However, he came to the point at once.

"Mrs. Rowland, I've some news for you which I'm afraid is a little disturbing." He looked at her anxiously. "We've had a long and thorough investigation of your husband's affairs. I'd better tell you right away that the picture is not a cheerful one. The mill is not in the strong position which we had anticipated."

He paused. Mrs. Rowland sat upright, listening attentively. "I knew something was wrong," she thought, and felt quite triumphant.

"The fact is that your husband was carrying out a long-term expansive policy, justified of course if he had lived, but unfortunately one which left the business top-heavy – well, as I say,

Mrs. Rowland, putting it bluntly, we shall be lucky if we realize a bare three thousand net. Hardly more than a nest-egg, as it were. Fortunately there is a purchaser, otherwise things might be worse. But I need hardly tell you it isn't what we expected. Your husband had not confided his plans to me or anyone else, so we weren't aware that – well, if I may say so, he rather mistakenly sought financial support independently of the usual professional advice – "

" He wasn't a man to confide," Mrs. Rowland agreed.

" Well, precisely," the lawyer nodded, relieved by her calmness.

" What had I better do? "

Mr. Webber stared at his finger-nails.

" Not to beat about the bush, Mrs. Rowland, you'll have to cut right down. You'll have enough, luckily, but it won't be comfortable. You'll have to leave the Mill House for a start. It's as well to face the facts."

" Yes – of, definitely," she said. It was astonishing how pleased she felt. But she had been brought up to economize and she found it quite natural to return to the idea. It was wealth and ease that she had always feared. " And we ordered all those clothes the other day! " she exclaimed. " Do you think we could send back – " Then the children came to her mind and she panicked. She stared at him in consternation. " There's Denny and his articles, it would be awful if he had to stop – "

She was behaving normally now and Mr. Webber at once fell into his firm, paternal mood.

" Now, Mrs. Rowland, there's no need to worry yourself. You can keep the boy where he is, so long as he's careful. Fortunately the girls are almost grown up, so you can take them away from school – I'll write the notice, if you like. And it won't do the girls any harm to stay at home, they can study there if it comes to that, and in any case it won't be long before they're off and married. Then there's the house – how many maids are you keeping? I should cut down straight away, if I were you – "

Mrs. Rowland returned home vaguely excited, and at once found the courage to give Edith notice. There was a tearful scene, an offer to work for a lesser wage, not meant to be taken seriously, followed by the withdrawal of the notice. Mrs. Rowland was left feeling defeated. She had had to restrain herself from offering an increase in wages, let alone wiping them out.

The girls, however, were delighted to hear that they were to leave school, and were unconcerned by their mother's exhortations about economy. They had never had any money and did not associate it especially with their material well-being. They rushed about the house and could hardly eat their lunch. Both of them found immense satisfaction in the thought that they had become grown up. It was the beginning of life. They waltzed around. Isabel could hardly believe it. The biggest nuisance she had to put up with had been eliminated.

In the afternoon she asked her mother gaily, "If I'm not going to school, can't I go up to Mr. Durrell and have another lesson or two? I could go on the excursion."

"Oh, my dear child," said Mrs. Rowland, "it is out of the question! Didn't you understand what I told you both? We've got to cut down everywhere."

"But if we're not going to school – "

"You don't understand," Mrs. Rowland said. "Oh, dear, I thought I'd explained. Isabel, it's no good thinking of such things. We'll have our work cut out to exist."

"But I've got to go up some time, after all there's the Academy next year – " Then, seeing her mother's hopeless expression, she felt a chill come over her. She began to tremble. "I *am* going to the Academy, surely – "

Mrs. Rowland sighed.

"You must try to understand, Isabel. It's all to do with your poor father's policy, he was building up – the money isn't there – "

"But I've got to go!" she cried desperately.

"We can't possibly afford it, dearest."

"I've got to!"

"You mustn't think about it."

Mrs. Rowland was conscious that the advice was inadequate, but she was startled by the terrible expression on Isabel's face. She did not understand her ambitions and had never been quite comfortable about the plan for her to go to London. It seemed altogether too daring a project. Confronted by this burning anger, frustration, perhaps even contempt, she merely sighed inwardly and then, as if to make things clearer, she pointed out:

"You see, dear, it will be hard enough to keep Denny on with his articles."

But Isabel paid no attention. She suddenly had an idea.

"Mother, we could go to London. Why shouldn't we *live* in London? Then it wouldn't cost—"

Mrs. Rowland smiled sadly at this unthinkable plan.

"But why not?"

"You know we can't, dear. We live here."

"Good heavens, people live in London, too!"

Mrs. Rowland became irritated.

"Don't raise your voice to me, young lady. Of course we can't. Things are much more expensive there, and this is our house, and then Denny—"

"Denny," Isabel said bitterly. Before her mother could speak again she rushed upstairs to her room and slammed the door.

Mrs. Rowland, regretting her abruptness, came up to make friends, and stood listening outside the door for a moment. She felt helpless at the sound of sobbing. With Sarah it would have been simple to take her in her arms and whisper soothingly. But with her elder daughter she was not at ease.

"A good cry may be the best thing," she reflected, and went downstairs again, without accomplishing anything.

CHAPTER TWENTY

They had been in the new house a year. 12 Brook Place was small, with only one room capable of holding a piano, and a desolate little backyard. There was also a desolate little front garden and beside the iron front gate, which had a very dreary and relentless clang, there was a small brass plate that read " Miss I. Rowland ". For Isabel now had some pupils, enough to make a little pocket money and help the financial strain. Miss Treddye's departure had left an obvious opportunity and the capital expenditure on the brass plate was in imitation of hers. The house was quite close to the Promenade and to their old street. The rent was eighteen pounds a year.

The summer had really been the worst time, because up to then there had been a certain fascination in the changed background. With the warm weather the loss of the garden at the Mill House and all that went with it was hardly endurable. All the same, as Mrs. Rowland never ceased to point out, it was very convenient not to have to take the train in order to reach the shops, and, of course, it was convenient for Denny, who could walk to his office, and convenient for Isabel, if anything were to come of her teaching – in time, Mrs. Rowland said, she was bound to be as busy as Miss Treddye had been.

So they had become more or less used to the new situation. Sarah, who had nothing to do except to help with the housework, surveyed things coldly and objectively. She saw how her mother was obsessed by her responsibilities and that she was sadly incapable of shouldering them. Sarah was constantly irritated by the feeling that in spite of her worries her mother was quite pleased to be living at a lower level and anxious that her family should not be too big for its now shrunken boots. They were always seeing the Mathers, not merely Aunt Ada and Aunt Phyllis, but the whole flock, all of them nowadays, of course, very smug and relaxed in the presence of the Rowlands. They tried to ignore the fact that, though they were now the better-off family, the Rowlands were still their superiors. Sarah detested them and was wild with annoyance when she realized that there was a mild complicity between her mother and Aunt Ada to bring herself and the second Mather boy, Ronald, together. Ronald could not dance, did not play tennis and worked with evident complacency as a clerk in one of the town's big breweries. It appalled her to think that her mother imagined she might like Ronald Mather.

One Sunday afternoon in October when he came to tea Sarah behaved to him with chilling grandeur. Isabel was playing at someone's house and Denny was also out. Mrs. Rowland was forced to run a difficult conversation about the weather, the health of Ronald's brothers and sisters.

He had been quite huffed when he left and Mrs. Rowland spoke angrily.

"I don't know what's come over you lately. Ronald is a very nice boy and you made him thoroughly embarrassed. Let me tell you, young lady, that if you behave like that you'll soon find yourself in the cold."

"I should be delighted to be out in the cold as far as Ronald is concerned. Mother, he's impossible!"

"He's a very nice boy," Mrs. Rowland repeated.

"He's so *boring*, mother." She refrained from saying that she meant he was socially impossible.

"Perhaps you were the one that was boring. You didn't make any attempt to draw him out. All I ask is that you should be polite. He must think you weren't brought up properly."

Sarah turned a little pink and sniffed. The summer had made her very sensitive to certain things. The long pleasant series of tennis parties and picnics which she had imagined lay ahead had somehow not occurred. There had been tennis, yes, and there had been picnics, yes, but they had always seemed to be rather humble occasions. If one did get invited to some fairly substantial house, one went and found that half the family, the more attractive half, was away. There were all sorts of people, the Longdens, the Dellertons, the Carrings, people whom they had seemed to know quite well when her father had been alive, whom Sarah had anticipated providing backgrounds for her to shine against, whom maddeningly her mother made not the slightest attempt to cultivate. The resentments she was now experiencing were new. When she had been certain of her place in the world and used to approval, it had been her pride to be nice to everyone, she had been pleasantly conscious of it – it was a different matter when she was no longer sure of herself, when instead of resolutely refusing to look down, one found that one was being looked down upon, or at least – and it was an equally bitter realization – that one's mother thought this was the case, and thought it was natural. It was no use being nice to people who didn't care whether you were or weren't. The Talbots were the sorest point of all in her present outlook. This was not because they had played much part in her anticipations. The Talbots lived on a stratum high up beyond her world, and there was no question of having any illusions about belonging there. The Longdens and so on were merely richer Rowlands. But the Talbots were another race, and she hadn't thought about them at all. Had it not been that Denny had known him so well, she would have regarded Edwin Talbot as someone far too grand for her to think about, except in a dream, of course. But still they *knew* the Talbots and the year before they had been to their garden party, which was not exactly private but really put on for the Primrose League. Still not everyone was asked and she and Isabel had been schoolgirls then and this year they were grown up. So they had looked forward to the event with some excitement. Then Denny could not go. They had to walk, hot and uncomfortable, the whole two miles from the station to the house because Mrs. Rowland refused to hire a car or a carriage, a terrible comedown from the year before when they had gone in their own car. So they had looked at their worst. Mrs. Talbot had given them a barely discernible nod. Mr. Talbot appeared for five minutes looking immaculate, and looking also as if something was smelling under his nose; he had disappeared for good in five minutes. Edwin Talbot, whom Sarah had longed to see, was in France. And her mother had forced them to spend their time talking to the most uninteresting people whom they knew already. In any case she had been green with envy at the clothes worn by the Talbots' friends, who paraded about with loud voices, making it perfectly clear who was who and who wasn't. Oh, yes, that had been an afternoon better forgotten, but Sarah had not forgotten it. She had never disclosed her feelings. Nowadays, in fact, she did keep things more to herself, and now as her mother spoke to her about Ronald Mather the whole unsuccessful, disappointing summer was present in her mind. She said nothing.

Mrs. Rowland went away to the kitchen. Sarah heard her crying, " Milly! Oh, you thoughtless girl! You've left the cork off the methylated spirit! Don't you know it will evaporate? That bottle cost threepence, kindly remember. Oh, and while I think of it you'll want a pint of cream to-morrow."

Sarah smiled to herself. She had noted that in spite of her mother's delight in economy, the years of prosperity had left her with some expensive habits of which she was not quite conscious. Trifles had to have plenty of cream. Coffee had to be strong, and so on.

" She's hopeless," Sarah thought, more affectionately, that her mother had redeemed herself a little.

Soon Isabel was back. She was brought to the door by Mr. Hawthorn, a tall, drooping man with one of those old-fashioned handle-bar moustaches that one never saw now-adays. Sarah, in a better mood for the moment, was watching from behind the window, and Mrs. Hawthorn from the victoria drawn up outside the house. The diversion was mild, but Sarah exaggerated it to the heights of comedy. Isabel found her doubled up. The moustache, the victoria, Mr. Haw-thorn – Isabel at first did not see the joke, and, in fact, she rarely giggled spontaneously with Sarah nowadays, as she used to, but then she too obligingly saw that the Hawthorns were ludicrous. However she stopped being amused almost at once, and began on a favourite theme, which Sarah found both fascinating and tedious.

This was a growing consciousness of the general malignity which the talented had to deal with. Only this afternoon, she now told Sarah, she distinctly overheard Kitty Fritch, supposedly the friendly daughter of old friends of the family, and possessor of the flattest voice in the society – of which her mother was a vice-president – whispering to the girl next to her, Hilda Bennett, who had been at Miss Murray's with them and who had rabbit teeth, " Ask her to play something she doesn't know."

" How do you know it was you? " Sarah asked, reserving her indignation – though she was ready to be free with it in the end, for she thoroughly enjoyed a good hate.

" Who else could it be? " Isabel snapped. " Anyway Hilda

did ask – for the Scarlatti I made a mess of last year, you remember – and she remembered, evidently – but then Mrs. Hawthorn made me go on with the Brahms, so it didn't matter."

"She's a poisonous girl, Kitty Fritch," said Sarah. "Simply poisonous! She used to keep making remarks – "

"But why should she *bother*? That's what amazes me."

"As for Hilda Bennett, don't you remember me telling you how she told Miss Malford about those flowers just after she had thanked me – "

Isabel lost interest. "Where's mother?" she asked, and went on, after Sarah had pointed, "How was the tea-party?"

"Awful. Painful. Mother, of course, trying to be bright. I was really quite sorry for him."

Isabel was smiling.

"It was rather funny," she said. "I mean, about Kitty – because there was a bit where I got my phrasing all wrong and nobody noticed. They would have enjoyed it if they'd known."

Still wearing her hat and coat she hurried to the piano and began to play the passage, over and over.

"It sounds all right," Sarah remarked, shrugging her shoulders.

"All right? It's awful! It's ghastly!"

"Keep your hair on."

Isabel played a despairing chord.

"It's ghastly," she repeated furiously. "I'm hopeless. I'm no good."

"If you're going to go off the deep end, I'm going upstairs."

Isabel ignored her, and went on repeating the passage, commenting angrily below her voice. Sarah heaved a sigh. Her sister was developing quite a temperament. She was becoming accustomed to her moments of despair, which were now a good deal commoner than the old bursts of happy arrogance.

Isabel gave it up again, with another chord.

"It's really hopeless. One's got to study under somebody or it's a waste of time."

"Don't be so absurd," Sarah said. "You said yourself nobody noticed, it can't be all that bad."

"Just because all those fools—" Isabel was speechless with annoyance. Then she swung round on the stool and began taking the pins out of her hat. "I shall just have to go up to London and have another lesson—"

"If I could play like you, I'd make the grass grow without any more lessons."

"How?"

"Well, you don't use your opportunities. You can get into any house with your playing. You know you can."

"Oh, yes, a lot of people who don't know one note from another. I hate that sort of thing, unless it's a professional engagement. Not for me, thank you."

"More fool you. What's wrong in singing for your supper if it gets you into good society? Oh, how I loathe having to talk to people like Ronald—"

"You really are becoming a dreadful snob," Isabel said.

"If liking more amusing people and better manners is what you mean, then I'm willing to admit it. They say money doesn't matter, but from what I've seen people are a good deal happier, and pleasanter, what's more, when they've got it than when they haven't. In fairy stories the miser's always a wretched old man, but in life he can't stop laughing for thinking about his hoard."

"Well!" Isabel looked quite startled.

"Not that what I think is worth anything," Sarah continued. "I'm just a dreadful snob. How silly, when you think of our position."

Isabel turned back to the piano and played a scale, gathering indignation.

"That is ridiculous," she said. The tone she used belonged to an irritated elder sister, a status which, though undeniable, had been for some time disregarded between them.

"Thank you." A stony look had come over Sarah's face, which at once disappeared as Mrs. Rowland came in, demanding to know what Isabel was doing with her coat still on, for this was not a cloakroom, and who had been there and how had it gone.

"All the usual, mother. It was all right, nothing special. Mr. and Mrs. Hawthorn brought me back."

"How awfully nice of them," cried Mrs. Rowland, amazed when anyone else was kind. "We had Ronald to tea."

"So Sarah was telling me."

"I like him very much," said Mrs. Rowland earnestly. "Such a good, sound type. A little on the dull side, I know, or Sarah pretends she thinks he is, but I'm sure he'll do very well."

"Tell mother about Kitty Fritch," Sarah said.

"Oh, it wasn't anything – "

"What was it?" asked her mother. "I don't see why everything has to be dragged out of you."

"It was just that I overheard her telling Hilda Bennett, 'Ask her to play something she doesn't know.'"

Mrs. Rowland did not believe a word of it and was quite ruffled.

"What nonsense! Kitty is a very nice girl. I'm quite sure you misunderstood. Why go through life thinking the worst of people? I assure you that doesn't pay."

Isabel turned pink and was silent.

"I wish we knew what did pay," Sarah murmured.

"Counting your blessings," said Mrs. Rowland sharply.

Sarah shrugged her shoulders. However, her mother was not always annoying. There was another time, not long afterwards, when Mrs. Mather herself came to tea. The darkest moment of Sarah's year was the one in which her aunt suggested, with smooth effrontery, that she might "help" by becoming a nursery governess. How she wished she had Isabel's temper! She wanted to scratch the old bitch's eyes out, for she knew quite well it had only been said for cheek. Unlike her mother, Sarah was under no illusions about how the Mathers were enjoying the Rowlands' situation. Their only annoyance was that Denny was still being prepared for a profession. It was quite fascinating to see such whole-hearted malice. Aunt Ada always looked delighted nowadays when she visited them and this afternoon was particularly pleasant for her, for she had learned that the Rowlands now were reduced to a daily charwoman – dear old Milly, the last of their former staff, having been found a place, and having left behind her a last line, tearfully spoken, which had been heart-warming.

" I don' wan' t'work for ee, ee ant no berrer'n me," she had said of her new employer, and had now been quoted with some pride by Mrs. Rowland. Sarah giggled dutifully, eager for any straw that kept up one's self-importance, but her aunt, usually an avid discusser of servants, gave only a frosty smile and presently asked, " So what is Sarah going to do? "

" Do? " said Mrs. Rowland. " Oh, she does lots of things, don't you, my pet? "

" Yes, I work terribly, terribly hard," Sarah cried, with an attractive blush, and also the tone and air of smart gentility. She went on with calculated, gay vagueness, " I dust this – and dust that – I *never* stop – "

" H'm," said Mrs. Mather, making it clear that she was not impressed. " It seems to me, though naturally I don't wish to interfere, that she would be better occupied doing something that earned a little money, and so *helped*, like her sister."

She often spoke quite frankly of Isabel, since it seemed now that after all she was getting nowhere.

" Oh, aunt, if only I could! " Sarah smiled prettily. " But you know that poor little me has *no* talents – "

Then had come that appalling suggestion. She reeled under it, and was glad to see that her mother didn't like it even if she said nothing against it, which she should have. Mrs. Mather continued on her awful path. She fully intended that her own girls should do something of the sort. If one found a good, respectable home it would be a fine education. It was bad enough, Sarah thought, to be related to someone who thought in such terms, let alone having the idea suggested to oneself. A nursery governess! Little better than a servant! It required all her self-control to keep her end up.

" I'll think about it, aunt," she smiled. " It ought to be the very thing. I'm *so* fond of children."

Mrs. Mather's lips showed her dislike of Sarah's affected way of speaking, and Mrs. Rowland laughed at Sarah for talking about children when she was hardly more than a child herself. Sarah, who occasionally enjoyed being " young ", felt that she had not come out too badly. All the same she was very conscious of her danger. Her aunt might easily take it into her head to press the matter and none knew better than

Sarah how easily persuaded her mother might be that it was a sound idea. She did not mention the matter to Isabel, but she thought about it hard for the next day or so. She even thought about doing it. If one went to a large enough house, after all, who knew that one would not be Cinderella to some Prince Charming and emerge to infuriate Aunt Ada with a title and a thousand acres? What bliss it would be! She spent quite a time with such pleasant day-dreams. On the whole, however, it did not seem likely. But she did not see what alternatives there were, if it were felt that she had to make money. Activity, anyhow, seemed essential. Before the end of the week she was taking a practical interest in church work.

Their new Rector and in particular one of his curates, Mr. Selby, who was unfortunately very poor, were delighted with her. Sarah plunged enthusiastically into easy " visiting " tasks, and she was indefatigable, at least to begin with, in taking jellies and beef dripping to smelly little back bedrooms where she was treated as a very grand young lady. She had discovered that it often went down quite well to be very open about their own financial position and poor young Mr. Selby went red with amusement when Sarah told him, " As a matter of fact, far from us visiting, we ought to be visited! " She had discovered that if she looked straight-eyed at people with her eyes wide and innocent she could create quite an effect with some almost shocking remark. Of course she was not sent to the rough streets, and for the most part she worked in the blanket depot, to which poor persons could come with a blanket ticket obtained from a subscriber, and she also helped at the Mothers' Union teas. After two or three weeks even Aunt Ada had to accept that Sarah had an occupation that was above criticism, in spite of its lack of profit.

So Sarah battled her way along, prettily but firmly. Mrs. Rowland continued to be worried because the girls mixed so little. It was her quite open and only hope for them that they would meet suitable young men. But gradually she gave up her attempts to induce Sarah to take part in the wide social life which was available if she would lower her standards. Sarah remained scornful of all the Ronald Mathers. She was more than conscious as she went about the town of the side-wards glances she attracted. She did not intend to waste her-self. It infuriated her all the more that Denny, for whom they were all making such sacrifices, refused ever to get in touch with people he used to know, like Edwin Talbot, who, after all, was once supposed to have been his best friend, and if he ever went out with anyone, went with the clerks at his office. He was generally in a bad mood and, though Mrs. Rowland idolized him, Sarah could see that he had lost most of his boyish charm. It was a pity, since a brother could be so useful.

Still, life was not so bad. She was just seventeen and there was plenty of hope. Others, after all, were worse off still. She was always moved to tears when the crocodile of orphans passed by on the Promenade, with their little red scrubbed faces, long skirts and aprons, a dress which would have been charming if it were not the badge of a crime. Sarah saw clearly that it was a crime to be poor. People hated and feared the poor. And when you saw the orphans – they were on the Promenade almost every day – you hated the thought that but for the grace of God – ah, how much pleasanter it was to see the comfortable and privileged. There was one little scene which made a strong impression on her. Two attractive and wonderfully-dressed children came along, each with a hoop, and though they were clearly a brother and sister, each was attended by a nurse. And suddenly an elegant woman appeared walking across the Promenade towards them. She was quite young and pretty, and her furs were superb, but it was her matchless air of confidence and superiority which made Sarah catch her breath; she was the embodiment of what she imagined a London society woman should look. Then the older nurse, seeing her, hurriedly told the younger nurse to keep at a distance, and the older nurse had the privilege of standing there while the mother charmingly greeted the children. Sarah was so spell-bound that she hardly realized that she had stopped to watch. She felt quite weak, not with envy but with excitement. She thought about it for days after-wards.

Whenever the little scene came into her mind she would close her eyes and shiver luxuriously.

"That's how it should be!" she would murmur, under her breath.

CHAPTER TWENTY-ONE

All that year Isabel had been waiting for a miracle, some event – heaven knows what – which might save her. But everything went wrong. She had a feeling that she was trapped in quicksands, going, going. Her unhappiness came in waves, depression followed by optimism, followed by depression. The worst of it, possibly, was that she could talk to no one about it. Miss Treddye, who, in a way, was responsible for most of her dreams, had deserted; had perhaps even given her up already as a lost cause before she went; but with her had gone the last person who even dimly understood how she felt. Her father, Nicky, Miss Treddye – without them she no longer belonged. She loathed the teaching she had begun, her pupils were the unmusical, unwilling children of friends of her mother's friends. But it hardly mattered what she did, for she loathed – in the depressed periods – everything and everybody in the town, except her own family circle, the three fellow survivors. Or it was not so much loathing she had for her environment as a more deadly feeling, indifference. She told herself at least that she was indifferent. But it was hard – nobody knew how hard – to go about the town and see the same question in everyone's eyes: what's happened to the success we heard so much about? She was unconscious of it only at home.

There was the business of Kitty Fritch and "Ask her to play something she doesn't know". It was so childish, if you could call such a thing childish – it was unimportant, and yet she couldn't believe that if their positions had been reversed, she would have said such a thing. It was far from the only instance.

There was Dr. Preston, the organist at St. Mary's, a Doctor of Music (Oxon.), the acknowledged and natural leader of the town's musical affairs. She knew him quite well, it was he who ran the annual symphony concerts in the Town Hall, he had been the conductor when she had played the Saint-Saëns concerto – her last public triumph, which seemed to recede further and further into the past. A delightful man, small, white-haired, a wrinkled face made distinguished by a pince-nez, he had always been pleasant to her, and full of praise on that famous evening. And yet this same man, giving the town's newspaper a review of the music of the year, had left out her name altogether. (She hadn't known at the time, but one found out everything in the end.) Next, he had insisted that there should be no pianoforte concerto in his concerts this year and last year. More recently still, when a Covent Garden soprano had arrived to give a charity concert under his auspices, without an accompanist, Dr. Preston had not suggested Isabel, but a middle-aged woman called Mrs. Gerald Scott who was worthy but mediocre and in any case had no career to make – whereas it might have been a wonderful opportunity for Isabel, and Dr. Preston knew that quite well. He knew, too, that she was a good accompanist and ten times better than Mrs. Gerald Scott. Why should Dr. Preston care? Was it simply that he hated to acknowledge her talent publicly? And Kitty Fritch? And the Mathers, her own relations who she knew were benevolent towards her nowadays because they felt they need not envy her? Or was it all imagination?

Sometimes she thought that perhaps it was. But there was too much evidence, and the consciousness of it made her realize the nature of the world. Still, playing the piano was still the most important thing in that world and she had kept faithful to Mr. Durrell's insistence on daily practice through thick and thin. Some day her luck would be good instead of bad. It was even possible that good luck was already beginning to show its face again. Webster's, the music shop in Peter Street, had written to ask if she would be free to play at At Homes and other private functions during the coming winter – which meant a few guineas and good experience that no concert pianist need despise – and she was given several engagements. She could therefore feel that she had at least begun her professional career.

At Webster's a man called Mr. Rich dealt confusedly with the local concert bookings. He was fond of Isabel, who had spent hours hunting out music which they kept in untidy heaps and piles. He was elderly and wore a high paper collar which seemed to be strangling him. In the windowless cubicle at the rear of the shop into which he would take her when she called there were signed photographs of Rachmaninov, Melba, Busoni and Ysaye – they had all performed in the town – and several filing cabinets. Only one drawer of one of these in fact dealt with bookings, the rest concerned the business of the shop, which had sold music, pianos and all sorts of instruments for a hundred years. But Mr. Rich always managed to give the impression that it was all agency business, most of it to do with Rachmaninov, Melba, Busoni and Ysaye, although the negotiations Mr. Rich undertook for such celebrities were mostly confined to hiring motor-cars to meet their trains. All the same, Rachmaninov (Sergei) and Rowland (Isabel) had their cards together in the file, and the sight of this happy juxtaposition was always exciting to Isabel. Her first engagement was in November and Mr. Rich had put down the details on the card. " Mrs. Hatch-Edwards, Melton House, Lavernoke. Transpt prov Lavernoke stn. Spr. P. 8-30-9.30. GI." This meant that Isabel would be met at the station, be given supper on arrival and would play from eight-thirty to nine-thirty for a fee of one guinea.

Although she had appeared in public so often as a child, this was the first time she had ever gone anywhere as a professional. The day which preceded it was full of tensions. She was sure she was playing badly. There was a pain in her left hand. She knew they would not like the Chopin, although her programme had been approved. If people talked when she played she was determined to get up and leave the room. There was a spot on her frock. Her gloves looked soiled. She could not go. Mrs. Rowland shared her worry, for she seemed to feel it remarkable and impressive that anyone was prepared to pay Isabel a guinea, and moreover Sarah spent the day insisting that she should go too.

"I don't think it looks right, travelling by yourself."

Isabel was accompanied, however, only as far as the

station. Sarah was annoyed, for she said that there was no reason why she shouldn't have waited somewhere while Isabel did her job, and as it was Isabel was giving the impression that she was just anyone.

"I am just anyone," Isabel said, with a curious little smile of satisfaction.

"You don't push yourself enough," Sarah insisted. "When I think of how everyone was all over you in London – you know, Isabel. I often think it's sad that I didn't have your gift and you were just useless like me. I wouldn't have hid *my* light under a bushel, I can tell you. I'd have taken you along and said you were my secretary or something and not just be a mouse – "

"You're just being ridiculous," Isabel said.

Sarah was carrying her bag, which contained her shoes and her brush and comb, and she swung it about excitedly as she walked beside her sister, bobbing up and down on her toes, speaking a rapid monologue and stopping only when she lost her breath.

When Isabel was at last sitting in the train she had been brought to an almost unendurable pitch of nervous tension and exasperation. If she had not lost her temper with Sarah, it was simply because she couldn't think of the right words to express her feelings. The trouble was, she knew that Sarah was right. Of course she was only right more or less by mistake. Sarah could be right because she knew so little. Isabel leaned back against the hard-cushioned upright seat and sighed. Once again she was considering her situation. She had spent many hours doing so in the past few months. The fact was – unless some marvellous piece of luck came along, but it showed no sign of doing so – it was hopeless. She knew perfectly well that she had to go to London, Academy or no Academy – as to that, she had never contested that Denny should come first, she had been brought up in an atmosphere of male superiority – and that unless she went to London she could forget any hopes she had ever had. Although she was still confident that given the opportunity she could reach the top, she was too aware of her limitations to imagine that London would come to her. At

168

the root of it, she was also aware, was the pity she felt for her family, love and pity mixed up, that was the disastrous thing. If only she were by herself, nothing need have stopped her – the world was yours if you really wanted it, Mr. Durrell had said, and she believed it – but of course circumstances had to allow you freedom of action. Or, if only they had even less money it would have been a help, for the talented poor could always find patrons and Sarah and Denny would have had to be earning money; as it was they had too little and just enough, so that the pin-money she earned from lessons and engagements like this evening assumed importance. The fact was, she had no chance at all.

The train journey lasted for forty minutes, and she was in a despairing mood when she got out at Lavernoke Station. A groom with a pony and trap was waiting for her. There followed a moonlit drive of two or three miles. The lodge gates through which they finally went were rather impressive and the house itself, with lights in dozens of windows, took her breath away. At once all her nervousness returned. She was given a front-door entrance and whisked away by a butler upstairs and out of sight. A door opened and she was met by a short and very erect woman in a dinner frock, whom she first thought must be Mrs. Hatch-Edwards, but who introduced herself cheerfully, "Miss Rowland? My name's Matthews. I'm the governess. We're dining together." Inside was a cosy sitting-room where their meal was served by a maid. Isabel was very impressed and Miss Matthews reminded her of Mrs. Slocombe, especially as she talked non-stop, first in very familiar terms about the Hatch-Edwards family, and then in more general terms about the aristocracy, some representatives of which were apparently at the party downstairs. Isabel was interested to meet Miss Matthews. This was evidently the kind of job Aunt Phyllis used to have and, if so, it was rather grand. In any case the governess's non-stop talking helped her to become relaxed, her mind was reeling with all the duchesses and countesses that Miss Matthews appeared to have known intimately as she went downstairs to meet Mrs. Hatch-Edwards. The latter was a mild-looking, worried looking, youngish woman, dressed in lots of grey satin and a diamond necklace. She gave Isabel two fingers and said that it would be all right if she only played for half an hour.

"Very well," Isabel managed to say, her voice shaking.

Then everything went out of focus and she heard Mrs. Hatch-Edwards announce nervously, "Miss Edith Rowland", far away in the distance. She had been led into a large and sumptuous room, full of large and sumptuous people in evening dress. There was some mild decorous little clapping and she didn't know how she ever found herself sitting at the piano, which was an Erard and fortunately in tune. But she had hardly begun her first piece a minute – it was Grieg's enchanting, light-as-a-feather *Papillon* – before she knew that she was going to play brilliantly. That was how it had always been – once she was in action, all the problems vanished. The scene before her belonged in one of those oil-paintings of a gala night at the opera, the white ties and the jewels, and the flowers in profusion everywhere. There were about thirty people present, mostly rather middle-aged, and standing or sitting statuesquely – she felt as if she were performing before the crowned heads of Europe. She tried to remember everything for Sarah's benefit, and wished she knew who were the aristocratic ones Miss Matthews had referred to. One man in particular dimly caught her attention. He was big, with a fleshy but rather fine face, suitable for a duke, and a ginger moustache. He stood by a glass cabinet listening attentively and looking now and then at his reflection. At the end of the piece he clapped enthusiastically and there was warm applause all round. The recital continued. She found herself playing at the man with the ginger moustache and it brought on the tendency she always had to thump a little. She forced herself to stop doing it and settled down again. At the end of the half-hour her reception was so warm that Mrs. Hatch-Edwards hastily cancelled her instructions and asked her to keep going. "Everyone is enjoying it *so* much!" she smiled at Isabel and looked both surprised and relieved. Isabel felt the glow that always came with success, and it was especially agreeable in such a luxurious atmosphere. The enthusiasm was so marked that she had a vague idea that she might be toasted in champagne and wake up famous.

When the end did come, however, nothing happened at all. The little burst of clapping was merely decorous, and then there was a moment's silence before everyone began talking to each other. She might have left the room already. Feeling not exactly humiliation but a strong sense of anticlimax, Isabel slowly pulled on her gloves, considered closing the piano and decided not to, and went to the door. She was not quite unnoticed, for Mrs. Hatch-Edwards nodded and smiled at her, without, however, leaving the guest she was talking to. They had had their guinea's worth and that was that. Outside a servant led her to a small room where there was a telephone. There was a very small fire which gave out no heat. Her coat and hat and shoe-bag had all been brought down and were on the table beside the telephone. She changed her shoes and put her coat on. The servant returned with a tray on which was a plate of biscuits and some coffee. He said he would tell her when the transport was ready. It was rather irritating to listen to the murmur of the party. She thought it might be rather superior to leave the tray as it was, but when she had waited a few more minutes she nibbled at one biscuit and then ate the lot and two cups of coffee.

"I'm a professional," she thought. There was nothing at all to complain of in her treatment, but she had never been treated like it before.

After a time there were sounds outside and she heard voices raised in ecstatic farewells. Then the servant appeared again. "The car's ready now, miss." He picked up her shoe-bag and she followed him out.

In front of the steps a large saloon stood waiting, and beside it a chauffeur, and beside him with his white tie showing behind his coat the guest who had been standing by the glass cabinet. He bowed to her. Close to, the fleshiness of his middle-aged face showed up. There was something about him she did not like, a kind of radiant self-satisfaction.

"Miss Rowland, I'm to have the pleasure of your company on the way. My name is Bochard." His voice was astonishing, small, high-pitched and lisping, and immensely affected. He

171

said "pl'shah" and "weh". She detested him even more. "I'm so glad to be able to thank you for your charming performance."

"Oh," Isabel said. "Thank you." And she detested him less.

She stepped into the car and sat down with her eyes straight ahead. She could not imagine what her mother would have said about this, but presumably anything done at Mrs. Hatch-Edwards' house was in order. He settled in after her and waved away the chauffeur and a servant who were at once trying to put a rug round him – they ignored Isabel.

"Buck up, now, let's be off."

"Yes, my lord," the chauffeur said.

Isabel felt her stomach turn over. She remained rigidly in the position she had taken up. She had never heard his name – Boch – Bosh – what had it been? Not that that mattered.

The car moved off and the voice beside her began again very affably.

"I have to catch the night train back to London, a confounded nuisance. I detest travelling anywhere by night, particularly in discomfort, unless the discomfort is so outrageous that it becomes interesting. I really did enjoy listening to you, you know, it was an unanticipated degree of pleasure, all the more to be thankful for – and I can assure you my judgment is to be respected enormously. I know a very little about music. A very little. What was it again – 'she didn't care for music, but was fond of musicians'?" He laughed gaily, and coughed. "You're rather a young thing to be out like this, aren't you?"

Isabel was slightly overwhelmed by his flow of talk, but with his last words her dislike of him returned, whether he was a lord or not.

"I don't think so," she said, still looking straight ahead. "I'm eighteen."

"Oh, really?" He was delighted and a little confused. "I say, forgive me, I wasn't daring to enquire –" A bump in the road cut him short, upsetting her rigidity and throwing her against him. She hastily drew back to her corner as far from him as possible, but his hand was supporting her elbow on the way and let go reluctantly. She could feel her heart

172

thumping. She was terrified. Was he going to travel with her in the train?

She was so anxious that she couldn't give full attention to what he was saying.

"Do you do much of this sort of thing?" he repeated. "I'm really interested. As I said, I do know a very little about music."

Calming down, she realized that he did sound interested. After all he looked old enough to be her father. She answered nervously that she did a little of it.

"Where have you studied? Where do you live? Forgive my impertinence. I'm really interested."

Then she wanted to tell him everything, but of course it was impossible. She said in her stiff, tensed-up voice, as if unwillingly, "I live with my mother and sister and brother. I have had some lessons in London with Mr. Durrell – Clement Durrell –" He showed no recognition. "I teach also. I did hope to be a concert pianist –" she went on.

"Don't you still?"

"Oh – yes, of course." Why had she said "did hope"? It had slipped out. Annoyed with herself, she hurried on, "I've played concertos at the town symphony concerts. I was going to the Academy in London, but – my father died – and things have gone wrong since then –" She dared to look at him and saw with a shock that his eyes were closed. She said angrily, "I'm afraid it's not very interesting."

"Not at all; I adore tales of disaster." His eyes remained closed. "Tell me about your family and what they do."

Isabel mentally shrugged her shoulders. He seemed unpardonably intrusive, but there was no reason not to tell him that her mother looked after the house, aided by Sarah, and that Denny was learning to be an accountant.

"I find it absolutely fascinating," he said. "Extraordinary."

"Not extraordinary," she answered at once. "Ordinary." She knew what he meant and that he was looking down on her from a great height, but she did not resent it. She had a curious feeling that she was talking to an equal for the first time in years.

"Not *very* ordinary, I think." He was amused and his eyes

173

were certainly open now, regarding her with a bright, staring look. "You know," he said, "you seem ripe to be rescued — we'll have to put this family of yours out to grass or something. Forgive me again for being personal, but you shouldn't be giving piano lessons — what lunacy, they should all be slaving to support you —"

"That's quite impossible," she interrupted furiously. She had grown rigid again. His languid, authoritative voice was like a dentist's probe touching a nerve. She perceived the truth through a mist of pain and at once she regarded it as an enemy not to be recognized. She was overwhelmed with loyalty and love for her family. She would not allow them to be insulted.

"If it's impossible, it's a pity," he said, unruffled. She was aware of his odious, straggling ginger moustache closer to her. No doubt he thought he could say and do what he liked. "One can always get help, you know."

"I'm quite happy as I am," she said, and thought, "If he touches me I'll scream."

"Ah, then I congratulate you —" The car drew up. "Hullo, what are we stopping for? What have we stopped for?" he repeated after the chauffeur had jumped out and was opening the door on Isabel's side.

"It's Lavernoke station, my lord, for the young lady."

"Oh, but you're not getting out here, are you? That's quite absurd. He's driving me to Peter Street, why should you go by train?"

Isabel was already outside, relieved and breathless. She took her shoe-bag from the chauffeur.

"I'm being met, you see. But thank you very much," she said quickly.

"It seems quite ridiculous." He was half-way out of the car with one foot in the road, but he paused. He looked at her reflectively. It was as if he had suddenly decided not to continue with an original plan of action. His big oval face was pale-white in the gloom. She was conscious that the coat she wore must look rather humble, but she held her head proudly or thought she did. Then he said, "Well, it's just as you like. What do you have in that bag?"

174

"My shoes."

"Oh, of course. Good-bye, then."

"Good-bye." She stood for a moment irresolute, unsure whether he was coming out and whether she was supposed to shake hands. But all he did was to nod and then sit down inside again. This time the chauffeur did cover his legs with the rug. Then the chauffeur touched his cap to Isabel and said, "Good night, miss." He climbed into the driving seat and the car rolled away, a gleam of white scarf in the back. It was as if she had never been in it at all.

"One of them might at least have carried my bag," she thought as she went into the station. It was a sleepy little place and there was no one to look at her ticket. It had been quite an evening. She walked up and down the platform, thinking about it, and then about this extraordinary incident with Lord whoever-it-was and how lucky it was that the car had stopped just then. She was sure that he had been about to hold her hand, or heaven knows what – she could still feel the pressure under her elbow after she had knocked against him. The thought of being touched by a man of that age and that awful moustache – she didn't care who he was – was revolting.

However, it was possible to think in two ways at once. It was possible to tell yourself that you were thinking in one way, when all the time, underneath, you were thinking in another way. Underneath she felt like crying. Underneath she knew that there had been nothing more than kindliness in his behaviour. When you considered how high was his position and how small hers – she had never heard anyone called "my lord" in her life, except in a speech – he had been amazingly nice. Moreover, he had appreciated her playing as no one had in months, on the scantiest information he had seen what was wrong with her life, and perhaps he had also meant that he thought of helping her personally, introducing her to someone in London – a man like that knew everyone. Oh, God, what a fool she was! What a fool, what a fool! Sharing the car with him had been the remotest accident – a chance like it might never come again, and she had thrown it away.

The train arrived twenty minutes later, ten minutes late –

the trains on this branch line which made a circular tour of the countryside were famous for being late. No wonder he had failed to understand, and indeed, for it was obvious, had at the last moment lost interest and given her up. She sat by herself in a third-class *Ladies Only* compartment and stared in the dim light at the photograph of the front at Paignton beneath the luggage-rack opposite, while inwardly she fought for the first way of thinking – he had been patronizing, she told herself angrily, he would have behaved improperly, she knew the look in his eyes, she had done the only possible thing. All the time the sound of the engine was making a chorus in her ears that went, "You've lost your chance, you've lost your chance, you've lost your chance –" Sarah would not have lost it, that was another thing. Her sister's words at the beginning of the evening seemed frighteningly right now. "You don't push yourself enough –" It was true, and she recognized the no less frightening probability that it would always be like this. But she could not bear pushing, and after all if you didn't push you also kept your self-respect.

She felt better as soon as she saw Sarah. Her sister stood by the ticket barrier, looking, as usual, young and pretty and excited.

"Were you all right? Thank goodness – I was thinking – suppose you didn't get away in time and missed the train! I'd have had to wait another hour and ten minutes!" Sarah said all this leaning half-way across the ticket collector, who did not mind at all.

"Yes, everything was all right." She looked round the station, but there was no sign of any ginger moustache, and of course the London train would have gone by now.

"Denny's in the waiting-room." Sarah took her arm affectionately as they walked through the booking hall. "Was it a lovely place? Anyone interesting there?"

"I had a lift in a car with Lord somebody –"

"You *didn't*! *Lord* somebody – oh, how marvellous! Who? Oh, why didn't I go? How wonderful!" Sarah almost danced with excitement.

"I don't know his name, but the chauffeur said 'my lord'."

"You don't know his name? Oh, you're hopeless!" Sarah cried, in amazement.

Isabel was relieved. It now became a mild little triumph that the episode had happened at all. She was glad she had mentioned it at once.

"Now start at the beginning," Sarah said. "Tell me all about everything, what they were wearing and everything. Don't leave anything out. Do you mean you sat *with* him?"

They picked up Denny, who seemed to be in a better mood than usual, and walked home. Isabel tried to give her sister an imaginative description of the frocks and jewels, which Sarah interrupted with exclamations and sighs. Even Denny was quite impressed that she had shared a car with a lord, although he resolutely tried not to be.

"Why shouldn't she?" he said. "What's so remarkable?"

"Oh, but of course it wouldn't be remarkable for you!" exclaimed Sarah.

"'I'm Jones of the Lancers – well, rather,'" Denny half-sang, from a song which was a favourite with them. "'By Jove, I'm the pick of the bunch!'" He went on to Isabel, "Has she told you we have company at home?"

"No, I haven't told her. When did I get the chance?"

"Not Aunt Ada?" Isabel said.

"It's a he. You'll be extremely surprised," Sarah said. "I'm quite sure you'll be pleased as well."

"Even though he's not in the peerage," Denny put in.

Something had certainly pleased them; she had been conscious of it even at the station, but they refused to give any more information and made a mystery of it. She tried hard to imagine who it could be. There was no one alive whom she knew and also wanted to see at that moment. The only person who came fleetingly into her mind was the unspeakable Sadler – who had kissed her at Mrs. Slocombe's and then had never written. At home Sarah insisted that she went into the sitting-room with her eyes shut and it was not Sadler whom she saw with delight when she opened them but a white smooth-haired fox-terrier puppy, which was being nursed by Mrs. Rowland. Isabel swooped upon it.

"How lovely! Is he really ours?" she exclaimed. "Oh, his teeth are like pins!"

"Denny brought him home," said Mrs. Rowland, for whom this made it more agreeable still. "He's a present from Mr. Teape." Mr. Teape was the partner in Denny's firm whom Mr. Rowland had known, and of whom Denny was now giving a memorable imitation.

"H'm, young Rowland, we have a littah at hom, h'm, and I wondah if your mothah would ceah for a puppeh?" said Denny, bending backwards in front of the mantelpiece and screwing up his face.

"You shameless boy!" His mother found him enormously funny. In fact, for the first time since they had been living there, the room was full of happy people, the mother, the two daughters, the son. Sarah talked excitedly about Isabel's evening, and Isabel confirmed that her playing had been successful and that the chauffeur had said 'my lord'. But the puppy was the centre of all their attention. They played with it and nursed it and prodded it and rushed it with screams to the prepared tray of earth when it settled down on the carpet to defecate. They discussed animatedly what it should be called. They would not have Jerry, the name of their old dog, buried long ago at Landen's Mill. They decided on Boxer. Only when Sarah cried "Think how Nicky would have loved him" was there a fleeting moment of pain, but it served to point all the more that the small sleepy puppy represented new life.

CHAPTER TWENTY-TWO

The first professional engagement was followed by half a dozen more over the next two or three months. At one of them she accompanied a soprano from London before a society of ladies concerned with the moral uplift of the working classes. The soprano told her that she ought to move to London. "If you could stick it for a year, dear, you'd be out every evening – masonics, clubs, dinners – a good accompanist is a real gem – " Isabel was not impressed. She knew she was a good accompanist, but she thought it rather an insulting suggestion. It was, in any case, out of the question. She seemed to be busy all and every day as it was, what with her pupils, and with playing everywhere – over Christmas Sarah, busy with her welfare activities, had involved her in numberless parish concerts. Sarah also began to receive many invitations and she generally managed to see that Isabel was included, which meant that at some time during the At Home or the tea-party or whatever it was, Isabel would be asked to play. Now that she had begun to earn money she was always a little exasperated at playing for nothing, but she knew that she was a considerable social asset to Sarah and she never complained. By the end of February pupils and engagements had brought her in nearly thirty pounds.

Mrs. Rowland was both delighted and impressed, and though much more money or a more starry success would have impressed her more, it would also probably have delighted her less. Thirty pounds was good, but it did not disturb anything or anyone, except possibly Denny. Isabel had become conscious that her brother hated the idea of her earning money while he earned nothing, it was a constant nagging blow at his pride; she tried to make no reference to it when he was present. She also dimly perceived her mother's attitude and, though it irritated her, she could understand the pleasure of non-disturbance. If you did well, but not too well, you would stay in the same rut and yet make it a pleasanter rut. Climbing out involved all sorts of discomfort, and all the forces of love and pity were ranged against it. She found her greatest ease of mind in the contentment of the other three. If they were happy, she was not unhappy. It was only when there was an "atmosphere" that she could not bear it, and it was then that the desperate dreams of fame returned.

There were many reasons for "atmospheres" – Mrs. Rowland would be upset if Denny or Sarah had been rude to the Mathers, Sarah if she had been snubbed or patronized during the day, Denny if his mother asked him to run an errand when he was trying to study. Tempers were lost, voices raised – all except Isabel's, for at the first sign of trouble she would withdraw into a shell, apparently poker-faced and maddeningly superior, or she would pretend to be absorbed by playing with the puppy. In fact, she was more emotionally affected than any of them, and the more the quarrel went on, the more the thoughts pounded in her mind, stirring her to an anger she never showed, "Why am I here? I don't belong here. They're killing me, I'm becoming nothing." Later, inevitably, she would pursue a dream which had first taken shape one afternoon when she picked up the woman's paper which Mrs. Rowland read for the serial and the household hints and Sarah for its weekly account of high social life called "Deborah in Society" and the articles on servant management – "Duties of a Parlourmaid" – and etiquette – "When a house is taken for the Season, it is the usual custom to have the town address printed as well as the permanent one on the visiting card." "Quite a number of people are in Paris this week," Isabel read. "The Princes Gabriel, Philippe and Gennarro of Bourbon-Sicily, the Duke of Westminster, Lord and Lady Charles Beresford, the Grand Duke and Duchess Cyril, Lord Bochard and many others were congregated at the Ritz –" Then she stopped and stared at that list of august names. Bochard – it came back to her now, the name that had passed over her at the time. "My name is Bochard," she could remember him saying as clearly as if it was a minute ago, and immediately she began to wonder what might have happened if she had stayed in the car. Various sequences suggested themselves. In some he was an Ethel M. Dell hero and in next to no time was grasping her in his arms. In others they had a serious conversation during which he became more and more enthusiastic as he realized that in her mental approach to music she was as impressive as in her performance and interpretation. But whatever happened there was always a later scene in which Lord Bochard had arranged a private audition for her with Sir Henry Wood, which was followed by a brilliant appearance at the Queen's Hall at a Promenade Concert; or more exotically she was playing in some wonderful town house, probably Lord Bochard's, before a group of people like Mrs. Hatch-Edwards' guests, and when she had finished a man with long hair and the eyes of a saint bent over her hand, murmuring "Mademoiselle, you must make your début at once!" and this was Paderewski.

This was Isabel's dream, a small world of escape which she built up from day to day, changing details but not the essentials, and into which she could retire. It became like an old friend she could depend on. Sometimes she would find herself in it, and sometimes she would deliberately decide to enter it. But always, when it was over, she would think bitterly, "Time spent in dreaming is more time wasted." To dream was to confess failure. "But what a fool I was." And then: "What a fool I am." And she would go on quite cheerfully with whatever she was doing. Sometimes her lips formed a little ironical smile, directed against herself.

Spring came, summer came. There was a period of great tension while they waited for news of the result of Denny's intermediate examination, for which he went to London with a fellow articled clerk called Proctor – a dreary, round-shouldered young man with a blotchy complexion and spectacles. Denny's gloom prepared them for anything and it was almost a relief when they learned that he had failed only in one subject, company law. But it meant that he must take it all again later in the year. Proctor, of course, had passed. Mrs. Rowland pretended that it didn't matter at all; Sarah and Isabel exchanged tirades against the examiners, whom they held to be unfair and prejudiced, and dissuaded their brother from a plan of disappearing to Canada. But after this he was more sensitive than ever. He grew very pale and refused to spend money on himself.

Also, during the summer, they had attended the wedding of the oldest Mather girl, Edith. Isabel and Sarah were, of course, bridesmaids together with the other two Mathers. The bridegroom was in the shoe business and took Edith Mather back to Northampton. He seemed well off, which was quite a shock to the Rowlands, and in fact the comparative prosperity of the Mather family was in evidence throughout the affair, and though Denny and Sarah, in particular, tried to behave with remote superiority – the bridegroom's relations had to be seen to be believed, Sarah kept on saying – it seemed that the Mathers were more than ever having the last laugh.

However, there was an event on the credit side, for Dr. Preston appeared at the house one afternoon to invite Isabel to play a concerto at his October concert. What had caused this change of front? Possibly the simple reason that no one else was available. Or had he never been hostile to her at all? She dearly wanted to snub him, but it was not worth it. They settled on the Schumann and had a long and interesting conversation. Dr. Preston was full of knowledge about the Schumann marriage and old Wieck, the father-in-law, and about Dresden and Leipzig. Isabel, starved of such things, enjoyed herself – but she was conscious at the end of it that never once in the conversation had Dr. Preston inferred that she was more than the good local amateur. When her mother said afterwards, "There you are, dear, you said he was against you or some nonsense – I distinctly remember – and this shows he isn't," Isabel did not take her up; but it occurred to her that Dr. Preston could now afford to be her patron again, since she had come to nothing. All the same it was a chance, and if she did as well or better than before, who knew what might not happen or who might be there in the Town Hall audience?

Moreover this particular concerto was ideal for her, it seemed to represent life as she now knew it. The nostalgic mood of the lovely and romantic first movement was almost unbearable, all her own losses and frustrations were so completely expressed. And then in the second and third movements hope came in, and determination – and fulfilment. But was the fulfilment as convincing as the sadness? She tried to convince herself that it was, but it seemed to her no more than a brave show. The more she worked at it, the more it thrilled her, and the more she disliked wasting time teaching – she was not, in any case, a particularly good teacher. She was determined to make the most of her return to the public eye; the thought of playing again with an orchestra before a large audience was intoxicating. At heart she was an exhibitionist, and now all her buried lust for applause came out of hiding and brought a light to her eyes. So also her outbursts of

182

temperament returned. Mrs. Rowland and Sarah never knew whether they would find her in ecstasy or despair. It was, of course, despair immediately before the concert. There had been two rehearsals. She said they needed ten. She had quarrelled with Dr. Preston about tempo, the orchestra was ragged, everything would go wrong.

The evening came. The Town Hall was packed, as before. Everybody who was anybody in the town came to the subscription concerts, it was an evening-dress affair – which meant that the Rowlands had been forced to an impossible expenditure on clothes. Isabel was filled with wild hope; she could not repress the thought, "To-night everything will change." The Egmont overture was received warmly. When Dr. Preston came to fetch her to the platform, wearing his frosty smile, she felt, in spite of her tension, a sublime confidence.

She played superbly. Although Dr. Preston insisted on taking it as unromantically as possible – and she had enough discipline by now to know that he might be right – nothing could stifle the bitter-sweet sadness of that first movement, and in the glorious, controlled cadenza when the piano by itself caught together and summed up all of life's regrets and memories of other days (they were her regrets, her memories) she was almost astonished by her performance. At the end of the movement, she was conscious of a gasp and sigh that seemed to come from the whole audience, and there were one or two involuntary claps. She felt purged, she felt triumphant – the whole atmosphere of silent acclamation, the feeling of being looked at, the air, the sounds, the place, all was magic. This was where she belonged. This was how she must live, or there was no point in living. And she waited like a voluptuary for the two little taps of Dr. Preston's baton. Just as she had herself belonged with all her soul in the first movement, so she was now perfectly attuned to answer sadness with action in the second and third movements, which ran together, ending in the firm declaration of gaiety and happiness. Her playing was inspired, and Dr. Preston and the orchestra, mixed amateurs and professionals strengthened by a few military bandsmen, were inspired with her. If only she

183

could have stayed there for ever! But the coda came at last, Schumann's final affirmation, and her hands were still. It was over, as everything had to be over, and the applause stormed. Some people rose to their feet – a bouquet was presented to her, and another one. She left the platform, she was back again – again – and gone. It had been an ovation.

Then she was by herself in the smaller of the cold artists' rooms, feeling that queer unpleasant emotion of anticlimax, the inevitable companion of any sort of triumph. But almost at once Dr. Preston was there shaking her hand again and saying with what was for him extravagant warmth, "Better than I dared to hope!" And then the rest of the orchestra returned – it was the interval – and she was surrounded by those who belonged to the music society, the first violin, a professional, was telling her that he had never heard anything better, and there was her mother and Sarah who told her with sparkling eyes what notables were in the audience, the Debeyers, the Admiral, Lord and Lady so and so. Aunt Ada and Aunt Phyllis were outside, as also was Denny who was self-consciously wearing his father's evening dress – which had been altered for him after much moral soul-searching. Afterwards they went back to their seats, and the orchestra returned to the platform and Dr. Preston, with a new collar, followed, a moment after the first violin – she had noticed how heavily he breathed when he spoke to her, his face had been damp with perspiration and somehow this had been rather depressing. She stayed just off the platform, hidden from the audience by some ferns, and listened to the rest of the concert, for she could not go home until the others. She heard nothing, and kept nervously pinching her lower lip. She felt both exultant and depressed. It was wonderful to have proved that she could still do it, after three years. It was dreadful that it had to be in the same place, in the same circumstances.

The next day she was able to read "the well-known local pianist, Miss Isabel Rowland, had a great success with Schumann's *Concerto in A minor* –" There was at last another clipping to put with the rest. And surely something else would come of it? Surely there had been someone of

184

influence, another Lord Bochard, someone interested? But there was no one – nothing. Twenty-four hours after that brief, intoxicating applause, she might as well not have appeared at all. Everything went on as usual. And for the next week or so she had to conceal an intense disappointment. But what had she hoped for? She did not know herself.

Denny went off to London to take his exam again, and once again there was an atmosphere of tension and excitement in the house, not so much on his account as on Sarah's. For Isabel's sister had brought off a great *coup*. She was to appear in some Tableaux Vivants in aid of the Parish Hall furnishing funds, and the *coup* consisted in the fact that all the others in the show were people belonging to the *élite* of the town – except Isabel, who was to provide the musical accompaniment. Hours were spent in dressmaking, there were countless rehearsals during which Isabel sat woodenly at the piano and watched her sister flirt with Mr. Selby, the curate, and also masterfully force her acquaintance on everyone worth knowing. The performance took place at the end of November in an overheated church hall, hung everywhere with Union Jacks, and seemed to last for several hours. It consisted of twelve Tableaux with agonizingly long intervals between each while the scenes were arranged. The curtain would go up and two or three performers would maintain their poses heroically for two or three minutes while the distinguished audience, which as usual included Mr. and Mrs. Debeyer, the Admiral and his wife and a local Countess, clapped enthusiastically. The climax was a portrayal of "Nelson's Death", for which Isabel played "Rule, Britannia". Sarah's Tableau was the seventh, "Between Two Fires". Mr. Selby was the Puritan, dressed in severe black, and on either side of him were Miss Annesley Farquhar, in cinnamon-brown and white, the younger daughter of the Marine Commandant, and Sarah, who looked bewitching in a lily-leaf-green polonaise, striped shirt and white coif.

When it was all over, however, the only real satisfaction was the annoyance which had been caused to the Mathers, who could not hide their jealousy. For the Rowlands knew no one that they had not known before and Sarah was cut

185

dead in Peter Street by Miss Farquhar, an incident which she described furiously. Moreover, Mrs. Rowland had had to find money for Sarah's costume and what with Denny's second London trip, things had become very difficult. Isabel's teaching helped a little, but not enough. However, a fortnight later, she was in Webster's, desultorily browsing amongst their large collection of scores, when Mr. Rich called her into his compartment.

"I've got something that may interest you!"

She followed him in, suppressing excitement, for his tone indicated that it was something out of the ordinary, not merely another At Home, and since there were posters everywhere proclaiming a concert by Clara Butt, she wondered if her moment had come unexpectedly and she were to be invited to accompany the world-famous contralto. After all, there had been such a chance before, and Dr. Preston had robbed her of it. This was her hope as she sat bolt upright on the edge of the small cane chair, and she could hardly believe it when Mr. Rich went on to say that the Rotunda Grill Room needed a pianist to complete the trio which provided light music from seven to nine every evening. It was a regular job and she would get two pounds ten a week.

She sat there more tensely than before. It seemed to her the most bitter and mortifying impudence. Mr. Rich wiped his nose and regarded her through his pince-nez.

"They're a violin and 'cello, of course – and if they don't get a pianist, their jobs are gone too, of course. It seems one of them, the violin, he was in Dr. Preston's orchestra the other day and he suggested you to the manager, Mr. Chapman, and Mr. Chapman came here personally. I said I'd see how you felt about it."

"But I couldn't possibly –" she exclaimed. "Mr. Rich, how could you – of course I can't! "

"It wouldn't be hard work," he said, as if he were surprised.

"No. No. It's impossible! "

"It's a pity," Mr. Rich said, shrugging his thin rheumaticky old shoulders. It was as if he hated the idea of anyone ignoring regular money. "Perhaps you'd like to think about

186

it – but Mr. Chapman'll want an answer fairly soon, because of the other two. It's just from seven to nine in the evenings."

A dead weight of hopelessness had settled on her. Her lips quivered for a second into an ironical smile. There had been a result of her concerto after all, and this was it. There was an ache in her throat, but she could not burst into angry tears or even angry words. A wall had been built up to prevent her emotions from being expressed, except through the piano, and the solider the wall became as the months had gone by the more intense became the loneliness inside. She tried to tell herself that Mr. Rich was of no importance and it did not matter how he estimated her, but it did not stop the humiliation, and the dread.

"Well, I'll think about it – I'll have to speak to my mother," she said, and with those words she knew in her heart that the career she had hoped for was no longer possible. On her way home she took a detour to the front and there on the Promenade she sat on one of the benches, staring out at the sea, a trim figure, hands clasped inside a muff, her face pale. She sat there for a long time, brave, young, desperate.

"I could write to Mr. Durrell," she thought. "I ought to have before. I've meant to go for another lesson all this year. If I've improved enough, he may be able to suggest something even. If I go to the Rotunda, I'm finished. A grill-room pianist strumming out waltzes – I can't do it. I won't do it. Why should I be the one to make the sacrifices?" But she knew the answer: she was the one who had sacrifices to make. Tears burnt her eyes. "Why don't I ignore it and not tell them? No, I can't. But I must go and see Mr. Durrell – or a London agent – I could stay at Mrs. Slocombe's or take the excursion – no, I won't, I won't do any of it – it's hopeless – "

When she got up to go home she felt better and there was a faint smile on her lips, as if finally she were amused by her situation. It was true that she did get some satisfaction from it. What she was doing was not only right but it was also in a way dramatic.

At home Mrs. Rowland said, "My dear child, I don't like

the idea at all. There are bars there and one hears all sorts of things – it would be most unsuitable – "

Sarah frankly expressed a slightly different anxiety. "If you do it everyone will hear about it and look down their noses – "

"Sarah, you really are the limit!" Denny said furiously. "Who the devil cares what anyone thinks? Look down their noses – ugh – you sound like a shop assistant. Though I must say, having been there, I'm not keen on the idea of my sister – "

He, of course, was in any case sensitive about Isabel's earnings. None of them appreciated what she might feel as a pianist. But they all knew, as she did, that the money would be too useful, it could not be thrown away. However, they refused to show enthusiasm and she was forced ironically to persuade them that she ought to go, like an aristo insisting on mounting the tumbril. Mrs. Rowland went with her the next day to see Mr. Chapman, the Rotunda's manager, a shrewd, plump man with a charming Devon burr, and was easily assured by him that her daughter's respectability was in no danger at all. He seemed to be amused by the visit. Denny was placated by such remarks as, "Don't worry, we'll all be living off you for years." Isabel met the violinist, Mr. Silvester, and Mr. Halton, the 'cellist. They seemed drab but agreeable. And the affair was settled, she was to start the following week.

Aunt Ada came to tea and heard about it. She remarked, not without satisfaction, "All I can say, Bessie, is that no daughter of mine would work in such a place."

And this enabled Sarah to face the matter with resignation.

CHAPTER TWENTY-THREE

At the end of her first night at the Rotunda Isabel was not sure whether it had been a dreadful experience or whether in fact she had liked it. They had had a rehearsal in the morning when the grill room was empty except for cleaners, but when she entered it in the evening it was entirely different, not so much because of the people as of the warmth and the smell of food. She had a sensation of horror and also she felt enormously embarrassed as she, Mr. Silvester and Mr. Halton made their way to the platform, which was raised only a few inches off the floor and had a protective chest-high rail at either end, as though she were publicly doing something rather disgraceful. Then as they played she couldn't get over the fact that the noise of talk and plates rattling didn't waver for a second. She couldn't get over the fact that nobody appeared to look in their direction at all. The three up on their little platform might have been in another room. She was angry and yet together with her anger she felt a certain satisfaction; if you weren't observed and applauded, you weren't criticized; if this were the grave of her musical career, the great thing about a grave was that there was nowhere deeper to fall. And anyhow, after she had been going for half an hour, she found the necessary calmness to look round and watch the people who were not bothering to watch her. It certainly made a change from home. She played her solo beautifully, with great care, and inspired two or three desultory claps. At nine o'clock when the grill room was half empty they left as inconspicuously as they had come. But any tendency she might have had to burst into tears was neutralized by the evident pleasure of Mr. Silvester and Mr. Halton. Both felt that it had been a night of triumph.

"Well, it went very nicely, Miss Rowland," said Mr. Silvester, who had a dark moustache and long hair; he was recognizable as a musician both off and on the platform. The only time Isabel ever saw him not looking tired was when he was going home to bed.

Mr. Halton, the 'cellist, a man entirely colourless and nondescript, also bowed to her gratefully.

"See you to-morrow, Miss Rowland."

They went off to remove their dickeys. Isabel went to the small cloakroom which had been set aside for the use of the lady cashier and Mr. Chapman's secretary. Sarah was waiting for her there.

"A man spoke to me," she said excitedly. "I was waiting

189

just inside the swing doors – and he stood by me; I had a feeling he was going to speak – and he asked me if I'd like to have a drink!"

"How awful!" Isabel gasped. She was horrified. "Whatever did you do?"

"Oh, it was quite all right – I just looked at him and he said he was awfully sorry, he thought I was someone else."

"You ought not to have been standing there. You ought to have come straight in here."

"Well, I came after that, but of course I wanted to hear how you sounded – I could hear every time the doors opened – it sounded very good."

They went out into the vestibule just as a party of four came along from the door at the end which led to the long bar at the back. It was a gay party. There were two young men being refined and gay and two girls being vulgar and gay. Powder, paint, furs and scent passed by the sisters. They went out loudly through the swing doors. Isabel and Sarah exchanged a glance which was both disapproving and excited.

"I bet they were naval officers," Sarah whispered. "I think the one that spoke to me was, too. Those girls were t-a-r-t-s. How disgusting!"

"How can you possibly tell they were naval officers?"

"Oh, well, there's a look about them, isn't there?" said Sarah, shrugging her shoulders.

There was a look about naval officers, it was perfectly true, but neither Isabel nor Sarah had ever taken much notice of it or of them. The Navy and the dockyard had always been a separate kingdom in the town. The town came into contact with it, as also with the Army and the Marines – but these were smaller entities – at the higher and lower social levels, but hardly at all in between. Aristocracy came to Admiralty House from the surrounding countryside, dancing men from H.M. ships and the Naval barracks graced the Assemblies and the important private dances, and every Thursday night one or two rows of the circle at the Royal Theatre were taken for officers splendid in mess dress and their guests; on the other hand the lower deck crowded the public bars, and boldly visited streets which the genteel mentioned in hushed tones, if it were necessary to mention them at all.

Apart from being aware of its existence they had never thought very much about the Navy. Isabel knew vaguely that naval officers came to the Rotunda, but it was only after she had been there a week that she began to realize what a popular place it was with them. Almost all of them who came ashore and did not live locally tended to congregate in the bar downstairs, which was respectable, or in the long bar at the back, which was not. Ladies of the town also congregated there – the commissionaire did not allow them in at the front. It was quite an education for Isabel. In her first few weeks there she learned a great many things that she had never dreamed of, and so did Sarah, who sometimes came and waited for her on the first evening. They were conscious of the naval officers as a type, for in some queer way they did all look the same. They had an open-air look, of course, that was one thing. They all sounded excessively refined. They all wore untidy old clothes, the shabbier the better. They all gave the impression of despising everyone they saw except other naval officers. It amused Isabel to watch them.

After the first few evenings, however, she realized that it also amused some of them at least to watch her. The first request she had was for the waltz from *The Chocolate Soldier*, a tune she detested. But before that there had been established a habit of people to come and lean on the rail behind her when she was playing her solo. The fact was that within a few nights Isabel had made quite a considerable success. Suddenly she was conscious that people were listening when she was playing; by no means all, of course —it was a grill room; but some, and they supplied her with new hope, and a new dream that one evening a London agent, or somebody influential, would come in for a meal and listen and – but for the moment *The Chocolate Soldier* request was important, for the young man who asked for it also asked her out to lunch. She refused and the next evening he brought her an expensive box of chocolates. Unfortunately he wanted to hear *The Chocolate Soldier* again. She took the chocolates home where they were eaten by Mrs. Rowland, who disapproved but had a sweet tooth, by Sarah and the dog Boxer, who discovered them behind a cushion. The next evening he brought flowers. He was a Paymaster Sub-Lieutenant. She agreed to have tea with him in the Winter Garden of the Imperial Hotel, so long as Sarah came too.

His name was Mackintosh. He was twenty-two, he had thin fair hair and a thin agreeable face. He told her that he had never seen anyone with such expressive eyes. She found him absurd but pleasant and well behaved.

She always remembered that Saturday afternoon in the Palm Court. It was crowded. People came there after the theatre matinée, on Saturdays there were always some of what the Mathers called the *élite* who took the opportunity of watching the *demi-monde*, for some notorious girls were there as well, with their escorts. Some of them were extremely beautiful and made remarkable marriages. It was quite a fascinating scene and Isabel also found it a luxury to listen to the Winter Garden orchestra. The Paymaster made shy conversation, at first to Isabel and then more and more to Sarah, who was all agog and looking very attractive; Isabel was too busy watching everyone to pay much attention to him. She saw one couple, a very starchy mother and daughter, whom they had known when they had lived at the mill; but the starchy couple did not or would not look in their direction. Two officers from the Paymaster's ship, however, stopped by their table for a minute – it was a new and flattering experience. Sarah was in the seventh heaven when they went home.

That was all there was to the Paymaster except for a letter from Malta a few weeks later, but by that time others had taken his place.

The fact was that the Rotunda job had unexpectedly caused a revolution in the sisters' lives. A succession of lieutenants and sub-lieutenants appeared. They were not at all backward in getting to know Isabel. Although the grill room itself was respectable the reputation of the Rotunda long bar naturally led the customers to suppose that any of the staff might be susceptible to a friendly approach. Isabel soon learnt how to deal with this, either with indifference, or with purposeful failure to understand. It came naturally to her for she despised

192

them, just as she despised herself for being there. How could they guess that privately she had a mild but shocking envy of the tarts? In any case some of them were entranced to find her so chilly, and were still further entranced, if they succeeded in taking her home, to find her sister equally attractive and a good deal more enthusiastic.

Sarah was astonished and delighted at what was happening. She fell in and out of love regularly. Most of them were about the town only for a short time – they were at the barracks waiting for a new appointment, or their ships might be in for refit or coaling – and Sarah changed from one to another, showing remarkable powers of adjustment. Isabel could not share these emotional ups and downs.

Sarah made no bones about it, however, that it was in her mind to marry into the Navy.

"There's something attractive about them, Isabel, don't you agree – it must be something about the life which makes them so nice – and as a wife you get asked everywhere, and of course you can go abroad. They have the most marvellous time at places like Malta. The only trouble is you want one who has money. Oh, you needn't look like that, I know it sounds awful, but it's the truth, isn't it? It's all right if they're single when they've only got their pay – but awful to be married to one; it would be like marrying poor Selby –"

Mr. Selby, her curate, had recently become engaged and Sarah had been showing a noticeable lessening of enthusiasm for her church work.

Denny had a different view of their new acquaintances. He was jealous of them, he disliked them and he was depressed by them. If one of them were brought home when he was in the house he disappeared morosely to his bedroom.

"A stinking snobbish bunch of poops," he described them. It was as well that his morale was temporarily raised by the news that he had passed his exam at the second try – news which of course made Isabel's stay at the Rotunda permanent, for he could not earn anything for another two or three years.

Mrs. Rowland, on the other hand, got on well with them, she made almost no attempt to chaperone and was merely relieved that her daughters were no longer social recluses.

Sarah' had never been so gay and optimistic. Although the attitude of the naval men to Isabel was uniformly admiring and respectful – after all, it was her playing and the sight of her playing which first attracted them – she knew they often found it difficult to get on with her and in the end they usually spent more time with Sarah, who in any case had more time. Pupils and practice took up most of Isabel's day. But for her, as for Sarah, it was a relief that a life which had largely consisted of preserving a front with which to face the Mathers was over. Hard up they remained, but now the house was often full of noise and guests. They were taken to theatre matinées, they were guests in wardrooms on board H.M. ships, they went to the skating rink and almost every Saturday afternoon to the Winter Garden for tea.

Isabel enjoyed watching her sister. She was fascinated by her effortless sincerity. At the skating rink, for example, Sarah was, like herself, quite a competent performer – for some years skating had been a rage in the town – but when they went under naval encouragement and esecort Isabel noticed that all her sister's enjoyment was in the spilling over and being helped up department. As you skated past Sarah you heard a naval voice saying, "I'm sure I absolutely crushed you! " or "How light you are! " or merely peals of laughter. Isabel also could not and on the whole did not wish to compete with Sarah's moments of whimsy which appeared to be so endearing to the masculine mind – the bold mention of words like "stomach" or saying airily, "Do you know, I was thinking in my bath this morning – " It was not that these things shocked anyone in the year 1913, but it was charming to pretend that they did.

It was just the same as at school when Isabel had often wished she could imitate Sarah's wonderful friendliness. Now she wished she could get the same harmless enjoyment out of the game of sex as her sister did.

"But they're all such bores," she would think. And yet – it was not that. If she could have behaved like Sarah, she would have. The constant affirmation of feminine innocence was Sarah's line, and it was hard to know to what extent she was doing it on purpose and to what extent it was instinctive.

194

Once, when they were invited to tea on board a cruiser, Sarah caused a sensation by insisting on knowing what those men were doing who kept leaving the ship to go to a dockside hut. The half-dozen officers present subsided into schoolboy hysterics. The men were going to the lavatory. Afterwards, Isabel accused her angrily of knowing all the time and Sarah was most indignant. But her most noteworthy innocent remark was at home when she pointed to the pelmets over the drawing-room curtains, which were her own work.

"I made those pelvises," she said.

Lt. Crindle, R.N., and Lt. Jeavers, R.N., were with them that afternoon and at once became Sarah's devoted slaves.

CHAPTER TWENTY-FOUR

A week afterwards Sarah came home to tea with Crindle, Jeavers and a new young man, whose name Isabel did not catch. They had met at the rink and the new man had been at Osborne and in the old *Britannia* with Crindle and Jeavers—the same year's intake always knew each other for good. Sarah was not showing much interest in him. He was rather squat and broad-shouldered, he had very thick, dark brown hair, and a smile which displayed very white and even teeth. He told Isabel that he hadn't heard her play at the Rotunda because he was so broke that he almost never came ashore.

"It's the truth, don't laugh."

"I'm not laughing," Isabel said. "It just seems to me to be so ridiculous. It only means you must have spent more than you could afford."

"Really? Aren't you rather severe, Miss Rowland?" He was half-amused, half-bored. He was not precisely good-looking, but he had a great deal of charm. His voice was husky and mildly arrogant. His clothes were terrible. In fact he was very like all of them, and probably nothing would have happened had not Denny come in later on. By that time she was at the piano, accompanying Crindle who was an enthusiastic tenor and wished to sing them "Songs of Araby". Sarah and Jeavers sat giggling quietly on the sofa and the new man sat looking reflective. His face in repose was rather mournful, but it would light up immediately if he spoke or anyone spoke to him. As the song was ending Denny came in. He glanced at the guests with his usual unfriendliness. It was always particularly irritating to him to meet them when he was in his sober, neat office suit.

Isabel hit the final chord and heard Sarah's best party voice behind her. "Oh, Mr. Nunn, this is my brother –"

"Hullo, how d'you do," Denny said, as rudely as possible. "I was looking for a book."

"What's it called?" asked Sarah.

"What does that matter? *Principles of Banking*, if you want to know –"

"Denny's learning to be an accountant," Sarah explained.

"I've met you somewhere," the guest said. Isabel turned and saw him frowning thoughtfully. "My name's George Nunn," he went on. "I'm sure I've seen you."

"Mr. Nunn, Mr. Rowland," Sarah said. "Mr. Rowland, Mr. Nunn."

"Probably someone else," Denny murmured. "Oh, there it is – excuse me –"

"Accountant, accountant –" Mr. Nunn said. "I know it! By Jove, what a memory! I met you with young what's his name – Talbot."

"Talbot?" Sarah said. "Do you mean Edwin Talbot?"

"Why, yes, Edwin," said Mr. Nunn, and it was one of those vaguely important moments. Isabel, listening to them, was perfectly conscious that Sarah's voice was high with new interest, and that Mr. Nunn also had in a second subtly changed his attitude.

"Denny was at school with him," Sarah said. "They were very great friends. Edwin used to come to the Mill – that was our old house, Mr. Nunn –" Sarah never lost an opportunity of bringing the idea of departed glory into a conversation, and as the months went by the Mill House became larger and larger.

"Nice people, the Talbots," Mr. Nunn said.

"Awfully nice!" Sarah agreed.

Denny found his book.

"Don't you remember, though?" Mr. Nunn said, turning to him. "It was in the Rotunda – I say, it is a coincidence – oh, yes, and not only in the Rotunda – "

"What were you doing in the Rotunda with Edwin Talbot?" Sarah asked her brother in amazement.

"Do shut up, can't you?" Denny whispered to her furiously. He was flushed and embarrassed.

"Now I come to think of it, it must have been someone else," Mr. Nunn said.

Denny mumbled incoherently and retreated.

"It seems extraordinary him not telling us – when could it have been?" Sarah said. She smiled radiantly at Mr. Nunn. "Brothers are awful! As a matter of fact I think men are awful, the whole lot of you. You all stick together."

"We all stick to-geth-er!" Crindle sang.

"It's so strange your knowing the Talbots," Sarah said.

"Play something for the good of our souls, Miss Isabel," Jeavers requested.

"*The Moonlight Sonata,*" Crindle said.

"No, too morbid."

"Don't let's get the morbs," Sarah exclaimed. "Don't you hate getting the morbs, Mr. Nunn?" It was always fascinating to watch the perfectly open way Sarah removed all her attention from one young man and gave it to another. From the moment George Nunn had mentioned the name Talbot he had become the centre of Sarah's interest. "You must have your fortune told," she said. "Isabel tells wonderful fortunes. I wish I could, but I can't do anything."

"Who cares about George's fortune?" Crindle said. "Let's have some music."

"I don't know that I want to know my fortune," George Nunn smiled. "I'm the sort of person everything happens to. Sufficient unto the day is my motto. It's better not to know about to-morrow."

"But to-morrow may be wonderful, I'm sure it will be – and Isabel's wonderful at it!"

"I certainly am not—" But in the end Isabel did tell his fortune, because people generally did what Sarah wanted them to do, and Mr. Nunn watched, smiling, as she laid the cards out on a private system, counting under her breath. Then she told him whatever came into her head. "You're a person who gets on well with everyone, but you're rather lonely underneath; you're deeper than other people imagine; I see a good many love affairs; oh, yes, and there's money coming to you. I don't see any illness. If you have any worries they'll be resolved, I mean cleared up. That's all."

"I liked the bit about the money coming," he said.

"Now tell me mine," Jeavers demanded.

"No," Isabel said seriously, "you had yours last week in the tea-leaves and it would break the luck."

The party was soon over, for Mrs. Rowland came in murmuring about the time to Isabel. The guests departed, after George Nunn had written in Sarah's autograph book. He had lazy, untidy handwriting. He had put down:

"Miss Isabel and Miss Sarah
    Are as fair as the morning sun.
    I can't think of anything fairer,
    So will sign myself simply George Nunn."

"Rather cheeky," Sarah remarked. "He was rather nice, though, too. He wouldn't skate, he just watched—he said it was too much bother to put them on. I hope we see him again."

"I don't expect so," Isabel said. "He looked bored, I thought."

A couple of hours later, however, she was astonished to see him in the grill room. He was having a chop at a table by himself. He was some distance away and she kept looking towards him, but never caught his eye. It was a curious thing, but she felt vaguely stirred by him. He was quite attractive and charming in a distant way, but a good many of them were that. It was not that he knew the Talbots, because, unlike Sarah, she had never cared about the Talbots. But she wished that she were not part of the Rotunda trio and that she were

198

sitting with him. It was so rare for anyone to attract her that she was quite excited and pleased by the wish; it meant that for once she was reacting normally, like Sarah. She was glad that her solo to-night was to be Chopin's C minor "Revolutionary", full of fireworks and emotion. When Mr. Silvester and Mr Halton left her to it, she improvised for a minute or two and, as usual, two or three men came up to the rail to watch her. He, however, seemed to be still busy with his chop. Annoyed, Isabel set about the Chopin and determined to make enough noise at least to disturb his concentration. She played with everything she had and consequently forgot all about him. She created sadness, fervour, magnificence – there were a dozen at the rail at the end, and clapping came from all over the grill room. Mr. Silvester and Mr. Halton took their places again, looking surprised. But he was still sitting at his table.

"That's what he thinks of me," she thought, humiliated, and she chatted to two of the listeners at the rail who were expressing appreciation. Then the trio went into action again. When the number was over a waiter handed her a folded note. She opened it and read : "Wonderful! G.N." She felt an immediate, absurd glow of pleasure. Her head had jerked up and she was smiling across at him. He was watching her this time and he half-rose in his chair and grinned back at her. But a little later on, when she looked again, he had gone.

"To the Empire, I suppose," she thought, disappointed.

The trio packed up, and she went away to change her shoes and put on her coat. Sarah was not waiting for her and she was quite relieved, for she wanted a few moments on her own to think calmly about Mr. Nunn – how strange it was that someone could come out of the blue and mean something to you – or was it some nonsensical imagination on her part, which, once having been imagined, was like a spot on a carpet that couldn't be got rid of?

When she went out into the vestibule there he was, talking to Sarah. She was relieved, ludicrously relieved, to see him.

"He wants to walk home with us," Sarah said. "Shall we let him?"

Isabel nodded.

"I hope you enjoyed your chop," she said. "But thank you for the note."

"I didn't know you played like that," George Nunn said. "What are you doing here? They said you were good, but I didn't expect anything like that."

This kind of thing had been said so often to Isabel that she was more surprised if people didn't say it than if they did. That *he* should say it, however, thrilled her.

"I'm glad you liked it," she said. "I'm afraid it wasn't very good really. But why are you here? You said you couldn't afford to come ashore."

"My presence is financed by a small loan from a brother officer, a trusting, well-deserving soul," George Nunn said.

He walked home with them, Isabel on the inside and Sarah in the middle. Isabel told herself that he was only like the rest of them. They all looked the same and sounded the same. The only point of variation, as Sarah said, was that some had money and some hadn't. George Nunn wore an old trilby hat with the brim turned down, a scarf round his neck and no overcoat, although it was chilly. She glanced sideways at him past Sarah's smiling face and she thought that if she were to meet him in some town a hundred miles from the sea she would still know at once that he was in the Navy. He told them, however, that he loathed it.

"I'm simply not fitted for it. It's perfectly monstrous the way people take some poor innocent little boy and pitchfork him into an unutterable place like Osborne."

"What are you fitted for?" Isabel asked.

"That's the tragedy, of course. I'm fitted for nothing else."

However, he was very entertaining about it. He kept up a flow of chatter all the way. He loathed the Navy, he liked golf and fishing, he also liked music. He was surprisingly knowledgeable about it. He detested Wagner, he was fond of Liszt – "I suppose mainly because I admire his private life." He had heard Busoni, Paderewski, Melba, Ysaye; he had seen the Russian Ballet. He had a brother, married, who lived in town, but hardly any other family at all. His parents had died in India when he was a child, but not before they had sentenced him to the Navy.

200

"Thank heavens there'll be a war before long. It won't be so bad in a war."

He was in a destroyer which was in for a refit. They saw a good deal of him in the next two or three weeks. He was often in the Rotunda, and now he always came to the rail and listened admiringly. His presence gave her a peculiar thrill. However much she told herself that he was like the others, he became less and less like anyone else. He had a way of looking at her, as if he were a doctor from whom no secrets could be hidden. She did not flatter herself that he really came to see her. He enjoyed listening, but the real purpose was to accompany Sarah on the way home – that was the way it happened with everyone and she was under no illusion that now, when for the first time she had fallen in love herself, it would be any different.

It was not. Sarah had one of her bursts of romantic enthusiasm and her world became suddenly all George Nunn. The three of them were often together, but sometimes he had free time during the day and then usually Sarah went out with him – it was always impossible for Isabel to join them, she would be going to a pupil or having to practise. He bought flowers and chocolates for them both – all on borrowed money, he said – in any case whatever he had he was only too willing to spend. Sarah admired his lordly way with everybody and everything not of the Navy, especially waiters, who always gave him affectionate attention. When he came to the Rotunda he walked back with them both afterwards, being flippant with Sarah and politely serious with Isabel. She knew he liked hearing her play, but she had the feeling that she was in the way after that. One evening, however, he was there at the rail and she knew that Sarah was not coming. She was out with her mother at a church whist drive.

She would never forget that walk home. First of all, while they were still in the Rotunda, to ease her conscience she had urged upon him that he needn't feel obliged to accompany her. He seemed to be rather annoyed, and she hoped for his sake that he wasn't too fond of Sarah. She knew from experience that her sister's enthusiasm was waning and her absence at the whist drive was a symptom. The fact was, Isabel knew, that Sarah had been disappointed to discover that George Nunn's acquaintance with the Talbot family had been slight, and that he had no intention of renewing it. The mention of that name had set old dreams going and she knew that Sarah had seen herself meeting, in particular, Edwin Talbot again.

Then after they had been walking for a few minutes, exchanging a few banalities—when Sarah was present, there was nonstop chatter—he made a curious remark.

"You know, you baffle me," he said. "No one would really take you for a breadwinner."

"I'm not the breadwinner," she retorted.

"Well, you don't play at the Rotunda because you like it, do you?" George Nunn said, unperturbed.

She was still very tense.

"One doesn't do everything because one likes it."

"Haven't you ever thought that but for your family you could have made a name for yourself?"

She was not going to have him disparaging the family.

"Certainly not," she said, angrily.

"I apologize. I was just thinking aloud. It seemed to me that your place is the concert platform not a grill room. It's perfectly monstrous. I had to go and tell a table of stiffs to keep quiet to-night, while you were playing."

Isabel was startled. She had seen him do it, without realizing what he was doing. It was a perfect example of his impudence.

"I shall be sacked if you do things like that!"

He seemed surprised.

"Nonsense. They didn't mind. They merely didn't realize—no, what I meant was, you seem to me to get the dirty end of the stick. I mean, your mother's a perfect dear, your sister's a pippin, your brother's a good chap—"

"They've got nothing to do with it," Isabel exclaimed. She felt overwhelmed. He came out of the blue like this and tore apart the covering to her innermost private feelings—so private that she refused to acknowledge them. She hurried on glibly, "I did think about it once, but it means a terrible amount of work, and then without influence—well, you have to give a recital and pay for the hall and everything and hope the critics notice you—but the trouble is, you may have made a

202

stir in a town like this, but if you go to London you just find you're one amongst hundreds. No, I'm very lucky really to be able to make what I do."

She was quite breathless. George Nunn laughed.

"You're a very attractive liar, Miss Rowland, if you permit me to say so, and you're a very nice person, but, frankly, I don't think you enjoy yourself as much as you should." He was silent for a moment. "However, I suppose you'd like to tell me to concentrate on my own worries rather than yours."

It took her several seconds to pull herself together. Then she burst out, "Have you any? Yes, if you had any, I certainly should, Mr. Nunn."

"My name's George, please. Sarah calls me George."

"It's very forward of her." But she felt extraordinarily happy. It was a pleasant shock to realize that he regarded her as a person with whom he wished to be on intimate terms. She was not merely a pianist with a frustrated talent; she was glad that that subject had been changed. She went on in an easier tone, "Have you really worries? It's hard to believe."

"The situation is hopeless, but not serious – but you know I have, anyhow – don't you remember seeing it in the cards?"

"Oh, that's only Sarah. She makes me do it. I don't see a thing, really."

"More's the pity, because you said my problem would be solved."

Isabel screwed up her nose.

"Oh, bills," she said. "Well, you could easily pay them if you were economical."

"That's all very well, but one's got to live," he pointed out.

"I think that's a disgraceful attitude!" she said.

"It probably is. You know, I really need someone like you at my elbow to keep saying 'stop' – to give me a moral yardstick –"

"Oh, you can laugh at me, if you like," she began indignantly.

"I'm serious." They reached the Promenade, for they had taken the long way back, rather to her surprise. The lights of a cruiser flickered prettily out in the harbour, and the sky was full of stars. It was beautiful, but too cold for walking

203

slowly. George Nunn, however, seemed to be in no hurry. When he spoke again, he did sound quite serious. "The trouble is," he said, "these trades-people give you credit because they know they can always squeeze you – I think it's a bit monstrous when you consider what they get out of the Navy. But what's particularly ticklish at the moment is that my tailors have threatened to write to my skipper."

"I'm not surprised," Isabel said. "What would happen then?"

"Well, it's taken out of your pay – they know they're quite safe, you see – but, of course, I go on the black list and probably spend the next ten years amid the excitements of Invergordon. Not a funny prospect."

She saw that he really was worried and her righteous mood changed instantly to tenderness. He was so appallingly wrong and so helpless. He was a man made for a private income. She thought for a moment.

"Why don't you write to your brother?"

"My dear brother," George Nunn said, recovering some gaiety, "wouldn't give me the parings of his nails."

"Isn't there anyone else?"

"Hardly anyone. There's one decrepit uncle in Cumberland who can't stand me. He's dried up, anyway. I've touched him before."

"But is it so much then?" she asked. A mad idea had occurred to her that possibly she could lend –

"My tailor's bill? Oh, about a hundred and sixty."

She thought that she could not have heard correctly.

"*How* much?" she exclaimed.

He amplified the figure, "I think it's a hundred and sixty-seven."

She stopped still in amazement.

"But it's impossible! Do you mean *pounds*? I've never heard – why, that much hasn't been spent on me in my whole life! Why, it's terrible!" She could not get over it. She would never have dreamt of such an amount.

"Well, now, be reasonable, my dear soul –"

"Be reasonable!"

"Uniforms cost money, and then one must have a suit or

two now and then. I know I'm a complete fool where money's concerned," he said humbly.

Isabel sighed and continued walking. What was the use of trying to explain to him that he had been using the tailors, and doubtless others, to gain a higher standard of living than he could afford and therefore was entitled to? But a terrible thought occurred to her, "Still, that's what Denny and Sarah do to me." She was shocked at herself.

"I don't see what you're going to do," she said.

"Nor do I, frankly."

And they said no more about it. She told Sarah when she and her mother came back, and Sarah was so astonished and impressed by the grandeur of the tailors' bill that she again began to feel warmly towards George Nunn.

"People with big faults have big virtues," she said.

"No, the virtues only look larger."

"Well, there's the Prodigal Son, after all," Sarah laughed. "I must say, it's no wonder he hasn't seen the Talbots much. But he is nice."

They both went to bed thinking furiously what could be done to save him.

"He must write to his uncle," Isabel decided. And the next day Sarah agreed with her. They discussed the matter a good deal, although they did not, of course, mention it to Mrs. Rowland or Denny.

When George Nunn came to tea the following Sunday afternoon, they presented him with an ultimatum. He must write his begging letter, he must promise to reform, to live within his means – in this way only could he be sure of maintaining the interest and friendship of the Rowland sisters. They were both breathless and excited as they talked. The bill for a hundred and sixty-seven pounds had struck their imagination; it was in the grand manner and added a new dimension to him.

He agreed, very reluctantly.

"I tell you, it won't be the slightest use. He's made it quite plain he didn't want to have anything to do with me."

"Oh, you're ridiculous!" Sarah said warmly. "Goodness, if only we had an uncle –" For they had been further impressed to learn that George Nunn's relation was a retired manufacturer of steel tubes.

"He's a ghastly, pompous old fool. What on earth can I say to him?"

They spent the whole afternoon and evening concocting a respectful appeal, gradually persuading him to be more humble and apologetic. It all went against George Nunn's grain, but he was prepared to accept advice in the end. "My dear uncle, you will probably be surprised to hear from me after so long an interval – I find myself in a very unfortunate position –" or "Dear Uncle Frederick, I am forced to write to ask for your assistance – I give you my word that –" He covered sheets of notepaper under their dictation. Mrs. Rowland was resting upstairs, she had become prone to headaches. Denny looked in once and Sarah ordered him to go away. In the end it was done, the envelope was addressed, Isabel supplied a stamp and they insisted on seeing it put into a letter-box.

"You're both extraordinary," said George Nunn. "If it works I'll never forget it – I'll never forget it anyway. I couldn't have written such a frightful thing by myself to save my life. Anyhow, I'm terribly grateful."

Two weeks went by, a time of painful anxiety for Isabel. She prayed that this absurd uncle in Cumberland would come to his rescue. When George Nunn came into the Rotunda he at once looked towards him enquiringly, but was always disappointed by him shaking his head.

Then one evening he said, "I'm afraid I shan't be seeing you for a bit. I'm off to Devonport to-morrow."

"Oh." She felt like choking. But they always came and went suddenly – it was nothing to be surprised about.

"With any luck I'm due for a spell in a hot sunny clime." He seemed to be very pleased with himself.

"Is it to do with the bill?"

"No, they're still holding their fire. What I hope is to be a few thousand miles away as soon as possible."

He walked home with them. He and Sarah were in very bright form. Isabel hardly said a word. When they reached Brook Place, he turned to them both. It was a picture she always kept of him, his face pale in the gas-light, the scarf, the awful old trilby.

"I had some other news to-day," he said.

"Oh, George!" Sarah exclaimed. "You mean he's sent it? How dare you not tell us before! Has he?"

"The old boy has coughed it up. Two hundred quid! He wishes never to hear from me again, etc., but he's turned up trumps, that's the main thing. I'm solvent, hurrah! The tailors will love me again. I sent them off eighty straight away."

"Eighty?" said Isabel, who was trembling with a mixture of happiness and sadness.

"Well, it doesn't do to comfort them too much. I thought about half was right. I must say it broke my heart to write the cheque."

"You must send the rest at once!" Isabel exclaimed, shocked.

"Oh, lord!" George Nunn said, smiling at her. "What have I done now? I was expecting to be praised. Do you realize that I acted within minutes?"

"You must promise to send the other eighty-seven pounds," Isabel said. She felt deeply about it.

"I expect he means to," Sarah put in. She also had been taken aback. The Rowland family had been brought up to believe in the prompt settlement of accounts.

"You must promise!"

"Good heavens," said George Nunn, looking for a second very bored. But he brightened immediately. "Certainly I promise. By all means. First thing after breakfast; I shan't be able to withstand the thought of your accusing eyes. I swear it. Well, good-bye, Isabel. Good-bye, Sarah. Say good-bye for me to your mother and to the esteemed accountant, whose bedroom light I see is on —"

And a few minutes later he had gone, with a last charming smile and a wave of his hat.

"I'm sure he'll send the rest of it," Isabel said. She felt unbelievably miserable.

"I suppose he will."

The next day a large box of chocolates arrived from him. And later there was one postcard — from Gibraltar — which the sisters tore up ceremonially and threw into the fire. For a fortnight after his casual departure Sarah had met Crindle when she was shopping in Peter Street. She returned home full of indignation. She could hardly wait for Isabel to send a pupil away.

Crindle had told her as a piece of interesting gossip that before he left George Nunn had had a tremendous stroke of luck. An uncle had sent him two hundred pounds in response to a begging letter.

" Well, that was true," Isabel said.

" Yes, but do you know what else I found out? He didn't go straight to Devonport from here, he went up to town on leave! You see? He daren't tell us. ' I should think he's blued most of it by now!' Crindle said. Isn't it despicable? He wouldn't have had a penny of it but for us! And all *we* got was a measly box of chocolates."

" It is disgusting," Isabel said in a low voice.

Hence their attitude to his postcard – on which was a formal, frivolous message. They had a few heated discussions about his outrageous behaviour. What they would say to him if he dared to turn up again! But gradually George Nunn ceased to be a topic of conversation. He did not fade, however, from Isabel's mind, but took his place there with other ghosts, her father, Nicky, Sadler, Lord Bochard. She remembered his smile, his trilby, his feeling for music, his sudden discomforting perception during that walk along the Promenade. Then another year began. There was the crowd every night at the Rotunda, there were two more Mather marriages, Denny joined the Territorials, Sarah found an occupation teaching the first steps in French to children at a kindergarten. A local child violinist of great promise played at one of Dr. Preston's concerts and not only did everyone Isabel met for days mention him to her – Aunt Ada went almost into ecstasy about him – but it transpired that, as a result of hearing about this very performance, a London agent had written to the boy's parents, and there were great things ahead for him. She knew now, and everybody knew, that nothing of this sort would ever happen to her.

CHAPTER TWENTY-FIVE

I t was October, 1915, a month in which the Austrian Third
Army took Belgrade and Servia declared war on Bulgaria;
Japan joined the Treaty of London, and M. Briand became
the Premier of France; there were battles in Artois and
Champagne, and the British made progress near Loos; Nurse
Cavell was shot in Brussels, five German transports were sunk
in the Baltic, the British and French landed at Salonika; and
God knew how many were killed, how many legs and arms
were blown off or amputated, how many eyes became blind,
how much pain there was, how much fear, anxiety, unbearable grief; it was another month in the war. Every evening the
Rotunda was crowded.

It was a Saturday. The trio were playing "Destiny" and
then a selection from *Veronique*. Mr. Silvester was still the
violinist, as he had a weak heart, but Mr. Halton, the 'cellist,
had gone into the Army and had been replaced by Mr.
Epworth, who had silvery hair and bloodshot eyes. His breath
smelt of whisky or peppermint. He could hardly play the 'cello
at all and often when a difficult piece began he would make
an excuse to leave the platform, and come back when it was
over. Isabel admired his nerve, although Mr. Silvester often
indignantly confided to her that before the war he wouldn't
have lasted two days. But Mr. Epworth was a good-humoured
and interesting man, who often entertained her with
reminiscences of a highly unsuccessful but varied life. He had
begun as a boy bugler at Woolwich and he had been all over
the world. He was always very courteous.

Isabel played absent-mindedly, automatically. She could go
through the whole of the two hours between seven and nine
without a single conscious reflection that she was there. Mr.
Silvester would nod to her or speak to her and she would nod or
reply in the same way that one wound a wrist-watch – the kind

209

of action that one realized must have taken place, but couldn't remember performing. Other things absorbed her this evening, the meaning of the tea-leaves in somebody's cup, whether Sarah would remember to give Boxer his yeast pill, a newspaper article she had read that morning. Mr. Silver nodded. Isabel began *Veronique*. The music was part of the atmosphere, like the smell of food – the Rotunda mixed grill was famous – and the noise of plates, the calls of the waiters. She glanced round as she played to see if she knew anyone. The place was packed with officers and girls, women, ladies, wives, fiancées, tarts. Isabel knew all the tarts, the grand superior ones, and it was a game of never-failing fascination to watch their progress. She also had to report on it to Sarah. "Violet had new furs. Susie was with a Commander I haven't seen before." It was gaiety and noise and the smell of food, and it was all sadness, but often one felt sorry for the wrong people.

The trio came to the end of *Veronique* and were rewarded with a couple of desultory claps from the far end of the grill room. Mr. Silvester bowed acknowledgment and Mr. Epworth was already on his way out. Isabel remained to play her solo. This was still the moment which made the Rotunda endurable to her although she had long ago given up hoping that someone influential would hear her. It was still something to play a solo in public every day, even if most of the audience went on talking and eating. And there was still the satisfaction of giving unexpected pleasure to some of the thousands in uniform who now passed through the town. To-night she played Chopin's *Barcarolle*. While she played she was conscious that someone had come to the rail, as people often did. Every night at the Rotunda was the same, and yet every night was different – sometimes she could feel more people listening, and to-night was like that. At the end there was quite a burst of clapping for a few seconds, and from just behind came a well-remembered voice.

"Still strumming away?"

She turned incredulously and gasped with pleasure.

"Good heavens, was it you standing there –"

"It's wonderful to see you again," George Nunn said. "I

was hoping you'd still be here and here you are, I think it's perfectly wonderful. What a frightful mob of people they have here now, this damned war's ruined everything. Oh, God, it's so strange to walk in here and see you just exactly the same."

Mr. Silvester was back and looking at her, and Mr. Epworth was settling behind the 'cello, but for once she was not mechanically getting on with the job. She would not have believed that anyone could make her feel like this. She was shaking, trembling all over, she was breathless, her lips were frozen in a painful smile. Physically she was right out of control, mentally she was struggling hard. She was telling herself, "Don't – don't – he never cared a ha'penny about you – he doesn't now –" and yet the fact, the unbelievable fact was that he was leaning over the rail just as he had long ago, and he looked quite unchanged – except that now he was wearing uniform, of course.

"I saw you in the cards yesterday!" she said. "Now I think of it, a dark man – how funny, I didn't think of you."

"I'm glad you're keeping up the cards," George Nunn said. "I often thought about you and the cards. It's years since I've seen you, positively years. Isn't it curious? And here you still are."

"Yes, here I still am," she said, and then Mr. Silvester succeeded in attracting her attention. She nodded.

"How's your sister?"

"Oh, she's very well."

"Not married?"

"No." Of course it was Sarah that he was interested in, just as it had been before. She was remembering now how unpopular he had made himself – how disillusioned they had both been, and the hard things they had said about him. His behaviour had been appalling, but he didn't seem to have any idea of it.

"I bet she's having a good time."

"That's not a very nice thing to say," Isabel retorted at once, always over-eager to leap to her sister's defence. "She works at the Town Hall, in the town clerk's office, she helps in a canteen and she sells savings stamps –"

"All right, don't snap at me—"

"I may as well tell you, she was furious with you and so was I," Isabel said.

He looked amazed.

"Miss Rowland," murmured Mr. Silvester pleadingly.

"What did I do? What are you talking about?"

"Oh, nothing," Isabel said, turning back to the piano.

The trio started a selection from *The Rebel Maid*. She was intensely annoyed with herself for a clumsy outburst and she was terrified that he would go away. He stayed, however, leaning against the rail. It was fantastic that he should have no idea why they should have been annoyed with him, but also, of course, typical—it was what Denny had always said about the N.O.s, they were the world's vainest and most self-centred body of men. But it was no good. The nearness of George Nunn thrilled her, it couldn't be denied. What was so remarkable in addition was the fact that he didn't look any older, in fact if anything he looked younger. Of course that was because she had become adult, and he had been adult all the time. *The Rebel Maid* was still going on when he spoke again—and that husky, hearty voice of his had just the same effect on her as it had in the old days.

"How's your mother—and Boxer and everything?"

"Oh, mother's—well, yes, she's quite well," she answered over her shoulder. "So is Boxer. Fancy you remembering Boxer."

"I look forward to meeting Boxer again. I must buy him a bone or something. You know I can't get over your being still here."

"Oh, I shall be here for ever." She could talk and play with Mr. Silvester and Mr. Epworth at the same time. She was a professional. If a bomb had fallen on the grill room she would have gone on playing.

The Rebel Maid came to an end, and Mr. Silvester bowed to somebody. Isabel turned round on the stool, smiling.

"And how about his lordship?" George Nunn asked. "How's the great accountant?"

She remembered now that that was what he had always called Denny. A dreadful lump rose in her throat.

"He was killed at Ypres last November."

She saw his head jerk back, as if she had slapped him. Her tone had been flat, matter-of-fact. It was the only way she could get it out.

"Oh, my God," George Nunn said. "Not the accountant. I'm a fool not to have thought – I'm awfully sorry. How damnable!" He was very upset. Then he looked at her sharply. "So it was all for nothing," he added in a low voice.

"Nothing?"

"I mean your teaching and everything – so that he could – "

Mr. Silvester was nodding to her again.

"As if that mattered – " she exclaimed, turning back to the piano. "Nothing compares with being killed, does it?"

"Good God, I know that," he said.

He went on standing by the rail while the trio played their final number. It was as if the last two years had not happened and they were walking again on the Promenade. Casually and instinctively he seemed able to bring out to light precisely those thoughts which she tried to bury. Nothing compared with being killed, but it was true that Denny's death had given her cause – contemptible cause, she knew – for another complaint against fate. The war had begun before he could take his finals, and she remembered how gay he had been about it. Denny had been delighted by the war. He was the last person one would have imagined with a liking for the Army, but he treated it romantically. The fact was that the strain he had been living under was over. It was the sight of his queer happiness which made it clearer to Isabel than ever before how great that strain had been; how unhappy he had been for four weary years; how he had loathed his position. When Mrs. Rowland and Sarah wept for his death a few months later and spoke in hatred of the war as if it had interrupted a happy and purposeful life Isabel could not join them. She wept but she also could not get out of her mind those first weeks of mobilization when he was still in camp a few miles away and the charming, self-confident schoolboy had come to life again. Poor Denny, and yet – what about herself? It was primarily for him that her life had been ruined. The money spent on Denny could have sent her to the

213

Academy. She need not have given a lesson. She need not have played in a grill room. Nothing compared to being killed, but nothing could stop such ideas finding a small and shameful corner in her mind. They certainly did not occur to her mother or to Sarah, or to anyone else. And yet they had occurred at once to George Nunn.

"What is he doing here?" she thought. "He's the sort of person I despise – he has no sense of responsibility at all. He thinks everything he does is justified, simply because it is he who does it, simply because –" But deeper still other words were being sung.

"I shall put him in his place," she decided firmly.

The trio came to its final Saturday night *fortissimo* cadence. They packed up in relief, three people who were in a little world on their own, and as usual quietly departed.

He was waiting for her in the vestibule as if it were only twenty-four hours since he had last done it.

"Am I having the honour of your company, then?" she asked.

"Well, there doesn't seem to be anyone else hanging about, so you may as well put up with me. Doesn't Sarah come to fetch you?"

"Sometimes."

"I have an idea, let's take a taxi. I seem to have been doing without home comforts for too long. By the way, I liked the dress you were wearing – that's a definite difference from when I last saw you in action – I mean, skirts are wonderfully shorter nowadays."

She took a deep breath and faced him.

"I don't understand how you can talk like this. You – you come in here as if nothing – what makes you think that Sarah or I should be overjoyed to see you, after what you did? Oh, don't think we didn't know! We took all that trouble trying to help you – to pay that awful bill – not to spend money in London. You said good-bye to us and told us you were going to Devonport, and you went on leave. Then you sent us a postcard from somewhere. You know what we did with it? We put it straight in the fire."

"Oh, but look here –"

214

"And I am certainly speaking for Sarah, who was just as angry as I was. If anything, more." She paused. The instant she began her tirade, she had felt the strongest possible desire not to go on with it. It seemed empty and ridiculous. She waited for him to complete the work by leaving in annoyance.

George Nunn stared at her reflectively. Then he shook his head and smiled.

"I abase myself humbly. I'm a worthless creature. I'm my own worst enemy. I deserved every word."

"It's no good," she began, trying to speak impatiently.

"Don't say that. I'm terribly respectable nowadays, as a matter of fact. What would you say if I were to tell you I hadn't a debt in the world?"

"I shouldn't believe you."

"Am I really as bad as that?"

It didn't matter to her, whether he was or not. She was overwhelmed with relief that she had not succeeded in driving him away.

He forgot about getting a taxi. They walked slowly home, through the dull streets which were given a touch of wartime excitement by two searchlight beams which moved about in the darkness above the town, and they talked about music — he wanted her to play the *Barcarolle* for him again — while she hoped nervously that Sarah would not be shocked at the easy way she had given in to him.

Sarah was upstairs and Mrs. Rowland greeted him first, with her usual vague kindness. She thought she remembered him, she was not sure — she was interested in anyone who had known her son, however dimly. She had been reading, with Denny's smiling photograph close beside her. George Nunn at once picked up the photograph and looked at it for a moment, and then said to her quietly, "I'm dreadfully sorry." If anything finally made Isabel worship him, it was this simple and unembarrassed action. For it was one which most people seemed to find too difficult and it gave a brief moment of sad pleasure to her mother, who had aged ten years in the last ten months and lived in lonely misery.

"Who is it?" called out Sarah, on her way downstairs. "Is it who I think it is — ?" She burst prettily into the room.

" I thought it was your voice," she exclaimed. " George Nunn! Hold your hand out, naughty boy! "

He almost ignored her for a second in order to look quizzically at Isabel, who uttered a foolish little laugh of relief. A feeling of exultation she had tried to keep in check broke loose within her. She had thought of him for two years and here he was, a ghost become flesh again. More extraordinary still, he was just as she had remembered him, down to the precise lines on his forehead and the small reddened lobes of his ears, although she had never pictured him in his uniform. Most extraordinary of all was her feeling, her certainty that it was not Sarah but herself whom he had come back to see.

CHAPTER TWENTY-SIX

Six days later they were engaged and the following March they were married. He spent the intervening months in the North Sea. For Isabel it was a period of alternate ecstasy and anxiety. The anxiety began on the first Saturday afternoon, when she and Sarah went together to the far end of the Promenade to a point from which it was almost possible to make out the faces of the crew lined up on the deck of the outgoing ship. They had often done it when someone they knew was on board, and it was always moving—dreadfully so since the war began—but this experience, of knowing that one of those figures was to be her husband, inspired her with awe. Joy and terror were hopelessly intermingled.

Both her mother and Sarah also had mixed emotions, of a pleasant kind. On the one hand they were astounded, on the other they were delighted.

"Who knows, you may be an admiral's wife one day," Sarah said. " I wish there'd been time to show him off a little."

The Mathers had to be content with a sight of his photograph and of the ring.

She lived, of course, for his letters. They were to marry whenever he next had leave. Every morning she woke up with the thought, "Will I hear to-day?" To this was always attached, more faintly but insistently, "What will I do if he's killed?" For she was so happy that she could not believe it would last. The idea that her life was going to be different seemed incredible. And what a future it was to be, if the plan he had expounded to her came off! She had told no one about it for they were all too happy with the thought of her being a service wife – a situation financially unexciting, but socially splendid (Aunt Ada and, for that matter, her mother treated her nowadays with an entirely new respect) – but George's intention was to leave the Navy at the first possible moment after the war and to get a job in business. There was an agency concerned with Anglo-French trade – he had met a man. They would live in London or in Paris. Whichever it was, he had said, *her* concern was to be the piano. It was his dearest wish that as his wife she should make her concert début. Another ghost had come to life again. She did not take it too seriously, but it was what he had said. And there was something else she told nobody, something which, whenever she thought of it – and ten minutes hardly ever went by without her thinking of it – made her heart sing. In order to buy her engagement ring, so much admired by everyone, he had sold his gold cigarette case.

Meanwhile life went on normally. She still had her teaching and there was the Rotunda every evening. And then at the end of February – (in France the battle of Verdun was starting) – the telegram came. When she dared to open it, she read, "Ten days leave arrive Peter Street to-morrow evening love George." She cried like a child.

Frantic preparations followed, culminating in a short little ceremony – a small group of people in a large empty church, the Mathers, Mr. Silvester and Mr. Epworth. (She had played for the last time at the Rotunda, and like other occasions which ought to be moving but are not this had been full of anticlimax; she had been worried about them, and they were not worried at all; there was a young man, discharged from the Army owing to wounds, who was available to take her place.) They returned to 12 Brook Place for a modest celebration – Isabel had been insistent that there should be no extravagance. She changed the white hat she had been married in for a navy blue felt cap which went with her suit, and there were four days left for the honeymoon.

They spent it in London, and spent was the operative word as far as Isabel was concerned. She was thrilled and shocked by the ease with which he parted with money. They lunched, they dined, they went to theatres, they danced, they took taxis everywhere – the cost of it all appalled her, but she realized that he had always done it and it was surely excusable now in the near hysterical, wonderful London wartime atmosphere.

She saw him off from King's Cross and returned home, enraptured.

And she went on living as before, except that she did not go to the Rotunda in the evenings. Everyone said that marriage evidently agreed with her, she was no longer aloof and withdrawn and she looked radiant although she lay awake each night in fear. She lived for his letters and spent hours every day writing to him. She walked about in a cloud of happiness, and she became passionately interested in running the house. Often when she sat down to practise, honouring her husband's demand that she should think of nothing but the piano, a thought would occur to her which apparently overrode problems of phrasing, and she would hurry off to find her mother to put a question about the price of tapioca or coal, or what was the best way to cook kippers, or polish brass. All her life she had left things about and now she developed a fetish of tidiness, and was for ever dusting and putting things back. She was quite annoyed when Sarah found this amusing.

Very soon, however, there was another interest in the house, and Isabel and her mother discussed repeatedly whether or not Sarah's own engagement was imminent. For in her work at the Town Hall Sarah had met a young officer who was stationed at an R.A.S.C. depot a few miles from the town, and had been out tea-dancing with him two or three times, and had brought him home. And the remarkable coincidence was that this young man was that same Proctor who had been an articled clerk along with Denny, and had passed the exam that Denny had failed. This fact alone made Mrs. Rowland

218

warm to him and he entered the house as an old friend of Denny's, an idea he did nothing to dispel – although Isabel vaguely remembered that poor Denny detested him. He was certainly not the kind of young man Sarah might have been expected to fall for. He had none of the old naval officer graces which Sarah had always found so pleasant. He was not bad looking, but he seemed rather pale and unhealthy. He stooped, he moved awkwardly and had a tendency to upset things that were in his way. Most of the time he maintained a pink-faced, embarrassed silence, but if he spoke it was in a breathless rush of words. It was true, however, that he was a qualified chartered accountant.

" I think he's rather a pet, don't you? " Sarah said.

Isabel agreed, of course.

" I like him very much, dear," said Mrs. Rowland firmly.

Indeed there was nothing to dislike about him, but he was not the kind of young man Sarah might have been expected to fall for.

The engagement was announced and the wedding quickly followed at the beginning of June. It was not at all like Isabel's wedding, any more than Harry Proctor was like George Nunn. There had been time for the banns to be read out, there had been a visit from his parents – they had owned a laundry and were now living in retirement at Eastbourne – Sarah had taken Harry round to see everybody they knew, and Harry had taken Sarah to see old friends of his parents, and there had been Sarah's dress to think of. Sarah said that she hated having such a fuss, but Harry insisted that she should be a white bride. Afterwards an amazing number of people crowded into number 12 Brook Place.

It was all very successful. Mr. Proctor made a speech, Mr. Mather made a speech – all the Mathers were there in full force – Harry made a speech. The best man, an R.A.S.C. officer from Harry's depot called Captain Henderson, turned out to be an excellent comedian. There were quite a number of telegrams, almost entirely from Proctor friends and relations, and the best man drew roars of laughter as he read them out. He was a plump, good-natured looking man. " And here's a thoughtful one, ladies and gentlemen," said Captain Henderson roguishly. "Very philosophical, I might say – I say, that was a good word, wasn't it? Philosop-soph – never mind. This is from Joe and Doris. They have extraordinarily bad handwriting, but I can decipher – Just married – just wonderful – just wait! And this one's from Mr. and Mrs. Newcombe – Our best wishes for your future happiness – hurrah for Mr. and Mrs. Newcombe!" exclaimed the captain, flushed with his success; he had had plenty to drink and would have gone on for hours. "Here's another one – from – from –" He peered at it with a frown and slowly closed one eye. "Can't read that one – awful writing!" he said. "Here's another – this is better – from Uncle Ted and Aunty Mavis – Love and best wishes –" He finished a few minutes later, amid applause. Isabel clapped him happily, and it was only afterwards that she remembered him moving away from the piano, against which he had stood to read out the telegrams, and how he had put the one telegram he had not read out into a pocket of his service-dress trousers as he went. Afterwards she remembered him doing this, although it had meant nothing at the moment, and she always felt admiration for Captain Henderson, who had reacted to difficult circumstances with such sang-froid and efficiency. For it was right that Sarah and Harry should have their day unspoilt, that Sarah should go and change and come downstairs in her going-away outfit, a very pretty and most composed bride, and that everyone should crowd round them as they pushed through to the car which waited outside in Brook Place; and it was due to Captain Henderson that everything went happily and merrily along, and that Isabel did not know that the unread telegram had been addressed to her, and regretfully informed her that her husband had been killed in action – until later that day.

CHAPTER TWENTY-SEVEN

The memory of four days, each waking minute of which she went over again and again, of a few conversations and strolls, and of the sound of his voice – there was nothing else left to her of Lieut. George Nunn, Royal Navy. Nothing mattered any more. There was no point in living. When she saw herself in the mirror she looked very pale and composed. She broke down only at night, by herself, when suddenly, without warning, she would feel herself seized, and dreadful, silent, painful sobs would choke her. And so the weeks went by, and gradually her marriage began to seem more and more like a dream, something that had never really happened. Except that she was called Mrs. Nunn, and that she had her pension.

Her new interest in housework remained, however. The reason for it had gone but the habit remained. At the same time, when she had recovered a little, she began to remember George's hopes for her playing. Should she not take her ambitions up again? Was it not something she could do for his memory – to try to make what he had hoped for her come true? Once this idea had occurred to her it became an obsession. She said nothing about it, fearing that no one would take her seriously – only he had done that – but she began to practise regularly again. She was twenty-two years old, and though she could not think of herself as being young, it was surely not too late. Moreover it was now more practicable than it had ever been since her father's death had ruined everything; for there was no longer the same financial strain in the house. Sarah was an officer's wife. She was an officer's widow with a pension. She made plans. Why should she not have some more lessons from Mr. Durrell, if he were still active? With her savings she could pay him, with her pension she could survive. She would wait until she felt she had improved enough, and then – why should she not have success? The hard knocks she had had might have dulled her technique – work could deal with that – but they must also have added depth to her playing, and that was something good luck could not have done. And she permitted herself to dream again of playing a concerto at Queen's Hall and of hearing applause which would sound all the more sweetly, because it would be a tribute to George; and she could even feel herself thinking at this imagined moment, "There you are, darling."

However she did nothing for the time being. There was one other reason which stopped her from saying anything about her intentions, and this was the fact that her relationship with her mother had become closer. It had always been affectionate but it had always been equally clear that Mrs. Rowland got on better with Sarah and understood her more easily than she ever had her elder daughter. Now, however, things were a little different. They had all known grief, but Isabel and her mother, both widows, had a kind of grief in common; and this was reflected in their attitude to each other. She did not want to announce it too soon that a quiet and unambitious life was not going to do for her, that it was necessary for her to break away and get to London. Her mother looked old, although she was not, and there was something helpless about her. It was a matter of timing, and meanwhile of working and practising.

In any case there was plenty to do. She still had pupils, and though she had very little interest in teaching she did not dislike it quite so much as she used to. Since her evenings had been free of the Rotunda she had been available for the numberless concerts for troops and concerts for war-wounded at which the bass always sang "The Company Sergeant Major" and there were Cockney recitations by refined young women – "I'm very appy ere you see, but I wants me chip pertaters and me kippers fer tea" – which always seemed to Isabel to be rather insulting. Mrs. Rowland knitted comforts all day long and also went to knitting parties. Sarah had given up her job at the Town Hall and now concentrated on her Y.M.C.A. canteen, where she was efficient and enormously popular. One evening Isabel went to help her there and within an hour was exhausted and in a state of confusion. Her arms

222

ached, she hated the idea of asking service men for money, she forgot orders, she lost her place at the kitchen hatchway to more forceful co-workers. Mrs. Borley, who ran the canteen, said to her kindly, " I don't think you're cut out for this kind of work, Mrs. Nunn. Now we've lots of strong women with nothing else to do all day – I should go home, if I were you, my dear." However she went back again when Sarah had a chance of an evening out with Harry and also when Sarah went off for a week to stay with Harry's parents at East-bourne. And so the war continued for the three ladies and Boxer, the dog, at 12 Brook Place.

Then Harry Proctor was posted away to a depot on the east coast near Lowestoft and Sarah followed him. She was to take furnished rooms and Harry would be able to live out. On the whole it was not too terrible a war for Harry Proctor, although, as Sarah often said, you never knew that he might not be sent anywhere at any moment.

CHAPTER TWENTY-EIGHT

S uch an annoying accident, and coming at such a time – when at last everything except the 'flu epidemic was good news, and the headlines spoke of enemy retreats, and the little crowds in front of the newspaper office in Peter Street came away from reading the bulletins in the window with cheerful faces. It was an October afternoon of 1918 and the Promenade was quite crowded, for there were a large number of wounded service men in khaki greatcoats over blue suits walking and limping about. Isabel and Sarah walked slowly along, the former being dragged by Boxer, now a grey-white and rather plump terrier of middle-age, and the latter pushing a pram, in which slept David Charles Proctor, aged six weeks and three days, whose christening had taken place a week before. There had been a family ceremony, after which Harry had returned to duty at Lowestoft; his parents went back to Eastbourne and Sarah had stayed on for the pleasure of David Charles's grandmother and aunt. As they strolled, the sisters chatted – conversation was almost more or less continuous whenever Sarah came to stay or Isabel went up to the draughty maisonette at Lowestoft – and were pleasantly aware of appreciative glances, even of faintly ribald comments. Isabel thought that Sarah deserved them. Her sister had never looked prettier. She wore a very smart new hat trimmed in the front with merle feathers and duck wings, and a costume in the shade known as Joffre-blue. Harry had little money to spare her, of course, but Sarah always knew how to look three times as well off as she was. Since her marriage she had assumed a rather superior air which was at the same time rather provocative.

Sarah was discussing the future, a matter which was very much to hand in the general victory atmosphere, and there was an aspect of her plans which had come to Isabel rather as a shock.

"Harry says that if he's to get on, it's essential to get into a London firm, even if it means not being quite so comfortable at first. Of course you can do well here or anywhere, but if it's a matter of long-term prospects, Harry says, it's senseless to go anywhere but London. Well, I think he's right, don't you?"

"Yes," Isabel said. "Yes, I suppose so –" But she hoped very much that it was not so. It had always been assumed that Harry and Sarah were going to settle down in the town. He had, after all, started in Denny's firm and there had been stories of how much they wanted him back after the war – one of the partners had attended the wedding. Isabel had looked forward to this as the moment when she could leave her mother comfortably. If Sarah were not coming back, how was she ever to leave?

"As a matter of fact," Sarah went on, "just between us two, Harry's met a very nice man at the Command Depot who –"

"Boxer, do be quiet," Isabel said, for he was suddenly growling and straining at the lead. Another dog, free and unattached, came nosing angrily towards him. "Go away, please go away!" she said – like her mother, she always

224

addressed animals as if they were human. The next moment Sarah gave a cry of alarm and dived forward in an instinctive protective action over the pram, while Isabel tried furiously to separate the snarling, snapping dogs. Boxer yelped, Isabel cried furiously, "Oh, you demon – ! " and just as suddenly as it had begun it was over. The stray dog ran off, with Boxer straining to get after him, and Isabel exclaimed, "Look, my coat sleeve! " There was a three-inch tear between her left elbow and wrist.

When they got home, she found that her blouse sleeve underneath was untorn, but there were two or three little scratches on her skin – no more than a graze.

"Don't you ever dare growl at a dog again," Isabel told Boxer.

"I must say you were awfully brave," Sarah said.

And apart from the matter of the coat sleeve they thought no more about it. But a few days later Mrs. Rowland, who always went down early to make a cup of tea, returned indignantly from the kitchen with the report that Boxer had snapped at her. Just after breakfast there was a further commotion. There was a cat who often visited the backyard and with whom Boxer had been on friendly terms for years; that is, he never molested it, except playfully; this time, however, he had made a ferocious onslaught. There had been newspaper stories of outbreaks of rabies and now they remembered the dog on the Promenade. Boxer had always been good-tempered and easy-going. This was strange behaviour. Two hours passed during which they kept watch of the animal with growing anxiety. He lay about as if he were in a slothful daze, and now and then howled in a peculiar high-pitched way, almost like a hurt child.

"He'll have to go to the vet," Mrs. Rowland said, with a shake in her voice. "In any case with the baby in the house we don't dare not make sure – " She sat down heavily, looking old and grey and weary. "Everyone, everything we love is taken from us! " she exclaimed bitterly.

Isabel stared at her. She had never heard her mother use such a tone. She and Sarah took the dog to the vet. It was a nervous business putting the lead on him. On the way there

Sarah made the one mention between them of Mrs. Rowland's outburst.

"Mother shouldn't have said that."

The vet confirmed their fears as soon as he heard the story.

"If he's got it he'll be dead within twenty-four hours. It's very serious, of course – we have to notify the authorities – and send the brain to be examined. Mrs. Nunn, you said your coat was torn? Did the teeth reach your skin?"

"Just a tiny scratch," Isabel whispered. She could hardly speak for the thought of poor Boxer, and in fact she had forgotten all about her scratch.

"Well!" the vet said. He was an irritating but efficient little man, who seemed to enjoy making other people face facts. He sighed and went on briskly, "You know what that means, my dear Mrs. Nunn? If the dog is rabid, you'll have to go to Paris and be treated at the Pasteur Institute. They've been sending over dozens of people. But there's no need to be alarmed. As a human being you have at least six weeks' grace."

That evening the dog was dead. The sadness of his going was swamped by anxiety for Isabel herself, and several busy and agitated days followed. She had to go and see an official of the Local Government Board and an official of the Board of Agriculture, she had to be photographed and she had to go up to London to get a passport. Everyone kept on telling her that there was no need to be worried, because it was certain that nothing would happen so long as you had the treatment. All the same it was difficult not to be slightly perturbed by the fuss. She had been to the town public library and looked up hydrophobia. She learned that if you did not have the treatment, there would come an itching where the scratch had been, and then a dreadful succession from feverishness and excitability to choking paroxysms and indescribable suffering for two or three days before you were released by death. All because of thirty unfortunate seconds on the Promenade.

"Just what would happen to me," she thought. However, if it had not been for their sadness about Boxer, the fuss would have been almost enjoyable. It made a change.

226

She went over on a night crossing from Southampton to Le Havre. They were winning the war now, but the war was still on and there was still danger from U-boats. She shared a cabin with two plump, agitated Greek women and a young English mother with a baby of two, who was also being sent to the Pasteur Institute. Her name was Mrs. Palmer and her husband was an infantry captain, at present in Palestine. The baby's scratch was a nick on his nose and Mrs. Palmer was doing her best not to show her fear. She had come on to the boat after fifteen hours in different trains and she was nearly prostrate with exhaustion. Isabel took the child from her and spent the night in her berth holding him in the crook of her arm. The Greeks chattered, the baby woke now and then and cried, and outside the cabin a conversation went on interminably between a girl and some slightly drunk young officers. Then the ship began to roll and shudder. This put an end to the conversation outside, but soon there came a smell of vomit from the Greek side of the cabin. A stewardess came in, all starch and brightness, and said, " Oh, what a mess, you naughty girl! " She told Isabel that it was three o'clock. " I see you're like me, looking after other people's troubles," she said, for Mrs. Palmer slept through everything. " Well, I always say it makes you forget your own, doesn't it? "

Isabel fell asleep at last and woke up to the queer stillness of a ship in harbour and the still faintly pervading vomity smell. The two plump Greeks were not in the cabin and Mrs. Palmer, who had evidently just got up, was busy scraping the basin. She turned round and smiled.

" Oh, you're awake, Mrs. Nunn. I don't know how to thank you for helping me last night – I was all in."

" I was glad to. Do you feel better for your sleep? "

" Oh, yes, thank you," said Mrs. Palmer, although her babyish face still looked tired and harassed. " Those two have left this basin filthy. I don't know why foreigners are impossible when it comes to anything to do with toilet – "

" Yes," Isabel said, " there were some Belgians in our road at home for a time and I always heard they were dreadful."

" Belgians, yes, I've heard that as well – "

The bond between them grew, fortified by their nationality, while Tom, the baby, gurgled peacefully in the upper berth. They went to much inconvenience in the interest of hygiene – for there was hardly room to stand – and made a point of leaving the basin spotless. When they were finally dressed, however, they both looked rather untidy and Isabel felt grubby as well. It was mildly irritating, when, just as Mrs. Palmer was wiping Tom's face with a flannel, the two Greek women returned from breakfast, fresh and smart, all kindly smiles and bows and with a welcome scent of eau-de-Cologne. The two Englishwomen exchanged a baffled glance.

They had to spend the day in Le Havre, with the baby in a small collapsible push chair, for there was no train they could catch until the evening. They walked about the town until Mrs. Palmer said she was too tired. They were confidential in the way of people certain they would not meet again. Isabel found herself talking about her husband and she heard a good deal about Captain Palmer, who was a schoolmaster in Nottingham. Poor little Mrs. Palmer looked ill. She was overwhelmed by anxiety and she seemed grateful for Isabel's assurances. Her inexperience of disaster made Isabel feel old, but at the same time pleasantly maternal. In the afternoon they went down to the empty plage and sat there. She pushed the chair herself on the way back and Mrs. Palmer held her arm as if she were too tired to walk. Isabel looked at her face in concern.

" Are you sure you're feeling all right? "

" Oh, yes. I'm just tired."

The train was terribly crowded with troops who, together with their baggage, made the corridors almost impassable. They found seats finally and Isabel noted the immediate look of long suffering self-pity on every face in the compartment; this was caused by the sight of the baby. She took it in turn with the mother to nurse him, but then Mrs. Palmer's eyes closed and Isabel kept him all the time. A colonel and his wife, impressively furred, sat opposite looking very privileged and complacent. They discussed their private affairs in an uninhibited manner, the main purpose of which seemed to be to emphasize their general difference from their fellow

228

travellers. They opened a luxurious little picnic basket and the baby, observing food, spent the next twenty minutes repeating his demand for a share. " Bisk – 'bisk – bisk – " The colonel and his wife stonily ignored him. Isabel was furious – she was also hungry herself – and made no attempt to keep him quiet. Then there were two journeys with him to the W.C. along the packed-out corridor. The train was very slow and there were stops in the darkness when you could hear troops shouting and singing, full of vulgarity and sadness. At Rouen she thought they had reached Paris, it had seemed so long.

The colonel and his wife dozed at last, well satisfied that everyone knew who and what they were, and everyone else in the compartment's gloomy light sat back like grey statues, and outside in the corridor they were also motionless. The baby whimpered and gurgled now and then, but mostly slept. His mother seemed out to the world. " It's always the same," thought Isabel. " Why am I so easily imposed on? " All the same she enjoyed having the baby in her arms, in spite of his considerable weight. Then her own eyes closed and she awoke to see vague outlines and shapes of buildings – they were in Paris. But when they finally halted she was taken by surprise, for they were at the rear of the train and it was so long that they stopped beyond the platforms.

A kind of pandemonium broke loose. Everyone was reaching for baggage, except the colonel and his wife, whose things were being looked after elsewhere by a batman – the batman had been discussed for a moment earlier on. Mrs. Palmer was dully awake and Isabel was at last quite exasperated with her, a feeling which disappeared immediately when she realized that Mrs. Palmer was ill. Her face was flushed and she could hardly stand. It was a fine situation. Outside all was darkness and confusion, and of course there were no porters. The last man in the compartment, a second lieutenant who had not spoken since Le Havre, pushed past her, mumbling an apology. Isabel was incensed and snapped at him, " Can't you see how I'm placed? Can't you give me some help? "

" I beg your pardon – yes, of course." He was thoroughly taken aback.

"This lady is ill, and there are the cases, and the baby, and the pram—I can't possibly manage!" She was amazed to hear herself sounding high-pitched and arrogant, and he was obeying her without arguing. Without him it was hard to see how they could have left the train at all. He was good-natured about it, though slightly embarrassed. He took the cases out and then the push chair. She followed with the baby, which she handed down to him—they couldn't go further along the train because the carriage did not communicate with the next. She returned to the compartment and helped Mrs. Palmer up. The latter was weak and helpless and leaned on her heavily. Finally they were down on the clinker in the darkness. They left the bags where they were and made a slow, highly uncomfortable journey, passing by a huge engine belching out smoke and steam. When they reached the platform the second lieutenant supported Mrs. Palmer with one arm and held the baby in the other, while Isabel unfolded the push chair. They put the baby in it and he went back for the bags.

"Ripping way to enter Paris," he said, when he returned. "I suppose your friend has the 'flu."

"I'm afraid it looks like it."

"The 'flu seems to be doing more damage than the war," he said.

However, the war was there on the platform down which they now slowly made their way. The train on the other side, whose engine they had passed, was full of French soldiers going back to the front. It was a victorious front now but men were still being killed. The platform was crowded with people in tears, moaning, wailing, despairing. Fear, loss and sorrow were in the air. Faces of unaccompanied poilus stared out like ghosts from the carriage windows. No pack-up-your-troubles here, no smile, smile, smile.

"Do you think we can get a taxi?" she asked. Ahead she saw notices, "Sortie Amsterdam", "Postes", "Hôtel Terminus".

"We can try."

Beyond the barrier was a long narrow hall facing the tracks, packed with people in uniform. The light was better and she saw the second lieutenant properly for the first time. He had certainly not been more than fourteen when the war started. Nowadays she was always being surprised by the fact that grown-up officers or, for that matter, mothers could be years younger than herself – but with his pink cherubic face he looked more than usually like a child.

Five minutes later, however, he had put them into a taxi. "You've been wonderful. Good luck and thank you."

"You're the one that needs the good luck," he smiled at her perched uncomfortably between baggage, a sick woman and a baby beginning to cry.

"Oh, this kind of thing was bound to happen to me," Isabel smiled back, and as the taxi moved off she felt quite exultant.

CHAPTER TWENTY-NINE

The hotel at which they were to stay, at Government expense, was small and undistinguished. It was in a street off the Rue du Marché St. Honoré. A black-bearded Frenchman, who might have come from a school-book illustration, received them. They put Mrs. Palmer to bed and a doctor was sent for. Isabel stayed with her until he came. She took the baby and a tin of Glaxo with her to her own room. She went to bed herself, finally, exhausted but full of a satisfaction at having proved to herself that she could cope with an emergency. The baby woke her at six. She went to the window and drew back the black curtain. In the dull, grey light she saw thousands of chimney-pots and high slanting roofs and a narrow street below. The smell of Paris rose to greet her. She had a feeling of excitement. She hurried to Mrs. Palmer's room and found her sleeping quite peacefully. Relieved and also a little triumphant, she hurried back to the baby. She was delighted with her responsibilities.

Everything went smoothly. Downstairs she found that the black-bearded Frenchman had been replaced by his buxom wife, who was English and came from the Midlands. Her name was Madame Hebert and her lips were turned down as if in perpetual disapproval. However, she made no difficulties about providing Isabel with boiled water to mix with the Glaxo and she would see if she could find some coal for a fire in Mrs. Palmer's room. While Isabel was having breakfast of two rolls and black coffee, Madame Hebert came beside her table to comment on the morning's news.

"It won't last much longer. They're advising the Kaiser to get out for his own sake and they say they're more nervous of their population than of us. Mind you, if it really is over, there are some who'll be sorry around here. I know what I know. Well, I can hold my head high. There's no butter to be had in this hotel."

She went off to speak to someone else and it was curious to hear the quick flow of French, beyond Isabel's understanding. She was impressed that an Englishwoman could do such a thing. Madame Hebert returned to say that the French lady on the other side of the room would see her as far as the Metro station. Isabel bowed across to her gratefully.

It was one of those days when everyone was kind and helpful. The French lady, white-faced and dressed in severe black, insisted on carrying the baby part of the way. They walked up a number of uninteresting streets and turned into the Avenue de l'Opéra, and there was the great gaudy opera house (season opening November 3rd), and dense traffic, and excitement in the air, there were troops walking about everywhere, and more flags than in London – although Isabel was rather annoyed that most of these were French and American and very few British. The French lady saw her to the ticket office and down the stairs as far as the gate to the platform.

Isabel felt a mounting apprehension when she was left on her own with the baby, but there was no need to worry. At first she thought that everyone in her carriage looked sinister, and an old man, smelling of garlic, sat down opposite her. There were warts, it seemed, all over him and dirty white whiskers on his cheeks. She had to ask him, however, for her peace of mind, to confirm that she was on the right train. The old man listened to her slow and halting French.

" *Anglais?* "

"*Oui*," said Isabel.

The old man turned his head and spoke to someone else. The French language at once flew in all directions. Half a dozen persons became involved and all Isabel could make out for certain was that she was on the wrong train. At each station she made as if to get out and they all told her not to. Concorde, Invalides, École Militaire, Champs de Mars – then at La Motte-Picquet they all turned to her with nods, smiles and cries of encouragement. "*Correspondance!*" several of them exclaimed. Isabel stepped out, grateful but confused, and then saw the word above an exit and "Pasteur" among a list of station names beside it. After that there was no more trouble and it was rather absurd to have such a sense of achievement. But she was aware of having learned something profound, though simple; it was that one need not be afraid of asking people for help. She thought that it might very well have a general implication for her whole life – she had never asked people for anything. There had been Lord Bochard, for example, and there was Mr. Durrell himself – why had she never got into touch with him? And even Dr. Preston at home – when had she ever asked him for anything? To ask, you had to humble yourself, and she had always been rather proud of not doing that – Dr. Preston had always had to come to her. And there was her mother, and Sarah – it had never occurred to her to ask them to consider her situation. Never!

All this went through her mind between the stations La Motte-Picquet, Cambronne, Sèvres-Lecourbe and Pasteur. Here she was in the Paris underground, travelling with someone else's baby. From this surprising situation, which would have seemed the sheerest fantasy a week before, it was quite natural to find oneself all at once viewing life differently.

The Pasteur Institute was in the Rue de Vaugirard. Isabel found herself in an old house, crowded with people waiting on benches or in queues. There were a good many soldiers. It was queer that everyone present must have been bitten by a mad dog. Two French doctors were in a small, white-walled room, dealing with each case in turn. Isabel stood for a moment wondering what she should do and a brisk voice said, "Are

H*

you Mrs. Palmer? I'm Dr. Waters. Where have you been?"
A middle-aged Englishwoman in a dark grey suit stood beside
her. She had a long, big-boned face and the over-assured look
of a woman doctor. Dr. Waters was there to look after the
British patients and she led the way through the crowd to
the French doctors. Five minutes later the baby had had his
first injection and Isabel was having hers. It was a very
embarrassing procedure for the needle had to go in on the
flank between the ribs and the hip, and there were no
facilities at all for undressing and it was all very public —
in fact almost everywhere you looked there seemed to be men
and women equally half-naked; the French were very peculiar
about some things.

"Well, you have another fourteen doses to come," said
Dr. Waters, appearing beside her once more. "You've had
the worst one — I suppose you feel all right? Don't be worried
if you see a few nasty sights here, people with their jaws
snapping and so on. They're purely temporary spasms,
nothing like that will happen to you. Be here at the same
time to-morrow."

Isabel thanked her and, having made herself presentable,
again went out through the crowded rooms into the Rue de
Vaugirard, and then slowly back to the Metro. She had no
hesitation in stopping people to ask them the way and it was
very exciting when her French was understood. She had been
very good at French at school but she had not spoken any,
of course, since she had been there. It was something pulled
back out of her youth and she thought of it as another sign
making for optimism. No, life wasn't over yet.

She found herself on a train again, ridiculously proud once
more of being able to get about on her own in a foreign city.
The child behaved wonderfully. It was nice to have people
looking at her and thinking she was his mother. When she
emerged again at the Opera it was a long and difficult trail
back to the hotel. The baby weighed a ton before she got
there, hot and breathless. Mrs. Palmer still had a fever but
she was better, and touchingly grateful.

In the afternoon Isabel took the baby for a walk in the
push chair, and looked around as a tourist. She was fasci-

234

nated by the way the houses seemed bunched up, as if they had built too many and they had all had to squeeze tighter and higher to make room. They were all dirty and crumbling, and some had washing hanging out; there was nothing agreeable about it, it would be dreadful to have to live there, but she loved it. She wandered in and out of little streets and then suddenly was in the Place Vendôme, where she passed a British general and three of his staff, glorious with affectation and shining leather. Then she was in the Rue St. Honoré and a funeral went by – three undertaker's men in bowler hats, a hungry looking horse, a dozen white-faced French mourners walking behind, all chatting vivaciously. She came to the Rue Royale and turned towards the Place de la Concorde and then caught her breath at the first glimpse of the Champs-Élysées stretching away. She pushed round the Concorde to look at some of the captured guns. When her feet began to ache she went back slowly along the Rue de Rivoli and found a seat in the Tuileries gardens where there were other women with children. She unstrapped the baby and he played about on the ground. She looked at the outline of the Louvre against the sky, and at the buildings on the other side of the river, and at the Eiffel Tower, and the Rue de Rivoli, and thought it amazing that it had all been here all her life, looking just like this.

"I've let myself become provincial – shut in – dull," she told herself.

But things would be different now. She resumed the thoughts she had had in the morning, she resumed also the intentions she had kept secret for the past year – but now with the feeling that she would definitely take action. She would go to London, she would have lessons, she would work, she would succeed. Her mother would be happier in the end and in any case there was no reason why she should not herself prefer to come to London, since Sarah was evidently going to be there as well.

"The main thing is not to allow myself to stay in the old rut," she determined. It had been worth the trip to Paris if only in order to be able to see things clearly.

Back at the hotel she found that a nurse had arrived to

look after Mrs. Palmer, and there were a dozen more British people who had come for treatment at the Pasteur Institute. The baby had to be fed and washed, played with and put to bed. Isabel was tired and very content. She chatted to Mrs. Palmer for half an hour, and later Madame Hebert came to her table while she had dinner and explained what she would do to the Kaiser were she to meet him face to face, and complained also of the behaviour of some of her British guests. Afterwards Isabel looked through some old magazines in the dreary little *salon* and went herself early to bed.

The fortnight passed quickly. The Pasteur Institute in the morning, a walk ending in the Tuileries gardens in the afternoon, a quiet evening, dinner, bed – this routine lasted for the first four or five days, while she was still looking after the baby. She was quite disappointed when his mother was well enough to take him over again – although Isabel still took him for the morning injection. But now she was free to explore Paris by herself and she walked everywhere, tirelessly. She spoke to very few people, except Sheila Palmer, of course – who never stopped talking about her husband – and Madame Hebert and the thin, ageless maid who appeared to be the hotel's entire staff. Her new mood of firm optimism stayed with her, and it was helped, of course, by the constantly cheerful news headlines: "Republic proclaimed in Vienna and Budapest. The Emperor has left Vienna" – "Armistice with Turkey" – "(1,554th day of war) Armistice with Austria" – "Mutiny in the German Fleet." She spent evenings quietly, for it was hardly possible to go out by herself and in any case too expensive. The only night out was towards the end of the second week, when Madame Hebert offered to look after the baby and Isabel went with Sheila Palmer to a musical show called *Pa-Ri-Ki-Ri* at the Casino de Paris. They saw Mistinguett and Chevalier and a dancer called Oy-Ra, and "the 76 Tiller's Beauty Girls" and "the 200 most beautiful women of Paris" and the orchestra was called "le grand orchestre américain". The big scene was hung with large French flags and large American flags, and other allied flags, modestly amongst which was a small British Union Jack. The girls were incensed by this, taken aback by the nudes and
236

baffled by humour which seemed to consist largely in spitting. But it was all very enjoyable.

"Won't Archie be amazed when he reads where I've been!" said Sheila, on their way to the hotel. She sighed happily. "One thing that's certain, I won't ever forget coming to Paris, and I won't forget your kindness, Isabel, and all the talks we've had. When I've settled down with Archie – there I go again, but it must be over soon now, mustn't it – I hope you'll come and stay with us – "

Isabel said she would look forward to it. She had become fond of her friend. The more Sheila recovered from her influenza the duller she seemed to be. But it was a placid dullness. There was something excessively ordinary about her. She radiated contentment. Isabel admired her for it.

The last days went by, Saturday, Sunday, Monday – the final injection was like the last lesson on the last day of term. This evening they would be on their way back to England. Sheila came with her, bringing the baby. She was very excited. For there had been rumours at breakfast which added a peculiar force to the end of term feeling. The rumours were also at the Pasteur Institute. The English woman doctor came over and said, "I believe it was signed at five o'clock this morning." One dared not be too convinced, and on the way back from the Opera station to the hotel everything seemed much as usual. But they had not been back fifteen minutes before the guns went off, and then almost at once came the dim sound of church bells ringing. There was no doubt about it – the unbelievable had happened.

Isabel was alone in her room. She hurried to the window and stared out. Everything, of course, looked as usual, the forest of chimney-pots, the dirty-white, dirty-yellow shutters and flaking plaster of the houses opposite, and the shops below which no one ever seemed to enter – *Articles de ménage – Teinturier (Stopper au 1ᵉʳ) – Comestibles – Vins – Fins Liquers.* Nothing was happening. Then a man came out of the café at the end of the street – *Café – Bar – Bière* – and started fixing up a tricolor over the entrance. Suddenly one of the firemen from the station round the corner appeared. He ran across to the café and the two men embraced, kissed each other's cheeks and stood there gesticulating. Tears had come into Isabel's eyes. An unbearable wave of emotion overwhelmed her.

All the things she had been calm about for months, all those agonizing treasures of memory, sprang out of their locked places and sent her stumbling back to lie on the bed with her face in her hands. She was back in the Rotunda with George leaning against the rail, she was in London with him, sitting opposite him at Oddys while he explained what the future would be, she was listening to his low, fervent "Oh – you dear!" She was back on the platform at King's Cross in the last minutes of their four days.

"George," she whispered helplessly – and then she remembered Denny and was ashamed that her brother had not come immediately to mind. But her mother would be weeping for him at this very moment, she knew. Four years now since he had gone, almost two and a half since George – it was unfair and vile and hideous. How could anyone embrace? She thought angrily of the two joyful men in the street. What about all the others? What about all the loss and pain and sorrow – it was all too frightful, too ghastly.

She heard footsteps approaching quickly and she forced control of herself, just in time for Sheila Palmer to burst in, crying, "Didn't you hear? It's over! Let's go and see the crowds – Madame Hebert's going to keep her eye on Tom – she has to stay at the desk –" She threw her arms round Isabel, who had not the will power to break away, and kissed her excitedly. So the scene the latter had observed from the window and which had revolted her was now repeated in her own room. For a moment she loathed Sheila and anyone else who had survived the war without a personal loss.

"Well, I've a headache, I don't really feel like it," she said. "Oh, do come."

Isabel allowed herself to be persuaded. The lump was still in her throat but it was hard to struggle against someone else's happiness. And what use was it to do so? Besides, she did not want to be alone.

Five minutes later they hurried round the corner of the street. The firemen called across to them. A taxi went by,
238

crowded inside, and with two soldiers and a girl sitting on top, waving and shouting. They saw a workman who was putting up official posters on the walls that told everybody to put out flags. *Habitants de Paris! C'est la victoire, la victoire triomphale* – The order was hardly necessary, for flags seemed to be coming out everywhere already, and girls wore little ones in their hair. When they reached the Avenue de l'Opéra things were becoming crowded. People wandered about the road so that traffic had to go slowly, there were groups with linked arms going along singing the *Marseillaise*. It was wonderful how formal the French were while they were being gay. A woman with an undernourished face and a fierce expression cried out close to Isabel, "*Vive la France immortelle!*" It was quite certain that however much noise they might be making, people in London would not be calling out long live immortal Britain, and Isabel had to conquer national self-consciousness before calling back "*Vive la France!*" in agreement.

"*Anglais? Vive l'Angleterre! Vive l'Angleterre!*" cried the woman, swaying across the road.

"She's drunk," said Sheila half-anxiously. "Isn't it fun? I hope it's not going to be too rough, though – oh, I do wish Archie were here!" Hardly a minute went by without her mentioning Archie's name.

"Stupid little fool," thought Isabel, but her own mood was changing rapidly. The crowd was getting thicker all the time, and the feeling of feverish excitement grew with it. It was almost impossible to move in front of the opera house. Now she began to be affected by the mass elation. She saw that her first reaction had been appallingly selfish, and she determined to enter into the general spirit.

"Oh, look!" cried Sheila. "What's happening there?" A girl who seemed to be dressed in a flag was dancing to huge applause from a circle of soldiers. Another dense little mass was centred on an old man with a magnificent beard who was selling song sheets. Isabel was arm-in-arm with Sheila, who had found a flag somehow and was waving it. Ribbons and streamers flew through the air. Suddenly a British sergeant appeared in front of her, said, "*Permettez-moi,*" and kissed

239

her – he disappeared at once and she burst out laughing. She felt dizzy. She couldn't hear what Sheila was saying. They moved with the crowd as it spread down the Boulevard des Capucines. Suddenly Isabel felt Sheila's arm jerked away from her and then found herself linked in a chain of twenty soldiers and girls doing some sort of crazy dance. The girls screamed, the men laughed. When she was released fifty yards down the street there was no sign of Sheila. Of course it was hopeless to try to see her. She hurried back to the spot where she had lost her, but it was all too crowded and confused. Some French soldiers and girls went by chanting, " On les a! On les a!" in happy delirium, and all at once there was more excitement caused by the sound of pipes. There was wild cheering as some Scots came marching by. Then there was a gay parade from the Leave Club headed by a Tommy dressed in a Union Jack. Everyone was heading for the Place de la Concorde. Isabel was very anxious about Sheila, and considered going back to the hotel – and then was annoyed with herself for thinking like a nursemaid, for, good heavens, Sheila could look after herself – " This is the place to be to-day, and I shall see everything," Isabel thought, and at once felt free and happy. Why should she bother about Sheila Palmer? That cramping and familiar feeling that there was a duty, a loyalty, an obligation to keep her from what she wanted – she had done with it! She would stay and see what went on, she would celebrate the end of the war like everybody else. And she drifted along with the riotous crowd, a little headachy, a little dizzy, a little hysterical.

The wonderful day went by. The whole vast space of the Concorde seemed to be a mass of people and there were little boys on each of the thousands of captured guns. There were different excitements everywhere. An English band was marching across towards the Champs-Élysées, a crowd of students in another part were pulling a field-gun away as a prize. There were screams and yells and pandemonium and general content. " On les a!" they were still shouting. There was cheering when a few musicians climbed on to some big guns and began to play waltzes and polkas. Isabel found herself dancing with a young American soldier who had a soft,

240

charming accent. He had short, stubbly, fair hair and an immature look and the firm intention of enjoying himself. When they stopped dancing he kept his arm round her. She didn't mind, for her legs felt weak and she needed someone to cling to. Besides there was nothing like the fine old French custom of dancing in the streets to make you feel free of all restraint – unusual circumstances led to unusual behaviour. " Shall we go across the river and cheer Clemenceau? " he asked, and they joined a mass movement in the direction of the Chamber of Deputies. It was amazing how you could keep going if you were part of everything.

They missed Clemenceau and caught the Metro back – it was packed with people coming into the celebrations and the American was overwhelmed with hugs and kisses, but he never let go of her. When they got out at the Madeleine, with almost everyone else, the general movement seemed to be towards the Opera. It was already dusky and another great excitement was the appearance of unshaded lights. The American told her that he wished her to call him Morton, and that he came from Valley City, North Dakota, and he was going back there to State Teachers' College. " I'm a teacher, too – a piano teacher! " Isabel exclaimed delightedly. Morton said she was a very pretty one and every few yards he turned and politely kissed her.

At the back of her mind she was vaguely conscious that this could not go on, that she must return to the hotel and pack her things, that Sheila might be worried about her – but she ignored this and went on in a blissful, light-headed glow. It was nice to be told one was pretty, it was nice to forget everything, it was nice to be happy, it was nice just to belong to the crowd – and the crowd, when they reached the Place de l'Opéra, was one vast mass of jubilation, flag-waving and cheering. Morton uttered high-pitched yells to help things on.

Then something wonderful occurred which snapped her mood. They had been there about a quarter of an hour when all at once quietness spread rapidly over the crowd and a moment later there came the small but clear sound of a man's voice singing the *Marseillaise*. It was stirring and unbearably sad. All heads were turned towards it – the man was up on a balcony somewhere quite close, but Isabel could not see where. Then the crowd began to sing with him. Relief had been the note all day in the streets, but now for a moment triumph and tragedy were in the air, and a solemn feeling of the magnitude of events. Only for a moment, for it was not in human nature to face such things for longer than necessary and almost immediately the shouting and flag-waving began again. But the nervous excitement which had kept Isabel going had disappeared. Dimly she heard Morton's voice in her ear: "What's wrong? Hey, what's wrong?"

She clung to him. It was not only the sense of overwhelming sorrow which had come back to her, but that her head was throbbing, there were pains in her legs, she could hardly stand.

"I think I'm ill," she whispered.

"You need a drink. Something to eat, anyway. We haven't eaten for hours. Come on, we'll find a place."

"No, I must go back to my hotel. I have to catch a train," she said, like a drunk trying to speak steadily. The Place de l'Opéra was turning blue in front of her. "I must go back."

Afterwards she always thought that it was very bad luck on Morton that he should have been saddled with her. He behaved splendidly, however. As soon as it was possible to move he half-carried her to a bar and gave her a cognac. He was very patient and kind, and sat there with his arm round her for almost an hour, but there was no doubt that she was ill. Finally she made an effort and they went out again and she staggered along, supported by him, until he was able to find a taxi. It was just the kind of thing that was bound to happen to her, to come down with the 'flu on Armistice Day, and it was very bad luck on Morton. She always hoped that he had a good time that night and it troubled her for years that, although she could remember his soft, boyish and charming voice, and his light fair hair, and the feel of his arm round her shoulders, she never could remember his face.

CHAPTER THIRTY

M adame Hebert also behaved very well. She helped her to her room and sent for the doctor who had earlier attended Sheila. The latter, of course, was also on the scene and Isabel was dimly conscious of her anxious, flushed face. But she felt too ill to pay attention to what anyone was saying, she merely nodded agreement that there was no reason why Sheila should delay her own departure, although the next morning Madame Hebert was indignant about it. "When I think of all you did for her and that child – well, I suppose that's the way people are nowadays. I'll get some coal for you this morning, though it's like gold dust. You'll soon be all right." This, however, was over-optimistic. Isabel lay in a fever which grew worse rather than better. The doctor arranged for a nurse to come in. That evening there was a crisis – but suddenly the fever broke and she was wringing wet. Madame Hebert and the nurse rushed about finding hot-water bottles which they planted all round her. The crisis was past and she went to sleep. In the morning, however, she was coughing badly. She was conscious of some mildly frightening French conversation. The doctor listened to her chest through an antiquated-looking horn affair – the French always had to do things differently. She was to go to hospital, and when the ambulance arrived she made a dramatic exit from the hotel, carried on a stretcher and seeing the faces of other guests, all with expressions of sympathy mixed with foreboding. The drive lasted a good half-hour, and at the end of it she had a brief glimpse of " Hertford British Hospital " in gold letters over a brown front door. She was taken up to a ward where there were fourteen other women.

Here she spent the next six weeks, while her illness followed its course – 'flu, pneumonia, pleurisy. There was nothing like a period in hospital to make a change from ordinary life. How amazing to have to lie there coughing up blood and goodness knows what else, somewhere in a north-western suburb of Paris, all because of that wretched moment on the Promenade! In spite of everything it was not an unhappy period for her and certainly there would always be lots of things to remember. There was the daily cupping ceremony, when a nurse brought in a tray of sinister little wine-glasses. You had to lie face down while she burnt a little methylated spirit in each glass and plopped it dexterously upside down on your back. There were the quantities of delicious bread and butter to enjoy and of repulsive cabbage or onion water which had to be forced down. There was paper-chain making for the ward Christmas decorations. There was endless conversation with the woman in the next bed, who was the secretary of a South American diplomat's wife. The patients were either British or the French wives of Britons. There was the afternoon somebody died. There was the visit from the British Consul, who gave them all calendars. There was a word game invented by the woman in the next bed, in which you had to make as many words as possible out of the text hung on the wall opposite: Seek Ye First The Kingdom of God. The long hours of silence and doing nothing, which seemed to be unendurable to the others, were almost pleasant for Isabel. She gave herself up to reflections on her life. Was there not some strange sort of pattern to be discerned, some fate which forced events, pleasant for some, disastrous for others? Things had always gone wrong for her – at all events had never gone right for her. Surely there was some point in it, some heavenly design? When she heard other women talking in the ward they seemed to her like inexperienced children. But she felt more strongly than ever that now was the moment when she must strike out again; it was amazing to spend so many weeks without touching a piano. She said nothing about this in her letters. In any case she must get back to work and then have Mr. Durrell's or somebody's opinion before she took any drastic step. Meanwhile, Mrs. Rowland wrote in loving anticipation of her return – she wrote, rather surprisingly, in more affectionate terms than she was accustomed to use in speaking. And it was made clear to Isabel when she was first allowed to take exercise, up and down the ward and then in the bleak hospital

244

grounds (to shouts from the soldiers in the big wards) that she must take things very easily for some time.

Sarah came over from England to fetch her in the middle of January, for they would not permit her to travel by herself, and was shocked by her appearance. For Isabel, though hardly aware of it, had lost two and a half stone – and she had a cough which sounded as if it were likely to persist for years.

"I must warn you about Mother," Sarah said. "It's nothing to worry about, but she had some kind of attack – pains in her chest and so on – it must have been the armistice and then hearing about you; evidently it's something with her heart. Well, it's to be hoped that the time of shocks is now over, but she mustn't run for a bus or that sort of thing. So you'll both have to take it easily for a while. Oh, dear, how awful it is just to come here and go straight away. Isn't Paris too marvellous for words? How I loathe having no money! One day I shall come here with Harry with my bag bursting!"

There was one incident Isabel did not see, but heard about from her sister, which perhaps supported those bed reflections about destiny and living to a pattern; on the way over, it appeared, Sarah had met a War Office colonel on the boat. Sarah had asked him for information about the length of the crossing.

"He really was a most charming man, Isabel. We must have talked for three-quarters of an hour. He took Harry's name and unit and everything – because, of course, I asked if he could help to get him released."

Whether or not it was due to the colonel, two months later Harry was out of the Army. They went at once to London and settled down in a boarding-house off Ladbroke Grove, while Harry began work in a firm of city accountants. Isabel was by now putting on weight and she too was settling down. Her life was uneventful and monotonous, but not unpleasant, and every day that passed made it more certain that it would continue indefinitely in the same way. She was still determined to go to Mr. Durrell again and she began to practise regularly. But the weeks went by and she constantly put off the test. "I'm not satisfied with myself – I'll write next month." And next month it was the same. Meanwhile, pupils began to come again. It happened that there was a shortage of music teachers in the town. She was invited to give private lessons at the High School, to which the Mather girls had gone, and it seemed impossible to refuse, although every step of that kind was another little chain binding her down. Moreover, the money, of course, was useful – Mrs. Rowland's capital was shrinking, but with Isabel's pension and earnings the two managed to live fairly comfortably. And that was another trouble: since they were living comfortably, why take a step which would disturb everything? The pros and cons of the matter waged an endless battle in her mind. Another trouble was that she and her mother got on tremendously well, in spite of the fact that, or perhaps because, they never had an intimate conversation. The uneasiness that there had been between them in her childhood had gone now that she was no longer a prodigy. The change had really begun when she first went to the Rotunda, and now they had an easy and affectionate relationship. Isabel did not wish for anyone else's company. She had no interest in local contemporaries. As she constantly reminded herself, but for her mother she would not have stayed another minute in the town. She therefore joined in her mother's meagre social life with Aunt Ada, Aunt Phyllis, and a few other friends of the same age. They played a good deal of auction bridge, and no afternoon was complete unless Isabel told someone's fortune in the cards or tea-leaves. There was no reason for anyone to think her discontented, and for her mother's sake Isabel felt herself obliged to maintain the illusion. Next month she must face things. Next month she would write to Mr. Durrell (she had at least discovered that he was still in practice at the same old studio). Next month, next month, next month.

Yet the illusion she purposely maintained was not all illusion. She was often happy. There was something satisfying to her in being accepted by her aunts as a woman of experience, one who had suffered and knew "life". Her illness in Paris had given quite a morbid thrill to that sheltered circle. And it had another effect on herself which she came gradually to notice. It acted as a sort of screen dividing her from the past, simply because it was the first event which George, inexorably dead, had known nothing about. Nowadays she was able to think about him almost dispassionately. And she fell into the habit of making solemn pronouncements, delivered with a cheerful sigh of resignation, like "That's life, though, isn't it, Aunt Ada?" or "Life is a struggle and the odds are against you unless you have luck – but luck only goes to the lucky!" Also, she began to take every opportunity of giving pupils advice of a general nature, although anyone who knew her might have found some of this advice rather astonishing. "Don't forget that your greatest duty is to live," Isabel would say. "You mustn't be afraid to seem selfish." And the child who listened was unaware that Mrs. Nunn was talking to herself. Isabel would even be stirred by her own advice; but, of course, did and said nothing. So the months went by, and Paris, the war, George, Denny, the Rotunda (quite a changed place nowadays, colourless, half-empty and the food bad – it was the post-war world) – all receded, as the two widows, mother and daughter, went on living their quiet, uneventful and by no means unpleasant lives.

Their relationship was one of affection and familiarity, but it was not one of intimacy. They could share a silence without strain. They passed many evenings with Isabel playing while Mrs. Rowland knitted or read. And there were other pleasures. Mrs. Rowland, especially now that she was much less active – she never went anywhere without her box of pills, but she had no more attacks – had become a great watcher from the window of all that went on in the road. If some neighbour bought a new coat, Mrs. Rowland had determined its price and place of purchase on its first journey past 12 Brook Place. Such items had an insidious fascination for Isabel, who never noticed anything herself. Her mother was also an excellent mimic of tradesmen and could make a very funny story out of a morning's shopping – they had the same sense of humour, and could share jokes which would be incomprehensible to anyone else. But there were hours when Mrs. Rowland would give herself up to sad memories and sometimes when she came into the house with red-rimmed eyes, Isabel would know that she had paid one of her long, lonely visits to the cemetery. In her turn, Isabel would sometimes be so overcome by her

247

feeling of frustration that she could hardly bring herself to speak a word all day. Her mother never seemed to notice – was it selfishness? Or was what Isabel liked to think was her own compassion merely a cover for lack of confidence or cowardice? But the mood passed, as did her mother's periods of grief. There were lessons to give, or a bridge drive to go to – dreadfully uninteresting people, but quite an amusing past-time – or they were to meet Aunt Ada for tea at the Winter Garden (which also was not what it was). Soon another month was gone. And Isabel, at twenty-five, gradually felt herself to be middle-aged.

One pleasure they shared was hearing the news from London. Letters came in Sarah's bold, excited handwriting, in which she reported the progress of the baby and of Harry, who had at once made himself felt in his firm. She was always urging her mother and sister to come up and see her. It took a long time before anything came of this. One had to decide on a day free of engagements. One had to discuss whether they should go together or separately. The duller one's life the more difficult it was to do anything. But finally, Isabel went up by herself. Sitting in the train she was amazed at the grotesque fussing about which had had to precede so simple a journey. And it was not only her mother, she had been as bad herself. As the train went by Landen's Mill – the London trains did not stop there – she noticed in those two or three seconds that everything was just as it used to be. One could have gone back ten years and altered nothing. Even the porter she glimpsed had a familiar face. There was a truck being unloaded in the mill siding, as usual – and there were the tops of the elms at the bottom of the garden. Had they really had that garden? Father, Nicky, Denny – it was unbearable to think about. How wonderful the future had looked! The last, the very last thing she would have imagined was that in ten year's time a trip to London would seem like an adventure.

"All the same," she thought, "if it hadn't been for falling ill in Paris, things would have been different."

Sarah was at Paddington to meet her and she made Isabel feel like a provincial aunt; provincial because Sarah already

248

had a tremendous air of being a smart Londoner and chatted away excitedly in her high-pitched voice, full of new affectations; an aunt because the most profound impression that Sarah had on her was her air of being young. She spoke quickly and walked quickly, dodging about among the crowds and pulling Isabel with her. As usual, she had some news of progress.

"I didn't tell you in my last letter, did I — no, I didn't — we've been to dinner with one of the partners! Honestly, they must think a lot of Harry, mustn't they? It was a house at Hampstead, quite small, but old and everything — everything *good*, you know what I mean. And they weren't a bit stuffy. They seemed to know all sorts of interesting people — *she* had met Marie Tempest, for instance. Honestly, it's too marvellous living in London — if only we could find a flat — but they're terribly expensive or pigstyes — And it's so difficult in a boarding-house with a baby. 'Here's the little fellow that keeps us awake,' is what you get flung at you — I've had some pretty sharp arguments. Honestly, if you don't stand up for yourself, you'd be out in the street for all other people care. Though Davy's a lamb of a baby really — aren't you dying to see him? I would have brought him, but I wasn't sure about getting a pram on the platform — that's one advantage of the place, I can always get one of the maids to keep an eye on him. Let's jump on this bus."

When Isabel returned home the following night — they had been to a matinée (*As You Were* at the London Pavilion) and she had gone straight to the station after it — she was able to give her mother an encouraging report. Mrs. Rowland listened eagerly to a description of the long walks in the Park pushing David, and of how surprised Isabel had been, when Harry returned from the city in the evening, to see how much more impressive he was as a civilian than he had been in uniform, which, of course, was quite the reverse with most men. The boarding-house itself was also rather impressive — like a hotel and with quite a number of entertaining people. There was even a gramophone in the basement, which was fitted up as games room, and a party of them had danced there until almost midnight; according to Sarah they had a dance at least twice a week. There was also a piano in the basement and Sarah persuaded her to play. She did so unwillingly, but her ten-minute performance was a great success. (It was pathetic how easily you could get applause from people who knew nothing.) What else had they done? Oh, yes, lunch at the Strand Palace.

"Heavens, you must be tired out!" said Mrs. Rowland, looking as if she were exhausted at the thought of it all. "You must have a long sleep. Still, it was good for you, a really good change."

"No, I don't really feel tired."

"Ah, well, of course, you're young," said her mother, and upon this Isabel at once did feel tired.

Then things went on as before. A few weeks later Sarah and Harry came with baby for a week-end. Some time during it Sarah said to her, "Honestly, Isabel, I don't know how you stand it, it's such a pity you can't come to Town and be near us – but, of course, there's your teaching and everything –" Isabel was rather angry at the sublime way in which Sarah ignored the necessity of someone staying with her mother, as well as at the realization that Sarah thought of her merely as a piano teacher. She replied sharply that she was entirely happy where she was, but when she was calm again she reflected that Sarah had no reason to think anything else; it was a very long time since her possible future as a performer had been even a matter for discussion. She could not say, "If only you and Harry had settled down here as I expected, I'd be in London now – I might already be a success." The matter was closed. A month later Mrs. Rowland herself had two days at the boarding-house, and then Isabel went again. These were the exciting events of their life. At Christmas they were disappointed when Sarah and Harry went to the Proctors at Eastbourne. But at Easter they came to Brook Place, with the great news that they had at last found a flat at Earl's Court. They were like two visitors from the big outside world. It was only to be expected that the baby, David, should be unusually large and showing signs of great precocity.

"Exactly like Denny," Mrs. Rowland said happily.

The months went on. Now, of course, there were visits to

the flat. Her mother returned from her first inspection clearly disappointed. She could not understand why anyone wanted to live in London and especially Earl's Court. The flat, with its dreary, terrible gas fire, and dreary, terrible outlook, seemed a nightmare to her and so were the stairs which led up to it – it now became her constant effort to think of what items she could give Sarah to cheer things up, doilies, table-napkins, towels, sheets, knives, glasses – anything that could go went, and any time Mrs. Rowland thought of something she and Isabel could do without she had a moment of contentment. Isabel felt quite differently about the flat. To her it seemed a wonderful kingdom over which Sarah reigned, glorious with all the troubles of being a housewife and mother.

Incredibly soon it was Christmas again. This year Sarah and Harry came to them, bringing with them a distinct air of prosperity – or more exactly, of prosperity to come. Harry, it appeared, was doing brilliantly. Everything was centred on David, now two years and four months old. His future was rosy and he had already been put down for the school Harry's senior partner's son had gone to – a fact which Sarah was careful to let drop in front of Aunt Ada, whose face at once froze into her old look of disapproval. Mrs. Rowland enjoyed herself a little too much, for on Christmas afternoon she had a slight attack – but she had her pills, which seemed to work, for she was all right again within an hour. Otherwise everything went well, and they looked forward to when David would be able to enjoy it. Next year the visitors would go, of course, to Eastbourne – alternate years was to be the procedure. Isabel put up a show of enjoying herself, but occasions like Christmas or birthdays rather depressed her; all anniversaries reminded her of time passing, opportunity passing, although by now her private ambitions had gradually faded. When she lost herself in reflection nowadays it was of what might have been rather than of what might be. She was back where she was before and the inspiration George had given had almost died.

So another year began. In August a daughter was born to Sarah. She had, of course, wanted a daughter. Otherwise life continued uneventfully. Bridge, piano lessons, walks on the

Promenade, an endless discussion whether or not to have another dog.

One evening in the following March, Isabel was at the piano playing while her mother knitted, making something for Sarah's baby. This was their normal evening, some music, a few words exchanged now and then and finally Mrs. Rowland would go to the kitchen and make a cup of tea. They spoke about the cottage Harry and Sarah were going to take for the summer holiday. It was near Felixstowe and Sarah was to go down with the children for the whole of August, while Harry came at week-ends. Mrs. Rowland and Isabel were expected to go for a week at least.

"In my opinion Sarah's a fool," said her mother. "She's taking on much too much. She thinks she can do anything — though the flat would be horrible in August — but really the idea of going away for a month! Sarah does everything she wants — she gets it from her father. That was a charming thing, dear."

"I made a mess of it, really. I haven't played it for months."

"It's always a mess, according to you, and it always sounds lovely. You know I have a feeling in my bones that this is going to be a failure; I ought to have known it was doomed from the start when Mrs. Hitchcock hadn't the right blue — and gave me the wrong change, you remember, I told you, dear —"

"Yes, you gave her half a crown and she said it was a florin," Isabel nodded. She knew the story well.

"I remember quite distinctly it was half a crown, and in any case I knew, because I had fifteen shillings and a pound note when I left this house, I had to go to the Post Office to buy stamps — three three-halfpennies, which I paid for with a sixpence —" She sighed good-humouredly. "You know, I never have been able to complain. Children ought to learn how to complain at school, it's the most valuable asset I can think of. Are you busy to-morrow, dear?"

"I've two brats at the school I'm trying to prepare for the harmony exam next week, that's all. Shall I go and put the kettle on?"

"No, I will, you go on playing."

Mrs. Rowland put down her things and left the room. Isabel played some more, a Brahms *intermezzo* she was particularly fond of. The piece absorbed her. Only when she had finished and she sat there idly improvising did it occur to her suddenly that her mother was taking a long time. A chill went through her, a sense of alarm. She hurried out and down to the kitchen, and there found what she knew she would find – Mrs. Rowland on the floor, unconscious, her face white and clammy, her right hand resting on her left side, where the old pain had struck.

"Mother!" Isabel cried. "Oh, how frightful – "

She flew. For the pills, which were in her bag by the fire, for a rug to cover her with and then out of the house to next door where they had a telephone. A frightful, agonizing fifteen minutes. All in vain – when the doctor arrived, her mother was dead.

CHAPTER THIRTY-ONE

Once again the two sisters walked along the Promenade, a final walk before Sarah caught the train back to London. Yesterday had been the funeral, a quiet, sad little affair, and, as usual, it was Sarah who could not control herself – she had sobbed the whole time, and a cold drizzle had made the ceremony uncomfortable as well. To-day there was a sharp wind, and the sun appeared occasionally behind the fast-moving clouds and lit up the Promenade for a minute with an unreal brightness. There was a destroyer out in the harbour – everything was much the same as it had been almost eleven years before, when they had walked here after their father's funeral and discussed the future. The future itself had changed, of course. There was less of it and its course seemed more determined. They would presumably go on as they were. That was what Isabel suggested.

"Will you mind living alone in the house?" Sarah asked.

"Oh, I shall be perfectly all right. I can always go and see the aunts, and they'll be coming in – besides, I've lots to do."

"I'd get a maid to live-in, if I were you. You can afford it now." They were each to receive, Mr. Webber had said, about seven hundred and fifty pounds.

"Well, I'll think about it."

"But you really ought to have a holiday – after the shock and everything – honestly, Isabel, I don't think I could ever have gone through such an ordeal. I wish you'd come up to town and stay for a week or two. Oh, this wind! It's no good, Isabel, I've become a Londoner. Sea breezes are not for me, except in August – or the south of France, *that's* where I'd like to be – but, anyhow, I shall be expecting you for all of August at Felixstowe. But do come up as soon as possible."

It was equally typical of Sarah that just as she had shown more emotion yesterday, she should be almost cheerful to-day. When Isabel saw her off at the station, however, her sister's eyes were again filled with tears.

"Heavens, it's so appalling – just the two of us left now – "

Isabel went home. In all the long conversations she had had with Sarah over the past three days she had not mentioned the most important of her plans for the future. This was, of course, the hope of taking up her serious playing again. Was it possible or was it too late? She dared not hope too much. She had said nothing, in case other people – including Sarah – would find the idea ridiculous. Mr. Durrell must judge, and if he judged against her it was better to keep the disappointment secret. And another reason for keeping silence was that it hardly seemed proper to act like a jack-in-the-box, released by her mother's death.

Yet it could not be denied that mixed with her very real grief was a feeling of release. At last it was true that no one stood between her and what she wanted to do, she had no duty to perform, no obligation bound her morally – she could now take the advice she had found such pleasure in giving. And her mother's money made the whole thing simple. For the moment she would go on as before. But as soon as a decent period had intervened she would write to Mr. Durrell.

"Although, I suppose, something's bound to happen to stop me," she reflected.

It was not so. Six weeks later she sent off her letter. She made so many attempts, first of all, that she was reminded of that Sunday afternoon long ago when Sarah and she had composed George's appeal to his uncle – there was no doubt about it, there had been happy times even in those days; and she remembered with amusement how angry they had been with the chocolates he had sent as their reward. She wrote finally: "Dear Mr. Durrell, I don't expect you will remember me, as it is so long since I came to you, and I hope you will not think I have taken leave of my senses in writing to you now. I came to you for a week in April, 1910, and you wrote to my father recommending that I should be sent to the Academy with a view to a concert career. Unfortunately, the death of my father and many subsequent troubles prevented my hopes from being realized. I played in a restaurant and for some years I have been teaching. I know it may be hopeless to think of going on seriously, but I have never given up the idea and have maintained my work. I am now in circumstances that would make it possible for me to devote myself entirely to work and practice, at any rate for a period, and I could stay in London. The question is – as before – is it worth while? Can you give me an appointment perhaps the week after next, so that you can tell me your opinion, one way or the other? It may be, of course, that at my age it is pointless, for I am now twenty-seven years old, which is very different, I am afraid, from sixteen. If this is the case I should be grateful if you would say so, and I shall quite understand. Yours sincerely, Isabel Nunn (*née* Rowland. I am a widow, my husband was in the Navy)."

Three days later she received his reply, which ran: "Dear Mrs. Nunn, Of course I remember you and am delighted to hear from you. Moreover, I shall look forward to hearing you play again. Can you manage Thursday week at 3 p.m.? Be sure I shall give you a frank opinion. As to your age, I assure you that this is entirely a relative matter. From where I sit it is quite hard to distinguish any difference between sixteen and twenty-seven. Both ages seem to me to be extraordinarily young. Yours very sincerely, Clement Durrell." Isabel was so delighted that she felt like jumping up and down like a child –

and she looked round as if in search of someone to show it to, but, of course, she was alone.

"He remembers me!" she exclaimed softly, and was already more confident. But confidence came and went in the next few days. Lessons had to be given, of course – for until she knew, it would be foolish to cut down on that – but she couldn't wait for them to be over so that she could settle down to practise, and several children were surprised and pleased at being ejected dead on the hour (for Isabel, though she continued to loathe teaching, was always free with her time, since she never noticed it going). In the recurring periods when her confidence left her and she felt certain that, in spite of his politely remembering her, Mr. Durrell would be forced to turn his thumbs down, she became quite desperate. What on earth would she do? For life in the town without her mother had no meaning at all. She had no friends of her own there. The old musical life of the town had disintegrated in the war. People she had known in the old days – not that she had known anyone intimately, for she had never had time – were all married with families or simply gone away. Dr. Preston's society no longer existed, and he himself had gone into retirement. Neither Aunt Ada nor poor Aunt Phyllis, now a decayed, kindly and uninteresting wreck of sixty, had any point for her without her mother. It was difficult to maintain conversation with them for more than a few minutes. And yet what would be the point of going anywhere else? The future looked lonely and boring. It was not as if she were a particularly good teacher.

But soon a wave of confidence would come back, and nothing mattered. She had decided that she would play him the same Debussy piece that she had played eleven years before – it would be a symbol of taking up where she had left off, on the one hand, and on the other, it would illustrate sharply whether she had gained anything in the eleven years or, of course, how much she had lost. She practised feverishly every day, hardly bothering to eat. She was constantly panic-stricken. Why had she asked for an appointment so soon? She needed another month at least. Several times she was on the point of writing to postpone the date. Had there been the

256

smallest excuse – but there was none. She was on her own.

The Thursday came. She caught the early London train from Peter Street. She had an absurd guilty feeling because she had told no one what she was doing. At Paddington she looked round nervously, in fear that for some extraordinary reason Sarah or Harry would be there – just the kind of thing that would happen. She took the tube to Baker Street, which was only five minutes' walk from the studio. She had too much time and she went to an A.B.C. café. She was far too nervous to eat anything. She sat tensely in front of a cup of coffee. When she lifted the cup her hand shook. She felt desperate – what a state to be in!

She realized that it was no use going on. The best thing was to go straight back to Paddington. She could send him a wire pleading illness; and, of course, she would pay for the lesson, so it wouldn't matter to him; and no one would know.

Dreams were best kept as dreams. When you tried to turn them into reality – especially when you tried too late – they suddenly wore a strange and uncomfortable aspect. All at once the life she was hoping to give up became more attractive. She had her small capital, she had her pension – in those circumstances it wouldn't be at all bad to go on teaching at Brook Place. She would always be coming up to town to see Sarah. She could take a holiday when she chose.

"Yes, the sensible thing is to go home," she thought. But the minutes went by and she sat there, unable to do the sensible thing. Finally, she picked up the bill for her coffee, which she had hardly touched, paid at the desk and went out into Baker Street. Ten minutes later she had reached Mr. Durrell's mews off the Marylebone Road. She thought herself mad. The only reason she could imagine why she was there was that her body must have felt bound, in deference to some well-taught moral scruple, to keep an appointment, if an appointment had been made.

It was odd to see everything looking so terribly the same, a little dirtier and older and smaller, as places always looked when one returned after a period. A chauffeur was looking inside the bonnet of a car; the stables, of course, had become garages. But Mr. Durrell's door was on a latch, as it had been eleven years before, and from upstairs came the sound of a piano – someone else having a lesson, probably some hopeful young girl. There was still time to retreat. What was the point of going in? Feeling old and depressed and unbearably agitated – for one thing she couldn't remember a note, not a single note, of the Debussy she had intended to play – she pushed the door and went in.

An hour and a half later she half-ran into Baker Street Station, made for the telephone kiosk and rang up Sarah. Her sister answered.

"Isabel? Good heavens!"

"I just wanted to make sure you were in!"

"Where are you? Are you in town? What on earth are you doing?"

"I'm going back this evening – I've been having a lesson from Mr. Durrell. You'll be amazed when I tell you – well, I'm coming right round to the flat – I'm so excited I can't speak –"

"What*ever* has happened?"

"I'll tell you when I get there!"

She went by an Inner Circle train to Earl's Court. She sat in a daze, while Mr. Durrell's words repeated themselves. "If you can come to London and work with me for a year, you will be first class."

The miracle she had longed for over so many years had finally happened.

CHAPTER THIRTY-TWO

S arah was amazed. She was also pleased. And for the next few months she remained amazed and pleased. Isabel had poured out her hopes and plans on that May afternoon. Sarah couldn't get over it – she had thought of her sister as stuck firmly in the mud. It still didn't occur to her to take the matter seriously until Isabel started talking about where she was to live – would Sarah find out if there were a room at the boarding-house where she and Harry had stayed?

" You mean you're going to leave Brook Place? "

" As soon as I possibly can."

" But your teaching and everything? "

" Don't you understand that I loathe it, and I've always loathed it ! " her sister exclaimed.

Sarah had not understood and she was very surprised to hear it. " If that's so, why did she do it? " she wondered. But in any case there was no doubt about Isabel's happiness at the idea of giving it up. She was positively bursting with her news. Well, Sarah thought, looking at her sister critically – Isabel's clothes were rather old-fashioned; in fact she was wearing the same costume in which she had gone off for her honeymoon – it would certainly do her no harm to live in London for a while. Furthermore, if Mr. Durrell meant what he had told her, and was not merely anxious to collect some tuition fees – a thought she considered voicing, but decided not to – that, of course, would be splendid. In any event it was a bold and rather Bohemian course to take, and one which would commend itself to the Dessletons – these were the partner and his wife with whom they had dined, and it was Mrs. Dessleton who had met Marie Tempest. Isabel might very possibly become a social asset. Though this thought did nothing to increase her support for her sister's plan, it certainly did nothing to lessen it.

Isabel, of course, was right up in the air. What to do about the house, the furniture and so on hadn't occurred to her at all.

" You'll have to put everything in store," Sarah said. " Or sell it – what about the piano, though? Where are you going to practise? "

But everything had turned out to be quite simple. She was impressed by Isabel's determination once her mind was made up. In the middle of July she had arrived in London for good, and was installed in one of the smallest and cheapest rooms in the Ladbroke Grove boarding-house. She went twice a week to Mr. Durrell. The incredible thing about the little man was that he looked exactly the same as before, although they had thought him old in 1910, which only went to show how fatally wrong you were about everything at sixteen – and

259

every day she practised in one of the rooms available for this purpose at a Wigmore Street piano shop. She seemed to have altogether ceased being the shy and withdrawn and moody person Sarah had known. Everything was going well with her. As for 12 Brook Place, she had given notice, of course, which could take effect at the earliest at the end of next quarter – but meanwhile it had been sub-let, furnished, to a retired couple who were waiting for a bungalow they were building to be finished. As for Aunt Ada and Aunt Phyllis, they and all the Mathers had become names in the past; they no longer existed; this was a considerable relief to Sarah, and even if there had been no other advantage to Isabel's removal to London this alone would have made it worth while. But there were many other advantages. It was pleasant for Sarah to have her sister's company again – for she was rather lonely during the day – and fortunately nothing delighted Isabel more than to help with the babies, she was always prepared to take David off in the pram – she said it reminded her of Paris. Ahead also in Sarah's plans was a move during the coming winter to a house in the suburbs – for this miserable Earl's Court flat grew smaller and more uncomfortable every day; and the fact that the Brook Place furniture would be released at the end of September would be most convenient. Furniture was always ruined in store, or, alternatively, sold at a loss – and it would be especially convenient for Isabel to have her piano somewhere accessible. All this was discussed between them amicably, and it was very useful to have Harry there to write to Mr. Webber hurrying up the final settlement of their mother's rather pathetic little estate. Harry knew just how to do that sort of thing.

But it was at Felixstowe, in August, that Sarah really became conscious of the change in her sister. They had a coastguard's cottage about a mile away from the Dessletons' seaside bungalow; and of course it was through the Dessletons that they were there at all. Sarah knew what it was all about and though in terms of comfort she would have much preferred to go to an hotel somewhere she was more than willing to play the game, in spite of outdoor sanitation and heating by oil stove – and the Dessletons had arranged for a local woman called Mrs. Fletcher to come in and help. The game, quite simply, was that the Dessletons were having a close look at them before Harry became a partner, a step which it was accepted was to happen within the next twelve months. You couldn't get to know people better than by observing them enjoying a Spartan holiday on the east coast. You could decide whether to move over to a first-name basis – or never under any circumstances to do this. Sarah was aware of the importance of things going well, and was rather more sensitive to it than Harry – who mistakenly thought that being brilliant at the office was enough. She was also sensitive to the fact that though the Dessletons certainly wanted to retain Harry's services, they considered him to be not quite a gentleman. Harry was improving all the time, but Sarah knew that there was some way to go. Of course the Dessletons saw the pure gold in him, just as she had herself, but when Harry talked about " the kiddies " or " the wife " she knew it was very hard for the Dessletons to take, and it all want to show what a very high opinion Gordon Dessleton had of Harry's work.

He was a large, florid-looking man in his early forties and his wife, Margery, was inclined to be arty, in a severe sort of way; fundamentally Sarah approved of them, they were exactly what she thought of as nice people. There were quite a number of equally nice people in the neighbourhood – holiday friends of the Dessletons – whom they met at the Glory Hole, which was just the amusing name given to a club, a converted barn with a bar that was run by some very nice people. It was very unfortunate that Harry not only looked out of place, but made no bones about his detestation of everything and everybody. Sarah almost lost her temper with him when he came near to refusing point blank Gordon Dessleton's offer to give him his first golf lesson. There was a golf course running along the coast which came quite close to the coastguard cottage, and of course it was a splendid opportunity. When he did, reluctantly, have the lesson, he looked hopelessly wrong – he had an insidious desire to be neat which had been fine in the Army and was fine in the city, and in informal clothes this somehow always made him look like a tripper – of course, he couldn't be made to see it.

So it was very important that the Dessletons realized that Sarah did understand, and that therefore they could feel hope for the future. She got on well with Margery Dessleton and let slip many a hint about her own childhood and background, designed to help round-out the picture – and in the memories on which these hints were based the old Mill House grew larger and larger and its grounds ever more extensive. The Dessletons were really very kind to her. Harry went back to London after the first week-end, and since she was very much tied with the children they were always dropping by in the car. If Mrs. Fletcher were there to look after things they would take her off to the Glory Hole for a drink. They came two or three times with a picnic basket and bathed from the coast-guard cottage. Things really went much better when Harry wasn't there – and incidentally he was also no enthusiast for the beach.

But there was an incident on the Thursday of that week which was most unlucky. It was the middle of the morning, about half-past eleven. Mrs. Fletcher had just gone for a walk with the baby, and Sarah was about to go down to the beach with David, when she saw Gordon Dessleton approaching from the direction of the golf course, his bag of clubs slung over his shoulder. He had never come alone and Sarah was aware of a certain mild excitement. She waved.

"Are you in?" he called.

"Only just."

"Any refreshment for a poor thirsty golfer?"

"Oh, dear," Sarah exclaimed. "I'm afraid we haven't any drink. Shall I make you some coffee – heat some up, rather?"

"Coffee would be perfectly wonderful," Gordon Dessleton said. "It's a ripping day, but a shade *too* warm for this customer. Think of your poor husband slaving away in the metropolis." He followed her into the cottage, breathing almost on her neck. He put down his bag on the floor and looked around. "By jove, you're very snug in here."

"You've seen it before," Sarah said coolly.

He chuckled, and sat down, pretending exhaustion.

"Yes."

She was not altogether surprised by this visit. She liked

what he stood for, but she had summed him up personally as rather vain and stupid – although shrewd enough to realize that he needed good brains to support the privileged position he had inherited. He had a big man's vanity, he was tremendously courteous to women, he clearly thought his eye-crinkling smile was very attractive. Her experience had been that it was difficult to talk to him for three minutes without having her elbow pressed or her hand or shoulder touched – purely to help him make a conversational point. This being the case, Sarah, busying herself with the coffee, was thinking hard what her action should be if he made some sort of advance; and she had no doubt that that was why he was here. She must in any case be very diplomatic. He was, after all, Harry's boss, and the firm, through no fault of his, first class.

"Harry will be here to-morrow evening, anyhow," she said.

"He must be very lonely for his pretty wife," murmured the guest, in a slightly whimsical tone that he often adopted.

"I hope so."

"He'll find her looking wonderfully brown."

"Do you think so? Good," said Sarah, keeping carefully out of reach. And that was as far as anything went, for there came the sound of a car stopping outside. Mrs. Dessleton had arrived.

Five most embarrassing moments followed. Nothing, of course, was said, but there was no doubt what Mrs. Dessleton thought – and no wonder, for her fat-headed husband looked as guilty as a naughty schoolboy. Sarah was beside herself with annoyance. How was it possible to suggest that this was the first time he had come there alone? What was to stop Mrs. Dessleton assuming that he made a habit of it? It was infuriating. Coffee for three was served in an atmosphere of cold politeness. The carefully-built-up relationship was in ruins. Nothing altered on the surface, they still came to see her – but not Mr. Dessleton alone – and over the week-end she and Harry went to the Glory Hole, and Harry had another golf lesson; but between her and Mrs. Dessleton there was now an unbridgeable gap, with heaven knew what consequences for the future and the partnership – until the following week-end when Isabel came down with Harry. She was to stay for the remaining fortnight; but she had repaired all the damage within twenty-four hours, without of course knowing anything about it. This miracle occurred for the simple reason that Mrs. Dessleton admired all persons who were connected with the arts. It would not have mattered very much what Isabel was, she could have been a worker in ceramics, a sculptress, and Mrs. Dessleton would have been equally enthusiastic. But that she was devoting her whole time to the piano, and that she had given up a most comfortable home – as Sarah pointed out – in order to do this, seemed to Mrs. Dessleton the height of romance. She was delighted with Isabel.

"Why have you never told me about your wonderful sister?" she exclaimed to Sarah. "We have a divine piano at Hampstead. You must persuade her to come and play for us there. And what a charming person she is!"

It was one of Sarah's virtues that she was always willing to join whole-heartedly in praise – of anyone or anything. She had not really been conscious of Isabel's charm, but now that it had been pointed out she was always noticing it. It was a charm based on what seemed to be an amazing simplicity of outlook; she played the piano and she wanted nothing else. She was looking younger and more attractive than for years, but was apparently unaware of it. She told all their fortunes at the Glory Hole; as for her own, she told Sarah, "Well, of course, all I need now is luck."

For the rest of the month Gordon Dessleton went back to London during the week as well as Harry. Sarah and Isabel spent a good deal of time with Mrs. Dessleton, and the holiday ended as a great success.

The autumn came and with it the business of moving. Suburban life began for the Proctors. It was, as Sarah regarded it, a new chapter and a breathing space. She had been able to say "my husband", then "my children" and now "my house". It was a small house in not too distinguished a road in the suburb called Watham Heath, which was just beginning the relentless going-down process but was very convenient for the city. Sarah was also at last able to have a servant problem and next year they planned to have a car. Thus it seemed to her privately – it was a thought which gave great satisfaction

– Harry was leading her back to the old original Rowland standard of life. The garden was going to be a wonderful boon to the children and meanwhile it was already giving Harry an outdoor interest which he was a good deal more enthusiastic about than golf. Next year also, however, she proposed to insist on him joining the golf club. The surroundings were much pleasanter than they had been at Earl's Court but Sarah was sensitive to the fact that though the Dessletons approved of their move there was something faintly patronizing in their approval. Even Isabel at her Ladbroke Grove boarding-house seemed to have a metropolitan edge on the Proctors. Sarah realized that as soon as it was possible they must either move back or further out. There was nothing to be said against Watham Heath, but it must be firmly regarded as somewhere to stop on the way. Such was Sarah's outlook, and meanwhile she was a happy and efficient wife and mother. But she had so much to do that she often quite envied the simplicity of Isabel's life, the bi-weekly lessons from Mr. Durrell, the hours of practice every day and all the concert-going – for her sister was now in the way of getting many free tickets, which Sarah sometimes used. They often met in town for a concert or a matinée, and every week-end Isabel came out, and played her piano, which was in the Proctors' drawing-room, amid much of the Brook Place furniture. And on three Sundays during the winter she went with Harry and Isabel to supper at the Dessletons in Hampstead.

There were always a dozen or more people present on these occasions, and they were always people who did interesting things or had interesting connections. Years afterwards it was easy for Sarah to look back and realize that poor Margery Dessleton was rather pathetic, but she certainly didn't seem so at the time, and you never knew who you would meet at her house – a man whose brother was in the Foreign Office, or a friend of the editor of the *Daily Mail*, or some actress's sister – it was very easy to laugh years afterwards but at the time it was impressive. There was a great deal of conversation about right up-to-the-minute trends in all departments, and it was very pleasant to meet people who knew important people. Harry, of course, was bored unless finance was being

I*

discussed, and Gordon Dessleton, the host, certainly would have been if he were not slightly intoxicated – and she would have a difficult moment with him sooner or later – but the guests were mostly friends of Margery, who clearly liked being hostess, rather as if this were her "salon". The Dessletons had money, the cold food was excellent and there was plenty of good claret. If the Proctors were there more or less out of kindness, Isabel on the other hand was definitely welcome. The hostess would force them all to stop talking and listen to Isabel play – preferably something difficult that no one really liked. When Sarah watched Isabel sitting at the piano, with her poker face, she was reminded sharply of her sister years before, it was just the same expression she used to have when as a young girl she had to play on all social occasions, because it was expected. And there was no doubt about it, she played brilliantly.

Some luck had come Isabel's way, moreover. Mr. Durrell had arranged for her to give a recital in January, a sort of début within a début. The real thing was to come six months later – the Wigmore Hall, some advertising and, it was to be hoped, some press critics at hand. This was merely a small affair with an invited audience and, unfortunately, no fee – at Schumachers in Bond Street; and the real star of the occasion was meant to be the Schumacher piano, of course. With any luck Schumachers might send a piano round to her when she became established, and all aspiring concert pianists hoped to be backed by a firm; so it was a very good thing to be introduced to their attention in this way. It was an example of what was to be gained by coming to London and working with a man like Clement Durrell, and heaven knew where she might be already if she had done it before.

"I would have if I'd been her," Sarah thought.

Isabel came out to Watham Heath for Christmas. Harry's parents were also there, so it was an orthodox family party – another sign, in its way, that the Proctors were settling well into the post-war world. Isabel was a fervent worker on such occasions, she slaved at the decorations, invariably taking five minutes where one was needed – in practical matters she was, as ever, hopeless – and secreted her carefully-bought parcels.

In fact she was looking forward more than anything to next Christmas, when David would be old enough to care. A series of wonderful family occasions lay ahead, to be inspired by a doting and perhaps very successful aunt.

"I must say, in your place I wouldn't be able to think of anything but the recital," Sarah said. "Goodness, I do envy you, Isabel! Think of poor dreary little me pushing a pram when you're hurrying from Paris to Rome—"

They were at the Dessletons on New Year's Day, which was a Sunday, and Margery Dessleton was very thrilled about the forthcoming recital. She seemed to regard Isabel as sort of protégée of her own, and she told Sarah, "I'm sure our girl is going to have a triumph! It's a curious thing but I've always had a great feeling for talent, I can *detect* it even though my knowledge of the subject may not be *profound*. But if one has an intuitive intelligence one can sense things. How beautifully she played that little Balakirev mazurka!" For Isabel had given some excerpts from her programme. Sarah left Mrs. Dessleton and crossed the room to her sister, who was talking to a slim, dark, attractive man. You never knew whom you would meet at the Dessletons and this was, of all things—she and Harry had been slightly shocked when they were introduced—a German. Sarah's general attitude to the former enemy was based on her reading of the Hun-hating *Daily Mail*—"Those Junkers will cheat you yet"—but as soon as she saw that Mrs. Dessleton was pleased to have him there as a sign of her progressive thought, and that he was more than well accepted by everyone, she had to make a quick adjustment; she saw almost at once that her general attitude must be thrown out of the window. It was no sacrifice, for she had never thought about the matter, and still less of a sacrifice when she actually spoke to this German, who had the very British name of Peters and the most charming broken accent, although he spoke English quite fluently. In any case, as far as Sarah was concerned, all guests of the Dessletons were worthy of respect. She was glad to see that Isabel seemed to be getting along well with him.

He turned towards her and gave her a brilliant smile.

"You've met my sister?" Isabel said.

"Yes, a little," he said, delightfully. "Only for one minute.

Your sister? Yes, yes, I can see this. Where is it? The eyes? The nose?"

"Not the nose," Sarah said. "Mine's terribly snub. I hate it."

"Pardon me, Snub?"

"Like this!" Of course, it was always fascinating to talk to a foreigner and it was a pity that never in a hundred years would Harry, or perhaps any Englishman, learn to cock his head as elegantly as Mr., or rather Herr, Peters.

"Oh, but I like it so," said Herr Peters. "You also play like your sister?"

"Only the gramophone," Sarah told him, putting on her most provocative expression. "I'm afraid I haven't any talents."

"That is sad. I, too, play a very little but so badly! It is an insult to the piano in my little flat in Berlin –"

To Sarah's annoyance she was dragged away by Gordon Dessleton, and was not able to continue the conversation. Little flat in Berlin – heavens, how romantic it sounded! But then she forgot all about him, for the room was crowded. When it was time to go someone gave her and Harry a lift to Great Portland Street, where they could catch an Inner Circle tube to Liverpool Street and from there a train back to Watham Heath. Isabel, who had been staying with them for the week-end as usual, was making her own way back to Ladbroke Grove, a less long-drawn-out and tedious journey. It was only when they were waiting in the dirt and gloom of Liverpool Street that Sarah remembered the German, and asked Harry if he had spoken to him.

"Yes, I did," Harry said. "A very nice chap. Apparently he was a supply officer in Belgium in the war, doing, I suppose, exactly what I was doing at Lowestoft. Rather a coincidence. He told me he was very impressed by the friendly reception he's had here. He says it's the same in Germany – they have no feeling against us at all, and after all, with the blockade they've had a pretty rough time."

"Yes, I suppose they have," Sarah agreed. "What is he doing here?"

"He said he was re-establishing contacts his firm had before the war. You know, to speak quite frankly, when you meet these fellows – though I must say, I wish he'd get his hair cut – sometimes it makes one wonder if we fought the wrong people."

"I thought his hair was nice," said Sarah. "Oh, God, Harry, I'm frozen – we simply must get a car."

"That's the next thing on the list, dear, you know that."

Ten days later the recital took place. Sarah arrived with Margery Dessleton. She had so often been to hear Isabel perform, and it was like old times, but this was London and she only hoped that Isabel was not as nervous as she was herself. She had sounded quite calm on the telephone earlier. Schumacher's small hall was quite crowded with their free list patrons. The platform was decorated with flowers, and the piano – Schumacher Grand (British Manufacture) – stood waiting. Sarah read and re-read the programme. There at last was printed the name MISS ISABEL ROWLAND – in London! It had taken Isabel longer than had been expected, but here she was, and there was no denying it.

"I'm so looking forward to the Balakirev," Margery Dessleton said, looking round bright-eyed at the audience. "Good heavens, there's my charming little German! You met him, didn't you?"

"Yes –" Sarah followed her stare and saw Herr Peters sitting at the far left of the front row. "Isabel must have given him a ticket."

"I think it's extraordinarily nice of her," Margery Dessleton said approvingly.

Sarah was so interested in looking across at Herr Peters that she almost missed her sister's arrival on the platform. He clapped enthusiastically. Isabel was looking highly attractive in a pale green afternoon frock. She was nervous, of course, and showed it by the stiffness of her bow. But she got on with the show right away and, it went without saying, everything was all right. She was in particularly good form. She began with the B Minor Ballade of Liszt (rarely played and very difficult), then Chopin, Balakirev, Debussy, Balfour Gardiner – the afternoon hurried by, the applause grew warmer every time, and every time Sarah was conscious of a remarkable thing. As she bowed Isabel's glance went towards the far

269

left of the front row, where Herr Peters sat applauding as feverishly as if he belonged to a claque.

Then all was over – not quite, there was an encore – and after the encore a bouquet was presented, which came of course from the management. So ended an entirely successful occasion. As the hall emptied Sarah and Mrs. Dessleton pushed towards the corner where Isabel, flushed and excited but convinced that she had been terrible, was the centre of a small group who offered thanks and congratulations. Among them was Mr. Durrell, bobbing up and down, his queer voice rasping out, "Wonderful! Wonderful! My dear, I was proud of you. I'm delighted, delighted!" Margery Dessleton wore her brightest hostess smile – for this was the world with which she felt she had affinity – and she kissed Isabel's cheek proudly.

"My dear, all I can say is *thank* you *very* much, you were perfectly marvellous. It was an enchanting afternoon – and I particularly loved the Balakirev –"

Mr. Durrell was introduced to her, and spoke to Sarah, and Isabel thanked two or three other people; and Sarah heard Margery saying "Hullo, I'm so glad to see you again" to Herr Peters, who had also stayed behind. Mr. Durrell seemed genuinely pleased. Sarah had met him two or three times in the last few months, for she had sometimes called for Isabel at his studio. He said, "Well, I think she's on the way now. A little more work, and then we'll let her loose in the jungle." Then he went off, and nothing remained but for Isabel to put on her coat and hat. It was always a little sad when something was over, whether it was a piano recital or a prize fight. They had arranged to go and have tea somewhere. Sarah had assumed that she and Isabel would be alone, but Margery Dessleton was still there and so was Herr Peters.

"You don't mind if he comes with us?" Isabel murmured.

"Heavens, no," said Sarah. She noticed that her sister still seemed excited. The incredible thought occurred to her that perhaps this was not entirely due to the recital. The scene at the Dessletons' house two Sundays ago came back to her in sharp focus. They certainly had been getting on well together. And she remembered, too – a thing that had meant nothing at the time – that when she had said good-bye to Isabel her

270

sister was still talking to Herr Peters, or he to her, about Bach or Brahms or something, so that she felt like a bull in a china shop when she interrupted. And, now she came to think of it, Isabel had been rather odd last week-end at Watham Heath. She came out as usual and practised on her piano, but she went back to town much earlier than usual, and she had behaved all the time as if she were lost in a dream – which of course Sarah had put down to preoccupation with the coming recital. It was all rather odd and she was slightly aggrieved at evidently not being so much in Isabel's confidence as she had imagined; not that it mattered, but it was one of those things it was annoying to be disillusioned about. She smiled at Herr Peters. " Are you going to join us, then? "

" That would be a fery great pleasure," he answered, with a bow. His attitude seemed to be that he had been waiting for nothing else but for her to notice him. Sarah found him, as she had before, extremely attractive. He had on a rather impressive brown overcoat and in one hand he held the brim of a trilby hat made of some kind of velour. He certainly might have been a musician. The general effect was at any rate continental and both she and Margery, wives of English accountants, were charmed by him. As for Isabel, there was no doubt about it, she could hardly keep her eyes off him. What on earth had been going on in these last ten days?

While her sister was away getting her things, Sarah asked him where he was staying. He named a hotel in Bloomsbury. At least, then, he had not moved to Ladbroke Grove.

" It is simple, but I am happy there," he said, in a way which suggested that normally he was used to something better than Bloomsbury. When Isabel returned, still all smiles and excitement, he went forward to meet her. " How is it possible? " he asked reverently. " How can you look so fresh when you should be exhausted? "

" Rudi, don't be such a fool," said Isabel.

Sarah and Margery Dessleton watched this exchange breathlessly and then glanced at each other. The easy use of the Christian name had been like a bomb exploding.

" Where are we going to go? " Sarah asked, for the outing was clearly out of her hands. " Stewarts? The Cri? "

"The Regent Par-lass," said Herr Peters, with his devastating smile. "I like it there fery much. You will do me the honour to be my guests?"

They moved out into Bond Street, where the quartette broke up, Isabel and Herr Peters went ahead, Sarah and Mrs. Dessleton behind. Thus they reached Piccadilly, with the pair behind observing that the pair in front never stopped talking.

"Did you know — ?" began Margery Dessleton.

"Not an idea!" What made it all the more astonishing was that so far as she knew Isabel had not looked at another man since George Nunn's death. But she was behaving for all the world like a girl in love. And when they reached the Regent Palace – in whose slightly cosmopolitan atmosphere Herr Peters seemed very much at home – and were settled round one of the little basket tables in the Palm Court, the impression grew stronger still. Isabel had no eyes and no ears for anyone but Herr Peters, who for his part blossomed under and returned the attention – although he did not neglect the other two ladies. He set out to be entertaining and succeeded especially because he spoke about matters of normal interest, as if they were men. He talked about Berlin, and Sarah wondered where she had heard that all the Germans were full of self-pity. But according to Herr Peters, "Things have been uncomfortable for us – it is quite natural, what else could one expect? But, you know, the strange thing is this, when you read about mutinies and revolutions and so on, life goes on just the same! One knows nothing about these events! You heard perhaps of the Kapp Putsch last year – no, no, let me think – the year before last?" Perhaps they had – it was unlikely – but they had forgotten. "Well, then," continued Herr Peters, "this was a big revolution, you understand, some lunatic of the old régime tries to destroy the new democratic republic – he brings in soldiers, there is firing in the streets, the President flies – we have a poor, harmless old President – then there's a strike and so on. And what happens to me, with my office and my flat in the centre of Berlin, during all these historic events? Why, I go from my flat to my office at the beginning of the day, to lunch in the middle of the day, and back from my office to my flat at the end of the day. Precisely

272

as usual! If you are not a President you are unaware that history is being made." And so on, with the little orchestra in the background playing "Rose in the Bud" and "Until" and "Absent", while they had mixed-Indian-and-China tea, and buttered toast and éclairs.

The first chance Sarah had of talking to Isabel alone was in the ladies' room. They had left Margery Dessleton, who was delighted to be left, with Herr Peters.

"Well, what do you think of him?" Isabel said at once. "Isn't he perfectly wonderful?"

"He's a dear, yes, and awfully good company, but – I'm flabbergasted, Isabel – how is it that – I mean, what's going on? You haven't mentioned him! I know we left you at the Dessletons' – "

"We walked back together."

"Walked? From *Hampstead*?"

"There seemed to be so much to say. Then he rang up the next day, you see – naturally I was surprised, but – well, we met again. You'll never guess where we went. The circus! Apparently Germans adore circuses. Another night we went to the Alhambra. It's most extraordinary, I feel as if I've known him for years! I've never imagined there could be anyone else after George – it's all very queer, I suppose – "

"My dear!" Sarah exclaimed. "Do you mean – this is really serious? You say 'anyone else after George' – do you mean – but I can't believe it!"

"Nor can I."

"But I can't understand why you haven't said anything – " For the moment what seemed to have been the deception involved was occupying her. It was not, of course, that Isabel was bound to supply her with a bulletin about her private life, but they had been to the sales together last Tuesday – and bought the frock for the recital – and there had been the week-end, and yet not a word had come out.

"I didn't know what to say, you see. I wasn't sure. It's all been so sudden – so – unexpected!"

There was a pause, for a woman in a fur coat came in to apply another coating of paint and powder to a fat, greedy face; her fingers, wrists and throat sparkled with diamonds.

273

What was the use, however, if you looked like that and breathed so heavily? The sisters pretended to look at their own faces, what was visible of them beneath the wide-brimmed hats which came down almost on top of their eyebrows. They had not bothered about the grim-faced employee in black who sat in the corner and obviously no longer cared what she heard; the fat lady's powdering was a long process, however, and Sarah couldn't wait. She went on in a whisper:

"Then – are you sure now?"

"I suppose so," Isabel nodded. "In fact, I suppose I've known for days. You know what it's like, the thrill when he's with you and then just living to see him again – "

The fat lady left, looking nauseated, and made a great fuss about putting twopence in the saucer. Sarah was conscious of a faintly uncomfortable feeling resulting from Isabel's last words. Did she know what it was like? She might pretend it was so, but the fact was –

She said in a bewildered tone, "You're not thinking of marrying him?"

"Of course."

"Isabel! How extraordinary! He's asked you?"

"Put it this way, we've talked around it – he doesn't have to ask so much as I have to answer. That's what I mean," she went on in a soft, enthusiastic voice. "We have this perfect sort of understanding – I daren't let it go, Sarah. I've let too many things go in my life. So – I think – I shall go with him when he goes – "

"Oh, my God!" Sarah interrupted, and in that moment – afterwards she was ashamed of it – she thought immediately that this would mean losing the piano and the Brook Place furniture. "When does he go?"

"About a fortnight from now, not more. It would mean a special licence, of course. He has to go up to Manchester for a couple of days – "

"Oh, my God," Sarah said. "You don't know anything about him!"

"I know a great deal," Isabel smiled. "After all, you don't really know anything about anybody – but as to the unimportant facts, his parents are in Hamburg, he was at Berlin

274

University, he's thirty-three, he's been with the same firm for ten years, barring the war, he was here visiting the same people as now just before the war, he earns – it's the same as about nine hundred a year –" All this came out with an obstinate, sublime certainty, as if from a great height. Sarah was terribly worried. It was up to Isabel to do what she liked, but she didn't want her to fall over a cliff if it could be avoided – this seemed to be the situation and she looked round desperately for rope.

"Couldn't you at least just go there and see first –"

"Of course not. If I go, I go as his wife."

"But, Isabel, you'd lose your pension," Sarah exclaimed.

"Naturally, but I shouldn't need one, should I?"

"All the same, it's so fantastic – they have all those troubles there, whatever he says –" She wanted to ask, but felt from Isabel's expression that it would be unwise, "Does he know you have some money?" Instead she ended weakly, "And after all a German –"

Isabel brushed this aside impatiently.

"The Kaiser wasn't his fault. He's a European."

"But living so far away – and amongst foreigners, anyway –"

"Good heavens, it takes less than a day to get to Berlin from here. Who do I live amongst here, anyway? Apart from you, Sarah – you must remember that you're in a different position, you have a husband, a house, two children – but what roots have I?"

"Music," Sarah said brilliantly. "Are you throwing that all away? You had such a success this afternoon and Mr. Durrell told me himself that in a few months –"

"I'm not throwing that away at all! Good heavens! I should think Berlin is a far more musical city than London – and don't forget I shall have an advantage as a foreigner, just as anyone with a queer name has an advantage here. Oh, no, my dear, if that's worrying you – no, Rudi is most enthusiastic that I should keep it up. After all, music is the one really international language."

"But you haven't spoken about it to Mr. Durrell at all," Sarah insisted.

"Of course not yet. But I know just what he'll say. He's always talking about the Germans – he has a great hate of the Leipzig *Conservatoire*. Listen, my dear," she said, taking Sarah's arm. "Not another word about it. Let me bring him over for the week-end. You and Harry can inspect him at leisure, and I know he'd love to come."

"Yes, of course," Sarah said, and smiled suddenly. "I was just thinking – whatever will Aunt Ada say when she hears?"

They each looked in their bag for a sixpence to put in the saucer, and then they returned to the Palm Court. Sarah was in a state of confusion. It was all too staggering and she really did not know what to think. One automatically regarded a marriage as wonderful and exciting, and she had to admit he was enormously attractive. He sprang up as they approached.

"Sorry we've been long," Isabel said.

"Has it been long?" cried Herr Peters, standing first behind one chair and then behind the other. "I have not noticed it! We have been having such an interesting conversation, have we not?" he bowed to Margery Dessleton, and took his own seat again. But the party broke up almost at once.

"I really have to go home now," Mrs. Dessleton said regretfully.

Sarah walked with her across Piccadilly Circus. They had left the happy couple still in the vestibule of the Regent Palace, and it was only possible to arrange to telephone Isabel in the morning.

"What a divine man!" Mrs. Dessleton said. "Compliments pour out of him like steam from a kettle, and he seems to be terribly intelligent. Is there something between those two?"

"Definitely something," Sarah agreed.

"Now that's what I call romantic, my dear!" Mrs. Dessleton said. "Perfectly marvellous."

Sarah went home, feeling better. What the Dessletons thought was for the moment one of her more important standards. She reached home before Harry, and when she broke the news to him later on, his first reaction was similar to her own.

"She must be mad," he said, and then, "My God, what happens about the piano and the other stuff?"

276

"Yes, I know," Sarah nodded. "But you have to admit it's romantic, darling."

CHAPTER THIRTY-THREE

T here had been a wedding luncheon with Sarah and Harry at the Troc on Friday, there had even been a honeymoon, two days at Brighton, where they had stayed at the Old Ship. Then the Harwich-Hook night crossing, and now it was late Monday afternoon and the long day's train journey across the north German plain was over. Herr Rudiger Peters and his wife had arrived in Berlin.

She was mad, of course, and dimly, contentedly aware of it. But it was also true that she had never been happier in her life. When they got out at the station in Berlin she had also never felt so excited, and she realized that, although Rudi was trying to appear calm, he felt much the same. She watched proudly as he spoke to their porter in a most peremptory way. The man treated him with reverence, which seemed to Isabel to be right and proper. It was reasonable that Germans themselves should recognize how wonderful he was.

"Well, we are here." He took her arm. "Think of Liverpool Street – isn't it wonderfully clean here?"

She glanced round, noticing nothing except the little chauffeur's caps of the porters, and nodded. She didn't think it did look especially clean, but she enjoyed Rudi thinking it did. The station was quite crowded and she looked vaguely at the faces, wishing she knew what everyone was saying.

"How far are we from the flat?"

"Oh, not far!" He had an intriguing, super-refined way of pronouncing "oh" which made it more like "eoh". "But first we will have a drink."

"Right away?" She was impatient to get to the flat.

"Yes, immediately! *Sofort!* We must celebrate our arrival without any delay!"

"Must we? All right."

They went into a restaurant-buffet where Rudi pushed a

waiter aside in order to pull out a chair for her. In spite of his claim to dislike the clicking heels tradition, his heels always seemed to be poised on the brink. As it was he managed to retain all the old romance and gallantry and yet to avoid the starchiness. And he looked at her with such candid pleasure! It seemed unbelievable that this wonderful thing should have happened to her out of the blue. It was astonishing that she should have been so favoured.

Beer came for him, vermouth for her.

"*Prost.*"

"*Prost.*"

"Our first Berlin drink together. I raise my glass to a happy life in my city."

"You'll make me cry if you're so serious about it."

"Oh," Rudi laughed, "that will be so nice, a woman should weep occasionally."

"I've wept too much in my life."

"So no more weeping, I do not mind. Oh, you look so beautiful, Isa, I'm quite worried about you meeting my friends. I am a jealous man, you know!"

He was anything he chose to say he was, as far as she was concerned. "How absurd and how wonderful life is," thought Isabel, and she looked round at the people at the other tables, wondering if they knew what she knew, or whether it was a rare secret. She turned back to find him looking at her.

He said, "I begin to blame myself, you know – I begin to understand – I should not have done this thing to you. You were among your own people, happy, successful – "

"I was nothing of the sort."

"Oh, yes." He leaned across the table and asked, "What do you feel, then, now you are here?"

"Young," she said immediately. "Younger than I am. Young and balmy. As if somehow I were just grown up and the world before me at last. A wonderful feeling, Rudi, dear."

"Balmy?"

"*Verstehst du nicht?* Well, it means sort of idiotic, up in the clouds."

"That's excellent. I am young and balmy, too. Less young, more balmy, no?" And he gave her his splendid smile. He
278

took her hand and pressed it. "Lulu also?" A German wife wore her wedding ring on the fourth finger of the right hand and he had whimsically declared, during their stay at the Old Ship hotel, Brighton, that he would call her fourth finger Lulu. It showed the power of love that she had found this amusing.

"Lulu also," Isabel said, faint with happiness. But the next moment he had released Lulu and she watched his face cloud over. The effect was aided by the dramatic way he put an elbow on the table and then leant his chin on his hand. He stared past her with a kind of hopeless gloom. At first she thought he was pantomiming and she smiled at him. His hand was bunching up the flesh of his cheeks and his chin, giving a comical, Punch-like look. The other hand drummed on the table. Finally he spoke, as if with reluctance.

"I have something to say to you, Isa."

"Something terrible?"

"I am afraid, yes, something terrible. You know nothing about me," he said.

Isabel laughed.

"You don't know much about me," she replied at once. "That's what's so nice about us. We're full of secrets and we've got years to find them out. Or ought one to find them out, Rudi, dear?" She was being gay and conversational. "I don't want to know anything about you!" she went on. "Take each other as we are. That was the agreement."

"But that is it," he sighed heavily. "As we are! As I am! You will despise me when you know. I have deceived you."

"How?" she asked, refusing to admit uneasiness; but she realized that he was not joking.

"I am not as well off as you think."

"Oh!" She almost laughed with relief. "Is that all?"

"Is it not enough?"

"You have your job, haven't you? I never thought of you as being well off. That doesn't matter."

"Listen to the angel!" he exclaimed, seizing her hands. The suddenness of his movement drew attention to them. There were not many people in the buffet, but in accordance with custom everyone was grouped together in one corner. Rudi seemed quite indifferent as to whether anyone understood

279

English and heard about his private affairs. He continued excitedly, "Yes, of course, I have the job, but it is in reality quite small, it is unimportant, I am, you must understand, an unimportant man! Yes, I have the job – and it is better to have one than not to have one – but it is something else, Isa – the flat – I have led you to expect – " He paused, suddenly unable to go on with his exuberant confession and self-abasement. He looked guiltily downwards.

"You mean there isn't a flat?" she said incredulously.

"Oh, yes, yes, there is a flat." His voice had sunk to a whisper. "But it is not mine, Isa. I have lied to you, I have deceived – "

"How do you mean, not yours?"

"Well, it is a flat belonging to a lady and her daughter and I have a room there. Her name is Frau Klockmann and you need not worry, she speaks very good English. I am sure we can have two rooms. And there is a living-room which we can use, a very fine, nice room, but – " He made a gesture of helplessness. "I am sorry, Isa."

Isabel was silent. It was too much to bear.

"You are angry? But of course. Lulu also?" But she could not be touched by any whimsical approach now. He said hurriedly, "Well, we don't have to go there, but it is cheap – and not uncomfortable, you know – " He broke off and sighed. "I have deceived you in thinking – you see, perhaps you should go back to England."

"Don't be absurd!" she said, in a low, sharp voice. But she did not know if it were so absurd. His disclosure seemed to be the embodiment of everything that Sarah, Harry and the stiffly formal note she had had from Aunt Ada had warned her against – she felt as if a ton weight were pressing her down. She knew, of course, that there was no question at all of not staying, whatever happened – although probably the wise thing was to take him at his word and catch the next train back to the Hook. But it was clearly impossible to go back, to acknowledge to Sarah, Harry and Aunt Ada – and Mr. Durrell, who had lost his temper with her when he heard about it – that she had been swindled like any other fool of a woman whose head was turned.

280

She was too paralysed even to free her hands from his, and they went on sitting there in a slightly unnatural pose, Rudi leaning forward, an anxious, hang-dog expression on his handsome face. She was tense and motionless, but the voices of three middle-aged Germans at the next table intruded on her thoughts. They were having a heated political discussion in which the name Rathenau kept being repeated. This and an ache which began in the small of her back had the effect of relaxing her. She was faced with the knowledge of having been swindled; it was no less than that. She was faced with it, and deep down she was aware of an astonishing thing, which was that, really, she didn't care.

" But why didn't you tell me before? " she demanded at last, and shifted her position to ease the ache.

" Would you be here if I had? " he said pathetically.

She was startled by such a direct answer.

" I don't know. I suppose not."

" Well, then? " he said, shrugging his shoulders.

" But you could at least have said something on the train," she pointed out. Not that where or when he had not said it mattered. Her remark seemed farcically unimportant. But somehow she could not rise to the moment with a proper sort of emotion. She felt so calm that she wondered herself if her calmness were hysterical. But what else was there to say? She tried hard to think of something, and failed.

" Yes, you are right, you are right," he said earnestly. " But I have put it off, put off the truth for as long as possible, because I have seen you looking so happy – I ask you to believe me I am sorry, but I love you, Isa. I love you."

" And is that the truth? "

" Why should you believe me? " he admitted sadly. " I have deceived you. I offer you a room, not a home. I have no money except what is in my pockets. But I love you, Isa. I swear by my honour that I love you." And he repeated it in his own language in a fervent whisper. " *Ich schwöre bei meiner Ehre dass ich dich liebe.*"

Indeed, why should she believe him? But she wished passionately that it was the truth, and therefore she decided that it was. After all, to be reasonable, he had not claimed such a great deal – it was not so much that he had misled her, as that he had allowed her to mislead herself.

"I can let you have some money, if you're hard up," she said. He had had to spend such a lot in the past few days – although, perhaps, not so much as she had. She wondered what was a suitable sum to suggest. Fifty pounds, perhaps? It was probably quite a lot with the mark at its present rate. Ah, whatever would Sarah say if she knew? And as for Harry – Isabel felt a sensation of guilty pleasure. She would really have given anything for Harry to have heard this conversation. She added almost lightly, "We don't have to starve immediately, anyhow."

Rudi seemed to be very moved. He let go of her hands and slumped back in his chair, as if unable to look at her.

"Ach, du wunderbares –" he began softly, but then sat up straight and exclaimed, "No, Isa! I am very grateful. But never – I take nothing from you." He became quite angry all at once, and rapped the table sharply. "Gott's Willen, I am a man – I can get money, I have my job. In Germany a wife keeps what she brings. That is the unbreakable rule. I take nothing. So, Isa, it is better perhaps that you –" He stopped short, looking, Isabel thought, like a handsome, desperate hero. She was not convinced that he meant what he said, but she was proud of him for saying it. She looked up. The waiter, mistaking the raps on the table for a summons, stood by their table.

Rudi glared at him and demanded to know what was owed. "Bitte zahlen!"

The waiter, a handsome fellow with a gold tooth and slicked-back fair hair, bowed. The cost of the drinks was three hundred and fifty marks. Rudi paid him with an air of disdain, and then said to Isabel with grim humour, "Now he has more than I."

She had an idea that he was dramatizing his situation more than was quite necessary.

"Are we moving? Rudi, there's something I must do at once. I must send a postcard to Sarah."

"Yes, of course," he said bitterly. "You have things to tell her. Very well."

They bought one at a kiosk outside the buffet, a view of the

Kaiser William Memorial Church. Isabel wrote on it at once:
" Arrived safely. Tired, very happy. Both send love. A kiss for
David and Betty. Love, Isabel."

" Put your name on it, too."

" My name? "

She handed him the card. He read what she had written and
stared at her.

" What's the matter? "

" Isa – this means we are still together? "

She nodded, and saw him mistily as he bent down to scrawl
his name. There was a lump in her throat. She was tired and
very happy. It was ridiculous, but it was so.

His mood was transformed.

" Isa, dolling," he whispered exultantly, " I promise you it
will be all right – I promise you we shall have our flat – it will
not be long – "

He took her hand and kissed it reverently.

" Does the – your landlady know I'm coming? " Isabel asked.

" No, that does not matter. Come on. We will get our bags."
Now his arm was round her, they were two lovers walking
along without a care. The only course open, Isabel saw, was to
let things happen as they happened.

Five minutes later they were getting into a taxi, which she
thought very smart with its black and white stripe. They had
two suitcases, and had left her trunk, which was half full of
music, at the station. She had her first experience of the cosy,
cigar smell of the Berlin air. It was very wintry and cold, but
as they drove off she noticed that the sky seemed to be an
exciting orange colour. This was the reflection of all the
lights from *Kurfürstendamm*, the pleasure centre of the city
which they crossed almost immediately. She had a glimpse of
crowded cafés and electric signs. Then everything was darker
and there were streets of heavy solid buildings. But the journey
was short, as he had said.

They went up two steps and Rudi pressed a bell beside
one of a list of names: Klockmann. Almost at once the door
made a noise and swung open an inch, as if by its own
agency.

" However did that happen? "

"Someone pressed a button, dolling. Please enter or the light will go out."

She entered. Inside was a bleak passage with stairs going up. It smelt musty. She was depressed and a little frightened. The heady, careless feeling she had had was gone.

"It's warmer here, anyway," she tried to say lightly. A few flakes of snow had been falling in the street.

"It is the third floor. You see it is all clean?" As soon as she put her foot on the stairs he suddenly put down the bags and flung his arms round her. "I love you, Isa," he whispered. "You are everything to me."

She clung to him, comforted, and they exchanged several kisses before going on. It seemed a very long way up the stairs. On the third floor they came to the name Klockmann again, on a card pinned to one of the two facing doors.

"Well, we are here," said Rudi.

He had a key this time, which was at least a proprietary sign and was almost a relief to her. But in the second before he opened the door she heard a woman's voice inside, talking to someone else. Nothing could have sounded more strange and foreign.

CHAPTER THIRTY-FOUR

They entered a narrow hallway, from which an inner door suddenly opened. A young woman's inquisitive face appeared, expressed amazement, retreated to explode in the interior a mass of German which caused further exclamations from someone else. Rudi whispered, "The daughter!" Isabel could distinguish nothing from the sounds inside but the words "Herr Peters". Rudi helped her off with her coat and engaged in a series of winks and gestures. He seemed all at once to be in high good humour. There was an elaborate hat rack and umbrella stand, part of which was a mirror. Rudi inspected himself with some satisfaction, combed his hair and smoothed down his lapels. All this time conversation went on inside at fever pitch. When Rudi had finished

284

with the mirror, he turned to her with his beaming smile and then pushed the door further open, upon which he collided with a plump middle-aged woman wearing a kimono.

"*Ah! G'nae Frau!*" he cried. "*Meine liebe g'nae Frau!*"

"*Glauben Sie nur nicht dass Sie hier herein kommen kön-nen, mein Herr!*"

"*Wass denn?*"

"*Geben Sie mid den Schlüssel, und dann bitte 'raus!*"

"*Aber Frau Klockmann! Liebe Frau Klockmann!*"

Isabel did not have to understand much of this to realize that her husband was not being given a hearty welcome. The woman stood with her arms folded, barring the way in. Rudi had been forced to step back a pace.

"*Den Schlüssel, Herr Peters!*"

"Whatever's the matter?" Isabel broke in anxiously, and the woman noticed her for the first time. She uttered a gasp.

"*Um Gottes Willen, wer ist das?*"

Rudi smiled, shaking his head.

"*G'nae Frau, darf ich Ihnen meine Frau vorstellen?* But we must speak in English. You speak very good English. May I introduce my wife? Isabel, this is Frau Klockmann, an old, old friend."

"*Ihre Frau!*" exclaimed Frau Klockmann, thunderstruck, staring at Isabel.

"In English, if you please," Rudi smiled, with a little bow.

"*Eine Engländerin!*"

"Yes, that is why we must speak in English."

"*Ach, mein Gott!*" said Frau Klockmann. She brushed past him and came to Isabel. She looked at her in astonishment and not without hostility. She had a wide, upturned little nose, heavily powdered. "It is true?" she said slowly. "You are his vife?"

"Yes," Isabel nodded, trying to look agreeable.

"*Mein Gott!*" said Frau Klockmann. "Is it true?" She turned round stormily, for Rudi had taken the opportunity to go inside. She shrieked, "*Herr Peters, ich verbiete Ihnen —!*" She took two paces after him, like someone wading through water, and suddenly gave way. She gathered the kimono round her rather large bosom and sighed theatrically. It seemed to

285

Isabel as though she were not really displeased at her failure to keep Rudi out. She nodded and gestured to the door. "Please to come."

Isabel then found herself in a sitting-room, where Rudi, acting now as a host, presented her to the owner of the inquisitive face, Fräulein Klockmann, the older woman's daughter. The Fräulein had quite an odd appearance, for though she had clearly been adult for some time she was dressed like a child, hair braided, a sloppy, shapeless frock, and bare feet, on which were scratches and minor abrasions. Moreover she went pink and attempted a very slight curtsy as she shook hands with Isabel.

"Good day, how are you?" she said in a harsh voice.

"*Wunderbar!*" cried Rudi proudly, clapping her on the back as if she were a man. "Isa, my dolling, I am very happy. You will have a great friendship. Anni is a wonderful person. She is my sister, my comrade, there exists between us that kind of relationship, the understanding, which gives life purpose! You will experience this, too, dolling." He put his arm round Isabel and hugged her. Fräulein Klockmann examined her hand, as if to make sure that it had not been contaminated in any way. Frau Klockmann came slowly across from the doorway. She was now gazing at Isabel thoughtfully. The light in the room was not good and she wanted to have a close look. Her eyes, which seemed rather small and sharp, because of the puffiness of her face, went up, down. Finally, she spoke in a friendly, but disconcerting way.

"You are more than thirty years?"

"No, I'm not," said Isabel. "As it happens I'm twenty-eight."

Frau Klockmann was not convinced.

"I sink so," she said with a gloomy smile. "Well, I am very sorry you cannot stay here. Man and vife here with my daughter is impossible. I do not like it."

Isabel, who wanted nothing more than to get away from this absurd and terrible place, felt nothing but relief, but Rudi was amazed and indignant.

"*Wiedenn? Was sagen Sie —?*"

"And z' room is also inhabited," Frau Klockmann added,

producing a trump card. She beamed at him, first with a kind of gentle malice and then with sheer amusement, as Rudi released Isabel, tore across the room and out through another door which led to the interior of the flat. Frau Klockmann called after him in German. He shouted back. Argument continued, with Fräulein Klockmann now and then putting in a thrust. Isabel stood there trembling. She couldn't understand a word that was going on. All she could do was to look round this sitting-room and realize that it was indeed very much as Rudi had described it in London except that there was no piano. The table, the red plush-covered chairs, the small flowered carpet underneath, the sofa by the wall that was never sat on, the bookcase with two or three large volumes that were never read – all that was true, and she clung desperately to anything true that he had said to her. She stood there helplessly, as if stuck to the floor where he had left her, trying to forget his grotesque claim to be the sole owner of this flat, while the German language, an unparalleled weapon of anger, filled the air with guttural sounds and sentences that never ended. The argument did end, however. It came to a shattering silence as Rudi grimly reappeared, his arms clasping a mass of shirts, underclothes, a jacket and trousers, on top of which perched a pair of shoes. He kicked along stray articles which had fallen off, some collars and socks. He came a yard into the room and, without glancing at anybody, raised his arms to let everything collapse on the floor.

" *Um Gottes Willen!* " cried Fräulein Klockmann, breaking the silence.

Frau Klockmann, as if coming out of a coma, uttered a long shriek and rushed at him, fists flying. Rudi seized her arms, smiling, and the two wrestled, one with the greatest calm, the other panting hysterically.

" *Mutti!* " cried Fräulein Klockmann, who showed no willingness to enter the fight. " *Das nutzt nichts!* "

Isabel tried to ask her what was the matter and, getting no answer, called to Rudi. He grinned at her over Frau Klockmann's heaving shoulder.

" Do not worry, dolling, it is not serious. Everything is all right, I have cleared our room."

" But we can't stay here! "

" We can and we shall, dolling—ach! " His voice broke suddenly into a scream, for Frau Klockmann had tried to bite his wrist. He was furious. He shouted and spat at her. A torrent of words came out and he forced her back into the room. Frau Klockmann gave up. She let go and hurried weeping behind her daughter, whom she treated as a defence barrier. Rudi, however, took out a handkerchief, dusted his face and hands, and pulled down his sleeves.

" Perhaps you'll explain what this is all about? " Isabel said. She intended to sound cool, but her voice shook.

" Later, dolling. It is a matter of principle, really. Nothing more."

He had clearly won the day, for Frau Klockmann was now sitting at the table, her head in her hands. Rudi whistled gaily to himself, then kissed Isabel lightly on the cheek and went out to bring in the bags.

" It's the door on the left," he said over his shoulder. " Go and see it."

Isabel glanced helplessly at the two German women, who took no notice of her, and then did as he told her, treading carefully over all the clothes on the floor. A short passage led off the sitting-room. She went through the door on the left. It was a small room, almost entirely occupied by the bed, which was very high off the ground. She had to squeeze against the dressing-table to get round. The wardrobe door and every drawer was open. A few stray articles lay scattered about, but a clearance had been made. A lace curtain covered the window, which was scarcely more than eighteen inches square and too high to look out of unless one stood on the bed. It meant that even by daylight the room would be as dark as it was small. It might have been a cell. This thought occurred to her, but she was too tired to care, and thankful to sit on, or rather lean against, the bed. She must improve her German as quickly as possible, that was the most definite thing. Nothing in the world was ever more exhausting than to listen to quarrels and complications of which one hardly understood a word.

Rudi brought in their cases almost at once.

"Isn't it comfortable?" he said. "Note it is all clean. Not luxurious, but very practical. I think it best if we unpack at at once. Ah, what a swindle! Come, please, I must have a kiss."

"What swindle? What was it about? It's horrible for me, just standing there – and you were so rough with her – "

"The swindle? Simply this. The old criminal has let this room to some scoundrel up from München when I have already paid for it for still another month! You see? When the cat is away, the mice will play. Not with me. Let her explain it to this gentleman when he returns. You cannot let a room twice at the same time."

"Well, I should think not!" she said indignantly. She was delighted that he had such a good reason.

He was already unpacking his own suitcase and flinging some of his belongings into an empty drawer.

"You do the same, Isa. It is good to take possession."

"But we'll move from here, won't we?"

"Yes, of course, but not at once, for it is crazy when I have paid for this room – and you can use the living-room, you see – "

"And there's no piano, Rudi," she said, reluctant to bring up another betrayal. But if anything it was the worst, for he had allowed her to agree to a deferred sale of her piano and the furniture she owned to Sarah and Harry.

"Ach, poor Isa!" He turned from the suitcase and put his arms round her. "This time I am not to blame. There was a piano when I left and they have sold it! They needed money, you see. That is how it is with us unfortunate Germans. But I promise you there will be a piano, there will be everything you want – "

"I don't know what Sarah will feel if I write and say I want it, after all."

"Ah, that is so much trouble, we will get one, I promise – "

"We can't stay here, though," she insisted. "With quarrel-ling going on like that, it's – it's impossible – "

He was not at all concerned.

"You'll see, we shall all be good friends in two minutes. I will go and have a talk to them."

Isabel was sceptical, but he kissed her and left the room. She set about tidying the drawer he had begun to fill – a drawer instead of a flat, that was apparently the situation. She thought, "This is a nice mess – typical of me, I suppose." She heard Rudi's voice outside, and then the two Klockmanns. Ten minutes went by; and then suddenly she heard laughter. The stray voices became gayer. Isabel went on unpacking, puzzled but relieved.

Finally, there was a knock at the door and Frau Klockmann's face looked round, wreathed in a smile.

She came in with an armful of thick white towels, which she dumped on the bed with a faint gasp. Then she looked at Isabel with good-humoured curiosity.

"You like to vash? Z' water is hot."

"Oh, thank you very much! *Danke schön!*"

"*Bitte!*" Frau Klockmann, with another smile, left.

Isabel washed happily. The bathroom was next door and reasonably equipped. The lavatory paper in particular was of excellent quality, and it occurred to her that though it was not the sort of thing one could ever talk about, this item was one of the most reassuring of all things. She reflected that it would certainly have been less amusing to be in the same circumstances in France. Feeling a good deal better and more courageous she returned to the sitting-room.

A party was going on, or seemed to be, for the atmosphere was festive. All three were seated at the table, all three were talking at once. There was a plate of sandwiches, beer in front of Rudi. He leapt up when he saw her and bore her across with his arm round her. The clothes of the new lodger had been removed, there was no sign of the battle that had taken place. The two ladies smiled a welcome to her and Isabel found herself sitting at the table. Conversation then continued at speed in German. She gathered that Rudi was describing his stay in London, but it was too fast to follow. Whatever it was he was not being over-complimentary. Every so often Frau Klockmann shook with laughter and her daughter smiled primly. Next to no attention was paid to the bride and it was all so far from the romantic first Berlin evening she had pictured that she almost forgot that she was one. Now and then Rudi winked at her and pressed against her or touched her hand, as if this was quite enough to keep her going. But he himself seemed different now that he was in the company of Germans. She saw that the reason for this was simply that he was no longer a foreigner. He was at home and very much so. It was the way he sat on his chair, the way he held his glass, the way they talked to him, and because of the fact of belonging he was somehow diminished, although not less attractive. But, however attractive he was, she realized more and more that she had made the mistake of her life. She wondered what was his relationship with Fräulein Klockmann. "I was mad, absolutely mad," she thought. And the flood of too-quick German continued.

After they had sat there for what seemed hours, Frau Klockmann disappeared. Isabel gathered that she had gone to the kitchen to prepare some supper.

"Well, how is everything?" Rudi asked gaily, tilting back on his chair. He blew out smoke from one of Fräulein Klockmann's cigarettes. The Fräulein herself was getting a tablecloth.

"Oh, fine," said Isabel.

"I have told them about your concert. They are so angry at having sold the piano. It stood against the wall behind you. Isa, is Lulu fine, too?"

"Oh, yes, Lulu is fine, too."

Supper was a plate of thin little sausages, *Wiener Würstchen*, and some *Sauerkraut*. There was more beer for Rudi, and coffee for the ladies. It was no banquet. Isabel could not help being surprised at Rudi's excellent appetite when she remembered how critical he had been in London. But there seemed to be general complacency, and there was even an attempt to bring her into the conversation, by trying to teach her how to say *"Würstchen"* correctly. It was so difficult, and the Klockmanns' friendly laughter so uninhibited, that Isabel felt certain she could never learn German properly, in spite of the fact that she had once won a prize in it at Miss Murray's. She was condemned to years of failure to understand or be understood. On the other hand it did not seem to occur to the Klockmanns, any more than to Rudi, that their pronunciation of English was not faultless. It was in the midst of their gaiety over her incompetence that there was the sudden low buzz of a bell from the hallway. Laughter ceased. Frau Klockmann drew her kimono round her tightly and looked deeply concerned; she seemed only able to register extremes.

"*Da kommt er!*" she said fearfully, and this was a sentence Isabel was equal to – the displaced lodger had evidently arrived.

"There is some interesting news for him here," Rudi smiled, nudging her.

Fräulein Klockmann went out to press the street door release and leave the door of the flat open. Then she returned and went to her neutral corner on the other side of the table, while her mother began addressing a number of short, urgent appeals to Rudi and, since he paid no attention, to the ceiling, with her pudgy hands clasped. She reminded Isabel of a distraught mother on the films begging for mercy from the man who was kidnapping her child. She would never have believed that there were people who behaved like that in reality.

Rudi helped himself to more *Sauerkraut*. Then steps could be heard, a grunt, a sigh; the rival lodger was in the hallway, doubtless removing his coat. Frau Klockmann braced herself and nervously called out, "*Sind Sie da, Herr Matthesius?*"

"*Jawohl!*" came a high-spirited answer.

"*Ach, Gott!*" said Frau Klockmann, under her breath.

The door swung open, pushed with more than usual energy, and Herr Matthesius appeared. He was a fair-haired man, perhaps in the late twenties. He wore a tight-fitting brown suit which, like his face, seemed vaguely to have been meant for someone else. He had the narrowest ears Isabel had ever seen, his nose turned up violently, exposing two larger than usual cavities, his cheeks were hollow, his chin small and pointed and also decorated by an honourable fencing scar. In fact it was a face so ugly that it commanded attention. He had, however, the relaxed air of the muscular and the smile which lit up his odd face, after his first faintly comic surprise, was engaging.

He spoke a few rapid words, and inclined his head to them

all in a vague bow. Isabel thought he had said that he didn't expect to come home to a party. Frau Klockmann then rose, with an effort, and went across to him, throwing herself, it appeared, on Herr Matthesius's mercy. She spoke at length, several times mentioning " *die Engländerin* " and glancing reproachfully, as she did so, in Isabel's direction. While she spoke, the three at the table waited to see how the new arrival would take the news. Rudi affected indifference. Fräulein Klockmann looked hopeful, her pale eyes seemed wider and brighter. Isabel, for her part, was visualizing a fight between the two men and as Herr Matthesius looked considerably stronger than Rudi, she felt extremely nervous.

But nothing of the sort happened. As soon as Frau Klockmann had finished, or rather had slowed down, the young man smiled again and replied that as far as he was concerned he did not care if he slept in a bed or on the floor. This was clear to Isabel, for he accompanied his words with gestures. It was as if he were so energetic that he seized every chance to make a movement. Then he stepped in a springy, quick fashion across to Rudi, holding out his hand.

" Matthesius! " he exclaimed.

Rudi stood up.

" Peters! "

They shook hands. Herr Matthesius then nodded to Fräulein Klockmann and turned to Isabel. He clicked his heels and bowed.

" How are you? " he smiled. It sounded charming. He had a soft, sing-song voice.

" Very well, thank you," Isabel said, " but we are terribly sorry that we have inconvenienced you so much – "

" Please, please! " cried Herr Matthesius, throwing up his hands in gay despair. " You speak too quick! I am not able to understand! " He became serious. " I am pleased to meet a lady from England. We have been enemies. We have suffered from the terrible cruel blockade. But now I think England behaves with honour. Between us, no more war! "

He shook her hand solemnly. Isabel could not help being impressed by his warmth and sincerity, although she was slightly put out at the implicit idea that it was England who had turned over a new leaf and required to be forgiven. Herr Matthesius's words, however, were seized on by Rudi enthusiastically.

"No more war! *Nie wieder Krieg!*"

"*Nie wieder Krieg,*" repeated Matthesius, "except perhaps with the French?"

"*La grande Nation!*" Rudi laughed.

"*Na ja, na ja!*" said Matthesius, sitting down with them. "*La grande nation.*" Though Isabel had no strong feelings about the French, one way or another, it made her feel a little uncomfortable to sit there while Germans were ironical at their expense, even if one of the Germans was her husband. The conversation, led by Matthesius, who was evidently stocked with theories and figures, gradually became spirited. The Klockmanns joined in. Occasional wit was supplied by Rudi and Matthesius would roar with laughter. He was ready to be exuberant over nothing, but the next moment he could suddenly become fervently bitter. At first Isabel tried hard to understand, but soon she let the words flow around, dinning in her head like someone scraping on a plate. Certain words were especially unpopular, "*Franzosen*" and "*Ebert*" and "*Juden*" and "*Demokratie*", and these were repeated endlessly. Talk, talk – she had never heard so much. It was almost unendurable. She felt near to tears, but smiled painfully as if she understood everything.

They went on until it was time to go to bed. Then there was a good deal of humour concerned with the making up of Herr Matthesius's bed on the sofa.

The Peters were at last alone in their bedroom. And Rudi at once cured all her distress. Determined not to complain, she was about to complain; he smothered her voice with a long kiss. He held her close and then as her tension died, he whispered, "That was terrible for you, I watched you all the time. You were wonderful. I was so proud of you. Did you feel me loving you the whole evening?"

"Were you?"

"Naturally. Were you?"

"Naturally."

"Isa, *Liebchen*, I swear we shall be by ourselves. A flat of our own. I swear you will be happy. You shall not despise me."

"But I'm sure Frau Klockmann and her daughter despise *me*."

"Oh, no! " He was shocked. "How could that be possible? "

In a few minutes he had half-convinced her that it was not possible. A little later, in bed, she said, "You were wonderful the way you beat them about the room. I don't know how you did it – I could never stand up for myself like that. Poor Herr what's his name, I feel quite guilty about him."

"What nonsense! He is comfortable enough."

"He took it well, I must say."

"Oh, he's a good fellow, I guess. He's a professional patriot. Dozens of bees in his bonnet. Myself, I think you get more done by helping to sell exports. But I am a European, not a German. He belongs to some ludicrous army or other down in Munich. They're all crazy in Bavaria. He thinks everything will be cured if you do away with interest. I ask you! Anyhow, he has to go to Dortmund to-morrow. I'd like to know who pays for these fellows to travel about everywhere."

"I'm a European, too," she said, lazily, feeling comfort steal over her.

"*Ich bin Europäer*," he whispered.

"All right! *Ich bin auch Europäer*."

Half an hour or so later, when she was about to drop off, and thought he had, she heard him say, "Isa, about the piano. You really must have a piano. It wouldn't cost much to get one. We could probably get the Klockmanns' back, but you want a really good one, you have your work, your career – I think you can get a very good one for a few pounds. You see, the mark is falling so much – "

"I'm going to send for some money," she said. The one precaution Sarah and Harry had persuaded her to take was that she should keep her nest-egg in London. Undoubtedly it was good advice.

"For a piano, yes. I don't object to that."

"All right," she agreed, smiling privately into the darkness. Soon Rudi was asleep. She lay awake, thinking, "Just like me, I suppose, to find someone like him." She sighed, and nestled cosily against him.

CHAPTER THIRTY-FIVE

When Sarah received the telegram Isabel had sent from the Zoo station most of the anxiety she had felt left her. If she had reached Berlin and was happy, all must be well. Sarah had always the greatest faith in good news. The implications of the first letter to arrive, which expressed in a reserved way the fact that the living quarters were not quite what had been expected, she did not bother about. Isabel wrote lovingly of Rudi and also sent a long description of what she had seen of Berlin – " long wide streets and solid buildings with decorated balconies and turrets and stone eagles ", " lots of people who look very pale and hungry ", " prices are very high because of the inflation " – so whatever had happened it couldn't be very serious. And the third or fourth letter Isabel sent was bursting over with pleasure. She and Rudi were moving into another flat which was perfectly marvellous and not far from the Tiergarten – " our Hyde Park, quite nice and full of lakes and amazingly ugly statues ". A few weeks later she made a reference to her piano, " a really good Bechstein, and I'm getting down to practice again ". Sarah read out these bits to Harry in great approval.

" So it's a success – heavens, I'm so happy for her. I think it's perfectly wonderful," she sighed, quite enviously. Her own suburban life seemed rather flat compared to living in Berlin. And this remained her attitude. Months later Isabel was writing, " When we went to the opera last night two men, both quite respectable-looking, almost fought to open the taxi door for us – it makes you feel quite guilty that your own head is so far above water; but Rudi is very clever. . ." or " I was hoping to come over for a holiday, I am always wishing that you were in the room with me, but I'm so busy, it won't be possible for the moment – but Rudi says he'll probably have a business trip next year, so perhaps I'll be coming then . . ." or " You can't believe what it's like to go shopping now – yesterday I paid a hundred and fifty thousand marks for a pound of veal, and it's the same for everything – if you go to the theatre your seat costs thousands and thousands of marks, and it seems to get worse all the time – how they all hate the French who are causing it all. To-night we are going to a very rich dinner party – "

Rudi did come on his business trip again, but without Isabel. She didn't want to travel at that time of the year, he explained – and Isabel also explained in her letters; also they were now in a new flat – they had moved from Matthäi-Kirch-strasse to Motzstrasse – and there was so much to do. Rudi was just as he had been on his previous visit, very charming and talkative. He was only staying for ten days, but he managed a week-end with Sarah and Harry, which included a golf club dance, where his continental accent and manner made him quite a lion. Harry found him very interesting. With the inflation over, Germany was settling down to peace and progress, Rudi said. "There are more bankruptcies, but fewer suicides." He told them stories of the inflation, there was the butcher of Hanover who was supposed to sell human bodies, there was the scandalous moral climate due to the east European profiteers and the story of the rendezvous party at which a well-known Berlin banker, out for an evening's illicit love, had been introduced to his own daughter, also out for an evening's illicit love – and many other stories, which made him a much appreciated guest. He played enthusiastically with the children, and Sarah saw more and more clearly how justi-fied had been Isabel's romantic decision. She wrote to Berlin telling her how much they had enjoyed having Rudi.

Isabel's own visit kept being postponed. In fact Rudi was back again two years later without them having seen her, and in spite of the occasional letters they exchanged she was already becoming a somewhat mythical figure from the past, a wonderfully talented and romantic figure – Sarah began to talk about her "sister in Berlin" in the same sort of way that she occasionally mentioned the Mill House, the size of which seemed to become larger and larger. She felt respect and a pleasant envy for the life Isabel appeared to lead, theatres and concerts, much society, the Berlin lakes and woods to enjoy in summer – Rudi had been poetical about them.

Meanwhile, Sarah had to admit, their own life wasn't so bad. Harry, of course, had been a partner for years and you had only to see the way Gordon and Margery Dessleton treated him to know how valuable he was. But their whole financial position had been improved, in 1925, by the sad death of his parents, within three months of each other. The Proctors had suddenly found themselves richer by twelve thousand pounds. Of course Harry would have had it in the nature of things some time but, coming as it did, it really could not have been better timed – leaving out the sad aspect of the matter. It was very pleasant to have a reasonable lining of money when you were still young enough to enjoy it. However well Harry was doing it was difficult to avoid being mildly loaded with debt, and having some capital made all the difference, especially with the children's education to be faced in no time at all. As it was they were able to regard such problems with equanimity and two years later they moved to a new house. They left their suburb and went right out of London to the Essex coast. The new house was quite small, but it had a golf course on one side and the sea a quarter of a mile away on the other. It meant a rather lengthy journey for Harry every day, but it was worth it. Sarah was extremely happy. They were soon accepted into the local social life, which included a number of quite rich people and in the summer was distinctly fashionable. In fact, the Proctors found their resources extended, but not too much so. It was in 1930 that Harry took the risk of joining a bigger firm.

The opportunity arose most fortunately, and just when he was beginning to have the feeling that, though he was doing well, he wasn't doing well enough. He was a big fish in a small pond, but he had an idea that he could be a big fish in a big pond as well. Then there was a bridge four at the golf club in which Sarah happened to be playing with the wife of quite a well-known K.C. who had a house locally, and they were invited round for drinks, and the K.C. had a guest staying with him, Sir Graham Hadden, an energetic, beetle-browed little man, who was the number two in one of the great firms of chartered accountants, Secker, Hadden & Caulfield, an affair of world-wide reputation. It just happened to be a fact that

298

Harry got on very well with him; he had the knack of getting on well with eminent men, and there was no doubt that he had plenty of talent for the eminent men to recognize. That week-end merely started the thought in his mind that it would be a good idea to move to Secker, Hadden & Caulfield. As it turned out the process took about eighteen months. When he took the final decision, he knew it was a risk – and you could never really calculate risks, a fact which Gordon Dessleton, who was very upset, pointed out repeatedly. Again it was rather hard to part from the Dessletons, who had been so helpful, but after all Harry had given as much as he had received and, as Sarah said when she found him worrying about it, that was not the kind of thing to be sentimental about. They had always remained great friends of the Dessletons, which proved that she was right. In 1932 they built a hard tennis court in the garden and a second garage, not that they could really afford it.

And when Sarah saw her children, now – how dreadful – thirteen and eleven years old, playing tennis on the new court, it was a source of peculiar and private satisfaction to her; for this, she reflected, was what it had been like at the Mill House. It was amazing how well things had turned out and she was very grateful to Harry for being such a wonderful husband.

Of course there were aspects of Harry which one had to put on the debit side. There were times when his obstinacy about some small point nearly drove her mad. Then he could sometimes be surprisingly mean – he was, for example, quite prepared to hand out the money to build the tennis court, but a positive campaign was required before he would allow reasonable expenditure on racquets and balls. She always thought he was too strict with the children, who tended not so much to be frightened of him as to keep out of his way; and he was very firm about keeping their pocket-money down, and in fact any expenditure on them except school fees. It was quite sound, of course, but it meant that she often had to poke about in her own resources when she couldn't afford it at all, for Sarah could never keep money. And both children grew so fast, poor David was like a bean pole, already looming above her, and complaining bitterly about the appearance of his pyjamas. "If he *wants* me to have an inferiority complex —" But the absurd, and nice, thing about Harry was that when after endless cajoling or private sacrifice the money was spent, and the racquets or the pyjamas bought, he was always delighted with the result. He liked asserting himself and having to be worked on. But he was really angry with her once when he learnt that she had lost five pounds at bridge — he hated playing anything for money. It was only with difficulty that she restrained herself from pointing out that but for her bridge he might never have got to know Sir Graham Hadden; and she was glad she did restrain herself, for she knew that Harry would probably have met him somehow. Dear Harry — just as with the tennis court, when he had brought her a little car of her own he didn't want her to use any petrol. But of course the things which exasperated her were the things which, regarded afterwards, made him lovable. For example, again, he always went to sleep in the theatre — when she could get him to go.

She did wish, though, that there was a little more of her brother-in-law about him. Once a year, or sometimes it was every two years, Rudi put in an appearance, complete with his brief-case, German-style mackintosh, his heel-clicking bows — more and more military as time went on — and his always charming accent. Of course he had aged a little, but not as much as Harry, who had gained assurance with his success but was putting on too much weight — it was difficult for him not to, he had too little exercise and too many big city lunches. All the same Rudi retained most of the small elegances which she had found endearing years before, and it was always pleasant to have someone in the house who knew how to behave towards women. David was dreadful in this respect, in which he took after his father, and she was always having to correct him, for not getting up, or not standing aside, and so on. He was a shy, overgrown boy, and though he did have an enviable capacity for scraping through examinations she felt that Harry was a little disappointed in him. But you could not enter a room without Rudi bouncing up, nor go towards your coat without finding Rudi wrapping it round your shoulders, nor take a cigarette out of the box before Rudi was
300

at the ready with his lighter going. Small things, but rather nice, and with it all he talked as racily as ever. "Lucky Isabel to have a man like that all the time," Sarah thought, especially in moments of irritation with her own men. But she was, of course, most glad of Rudi's short visits – he never overstayed his welcome – one or two nights at the most – because it was the one contact apart from her occasional letters that she had with Isabel. How the time had flown! It was terrible. And the visit had never come off, though they wrote about it every year. On the one occasion when Isabel seemed on the point of coming she had gone down with the 'flu – but there was always something. Sarah fully understood. Berlin, after all, was a long way away, it was doubtless just as inconvenient for Isabel to come to England as it would be for her to think of going to Germany. One was always meaning to do it and always putting it off. According to Rudi, Isabel was much the same as ever, and still played the piano beautifully. She had certainly been living through an interesting time and Sarah envied the glamour of her cosmopolitan life. Sometimes the headline news from Germany, the street fighting, the Communists, the Nazis, made her nervous for her sister, but Isabel made no reference to it in her letters, which mostly referred to Sarah's own news.

Rudi arrived again while he was on a business trip in September 1935. In some ways it was a less satisfactory visit than usual, although he was his normal charming self when he had a chance to be – but most of the time he had to spend in argument, supporting the Nazis, not so much against Harry, as against David. It was depressing to Sarah to realize that her son, now nearly seventeen, was old enough to be concerned about such matters, and whether or not his angrily-expressed opinions were sound he was certainly often extremely rude to his uncle and annoyed his father. All that week-end one heard nothing but the Reichstag Fire Trial, Concentration Camps, Purges, Anti-Semitism, Hitler – while Rudi spoke glowingly about national honour and regeneration, and kept his temper, because, Sarah suspected, he didn't really care. But it was sad to talk about such things when there was golf and tennis, and the sea looking blue, and a dance at the golf club that night.

It was also unfortunate for David to have put his foot in it with his father, for he had been conducting a campaign to leave school and go to France. After Rudi had left, this was the main discussion in the house.

"It's such a frightful waste of time, just going back to be a prefect and play rugger. Shall I get into the XV? How exciting! Much more useful to really learn French."

Sarah was sympathetic, as she always was with her son, but this project did happen to strike another chord. She was reminded suddenly of a hazy figure from her childhood, hazy but full of significance, Denny's friend Edwin Talbot, who also had gone to France for this purpose. It pleased her to think that her own son might do what Edwin Talbot had done. Harry was difficult about it, not to say impossible. David sulkily returned to school. But a week after the beginning of the term Sarah had an idea, which had eluded her perhaps because it was so obvious. Why shouldn't he go to Berlin? His aunt and uncle would be there to keep an eye on him, and it would certainly be educational. "And we can go and visit him there." She brought it up at a time when Harry was too busy to pay much attention, and so he did not object. She wrote at once to Isabel.

The latter replied after an interval that she and Rudi were delighted with the idea and Rudi suggested that David did a German language course at the university. This satisfied Harry and so the matter was arranged. Only David's headmaster was annoyed. David himself was eager. He wrote to Sarah, "I should have preferred France, which is civilization, but I suppose neo-Gothic barbarism will be just as instructive —"

Sarah was very happy about it, and she was glad of something to be pleased about, for during this period there occurred an event so depressing that she could hardly bear to think of it. Afterwards, of course, it mattered less, or at least she was used to the fact that it had happened, but at the time it seemed a catastrophe. Neither the unexpectedly wonderful present from Harry, a diamond brooch, nor the theatre and supper for which she joined him in town in the evening made up for it.

It was her fortieth birthday.

PART TWO

CHAPTER ONE

"**D**arling," Sarah said, looking up and down the Boat Train platform at Liverpool Street, "you must write to me immediately, don't forget, or I shall be prostrate with anxiety."

"Yes, I will, mum."

"I'm perfectly sure I recognize that man," Sarah said.

Her son did not bother to follow her gaze. She was constantly being sure that she recognized people.

"P'raps I'd better be getting in," he suggested.

"No, there's still heaps of time, darling. You're as jumpy about trains as your father. He can't *bear* the thought of being left behind. It's never worried me in the slightest – I'm perfectly sure that man was in the Navy, oh, he's coming up –"

Sarah's lips remained parted expectantly, ready to flash into a smile. The man under observation passed close by, talking to someone in German.

"Wrong navy, mum."

"How infuriating!" Sarah laughed, unperturbed, and squeezed his arm affectionately. "He looked rather attractive, too, didn't he? That clean-cut Noel Coward look – just what you'll be like, dear, in years and years."

Her son, who hoped that he had this look already, was not altogether pleased. In fact they had been, that afternoon, to a matinée at the Phoenix of Noel Coward and Gertrude Lawrence in *To-night At Eight-Thirty*, and immediately afterwards, walking down Charing Cross Road, he had worn his trilby at an angle demonstrated in a foyer photograph of Mr. Coward.

"Mum, I'm sure I ought to get in. Someone may bag my seat."

"You are *exactly* like your father. Give me a kiss, then – don't draw away in agony, damn you –" She held out her arms and her fur coat fell open. They kissed, not without emotion. Then she said, "All right, go on in – but hang out of the window –"

Two minutes passed while he upset some luggage, waited pressed against the corridor for three clergymen to squeeze past, went into the wrong compartment, apologized and finally arrived at the correct window, watched with interest by fellow passengers.

"What *have* you been doing, darling?" asked his mother from the platform. "Everyone looks nice that you're with, anyhow – though I do wish your uncle could have been with you – mind you give my love to him. I'm still worried at your going half-way across Europe by yourself –"

"Oh, cut that out –" he whispered, furiously conscious of eavesdroppers behind him.

"And, David, write at once."

"Yes."

"You've got your passport and tickets and everything?"

"Yes."

"Have a ginger ale to settle your stomach."

"Oh, yes, all right."

"I shall feel so lonely, you gone and your father still at Leeds, bless him. Old and miserable and tired, that's me." She gave a pathetic look around and then smiled brilliantly at a middle-aged man in a baggy tweed suit whose seat was opposite her son's. This gentleman, who had been admiring her, and had already been flattered by the "everyone looks nice", returned the smile and bowed. He looked prepared to enter the conversation, but a whistle blew and she at once said quickly, "Oh, dear, off you go – I'll wire Isabel right away – good-bye, darling –"

The train was suddenly moving.

"'Bye, 'bye, mum –" He waved, slightly annoyed at the constriction in his throat. He had a sentimental streak which made him loathe partings. But as soon as she was out of sight, he sat back in relief. There were four others in the compartment with him and he had a strong feeling that they were all looking at him. He wished his mother were not so uninhibited in public, although he had to admit that she could behave superbly when it really mattered – as, for example, which happily no longer mattered, when visiting him at school. But on station platforms, as in restaurants or theatres, she seemed to be quite unconcerned at drawing attention to herself. His own almost desperate shyness was probably, he thought, a natural reaction.

He felt in his pocket for his notebook and pulled it out. Then he took out his fountain pen, opened the notebook on its first page and wrote the date: *26.1.36*. Under this he put, rather shakily owing to the movement of the train: *Wie froh bin ich, dass ich weg bin!* He gazed at this for a moment with satisfaction. It was a gesture that he had rehearsed in his mind, and he had learned the words by heart so that he could make it. If he happened to die during the next few months, the notebook would be found and people would recognize that first line of the *Sorrows of Werther*. It might be that, like Werther, he would commit suicide owing to frustrated passion. This seemed to him – for he knew himself well – quite probable. Equally he might find death when trying to smuggle some fugitive across the frontier, a twentieth-century Scarlet Pimpernel. To no one alive would he have confessed that this sort of thing was a minor ambition. At school he was under the impression that he had built himself up as a quiet, cynical, witty character. He had been well known for reading the *New Statesman and Nation* – it was quite a progressive sort of school, and that kind of thing was almost encouraged. Only the fact that he was a keen cricketer might have been a clue to the hidden Pimpernel. They seek him here, they seek him there – and here he was, cynical, witty, secretly adventurous, on his way to, of all places, reactionary, nationalistic, totalitarian Nazi Germany. The land of secret police and concentration camps was all unaware of the nature of this Proctor. It had better look out.

Wie froh bin ich, dass ich weg bin! – how delighted I am to get away – from school, of course, a totalitarian state in itself, but equally from an almost obscenely comfortable home. It was a fact that neither of his parents had any true idea of the society in which they lived. They adored Mr. Baldwin. His father was pretty successful it seemed, and his mother, gay and charming as she undoubtedly was – though

306

it was time, he felt, for her to be rather less gay – had the mentality of Marie Antoinette. To hear either of them talk about the unemployed or the workers generally, one would think they were discussing a national enemy – though enemy by itself was perhaps right enough. Not that he wasn't fond of them, of course; that was another matter. And as for Betty, his fat younger sister, at fourteen she could presumably be excused, but it wasn't exactly *brilliant* to divide her time between dreaming of the Prince of Wales, who was now the King, and of her future place in the British lawn tennis team for the Wightman Cup – a wildly unrealizable ambition, poor girl; after years of practice she still had no back-hand. Yes, they were a splendid family to get away from. He glanced once more, contentedly, at what he had written before putting the notebook away.

He became conscious that the man opposite in the baggy tweed suit was looking at him. He had a large stomach and was rather elderly. Thick grey hair, cut short, and in a quiff – a style David detested.

"Goot vadder to-night?" the man said.

David was startled at being addressed. He did not at once understand what had been said owing to the heavily Teutonic accent. By the time he did he had already blushed with embarrassment – a highly annoying moment. Finally he managed to nod.

"You are going to Germany?" went on the man, whose expression was kindly.

David nodded again. It could not be denied. Above his head was his suitcase, plastered with D. C. PROCTOR, Harwich – Hook – BERLIN.

"You have not been before?"

"No," David said, uncomfortably aware that the other passengers – three middle-aged men in very drab suits – were listening with interest. Amused by him, also? It was possible. Grimly he waited for more questions.

"You are going to study?"

"Well, I'm going to try to learn German."

"That is wonderful. You will love our country. It is fine that youth comes to mix with youth," said the man fervently, his accent heavier than ever. "We are proud of Germany nowadays."

Well, really! He was hardly ten minutes out of Liverpool Street and already Nazi propaganda was being tried on him! David became excited. His Uncle Rudi had been full of this line on that last visit which had resulted in the present journey. He leaned forward. He was determined to stand no nonsense from Nazis.

"What is your attitude to the persecution of the Jews?" was the question he was on the point of asking, but before he could get it out the benevolent German looked round the compartment and enquired if anyone had any objection to his smoking. It was a non-smoking compartment.

Nobody had. The other men, two Dutchmen and an Englishman, bowed, smiled and immediately small cigars and cigarettes were produced. The compartment became alive with good fellowship. The German offered David a cigarette, which he rather shamefacedly accepted. Having done so, it was of course out of the question for the moment to refer to Nazi persecution.

The German nodded to him.

"One thing you will see in Germany, everything is clean! See the dirt on this window? Not on a German train. And Liverpool Street – terrible, terrible!"

David smiled politely. Everyone knew that Liverpool Street was terrible but it hardly seemed necessary for the German to say so. The ticket inspector arrived and there were jokes all round about the illegal smoking. The inspector returned with a board to hang over the non-smoking notice, and left them all in a very good humour. A business conversation ensued. They were all, it seemed, commercial travellers. Listening in, David felt himself to be rather in the swim of things and he wished he, too, were earning his living so that he could join in. On the other hand he reflected that it would be a sad thing if he were to reach the age of these men and still have to travel third-class. How awful if that *did* happen. How awful, equally, to be so shielded from life as he was – the plan laid down for him was six months in Germany, three years at Cambridge, two years as an articled clerk and finally

308

a privileged entry into his father's firm. He had not, of course, the slightest intention of carrying out this plan. The only trouble was that as yet he had no clear alternative in view. After a time he got up to go to the W.C., and noticed as he did so from the suitcase label that the German's name was Princkel. In the delightful privacy of the W.C. he inspected himself in the mirror. Apart from his protruding ears, his appearance was, he thought, quite elegant and mature. He did not, thank God, look particularly young. That was partly owing to his dark-blue lounge suit – what a pleasant change it was from the school blazer – but his chin and upper lip were satisfactorily darker than the rest of his rather sallow skin. The beard was coming along nicely. He looked at himself in the mirror with raised eyebrows and murmured silkily, " You say you are proud of the new Germany, my dear Herr Princkel. Are you also *proud* of the persecution of the Jews? Of the concentration camps? Of the outlawing of liberalism and freedom? Proud of the contempt of the civilized world? " He did not want to be hard on Herr Princkel, but he intended to take the first opportunity of showing him where he personally stood.

Back in the compartment, however, Herr Princkel was reading some business papers, an open brief-case at his side, the Dutchmen were eating some extraordinary unattractive-looking sandwiches – the middle layer seemed to be merely another kind of bread – and the Englishman, a very insignificant fellow, dozed. Hardly a word was spoken all the way to Harwich. David felt disappointed, though he was also relieved at not being put to the test.

CHAPTER TWO

The next morning he was in another train, far more glamorous, with Mitropa coaches and notices like " *Nicht hinauslehnen* " instead of the dull " Do not lean out ". It was a cold day, there had been biting sleet at the

Hook, and Holland looked most dreary and uninviting. At Bentheim, shortly after the train had crossed the German frontier, there was a stop and the Customs men and passport inspectors arrived.

"*Heil Hitler, Pass Kontrolle.*"

David sat in his corner, concealing an immense excitement and some nervousness. The overnight trip had not been without incident. He had gone to the ship saloon to have his ginger ale and had found himself sitting next to the Englishman from the train compartment. They had had quite a session, and he personally had drunk three whiskies and ginger ale, and been unaffected by them. Furthermore, he had talked most fluently. The Englishman, who belonged to the lower *bourgeoisie*, for which stratum David felt no protective interest, was nevertheless good-natured, and had queer interests like motor cycle racing, about which he was full of information. He had some job which took him to Amsterdam and also frequently to the Rhineland. So they had become political. The Englishman was very anti-French and, it seemed, totally ignorant of Nazi excesses. David was able to give him the substance of the speech he had prepared for Herr Princkel. The Englishman said, "Well, old boy, that all may be true, but the fact is he's given them back their guts, and if a Jerry gives you his word, you can depend on it – a bull point, to my way of thinking." David then did his best, his voice becoming more highly pitched than he intended, to alter his way of thinking. He spoke scornfully of the Austrian housepainter, he tried to remember facts from Victor Gollancz's Brown Books, the Reichstag Fire, Dimitrov, Gestapo, the fate of the trade unions, the press – and at the end of it he suddenly realized that Herr Princkel was sitting hardly more than a yard away, and presumably had heard it all. Nothing happened, of course, although Herr Princkel, getting up to leave the saloon a little later, gave him a glance that was not exactly affable. David had felt a considerable sense of victory, which was not even spoilt by the Englishman's phoney wisdom, "I expect there are two sides to all that, old boy." He would soon be making the same speech to Uncle Rudi, who no doubt expected him still to be an uncommunicative schoolboy. The feeling of satisfaction had lasted until a few minutes before the train left the Hook, when, of all people – he had seen no more of the Englishman or the Dutchmen – Herr Princkel came into his compartment and took the empty corner seat, diagonally opposite him. David was at once conscious of a good deal of inward thumping. They gave each other a nod of recognition. Was Princkel, then, after him? Was he about to denounce him to the passport man? They were in Germany now, a very different place to the saloon of a British ship, and he was alone. The other people in the compartment were Germans. Why had Princkel come into this compartment, anyway?

"*Dank' schön. Heil Hitler!*" Slowly the passports were being examined and collected. Now his own – a pair of official eyes looked down at him searchingly. He could only hope that his terror would not be guessed. There was a second official, armed with a revolver, of course, who was at present out of sight, possibly receiving a confidential whisper from Princkel.

"Where are you going?" the passport man said benevolently.

David swallowed.

"Berlin."

"For how long?"

"Six months."

"Thank you." And the passport was added to the collection.

The two officials retreated to the corridor. David sat frozen. He dared not look at anyone, but he could feel Herr Princkel's gaze. Outside the passports were looked at, held up to the light, discussed, stamped. One of the men brought them back and distributed them.

"Have a good time," he nodded to David with a smile. Then at the door he addressed them all. "*Heil Hitler!*"

"*Heil Hitler!*" murmured one or two of the occupants.

David felt almost ill with relief. But the dreadful thing was that the official's tone of friendliness had been welcome. He had been pleased at being spoken to in a pleasant way by a Nazi. "I am a Judas," he reflected gloomily. Then he took out his notebook and wrote down another prepared phrase. "Passed German frontier. Passport man came and went, no trouble. Heard my first *Heil Hitler!* Sounded like the history of Europe." He was relaxed again now, and he looked straight at Herr Princkel; but the latter was glancing through the Nazi daily newspaper, *Völkischer Beobachter*, looking smug and sardonic. David now began to consider very calmly what might have happened if the little man with the pince-nez opposite him, scenting arrest, had dived for the window while he himself tripped up the passport man.

The Customs man arrived. He almost wished something would happen now, but of course nothing did. He managed a cynical smile in answer to the final "*Heil Hitler!*"

As the train continued into Germany he noticed that the landscape was a good deal more dreary even than the Dutch had been. Bare earth, sometimes brown, sometimes grey-white with a thin layer of snow, stretched away for miles. It was all very murky and the small towns they went through seemed murkier. The few swastika flags on the station platforms brought some sinister colour, but the people who stood waiting looked pale and cheerless. "No sign of a storm-trooper or even of a book being burnt," David thought ironically. But still, at one station where the train stopped for a minute he was able to lean out and buy a bar of chocolate and some coffee in a thin, hot, cardboard mug. When he had finished both, feeling pleased that he had managed a little German, he lit a cigarette. It was bliss to be free! And amusing that in order to be free he had had to come to a dictatorship. Was that worth putting down? He considered bringing out his notebook, but decided against it. He blew out smoke and, glancing at his fingers, imagined that he already saw signs of an honourable nicotine stain. At the same moment he felt a tap on his knee.

"You moss not shmoke!" The little man opposite with eyes shining disapproval. He pointed to the *Rauchen verboten* notice on the window.

"Oh, God!" said David, flushing at once. "I'm sorry! *Entschuldigung!*" In great confusion he looked for an ashtray. None was available. Everyone was gazing at him critically, except Herr Princkel who remained behind the *Völkischer Beobachter*.

"Shmoke out zere," said the little man, pointing now at the corridor.

"Oh! Right! Yes! I'm awfully sorry – " He got up quickly, his cheeks burning, and on the way out his long legs seemed to get in everybody's way. What a ghastly, schoolboy performance – in the corridor, out of view of the compartment, he swore silently at himself. As he cooled down, he excused himself with the idea that the embarrassment had been due to knowing so little German. He had only done it for a term. If he could have answered fluently – "*Es tut mir Leid, meine Herren*" – he would have begun – and then the memory of Herr Princkel in the train from London to Harwich struck him. Really! It hadn't mattered about No Smoking notices in England! He recalled the happy confidence with which not merely cigarettes but those stinking little cigars had been produced – the winks, the smiles! And the amiable railwayman changing the notice! A very small thing, perhaps – but it certainly showed the difference between the two countries.

He smoked the cigarette calmly now, looking out at the dreary unending landscape. There had, after all, been something rather daring in his lighting up. He saw himself returning to his school on a visit, perhaps giving a lecture in Hall on his experiences. He would stand on the platform, his face a little drawn with pain – the stick he leant on was the indication of that last scuffle with the Gestapo, when he was helping a refugee over the mountains into Czechoslovakia – and with that look in his eyes, to be seen only in those who have been through much, which set him apart from others of his own age. At the end "Three cheers for Proctor" were called by the head of the school, and perhaps "Land of Hope and Glory" was played.

David stubbed out the cigarette, smiling tolerantly at himself, just as there rose the sound of gong banging and a white-coated steward came along announcing lunch. It was a splendid opportunity of saving his face in the compartment. He decided to go to lunch right away.

CHAPTER THREE

He had to go through about eight carriages to get to the Mitropa restaurant car, and when he got there he had to join a small queue. Ahead of him was a tall bullet-headed man with scars on his cheeks, a real Prussian and infinitely more impressive than Herr Princkel. He was accompanying a most severe-looking woman, perfect emblems of the new Germany. David felt himself becoming more and more of an experienced cosmopolitan observer. All the women he had seen were atrociously ugly. However, when he was at last directed to a seat, he was at once obliged to reverse this opinion.

The woman he was to sit opposite, at a small window table for two, was both blonde and glamorous. She was not young, or he would not have been able to move his limbs at all. As it was he managed to bow and sit down. He could then find nowhere to put his feet, tried crossing them, but the table was too low, tried spreading them apart, and met hers – he withdrew as if electrified. She appeared not to have noticed. Where exactly to rest his hands was also a problem. He adjusted his tie once or twice, and touched the top of his handkerchief in his breast-pocket.

She was looking quite calmly out of the window, and he had little doubt that she was scornful of him. When the wine steward came up she ordered a cocktail of some kind. He, of course, shook his head convulsively. All round he noticed that at every table people were talking gaily to each other. Only at this table was there total silence. He pictured himself on his return journey in six months' time, effortlessly pouring out witty and fluent German small-talk.

When the soup was brought, he said firmly, "Thank you," in English. But even that didn't stir her. She just went on staring out of the window, and sipping at the cocktail. She wasn't having soup – an elegant piece of business, he considered, since she had to pay for it. He happened to be feeling hungry or he would have been tempted to imitate her. Then there was some fish and she went into conversation with the wine steward again, too fast for him to get an idea of it, but the result was a half-bottle of white wine. David was impressed. She also toyed with the fish. She had a lot of make-up on, and her skin had a kind of athletic-looking suntan, rather odd at this time of year. She had a fur pill-box hat tilted over to one side, and a plain light-grey suit with a vaguely masculine cut about it. By now he was beginning to feel calmer. He noticed that there were quite deep wrinkles at the side of her eyes; she was probably not much younger than his mother, if at all. When the steward came along next he asked him to translate the meat items on the menu. He chose roast veal. All at once she was looking right at him.

" Hey, are you English? " she said.

" Yes." He was taken aback and, of course, his ears began to burn.

" Why, that's cute," she said. Her voice was warm and a little husky, and had a surprising transatlantic accent. " What are you doing, then – on business or holiday? "

" I'm a student," David said, extremely flattered at the suggestion that he might be on business.

" Well, isn't that interesting? What are you a student of? "

" Oh, just German, I suppose," David said, a little deflated.

" An Englishman learning a foreign language! " she smiled, displaying a mouth of perfectly white, perfectly even teeth. " How amazing! "

" Are you – " He paused momentarily. She spoke so well that she might even be English, in which case it would obviously be an insult to suggest that she was anything else. He gave her a sideways glance. " Are you an American? "

" No, no, I'm German, but I've lived for years in the States. That's how I got my accent. Where are you going? Hanover? "

" Berlin. I have an uncle and aunt living there. My uncle is German."

" Is that right? Where do they live? "

"Wilmersdorf."

"Uh-huh." The words she used didn't seem quite right for the soft and elegant manner in which she used them. She would have fooled him if she hadn't told him she was German; but since she had he realized there was something not quite right about her English, although she was uncannily good.

"I hope I'll learn to talk as well as you can," he said with frank admiration.

She smiled again. She really was a beautiful woman.

"You're cute. Will you have a drink? C'mon."

"Oh, no thank you very much –" he began, embarrassed. If he accepted, wouldn't he as a gentleman have to pay for the bottle?

"Oh, now, don't be so damned coy. You Englishmen are all the same."

"Well, you have one with me –" he said uneasily.

"Look, dear, I'm old enough to be your mother. You don't have to stand on your dignity with me. What are you – nineteen? I was thirty-seven last week."

The innocent compliment about his age together with her staggering frankness overwhelmed him. He said he would have a whisky and ginger ale. In a way she was not unlike his mother, and also not unlike the picture he had of his aunt, except that this woman did not seem to be particularly artistic, and he did not think his aunt would have any suntan. In the old photograph of her at home she seemed distinctly pale.

The whisky and ginger ale came. It seemed to go well with the roast veal. Then they had cheese and she ordered coffee and a brandy. Meanwhile she had been full of questions about himself and his background, which she asked with such unashamed curiosity that it would have seemed as if he had something to hide if he didn't answer. He became quite talkative, but flattered himself that he said nothing indiscreet. He must have made a good impression, however, for the woman suddenly dived into a most luxurious-looking handbag, python skin, and gave him a visiting card. He read an address in Berlin and her name, Frau Dr. Bürckel.

316

"That's so you know who I am, and maybe you'll want to call me up some time."

"Thank you very much," he said, concealing a good deal of excitement. Was she making a pass at him? He would have given a lot for certain members of his late school to be observing this scene. Casanova was also one of his private selves, along with Pimpernel. An immensely smooth and sophisticated David Proctor was as desirable as the wounded anti-Nazi hero. Frau Dr. Bürckel certainly was attractive, and this might very well be the start of one of those youth-and-mature-woman affairs so much recommended as an introduction to life. All this went rapidly through his mind and he was thinking about it so hard that he was late in offering her a cigarette – she was opening her own case. He practically upset the table in trying to get his packet out. Then she shook her head, anyway. Hers were a special brand, with a filter end, and scented. He hadn't come across scented cigarettes before.

"You have one of your own," Frau Dr. Bürckel said. "These are strictly feminine."

David, feeling masculine as a result of this remark, took one of his own and struck a table match quickly to light hers, but she had already produced a little jewelled lighter. However she gave it to him to hold, and kept her hand on his, pressing firmly, while she lit up. Not only that, but she looked straight into his eyes. He felt his heart thumping. This really wasn't bad, less than twenty-four hours from home. He wondered if she knew how totally inexperienced he was and, if she did, whether that was what she liked. Ought he to be innocently youthful or continue to be suave? He was not sure.

"Tell me all about your aunt and uncle," she said. "I just love hearing about people, don't you? Especially if you have a feeling of real interest. You interest me a lot."

He had to think. It was one thing to talk about parents who were safely behind in England, but his aunt and uncle might both be at the station. It was infuriating that he had to be met.

"Well, I really don't know much about them." Then he

317

thought of something brilliant; it would enable him to see how she reacted. He went on, " My uncle's an enthusiastic Nazi – "

" Is that so? What is he? "

" He's – he's something to do with textiles, I think – "

" No, I meant has he a rank of some kind? Is he in the S.S.? " She showed no disapproval.

" Well, he's a member of the Party – " He was taken aback. That his uncle sympathized with the régime seemed shameful enough.

" Oh, is that all you mean? Or is he one of the first hundred or something? "

He shook his head.

" Not as far as I know," he said. He was considerably shocked that she should turn out to be a Nazi.

" Well, that's a relief. I find the old guard and all that very tedious, even after they were all put in their place last year – no, the year before, wasn't it? But I do like the S.S. uniform, apart from the fact that it's the only thing for what you call a gentleman to be in. My husband wanted to join, but General Goering himself told him not to. Now, there, I must say, is a delightful man."

" You *know* Goering? " David exclaimed.

" Well, I've met him," said Frau Dr. Bürckel, blowing a ring of smoke towards the window. " I've met them all, my dear, even the Führer, though that was before he came to power. Just a quick presentation, you know. Bless his heart, he was very gallant and polite. I don't believe a word, not one word, of what they say about him and women. I do hope he'll be down at Garmisch next month; I'm going for the Olympics. Such a lot on his shoulders, poor man. Do you like ski-ing? "

He tried to seem as if he were accustomed to this sort of conversation, but in England he had never met people who knew the Prime Minister, his father had no dealings at Cabinet level. Was she putting up an act? But everything about her was rich, the cigarettes, the lighter, and not least her air of confidence. Furthermore, he was experiencing very mixed feelings – he wanted to stand by his firm anti-Nazi, anti-

318

dictatorship principles, but in the circumstances it seemed rather silly not to forget these. You never knew, he might even meet some of the Nazi big-shots through her. "English boy speaks his mind to Führer!" – he could see the headline.

"I've never done any," he said, apologetically.

"Oh, you must! I adore it. Go on about your uncle."

"Well–" He was even more embarrassed, now that she had put herself on such a high level, and he felt the need to bolster himself up. "He's a very amusing man, I think – I haven't met him much, you see, I mean I've been away at – I've been away often when he's visited us – he's come to England on business now and then." In spite of his uncle's Nazi enthusiasm, he had liked what he had seen of him, and his parents adored him – Uncle Rudi tended to be the life of the party, with his flow of small-talk, charming accent and habit of clicking his heels gallantly with an elegant little bow, which greatly intrigued his mother. But he did not want to build him up too much to Frau Dr. Bürckel. He was fairly sure that Uncle Rudi had not met Goering, for example, to say nothing of Hitler, or he would undoubtedly have heard about it.

"It's your first time away, is it? Or have you been abroad before?"

"Actually it's the first time," David admitted, flushing.

She gave him a quick smile, as if to say, "I understand."

"Well, I think that's just fine. What about your aunt?"

"Oh, I'm afraid I don't know much about her."

"Why not?"

"Well, I've never met her, at least not since I was about three. Since then she's always been nearly coming for a holiday, but it's never come off." He had a theory why it hadn't, too, not that he proposed to mention it – the fact was, as he had lately come to realize, his household was extremely stodgy to anyone who was even vaguely Bohemian or used to a metropolitan life. He had no memory of his aunt, except of an unwanted kiss – nothing which had any relation to the old studio portrait of her, and everyone looked farcical in old photographs – she was supposed to be a young girl in it and looked about sixty. But still she had been part of his life, the

319

romantic relation, the proof that there was, as he suspected, something artistic in his blood. In fact he was rather proud of her. She'd have something else to talk about than bridge, golf and scandal. He added, "She's a brilliant pianist."

"A concert pianist?" Frau Dr. Bürckel said.

"Well, yes—"

"What is her name? I know Fürtwangler and dear old Strauss and Gieseking—"

"Well, I don't mean now, you see. I mean she used to be, I believe." He became confused, having apparently claimed too much. Things he had dimly heard about came back to him. "But I suppose when she got married—actually my uncle is her second husband—I know she gave a concert in London, though—"

"I suppose that's where you get those long fingers from," Frau Dr. Bürckel said, and she touched his hand lightly.

"Yes—are they—perhaps," he nodded, with a tremendous attempt not to appear awkward. She really was flirting with him, there was no doubt about it.

"It's always fascinating to hear about other people's lives. And yours is ahead of you. I wonder what will happen to you. What do you intend to do?"

He was going to say, automatically, "I'm going to be an accountant," which was what he always said, and always satisfied everybody, although he had no intention of being an accountant at all. But he felt it wouldn't be a suitable answer just now. He shrugged his shoulders.

"Well, try to be something creative," Frau Dr. Bürckel said. "Whatever you do, don't be a banker like my husband."

"Not if I can help it!"

"It's not for your sake I'm thinking, but your women. I'll give you a great life secret, one of the secrets the young just never know. It's this, the duller an occupation seems, the more interesting it really is. If you're married to a banker, you never see him. Why? Because his job is so fascinating—power and intrigue and politics, you know? And it absorbs all their sensuality—it's getting as bad here as in the States."

He was amused.

"That might apply to my father, as a matter of fact."

"There you are." She leaned slightly across the table, so that her face was quite close to his—it was a pity her neck was rather scraggy; and beneath the table he felt the pressure of her ankle. "It's all so stupid. One wants comfort of course, and a little luxury here and there. But it's a fact that the only thing that matters in life is 'I want you and you want me', isn't it? Do you agree?"

"Oh, I certainly do," David said, swallowing.

He couldn't imagine what might happen next, but a steward was coming along with the lunch bills and also the train was entering a built-up area which went on and on.

"Hanover," Frau Dr. Bürckel said. "That's where you ought to be getting out, my dear. They speak the best German." Then she was busy with the steward, talking, of course, in German, and he noticed that the steward was paying her the exaggerated attention which one always hoped to inspire but rarely did. Once more he was impressed by her elegance. Her features were coarse, really, the nose was quite thick and there was a strength about her, but at the same time he was conscious of immense femininity. She was making herself attractive to him all the time, he was sure— even when she was talking to the steward. And he wasn't attracted, and yet he was. He paid his bill, attempting unsuccessfully to imitate her manner. The steward, of course, was polite but off-hand with him, as if he knew he hadn't much money. He certainly hadn't, after buying drinks and cigarettes on the boat. His parents weren't ungenerous, but they didn't throw money at him. In fact he knew that his mother often had the devil of a job getting it out of his father for herself, let alone him.

Then suddenly they had stopped in the main station and at last there were real signs of Nazi Germany, swastika flags everywhere, one or two jack-booted storm-troopers walking about, an S.S. man in black, and a group of Hitler Youths, jack-booted, armed with short daggers, swastikas on the left sleeve of their brown shirts. The ordinary civilians looked very drab in comparison. A long banner was strung over the main exit, declaiming "*Ein Reich! Ein Volk! Ein Führer!*" One country, one people, one leader—he remembered guiltily that this was enemy territory to anyone who claimed to be civilized. He coughed.

"What do you think of it all?" he asked, nodding towards the Hitler Youths. He proposed to make it plain where he stood.

Frau Dr. Bürckel followed him perfectly. She smiled and tapped her second special cigarette against the ash-tray.

"My dear, it keeps the workers happy. *He* knows how to do it. What more can you ask of any man or any government?"

At once he found himself raised up to the privileged classes. He saw that idealism was foolish. The storm-troopers, the Hitler Youths, were playthings to be manipulated.

"Obviously nothing!" he smiled in return.

But the next moment he was very much taken aback. Frau Dr. Bürckel was busy pulling her fur coat over her shoulders – he was late in remembering to help – and then she stood up. She held out her hand. He got up hastily.

"Well, it was nice to meet you," she said. "I hope you enjoy yourself in Berlin."

He touched her hand, speechless, and he was left staring after her elegant, arrogant back. It was an unexpected development. He felt sure that he looked a fool, and that people, waiters and stewards were staring at him with amusement. The head steward was already directing someone to his place. The only thing was to follow her in as dignified a manner as possible, but this was not easy. He felt his ears burning and his body seemed a mass of unco-ordinated bones, so much so that he almost tripped himself up twice before he got out of the restaurant car.

He was so annoyed with himself that he almost forgot about her as he walked down the first corridor. Then, free of the restaurant car stares, he became merely deflated. Just when he was feeling himself sophisticated he had become the gauche schoolboy. There were two first-class carriages to go through. He hurried along looking away from the interiors, in case he should catch sight of her and be further humiliated. When he was through to the second-class and the ordinary passengers he relaxed. Meanwhile the train was on its way out of Hanover. He slowed down and had a look at the roofs. It was all neater and solider than the outskirts of an English city, although there were some allotments which looked like the home variety.

He felt in his pocket for his cigarettes and touched the card she had given him. At once his mood changed again. The card had been a definite invitation, there was no doubt about that. Perhaps he had made another kind of fool of himself, and really he ought to have followed close after her, accompanied her to her apartment. It was the curse of being inexperienced. She might very well have a compartment of her own and perhaps even now, if he had known the thing to do, they might be continuing their conversation in a far more intimate way.

"But not to-day, Josephine," he thought, as if he had considered the idea practically and had turned it down.

When he got back to his own compartment he was feeling very pleased with himself. They were all still there except Herr Princkel—he had forgotten that the latter, of whom he had been foolishly nervous, was due to get out at Hanover. His seat was waiting for him and the little man opposite dozed. In Princkel's place, however, was a large bull-faced man in storm-trooper's uniform. David trod warily over his jack-booted legs. He settled down in his corner wishing they could all know what a gay dog he had been, and covertly examined the storm-trooper, who had—it seemed rather incongruous—two brief-cases, from one of which he kept selecting papers to study. He was fat, powerfully built and middle-aged; his stomach and legs seemed to be bursting out of his uniform.

David pulled out his notebook and put down "Storm-trooper in compartment". For discretion's sake he decided to make no mention of his luncheon companion. Then he put down simply, "Met B." Who knew how significant that little entry might eventually be? He wondered if, snug in the first-class, she were thinking of him. Then he had a moment of panic when a woman went by down the corridor and for a moment it looked like her; but it wasn't.

The storm-trooper finished with his papers and closed up

his brief-cases. He took off the spectacles he had been wearing and changed them for another pair. Then he began to converse, in a hard, guttural voice. The little man opposite woke up, his head seemed to pop a few inches out of his high stiff collar. Soon three or four of them were talking. David tried to make out what it was about, but it was impossible. He kept his notebook open, but there was nothing to put down – no mention of Führer, or Baldwin, or Mussolini to give a lead. There was laughter – not at himself, he hoped – and the storm-trooper kept slapping his revolting knees. The little man told some story in an amazingly dry voice. Evidently he was a wit. David found it very irritating not to understand. He stared out of the window at the gloomy, cold afternoon – the daylight was beginning to go – and managed not to listen. He thought some more about Frau Dr. Bürckel, and also about Herr Princkel, and the Englishman on the boat – it seemed as if he had been away for months and that he was already slightly cosmopolitan. To-night he would be dining in a Berlin flat. All this was certainly pleasanter than going back to school.

After a time he became bored, and then he dozed for a while himself. It was late afternoon and lights on everywhere when the train reached Berlin. He had a shadowy view of lakes and pinewoods which looked as if they might be pleasant at some other time.

He knew that there were two Berlin stations and that he had to get out at the first, the Zoolog. Garten – the instructions had come from Uncle Rudi, and he glanced at the piece of notepaper carried in his wallet to make sure. Up on the signal box he saw " Berlin " – it was exciting. This was now his city. As the train came into the station he saw lots of people, uniforms, flags. He leaned across to the little man and spoke a sentence which he had been practising for some minutes, in German: " Excuse me, here is Berlin Zoological Garden? " The little man gave him a sharp look and then nodded. The storm-trooper got out at once, saying good-bye with a cheerful, gruff " *Heil Hitler!* " The others were not moving. David got down his suitcase and coat, put on his hat and staggered clumsily to the corridor. Nobody said good-bye

to him – perhaps, after all, Herr Princkel had talked when
he was away at lunch. He didn't hurry too much to get off,
because he wanted Frau Dr. Bürckel to have a clear start. He
stood aside at the doorway, looking out, and then had the
pleasure of seeing the back of that fur coat and the pill-box
hat receding elegantly towards the exit, followed by a porter
laden with bags. Now that she was safely away it gave him
a considerable feeling of satisfaction to think that he had
lunched with her. If only he were not being met, he might
very well be leaving the station with her at this moment. He
got down to the platform and put on his coat. The air was
extremely cold.

For the moment there was no sign of Uncle Rudi, smart,
confident, ebullient. Nor, alternatively, of his aunt. He was
expecting someone rather like Frau Dr. Bürckel, only, of
course, older. The train remained still. He moved up a little
so that the compartment should not see him looking lost.
Ten minutes later the train moved slowly out of the station
and he suddenly wondered if there had been a mistake and
they were at the other station, the Friedrichstrasse. His ears
were getting frozen. Perhaps he could telephone, but he
wasn't sure that his new-found confidence was equal to tele-
phoning. Did they have directories as at home? The name
was Peters, presumably under Rudiger Peters – he was thinking irresolutely about this when he had a curious sensation.

He thought he saw his mother walking towards him.

It wasn't, of course, and the possibility which naturally
followed, that it was his aunt, he dismissed at once because
this person was altogether too drab. As she came closer the
resemblance to his mother disappeared altogether. It had been
an optical illusion. This woman was just one of the Berlin
four million with a shabby coat and a shopping carrier-bag.
There was a depressed, colourless look about her.

She came up to him nervously and asked, "Are you
David?"

"Aunt Isabel?" he said, privately aghast. Then he remembered to raise his hat.

"Yes, of course." She not only looked but sounded
depressed. She moved towards him and dryly kissed his cheek.

325

"I didn't think it could be you," she went on. "I suppose I was expecting someone younger looking, more like a boy. You're tall, aren't you? What a queer hat that is." She referred to his rather wide-brimmed grey trilby.

"It's just an ordinary hat," he said.

"Yes, yes, I suppose so. You know I thought I must have gone to the wrong station but Rudi said the Zoo, I was sure. Still it would be just like me to go to the wrong one."

"You've been here long?" He kept telling himself that she couldn't be true.

"Just a few minutes. Is that your bag? It looks a good one. Well, we'd better go along, I suppose."

"Yes," he said, thinking, "God, this is too awful." He picked up his suitcase, which was quite heavy. There was no question of a porter and equally he was sure there would be no question of a taxi when they got outside.

"How are Sarah and Harry?" his aunt asked despondently, as they walked towards the Ausgang, beneath the hanging swastikas. "Very well, I suppose. It must be a big expense sending you here. Everything's so expensive nowadays. I suppose you're very hungry at your age." She nodded down to the deplorable, black, oil-leather carrier bag. She seemed to be quite on edge. "I've got in more bread."

CHAPTER FOUR

Outside the station they caught a tram, which was crowded. His aunt took two ten-pfennig tickets. He had a feeling that he ought to offer to pay, but it didn't seem to occur to her. He had never felt so depressed. They were surrounded by people so he couldn't look out. The tram clanged away like an English tram, except that it was just a single-decker. Fortunately it was impossible to make conversation. The other passengers were mostly workers going home, he presumed. They looked pale and not especially gay.

He noticed the extraordinary length of a man's raincoat, buttoned up at the neck it reached down to his ankles. No one was in uniform.

They passed what was certainly a brightly-lit quarter – he had glimpses of cafés full of people, whom he envied. Then he was sitting next to his aunt, with one hand guarding the handle of his suitcase. He kept trying to think of something to say, but when it came to it he couldn't get his mouth to work. He realized that she was in the same sort of difficulty. Anyone more unlike his mother was hard to imagine. Moreover she was the last person one would expect to be Uncle Rudi's wife. She spoke finally, in the same subdued, hesitant voice as before.

"The trams aren't always as crowded as this, it's just the time of the day. We've struck the worst time."

"I suppose it's the rush hour."

"Yes, the same as in London. Only they go to work earlier here. They work harder here. All the offices start at eight."

This also seemed a vaguely depressing piece of news, although it did not affect him. He wasn't, thank God, going to an office.

"What part of Berlin is this?"

"Well, it's the west, or south-west, at least we're going south now. You can see it's all clean, nobody throws papers about. They're very litter-conscious."

"Yes." He glanced sideways, suspecting that there had even been a touch of irony in her voice. But she looked quite solemn. She had, however, sounded a little more lively.

"Rudi's been to the university and found somewhere cheap where you can live."

"Good," he nodded. That was what he had been looking forward to most of all, the *pension* where he could begin to live – nothing could dim the idea of that. "It's awfully kind of him," he added politely.

"I don't know what it's like myself."

"Oh, anything will do me." He found himself already talking down to her, trying not to put on side. But a queer, uncomfortable thought had struck him: "She didn't want me to come."

"But, still, I suppose you haven't been used to luxury and breakfast in bed at school."

Again he detected irony of some sort, but she seemed to be quite serious.

"Not exactly!" he smiled. But she did not smile back.

"We get out here."

"Oh, good." It had at least been a reasonably short journey. He pushed his way out with his suitcase, followed by her. Buildings rose dark and high on either side of a wide street, and the lamplights seemed to shine for miles in either direction.

"We ought really to have waited for the next tram, it goes nearer home," she said. "It's always the wrong one that comes first. But still, you're young and strong, I suppose, you don't mind a little walk."

"Not at all." They crossed to the pavement and walked some way down the street, while the suitcase became heavier and heavier. He kept going out of vanity, acting the part of being young and strong. They turned into a side street, which was narrower but also seemed lengthy.

"In summer when the trees are out it's quite pretty," she remarked. "It gets very hot, of course."

"Oh, yes?" He changed hands desperately. The idea that summer merely meant trees in leaf in the street was almost unbearably depressing. The months rose up before him like huge mountain ranges of boredom and dreariness. The sooner he got away from her and into his *pension* the better.

They turned into another street, exactly similar, it seemed, to the last. The street lamps showed up decorated balconies on either side. Some of the designs of the front doors were grandiose and fantastic, and yet the general impression was that they were all the same, old-fashioned, and dull and solid.

"Well, here we are," his aunt said, in front of one of the less pretentious front doors. It was open and she led the way in to a bare vestibule with a staircase. She pressed a button to switch on a light. "We're on the third floor." There was a stale sulphury smell in the air. Sweating and aching he forced himself up after her, infinitely relieved that he could soon put his suitcase down.

328

Finally they were there. She produced an outsize key and they went through a door on which there was a slot for a card that read simply: Peters. Inside was a passage equipped with a hatstand. He put down his case. He felt dizzy.

"You can hang your coat up there," she said. "I'll make some coffee. I expect you'd like some after that long train journey."

"Thank you very much."

"This is our sitting-room. Make yourself at home."

The sitting-room was gloomy and sparsely furnished. It was, in fact, rather like a wide passage, somewhere to go through rather than stay in. It was entirely cheerless. His aunt disappeared through a door which apparently led to the kitchen, for he heard vague kitchen sounds immediately afterwards. The window, at present locked, served a balcony which overlooked the street. Beside it was an alcove – really a small room, almost filled by a large pianoforte. This was a business-like section – there was a pile of music beside the stool, but otherwise it was bare. He sat down on a rather hard sofa which stood against the wall facing a table, but got up at once to investigate some photographs on the other side of the room. They were of his mother, one fairly recent, the other old, of Uncle Rudi and his aunt, years ago – in spite of the clumsy dress and ugly hair style, one could see that she wasn't quite so dim looking then – and there were his mother's parents and her brothers Denny and Nicholas. Except for the old one of Uncle Rudi and his aunt, they were all to be found at home, and it was uncanny to see them here, somewhat disconcerting to think that they equally belonged here – in an atmosphere of what seemed genteel poverty. Those shoes of his aunt, the awful coat – he was sure his mother had no idea of the state she was in. It was certainly not the impression Uncle Rudi had given.

His aunt returned. She put the coffee pot on a table and brought it over to him. Then she went to the cabinet and produced a cup and saucer.

"You must have our best china in honour of your arrival," she said with her nervous smile, gone almost before it had come.

L*

"Can't I help at all, Aunt – Aunt Isabel?"

"No, no, just sit there – it's all so curious, you must excuse me – David – is that what you're called, David?"

"Yes."

"I'd better wash that cup now I think of it, it must be dusty – though everything's cleaned – would you like a biscuit?"

"Well, yes, I would. Don't bother about the cup."

"It won't take a second." He noticed that her hand trembled a little and was slightly anxious that there might be an accident to the cup. She disappeared again and there were more sounds from the kitchen, a brief reappearance for another visit to the cabinet – a plate was extracted – then back to the kitchen, and more sounds. He warmed to her a little for being so enormously inefficient. But the coffee, when at last poured out, was unaccountably cool and the three thin biscuits, for which the special plate had been procured, had a touch of staleness. She also had a cup, one of inferior quality as if she wanted to insist that that was good enough for her. She stood sipping about a yard from him for a minute. Then she made an effort and sat down on the sofa.

"Mother sent her love, of course," he said, remembering the farewell message.

"Yes?" She seemed to be quite surprised and pleased. "It's such years since I've seen her. Have another biscuit."

"I don't think I will, thanks." Embarrassed, he felt for his cigarette packet. "Do you mind if I smoke?"

"Won't it stunt your growth?" And again he could not imagine that she was not being ironical, but she seemed merely anxious. It was as if she were completely out of touch.

"I don't think so. Will you have one?"

"Well, perhaps I will – I'll get an ash tray –"

"Let me –"

"No, you sit there." She got the ash tray and took the cigarette he offered. Then she held it like someone who had never smoked before. He took notice of her dress, which had a flower pattern; it was full-sleeved and did up at the neck. She had on rather thick stockings and black shoes, and of course she wore no make-up, except perhaps a little powder.

330

She might be his mother's aunt, let alone his. He lit his own cigarette. This really was a far cry from the Continental-Bohemian evening he had been expecting. Frau Dr. Bürckel, he felt sure, was at this moment having a dry martini or something. She went on, "Rudi will be back soon, I hope. Of course it isn't long ago you met him."

"He's awfully amusing."

"Yes." She smiled bleakly.

"Do you agree with his political views?"

"Yes – well – women don't have political views here," she said, taken aback. She took a deep puff at her cigarette and began to cough. It was rather a hard cough, uncomfortable to hear. Her face went pink and she became quite breathless. He suspected that she had done it on purpose to change the subject – though he thought he had brought it up diplomatically. "Excuse me," she said breathlessly. "Some smoke went the wrong way, I ought not to have it really." She sounded a little more cheerful. "By the way, we've fixed a bed for you to-night in the street floor flat – we thought you might as well have a proper mattress, and they have a second bedroom, just a plain little room, of course. Then you come up here for breakfast in the morning."

"It's a lot of trouble for you." At least he wouldn't sleep here, that was something.

"Of course we could put you up all the time if we moved the piano," she said with a return of her hesitancy. "But people come here for lessons – and besides you wouldn't want – I don't know what to do for boys."

He was extremely relieved that such a ghastly idea was impossible.

"I must be an awful nuisance."

"Oh, no, after all it's all in the family."

"Yes," he said, grimly accepting the fact.

"Now I'd better lay the table for supper. If – if you want to go somewhere, it's the second door on the right."

Once more she set about domestic tasks, using up a great deal of energy. If she wanted to bring in two plates it seemed that two separate journeys were required. Furthermore, she reproached herself every time for her forgetfulness. The whole process got on his nerves. Of course he was not at all critical because they evidently had no money. As a reader of the *New Statesman* he had considerable Socialist leanings, and he felt logically that it was a good deal more honourable to set one's own table than have some under-privileged, exploited person to set it for you. It wasn't that, it was the way his aunt was doing it. She looked to be an inefficient drudge, not a carefree Bohemian. And that awful cough – she couldn't help it, of course – but he couldn't help it either if he were always faintly revolted by signs of physical decay. There had been a master at school whose inside constantly rumbled, which most people thought extremely amusing, but always nauseated him. He both hated the master for doing it and felt terribly sorry for him for being like it. He had this mix-up of feelings, but more so, now.

He went to the bathroom. It was old-fashioned but, he was relieved to see, properly equipped. Hot and cold taps that worked, a small-sized bath that needed a new coat of enamel, a W.C. and a decent supply of toilet paper. Well, that was something, and it was all very clean. Feeling some relief – he had expected anything – he fetched his suitcase and took out his wash-bag. He had to admit that he didn't look too hot himself in the mirror, and his suit was rather crumpled. It was a reach-me-down from Harrods' sale, going very cheap owing to his peculiar size – he just couldn't put on weight, his legs and arms seemed to become more like matchsticks every day, and he was rather sensitive about it. If in addition the suit was slightly too big everywhere, for he was still growing, it was all too easy for the crumpled effect to set in – a most irritating reminder of adolescence. After he had washed he put in some hard work with his clothes brush. Then he slicked back his hair, which was long, straight and dark brown. Finally he removed a couple of blackheads, which he hoped Frau Dr. Bürckel had not noticed – and replaced his breast-pocket handkerchief.

He returned to the living-room, to find his aunt still flurrying to and from the kitchen.

" Are you sure there's nothing I can do, Aunt Isabel? "

She seemed quite taken aback.

"No, no, of course not, you're a man – you just sit. There are some picture papers you can look at. I forgot to ask, do you speak any German yet?"

"No – well, very little."

"I suppose it's a good thing to learn." She had paused by the kitchen door, cloth in hand. "Lots of Englishwomen who live here don't speak a word of it, but then they don't have to get a job. It's very beautiful really – Schiller and Goethe and everything – on the other hand Frederick the Great would only speak it to his horses."

This time there could be no doubt about it, she had said something amusing. She allowed herself a brief flicker of a smile while he shook with laughter. For some reason she seemed more self-possessed with the dishcloth in her hand. She stood there rather like a woman in a poor street who gossips with the neighbours from her doorstep.

But the next moment she looked anxious again, as the sound came of the front door opening.

"Hallo! Hallo!" his uncle called in German style. "You are there, David?"

David stood up. He felt rather embarrassed. It was not his fault that he had had this glimpse of his uncle's humdrum living standard, his uncle had indeed brought it on himself. All the same David felt vaguely sorry for him.

Uncle Rudi, short and dapper, came in smiling and raised his hand in the Roman salute of the Nazis.

"*Na! Heil Hitler! Wie geht es denn?* How are you, David?"

"Very well, thank you." While his hand was being shaken vigorously he noted that his uncle did not in fact look anything like as smart here as he had in England. This was not the star of the cocktail party, the lion at the club dance. The long, thin, grey hair was brushed back, but his suit was of some thick material, the necktie was cheap. Furthermore David resented the *Heil Hitler!* and was damned if he would return it – his uncle had never used it in England, he recalled. Furthermore he looked older, paler. But of course the time of the year was to blame. The *Heil Hitler!* had destroyed his vague feeling of sympathy, anyway.

"*Na!*" said his uncle. "I think you must have grown

another six inches since September! Then you were a school-boy. Now you are a man!"

"I don't actually think I've grown at all," David said, blushing. He was glad about his height, but disliked references to it.

"Eh? Not? Pfui! Look, you are a foot higher than me."

"It's a pity he's dark," Aunt Isabel murmured – she had not moved when his uncle came in, and he had not so much as glanced at her. "Otherwise he'd be a fine Nordic type."

"Yes, the dark hair is from his father. Well, David, is everyone well at home? When you write send them our love – you like our flat? It's small, of course, but very convenient, I think. Pfui! I'm hungry. You like beer, David? Let's have some beer. In England, cocktails, here, beer. Beer, beer, glorious beer, fill yourself up with right up to here – you know that?"

"I don't think there is any," came from the kitchen doorway.

"What's that?" Uncle Rudi stared at her in angry astonishment. "You knew David was coming and –"

"It doesn't matter, uncle," David said hastily, shocked by his tone. "I don't actually care much for –"

"*Mensch, Mensch!*" Uncle Rudi switched into German and spat a torrent of contemptuous words towards the kitchen, into which Aunt Isabel had retired. Her voice occasionally replied. David listened without understanding a word, horror-stricken. It seemed the most appalling behaviour he had ever witnessed. He stood in extreme discomfort, not sure that he should not interrupt and come to her rescue. This was a side of Uncle Rudi they had no conception of at home – where he had spent half his time leaping up to open doors for ladies and lighting their cigarettes. Finally the tirade stopped, Uncle Rudi turned to him with a shrug of his shoulders and gave a huge wink. At once they became a conspiracy of men. David grinned feebly back. Uncle Rudi clapped him on the back. "Women are fundamentally impractical, my boy," he whispered. "Well, I must get some supply."

He went out and David heard him putting on his coat. The front door slammed. Sounds of meal preparation went on from the kitchen. David went to the small bookcase in the corner.

334

It contained two shelves and among the books were Hitler's *Mein Kampf* – his lips curled derisively – *Kleiner Mann Was Nun, Volk, Ohne Raum*, a few yellow-backed cheap editions, probably detective novels, and a couple of *Tauchnitzes, The End of the House of Alard* by Sheila Kaye-Smith and *Thou Shalt Not Kill* by Mrs. Belloc Lowndes. Nothing there for him. On top were some newspaper magazines, the *Berliner Illustrierte*, and some old English women's papers – surely his aunt's taste was better than that? He took the *Berliner Illustrierte* back to the sofa. They were full of propaganda, of course – pictures of Hitler opening something or other, surrounded by smiling thugs in uniform. He tried translating the sentences, but it meant opening his pocket dictionary at every other word and even then he didn't get very far. When his aunt reappeared he glanced at her surreptitiously but the argument seemed not to have disturbed her at all.

" Aunt Isabel, have you read *Mein Kampf*? "

" Oh, dear, no, I'm afraid not. I ought to have, I know. It's such a long book."

" But isn't it the biggest collection of tripe ever got between covers? "

" Well, he's done a lot for them, you know – their self-respect and everything."

" But the concentration camps, and the stopping of freedom, and all the refugees – surely you don't *approve* of all that – ? "

" Well, you see, I don't know. I'm just a housewife. I wish he wouldn't shout so much – it's not good German. Goebbels speaks beautiful German, though."

" The Nordic Goebbels," David commented, giving his aunt up. She was evidently all at sea and as she was so anxious to please him he did not want to say anything unpleasant.

Then he heard the front door opening again and she went back rather hurriedly to the kitchen. His uncle returned with two very large bottles of beer.

" *Na*, here we are, David! Now! Your Berlin life is permitted to begin! "

A voice answered him in German from the kitchen – she certainly could speak it, David had to admit. The ping-pong match of quick incomprehensible sentences went on. His mother and father often had rows, of course – principally when his mother wanted to spend too much money – but even when they were on there was always a façade of politeness in front of himself and his sister. This awful lack of restraint baffled him. They must be extraordinarily unhappy together. It was distressing, quite apart from their circumstances. It was also life, of course, he reflected. He was seeing life at close quarters. Once again, however, the storm blew right away and might never have happened. Aunt Isabel brought in two glasses, and his uncle filled them.

" *Prost!* Cheerio! "

" *Prost!* " David said. " Is it true that you've found a *pension* for me, Uncle Rudi? "

" Yes, of course! We are looking after you here! I promised your mother! It's a fine place, isn't it, Isabel? "

" I don't know, I haven't seen it, but there'll be young people there," his aunt said, without enthusiasm. She had appeared with a bowl of mashed potatoes which she set down on the table. " I hope he's not expecting anything *de luxe*."

" *De luxe?* He is a student! A young man! "

David took a deeper gulp at his beer. He was a little disturbed by the trend of the conversation. He was by no means so opposed to *de luxe* conditions as they seemed to think.

" Perhaps he would be able to do a month with the Labour Service," Aunt Isabel suggested. " The *Arbeitsdienst*. I don't know if they allow foreigners."

" No, thank you," David said. He was shocked at the idea. The Labour Service referred to the hard six months on the land, road building, and so on, which all Germans had to do before entering the Army.

" Well, I was just thinking if he wants to get to know what things are like here – "

" He is too young for the *Arbeitsdienst*," Uncle Rudi said.

" He can't go in the Hitler Youth, he's too tall."

" As a matter of fact," David said in a rather strained voice, " I disapprove of all militaristic organizations, so I couldn't possibly go in one. Actually, if there were a war, I should probably be a conscientious objector."

" Militaristic! " Uncle Rudi shook his head good-humouredly.

336

"There is nothing militaristic about German youth! Why, we are all conscientious objectors, my dear David. *Prost* again – down with militarism!" No room in which Uncle Rudi was present could be precisely dreary. Having warmed up a little, he reminded David more of the guest he had been the previous September – when they had had all those arguments about the Nazis. "Of course," he continued gaily, "we are also all conscientious objectors to the Treaty of Versailles, but in that respect you can hardly accuse *us* of being militaristic – the Führer is the greatest influence for peace in the world – "

"I don't think!"

"You will learn, my boy! You will see!"

"I intend to see, Uncle Rudi."

David felt he had come rather well out of this. He had made his position clear. It was amusing to realize how little they understood his quality. It occurred to him, however, that if by chance he were involved in underground activities, say by helping Jews to flee the country, or acting as a courier for hidden Social Democrat leaders, it might be no bad thing to have this open connection with a solid little bourgeois couple.

Aunt Isabel brought in the main dish – he was relieved to see it, for the mashed potatoes had been standing unattended for some minutes. It was a plate of small boiled sausages, enclosed by cabbage.

"*Wiener Würstchen* and *Sauerkraut mit Kartoffeln!*" exclaimed his uncle. "Is this all for David? Isn't there some for me?" He laughed happily at his joke, pulled two chairs out from the table, pushed David into one and took the other. Aunt Isabel had to pull her own out. When she had sat down, Uncle Rudi said to her rudely, "Mustard, mustard!"

"Oh, now, why wait till I've sat down?" She sighed and got up again, while David half rose uncomfortably.

"Go on, help yourself," Uncle Rudi told him heartily. "A real German dish."

It was a real German dish and also a very simple one, David considered. He liked the sausages, and he had a good appetite, but it was certainly a long way from the home standard. Surely his uncle must be conscious of this? Fortunately he did not seem at all embarrassed; in fact to judge from his attitude a rare banquet was being offered. David was moved to emphasize how much he was enjoying it. It fitted in with everything, so far, the shabbiness, the tram ride. He was certain his mother would have a fit if she knew they lived like this. The potatoes were tasteless and the plates were cold. He had had better meals at school, and that was saying something.

Afterwards he had a thin sliver of cheese – he would have liked more, but restrained himself – and dreadful coffee. He had to force himself to ask for a second cup in order not to seem critical.

The rest of the evening he found agonizing. They remained sitting at the table. Another quarrel began when his aunt was washing up. Uncle Rudi went to the cabinet and brought out what looked like a mustard pot. On it was painted in little black letters, "*Die Saar gehört wieder dem Vaterlande!*" David translated, "Once more the Saar belongs to the Fatherland." It clearly referred to the Nazi triumph of the previous year, when at the end of the League of Nations mandate the Saarland population had voted overwhelmingly to return to Germany.

"Excellent! And you see what is inside?"

"What is it, black pepper or something?"

"Saarland earth!" said his uncle emotionally.

David coughed, a half splutter of amusement. But he saw that Uncle Rudi was quite serious.

"Twenty-five marks for Winter Help," came the voice from the kitchen, tonelessly. "That was the biggest swindle –"

"It was not a swindle!" Uncle Rudi snapped.

"How do we know it was Saar earth, you just have an S.A. man's word –"

"An S.A. man's word is good enough!"

"Twenty-five marks – that's what the rich give –"

This time the switch from English which David could understand to a prolonged slanging match in German which he could not lasted for about twenty minutes. He thought it was about money. Then Aunt Isabel returned to the table, murmuring that she supposed his mother hated washing up, while Uncle Rudi sighed and lit a small cigar.

"Oh, yes," David said – indeed his mother never did any,

338

but he did not add this. He felt far more exhausted by the quarrel than the other two looked, although he had only been the audience. An hour of difficult conversation passed. Uncle Rudi's manner remained rude and abrupt, except when he was talking directly to David. When there was a silence, he exclaimed to her, "Why don't you play to your nephew? You are a great pianist. There is the piano. He could live here but for the piano. Let's hear the piano."

"No, no, I don't feel like it, Rudi."

"Ah, you never feel like it. She never feels like it, David."

"I'd like to hear you play, Aunt Isabel," David said.

"Oh, dear, I'm afraid I'm not in practice—"

"Ach!" Uncle Rudi said. "She's always practising but she won't play for anyone else."

"Rudi, that isn't true—"

"Well, play us something now. Go on." He looked at her as if he were half fascinated, half exasperated. It made David still more uncomfortable. "She won't." Aunt Isabel, however, rose without a word and went to the alcove.

"I don't know what you want to hear—" she said vaguely.

"I'm afraid I'm not awfully musical, Aunt Isabel." He realized too late that this was not exactly the right thing to say, but she seemed if anything to be pleased.

"Nobody in the family ever was," she said. "Except Nicky, perhaps. He liked to listen."

He did not know whom she was talking about. All he really wanted was to leave them and go to bed. Instead he twisted awkwardly on his chair so that he could watch her, and because he was afraid to move during a performance of "good" music he soon developed an ache in his neck. Meanwhile, his aunt sat at the piano and played. Her face was as lifeless as if she were peeling potatoes, but her fingers pounded away and ran up and down expertly, making, as far as he was concerned, a fairly meaningless noise. He glanced once at his uncle and was surprised to see him listening intently. "How queer life is," David reflected, and it seemed to him that he was learning something profound. The music came to an abrupt stop.

"Um Gottes Willen—" Uncle Rudi exclaimed.

"I can't do any more, Rudi. My fingers aren't right. I caught my elbow such a knock this morning. I think that must be it."

"There you see." Uncle Rudi turned to him. He sounded contemptuous. "I told you, David. She's always making excuses. The room is too warm. The room is too cold. She has knocked her elbow."

Aunt Isabel was closing the piano, taking no notice – she might not have heard him.

"It was awfully good, I thought," David said, as soon as he was confident that she wouldn't play any more. "What was it, actually?"

"Well, it was Chopin –"

"Poor Chopin," Uncle Rudi interrupted. "You hear a little tinkle of dust? He is turning in his grave. She doesn't play him, she thumps him."

"Well, I haven't played it for months, Rudi – oh, now, I've just remembered – there's your shirt to iron, you want it for to-morrow. I must go and do it right away."

"*Ach*, her excuses!" Uncle Rudi gazed after her sardonically as she disappeared again into the kitchen. "What about another glass of beer, David? *Noch ein Bier?* We must speak German now. *Wir müssen jetzt immer deutsch sprechen, nicht?*"

"Well, give me a day or two," David said. He looked at his wrist watch. It was only a few minutes after ten, and he couldn't very well suggest going to bed yet. Another boring hour went by, while his uncle prattled away, and then the latter began to yawn ostentatiously himself. David went into the kitchen to say good night to his aunt. She was still busy over the ironing board, having found several more things to do. She seemed to be quite embarrassed at the sight of him, as if this was territory she had not expected him to enter. The kitchen was untidy but quite well equipped. He noted a calendar on the wall with a picture of Hitler and the late President Hindenburg facing each other in Potsdam Garrison Church. His aunt looked far more in keeping with her surroundings than she had when seated at the piano. It was a curious thing, but his uncle's rude and cursory attitude to her no longer shocked him quite so much.

"Are you going down now? Excuse me for being in such a state, but Rudi has to look well turned out – you know how it is with a business man."

His uncle accompanied him only as far as the landing outside the flat and pressed the button for the stair light. He sent a cheerful "*Heil Hitler!*" after him, as David hurried down with his suitcase bumping beside him. He had to hurry as the light only lasted a few seconds. Both his uncle and aunt, it seemed to him, were rather casual about his welcome when one considered how close was the relationship. They had certainly gone to the minimum of trouble, although that was better than being all over him – good God, what a dreary set-up it was!

"If they were workers, real proletarians, I wouldn't mind," he thought.

With this reflection he rang the bell of the ground-floor flat. It was opened by a woman dressed in much the same dim way as his aunt. She was older and did not look friendly.

"Good evening, I am Frau Peters' nephew," he recited self-consciously in German.

"Frau Peters – oh, *ja – ja –* "

She seemed nervous, too, and he thought, "Of course, knock on the door late at night – could have been Gestapo – " Inside there was a tremendous smell of must. She led him at once to a small bedroom. A single bed filled most of it. He said – Uncle Rudi had given him his lines – "Thank you, madam, please wake me at half-past six."

She nodded. Five minutes later he was asleep.

CHAPTER FIVE

The next morning after breakfast – breakfast had not been too bad, although he learned that the small quantity of butter was the first his aunt had been able to buy for three weeks – he left with Uncle Rudi. The latter was equipped against the cold. His wide-brimmed trilby was covered with oilskin, he had ear-muffs and a black raincoat glistening with buckles and straps, and on his feet were goloshes. David, staggering along beside him with the suitcase he was beginning to hate, felt wet through and freezing before they reached the bus stop. An icy rain was falling. To add to his discomfort his bowels had been resolutely closed.

The first stop was at his uncle's office, which was reached fairly quickly, twenty-five minutes in a crowded bus. Once again David's view of the city had been restricted. He was conscious of a mass of solid buildings and a large number of swastika flags. His uncle left him in the ground-floor vestibule, sitting on the suitcase. He promised to be no more than a few minutes. Half an hour went by. At first a stream of people had been coming in and going to the lifts and staircases, most of them apparently clerks or secretaries. David was fascinated to see some of the men pause as soon as they were inside to comb their hair back. He heard a few "Heil Hitlers" used in the place of "Good morning". A large picture of Hitler hung in the centre of one wall. The girls who passed were mostly plump and as dowdy as his aunt. None of them seemed to wear cosmetics. Another half-hour went by. Men began to arrive who looked more like executives, more like his own father. Sometimes the doorman came to attention, bowed, saluted – and there was the jocular interchange of how-are-yous between top and bottom. "Obsequious ass," David thought, but it would have been pleasanter all the same if Uncle Rudi had received this attention. Then the doorman came over and asked him what he was doing. David answered in German that he was waiting for his uncle, and felt pleased with his performance. The doorman spoke some more, louder, then shrugged his shoulders and returned. A messenger arrived, delivering a note. There was an exchange of salutes and "Heil Hitlers". "Bloody fools," David thought, watching them morosely.

Then his uncle appeared again. He was flurried, perhaps, but not apologetic.

"You are all right? Fine. We go on."

The doorman ignored them. Outside they caught another bus. Traffic was thick. After ten minutes they turned into a wide, magnificent street and got out. It was Unter den Linden. In the distance on the left he saw the Brandenburger Tor, the Berlin trademark. To the right were palaces everywhere, among them the university. It was a good deal more impressive than anything he had seen so far. They crossed in front of the statue of Frederick the Great. Uncle Rudi identified the various buildings, but he was getting a move on. The rain had now turned to a light snow.

They went across the big courtyard into the principal hall. It was crowded with students, most of whom David noticed, rather conscious of his recent schoolboy status, were at least twenty. They strolled arrogantly or busily around; he was impressed by a few whose faces were scarred. The majority wore some sort of plus-four outfit, but some were in storm-trooper's uniform, with brown shirts, belts and jack-boots. Some posters depicted a smiling, blond young man and a caption which was within David's scope: "The German student fights for Führer and People." Behind the building was another courtyard. They went to an office where David was signed up for the section which dealt with training foreigners to speak German. They crossed the courtyard again to visit another office, which dealt with students' living accommodation.

"We just call up to make sure they are waiting for you," Uncle Rudi said.

The telephone call was made by a girl with plaited fair hair, who said "*Heil Hitler!*" into the mouthpiece. The result was positive.

"Yes, they have a bed for you," she told David in English. He put down the fact that she said bed, and not bedroom, as a fault of language.

"Now we go to the bank, uncle?" he said, when they were outside. He was to have two hundred marks a month, a modest sum, but one larger than he had had in his possession before. "I'm fairly bankrupt at the moment."

"Right away," Uncle Rudi said breezily.

They walked down Unter den Linden as far as the Dresdner Bank. The snow had stopped, but once again the suitcase was becoming heavy. Inside the bank his uncle took charge, "*Heil Hitler*"-ing everybody, and it occurred to David that in spite

343

of the language difficulty he might probably be doing just as well on his own. It was not as if his uncle were anything but an underling himself. This new attitude enabled him to take a firm line when, after a good deal of formality and passport stamping, the two hundred marks was handed over, his uncle suggested that he held the money and gave David an allowance from it.

"I think I'll keep it all, thank you, uncle."

"Are you sure? It's a lot to carry about."

"Quite sure." His decisiveness surprised himself. He could see that Uncle Rudi was slightly put out, and he hoped he had not offended him. He did not want to give the smallest hint that he in any way looked down on his uncle or his aunt because of their condition.

They had a beer at a café on the corner of Friedrichstrasse. Through the window they could watch half a dozen men working on the roadway in Unter den Linden. They were busy doing something to the drains or telephone wires and they were all going at it hard. Above them there was a banner on which was painted in large letters: "We thank our Führer that we are working here."

"I'd like to see a bunch of navvies in London with a notice thanking Mr. Baldwin."

"Ah, there is not our spirit in England," Uncle Rudi agreed, quite seriously. "You see there is no slouching about here. That is the feeling the little people have for the Führer. He had reduced unemployment by over two million. You have no idea what it was like before he came. In here there would be only Jews, and outside, hungry, decent Germans—"

"Oh, but really," David protested. "You're not trying to say that those workers really mean that? Wouldn't the road have been dug up sometime, Nazis or no Nazis? And isn't that banner thing handed out by some minion of Goebbels?"

"No, no, no. In any case it is what they think."

"How do you know what they think, Uncle? Really—" He was losing his temper, but he breathed deeply and paused. What else could his uncle say, after all? One had to be sorry for him. He smiled weakly. "I'll resume the argument in a month or so."

344

Uncle Rudi paid for the beers, " *Heil Hitler* "ed the waiter, who " *Heil Hitler* "ed back. Outside in the Friedrichstrasse they caught another bus – David noticed that his uncle had a way of treating a bus with the same proprietorial air as if he were hiring a car. It was quite a short journey, they were still in Friedrichstrasse when they got out. They crossed the road and went through a gateway which led round the back of a shop to a small courtyard. Here was a door and a row of three windows, the ground floor of a grey, barrack-like building. It was not precisely the *pension* David had imagined.

" Here we are! " Uncle Rudi said enthusiastically.

David was not too impressed. However, he followed his uncle through the door, which was on a spring that creaked badly, and down a corridor to a small bare hall, where there were stairs, a plaque on the wall close by a small frosted-glass window high above the ground and a kind of pantry hatch-way. From here evidently came the smell of stew which permeated the building. Uncle Rudi rapped on the counter. A woman's voice answered raucously. Uncle Rudi said that he was Herr Peters who had just rung up from the University. The woman appeared, short, fat, snub-nosed, middle-aged, aggressive. David immediately detested her, all the more because the sharp look she gave him seemed to be critical. He figured largely in the conversation that followed as " *der junge Engländer* ". Then the woman raised the counter and came out. She wore a dirty white coat.

" A real Berliner," Uncle Rudi whispered. He seemed to be favourably impressed by everything.

The woman went ahead up the stairs, and on the first landing flung open a double door. David was horrified to see a large dormitory, a cross between the school variety he had just left and a dosshouse. It was largely empty, but four young men sat round one bed playing cards, a boy in Austrian costume sat bare-legged on another bed adjusting a banjo. A photograph of Hitler looked down on the scene. More small photographs of Hitler were pinned to the walls in various places. The central-heating system was efficient and the windows were closed, so there was a tremendous fug, mixed up with the all-pervading stew smell and tobacco smoke.

Nobody took any notice of them. He didn't care what happened, he wasn't coming in here. The woman advanced to a bed and indicated to them that this could be his. David caught his uncle by the elbow.

"This is no good to me, Uncle Rudi – "

"No?" said the latter in astonishment. "But you would have comrades and it is cheap – forty-five marks!"

"I expected a room to myself." Surely it was reasonable but it sounded childish and spoilt. He felt most uncomfortable. He added weakly, "Besides, I need a table for working – "

"A room! But a room would cost much more——"

The woman returned and another long conversation took place, during which *"der junge Engländer"* was clearly regarded as incomprehensible. David was furious, both with himself for not being able to carry off this thing with greater aplomb and with Uncle Rudi for having brought him into it.

As they went downstairs again he learnt that a compromise was possible. There was a vacant bed in a room on the ground floor which he could share with only three others. The woman knocked at a door this time.

"Sind Sie da, Herr Köhler?"

There was no answer. They pushed in. It was a tall, bare room, with the same thick air as the dormitory. The window was tightly closed and clouded over. There were four camp beds, two on either side; in one of them lay a motionless sleeper. Three pictures of Hitler and one of a monster Nazi rally were the decorations. There was a table beneath the window. On it were some books, boot-polish, a half-eaten sandwich, a mug and a shaving-mirror. Beside one of the beds on the left stood a pair of high jack-boots. The bed on the right inside the door was available for David for sixty marks a month, including breakfast, supper and a ticket for a midday meal at the students' club. The bed had been vacated that morning by a baron. The "Herr Baron" was mentioned several times with great emphasis and respect by the woman and when Uncle Rudi, himself not unimpressed, passed the fact on, David knew that there could be no further argument. What was good enough for a baron was good enough for him. "Herr Köhler", who was not present, was also a man of

346

standing, he gathered. He nodded. The woman said he must pay in advance.

They retired down the corridor to the hatchway and did business. Under the somewhat resentful eye of his uncle he took out his wallet and paid with one fifty mark and one ten mark Reichsbank notes. The woman went behind the counter and wrote out the receipt, laboriously.

David thanked her.

" *Danke schön.* "

" *Bitt' schön,* " she said. Then she gave him a large key. This was for the street gate which was closed at ten o'clock every evening.

The suitcase was dumped in the new room. The sleeper remained undisturbed.

" *Englischmann!* " the woman called after him.

She was leaning over the counter on her extremely plump elbows.

" *Leihen Sie kein Geld! Versteh'n Sie mich? Solange Sie hier wohnen, leihen Sie niemand hier nischts!* "

"She was telling you to lend no one any money," Uncle Rudi explained on their way out.

CHAPTER SIX

They walked down Friedrichstrasse. It was a busy, long, unattractive street, something like Tottenham Court Road. Every few yards, however, Uncle Rudi clutched his elbow and pointed out how clean the pavement was, how hygienic a shop was, how splendidly two young storm-troopers walked along, heads high – not slouching with hands in pockets after the manner of English youth. They crossed the bridge over the Spree, an unimpressive narrow stream, passed the Admirals Palast variety theatre, went under the railway bridge. There were a good many hotels, restaurants and beer places. Every other window had a picture of Hitler. Soon they were down by the workmen who worked under the banner which said that they thanked the Führer because they were working, and Unter den Linden stretched away in either direction. Uncle Rudi said that the lime trees that ran all the way down the centre, and gave the street its name, looked beautiful in summer. They paused at a bus stop. Uncle Rudi was to go back to work and David to return for the afternoon with his aunt.

" Are you sure you won't let me keep a hundred marks for you? "

" Quite sure, uncle, thank you. Thank you for coming with me like this and everything. I know I'm a terrific nuisance."

" A nuisance! Aren't you my nephew? You are sure about the money? "

Something in his tone made a ludicrous thought occur to David. " He wants to borrow it himself, the bastard." But he couldn't be all that badly off, surely? The dreary flat was already seeming a comfortable haven in comparison with the hostel, and his uncle had it, owned it or rented it. He must make something at his job. David turned up his coat collar to protect his ears. The breeze was freezing. He noticed the café where they had stopped for a beer and saw a card in the window: Jews – no entry. How charming!

" Well, then – " His uncle shook hands, continentally. " Now you are a Berliner! Here is the bus. Just say twenty-five – *fünf und zwanzig*. Get off at Wittenberg Platz and walk down the Bayreutherstrasse and you are there! Shall I see you for supper to-night? "

" Well, I thought perhaps I'd better settle in at the – "

" *Na*, yes! Yes, I think you are right! Well, *Heil Hitler*! Good-bye."

" Good-bye," David said, pretending a confidence he did not feel at all as he got on the bus. He caught sight of his uncle crossing to the continuation of Friedrichstrasse. There was something queerly pathetic about him. An office worker, a wage slave, how awful to think how many thousands there were like him, everywhere, in every city on the earth, how great the danger of becoming like him. He had never felt such respect for his father, who had avoided the fate so efficiently.

348

"*Fünf und zwanzig*," he said to the conductor. Success – he was understood. He had finally begun his cosmopolitan career. The bus went under the Brandenburger Tor and plunged to the left down the Hermann-Goeringstrasse alongside the Tiergarten.

He was suddenly in an excellent mood. He was free, alone and with money in his pocket. If only he were not young – it was the sole disadvantage. But he might easily be doing P.T. at school at this very moment, it was about the right time; and after P.T., it was the right day, would be the weekly New Testament period taken for the sixth form by the head-master, that august triple Blue. He was out of it! D. C. Proctor's desk was being used by someone else. "Damned lucky I'm tall," he reflected. For without that he might not have got out of it.

He had recovered from his shock at the sight of his living quarters, so different from the elegant *pension* of his anticipation. The cost of it, when one reckoned it out, was so little that there were great advantages – one couldn't have everything. And the curiously neutral attitude of his uncle and aunt was a good thing. It was amusing to think of the vast protective mantle his parents would automatically have spread over a boy coming from Germany – there would be theatres, parties and heaven knows what arranged for him.

There was no difficulty at all in getting off the bus at Wittenberg Platz. No one even looked at him. He felt very complacent. And walking along without the suitcase – and the fact that the suitcase was planted somewhere, giving him a stake in the city – made for a further sense of freedom. This afternoon with his aunt was more or less inevitable. One couldn't *ignore* one's relations altogether, but he was certainly going to see as little of them as possible. He noted a more cosy and yet fashionable atmosphere as he looked up a street from the square, and it occurred to him that he might very well become bilingual quite quickly, and then through some good fortune send a brilliant dispatch to one of the London papers which would promptly offer him a job as foreign correspondent. Why not? It was perfectly possible. He would have a really sumptuous flat, with several telephones. It would

349

be rather pleasant. Perhaps also he would be in a position to help his uncle and aunt.

He reached the house after quite a walk and pressed the bell opposite "Peters". He watched the door spring open as of its own accord, a fascinating occurrence at first sight. It seemed a drearier place than ever, though its air was more refined than his own new quarters. "Everything is relative," David thought, still in his improved mood. On the first floor landing he saw a poster on the wall. It showed a happy young uniformed woman with glistening white teeth, a shiny nose and a German army helmet. "*Frau in Luftschutz!*" said the caption. David consulted his pocket dictionary, he was becoming quite expert at pulling it out and turning to a word. "Woman in air defence" was the meaning. "Militaristic swine," he murmured to the empty landing, but he was then conscious of something even more ominous. The unmistakable sound of a piano lesson was coming from upstairs.

When he reached the Peters' landing he found their door open. Aunt Isabel's voice was intoning wearily, "*Eins zwei drei, eins zwei drei –*" But she heard him enter and interrupted herself. "Is that you, David?"

"Yes, it's me."

"Make yourself at home. I won't be long. *Nun, weiter, Gerda – eins zwei drei, eins zwei drei, immer leise, immer leise –*"

When he entered the living-room he had a glimpse of the pupil, a small girl. Aunt Isabel sat beside her with her usual wooden expression. She glanced sideways at him, as if she were trying to smile a welcome, but couldn't quite make it.

"Any letters for me?" he asked.

"*Eins zwei drei, eins zwei drei, na! runter mit dem Daumen!* No, no letters. *Eins zwei drei, weiter weiter –*"

He sat down on the sofa, feeling unexpectedly depressed and homesick. Perhaps it was the familiar photographs on the other side of the room. It was not that he cared whether he had any letters or no, but it was annoying to depend on something and then to be let down. Oh, God, what a dreary place this was! His mother had never mentioned about Aunt Isabel giving lessons, nor had Uncle Rudi. The whole set-up appalled

350

him. If they had been poor and proletarian it would have been fine, but it was horrifying to be so closely associated with the shabby genteel.

The lesson continued relentlessly. When it was finally over, his aunt led the little girl out and returned apologetically.

"I'm sorry you had to listen to all that, but her father is a captain in the Army – they don't like to be given short time, you know."

David shuddered. A captain in the Army – fancy having to care about *that*.

"Do you do much teaching?" he asked.

"Not a great deal. But you get recommended, you know. A few. It all helps."

"Yes, of course."

"It's tiring, of course, and I'm not good, really, with children. One wants to be young and hearty. Well, I suppose Sarah's beginning to feel her age." She kept on patting a wisp of hair that remained defiantly out of place. "The years go by and nothing can stop them."

"Well, she –" He was about to defend his mother, who would have turned pale at the remark about age, which she emphatically did not feel, but he thought it might be unkind. He said instead that perhaps he ought to write home, if Aunt Isabel could find him a stamp.

"Yes, that's a good idea. They'll want to know how you are. I was going to write, too. But you can busy yourself doing that while I get some *Mittagessen* for us – what would you like to eat?"

It was an embarrassing question. He said hopefully, "Well, those sausages last night were very nice –"

"You liked them? Good, I was so afraid – I have a few left – I'm glad you liked them. I'll get you some paper and an envelope –"

He could see that she was delighted. It was vaguely pathetic. In his letter all he wrote about her to his mother was: "She looks rather tired." Equally, he said no more about the flat than that it was "small". He felt rather smug about his restraint. All through the lunch that followed his aunt seemed unwilling to sit down, and hovered about like a waitress.

He couldn't imagine how they would spend the afternoon and he was relieved when she suggested the pictures.

"It's a cold day for walking about. It would be bad for my chest."

"Oh, but I'd like to go to a picture, Aunt Isabel. Jolly good idea."

"We ought really to go to a museum, I suppose. For your education. They have wonderful museums here."

"Yes, but I've lots of time for them. Do you go to the pictures much?"

"I haven't been for about — about a year and a half, I think. Rudi doesn't like it much."

She put on the shapeless coat and hat and goloshes, a process which seemed to take about an hour. Then they walked for a further hour, along one identical street after another. But the atmosphere became increasingly proletarian, and some of the inner courts had not the cleanliness Uncle Rudi said was so widespread. There were not so many uniforms about in this quarter. But when they reached a main street again it was just in time for a march past of some Hitler Youth, preceded by a band and a flag bearer. They marched extremely well, with sullen, unenthusiastic faces. As the flag went by passers-by raised their hands in the Nazi salute. Not everybody did it, and fortunately not Aunt Isabel. He hoped that the leading Hitler Youth noticed his expression of contempt.

"I notice you didn't salute," he said, with satisfaction. Uncle Rudi, he was sure, would have stood to attention and shouted "Heil!" He was glad to have been spared the shame of that.

"Well, I don't think they bother much about women."

"Really, I thought the women were the most fanatical followers."

"Oh, yes, some of them are."

"But not you."

She would not be drawn. Perhaps she hadn't understood that he was hoping she would be. In any case they had arrived at the cinema, which was showing an American film with Jean Harlow. The seat prices were 45 pfennigs and 60 pfennigs. Aunt Isabel bought two forty-fives. He had tried to summon the courage to offer to pay himself; it was depressing that even in a cheap place she automatically asked for the cheapest seat — it wasn't that he minded the cheapest seat himself, it was that terrible automatic attitude, there were years of the cheapest seats behind the way she opened her purse. Inside was the smallest cinema he had ever seen. It was no more than a large room, but it was pleasantly decorated and well equipped with about a hundred and fifty tip-up seats. It was interval time, for the lights were up. About twenty customers were seated, and there was an animated buzz of conversation. Then the show came on, consisting of advertisements — one of which demonstrated a pair of scissors for cutting off nose whiskers and caused great amusement — a news reel devoted to the celebrations in the Saarland on the anniversary of its return to the Reich, a long speech from a big-shot Nazi, a parade of brown-shirts which lasted as long as if one had been there, and finally a little blurb for the Winter Help campaign — an old man happily eating soup given out by a cheerful storm-trooper. Sighs of relief greeted the appearance of the main film and more sighs the appearance of the blonde Miss Harlow, whose racy native speech had been dubbed into German. David understood almost nothing. It seemed to go down well, and there were occasional bursts of laughter from some of the small audience, though not a sound from his aunt beside him.

Afterwards, she claimed to have enjoyed it, as they walked along in the bitingly cold evening.

"It was an American comedy," she said. "Didn't you think the girl was beautiful?"

"Not exactly a National Socialist type."

"I don't know. She was very blonde."

It was curious, but always in the moments when she seemed to be speaking ironically he felt a strong bond of sympathy with her. It always disappeared at once owing to her remoteness. He suggested a cup of tea at a café they passed. It fitted in with the neighbourhood and looked dowdy, although well lit up.

"Well, it will be cheaper at home," Aunt Isabel said. "These places all swindle you."

"I thought I ought to go straight back to the hostel, really. So that I can settle in."

"Yes, and there'll be supper for you there, of course." Her approval was slightly disconcerting. He needn't suppose that she was disappointed that he would not spend the evening with them, David was forced to reflect. In fact she became all at once a good deal more cheerful. She agreed to go into the café and smiled at the girl who served them. For the first time she showed some sort of curiosity about his mother and home in general. He was encouraged to take out his wallet and show the snapshots he carried. She was full of admiration.

"Only last summer? Why, she's still girlish, she still has a girlish figure. Oh, dear, it makes me feel very elderly."

David was uncertain whether she was fishing for a compliment. He opened his mouth to reassure her gallantly, but found it impossible to say anything. He knew she wasn't much older than his mother, but, there was no getting away from it, she looked it. Aunt Isabel, however, seemed quite content with his silence. She went on inspecting the snapshot.

"Such a pretty face. She's deserved to have everything go so well."

"So well?" David said questioningly.

"A family, you know, and a house and everything."

Evidently she was conscious of the difference in the way they lived. David felt uncomfortable. His aunt was still looking at the snapshot. Then she put it down and picked up one his father was in and one of his sister, supposedly serving an ace. They had all been taken when they stayed at an hotel in Scotland. It was a holiday he remembered with favour because, in spite of considerable argument from his father, it had caused him to be provided with his first dinner-jacket.

"It's funny to think you were brought up together," he said, and at once saw that the remark was not well chosen. He added hastily, "You ought to come and visit us."

"Yes, but the fares are so expensive. Rudi has the firm to pay for him when he goes. And then it's difficult to get away —something always happens, you know. I did try about three or four years ago, but a neighbour downstairs, her mother died, an old friend of ours, and she was so upset I couldn't really think of going away. Something always happens."

He couldn't see that a neighbour's mother dying should have all that effect, but his aunt sounded queerly pleased as she thought of her ruined holiday.

"It must be odd not having been in England for so long."

"Oh, well, there are plenty of English here, you know. There's the church, too, I go now and then. Perhaps we'll go one Sunday."

"Yes," he said, without enthusiasm. He had only recently been a strong atheist. "Mother was vaguely hoping that she and Father might come over for the Olympics."

"I know, yes, she mentioned it in a letter. Rudi and I could give them our bedroom."

"Oh, they wouldn't want you to do that, they'd go to a hotel, of course — "

"But they'll all be full and they're so expensive," his aunt said, as if the idea was so impractical as to be hardly worth discussing.

As it was dark she was prepared to waste fifteen pfennigs on a bus ride. He had to pay twenty-five as he had a longer journey. She left half-way and he felt a tremendous relief. He couldn't help liking her, but she weighed down on him somehow. It wasn't her poverty that depressed him, and anyhow, she wasn't exactly poor, it was her acceptance of things, as if she had reached a stage further than resignation. He could not stand that attitude.

He got out in Unter den Linden at the Friedrichstrasse corner. He felt already as if he were a native, although he was a little uneasy what the hostel would be like when he made his entrance unescorted. He hoped there would be no similarity to the first day at school or anything like that. He crossed to the other side and began the long walk — he wasn't confident enough to take a bus on his own yet, in case it suddenly went off in the wrong direction and he found himself lost. The street was very lit up and full of activity. There were plenty of storm-troopers and S.S. men walking around, a few soldiers, a great many slightly drab-looking, ordinary citizens. Through a lighted doorway, where a fat man dressed as a chef stood with the menu written on his apron, came the sound of an accordion mixed with people's voices. It seemed to be pretty gay inside. He listened for a moment, feeling very lonely. Then he walked on, telling himself what a terrible job the man on the door had. But that didn't make him feel any more cheerful.

The hostel gate was open. He went through into the courtyard and saw a few lights on. Voices floated down, presumably from the dormitory upstairs. He certainly did resent being forced into this semi-school atmosphere. The door clanged open and three of the residents came out, talking loudly. Two were in some sort of uniform, the third had a wind-cheater jacket and riding-breeches. They glanced at him curiously and he felt rather effete in his civilian overcoat and trilby, especially as they looked a good deal older than he was, and also as his feet were tired.

Inside there was a small crowd at the end of the corridor in front of the hatchway, and he hadn't the nerve to join it in order to greet the woman again. When he came to the door of his room he pushed it open and nervously entered. He was faced by a wiry, dark-haired youth of nineteen or twenty in jack-boots, breeches, and a brown shirt, who fiercely spat out a number of incomprehensible words.

" Hallo! Hallo! *Was suchen Sie? Heh? Wie? Wass denn? Heh?* "

" Er – " David began, shattered.

" *Der Engländer!* " said the other, at once changing his attitude to one of extreme friendliness.

" *Ja!* " David said, blushing.

The dark-haired youth clicked his heels, bowed, seized David's hand and shook it.

" Köhler! " he exclaimed.

David appreciated that he was introducing himself and answered self-consciously, " Proctor." Behind the youth now appeared the occupant of the second bed on the left, a tall, broad young man, also in uniform, who had been busy polishing his boots. He had not yet put them on. He also shook David's hand, but his approach was more phlegmatic. He murmured, " Habraschka," to which David again replied,

"Proctor." The room was warmer and the air staler than ever. Socks and underclothes seemed to have been thrown around without any regard for the supposed German tradition of tidiness. Some half-eaten sandwiches were on the table. The occupant of the third bed, who had been sleeping that morning, was not present; judging by the state of his bed he had just got up. Habraschka, having introduced himself, retired to continue polishing his boots. The other made David a long speech, not a word of which he understood.

"Do you speak English or perhaps French?" David said in his halting German.

The dark-haired youth threw up his hands in despair.

"I can understand a little German if you speak slowly," David continued.

"It iss a long vay to Teepereery!" sang Habraschka, suddenly and triumphantly, in English, without ceasing to polish. However, this turned out to be the extent of his knowledge and conversation for the next ten minutes – Habraschka took no part in it, he had had his say – was carried on in a mixture of elementary German, French, English and sign language. From it David learned that the fourth member of the room was a Pole and that supper was now available. "Essen! Trinken! Manger!" Köhler exclaimed, making a dramatic imitation of a starving man eating and drinking. He took David by the elbow and led him outside along the corridor where the small crowd stood in front of the hatchway. The woman was there, hard at work cutting bread and shouting at a secret member of the staff out of sight. She gave David a glance of recognition, quite devoid of pleasure, but at once dropped everything to take notice of Köhler. She handed David a plate on which were two large brown bread sandwiches, one jam, the other sausage meat, a knife and a mug of coffee. There seemed to be no complaints that he had jumped the queue.

When they returned to the room his companion had to go to the assistance of Habraschka, who was at last pulling on his boots. David sat on his bed and ate the sandwiches. They were solid rather than tasty, and so was the coffee. The other two were talking to each other and were no longer interested

357

in him. When the boots were on Habraschka stood up and with a self-satisfied air began smoothing his breeches and his shirt. Then they both put on military-looking raincoats. David was trying to think of an appropriate phrase for asking where the lavatory was – delicacy had shrouded the information that morning, although he knew that a wash and shower-room was close at hand – when the door opened and the Pole came in. He was thick-set, a little older than the other two. He wore an embroidered shirt, light-blue trousers and red bath-slippers. He glanced at David without surprise and murmured gently, "*Guten Abend.*" A wave of eau-de-Cologne passed with him as he went to his bed. He sat down, sighed and began to comb his hair. It was long and fair and already neatly combed back from his forehead, but he went on combing it back some more. David lay on his bed watching with his head up against the wall, his arms clasped round one raised knee. The Pole stopped combing. He searched in his toilet bag and drew out a bottle which turned out to be hand lotion.

"*Heil Hitler! Heil Hitler!*" said Habraschka and Köhler, more or less in unison, at the door. They were going somewhere, doubtless to a parade.

"*Wo ist die Toilette, bitte?*" David asked hastily, jumping up.

The dark-haired youth raised his eyebrows in congratulation at the sentence, then led him through the door and along the corridor to the foot of the staircase. He pointed to a door half-way up to the first landing.

When David returned to the room, the Pole had finished with the hand lotion and was manicuring his nails with great care. He looked up with more interest than he had shown before.

"You are Englischmann?"

"Yes."

"I spik a little. You are National Socialist?"

"No, just a student."

"I also. I am hungry. You will come out with me to eat? It is too little zey give you here. I always must go out."

David was nervous of saying yes, for the Pole's great elegance suggested that he would go somewhere expensive and his allowance would not run to that. The hundred and forty marks he had left had to last for a month. But he did not care to be left alone, and he certainly was hungry.

" All right."

It was some time before the Pole was ready. He rubbed some cream on to his face, applied some scent to a handkerchief, put on a necktie, changed his mind and replaced it with another. Then he took off the pale blue trousers and from his tall metal locker against the wall – there was a locker to a bed – he withdrew a smart dark suit. When he was finally ready he looked as if he were about to appear as the juvenile lead in a musical comedy. He slipped a light raincoat round his shoulders, the sleeves hanging loose. David wished he had not agreed to go with him, but he did not know how to back out.

They left the hostel and walked down the Friedrichstrasse towards the crowded area. Shortly after they had passed under the railway bridge they crossed the street to a large café called Aschinger. David was relieved to see that it was not expensive. The Pole ordered a small light beer and David did the same. There was a small area where, instead of tables, there were ledges at which customers could stand. Each of these ledges was equipped with a basket of rolls. The rolls, it appeared, were free. The Pole ate six one after another. David had three. Then they went back to the hostel and the Pole undressed at once and went to bed. David opened his suitcase and took out his pyjamas and his toothbrush. He went to the washroom to clean his teeth. When he came back the Pole was snoring gently.

CHAPTER SEVEN

The next morning he got up at eight. The other three were still sleeping, and they had made no particular move when he left, having washed and breakfasted – the breakfast being identical to last night's supper. There was certainly no early to rise and a good cold bath atmosphere about the hostel. This was a cheering discovery; he felt somewhat more amenable to Uncle Rudi's choice of a home for him as he walked out into Friedrichstrasse.

He arrived at the university with twenty minutes to spare and found that his class was composed almost entirely of Japanese students. Some of them were quite old; he learnt that one was himself a professor in Tokyo; and all were charming. There were also three Turks and a Syrian. The teacher was a neat, agreeable man with a slightly oriental face and a Hitler moustache. David was more in practice at being a pupil than anyone else and got along well. At lunchtime he went with two of the Japanese to the students' clubhouse in the Oranienburgerstrasse, about fifteen minutes' walk. Here there were canteens, ping-pong rooms, writing-rooms. He was able to exchange a ticket given to him at the hostel for a plate of stew. The place was crowded. A few young men were in uniform, but the majority were in strikingly individual though sombre outfits of their own invention. "I am one of them, it's really true – I am a student in Germany," David kept thinking, rather complacently. The radio played all the time, there was a loudspeaker in every room. There were notices posted of Berlin entertainments, especially of the State Opera and State Theatres. Shakespeare, Goëthe, Schiller, Oscar Wilde, Shaw were the constant playwrights. Students could get in cheaply and David saw himself becoming splendidly cultured. In the second canteen, devoted to coffee and cakes, he sat next to a fat young man who enthusiastically welcomed him to Germany. Within a few minutes he was having a friendly argument with him and two or three others on the unreasonable attitude of the Western Powers to the Nazi experiment. They said that they were baffled by the hostility of the English to a man who wanted only to be friendly. Let the English have their empire, let the Germans have a free hand in eastern Europe, the fat young man said, for that was the historical necessity and to stand in the way of it was lunacy. They were also anxious to know if he admired the works of Thomas Wolfe. He left them for the afternoon session, happy but also ashamed of himself for having agreed to a weakly platitudinous peace-

between-our-countries resolution and for not having admitted
that he had not read, had in fact not even heard of the works
of Thomas Wolfe. There really was a lot he had to get
through – on economics, for example, they had been full of
facts, doubtless false, about their former colonies in Africa –
and he, of course, was quite unable to answer. Half-way back
to the university he found an agreeable little bookshop where
he bought a second-hand copy of Shakespeare's *Julius Caesar*,
German on one side, English on the other. That, at least, was
a start. After the afternoon session he strolled by himself
away from Unter den Linden, past the rather impressive little
Greek temple affair which was the national war memorial,
where two soldiers stood guard over the little lump of black
granite crowned with silver leaves, and across into the Lustgarten. It was a big square, hung with Nazi flags and banners,
overlooked by a museum, a cathedral and the Kaiser's old
palace. Traffic crossed the south side, otherwise it was almost
empty. Some workmen were busy attending to a couple of
flagpoles and in one corner a squad of Hitler Youths was
being drilled. A young harsh voice yelled out, "*In Linie
angetreten!*" David watched them from a distance. He found
the sight distasteful. But though he told himself that he hated
them for being militarists and Fascists, he knew also that
he envied them a little for not minding what they were
doing.

He walked back past the university and the statue of
Frederick the Great, back to the shipping line offices and
banks and cafés. When he came to the one he had been in
with Uncle Rudi he thought about having a coffee. But he
saw the price on the menu card, forty-five pfennigs, without
cream, and hesitated. It was ludicrous to pay four times as
much as at the students' club. "I really can't afford it," he
thought, and was rather pleased with this adult reflection;
if it separated him from the rich customers he could see
through the windows, it gave him a feeling of unity with the
struggling masses outside. He crossed the street with some of
the latter and wandered down Friedrichstrasse, window-
shopping. A brass band playing the "Horst Wessel" song
stopped him. He looked around for a parade, but found the

noise came from a shop. Large notices pasted on its window announced: " 1918-1933 Great Exhibition of the Time of Struggle. Entrance Free. Jews Forbidden."

No one seemed to be present inside, where the "Horst Wessel" song continued relentlessly. When it finished it began again, fed into the shop through a home-made loudspeaker up in one corner, high enough to be out of reach of maddened visitors. The exhibition itself was merely of photographs of the sinister or decadent post-war Germany, mutineering sailors, soldiers with clenched fists, Rosa Luxemburg and Karl Liebknecht addressing revolutionary crowds. David glanced at them with a cynical smile, telling himself that he preferred the Communists to the Nazis. Then there were pictures of injured storm-troopers, of negro dance bands, of Jews in Berlin night clubs having what seemed to be a very dreary good time with half a bottle of champagne – surely they could have produced more damning evidence? In the centre of the former shop was a showcase containing knuckle-dusters, revolvers and knives taken from Communist street-fighters. It really wasn't much of an exhibition, and yet there was a queer force to it. It was horrible and fascinating. Perhaps it was the awful repetition of the oddly nostalgic party march – "The Eton Boating Song of the thugs," David made a note in his little book – or it was the fact that most of the photographs were now old, so that there was a historical glow to them. But something more was there, a chill in the atmosphere – the place was haunted. When he found himself in the street again, it was with an absurd sense of relief.

His next call was at an automat, where one could have coffee for five pfennigs by putting a coin in a slot and watching the measure three-quarter fill a cup. He also had an excellent cheese roll for twenty pfennigs. He caught sight of himself in a thin strip of mirror as he passed to a table. With his hat on, at a more rakish angle than he would have permitted himself in England, and with his face looking extremely pale, he might easily pass for a revolutionary. "Definitely *not* a Hitler Youth," he smiled to himself. Another Hitler, on the other hand – that seemed more possible. Hitler had most emphatically not been a Hitler Youth.

Furthermore he had lived for some time in a dosshouse, and it occurred to David that his own present residence was much the same sort of thing.

He walked again for some time and passing a cinema decided to go in. It was wonderful to be able to make such a decision without reference to a single living soul. The cinema was almost as small as the one he had been to with his aunt, but it was dirtier and more crowded. The news film was exactly the same. The big feature was concerned with the career of an ex-officer of the German Army, who returned after the war to find his country in the grip of decadence, such as mutineering sailors, soldiers with clenched fists, Rosa Luxemburg, negro dance bands and all the various items David had seen at the exhibition back along the street. The hero was seen, a large-faced, burly man, not unlike a young General Goering, observing all these scenes with a brave sadness. Invited to drink by a hard-working night club hostess, the hero angrily dashed the glass to the ground and strode out of the club – though it was not clear why he had gone in in the first place. Then came mass unemployment, and suddenly the hero was confidently marching at the head of a troop of men in semi-uniform, and managing still to look bravely sad. There were street fights, and more marching, then dramatic shots of open-air meetings addressed by a highly energetic-looking Hitler, and more marching. Finally the story drew to a happy climax with the hero looking on contentedly at the rearmament programme. David came out into the brightly lit Friedrichstrasse almost breathless with contempt.

He walked back to the hostel. No one was in the room, but the sound of a camp-fire concert came from the dormitory upstairs, folk songs accompanied by an accordion. Just as with the boys drilling in the Lustgarten, he was revolted and yet envious. Those horrifying lusty voices belonged to people who were enjoying themselves. He collected his supper from the hatchway – the woman returned his *Guten Abend* with a smirk. He had learnt that she was called Frau Döring. While he waited for the coffee to be produced he studied the inscription on the plaque above, presumably the hostel's motto. The words, unsigned, undated, were carved in modern Roman letters: ICH ABER BESCHLOSS POLITIKER ZU WERDEN. He copied them down in his book and when he was back in the room translated the sentence: I HOWEVER DECIDED TO BECOME A POLITICIAN. It did not make much sense as a motto.

"Herr Proctor!" He was sitting on the bed, about to start his sandwiches, when he heard Frau Döring call him from the passage. He got up and went outside. She was standing with two letters in her hand.

One was from his mother, the other from a friend at school; they had been readdressed by Aunt Isabel. He thanked the Frau, who shrugged her shoulders and nodded, and retired with it to the room. His mother's letter was something of an anticlimax; in the first place it was largely devoted to her fears about the sea crossing – which he had almost forgotten – and in the second it was clear that she was writing to him as if he were still at school. There was that placid assurance that nothing of interest could really be happening to him. Otherwise the news was that his father was in Dublin. His father was always going somewhere. And his sister, back, of course, for her Easter term, had promptly caught mumps. She always caught anything that was going. The other letter caused him intense pleasure. It informed him who had been made a house monitor in his place, who now had his study, who had taken his place on the committee of the debating society, who had become secretary of the League of Nations Union branch, and the prospects of the writer of getting into the hockey team. How remote it all was! How like a bad dream! It was hardly conceivable that he might still be there.

"Mother," he wrote, "you see my address as above. The journey was perfectly O.K. as I said in my previous letter. I am sharing a room with a Pole and a couple of storm-troopers. My bed was recently occupied by a baron. It makes me feel like the history of Europe –"

"Dear John," he wrote, a little later, "Many thanks for your epistle. Here I am in the middle of the Brown-shirt nightmare, sharing a room with a Pole and a couple of storm-troopers. It all feels like the history of Europe. Remind me to tell you how I lost my virginity on the Harwich-Hook boat — "

The second letter was interrupted by the arrival of Habraschka and Köhler. Habraschka ignored him entirely. Köhler, who seemed to be constantly in a good mood, saluted and murmured some sort of greeting. Inspired by the claims he was busy making in his letter, David overcame shyness and determinedly made German conversation.

"How goes it?"

"Good, thank you!" Köhler exclaimed, amazed.

"I have been to the cinema."

"Good! You're speaking well already! Wonderful! Was it a good film?"

"No, it was not a good film."

"Not good! What was it called?"

"I don't understand."

"The name? The title?"

"I don't know."

"But you speak *much* better!" Köhler said admiringly.

David was enormously flattered, although aware that what had happened was merely that owing to the day in class the German he knew already was coming out more easily. However, after this excellent beginning, he went on talking. Habraschka went out to get their suppers. Köhler told him that he came from Austria, that he was studying law and learning to be a Hitler Youth leader. The Austrians were all Nazis and only the Jews and France prevented them joining the Third Reich. Köhler turned round and put his finger earnestly on one of the three pictures of Hitler that were pinned to the wall beside his and Habraschka's beds.

"He is our Führer," he exclaimed in a voice that almost trembled.

David nodded. He was not equal to trying political argument, but in a few weeks he would be letting loose a torrent of irrefutable facts on these madmen. For the moment, of course, the game was to humour them. Köhler was now pointing to the fourth picture on the wall, which showed a crowd of fabulous size with Nazi banners and eagles all over the place.

"Nürnberg last year! Party day! This year we hope to go!"

There was a charm about such unself-conscious fervour and David was affected by it. He hoped that the dark-haired youth would have his wish. Köhler had so pleasant a face that it was impossible to associate him with the dark side of the régime.

"And what do they think in England?" Köhler then asked, more calmly. "Now they have a young king, perhaps he will be a friend to the Führer. Youth understands youth."

"Oh, yes." Now was the moment to explain to this charming political moron the meaning of parliamentary government, but the project was beyond him. Before he could go on with the conversation Habraschka came back with their sandwiches and coffee, and almost immediately after him a boy of about sixteen in a fancy Austrian waistcoat and extremely brief leather shorts. The latter saluted Köhler with tremendous smartness and a loud "*Heil Hitler!*" Still at attention, he then barked out a series of questions. After this he was invited to sit on the bed beside Köhler, who now looked full of responsibility as he gave out a long series of orders. The boy kept nodding and murmuring "*Jawohl!*"

David continued his letter, vaguely resentful at being out of things. There was evidently no more time for conversation with him. Important affairs were on – it was rather ludicrous, but Köhler and the boy and also Habraschka radiated this feeling of importance. He left them to it and went out for a walk by himself, ending up with a beer and some free rolls at Aschingers.

The next morning he soon found out what it was all about. Rather to his concern both the opposite beds were empty. The Pole was fast asleep. He had come in late. David glanced hastily at his watch, but it was only just after eight o'clock. He had plenty of time to get to the University. In twenty minutes, when he had washed and dressed, he went to the hatchway to collect his sandwiches – breakfast and supper were the same and never altered. He could feel the general emptiness of the hostel.

"Good morning," he said to the fat Frau Döring, who gave him a nod.

"Heil Hitler!"

"Where are all the people?"

"Out! Gone! All out!" replied Frau Döring.

The Pole was snoring lightly when David left. Outside in the Friedrichstrasse he was conscious of something in the atmosphere which had not been there yesterday. There were more swastika flags flying everywhere and more uniforms about. He walked down towards Unter den Linden. There were a great many people about, and when he got to the Linden itself some of them were lining the opposite pavement. Coming along from the direction of the Brandenburger Tor was a company of storm-troopers. The front rows carried eagle-crested banners. Most people saluted from the pavement as they went by. The marchers were mostly round-stomached men who would have looked a good deal more attractive in lounge suits. Some had tough, gutter faces, the toughness enhanced by their close-cropped hair. From somewhere in the distance came the sound of military music. The storm-troopers disappeared towards the Lustgarten. Nauseated, David reached the university. Very little seemed to be going on there. He went through the main vestibule to the wing where his class was held, and found this to be quite deserted. He began to feel extremely silly. In the street behind, Dorotheenstrasse, there were several hundred policemen. They were standing about in rough formation, talking to each other. He felt far too self-conscious to ask any of them what was going on. He walked hurriedly by. The street led back to Friedrichstrasse. There he found a man selling papers and he bought a *Völkischer Beobachter*, the official Nazi newspaper. He took it to the automat across the street, bought himself a cup of coffee and found a seat. Then he murmured to himself at once, "Oh, God, what a fool!" For it was the 30th of January, the anniversary of the taking over of power by the Nazis. The *Völkischer Beobachter* was a Special Number. The Führer with his arms folded and in three-quarter profile, looking solemn, kindly and determined, was there on the front page to decorate the big article: "From the National

367

Socialist Revolution to the German Führer State: Three Years of Adolf Hitler's Construction Work: by Alfred Rosenberg."

David sipped his coffee, feeling rather deflated. He had thought that he was making quick progress and surely this event must have been mentioned yesterday in class – none of the others, the Japs and the Syrians, had put in an appearance, and obviously the boy who had come into the room last night had been discussing details of some parade or other. It was very annoying that everything had passed right over his head.

He took out his pocket dictionary and spent some time making something out of the opening paragraph. The contents of the Nazi newspapers might be sensational but the layout certainly was not, nor the style of Herr Rosenberg. "On the 30th January the National Socialist movement looks back for the third time on a period of its history which has introduced a new epoch of the great struggle of destiny. Whoever wants to estimate these three years comprehensively and justly must be clear that literally everything that had meaning in the in-between Reich of the November Republic had to be altered from the roots up, and that furthermore many thoughts which were handed down to us from the pre-war period, and which in various comradely and social forms still had value, must nevertheless undergo a decisive transformation. Naked misery had millions and millions of Germans by the throat, and in foreign affairs Germany, in spite of all the soothing speeches, was not a Great Power with equal rights but merely an object at whose expense other peoples tried to pay their bills." Two columns followed, surrounding the Führer's picture with small Gothic print. David was exhausted with looking up words, and he went out again into the street. The crowd was getting bigger towards Unter den Linden, and down Friedrichstrasse came more marching storm-troopers, headed by their banners and eagles. Every few minutes another lot arrived and made its way along the Linden, with salutes from the pavement all the time. Swastikas hung from every window, there was a constant echo of military music, a general undercurrent of excitement. It was not that people looked excited – most of them, except those waiting on the

Unter den Linden pavement, were behaving as usual – but there was something extra in the air. David at last plucked up the courage to ask someone if Hitler was going to go by. He found a kindly looking man who had a little grey moustache and a felt hat. He rehearsed his German and approached.

"Excuse me, sir."

"Please?"

"Please, can you tell me if the Führer is coming?"

"Yes, yes, I believe so. Are you a foreigner?"

"I am an Englishman."

"An Englishman! Give me your hand. I was a front-line soldier in the war. We two nations will never fight again – never!"

David was highly embarrassed to find himself shaking hands forcefully.

"Yes, yes, the Führer is coming. You will see him." The man beamed at him paternally, still shaking his hand. When he let go he patted David's shoulder.

"Thank you very much." He moved out of range.

"Not at all," the man nodded. "*Heil Hitler!*"

"*Heil Hitler!*" David said, and he had gone a couple of yards before he realized that he had said it. He flushed with shame, and walked quickly away, behind the backs of people who were waiting, now two or three deep, to put distance between himself and the scene of his undoing. It took him several minutes to recover. Even the use of "Führer" instead of Hitler – he had intended to say Hitler, only the misguided Germans said "Führer", acknowledging him as their God-given leader every time they did so; but he had said "Führer" and what was worse, there had been a faint tinge of pleasure in saying it. He had been allying himself with the man in the felt hat as he said it, admitting the dictator as if he, D. F. Proctor, was one of the believers, abasing himself in fact and getting the kick that came with abasement. What was so terrible, moreover, was that he had done it as the thing to do, the decent thing – like being reverent in a church if you were not a believer. The unfortunates who were at this very moment in Hitler's bestial camps, the Reichstag Fire trial, the bully Goering, the sinister Himmler, the awful

Goebbels, the pogroms – all this had vanished in that nasty little second. It was almost a quarter of an hour before he convinced himself that, in reality, he had not been weak but diplomatic, that it would have been unkind to take any other attitude with a benevolent little man who wouldn't know what was going on whatever régime was in power. His self-esteem refortified on these lines, David looked for a place in the crowd – for, after all, he might as well see Hitler, now that he was here. Meanwhile more and more storm-troopers went on marching by. Then there was a contingent of police – heavily armed, of course. An open Mercedes drove by importantly with four S.S. men inside. The crowd kept growing and waited humbly. After twenty minutes David became exasperated. Had he no self-respect at all? Why should he get cold and footsore as well in order to swell the crowd that would applaud this ludicrous, monstrous tyrant, this *petit-bourgeois*, anti-semitic, uneducated house-painter? "I'm damned if I will," he thought, and suddenly he turned away, elbowed his way through the crowd – which had been growing further while he stood there – and walked along. He turned left into Charlottenstrasse. He knew he really wanted to stay, and he got some satisfaction out of his self-denial. If enough people would do the same and refuse to stand to watch Hitler pass, he wouldn't last very long.

Eventually he reached the students' club. Rather to his surprise it was open, though largely empty. Everything was going on as usual outside in Oranienburgerstrasse. He sat in the canteen – closed for service – and went to work on a concluding paragraph of Herr Rosenberg's article. In half an hour he had achieved it more or less. "The Führer has also often said in his speeches that if it is possible for him to-day to stand at the head of the Reich, he owes it before anything else to the fellow fighters who unflinchingly struggled with him for Germany through these hard years. But the whole National Socialist movement and with it the whole German people knows only too certainly that all attempts, however well meant, and all personal sacrifices of the best Germans would have been in vain, had not a man sprung out of the struggling crowd who, with imperturbable instinct, unshak-

370

able faith and the greatest stubbornness, anticipated the deed, lived it inwardly beforehand and thus guided us all into a new life. To-day the whole National Socialist movement thinks of all this and together with the whole people thanks the Führer for his struggle up to 1933 and for all those deeds since that hour of January 1933 of which we are all thinking to-day. . . ."

"God, what a pack of morons!" David thought, boiling over with contempt. It was fantastic, unbelievable that this one nondescript man could get people to think and write in these terms. And just then there was a crackling sound and the canteen loudspeaker came into action. An excited but reverent commentator was explaining how thousands of Berliners were greeting the Führer. Then there was the long, apparently unending, unvarying noise of cheering.

"Thank God I'm not there," David murmured to the empty canteen, and was almost ill with annoyance at having been such a fool as to come away from the excitement. He wondered if one could hear the real sound of cheering in the street, for the great man was not much more than half a mile away, if that. He hurried out of the canteen and into Oranienburgerstrasse, only to realize that the street loudspeakers were all on, so that the noise was the same everywhere. Where the loudspeakers were fixed up there were little knots of people gathered. Suddenly that famous deep voice was speaking. Sarcasm, derision, feverish crescendo – all the usual effects came out. David could not understand a word, but he watched the street scene, fascinated. Then the Führer ended whatever it was he had to say, and cataclysmic cheering broke out, followed by the music, the "Deutschland Uber Alles" and the "Horst Wessel" song, with its terrible nostalgic sigh over the street battles and heroes of the long ago. And everyone in the street stood to attention with right arm raised in salute towards the nearest loudspeaker. David felt he was concealed by the doorway, so he had no moral battle to fight. "God, what stupid bastards!" he thought.

That afternoon he worked at his copy of *Julius Caesar*. In the evening he walked to the Potsdamer Platz and then went to a cinema. It was quite late when he came out and there was more excitement going on. Up by the Brandenburger Tor there was another huge crowd and a torchlight procession was passing under the great gate. Thousands of storm-troopers were marching, each with a flare. It was surely tragi-comic that grown men should play such a childish game, but David felt his cynical amusement weighed down more and more by the Wagnerian effect of it all.

No one was about when he got back to the hostel. He went to bed.

In the morning everyone was there, fast asleep. Köhler and Habraschka were immovable lumps. David went to the University and found his class again in being. At lunch-time he rang up his aunt – the arrangement was that he should keep contact every two or three days. He agreed to go to supper. When he arrived he found she was alone. Uncle Rudi, she explained, had gone to Leipzig on business. It was a boring, but not disagreeable evening. He was quite relieved to discover that she was hardly aware of yesterday's Nazi celebrations.

"Well, you see, there's always something going on like that."

"But it's so frightful!"

"They like that sort of thing." She shrugged her shoulders.

CHAPTER EIGHT

There seemed to be no more circuses for the moment and David's life began to establish a routine. Every third day he rang up Aunt Isabel. Once a week he wrote home. Almost every evening he went to the pictures, for the sake of hearing dialogue. Lunch at the students' club, class in the morning and afternoon. As his German improved he began to have arguments with Köhler. Habraschka also came from Austria, and so did most of the inhabitants of the hostel. They were all waiting for the big day when Austria went Nazi and claimed to regard themselves as refugees from

372

tyranny. The arguments were friendly but always ended in an outburst of mystical loyalty from Köhler, who appeared to be under the impression that the English – the British were an unknown conception – though brothers to the Germans under the skin, had committed crimes which made the Germans pale, in particular with their concentration camps in South Africa. David was still suffering from an inadequate command of alleged facts, especially about England's empire. He had, of course, no idea where the greater part of that empire was, let alone what it did. Köhler knew it all, from the population of Colombo to the exports of Nigeria. Habraschka took no part in these discussions, although he listened and now and then made *sotto voce* comments to Köhler which David could not catch. The Pole was asleep most of the time. No one ever spoke to him.

It remained cold, and often snowed. Every day David would spend a moment staring at the photograph of the Nürnberg rally. The fabulous size of that massed crowd fascinated him. The Führer was a bastard, but he was certainly a popular bastard. The inscription, too, by the hatchway – " I however decided to become a politician " – this, he realized, was a quotation from the great man. It wasn't even necessary to put his name. David stared at it every morning and every evening. What a fantastic achievement – you began by laughing at the phoneyness, but pretty soon you stopped laughing. There it was, morning and evening. " I however decided to become a politician."

Köhler said, " The three great spirits of the German language are Goethe, Schiller and Adolf Hitler."

A youth from the dormitory with an engaging, pleading smile stopped David every morning and explained at length that he was short of money, and that he would be grateful for a small loan. Every morning David refused firmly. It made no difference. The next day – sometimes the same day – the explanation would be made again, without a hint of discouragement.

Most evenings, and especially at week-ends, they sang folk songs or gay marching songs up in the dormitory. David loathed this sort of activity, or pretended to himself that he

373

loathed it. He was a determined anti-scout. He did not like the sentimental undercurrent, the linked arms, the invocation of comradeship. Insurmountable barriers stood between him and joining in. He went up with Köhler one evening when the latter encouraged him. It was an hour of agony. Fortunately no one took any notice of him after a few hearty handshakes. He watched Köhler exercising his leadership talents by being the life of the party and he tried to look as if he was enjoying himself and not being nauseated. The remarkable thing was that they all knew all the words of quite complicated songs. Köhler told him afterwards that it was the duty of a young National Socialist to learn them as a help to the ideal of comradeship.

"It becomes clearer every day that I live in a mad-house," David wrote in the notebook he still kept, for the benefit of posterity. He was working quite hard at the university, but the hostel was teaching him more than the class. He made no attempt to become friendly with his Japanese co-students, for it seemed as much a waste of time to try to talk German to them as to the Pole. They arrived smiling and agreeable every morning, all equipped with elaborate cameras which went everywhere with them. There were expeditions with their dapper little teacher – to whom the Japanese, Syrians and Turks reacted like a class of moderately well-behaved children, passing notes, whispering, laughing at his jokes and so on. They went to the Zeughaus to see Frederick the Great's uniform, Napoleon's hat and Hindenburg's death mask. At the Altes Museum they looked at Greek goddesses and Roman kitchen utensils, at the Neues Museum there were Egyptian vases, at the Pergamon Museum the altar of Pergamon. At the Deutsches Museum they stood respectfully before the works of Dürer and Hugo van der Goes. At the Schloss they inspected the Kaiser's apartments. The National Galerie, the Kaiser Friedrich Museum and various others awaited their inspection. The Japanese, unable to use their cameras, were very restive on the museum trips. One day the expedition was a mass visit to a dairy. Other classes joined them on a charabanc excursion to an enormous model farm a few miles outside Berlin. It was a day devoted to cows. After the free lunch a girl came up to

374

David. He had seen her at a distance a few times in the past weeks, looking slightly distrait and rather a Hitler Maiden type. He put her down as some sort of Scandinavian who was likely to go folk-dancing. He thought she was about twenty. She touched him firmly on the elbow.

"You are English, aren't you? "

"Yes, I am, actually," David said, in surprise. "Good Lord, are you? "

She shook her head indignantly.

"Certainly not."

"Well, you sound it," he replied, appalled by her.

"Then I'm extremely sorry to hear about it," the girl said, not looking, however, altogether displeased.

"Well, where *are* you from? " he asked, not that he cared. When she told him he went on, aware of the insult, "Well, a dominion's the same thing."

"Oh, that's typically English! As a matter of fact I could tell you were English simply because of the way you were walking round with a smell under your nose. The famous English reserve – "

"What nonsense! " David said, flattered.

" – covering the English sense of inferiority."

He was less flattered, and also speechless. Furthermore he felt nervous that his face was about to redden. In half a second she had made him conscious of his age, his awkwardness, his lack of experience. The fact was that she had hit the bull's-eye with dreadful accuracy. He had spent the morning with this mixed crowd of Japanese, Syrians, Brazilians and so on, and he had hardly spoken to anyone although they were all chattering to each other with the utmost abandon and gaiety. The only Englishman, he felt wildly self-conscious, too shy to speak to anyone or to encourage approaches. Accordingly he had decided that he stood out for his sophisticated appearance amongst this crowd of gabbling Orientals and Arabs. Now he lay in ruins, no longer the suave, mysterious man from the Foreign Office but merely the difficult boy at the party who wouldn't join in. The situation was agonizing.

"You're probably quite right," he said in a pathetic attempt to be sardonic. "You analyse my social reactions *brilliantly*."

Having made her point, however, she continued in a more amiable fashion.

"They're going to show a film now. What are you doing here, besides learning German, I mean? Where do you stay? I *live* here, you see. My father works at the legation. You know we have almost as much trade with Germany as with the United Kingdom – we'd really like to make it more. The Germans are very good to do business with – you English seem to have forgotten what work means."

"I'm at a hostel in the Friedrichstrasse."

"With Germans?"

"Mostly Austrians. Refugee Nazis."

"Oh, that's most exciting!" For the first time she showed approval.

"Yes, if you like Nazis," he said.

"But don't you?" she asked incredulously, and then before he could state his position they were all being shepherded out of the dairy's restaurant on their way to another spotless barn, with cows looking at them from either side of the spotless concrete runway, and then to the spotless bottling room where respectful workers stood around in spotless white coats. To David's relief he had found himself separated from the girl and he made no attempt to get close to her again. He heard her prattling away enthusiastically, in German, of course – there was something curiously depressing about girls who spoke German – in a party of Roumanians or Italians. It was also true that she didn't bother to come near him again, even in the charabanc going back to Berlin. He ignored the slight annoyance this caused him; for it seemed as if she had given him a trial and he hadn't done well enough. To hell with her. He wished, though, that he had come out of the affair more smoothly. When he was back in the hostel, sitting on his bed, watching Habraschka work at his boots, several answers occurred to him which would have done very well. The incident had upset him.

The following Sunday he lay in bed as usual watching the two Austrians preparing for their weekly sports day. They were out and about quite early, it was not much after nine – there was no desire to meet the dawn at the hostel – dressed in dark track-suits, doing a little running on the spot to limber up for the day. This weekly burst of enthusiasm intrigued him. For six days a week sport was a closed book to Köhler and his colleague, but on the seventh day the book was opened smartly. Football, handball, boxing, wrestling were all on the day's programme, David understood.

While they were all breakfasting – the running on the spot did not cease as they ate their sandwiches – and the Pole sighed and groaned in some private sleep agony, there was a knock at the door and Frau Döring's voice was heard.

"Herr Proctor! Telephone!"

David upset his coffee and hastily got out of bed, groping for his dressing-gown.

"It is a lady," Frau Döring continued from the corridor, with a note of disapproval. She was the only lady permitted at the hostel, apart from an old laundress who came to solicit trade every few days, and she inferred that a female voice on the telephone was an intrusion.

It was, of course, his aunt.

"I wondered if you'd like to come to church with me, David."

He met her outside the English church, a building and an institution he had avoided on the grounds of religious principles and the purpose of his stay. She looked cheerfully drab as usual, and she apologized because neither the Ambassador nor anyone of importance was there.

"I *would* pick the wrong Sunday. Sometimes it's quite impressive."

The congregation was small and consisted largely of elderly ladies. But David did find it strangely impressive, since he had not before experienced hearing the familiar words abroad. Listening to Aunt Isabel praying beside him he was overcome by a feeling of pity, not only for her but even more for the elderly ladies. It was pathetic that they should all be away from home, it was doubly pathetic to hear them repeating the words they had spoken as children. How awful life was, how terrible to be a failure – they all looked failures – and to be stranded abroad, keeping up a dreary façade of respectability – in Berlin of all places.

After the service he was agreeably surprised to find himself an object of great social interest. Aunt Isabel appeared to know everyone, though not intimately, and she made a few nervous introductions. David learned that she had formerly often played for the services but that his uncle had forbidden it after Hitler came to power three years before, as he had felt it unbecoming from a patriotic point of view. While they were still in the church porch two of the ladies struggled to tell him first that he had come far too late to Berlin.

"Before '33 – *that* was the time – oh, the night life then! It's a dead city now. They say it's a good thing Hitler's cleaned it up, but I don't know, a capital city ought to – "

"Perhaps our friend doesn't like night life! "

"Nonsense! All young men like night life, don't they, Mr. Belford? "

"Goodness, are you giving me a *bad* reputation? " said a demure voice at David's side. This belonged to a young or youngish man with a rather plump, cherubic face. His dark hair, parted with immense neatness, was brushed hard sideways as if it were glued down. His skin, where it was not white, was dark with beard, closely shaved. He was dressed very formally in a black suit, a black tie, black shoes, a white shirt and a white stiff collar. All this gave him a priestly look, and David was suddenly conscious that he had seen him singing with the six-strong, mixed choir. "Who is this? " continued Mr. Belford, giving David the friendliest possible glance. "Not a *new* face in Berlin, surely! "

It was very flattering to be regarded as a new face in Berlin. David was introduced.

"For my sins, which *they*," said Mr. Belford, looking roguishly at the ladies, "will undoubtedly tell you are *many*, which may or may not be true, and in any case shall be nameless, I am a teacher of English."

"I am a student of German."

"For *your* sins." Mr. Belford was clearly pleased with him. "It isn't a pretty city, is it? "

"No, it isn't."

"I was just telling him, Mr. Belford, that he came too late for the real Berlin – "

378

"So did I," Mr. Belford sighed, and went on smugly. "Too young, too late! The torment of it! Much as I admire *der Führer* I cannot easily forgive him for taking over power before I had tasted the joys of the Tauentzienstrasse."

"And a very good thing, too, believe me. Much better for you to be a pure young man."

Mr. Belford pouted.

"You say that, and yet not a word from either of you about how the anthem went – and after we *slaved* at it – "

"Here's the vicar!" whispered one of the ladies excitedly to David.

He was introduced again and invited with his aunt to the vicar's home, a flat where half the congregation also assembled within the next half-hour. English tea was available – it never tasted the same, of course, owing to the water – and Dundee cake. It was certainly very pleasant and David was again conscious of how much it all meant to the permanent inhabitants. It was a new angle on the function of the Church of England. For his part he certainly did not intend to come regularly, owing to his convictions, but he was favourably impressed. Moreover while the vicar held court in one corner of the room David was almost equally surrounded in another, an unusual experience. He was asked his opinion of the Nazis several times by ladies who were anxious to give him their opinion. This was in every case that quite shortly the Kaiser would return.

"I was told in confidence from quite a high quarter that there have been conversations at Doorn."

"A friend of mine who knows the Crown Prince – she was riding in Dahlem the other day and met him and he almost hinted – "

"Auwie is the one *I* should like to see on the throne, and in any case how can you imagine that a Hohenzollern would lower himself to put on S.A. uniform unless – "

"You'll see. Within two years if not less Hitler will have stepped aside. The people are dying to have a Royal Family again. I've lived here for thirty years and I know. In that they're just like us – "

Mr. Belford stood beside him again and wanted details about

why he was there, and what were his plans for the future.

"Well, I'm supposed to learn German and then what I'd like to do is to go to France for a bit and then I'm supposed possibly to go to Cambridge."

"Oh, but how exciting!" said Mr. Belford. "I can tell you all about France, I was in Paris for two years, and I can tell you all about Cambridge. I was at Queen's. Do let us dine together one evening. We'll go Dutch."

David hesitated for a second. His new acquaintance jarred on him a little, but in any case he would certainly be a rest from Köhler and Habraschka. It was rather weak to arrange to spend an evening talking English, but a man who had been to Paris and Cambridge could be useful – in fact he was faintly attracted to Mr. Belford and prepared to forgo his determination never to mix with English people if it could be avoided.

"All right."

"Don't be so flatteringly enthusiastic," Mr. Belford said, a little waspishly.

"No, I meant –" David blushed and smiled. "You see, I haven't much money and –"

Mr. Belford waved a plump, white hand.

"It will be most economical, I assure you! Do you like borsch? I always go to a charming little Russian restaurant, where I know everybody. Can you manage Tuesday? I can't do to-morrow as I have to do evening classes. Come to my bed-sit at six, and be prepared to tell me all about yourself – I promise not to listen. I live quite near Kurfürstendamm, you'll find it easily."

He gave David a card, on which was neatly printed his address and his name – Adrian Belford. "Don't be late," he added severely, moving away. David was joined by his aunt, who said that Rudi would now be waiting impatiently for his midday meal and they must go. After being such a hit David could not avoid the feeling that she was a social drag on him, to say the least, and it was almost with surprise that he remembered half-way down the stairs from the chaplain's flat to the street that but for her he wouldn't have been there at all.

CHAPTER NINE

On the whole, life seemed to have become one long argument. At the hostel he argued regularly for two hours in the evening with Herr Köhler. Now he spent Sunday afternoon arguing with Uncle Rudi, who was disillusioned that he had not yet become a Nazi but excited by his progress in German. They discussed the iniquity, according to Uncle Rudi, of the Franco-Soviet Pact, the iniquity, according to David, of a censored press, the iniquity, according to Uncle Rudi, of foreign Jewish interests stirring up unfair hostility to peace-loving Germans, the iniquity, according to David, of the smashing up of trade unions. And so on, from half past one to ten past four. During this time Aunt Isabel washed up and then was constantly going from the kitchen through the living-room to the bedroom and back again, busy with domestic tasks that seemed unending. David now took both his aunt and uncle for granted, and was himself an accepted part of the scene. Consequently he was only now and then aware of his uncle's sometimes fiendish rudeness to his aunt. Moreover he had half forgotten the very different expectations he had had of them.

At tea-time he went with Aunt Isabel to a cinema. They seemed to spend hours watching the same smiling, healthy, Aryan skier fly past them down a slope. The main feature film was an UFA production which for once did not refer to the terrible days when there had been negro jazz bands in Berlin and disillusioned ex-officers pacing gloomily about. It was about a gay mix-up between two bronzed and smiling young couples. There were sports cars and a comfortable but not enormous house, servants, champagne, a lake and a tennis court; everything was gay, clean and romantic. "This is what they really want," thought David. "Surely one can learn from a people's escapism what they are like at heart?" He made a note of the thought. Anyway the drab middle-aged Germans

381

sitting around were lapping it up. Aunt Isabel, however, was silent. Her only remark when they came out was about the luck one of the actresses had had to be made a star.

"Still, I thought she *looked* rather good," David said.

He felt like arguing, as he happened to have found the actress in question rather to his taste and had even indulged in a few mild fantasies, in which he instead of the fortunate actor was in the sports car, playing tennis, swimming and sipping champagne with her. But Aunt Isabel then said that she had a slight headache, the pictures must have brought it on. David expressed sympathy – God, how dreary reality was, headaches, cold and wet streets, people in goloshes – and said that he would just as soon go straight back to the hostel, as he had work to do for his class.

"All right," Aunt Isabel said. "Anyway it would be very dull for you, as I don't suppose Rudi will be back until late. He'll have to drink beer and play skat with the Blockführer."

Uncle Rudi had gone to a weekly local meeting of the party, that was why he had been unable to come to the pictures with them.

He left her at a U-Bahn station – he had lately taken to travelling underground.

"Well, thanks awfully, Aunt Isabel. I'll ring up on Wednesday."

"Yes. Give my love to Sarah if you're writing home."

"Yes, I will. I certainly will. Bye-bye." As usual he couldn't get away from her fast enough and then a few seconds later felt a touch of remorse at this feeling. The last glimpse of her always reminded him of the lonely tramp at the end of a Charlie Chaplin film.

That evening he read *Julius Caesar* to the sound of folk songs from the dormitory.

On Tuesday when his class had finished in the afternoon he attended a tea party at the foreign students' hostel. Here there were several English people, mostly teachers working for a diploma. They seemed to David a dull crowd, and one of them, an eager young schoolmistress from Sheffield, explained to David that the phrase "*Kraft durch Freude*" – three words which were on posters everywhere and referred to the Labour

382

Ministry's organization for giving workers pleasure cruises, cheap theatre tickets and so on, and which meant, literally, "Strength through Joy" – was typical of the way the foolish, good-spirited Nazis got themselves a bad reputation abroad. "You see," she told him, "it really just means 'Fun and Fitness' or something like that. 'Strength through Joy' sounds so heavy and militaristic to us, it's so unfair, don't you agree?"

"Well, perhaps," David said, doubtfully.

The purpose of the tea party was to hear a German poet recite from his works. He turned out to be the slightly emaciated, tall and stooping type of literary man. The quiet library atmosphere was blown up, however, as soon as he actually started. The glory of the bayonet, the pleasures of death on the battlefield, the immortal qualities of the front-line German soldier were all themes he had dealt with, and he shouted the hard-wrought verses at a somewhat anxious audience – there were only about two dozen present and it was not a big room. When the poet's voice became suddenly tranquil there was a noticeable wave of relief. The tranquillity, however, referred to the strange happy quiet, the moments of peace with nature and with the soul which preceded an important attack. Within a couple of minutes he was once more shouting at them hoarsely, and in addition banging his fists on the rostrum to help simulate shell-fire.

When it was all over David glanced at the schoolmistress from Sheffield. She was standing by the poet smiling eagerly as she waited for his autograph. He went over to her.

"Lots of fun and fitness?" he murmured.

She was very annoyed.

"He was sincere, and that's a wonderful quality," she said. "I hate cynicism." Then it was her turn to step up to the eminent visitor and her toothy smile returned, together with the glazed stare of admiration.

David remembered his appointment with Mr. Belford. He left the tea party and walked round to Unter den Linden to catch a bus. He was feeling rather pleased with himself, both for understanding a good deal of the poems and for his remark to the schoolteacher. He reflected that a month

383

or so before, when he was still a schoolboy, he would have been incapable of addressing a grown-up young woman with such abandon. "A definite sign of maturity," he thought contentedly.

Mr. Belford's address was in Ludwigskirchstrasse, two streets south of the fashionable Kurfürstendamm – a quarter David had seen little of. Mr. Belford was watching for him from a ground-floor window, and let him in.

"Really I thought you weren't coming. It's already ten past six," he greeted him disapprovingly. He didn't look quite so spick and span as on Sunday. The face and hair were the same but instead of the dark suit and white stiff collar, he was in a sports jacket, grey flannels, a check shirt and woollen blue tie.

"I'm awfully sorry, Mr. Belford – "

"Oh, my God, for heaven's sake call me Adrian! "

"I had to listen to a poet."

"Even that does not quite mollify me," Mr. Belford said. "Now come into my parlour, we'll have a glass of *vermout*. Why do you wear that awful hat? I shall feel I am going out with a commercial traveller from Wigan. Take off your coat and sit on the divan."

David obeyed in some astonishment. It was a small room and appeared to be in use as some sort of chapel, for the dimly-lighted walls were decorated with small sacred images and little mosaics, some equipped with candlesticks, in one of which a candle was burning. All this was so curious that he forgot his resentment at the remark about his hat.

"Ah, you're looking at my icons," Mr. Belford continued. "Aren't they lovely? My one extravagance, together with seventeenth-century prayer books."

"Aren't you a little High Church for the vicar? " David enquired.

"M'yes, I suppose I am a little," Mr. Belford giggled, opening a cupboard. "And I'm so glad to hear that my guest is witty."

David sat himself more comfortably on the divan, while the host produced a bottle and two glasses, which he set down on a table.

"It's a very nice room," he remarked.

384

"Yes, I'm rather proud of it, and it's wonderfully cheap. Thirty-five marks a month." Faint echoes of mild celebration came from within the flat. "That's my landlady and husband. They're Jews, poor dears. They're having a birthday party to-night with guests – I was invited in to drink a toast, a great honour. They're so nice – I feel that renting a room is at least one's tiny little contribution, you know."

"Yes," David nodded approvingly, and felt that a point in his host's favour had been established. He accepted his glass, hoping to look at his ease. Mr. Belford sat on a wooden arm-chair and smiled at him.

"Well, *à ta santé*, David, or as I believe we say in England, cheerio."

"Cheerio."

"Oh, dear, you make me feel more and more like Tonio Kröger every second, if you know who Tonio Kröger is? "

"I'm afraid I don't." He couldn't help it, he began to feel awkward again.

"Well, he's the hero of a wonderful short story who happens in a way to symbolize me, an artist with a sort of adoring envy of ordinary people – don't look so insulted, I don't mean you are ordinary, David, any more, alas, than I am an artist. Do you read? You see, I'm trying to find out about you. What have you read? Who is your favourite author? Henty? Captain Marryat? "

David confessed self-consciously to Aldous Huxley and Sinclair Lewis. Mr. Belford seemed less impressed than he had hoped.

"When we come back from dinner I shall show you my books and I may even permit you to borrow one. I'm already beginning to feel like Socrates with a young Athenian noble to instruct."

David sipped his vermouth and stared hard at the carpet. He found the idea flattering, though not entirely comfortable.

"You realize, of course, that the whole basis of Nazi Germany, whatever you may think of some of its manifestations, is a vast hellenistic revival? " Mr. Belford went on. "Fair, lovely Hellas lives again and of course the Olympics this year add the final touch. Over our *borsch* I may embroider this theme for you."

"I'm reading *Julius Caesar* at the moment in German," David said, feeling this was more or less appropriate. "Well, actually the German is one side and the English the other, I admit. But I must say it's frightfully good." He rushed on enthusiastically, encouraged by the sound of his voice. "It was rather funny last night. A chap in my room burst in just when I was reading some of it out loud. '*Ein Dichter!*' he cried— you know, 'a poet'— and he pulled my leg no end about it—" He tailed off rather weakly, conscious that the anecdote was lacking in strength.

"Shakespeare!" Mr. Belford murmured with a sigh. "I allow you the sonnets, of course, but *Julius Caesar*— you'll be telling me you like the *Pickwick Papers* next. Dear me, I can see I have a long way to go." Then he raised his tone a little. "A chap in your room, David, did you say? What chap? Do you share a room, then?"

"Oh, just an Austrian."

"An Austrian—but I thought you were with the Foreigners or something, you told me on Sunday—"

"Oh, I don't live there. I'm at a hostel place in Friedrichstrasse with a lot of S.A. men and students and Hitler Youths and people. I say, do you really only pay thirty-five a month? I wouldn't mind a room like this myself."

Mr. Belford leaned forward, much moved.

"David, you're *living* with S.A. men and Hitler Youths —what an extraordinary place to find! But how did you—"

"Well, it was through my aunt, or rather my uncle—"

"Oh, yes, Frau Peters, I'd forgotten—a charming woman—" Mr. Belford rocked to and fro, one hand against his forehead, alone with thoughts which apparently did not cheer him. Finally he sighed deeply.

"It's pretty uncomfortable, you know," David said, feeling rather at a loss. "There are four in my room altogether. There are a few other rooms, but none single, and there are stacks of people in a dormitory—they sing ghastly folk songs all the time, or marching songs like *Sturm! Sturm!*

386

Sturm! But there are quite good showers and of course it's awfully cheap."

"May you die at twenty," Mr. Belford said. "Are you hungry? Let's go and eat."

When they were walking along in the street David wished he were a little less tall. Mr. Belford, who wore a rather impressive overcoat with a big belt negligently tied in front, seemed to float along at a level two or three inches below his head, swaying neither up and down nor from left to right, while David kept bumping into him – an experience he often had when he was slightly ill at ease; he just couldn't walk straight. Mr. Belford wore no hat, and David had also left his behind, overcome by the criticism. Aunt Isabel had also mentioned it, he remembered. It would be hard to wear it again.

Mr. Belford's mood improved at once as they entered the restaurant, which was small, clean and cosy. He was greeted by the proprietress and a waiter in Russian, and he replied in Russian. It was enormously impressive. Everyone shook hands, and David was introduced by his companion rather as if he were a prize exhibit. They sat down at a table beneath a yellowing photograph of the late Tsar and his family. They had *borsch* – "the soup that has *everything*," Mr. Belford said gaily – and also a glass of vodka each. David enjoyed himself. He became talkative. He described the poet's recitation and the schoolteacher he had spoken to. Mr. Belford was amused and both were brilliant in diagnosing the German character.

"Fun and fitness! It's such a ghastly mistake! Strength through Joy really *is* the translation."

"Or Joy through Strength."

"*Freude durch Kraft,* yes!"

"Anyhow it must have some sort of mystical overtone. Heroism, comradeship, honour – the kind of things no one dares mention in England – "

"Yes, David, comradeship especially – like the Greeks – "

"And do you notice how if you argue with them they always blow up into some vague sentimental fog and absolutely lose the drift of what they're saying – "

"Well, sentiment is something I rather approve of, David; in fact if I have a soft spot for the party it is that they *do*

387

accept sentiment — I believe one of the most moving experiences one can have is to be at the Nürnberg rally when the Führer is dedicating the flags — with all those hundreds of thousands standing rock still, and a gun firing with that terrible sort of tense silence between each burst, and the 'Horst Wessel' being played softly — every second changed with tremendous significance—"

"I know exactly what you mean. There's a little exhibition in Friedrichstrasse I visited—"

They went back to the room afterwards and Mr. Belford lit the candles in front of the icons. They had arranged to meet again next week. Conversation had become literary and Mr. Belford spoke of the works of Gide. Then he insisted on reading aloud some French poetry. Verlaine and Rimbaud were the authors favoured. Half an hour went by. David was hard put to it to conceal his boredom and also his lack of comprehension of Mr. Belford's impressive French accent. In any case this sort of thing seemed to him most embarrassing — he understood getting worked up about poetry, but one had to be alone, it had to be private. When he could stand it no longer he began to look impolitely at his wrist-watch and to clear his throat.

"I really ought to be going, Adrian," he said at the first opportunity.

"Must you? All right. Just listen to one more."

"Well, only one."

"Really, I've seldom had a less flattering audience. I am accustomed to being asked to go on, not to stop."

David began to smile, but then realized that Mr. Belford was extremely put out, and, though thinking him an idiot, he was nevertheless concerned. He did not want to hurt his feelings.

"I was enjoying it, honestly," he said. "That last one was awfully good—"

Mr. Belford sighed furiously.

"Go back to your Hitler Youths, my dear boy. I'm sure you find them much more entertaining."

"Well, I really must go," David said, getting up awkwardly. "I've actually got some work to do for to-morrow and—"

388

" Of course, of course."

He put on his overcoat. Mr. Belford stood in the middle of the room, managing to look severe and hurt and pathetic at the same time.

" Well, I'll take that book you mentioned with me," David said heavily. He meant it as a peace offering, not that he could see what all the fuss was about. He was annoyed that his voice seemed tense and nervous. He picked up his hat.

" What book? " Mr. Belford asked in a distant voice.

" *Les – Les –* I forget the name –" David gulped. He refused to attempt a French pronunciation.

" Oh, *Les Faux Monnayeurs*? "

" Yes."

" Certainly." Mr. Belford jerked his head back, turned to his bookshelf and then handed the novel to David at arm's length. " Please don't turn down the pages. Use a bookmark. You can *send* it back to me when you've finished it."

" Yes, all right." David was uncertain whether the last remark meant that their proposed meeting next week was now cancelled.

Mr. Belford saw him to the street and murmured a stiff " Good night ".

" Thank you very much, good night." David tried to make his response unruffled and cheerful, but felt that he had only succeeded in being impudent. He walked along furiously. Mr. Belford was a bloody fool, but what annoyed him was his own ineptitude, firstly in being unable to bring the poetry reading to a smooth end and secondly in allowing himself to be the one who was in the wrong. He put on his hat, which he had been holding. To hell with what Mr. Belford or his aunt thought, *he* thought it looked all right. After he had caught his U-bahn train and found a seat, however, he took it off. He returned to the hostel in a faintly worried state of mind.

CHAPTER TEN

A corner of dissatisfaction about the evening remained in his mind for the rest of the week. On Thursday the Pole invited him out, but he had arranged to go with his aunt and uncle to an "evening of culture", organized under the Party auspices – at which a group of middle-aged Germans and their wives were harangued by a young man from the Ministry of Propaganda.

His aunt sat through it all with a placid expression on her face. The chairs were hard, the lecture, so far as David could follow it, was concerned with the racial origins of European peoples. There was something very sad in that audience of mature faces, mostly over-fat or criss-crossed with age lines, faces with discontented mouths or unattractively smug looks – no one there looked particularly nice, David thought, except his aunt, who was clearly not listening at all. And except possibly the lecturer, who was such a mass of words that there came no second of revealing ease in which his dark and curiously un-Aryan features might have disclosed a human being. When he finished, after a non-stop three-quarters of an hour, he wheeled round at once and saluted the portrait of Hitler which was on the wall behind him. Then he shook hands with somebody and marched quickly out of the room – they were meeting in a school. He was off, Uncle Rudi said, to address another local group. That, he added proudly, was the kind of energy that the movement generated in its young officials.

David noticed that his uncle was very attentive to his aunt in the subsequent coffee and biscuits period, and also to other women – in fact he was being almost as affectedly charming as he was in England. He introduced David to various rather dull people who were even discussing the lecture with interest and approval.

"I'm afraid he was rather bored," Aunt Isabel said afterwards. The three were walking together and she discussed him with his uncle in the third person, a habit mildly irritating to David.

"Not at all, it was very interesting," he said.

"It shows him what goes on," his aunt continued, with her faintly ironical note.

"Do you go often to that sort of thing?" David asked.

"About once a week usually."

"Once a week!"

"Well, sometimes it's quite – it's more interesting than to-night. It develops our *Weltanschauung*, you see. Our point of view. Besides, we have to go, you see, the Blockführer – "

"*Das ist ja Unsinn!*" Uncle Rudi interrupted her angrily, and one of their furious arguments sprang up, in which he repeated endlessly that she knew quite well there was no question of being forced to go to the lectures. It was embarrassing to David, although he was used to it.

The next day the Pole invited him out again when they met at the students' club, but he had to refuse once more. A great event had happened that morning. He and three of the Japanese had been told that, starting next week, they were to go to the higher class. The Japanese were quite exultant and invited him to go out that evening to celebrate.

"I'm awfully sorry, Stefan." He was on first-name terms with the Pole because the latter's surname was impossible.

The Pole looked dejected.

"You do not like to come?" He spoke in English and the broken accent helped to make his question pathetic.

"I'd like to come very much, really I would," David said, feeling ridiculous. It seemed that nothing would go right in his relations with people. He was always being put in the position of hurting their feelings. He hardened a little as he caught a touch of perfume. "I just can't, that's all." The Pole sighed tragically and he added, furious at his weakness, but with his conscience eased, "I'll come out with you to-morrow, if you like."

"To-morrow, very well," said the Pole, cheering up a little, though grudgingly.

David was left feeling angry. However, there was to-night's night out and he was quite excited about it. None of the Japs was young, but they looked as if they liked a good time. He was hopeful that there would be women, and a plunge into night life.

The meeting with his classmates took place by arrangement in the entrance of Haus Vaterland in the Potsdamer Platz. The Japanese were full of smiles as usual, which now and then made him feel uncomfortably that they were amused by him, and they had the look of prosperous tourists prepared to sample the pleasures of the town. David tried to be casual, as if he were always doing this sort of thing. He was a little chilly for he was not wearing a coat, and certainly not his hat, while the Japs were in luxurious teddy-bears. He had to pretend that the English never wore coats. In fact he had left it behind so that he could avoid any possible cloakroom charges.

It turned out that he need not have worried. After some discussion, they all walked up the street to the Münchener Löwenbräu Keller and there in a cosy atmosphere of dark wooden tables drank beer for the rest of the evening. It was enjoyable and to some extent a relief, but he returned deflated and annoyed.

The next evening was equally an anticlimax. The Pole spent an hour dressing himself and refused to commit himself about the night's entertainment. A brothel? "Or is he going to seduce me himself?" David thought. When they set off, to walk beside him was like wandering through a garden in July, so indulgent had he been with his bottles. The cuffs which protruded beyond his sleeves were of a whiteness never achieved by the laundrywoman David patronized. And, as before, they went to Aschingers. This time, however, it was not for beer and free rolls. They had a table and, the Pole recommending, ate a Königin Pastete each, a rather tasty pastie affair which David drowned in Worcester sauce. They were having a not too interesting discussion about the pronunciation of "Worcester" when the reason for the evening appeared, a friend of Stefan's, who came up with the confident smile of one who knew a place was ready for him. Stefan's

392

affected surprise was both amateur and pointless. The friend was also a Pole, unperfumed, brisk and rather hearty. The point was, it turned out, he was about to visit England. Could David change some currency for him? Would he estimate the cost of lodgings in London, in Birmingham, in Newcastle? Did he know of any addresses that might be useful? What was David's address, so that the Pole could take greetings to his family? It was all very irritating.

The next night he went proudly alone to a film called *The Lives of a Bengal Lancer*, at a quaint antiquated cinema like a ballroom in Unter den Linden. The dialogue was in English, but the audience was moved to tears, as if any form of military loyalty or glory stirred them, German or not. " God, what a bunch! " David thought at the end, looking round contemptuously at the handkerchiefs, hearing the chorus of coughs and sniffs.

The next day, a Saturday, the Führer sent his troops into the Rhineland.

David went to the students' club to hear the big speech. " The Führer speaks to the world! " said newspaper headlines on the way, with rather childish pride. " The whole world is listening to the Führer! " The speech went on and on, as usual, with groups in the street and everyone in the club looking serious and not particularly elated. David wondered uneasily if there would be a war and was rather ashamed when he realized that his unease was entirely on account of what might happen to himself. Sarajevo, lights going out all over Europe, dramatic interruptions of the garden party, a dreary man with an awful moustache pointing a finger out of a poster and, oh, God, white feathers – these were the vague associations his early education had provided him with for the word " war " and somehow now meant more than Beverley Nichols' *Cry Havoc!* or the Peace Pledge, or the realistic novels and exhibitions, the accumulated facts and literary experiences of the last couple of years. He considered: would he have the courage to be a pacifist? Would he be interned? In a concentration camp, perhaps, things might move very quickly. For a moment real panic seized him, but everyone looked so calm that it died away. If there were an ultimatum he could prob-

N*

ably get out—fly home and join up, and within a month or two become another—what were those old names—Jack Cornwall, V.C.? Or die with a bayonet in his stomach? But so marked was the absence in the students who sat around, even the ones in uniform, of any manifestation of belligerence or patriotic exultation that his anxiety died away altogether.

He rang up his aunt. She reported that Uncle Rudi was in a state of great excitement. She certainly was not herself, although David thought he could detect a hearty, almost cheerful note in her voice when she wondered if he ought to return home.

"I'll speak to the Consulate and ask their advice. After all, you never know what may happen. We don't know what Britain and France may do."

But Uncle Rudi interrupted her and took over the conversation.

"Pay no attention to her, David! She is being ridiculous! Of course nothing will happen! You heard the Führer's speech? The whole thing is justified, of course. France has broken Locarno! We can depend on England to take a correct attitude. This time surely the Führer's peace appeal will be listened to."

David did not have to answer, for his uncle seemed to have turned aside to reply to some comment made by Aunt Isabel. Angry German sounds came from the receiver, then his uncle's voice continued cheerfully.

"No, no! Everything will be all right. It is a great day, a historical day."

"Yes, uncle."

"There, you agree?"

"No, uncle, I think international agreements should be kept," David said. He felt it was rather brave of him to say so, even in English, since the line was probably tapped.

"But France—" began Uncle Rudi, who was, however, interrupted once more. Another background argument took place, it was rather like his first evening in their flat. He felt a certain respect for his aunt. Finally, Uncle Rudi said, "Excuse me. Your aunt—will you come to tea to-morrow?"

"Yes, thank you, if I'm not interned," David replied,

394

conscious of how splendid it was to be able to make such a remark, even a quarter seriously. After all it was possible.

Uncle Rudi was shocked, but at once laughed heartily. " Na, good, then! *Heil Hitler*, David."

" David, don't go about mixing with people," Aunt Isabel's anxious voice broke in. " It's so easy to get into some trouble, if they're in a mood – you don't know what it can be like – "

" Oh, I shall be perfectly all right." He was most irritated.

" Just stay in the hostel and don't argue with anyone, whatever you do."

He said good-bye almost curtly, appalled by so cowardly and defeatist an attitude. Moreover, he felt that he knew a good deal more about the mood of the streets than his aunt, busy cooking indifferent meals for Uncle Rudi.

He had another coffee – it was terribly easy to waste time in the students' club and already some expert time-wasters were playing skat again – and then went back to the hostel. No one was in. He read *Julius Caesar* for a time and then two pages of *Les Faux Monnayeurs*. Suddenly Köhler and Habraschka burst in. A good many others had returned with them and their shouts and their boots echoed over the building. They had all been to Wilhelmstrasse, under the Führer's balcony. Köhler shook hands with David and slapped him on the back.

" You ought to have been there, Herr Proctor! You would have seen the Führer! And Goering as well! "

" And Juppy," added Habraschka, who was in an unusually good mood. Juppy was their pet name for Dr. Goebbels.

" It will be Austria next! " cried Köhler, flinging himself on his bed with a great exultant sigh.

David was annoyed that he hadn't thought of going to Wilhelmstrasse, but consoled himself that it wouldn't have been in the best of taste for an Englishman to be there. To confound his aunt, however, he decided to go somewhere. On the way out he met the Austrian youth who was always trying to borrow money.

" Oh, excuse me, I'm very short – I wonder if you could help me out for the week-end? "

" I'm awfully sorry, I have no money either."

395

The Austrian bowed obsequiously like a waiter, then flashed a smile and saluted.

"*Heil Hitler!* So sorry."

"*Heil Hitler!*" answered David, who had now weakly fallen into the habit of using this formalized greeting, except with Uncle Rudi — it saved trouble, he told himself. But underneath, he wondered, was there not a secret conspirator's shame? Was he at heart treacherous? Did he not rather admire the self-sufficiency of Köhler and his Hitler Youth comrades? He worried about these questions in much the same way that he had worried once about survival after death.

There was no sign of any excitement in the streets. Only when he bought a bar of chocolate the plump, middle-aged Hitler behind the counter said, "Well, what will England do?"

"Nothing, I suppose, unless France does something."

"Then it is peace!" said the shopkeeper dramatically, as if the whole matter had now been disposed of. He shook hands effusively.

It was at any rate still peace the next day, Sunday. The usual sports meeting of his room-mates had been cancelled. Köhler explained that they would all be very busy with the coming election, in which the Führer was asking approval of his action — and the whole hostel remained indolently under the blankets. Occasionally a red-eyed, unwashed figure went to the hatchway to collect coffee and sandwiches. At tea in the afternoon, Uncle Rudi was almost unbearably complacent. He was particularly pleased that Aunt Isabel's advice had so far turned out to be pointless. She shrugged her shoulders.

"Anyhow, the most important thing is that I'm going to a new class to-morrow," David said.

On the way back to the hostel he saw an enormous picture of the Führer being erected over the entrance of the Potsdamer station. "I, however, decided —" he murmured appreciatively.

CHAPTER ELEVEN

The new class was on a floor higher, but otherwise there was little difference. There were a few more Syrians and Turks, but the general effect was still predominantly Japanese. The teacher was rather less sympathetic than the old one, a pasty-faced young man with a Prussian haircut and an unmelodious accent. For a time there seemed to be quite a bond of loyalty between David and the old classmates who had moved with him. Their smiles embraced him with paternal fondness.

Outside the university the election was already making itself evident. A lorry-load of storm-troopers shouting slogans had passed him on his way down Friedrichstrasse, noticed with vague, certainly not exuberant warmth by the going-to-work crowds. There were large posters on all the kiosks which advertised theatres and cinemas: "NSDAP Greater Berlin district – Minister of the Reich and Party Comrade Dr. Goebbels opens the Election Struggle on Tuesday, 10th March, in the Deutschland Halle – Admittance 18 hrs. – Start 20 hrs." The press was trying hard, the ponderously vulgar *Völkischer Beobachter*, the hysterical *Angriff*, the Roman-printed almost civilized *Berliner Tageblatt*, all shrieked banner headlines. It was already clear – to David's considerable relief, which he at once convinced himself was the opposite – that France was doing nothing, that England would do nothing, that Hitler had won again and that everyone abroad was settling down uneasily. He couldn't help thinking how wrong Aunt Isabel had been, and how somehow inevitable it was that she should be wrong. He hoped she hadn't disgraced him by ringing up the Consulate.

At the students' club there was a rise of enthusiasm in the atmosphere. Where yesterday and on Saturday the murmur had been low-pitched and serious, there were now bursts of hearty laughter, everyone was loud and manly, not least the beefy girl students, who were especially full of *joie de vivre*. In the evening he went to a cinema and Hitler's appearance in the news film was applauded from all over the theatre. Normally there were only four or five dutiful claps, always giving the queer impression that the clappers were teacher's favourites setting an example, and, shielded by the darkness, nobody else bothered. When he returned to his room there was the old G.H.Q. atmosphere centred on Köhler – a succession of uniformed or Austrian-costumed youths arrived to discuss what were apparently to be their duties in the election. Köhler had it all down on long sheets of squared paper, and the whole thing was treated with great seriousness, and much saluting. David lay on his bed watching it all for some time before he became conscious that something his head had dislodged on to the floor was in fact a letter. He picked it up and opened it. He read, "I shall expect you to-morrow evening (Tuesday) punctually at six-thirty. Adrian."

He was astonished and rather exultant. What a triumph! A man who could hardly be less than twenty-five had bitten the dust before the seventeen-years-old Proctor. Perhaps, after all, his behaviour last week had not been so boorish. He drew his knees up to his chin and rocked to and fro, feeling extremely self-satisfied, although the prospect of more French poetry was daunting.

The next morning he went along Dorotheenstrasse to the university's back entrance, smiled at the storm-trooper who stood on the corner with a Winter Help box, chatted brightly to one of the Syrians, whom he picked up on the way, a dark young man who spoke German fluently in a lisping, high-pitched, sing-song – he was an enthusiastic explainer of the faults of British Middle Eastern policy. Election slogans were posted up everywhere, looking rather ludicrous since there was no opposition, but this morning the horrifying comedy of dictatorship passed David by. He felt as if the world belonged to him more than it had before. The world was always slipping in or out of his grasp. It was absurd to be elated by such a trifle as Mr. Belford's letter, it gave him the same kind of pleasure that a chance eavesdrop at school had once given,

398

when "Oh, him, he's all right" had been an intoxicating phrase. In the same way, Mr. Belford's letter was a kind of acceptance into the adult world.

In class he was more talkative than usual and the Herr Doktor, who had been chilly towards him yesterday, gave him some benevolent attention. He went to lunch with the Japanese, and even his elbows and feet, always five per cent out of control when he was talking to people, became co-ordinated. He was already deciding to expand his social life – there was the plan, for which he had so far lacked the confidence, to ring up that woman he had met on the train. After all, she had given him her card. "Won't you drop in for a cocktail?" he could almost hear her saying. Frau Dr. Bürckel. He would do it this evening.

He returned to the class a little late. He apologized to the Herr Doktor, who was in the middle of describing a proposed visit to Potsdam, and though his new confidence sustained him he must have been slightly confused, for he did not notice the new pupil until half an hour later, when the Herr Doktor addressed her as "Fräulein Robinson". He did so with a certain unction and David, looking sideways, saw the girl who had been on the outing to the dairy. She sat at her desk sucking a pencil and frowning. She looked a good deal more attractive than the other day and he immediately forgot about not only Frau Dr. Bürckel, but the Herr Doktor's lesson. He was at once convinced that it was a stroke of fate, and at the same time he was worried about how old she was. Ideally, he wanted someone slightly younger than himself or, following a different dream, twice as old, a Frau Dr. Bürckel, who might be drawn by his inexperience and leave him a veteran. A girl of twenty or twenty-one, as he judged her to be, might be too much for him. He was anxious.

"Herr Proctor?"

His name woke him up.

"Will you continue now, Herr Proctor?" said the Herr Doktor, with a faintly resigned tone that seemed to announce that he was lost among foreigners.

They were reading an excerpt from *Wallenstein*. David found the place and performed nervously and badly. There were only two afternoon periods and in the interval, when they all wandered into the corridor, he went right into the attack, elbows and feet once more out of control. She stood talking to two Turks. David pushed in beside them, like someone at a cocktail party determined to begin a conversation, and since the three ignored him he fell immediately into a state of paralysis. He couldn't follow what they were talking about. Something was beautiful, they were all agreed – could it be *Wallenstein*? No attempt was made to enlighten him. But suddenly she turned, with her head imperiously up and back, so that she regarded him through lowered eyelids, although she was rather short.

"Hullo, are you in this class now?" She spoke now in English.

"Yes."

"I've been away for the week-end in Mecklenburg. Weren't you on that outing the other day?"

"Yes."

"I thought that was where I'd seen you."

They returned to the classroom. He was speechless with annoyance. She *thought* that was where she had seen him, while he remembered almost every word of the conversation they had had. He had been all ready with a racy remark about Robinson being a curious name for someone who disapproved of the English so much. It died before being uttered.

He spent the second period in a fury, glancing sideways only to reassure himself what a frump she was. In profile he saw a forehead normally creased into a frown as she concentrated on the lesson – German proverbs – a small, more or less straight nose, which shone a little, and a short neck. All this was topped by straight, yellow hair bobbed and cut in a fringe across the forehead. The effect was Hitler-maidenish. Furthermore, her voice had been queerly high-pitched and seemed to sustain one note all the time. He decided to ignore her.

They were finished at four. David was always fascinated that grown men, some middle-aged and highly qualified, behaved similarly to English schoolboys at this moment. The
400

same sigh of relief went up from Japanese, Syrians, Turks, everybody; there was a communal sense of escape.

He was on his way down the stairs when he realized that she was beside him.

"What was your name?" she said. "Proctor?"

"Yes."

"Thank heavens there's someone young at last."

"Oh?" he said, astonished. He was not sure how to take it. If she were bracketing herself with him in the matter, that was one thing. Otherwise he had no wish for youngness to be his trademark.

They reached the courtyard.

"I've been here for two months now, surrounded by dotards," she went on.

"At least they're not English, I suppose that's a comfort for you."

"Ha, ha," she replied, looking at him gravely.

"It amused me to hear you called Robinson. It must be most embarrassing."

"It's just what I said," she told him. "You English are so ridiculously sensitive."

"Well, I'm glad you remember what you said."

She was off-balance for a moment, and he saw it, but she recovered at once.

"I haven't any prejudice, as you seem to think. As a matter of fact, next year, when I'm seventeen, I'm hoping to spend some time in England – at least my mother wants me to – so you see, we haven't any prejudice. We're just not impressed by the English, that's all. You can be amused by my Christian name, too, if you like. It's Sophia."

"Sophia?" He was amazed that he had been so wrong about her age.

"Sophia," she repeated, rather defiantly.

"Not particularly amusing, any more than mine." He swallowed. "David."

Conversation flagged. His mouth felt painfully stiff, as if he were trying to smile for a photographer. They passed through the main block of the University and out between the statues of the brothers von Humboldt into Unter den Linden.

"You're going to Potsdam next week, David?" she asked. She was perfectly natural about using his name, a trick easy to the Dominions.

"I suppose so. Are you?"

"Are you?"

"Well, are you?" He tried to add "Sophia" but failed.

"Yes."

"Well, yes, too."

"Fine, here's my bus."

"Where are you going?"

"I have to meet my mother."

"Oh."

"See you to-morrow, then."

He murmured something incoherent and she got on the green double-decker. The bus continued down the Linden, bound for Halensee. He watched it until it was lost in the traffic beyond the Friedrichstrasse corner. Then he said to himself, "God, I'm in love!" He was delighted. He hurried back to the hostel and kept repeating her name under his breath. "Sophia Robinson, Sophia Robinson, Sophia Robinson." He said it aloud. "Sophia Robinson."

Half an hour later he sat on his bed and began to write up the matter in his notebook. "A Great Event. This afternoon at — what does it matter when? Love is timeless. Suffice to say that at last I am in tune with the whole world. At last I, David Proctor, belong to the human race. Ah, ecstasy! She spoke my name! Yesterday Werther was a character in a book. To-day I am Werther! 'See you to-morrow!' To-morrow! To-morrow and to-morrow and to-morrow! Question: am I in love, or merely in love with being in love? Answer: in love. Her eyes are an extraordinary sort of placid blue and a way of looking at you without blinking as if they contained all the truth in the world."

He read it through complacently and then lay back and stared at the grey-white ceiling.

When Köhler and Habraschka came in he was trying to read *Julius Caesar*. It was quite impossible. The conversation about the visit to Potsdam echoed and re-echoed, and he shivered with pleasure and excitement.

His room companions were to join a truck which was to tour a suburb called Lichterfelde that evening.

"We shall shout to the people!" cried Köhler enthusiastically, combing his sleek dark hair. "The voice of youth will give zest to the *bourgeois* folk! The Führer's battle was won on the streets and must be reaffirmed on the streets! Hurrah!" He waved his comb in triumph.

"Pfui!" said Habraschka, without looking up from his boots.

The Pole entered murmuring secretive "Good evenings" to the right and left. Hostel life continued. Folk songs began upstairs. Köhler imitated a man playing a concertina for David's benefit. Köhler was one of those comedians who thought pulling faces should send people into fits. David laughed politely. Habraschka's boots shone.

At ten past six David remembered his appointment with Mr. Belford and jumped up from his bed in a frantic hurry.

CHAPTER TWELVE

"Really this is quite unforgivable," said Mr. Belford. "You can take it that our friendship is at its lowest possible ebb. I was worried that you had had some sort of accident—"

"I'm awfully sorry, Adrian—"

"Some sort of accident, it was the only imaginable explanation. But, no—you *forgot*. It seems that I am to be spared no indignity."

"Well, I came as quickly as I could." David began to sound aggrieved, if not rebellious. He was still out of breath from running all the way to the bus stop. He felt Mr. Belford's fury, which had been sustained for several minutes, to be unreasonable. "I've said I'm sorry, I can't say any more, can I?"

"No, you can't say any more. In fact there's nothing you can say at all. I am very annoyed with you, David. You have done your best to ruin an evening I was looking forward to. Well, we'd better go and eat right away. There's no time for a drink."

Mr. Belford calmed down by the time they were eating their *borsch*, soothed by the practice of his Russian. David could not see that there had been any need to hurry, for people kept coming in long after them. However, Mr. Belford was soon in good conversational form. He discussed the life of Rimbaud, a subject David had to admit was of considerable interest. Boy genius, vagabond, Abysinnian merchant – how incredible life could be! What fascinating people there were to hear about! He saw himself as Rimbaud. Mr. Belford, carried away by his own brilliance, was similarly stirred. After their modest bill had been paid they returned to the street, two romantic adventurers.

"Who knows?" Mr. Belford said whimsically. "Perhaps you and I will set off on a journey through Europe. Verlaine and Rimbaud."

"Belford and Proctor!"

"I prefer Adrian and David."

"When you shoot me, select somewhere with a comfortable prison."

"What a material boy you are!"

Back in his room, Mr. Belford lit some icons and produced the *vermout*.

"Next time you come I'll make some Turkish coffee. Do you like it?"

"I've never had it, actually."

"Oh, David, such virginity! You know, you keep on depressing me so much, every four minutes at least you make me feel my age, just when I'm feeling *young*. Next week, then – the introduction to Turkish coffee. Roll of drums. It'll have to be Wednesday, by the way. We have a choir practice."

An hour of French poetry followed. David heard a word now and then, which interrupted his meditation on the pleasure of being in love. Occasionally also, in an interval between poems, there came a faint, distant buzz or a sound like a voice coming through a telephone receiver and heard some yards away – this was Dr. Goebbels' mass meeting,
404

relayed by surrounding radios. Selections from Baudelaire followed Rimbaud. David was relieved that his host had forgotten about the novel he had borrowed and so little read. Determined to be polite this evening, he did not get up until Mr. Belford himself was suppressing yawns.

"I *have* enjoyed this evening. Have you, David?"

"Yes," David said, rather uncomfortably. He could not very well say "no" or "well, moderately", but "yes" seemed to infer more than was in fact the case.

"You really have?"

"Yes, of course."

They stood on the step leading to the street. On the other side the sky was faintly aglow with the lights of the Kurfürstendamm. Mr. Belford patted his shoulder affectionately.

"If only it were four years ago we should now go on a tour of the bars. Oh, what a city it used to be! As it is, our fastidious gaze would light upon ageing ladies of the town intent upon pot-bellied provincials from Saxony or somewhere. So good night, sweet prince. May flights of angels, etc. *Schlafen Sie recht wohl*. Odious language. Shall I see you in church?"

"Well, no, I don't think so." He stepped down awkwardly on to the pavement.

"No sins to ask forgiveness for? Until Wednesday, then. *Au revoir*."

"Cheerio," David said, and walked along self-consciously, without looking round. When he felt that he was out of view he relaxed and was very pleased with himself. It was pleasant when you were happy to make someone else happy. Next Wednesday was going a bit far, however. "I think I've had enough of him for the moment," he decided. He mimicked a phrase of Mr. Belford's in the latter's slightly mincing tone for his own amusement — "Have you, David?" — and then, his mind concentrating on the world of love, forgot about him.

The next morning he was nervous that the sight of her would be a disappointment. It was not. If anything, she was more attractive than he expected. For example, how perfect was the way she sat. Her back was straight, leaning forward a little, her neck — admittedly short — a marvellously graceful continuation of the same even line. He himself was a mass of

405

sharp corners and irregular curves. He settled on to a seat like a collapsing tent. Her teeth were even. His were not. She seemed to know everyone by name. He hardly knew anyone by name, even in the old class. All through the morning he discovered new qualities in her and he made a note which pleased him : " Love is really a beautiful kind of envy."

When they went outside for a break he hurried across to her. He found himself talking rapidly. She asked him about his future. He told her at once that he was thinking of becoming an economist. It was an idea that had fleetingly occurred to him once. Having announced it, he defended it vigorously. The world was starving in the midst of plenty. They had burnt coffee in Brazil. The sensible thing was to learn how trade ought to be worked. He proposed to devote his life to this. He paused for breath excitedly and her wonderful blue eyes regarded him.

" Have you seen *Broadway Melody of 1936?* "

" No."

" I'm going to it with my mother this afternoon. Would you like to come? "

" Would I? Yes! Good Lord, yes! I mean I would, Sophia. I'd like to very much. Yes, I would."

" Meet us outside the Gloria Palast at two-thirty."

He followed her back into the classroom feeling quite faint. It was like some childhood joy, waking up on Christmas morning, deepened immeasurably.

At lunch-time he remembered to ring up his aunt.

" I'm awfully sorry I can't come this afternoon."

" Oh. Can't you? Never mind – you're not ill or anything? "

" Oh, no, it's just – well, there's a lot of work at the moment, though it's supposed to be our afternoon off, and – "

" Yes, of course, you must do your work. As it's such a nice day I was thinking we might have gone for a walk – perhaps in Grunewald." The disappointment in her voice was clear and for some minutes afterwards he felt guilty about it, until he remembered that somehow this was always the effect of a conversation with his aunt.

CHAPTER THIRTEEN

He was at the Gloria Palast at two. Six storm-troopers stood on the edge of the pavement barking out in unison, "The Führer gave us freedom and honour – our thanks are our votes on the twenty-ninth of March!" After this they relaxed for a minute or two, then drew themselves up and shouted it again. David was accustomed to the slogan. He had heard it being rehearsed up in the dormitory the night before. Here in the more fashionable part of the city, the Memorial church neighbourhood, Nazis looked almost out of place. David noted the resigned cheerfulness of the Berliners who were being shouted at. The smarter the people the more likely they were to ignore the storm-troopers.

Punctually at half past two Sophia came alone.

"My mother had an engagement."

He nodded. It was excellent, but created a problem. The Gloria Palast was rather an expensive cinema. He had automatically expected that her mother would pay.

"I've got the tickets," Sophia said.

As they went in, with the problem solved, he wondered if Sophia had known all the time that her mother wouldn't come. He glowed at the idea. They were shown to expensive seats, which was very satisfactory. *Broadway Melody* was the hit film of Berlin and "You are my Lucky Star" or in the German version, "*Du bist mein Glückstern*", the hit tune. There were contented sighs all around and even some applause for Eleanor Powell's tap-dancing. It was as if the audience was having an hour or two off from the régime. About half-way through the film, while he was offering half a bar of chocolate, Sophia took the opportunity of pressing his fingers. Intoxicated, he at once seized her hand, and spent the rest of the film wondering feverishly what further liberties he might now take. She gave him no further encouragement, but seemed to be entirely placid.

407

Afterwards they walked a little way up Budapesterstrasse. He was on the point of risking bankruptcy by inviting her to tea in the modish Eden Hotel. He understood now how men would stint themselves and lead hard dull lives in order to indulge their loved ones. But fortunately Sophia said, "You'd better come home to tea."

He bought her bus ticket. Buying something was really what mattered, and even fifteen pfennigs was not a meaningless item to him.

He was delighted to realize how much the film had impressed her.

"Wait till you get to London," he boasted. "The musical shows are marvellous, they really are. Much better than Hollywood."

"I don't believe it."

"Honestly. I mean, this is just a provincial city compared to London. For example there's hardly any traffic at all. I mean, compared to London." He glanced out at the hold-up which had developed at the Hitzig bridge.

"I suppose everything's comparative," she said meekly.

"Yes, of course. Then again the night life here hardly exists, though I believe it *used* to be pretty good. I mean there's just a few frowsy bars –"

"Have you been to the Femina?"

The question threw him hopelessly off-balance. He shook his head and blushed.

"I went to the Femina three weeks ago," Sophia said, in a documentary tone of voice. "My parents don't know, by the way. It was a party from the legation and I was smuggled along. They had telephones on every table and you could ring each other up. I thought it was rather silly. Do you go out much in London?"

"Well, you see, we live about sixty miles away, but, of course, one gets in –" He wished he had never started it. He was shattered by the discovery that she had actually seen more night life than he had.

"This is where we get out."

They were half-way along Tiergartenstrasse, with the park on one side and faded mansions on the other. They entered

408

through gates decorated with the royal crest and the Dominion flag. A porter bowed to them. Sophia led the way, marching briskly, with a proprietorial air. Inside the house they went up some stone steps to a thickly carpeted landing. She opened an impressive door and beckoned him to follow her in. The next moment he was in quite the largest and most comfortable living-room he had ever seen.

"No one about," Sophia said. She pressed a bell-button in the wall.

"Is this where you live?"

"Yes."

"Is your father the ambassador, then?"

"He's not an ambassador, he's a minister."

"Good lord."

David was slightly overawed. When she had said that her father worked at the legation he had assumed that this was in some respectable but subordinate capacity. Now it appeared that Sophia lived in a higher world altogether than his own. He was not at all displeased. The atmosphere here, though grand, was also cosy. He flopped down on to a wide, deep sofa, while Sophia sat on the arm of a chair.

A manservant came in and bowed a "*Jawohl*" to her request for some tea. David watched, fascinated. Menservants had not existed for him before, except imaginatively. He looked at her with even greater admiration than before.

When the man went out Sophia said, frowning, "I wish you wouldn't stare at me like that."

"Why not?" he asked happily.

"It makes me self-conscious."

"That's wonderful. I mean—" He was in a mood to be brilliant. "If I were you I should think it would be wonderful to *be* self-conscious."

"There's no need to be sarcastic."

"But I meant it!" He made the terrible discovery that she was lacking in humour. "All I meant was, if I were you—"

"I just wish you wouldn't stare."

"But I'm irresistibly compelled to."

"Oh, rubbish." She coloured slightly and made a pattern

409

on the carpet with her foot. "What I mean is, when some-one's in the room."

"Oh!" he said, in ecstasy. He wanted to spring across and fling his arms round her. But he could hardly do it with tea coming in at any moment. He was agonized at the thought of wasting an opportunity.

It was already gone. The door opened and a short, solidly built and grey-haired woman came in. Obviously her mother, but not at all the patrician diplomat's wife he had vaguely expected. She was more like a preoccupied school matron. He leapt up and fingered his tie, not sure whether to be young and respectful or suave. She smiled at him, but not as if she actually saw him.

"How do you do? I'm so glad you could take my seat. Was it good?"

"Awfully good!"

"Sophie tells me you're in her class, Mr. –"

"Sophia, Mother, *please*. His name's Proctor. David."

Mrs. Robinson blinked.

"Oh, yes. Well – make yourself at home, Da – Mr. Proctor. I have to rush along, I'm afraid. There seems to be so much to do in Berlin. Do you find that, too?"

"Yes, appalling," David agreed, and was so satisfied with himself, and so flattered by her question, that he wondered at once whether he should not try for the Foreign Office. Surreptitiously he pulled at his sleeves to remove their crumpled effect.

"Such a lovely day –" Mrs. Robinson gestured to the tall windows, through which, David noticed for the first time, the Tiergarten could be seen. "Though I don't like this tiresome election and all these men shouting everywhere. Sophie, dear, you have to come with us this evening to the Bolivians, so don't run away. I have to write some letters. Where do you live in England, Mr. Proctor?"

In spite of her vague manner, before she left the room, a minute or so later, Mrs. Robinson had drawn from him not only where he lived, but what his father was, where he had been to school, where he was staying in Berlin, and what he intended to become.

410

"An economist? My husband will be interested in that. It's his subject."

Tea came in as soon as Mrs. Robinson disappeared and two menservants brought it. David, who had lost all his self-possession while being examined, relaxed again into an enjoyment of high life. Sophia poured out. There were delicious sandwiches. It was all very different from the hostel and very different, too, from where he should really have been – at his aunt's. Viewed from here the latter, and his uncle as well, seemed more pathetic than ever.

"Your mother's awfully nice," he said politely.

"Yes. She will insist on calling me Sophie. I loathe it. It makes me furious."

David nearly disintegrated with love, he was so charmed by the outburst.

"Sophia's a beautiful name," he said sympathetically.

"Do you think so? If you want to know, I loathe that, too."

David understood exactly how she felt. He was not too satisfied with his own name. It always seemed to impose a character on him that he did not feel to be his own.

"It's amazing how much we have in common," he thought.

The illusion received a severe blow almost at once.

"David?" Sophia said.

"Yes?"

"What's your opinion of National Socialism?"

"Oh, God," he said, conscious of disappointment. He had not been hoping for a political discussion. "Well, I think it's repulsive, of course."

"I don't."

David put his cup down, shocked.

"You're not serious?" he enquired. "You don't think Streicher is repulsive, for example? *Der Stürmer?* Concentration camps?"

"*You* can hardly talk about concentration camps. What about South Africa?"

"But, my dear Sophia –"

"You shouldn't condemn what you do like just because there's something you don't like, anyway," she said rapidly. Her cheeks glowed. "I admit that some things – but look at the

wonderful spirit everywhere – in the summer I'm hoping to
go for a few weeks with the BDM in the country – to help
farmers' wives, all that sort of thing – "

"But listen! The whole point is Hitler doesn't have to allow
anything he doesn't like! "

"He probably doesn't know. He can't do everything at
once."

"Oh, my God! " he exclaimed. "Doesn't know – *Mein
Kampf* is full of – "

"You've read it, of course? "

"Bits of it," he lied, caught out once again.

"Have you read the Protocols of the Elders of Zion? "

"That's a forgery! "

"How do you know? "

"Everybody knows! " he cried. "Good lord, you don't
approve of what they've done to the Jews, surely – I mean it's
frightful, it's uncivilized! "

"Yes," Sophia said heatedly, "I know all about that, but
did you know that in Prussia, for instance, fifty per cent of
the lawyers – "

"Well, if you're going to swallow all that drivel – "

"I don't just disregard *facts*, as you seem to."

She stared at him angrily. He realized too late that the discussion had in fact been intimate. But it was clear to him that
he was faced with a moral problem. He must give in or he
must fight to convert her to decency. The ghosts of at least
fifty issues of the *New Statesman* hovered about him, giving
support to the latter course. She looked wildly attractive.

"And I," David said bravely, "don't happen to admire
persecution or militarism or all this bestial racial nonsense,
Aryans and Non-Aryans and all that, I mean it's absolutely
childish – "

"It isn't such nonsense. The Norsemen were in German land
after the ice age, they had beautiful wooden houses and tools
and everything, *long* before the Greeks, and, anyway, the
Greeks were Germans really – "

"Whoever's been telling you all this? "

"I can *read*. Also we had a professor here the other day, a
very eminent man, and *he* was telling me."

412

"A professor! Oh, my God! What was he, a professor of astrology?"

"Of history, if you want to know, from Heidelberg, and if you don't mind I prefer—" She broke off as a servant looked round the door.

"Excuse me, I thought his excellency was in here."

"I haven't seen him, Friedrich."

David was more impressed by this little exchange than by any conversation he had ever heard. It was something out of a costume film, but it was real and he was there.

"You prefer?" he said, still shaken.

"Oh, it doesn't matter. I can hear my father. He also disapproves of what I think," she said bitterly.

David jumped up as a short, brisk, middle-aged man came in. He looked like and was dressed like a business man. He advanced straight to Sophia, who had not turned round, and put his hands over her eyes. Sophia broke free, looking flustered.

"Daddy, I *wish* you—"

"You're coming with us to-night, did your mother tell you?" said the Minister, winking at David. The wink reassured the latter, who was wondering, rather panic-stricken, if he should say "Your excellency".

"You saw Friedrich?"

"Bumped into him just now," said the Minister, picking up the last two sandwiches, which David had reserved for himself. "Who's the guest?"

Sophia explained.

"How are you, Dave," said the Minister, shaking hands with great heartiness. "How long have you been here? Where are you staying?" He produced a gold cigarette-case and offered David a cigarette. He was constantly doing something—not a comfortable man to work for, David thought. There seemed to be a slightly disapproving note behind his harassing tactics. When David mentioned the hostel, however, he became both approving and interested. "That's good. That's the way to do it. Sit down and tell me about it. What do they think about everything? The Rhineland? What do you think about it? You've read Baldwin's speech?"

413

David was immensely flattered. After a moment or two of modest hesitation he became quite fluent. He remained carefully respectful, however, it was rather like chatting to a friendly housemaster.

He left about ten minutes later when, without ceasing to be hospitable, the Minister implied that the interview was over, and that since he himself was staying put, it was clearly necessary for David to go. Sophia, who had been silent, saw him as far as the stairs.

He turned to her eagerly.

"Well, see you to-morrow. Thanks awfully for letting me have the ticket."

"Thank you for going with me," she said with stony politeness. But she stood there, placidly waiting. He trembled with the suspicion that she wanted him to kiss her, but he was inhibited by the thought of her father behind the closed door two yards away.

"It was an awfully good film."

"Yes."

"Well—see you to-morrow." Unable to bear it, he turned and ran down the stairs without looking back.

He walked along beside the park towards Skagerrak Platz, despising himself. But very shortly he rationalized the whole thing. A casual unemotional good-bye had been the proper way. If she had been disappointed so much the better.

There was a whistling of sirens and three motor cycles tore along ahead of a large Mercedes flying a swastika. Some big Nazi—he couldn't recognize the face in the bad light. The car disappeared, an emblem, though unfortunately a Nazi one, of the sheltered comfort of which he had just been a part. How splendid it was to have power and position! His mind was full of exciting thoughts, not least among them the idea of being addressed by servants as "*Excellenz*". What prizes were available and how fascinating life could be! What fools people were to despise ambition! He noticed passers-by with new eyes. He felt in his bones that he was by nature a prince.

He stopped to read a poster that was being put up everywhere. The Führer, looking very earnest, one hand raised in salute, the other holding his cap against his chest, rose out

414

of a darkness on which white words were printed: "I now ask the German people to fortify my faith and through the strength of their will to give me strength to stand courageously for their honour and freedom and to care for their economic well being. And especially to support me in my struggle for a true peace."

"What a bastard!" David murmured, with a kind of friendly admiration, as from a fellow conspirator. The Führer's lonely eminence overpowered him less now that he too had glimpsed the land of *Excellenz*.

Sophia's opinions, however, worried him a little. A love affair with a girl who approved of the Nazis was going to be full of difficulties. In a way it was charming that she should be so wrong-headed, and it would, of course, be splendid if he could reform her. But equally he was aware – it was a disconcerting factor – that he sympathized with some of her feelings. His companions at the hostel might be bores, but they did not seem to be thugs, except possibly Habraschka. Some were charming and all were filled with a spirit of purpose and service. You could despise what they were serving, but not the enthusiasm with which they served. Sophia was merely trying to express honestly what he refused to admit.

Another new poster showed a youth in Labour Service uniform saluting with his shovel – in the Labour Service they drilled with shovels instead of rifles and the salute was like a military present arms. A few ghostly starving proletarians were in the background. Beneath ran the slogans: "Yesterday: Unemployment – Despair – Demoralization – Strikes – Lock-outs. To-day: Work – Joy – Discipline – Comradeship. Thank the Führer with your Vote!"

"No, it's ghastly," David decided.

The lights of a dance café in the Skagerrak Platz reminded him of Sophia's visit to the Femina and depressed him. It was maddening that he couldn't afford to go to such places. And even if he could, he reflected gloomily, he was still too adolescent, too unsophisticated, too inexperienced. The mood of unpleasant truth settled on him like a cloud. The lights of the expensive Esplanade Hotel down the Bellevuestrasse further depressed him. He was jealous of Sophia for the wonderful time she must have. The Bolivians, for example, to-night. The best he could do would be a frightful evening with Aunt Isabel and Uncle Rudi. He had been thrown a crumb, that was all. For him it was back to the hostel, which was hardly more than a home for young tramps, after all.

The mood vanished as soon as he remembered that the Minister had almost shown respect for him when he heard about the hostel. The normal thing was to stay with some awful family. To be interesting you had to be somewhere uncomfortable, David realized, and at once became cheerful again. The middle way had to be ignored. It must be the top or the bottom always. Once more full of a sense of destiny, he went on walking and turned into the Hermann-Goering-strasse. Ahead was the Brandenburger Tor and beyond it the burnt-out Reichstag. Opposite was the garden wall of the Presidential Palace and the Chancellery.

"I really am in the centre of things," he thought. "I must say it's damned lucky that Sophia is who she is. God, what an angel! How annoyed she looked! There's no doubt about it, I'm desperately in love."

CHAPTER FOURTEEN

The election became noisier. More and more storm-troopers – where they came from or what they did at at other times seemed to be a mystery. More lorries went by loaded with men shouting hearty slogans, now and then there would be a procession of private cars all fixed with ships' klaxons which blared away, the lamp-post loud-speakers constantly poured out speeches being delivered somewhere to cheering crowds, uniformed motor-cyclists screeched by, S.S. men in black, looking very conscious of their *élite* quality, drove mysteriously about, the Führer's progress – he was touring the country – was hysterically reported.

"I am not working for the rearmament of the German

people because I'm a shareholder. I believe I am the only statesman in the world who hasn't a bank account. I have no stock, no share in any business. I get no dividends. All — I — want — is — that my people should be *strong* — and able to exist in this world. If you're a decent German, have you any reason to be ashamed of these last three years — before the people, before history, before posterity? Haven't you reason to be proud once again? Can't you now say: 'Lord God, whatever little things we may still lack, over — all — we're once again — a fabulous people! Once again — we're an up-right people! Once again we're an industrious and skilful people! What — can't — we — now — do — in — Germany?' We have no desire to conquer anyone in Europe. We haven't any intention of doing harm to anyone in Europe — but we also haven't any intention of letting anyone do harm to us! For over three years I have done my duty — Germans — now go and do yours! For three years I have struggled for you, with devotion and fanatical faith. Now gather up your courage and stand as fanatically behind me!"

At the hostel things had become extremely tedious. The singing up in the dormitory with its camp-fire atmosphere, going on for hours at night or at any time during the day, the stamp of boots along the corridor, the constant Heiling and saluting, and, less clear but deeper, the cloying feeling of physical vanity all around, the awful youth emphasis — all this added up in the end to an impression of disease instead of, as it first seemed, health. The loungers on the street corners at home, whom Uncle Rudi was so fond of remembering critically, were surely more sound, David began to reflect. He was no longer so stirred by the "I however decided . . ." plaque. Not that the Führer required any plaques during those weeks. He was part of the air. David would not have been surprised to see Köhler praying to him.

All the same the hostel was of great benefit when he was invited to lunch at the legation. He was able to speak expertly on "what they are thinking" when the Minister questioned him. Enormously impressive young men on the staff and some business visitors were present. It was a most satisfactory experience, and he could not help thinking it remarkable that he could justify his place there – especially when he reflected that the Minister, according to Sophia's information, was a professor of economic history when he was at home, a doctor of economics, London, a doctor of philosophy, Heidelberg, and heaven knows what else; and that the business men owned factories; and that the young staff men also tended to be doctors of this and that, or to have been to both Harvard and Oxford – and yet here he was, the seventeen-year-old Proctor, listened to quite eagerly.

He was aware that he didn't really belong in their company. It was depressing to think how many examinations they had all passed, and in this, he was also aware, lay one of the most inspiring aspects of the Führer, the message of hope the great man brought to the lazy and uneducated that there was nothing in the world that could not be achieved by the simple exercise of will power. The Triumph of Will, that was the famous phrase. The conversation of the Minister and his staff and his guests in which Hitler was dismissed as an uncouth pawn was vaguely irritating to David. In spite of his own disapproval of Hitler he felt almost resentful of this patronizing attitude, while at the same time he was impressed by it. To the Minister, it appeared, Dr. Schacht of the Reichsbank and Herr von Neurath of the Foreign Office were much more important than Hitler purely because they had been educated in the same sort of way as the Minister. There was enough sense in this point of view for David to be swayed by it, although a more powerful argument was the simple fact that the Minister met and knew personally the members of the German Government, and of course had met Hitler himself. The affable, intelligent Dr. Robinson was really at the centre of things and David was influenced by his opinions since he had never known anyone in such a position. And he was fascinated also to observe the deference paid to the Minister by the rest. All the same he retained the suspicion that professors who respected only professors disclosed a weakness in their equipment.

This did not stop him from using her father's point of view to argue with Sophia.

"You see, your attitude is purely romantic and illogical. In fact, Hitler is just a Jew-baiting tub-thumper. The real policy is obviously laid down by the same people who've done it all along."

"If you knew how ridiculous you looked when you try to be superior –"

"You can't deny –"

"I do deny. Life *is* romantic and illogical, anyway."

"Oh, God, that's absolutely typical!"

"If anyone's typical, it's you. The typically absurd Englishman."

"Now, Sophia, don't forget that you can't please an Englishman more than by reminding him that he is an Englishman."

"Well, if you think those men are marching for Dr. Schacht, you must be out of your mind."

They were at Potsdam, standing in front of the palace called the Stadt-Schloss, inside which they would shortly be inspecting rooms used by Frederick the Great. It was a class trip. They had just been to the Garrison Church, where Frederick and his father were buried and where, above all, the first Nazi parliament had been held. They had looked at the hallowed spot where the Führer had stood, rather unsuitably dressed in morning clothes – it was a favourite photograph – addressing the giant old Hindenburg who sat in front of him. Now they were watching a squad of soldiers goose-stepping up and down the parade ground in front of the palace, where Old Fritz had drilled his grenadiers. David was annoyed at the admiration Sophia clearly showed on her face.

"A tub-thumping agitator," he repeated.

"Dr. Schacht with those awful old high collars," she said. "I hate him."

"At least he's less of a gangster than his so-called master."

"It would do you good if they had conscription in England."

"England is a volunteer country. Although, I may say, I have no intention of volunteering."

"It would certainly surprise me if you did. Oh, good, here come the others."

David perceived that it was a compliment to him when she descended to the schoolroom level. As the remainder of the crowd of Japanese and Syrians came up, all armed with their expensive cameras, he determined to risk everything.

Half an hour later in the garden at Sans Souci, at a moment when they were hidden from the others by one of the cone-shaped yew trees that lined the steps up to the enchanting little palace, he stumbled against her on purpose and quickly kissed her. To his astonishment and relief it was a success. Sophia merely looked breathless. Then she turned and pushed past him, but without a sign of annoyance. Having stumbled on purpose to begin with he was now so carried away with excitement that he stumbled by mistake and fell headlong. Nobody saw him. Bruised and happy, he hurried on up the steps to rejoin the party, which was inspecting and photographing the graves of Frederick the Great's greyhounds.

Later, when they were all back in Berlin, he rang up his aunt.

"Can't come to night, Aunt Isabel, I'm afraid."

"All right. I was only half-expecting you. We hardly ever see you nowadays. Are you keeping well?"

"Yes, of course, I'm fine – absolutely fine – I'm sorry I –"

"There's a lot of bronchitis about. The weather's so treacherous just now. Keep your overcoat on if you go out anywhere."

"We all went to Potsdam to-day."

"That was nice. I haven't been there for years. Here's Rudi to speak to you."

"Hullo, David, hullo! *Heil Hitler!* You are not coming?"

"No, uncle, I can't, you see –"

"That is all right! You are a student – enough said! Your stupid aunt thinks you are busy with your books. I tell her there are other things more entertaining than stupid relations! But don't hide completely. Don't forget we are responsible to your parents. Give my best wishes to them when you write next."

"Yes, uncle. Cheerio."

"Cheerio! *Heil Hitler!*" Uncle Rudi said.

David rang up Mr. Belford.

"Adrian, I'm awfully sorry. I won't be able to manage it this week – that is, to-morrow."

"It doesn't matter at all, I assure you."

"It just so happens there's something I can't get out of – "

"Which doesn't happen to be your engagement with me. I quite understand. Let me give you a little advice, though, David. It won't *pay* you in the end to sweep people aside merely to suit your convenience – "

"Oh, God, Adrian – "

"Let me finish, please. Of course I quite realize that we belong to different generations, though they're not so far apart as you may imagine – you will realize that all too soon, and I hope that when you do you will have no cause for regret, David – but I was certainly under the impression, a laughably erroneous impression, it seems, that we were friends. I suppose I'm just a fool. It's what one should expect in a hard, barbaric city. I am not used, David, to the kind of behaviour which is doubtless prevalent among your young storm-troopers – "

"Oh, lord, look here. I'm sorry. Next week – "

"No, David, I think we will make no more arrangements for the moment. Good-bye."

"Oh – well, good-bye."

Then he rang up the legation and asked for Sophia.

"Hullo!" he said, when she came on the line. "It's all right, I'm free to-night now."

"David, it's an awful nuisance, but there's a dinner party and they insist I have to be at it."

"Oh, damn!"

"Well, I can't help it."

"To-morrow, then – I've put off that ass I told you about – "

"David, that's no good either. I have to go to the Opera."

"But you said – "

"I didn't know then – "

"Damn, damn, damn."

"We'll go on Friday, if you like. They're going to the

French Embassy and I won't be in that. We'll go to 'Soldaten-Kamaraden'; somebody told me it was good."

"Friday, yes, all right, but Friday! God, can't I see you before then?"

"You'll see me in class to-morrow morning."

"I want to see you all day every day."

"Don't be such a fool."

"I shall go mad to-night."

"If you ask me, you're mad already."

Meanwhile Dr. Goebbels announced the rules for the last two days of the campaign.

"On Friday, 27th March, at 16 hours, the Führer will speak from the Krupp works in Essen to all German workers and soldiers. At 10.45 all stations will broadcast the command: 'Hoist flags!' On this command, flags will be hoisted on all public buildings, factories and private houses. At 16 hours the sirens of the Krupp works will proclaim for one minute long the beginning of the Führer's great call for peace. The sirens of every factory, ship and locomotive in the whole of Germany will join in the piercing sound from Essen. Then for the whole nation, for factories and their workers, for private persons, for vehicles, other than trains and airplanes in motion, one minute's rest and general stillness. The nation will use this minute for inward contemplation and thereby demonstrate to the whole world its determination to stand as one man behind the Führer and his policy for peace, honour and equality.

"In all factories and barracks there will be mass audiences. All shops will cease business from 16 to 17 hours to give their employees and the public a chance to hear the Führer's speech.

"On Saturday, 28th March, the whole German people will celebrate the German People's Day of Honour, Freedom and Peace. National Socialist formations will hold giant demonstrations. From 18.30 hours the streets will be filled with millions of people on their way to meeting places in order to hear the Führer for the last time before the election. At 19.45 hours the columns will stand ready. At all meeting places and gatherings there will be a solemn stillness.

422

At 19.50 hours the bronze mouths of the bells of Cologne Cathedral will peal to announce the Führer's call for peace, which will be delivered at 20 hours in the Cologne Messehall. At the end of his call the Old Netherlands Thanksgiving will be sung in the Messehall, and mixed with the sound of the singing of this hymn, which will be broadcast from Cologne to all stations even to the remotest village, will be the singing of the whole people. All Germans in the whole Reich will stand and take part in this singing. The words 'God make us free', sung by sixty-seven million people, will roar over the whole of Germany. Then bells will peal for a quarter of an hour, followed by a broadcast pause of fifteen minutes, with which the election struggle will be concluded.

"On 29th March the whole nation will go to the election urns, resolved to do its duty and to strengthen the Führer in his faith in the German people and in his brave and unshakable struggle for the honour, freedom and peace of the German nation."

And everything took place as the doctor ordered. David watched the sudden appearance of flags at every window of Oranienburgerstrasse where he was on his way to the students' club to hear the Führer's speech. It was incredible that in every street all over Germany the same thing had happened. The military precision with which people obeyed the order, as if they were taking part in a stupendous children's game, was amazing and impressive and chilling. In the canteen at the end of the speech, when everyone turned to the loudspeaker and saluted and "Deutschland über alles" and the "Horst Wessel" were being played, David stood as sloppily as possible, keeping his hands to his sides. He was aware that it could hardly be called brave, for as a foreigner he was under no social obligation to salute Hitler, but still he felt it was a small private gesture.

CHAPTER FIFTEEN

I t was April. Suddenly the election was in the past – with Köhler proclaiming lyrically, almost tearfully, "Ninety-eight per cent! That is what the people think of the Führer! Ninety-eight per cent! It is historic, Herr Proctor, don't you agree?" – and even the news reels of the mounted German soldiers crossing the Rhine bridge and of the symbolic sentries posted once again were allowed to fade away. The Olympic Games, due in August, became the next item.

David threw himself into his love affair with enthusiasm. He wrote pages in his notebook, heavily under the influence of Goethe's Werther, suffered agonies of jealousy when he knew that she was attending some legation function – for it was her duty to be nice to young officers and cadets who happened to be present – and equally trembled with pleasure when she was with him and in a good mood. If only he had more pocket money – if only he had evening clothes – it was sheer pain when he was once permitted to see her in a dinner frock, ready for yet another South American reception. However, he was constantly invited to lunch or tea and he made the most of it, shrewdly concentrating on behaving well in the presence of her parents. By the middle of the month they were taking him for granted and, if anyone else were present, introduced him as Sophia's friend. He supplied the Minister with a flow of the current opinions of the hostel, such as Köhler's strong disapproval of a Laurel and Hardy comic film about Scottish soldiers in kilts. "It makes fun of the military," Köhler had said critically. He went on two drives together with the Minister, Mrs. Robinson and Sophia, roaring out of Berlin in a large Mercedes that received flattering attention from policemen on point duty. His mother was extremely pleased to hear about it. "I'm delighted to know that you have met some nice people," she wrote. He introduced Sophia to the automat and Aschingers, taking some pride in his knowledge of the life of poor students. All in all it was a wonderful month.

Except at Easter, when the Robinsons went away to the Harz mountains, on a trip for which he had hoped for an invitation. He passed several days of misery. Even the hostel was half empty. Köhler had gone off with a party from the dormitory, all of them in shorts and decorated waistcoats and equipped ominously with mandolins and banjoes. He sat about suffering, giving a performance as a tragic lover. On Easter Sunday he went to church with his aunt, who commented on his pale appearance. This pleased him. Mr. Belford was there in his Sunday black and his nod was unexpectedly cheerful. David was rather nettled. There followed a long afternoon at the flat. Aunt Isabel played for an hour and his uncle dozed. After tea they went out to a café crowded with thick-armed women in flouncy dresses and heavy-jowled men with cropped hair and cheap suits – the middle-aged, *bourgeois* Germans were a dull lot. He kept silent about his new social life, feeling that it would be kinder not to let his aunt and uncle know in what superior circles he moved. He felt mildly patronizing towards them. Even when his uncle paid the bill, he degraded the occasion by bringing out a purse in which he kept his change. David looked away.

But Easter was over, and Sophia back, and she invited him to watch her riding. She did this with a German girl called Wanda Meissner who lived in the extremely smart suburb of Dahlem to the south-west of the city. Wanda was a plumper edition of Sophia, and perhaps a little older. It was with her that Sophia was proposing to do her voluntary labour service. David watched them ride round and round a ring at a nearby riding school. As a pastime it seemed to him boring.

However, here among the pine trees and comfortable houses he felt himself at home. It was a place where the air was scented pleasantly. Afterwards, as they went back to Wanda's house, it was pleasant to crush the pine needles beneath one's feet, while Wanda talked enthusiastically about life at a Nazi girls' camp. Her German was rapid and breathless and he was pleased to find himself following it.

o*

"We get up at six forty-five. Then we have a game of something before breakfast, it's such fun, and then the flag parade, of course; I mean we salute the flag – only you couldn't, Sophia, I suppose, not being a German. I'm not sure about that – and then we help on the land all the morning. Well, first of all, there's a National Socialist world-outlook lecture, it's always frightfully interesting, and in the afternoon we often go to a village to mix with the villagers and help the mothers – that's what's so wonderful about National Socialism, how our German youth is brought to understand its real roots. And then there's the evening flag parade and a sing-song – and I can tell you, Sophia, we're practically exhausted when we get to bed – "

David had an idea that Sophia was not really responding with equal enthusiasm. This was certainly to her credit. "Is she changing her mind because of me?" he wondered complacently, and he at once made himself as friendly as he could to Wanda. He asked her to tell him what she admired most about the Führer. The veteran of countless arguments with Köhler, he knew what question to ask when one wanted to please. Wanda took a deep breath.

"Oh, heavens, where can one begin? First of all, perhaps, he is a Man. Then, you see, he sacrifices himself so much, he has no thought for his own comfort – "

Wanda continued at full flood for the next quarter of a mile, until in fact they had entered the Meissners' sitting-room. This was large and modern, with Scandinavian tendencies, and included busts of both Herr and Frau Meissner and also of Wanda as a child. Architectural and art magazines lay about, carefully abandoned, and a plant grew up a trellis against one of the walls. Frau Meissner was on a sofa with her legs tucked under her, a pretty, slim woman with a shiny nose and nice ears, fully exposed. David understood that Herr Meissner, who was not present, was a successful lawyer. Frau Meissner welcomed him charmingly, rang for tea and complained that English newspapers were unfair to the Führer because they never showed him in a good-humoured mood.

"Well, that's possibly true," David admitted, balancing his conscience carefully. "I mean, they don't ever give the im-

426

pression that he makes his audiences laugh. But he certainly does quite often."

"Precisely," said Frau Meissner.

"He is the most wonderful man in the world!" exclaimed Wanda with a rapturous smile.

"Dear child," said Frau Meissner. "Well, Herr Proctor, you must tell us about what they are thinking in England – my husband often reads the English newspapers in spite of their inaccurate reporting of Germany – although I believe your Ward Price is a good man – my husband likes to meet English people. He will be here in a minute, he has been on a parade and he is changing out of his uniform. He is in the S.S." Frau Meissner announced this with the casualness of one who knows she has said something to impress.

Herr Meissner arrived downstairs in time for tea. He was tall, elegant and charming and he joked with the yokel-type maid. David had the impression that both he and Frau Meissner were anxious to put on a good show before the English guest, and were proud of knowing what sort of a show to put on. Herr Meissner wore a sports jacket and grey flannel trousers. He told David that he had his shoes made in London.

"You know you are an Englishman's friend," he said, "when he tells you the name of his tailor, his shoemaker and his shirtmaker."

David hoped that Herr Meissner would not inspect his own suit, shoes or shirt too closely. Some more people came, friends of the Meissners, all rather smart-looking. Herr Meissner opened a bottle of hock. David had a glass and also several cigarettes, although Wanda told him, "German youth does not smoke or touch alcohol." One of the guests began telling a funny story, which David could not follow, but the word "Jude" kept cropping up. He felt rather sick at the idea of being funny about the Jews in a country that was persecuting them. The impression he had had that they were all very agreeable people disappeared. He was sicker at the laughter that greeted it, and sicker still when Frau Meissner followed it up with another anti-Jewish anecdote. This one he did understand. It was all about the exquisite comedy of a middle-aged Jew being swindled at the customs and bursting into tears because of the money he was losing.

"Our tennis club was full of them!" Frau Meissner told David. "Oh, it is so much nicer now."

"And, you know, they are allowed to have a club of their own," put in Herr Meissner.

"Really? Where?" asked Frau Meissner in amazement.

"Oh, somewhere near the bottom of Kurfürstendamm. Near Halensee station. Do you want to join?"

There were shrieks of laughter and Frau Meissner said anxiously, "You know, sometimes I wonder if we are not too kind – it's just like the Führer –"

"I passed a Jew in the street the other day," Wanda confided to David. "He was walking along as bold as brass. Do you know a cold feeling went all over me? It was horrible!"

Meanwhile another story had started. The chill Wanda claimed to have felt was nothing to the chill which the conversation had inspired in David. He determined to tell them what swine they were, and how uncivilized and repulsive an impression they made upon their English guest. Why was he not doing it already? How could Sophia tolerate them? He felt himself trembling. He *must* say something. It was too awful to pay no attention, to smile politely and enjoy the freely available comforts – but now they were talking about Dr. Eckener, the Zeppelin designer, who was supposed to be in disgrace, and then the film actor who was supposed to have assaulted Dr. Goebbels, and on these subjects they were all surprisingly disloyal and pleasant and on the side of the angels. He was relieved that he hadn't made a fool of himself.

Wanda brought over a large book bound in blue and gold. It was all about the previous year's rally at Nuremberg. She opened it half on her lap and half on his. He could feel her breathing, and her hair kept touching his cheek. It was sad that she did not attract him. "How awful to be forced to marry her," he thought, while Wanda leaned hard against him.

"This is one of my favourite Führer pictures. He looks sc

kind, don't you think? Foreigners aren't allowed to see how kind he is. There, that's the railway station; oh, and there's something to interest you, some English Fascists."

"How awful! They look like unemployed chauffeurs."

"Awful?" said Wanda in surprise, and leaned harder. He leaned back. It was a sort of counterpoint conversation and he was not displeased by it. He wished Sophia had Wanda's enthusiasm. "Well, black is a silly colour for the English to choose, since you have a good deal of Nordic and Dinaric blood. Here's Gauleiter Streicher and Gauleiter Wagner waiting at the airport for the Führer – and here's the Führer stepping out of his plane." Wanda turned eyes sideways and upwards to meet his; but she seemed to stare beyond him, as if carried away. "The wonderful thing, David," she went on in a thrilled tone, pronouncing his name as "Derfid", "was the way the excitement kept *growing* all day, with the streets absolutely *packed*, and then as soon as they knew he had come, all the church bells started pealing and you could hear guns in the distance firing salutes, and of course all the bands began playing the 'Badenweiler' – that's his favourite march, you know – "

"Yes, I know. Were you there, then?"

"Yes!" Wanda said, pressing now against his ankle. "I was there with my parents. I think it was the happiest week of my life. Especially the first evening! We went to the special performance of *Meistersinger* and the Führer was there, of course, and in the interval I was as close to him as the width of this room! Everyone was crowding round him, of course, and he was so gay and friendly, just as if he were an ordinary person and not our Führer – at that moment, David, I tell you, I really wouldn't have minded dying. Have you seen him yourself?"

"No."

"You haven't? Oh, that's terrible! But you can see him next week on May Day. Oh, how wonderful to see the Führer for the first time!" Wanda seemed to be quite overcome. Her slightly blotchy but still babyish skin had turned pink. The Meissners and the guests who had overheard the last part of her ecstasy laughed approvingly.

429

Sophia, who sat by herself on the other side of the room, said, "I think David and I ought to be going now."

"If you like," Herr Meissner said to David, "I can arrange for you to have a ticket overlooking Unter den Linden. You get a good view and don't have to stand in the street for hours."

"That's awfully kind of you, Herr Meissner –" David said, and immediately thought, "God, I oughtn't to accept a favour from an S.S. man. How contemptible! But still –"

"Let me have your address and I'll have it sent to you. Do you want one too, Sophia?"

"No, thank you, Herr Meissner."

David was on his feet, telling Herr Meissner his address – he was impressed by the latter's gold pencil, embossed like his notebook with a swastika – and Sophia was on hers, firmly saying good-bye, and equally firmly refusing offers of a lift if she wouldn't go just yet. Within five minutes David found himself outside in the road, rather resentful at having to go just when another bottle of hock was being opened.

"I hope you didn't mind leaving," Sophia said.

"No, of course not."

"Wanda's a nice girl."

"Yes."

"It was lucky your getting a seat for May Day."

David nodded, a little guiltily.

"We can take the U-Bahn from Breitenbachplatz," Sophia said, after a minute's silence. He glanced at her and noticed that she was gazing stonily ahead. Something in her tone had led him to expect it.

"Is anything the matter?"

"No. Why?"

"Well, nothing." They continued walking along past the comfortable houses and well-kept gardens. It was twilight now and lights were going on, showing some very attractive interiors. It was all very different from the north end of Friedrichstrasse or, for that matter, from all the long, monotonous streets of the inner city. No clusters of stone eagles here – but these houses were just as much relics of an age that was gone,

430

the boom of the late twenties. "Which would you live in if you had to choose?" he asked.

"What?"

"I said, which would you – oh, forget it."

Puzzled by her attitude, he attempted clumsily to put his arm round her.

"Do stop banging into me," Sophia said, moving out of reach.

"Oh, God! What's the matter?"

"Nothing's the matter. I told you."

"You sound as if there was." A possibility occurred to him that she had been annoyed by Wanda's behaviour. It was obvious as soon as he thought of it. "I couldn't help sitting next to her, you know."

Immediately he realized that of all possible remarks this had been the most fatuously stupid.

"What *do* you mean?" Sophia enquired icily.

"Oh, nothing."

"You must have meant something." There was silence. She continued, "I must say I was rather amused when I heard you being so enthusiastic about seeing Hitler. I mean, in view of all your principles and everything. I was going to invite you to come with us into the country on Tuesday –"

"Oh, God, of course I'll come –"

"Certainly not. You'll have to use your ticket."

"Why? Meissner won't know."

"That would be quite impossible. In any case, I'm not going to invite you."

"All right, don't!" David said angrily. He was baffled. It was really too absurd and childish. They reached the Breitenbachplatz, a newish, attractive little square, still in silence. Then they caught the underground train back to the city and hardly spoke all the way. Sophia remained cold and aloof. After leaving her at the legation gate he returned to the hostel and spent the evening feeling exasperated.

The next day she was not in the class. He could hardly imagine that her absence was due to him and yet it would not be more remarkable than her ridiculous annoyance. At lunch-time he rang up the legation, but she was out. The

431

afternoon dragged away and he rang again. She was out again.

When he returned to the hostel there was a note for him from an office in Unter den Linden enclosing a ticket "by request of Herr Meissner". He considered not using it, as a sacrifice, but then decided firmly against any sacrifice.

Everyone at the hostel was busily preparing for various parades the next day. There was to be a youth congress of eighty thousand in a stadium a mile away and Köhler, who was going to it, was delirious with excitement and self-importance. Later on David went out with the Pole to Aschingers for beer and free rolls. Flags were out everywhere and down on the Linden people were already beginning an all-night wait. There was the same queer hypnotic something in the air that he had noticed on previous festival occasions. He almost forgot about Sophia under its influence. When he went to bed he realized that he was feeling quite stirred by the knowledge that he was going to see the Führer at last.

CHAPTER SIXTEEN

The room was on the third floor of an office belonging to a shipping company and it had three large windows; the view was excellent. David reached it in accordance with the instruction in the note by eight o'clock. About twenty people were already there taking coffee and sandwiches. Some Americans and Spaniards and a few German wives made up the shipping company's guests. The German wives were full of gossip about the S.A. and S.S. duties of their husbands – they exchanged it with complacency. Outside the pavements were crowded ten deep, with a narrow lane behind along which people with tickets could pass. It was most agreeable, David thought, to look down on the scene and feel oneself to be one of the privileged. S.A. men marched by and Hitler Youths and long-skirted Hitler Maidens, then a workers' guild, then more storm-troopers – all on their way to the

Lustgarten, where the Führer was to speak. The ever more enormous crowd watched and docilely saluted the flags as they went by.

He overheard a little American conversation.

"I'd say we can see a hundred thousand people from this window."

"More like half a million."

"Don't you admire their orderliness? Oh, now, did I hear you say you lived in Albany? Do you happen to know the Bishop of Buffalo? Or is it the Bishop of Upper New York?"

"Ma'am, I haven't even been to the Niagara Falls."

A loudspeaker interrupted this promising exchange. The room was filled with fervent speech. "National Socialist world view-point . . . the true German living in the name and spirit of his Führer . . . all folk-comrades to-day are politicians . . . fanatical will of millions . . . Versailles . . . the fundamental racial . . ." At first it drowned everybody, but after a time one became used to it, as to darkness in a cinema, and when some military music started it came almost as a surprise that the speech was over. A woman in a *cloche* hat, like someone from a ten-year-old photograph, began to chat to David. She was the enquirer after the Bishop of Buffalo, but her accent was strongly southern. She told him that she was forty-five and didn't mind who knew it, that she came from New Orleans, that her family had cut her off when she married a German, that it was years before she learnt the language because she spoke perfect French and her husband's family did too, that her mother had been a beautiful woman, that she knew confidentially that the Führer was going to restore the Hohenzollerns, that she admired the new King of England, that Boston and New Orleans were the only cultural centres in the United States, and that she wished to apologize to him, an Englishman, for the fact that Americans in general were vulgar, though less so in the South and hardly at all in New Orleans. She continued relentlessly with the negrer question – she begged pardon with a brilliant, humourless smile, she ought to say Negro – and how criticism of the Southern treatment of negrers was wicked, for she remembered perfectly that her mother and herself for that matter had always been on the best of terms with the negrer servants. David fidgeted, tried and failed to interrupt, despised himself, and smiled weakly.

The morning passed slowly by. Outside the huge crowds remained docile and slightly apathetic. There were no shouts or uninhibited cup-tie yells. Martial music blared out into the May Day air. David's companion grew tired of him and he heard her telling someone else, "So I didn't bother, as I spoke perfect French and my husband's family —"

Just before midday one of the German women screamed suddenly over her shoulder, "He's coming!" David craned his neck out to see as far as possible towards the Brandenburger Tor and felt himself struck by a noise so fantastically loud that it was as if a dozen aeroplanes were flying low along the street, then another dozen and another. The incredible sound was made by the "Heil – Heil – Heil" of the crowd, which had seemed so passive before and was now a forest of arms raised in salute. And here was the slow-moving procession of cars —

"Heil – Heil – Heil – Heil – Heil – Heil – Heil – Heil —"

Was this the Führer? Dazed by the shattering noise David saw the small black moustache, the white, grim face, the forehead hidden under a comically huge cap, the saluting arm held straight out at a right-angle, a long military coat, an immobile figure, larger than expected, looking ahead, ignoring the crowds, like someone trying not to be sick. Behind his car and between the bodyguard S.S. cars came an entirely unimpressive and unmilitary saloon on the top of which a man in an untidy lounge suit crouched behind a film camera. It was grotesque. Then came the stream of long black Mercedes containing the high and privileged, Goering, looking curiously small, Goebbels, Himmler — they received minor acclamation, the excitement was over, though it was taken up in a modified way by the loudspeakers.

David discovered that he was trembling. He felt exhausted. The symbol of greatness had passed by and had been frankly a disappointment. He told himself that he was glad, but in his heart he had not wanted to be disappointed.

"I have to say it," said the woman from New Orleans. "I

don't like him in that hat. It seems too big for him, doesn't it?"

"Perhaps it's bullet-proof," David said.

"The idea! Why, if anyone touched a hair of his head I believe I'd kill the scoundrel myself, even though I'm a poor weak woman! What worries me is if he has a cold."

Pandemonium was now coming out of the loudspeakers. The Führer had arrived at the Lustgarten. Below the shipping company's windows the crowd seemed to be moving about a little, so far as this was possible, as if a tension had been broken.

Dr. Goebbels was speaking.

"In all these years you were our example in courage and in work. It is no empty phrase if the nation says of you that you are our first worker —"

"God, they're all insane," thought David, and he felt a tremendous distaste for everyone in the room and the street outside. Why wasn't he out in the country with Sophia? He was mad to be here with this concentrated mass of imbeciles. God, the sound of that Heiling! He was still overcome by the shock of it. Nothing on the radio or the news films had prepared him for that fiendish, frightening din.

More pandemonium from the loudspeakers and then the famous voice was rolling out, deep and resonant. Benevolence was to-day's keynote.

" — and I am so proud to be your Führer, so proud that I cannot imagine what in the whole world could be equal to it — for it would be better, a thousand times better to be the least amongst you than a king anywhere else!"

Tumult.

"It's going down well," David said ironically to the woman from New Orleans, but she was bent forward, her eyes shining.

" — this pride fills me especially to-day. As I drove here through these long streets and saw to left and right hundreds and thousands and millions of fellow countrymen, from every kind of factory and works and plant and office, my heart was overfilled, and I felt truly — that this is our Germany! This our people, our magnificent German people and our beloved German Reich!"

435

Tumult.

On the return journey the noise was, if anything, greater. Hitler was now more relaxed, he allowed his arm to bend upwards at the elbow, he was smiling, though the enormous peak still hid his eyes from the spectators in the windows. And again David could not help a surge of feverish excitement. The thoughts he had claimed for himself in the interval were nonsense – he was as much affected as any of the screaming, heiling mob below. There were tears in his eyes.

It was another hour before they were able to leave the room and join the slowly-breaking-up crowds. He dodged the woman from New Orleans and made his way back to the automat in Friedrichstrasse. He bought a cheese roll and as he ate it he tried to make some sense of his reactions. He concluded that his emotion had been simply like the lump in the throat when you heard community singing at a football match – phoney and temporary. His disappointment with Hitler remained, but so too did the image he had received of that extraordinary figure. And how small the other notorious faces had looked! He changed his mind again.

"He didn't really look comic at all," he decided now. "It was really that I had a slightly wrong conception of what he would be like."

He was anxious to confirm Hitler's greatness to himself simply because, if Hitler were great, then he could be great himself by means of the Führer's own simple recipe – will-power – if not, then the long, tedious and also difficult road taken by people like Dr. Robinson lay ahead instead, an eternity of education still to come. "The trouble is I know nothing," he thought gloomily. "I must read –" He sketched out in his mind an immense personal reading plan, beginning with Gibbon and the whole of the *Cambridge Modern History*.

He left the automat and began to wander about the crowded streets. The atmosphere was gayer now and quite a few people were happily drunk. He looked at an enormous diagram in a shop window which indicated the insidious world power of Masonry. "Something else I know nothing about," he thought. He went down as far as Leipzigerstrasse

436

and past the giant stores and Goering's new Air Ministry, which was supposed to be bomb-proof. He decided to be extravagant and he went into the Leipziger Hof in Potsdamer Platz for a more expensive beer than he was accustomed to, to celebrate his reading plan. Once he was seated at a table with a huge mug in front of him he allowed himself to think about Sophia; he found he could do so quite objectively. Was there room in a dedicated life for such an infatuation? Was not being ascetic part of the price of greatness?

It was evening now and he was quite tired and hungry, but the menu looked too expensive. He left to go back to Friedrichstrasse. A meal at the students' club and then, as a first conscious move in his career, two or three hours of *Julius Caesar*.

But as he crossed Wilhelmstrasse he saw a crowd in the distance beyond the modern white Chancellery and he felt bound to investigate. He walked up the street. There were a good many police about and a few dozen people standing desultorily under Hitler's balcony and opposite by the Kaiserhof hotel hoping for an appearance. "Morons!" thought David, but he quickened his pace towards the crowd. Several hundred people were standing in front of the Presidential Palace, the pleasant eighteenth-century house where the heads of state had lived from Ebert to Hindenburg. Everyone was excited. It was thought that the Führer was inside. Half an hour passed. The crowd grew larger.

"When he comes out we must all shout our heads off!" said a middle-aged woman next to David.

"No, we'll leave that to the youngsters," said another, who looked as if her feet were hurting.

Another half hour. Some small boys climbed on to a window ledge and were called off by a policeman. They climbed up again and shouted at the police. The crowd, after a moment's shock at this indiscipline, decided to laugh. The police accepted it. Everything was good-humoured. Inside the forecourt of the palace cars waited – and suddenly started to move. In ones and twos leading members of the Government came out and drove away. Goering – a big cheer from the crowd; Baldur von Schirach, the youth leader, whose photograph was above Köhler's bed along with the Führer's – a mild cheer; Rosenberg – the Nazi theorist whose long book *The Myth of the Twentieth Century* was to be seen about almost as widely as Hitler's *My Struggle* – no cheer at all.

The last car rolled busily away – who was inside it nobody knew, but whoever it was kept his hand raised imperially – nobody in the crowd seemed to bother about saluting him back. Twilight was coming on. David realized that the whole street was now loosely packed with people. Groups of police and S.S. stood everywhere. Again he could feel an inner tingling of expectancy.

Suddenly a mounted police officer rode up, shouting, "The Führer is at the Chancellery!"

No time to breathe, no time to think – the whole crowd began at once to scramble and fight its way down the street towards the white, rectangular building with the balcony. David did as well as he could, and in fact surprised himself by being very efficient. He saw a cordon of S.S. men forming ahead and struggled sideways to get behind a cameraman's car which was edging slowly down the street. The cordon broke to let it through and David was through with it. He was swept on by a crowd of Hitler Youths and screaming women until, quite close to the balcony, it was impossible to get any further. He was pushed and trodden on and stifled, and then he became conscious of a huge enthusiastic shouting to a rhythmical beat going on all round and from far behind. It was like a war cry – "Daa da-de da-de-de da-de da-de," came the waves of sound, which he distinguished after a minute as *"Wir wollen unseren Führer sehen!"* – "We want to see our Führer – we want to see our Führer – we want to see our Führer" – Then a roar broke out and arms rose up in the air like thousands of birds, and there was the thundering shattering unison, *"Heil – Heil – Heil – Heil – Heil – Heil – Heil –"*

The Führer had come through the tall first-floor window and he stood there on the balcony, saluting back. There was the moustache, the white, plumpish face, the forelock – this time there was nothing comic about him, but there was the same curious immobility. David found himself choking with

438

excitement. This was a mass act of worship, the balcony was an altar, there was a dreadful hysteria in the air. The Führer retired and the tremendous chorus of " *Wir Wollen –* " began once more, louder than ever. When he came out again the tumult reached the sky. Not only the Hitler Youths, but middle-aged and even elderly men and women were screaming their adoration. All this, thought David, beside himself, for an ex-corporal of the German Army, son of an Austrian post office clerk, unsuccessful artist. The Manitou! That was the old storm-troopers' name for him – the man with supernatural powers, and now the living symbol of power on earth.

" *Heil – Heil – Heil – Heil – Heil – Heil – Heil – Heil –* "

And suddenly it was all over. The Führer went inside, it was made known that that was the end, the crowd obediently broke up. The hysteria had disappeared in two or three minutes. David heard a woman talking about stockings. He was bruised and exhausted.

He walked up to Unter den Linden. It was getting dark now and the torchlight marchers would be the next attraction. Finally Goering was to close the May Day proceedings in a ceremony at the Lustgarten, where the Führer had been at midday.

He went to the Friedrichstrasse Aschingers and ordered *Wiener Würstchen* and mashed potatoes. There was certainly a May Day atmosphere now, it was packed out with customers and there were bursts of rowdy laughter – David glanced at the parties with a feeling of exultation. There they were, the little people having their fun, unaware that greatness was sitting amongst them – a greatness without undesirable features, moreover, a liberal democratic greatness.

" I have decided to be a politician," he thought, and was overawed by the importance of the moment.

He was in the middle of his second sausage when he remembered having arranged to spend this evening with his aunt. Oh, God! The thing had gone right out of his mind – she was going to cook something, and his uncle had spoken about going to a beer garden – oh, God, they might still be waiting for him!

He ceased to be concerned with his destiny, gulped down the rest of the sausage and mashed potato, and hurried guiltily to the telephone.

CHAPTER SEVENTEEN

The bell rang for some time. Perhaps they had given him up and gone out. But just as he was considering putting the receiver back his aunt's voice was on the line.

" Who is it? " she asked in German.

" David."

" David? "

" Yes. I'm terribly sorry about this evening, but there's been the most tremendous – "

" Oh, it's you, David."

" Yes – I say, I'm awfully sorry about this evening – but I've been seeing Hitler – Uncle Rudi will be pleased – "

" Yes." As usual it was hopeless. She could dampen anything. " Where are you? "

" Where? In Friedrichstrasse. I've just – "

" Are you coming for some supper? There's some roast pork." Since the *Wiener Würstchen* had not made too filling a meal, this did not sound unattractive. It seemed much too late to make the journey, however. He was trying to think of an excuse when she added queerly, " Please come."

He felt he had to fall in, since she seemed to be so tolerant of his forgetfulness. A few minutes later he walked down to Jägerstrasse and caught the underground. There was a good deal of drunken singing in his carriage. David was beginning to feel pleased with himself again. He was not at all averse to roast pork and really it was much better to go as late as this to Aunt Isabel's. It cut down the time devoted to sitting around uncomfortably. " One must live ruthlessly, efficiently," he thought, as if he had planned it like this. The fabulous sound of the cheering crowds was still on his mind. He leaned back and closed his eyes, tired but exalted. Some sort of

440

Wagnerian music played – *Tannhäuser*, perhaps – and also the *Badenweiler* march. When he got off the train he felt that every step he took was towards some thrilling end. "How kind and friendly all these people look!" he thought. It was sad that to be happy one must be unimportant.

His aunt opened the door to him, neat and pale, a melancholy ghost. She gave him her quick, dim smile.

"You haven't been long."

"I got a train right away." He was embarrassed by a fleeting idea that she wanted him to kiss her.

"I hope you're hungry. Rudi's not here so you'll have to eat double. Aren't you too cold without a coat?"

He went past her into the living-room and saw the table laid for one.

"I had something earlier," she said. "I'm not hungry now."

He protested, but she didn't listen – it was the most boring aspect of one's family that no one ever did listen. His uncle's absence was also a bore. One could at least argue with him.

"Did you say you had seen Hitler?" Aunt Isabel said from the kitchen.

"Yes. This morning and about an hour ago. I got caught up in the crowd in Wilhelmstrasse."

"That was interesting for you."

"Yes, it was." The understatement amused him. How could his aunt conceive the fabulous drama of absolute power? It was not worth attempting to describe what he had felt.

"Whatever people may think at home," Aunt Isabel said, "he is the German of all Germans. He knows what they want."

"Yes," David said, conscious of the often recurring note of irony in his aunt's voice.

"What else have you been doing? Working hard, of course. Now the summer's coming you'll be able to go to Wannsee and swim. There's a nice beach there, though I think you have to pay – but there are lots of places where you can go free. I used to go with Rudi – years ago, of course."

She was very talkative and comparatively lively. David slowly became puzzled. He wondered if the day had stirred up his nerves to an unusual sensitivity. There was something different about his aunt. The flow of conversation had never been so sustained. She came in with the food and then sat opposite him, crumbling bread while he ate a huge plate of roast pork and potatoes and *Sauerkraut* and sprouts. It was all rather shrivelled, but still eatable. But she kept on wanting to know if he had had enough and if he liked it. The need for constantly repeating thanks and praise started to irritate him. Then she wanted to know if the light was all right for him and not too dim, and if he felt a draught. He reassured her, and a moment later she repeated the questions as if she hadn't believed him. He became more irritated. She went on with a series of aimless remarks about his mother, which she had made many times before. All the time she crumbled her slice of bread, gradually making little doughy balls of it. He found himself watching her fingers.

"Of course Sarah always was so lively, but I hope she doesn't tire herself too much – it must be such a responsibility nowadays, running a house. I do hope she can come to Berlin for a holiday – she always said she would come, but of course it isn't easy – and then your father being such a busy man makes it all so difficult. But she can stay here, hotels are so expensive. Have some more potatoes, David. A boy of – I should say a young man of your age, I suppose – should eat, you know, the growing frame demands –" Again the queer flash of irony that disconcerted him. But she went on, as if she were making aimless party conversation, "Until you're twenty-five, you know. At twenty-five you can look in the glass and say, 'Well – here I am.'" She laughed – a party conversation laugh. "Then of course decay sets in."

David glanced at her and looked quickly back at his almost empty plate. He felt very embarrassed. He hardly knew whether he was supposed to laugh with her or not. Out of the corner of his eye he was conscious of the fingers still nervously touching the bread.

"I won't have any more, thanks."

"Of course it's all dried up, I'm so bad at keeping things warm – it's quite an art, you know –"

"It was awfully good, really, but honestly I've had enough."

442

"I suppose Sarah's a good cook. Mother made her learn, but I never learned. I was always at the piano, practising. I had to learn afterwards. I've never been good. You have to learn everything when you're young or it's too late. But there are plenty of potatoes, David. I'll get you some more."

It was hopeless. He longed to have the courage to shout at her that when he said he had had enough he meant it. She had already hurried to the kitchen, still talking. He had never been so uncomfortable. It was as if he were shut up with a madwoman. Or was she ill?

". . . your mother would go down to the kitchen, she had such a winning way with her—I never had—even if she was a nuisance nobody minded. I was practising all the time, you see, David, practice, practice, practice—Nicky would sit on the pouf listening—he was such a sweet, clever boy, but there was death written on his face. He was an angel." She had brought back his plate, piled with potatoes and overflowing with gravy. He didn't want to touch it. His one thought was how soon he could get away. "An angel," she repeated, standing beside him. "I always knew somehow—"

"What time is Uncle Rudi coming back?" he asked.

"He isn't coming back."

David felt his heart pounding.

"How do you mean?"

"He isn't coming back. He's left me. He's gone." She began to tremble. She whispered, "He's gone. He's gone." She put her hands to her eyes and moaned.

David was appalled. He experienced the discomfort felt by the young when faced with a display of emotion by the mature. He would have been hardly more upset if an earthquake tremor had shaken the flat. His aunt looked and sounded grotesque and totally undignified. The only relief he could see in the situation was that now he would surely not be forced to eat the potatoes and gravy. He pushed the plate aside firmly and half rose—but he didn't know whether he should pretend to ignore or to show sympathy. It was horribly embarrassing.

She saved him from a decision by darting to her own chair. Still with her hands over her eyes she laid her head on the table and burst into a torrent of sobbing. A knife clattered to the floor. Her left wrist pressed on a plate so that its opposite edge was tilted up.

"Probably a damned good thing if he's really gone," David thought. He began to feel some excitement along with his distaste for the unnatural scene. One didn't see a marriage break up every day. He leaned across and pulled the plate out of contact. Mixed up with the sobbing now was his aunt's cough. It was a more suitable sound for one of her age and brought her back some dignity—he felt himself outside the whole thing, watching objectively. He reflected, "God, I'm a callous bastard. The artist makes notes as his mother dies. I am, after all, ruthless—" But he began to lose his ruthlessness almost at once. She continued to shudder. A sympathetic lump rose in his throat and he felt his eyes pricking with tears. Suddenly emotion swept over him. He could not sit still any more. He got up and stumbled round to put his arm on her shoulder.

"Don't cry like that—please—"

Her sobbing redoubled and she seized hold of his arm in a painfully tight grasp. Then she coughed for a minute. It was a dreadful sound. All at once there was silence. She breathed in deeply, sighed, relaxed her grip and sat up. She said, "Whatever can you think—lend me your handkerchief, please—"

"It's a bit dirty."

"It doesn't matter. I'm terribly, terribly sorry, dear. I'm afraid I was hysterical—it came over me." She gave him an embarrassed little smile and dabbed her face with his handkerchief. "I oughtn't to have—I ought to have told you not to come—it's not fair to make you—I mean you can't understand these things at your age—"

"Oh, I do understand," he said, a little nettled. He had only to think of Sophia to understand.

"Please forget all about it, dear." She ignored what he said, of course. "It's all over now."

"What are you going to do?" He hoped to God she wouldn't want him to move into the flat.

"Well—I'll make you some coffee, anyway. Oh, there's some blancmange if you'd like it. There's no need to spoil your meal because of me."

444

"I don't want anything more," he said tersely. He was annoyed at the way she had treated his question.

She seemed to sense it, for she put a hand to her forehead and added in a flat, weary voice, "I don't know what I'm going to do. I don't know. Whatever I do, it'll turn out wrong."

He thought she was going to collapse again.

"When did he go?"

"Last night." She set about clearing the table.

"Do you know where he is?"

"Yes. Yes, I know where he is."

"You mean he's with – another –" He paused, anxious to make no adolescent gaffes.

"Oh, he's not alone," she said, with the ghost of a smile. She went out to the kitchen with the plates, leaving him feverish with curiosity. "It's nobody you know."

"Will you divorce him?" He found it wonderful to be able to ask such a question. He heard the gas go on and tap water running. He added hurriedly, "But, of course, I suppose he may come back –" He followed her out. She was at the sink, her back towards him. "Aunt Isabel, isn't there anything I can do?"

"Oh, no, dear," she said softly, almost as if she were amused. She turned round, her eyes bright. He stepped towards her clumsily, hardly knowing what he was doing, but conscious of a queer illusion that he saw her as she must have been years before, young and attractive. He could not bear to speak. He put his arms round her and his cheek was pressed against hers. His eyes pricked with tears, but in spite of his sincere feeling of compassion, it occurred to him how divine it would be if this were Sophia and not his aunt, and at once despised himself for thinking it. He held her more tightly.

After a moment she said, "I've upset you. I'm sorry, dear. You see, this is only typical of everything that's ever happened to me. Perhaps you're right and you understand – it was all happening to me before I was your age. Things start as they go on, events and happenings pile up and you grow older, but it's always the same, things turn out for some people and not

445

for others – I pray you don't understand, David. It just seems that things have to go wrong with me. Whatever I touch, whatever I love even – it's almost a crime for me to love anybody, when I think what's happened – "

He was conscious of another feeling still, of admiration. She managed to sound almost cheerful. After the state she had been in, it was marvellous that she could control herself so well.

"As for your uncle," she said, "we should never have married. Do you know why he married me? Because it was the inflation time and I had some English money."

"Good God!"

"Yes, it's a surprise, isn't it? Life is full of surprises, I've found, most of them not too pleasant. What a glorious fool I was! But there it is, I was in love with him. Just when I was at last getting somewhere – ah, my dear, there it is, one can't go against fate. It's easy to look back afterwards and say one shouldn't have done this or that, but if fate's against you, it's against you, and that's all there is to it. You can't help falling in love. You know, I often think of your mother and how things have gone so well for her, such a gay, interesting life – "

David said, "She'd be surprised to hear that. I know she's always thought of you having the gay, interesting life. She always says there's no glamour in her life and she wishes she'd run off romantically – she's joking, I mean, of course, but all the same I guess she means it a bit."

"Run off romantically," his aunt repeated with a smile. "Well, yes, I suppose it may have looked like that – yes, it felt like it, of course it did." She shrugged her shoulders and sighed. "Fourteen years ago. Fourteen years of hell. That's what running off romantically did for me, my dear."

He stared at her.

"But I know mother's always thought you were very happily married."

"I've never told her I wasn't," she said wearily. "I've never told anyone – I suppose I ought to despise myself for telling you. But, still, there isn't any hope now and it does me good to talk, I expect. Not that there was ever any hope, although I always pretended. I suppose I knew that the first day we

446

were in Berlin. In fact, I knew he'd been lying to me before we even arrived. Rudi had drawn a pretty picture of his flat and his piano, you know, and of course I'd been looking forward to it – he described the pictures and the books and the carpets – and there was only one thing wrong, there wasn't a word of truth in any of it. We were half an hour from the Zoo station when he calmly let me know that he was really a lodger in someone else's flat. And *they* had the piano – but even that wasn't true, they'd sold it while he was in England. I ought to have left him then and there and taken the next train back, but of course he was so persuasive, and I was in love with him. I told myself that I'd married *him*, not the supposed flat. Besides, I wasn't a young girl. I should look such a fool, if I went back.

"I'll never forget that first evening, David. There were two women there, a mother and daughter, and a man who'd been sleeping in Rudi's room while he was away. There was a terrible quarrel about it – of course I hardly understood a word – I thought I'd go mad. There was a quarrel about rent as well. That was where I realized what my husband saw in me. I had a few hundred pounds and the great inflation was getting going. Anyone with a few pounds was quite rich. He'd seen his chance in London. A nice gullible Englishwoman. Yes, I have to admire the way he did it –"

"My God, Aunt Isabel!" David whispered. But he was less horrified than excited.

"We soon had our flat, of course – and the piano. The piano's about the one thing that remains from that time. Yes, inside a week we had a flat, it was in Matthäi-Kirchstrasse, much smarter than here, not far from the Tiergarten. We went into it fully furnished for fifty pounds. It belonged to a retired army couple and they couldn't keep it up, the inflation was crippling them already. There was a suit of armour in the hall – they love that sort of thing. But I was so relieved! David, I was so happy! Rudi was kind to me, I loved him – in fact things had turned out almost as he had said – except that the flat was much too big, and it was such a lot of work to run it, and with my practice to do as well, for I was determined to keep my playing up. We were spending much too

447

much – but it was quite simple. Rudi would borrow some money and pay it back when the mark had dropped another twenty-five per cent by cashing a few more of my pounds. All that year as the inflation got worse we kept buying things. I say 'we' but of course he did all the buying, I couldn't stop it, and he knew how to get round me for another ten pounds – which here was worth heaven knows what, a hundred or two hundred. Yes, when you hear your uncle turning on the National Socialist sermon about profiteers and Jews and everything, you can remember that we had about ten carpets for every one we could use; we had to use one room as a store; we could have furnished a mansion. Of course, by the end of the year my savings were almost gone, but Rudi was very confident. He was always saying it was sensible, after all, to use the pounds when their purchasing power was so enormous – it wouldn't last for ever, and when the German currency was strong again we should own some saleable commodities – 'Sachwerte' was the word, David. Yes, we were profiteers, we were 'Schieber'. I didn't see it then, but everything Rudi bought came from people who were forced to get rid of it. Yes, that's your great National Socialist, that's Rudi, that's what he was doing in the Fatherland's crisis. Not that I was having too bad a time at first. I was proud of our flat and it kept me busy. We went out quite often to concerts and the opera, in the summer we went bathing and picnicked – there's nowhere like Berlin for that – and you'd come across parties of nudists in the pinewoods, all sitting around calmly and singing – my dear, this was an amazing country. Yes, I say I was happy and Rudi was still pretending to be fond of me – or perhaps he wasn't pretending, I don't know. But there were always women; I know that. He'd been a gay bachelor and he didn't stop his habits. I had to accept it, that and other things. Sometimes he'd go out and get drunk – that's supposed to be frowned on since Hitler, but German men used to treat it as a kind of sport – it was something you didn't criticize, according to him. When he was in that state he could say the most terrible things. I'd keep telling myself that I ought to go – and then he'd be charming again for a period. And he did like music. He liked hearing me play, and I always prac-
448

tised, you see—I always have, heaven knows not for any reason, but I suppose it's kept me going. You always have to pretend that something matters or you're lost. Of course, *he* never took my playing seriously—it would never occur to a German that it was worth competing with other Germans. Of course it's different if you're one of the lucky ones. As a matter of fact, though, I did think about going to a professor, one of the famous teachers—that might have been my way in, you see, you have to be somebody's pupil, and if he's interested in you he may be able to use influence—one thing's certain, you can't do anything without influence, and of course Rudi knew no one. What happened was perfectly typical. As I say, I was on the point of going to see him—we were settled into the flat by then—when what did I do but slip on the kitchen floor and sprain my wrist. I was out of action for weeks, and when at last I was playing again I realized that our financial situation wasn't looking at all rosy—Rudi was buying things feverishly and there weren't so many pounds left, though to look at the flat you'd have thought we were rich. I did write to the professor, but that went wrong, too. He was away in Vienna.

"Then, of course, the inflation went mad when the French went into the Ruhr. It meant that Rudi had spent my money too soon. He couldn't get over what a fool he'd been—if he had only waited to do his profiteering, heaven knows what he couldn't have bought. He took it out on me. I wasn't any use to him any more. Sometimes I thought he hated me. Up to then he had always been drunk before he'd fling his sneering insults at me, but now even that wasn't necessary: He was quite capable of telling me to my face where he had spent the night. The only reason I didn't leave him was what people always say is the silliest reason: pride. But everything was mad that year. I can only remember one figure, that a pound in the autumn was worth five hundred thousand million marks—Rudi's firm were printing their own banknotes. It was like living in an earthquake. Then Rudi had a new game which made him feel better. He bought shares at a certain price and as the mark kept on going down, always faster than anyone thought, he sold them at a profit before he needed to pay for them. There were people making private empires in the same sort of way, but Rudi was very proud of himself, and we went on living comfortably – and then the currency was stabilized and Rudi was caught. Fortunately it wasn't an enormous amount, but everything we had had to go – he was suddenly facing a loss instead of the easy profit, and what was more it had to be paid in the new currency. We had to sell everything, all the carpets and silver, four full dinner services, all the carefully-hoarded ' Sachwerte ' – and we couldn't keep a penny of it. Of course we had to leave Matthäi-Kirchstrasse. We came here, with nothing left almost except the piano. Rudi was broken, collapsed. He hardly knew how to go to work. I'll say this for him; somehow he's managed to keep his job going, though he had to accept a thirty per cent pay cut in nineteen thirty-one, when they were cutting all the wages and salaries, if you were lucky enough to be working.

" I began teaching again, of course. All through the inflation I'd managed to keep a hundred pounds out of his hands, but that had to go now – and my hopes of a holiday in England. We had a hard time, though not so hard as some – I'll never forget some of the ghostly faces you would see in the streets in those years. But Rudi was very bitter. Not only against fate, but against me – he never forgave me for concealing the hundred pounds, even though it had come in so useful. ' You fool, we could have bought half a street with it last year ! ' – that was what he'd say and call me something worse. But sometimes a week would go by almost without him opening his mouth. Those times were unbearable. Then, of course, he went almost every year to England and your mother would write to me how charming he was – oh, he could still be charming, if he liked ! Even with me. He's come in here time and again, put his arm round me and whispered, ' I'm a swine to you, I know it,' and, God forgive me, it's given me pleasure. When things got better again, as they did, of course, he started enjoying himself again. There was a girl at the office – that went on for years. Now there's this woman, she's a widow with a flat in Zehlendorf, a strong Nazi enthusiast – Rudi, incidentally, joined in February 1933, just as he'd have joined the Communists, or the Flat Earth Society if they were coming into power, and his great complaint against me is that I haven't

450

fully integrated myself with National Socialist ideals – he's quite right, but he doesn't mean it, of course, it's simply the perfect line for him with a foreign wife, if there are any legal proceedings. That is my reward for fourteen years of trying to live with him. The real reason is that his widow has suddenly been left fifty thousand marks – so now he hasn't gone off for the usual two days, disguised as business – sometimes not even disguised – now he's gone for good, at least until he's spent the money, I suppose. Well, David, dear, that's it. That's been my life. If you want to know why I was in tears, it wasn't for your uncle – any fascination he had for me is gone long ago – no, it was for the mess, the mess my life has been. Fourteen years! It goes so quickly, and yet the days have been so long – well, that's the way life is, dear – now go and smoke a cigarette and I'll bring the coffee out on to the balcony."

He went back to the living-room, dazed by the long, calmly-told story. He couldn't get over the idea of a marriage for such a reason – above all between two people whom he knew. "Good God!" he thought. "How fascinating!" He opened the balcony window and stepped into the evening air. There was the faintest breeze, neither warm nor cool. It smelt vaguely and pleasantly of cigars, a Berlin smell. He stared up and down at the lights of the street. Was this the kind of thing that lay behind these other windows? "It's the way life is, dear." Life! God, what an exciting day it had been! He lit his cigarette and watched the smoke vanish. Then he turned and went through the sitting-room out to the bathroom. "How frightful that one has to piss," he thought. He noticed that there was only one toothbrush by the wash-basin and no sign of his uncle's shaving gear. He shook his head wonderingly, as if to say, "Well, it's really true." On his way back he glanced into the bedroom. It seemed in the dim light to be very untidy, and he hurriedly went on, with a feeling of guilt as if he had just opened someone else's letter.

She had brought in the coffee.

"Oh, there you are. Shall we have it on the balcony or is it too chilly? But let's have it out there, anyway, and celebrate May Day."

She took the tray out and put it on a little half-rusty iron table. David followed with two chairs. "There, that's right, thank you, dear. Well, it's summer again."

"Yes."

"Berlin is lovely in summer. The lakes, brown bodies, Nivea Cream. You'll have a good time." She poured out the coffee. "Let's see, you must go to the Pfaueninsel. That's quite attractive – "

"Yes."

"David – I don't like to ask you, but – it would oblige me if you didn't say anything yet – when you write home – "

"Of course not!" he exclaimed, although the idea of saying nothing had not occurred to him.

"I have to think out what I'm going to do, you see."

"Look here, Aunt Isabel, why don't you go back to England?"

"Well – " She shook her head. "It's what I'd like to do. If I could get work – perhaps with the B.B.C. as an accompanist – but of course I expect it would be hopeless – "

"Surely it's worth trying?"

"Well, as I say, it's all a matter of luck," she answered. "Luck is what you want in this world. Oh, it's no good thinking about it. It comes or it doesn't. If you could imagine the kind of dreams I used to have – oh, but it's such a long time ago! And there were so many things. There was a week I spent with your mother in London, when everything seemed – oh, but as I say, it's no use. For someone else it would have been different. Imagine, David, all those years I played at the grill room – you know about that?" He nodded. "I hated going there at all – but in the end I was almost giving a recital every evening, not grill room music at all and – it sounds very conceited, but it's a fact that people would come miles to hear me – they'd sit and just listen all the evening – and yet, in all those years nobody influential was there by accident – as you can depend on it they would have been with someone else. Some people wouldn't have been there a week before an agent or impresario, someone influential, walked in."

He didn't know what to say. He finished his coffee. He was very depressed by her recital, in spite of her courageous attitude to her misfortunes. For he could not help relating what had happened to her to what might happen to himself. Was this what it all depended on? The right person coming into the grill room at the right time? He would hate to believe it.

He said, " Well, I suppose I ought to be getting along."

" Yes, and it's much too cold for me out here, with my chest. I don't know what I'm thinking about to be sitting here. Shall I heat the coffee for another cup? "

He shook his head.

" David, I'm sorry – I oughtn't to burden you with my troubles."

" It's so damned unfair! " he said angrily.

When he left a few minutes later he was conscious of a dreadful loneliness which seemed to hover round her. She clung to him for a second and he was sure that as soon as the door closed her self-control would break down. He felt guilty at leaving her and overcome with such a wave of pity for her and anger with his uncle that he nearly choked over his good night.

She smiled from the door. " Don't worry about me, my dear."

He nodded. When he reached the street he murmured to the air, " God, how bloody life is! "

At the hostel there was a party's-over-now atmosphere. They were all exhausted and drunk with parades and torch-light processions. Habraschka was asleep on his bed, fully dressed. The Pole was still out. Köhler paused in pulling off his boots to say excitedly, as David came in, " Well, did you see the Führer? "

" Yes. Twice. This evening as well."

" Ah, you were in the Wilhelmstrasse? Wonderful! So was I! " Köhler sighed happily. " There's no doubt about it, Herr Proctor, he is the greatest man in the world."

CHAPTER EIGHTEEN

When he woke up the next morning, he looked across at Köhler and Habraschka, both dead with sleep – hardly anyone in the hostel was likely to get up before lunch – and they seemed to him not so much misguided political opponents as adolescents. He felt middle-aged. That part of their myth which he had accepted, that youth was the precious time, the active time, the passionate time and that after the middle twenties existence became vegetable-like for the majority, he now knew to be nonsense. It was clear that the dullest couples might be living feverishly complicated lives. When he went to collect his breakfast he glanced at Frau Döring's fat Slav face with a new interest, wondering what story her unpromising exterior concealed. But the plaque on the wall reminded him that the Führer was celibate. A life free of personal entanglements, yes, that was definitely involved in " I, however, decided – "

This thought had an immediately bracing effect on him. He drummed his fingers on the counter. Frau Döring gave him one of her most unfriendly and suspicious looks and positively snapped " *Heil Hitler!* " as she handed over his coffee jug.

Half an hour later he was on his way down Friedrichstrasse. Armed with his new perception, he looked at people sympathetically. Let them enjoy their mixed-up lives. For his part love must be cut right out.

" I renounce it," he murmured, opposite the Admiralspalast. " Single-mindedness, that's the thing."

When he entered the classroom, however, together with the Herr Doktor – for he was rather late – he saw Sophia and she smiled across at him. Instantly David forgot everything he had been thinking. He felt as if he had just run a hundred yards and he succeeded in knocking his chair over before he sat down.

454

During the mid-morning break she behaved as if there had been no chilly atmosphere at all.

"I think I've got a fearful cold coming on," she greeted him. "My head's all muzzy. You'd better not come near."

"It will be a pleasure to catch it from you," David said brilliantly.

"What was it like yesterday?"

"Boring. How about you? Did you have a good day?"

"Boring also," said Sophia, staring at him with her wide blue eyes.

David trembled. Did she mean that it had been boring because of his absence? He felt as if he could cry.

"Well, I saw the Führer," he said, with a great effort at casualness. "He looked bigger than I expected."

"We went to Müncheberg. Quite a pretty drive, all forest and lakes. I had a swim. It was freezing."

"I bet it was. How about a film this afternoon?"

"What film?"

"*Sehnsucht*. Marlene Dietrich, Gary Cooper."

"I don't feel much like it, but all right. You'd better come back to lunch."

It wasn't until the middle of lunch, during which he was questioned by the Minister about crowd reactions the day before—he felt that he answered impressively—that he remembered his aunt. He had meant to ring her up, but from the moment he had seen Sophia he hadn't given her a thought. It didn't matter, of course, but he felt guilty and determined to ring her before they went into the cinema.

One of the legation secretaries, an agreeable young man, was at lunch with them. He asked what film Sophia was going to see.

"*Sehnsucht*."

"Good heavens," said Mrs. Robinson, "that doesn't sound at all suitable, dear. *Desire!* Really!"

"Oh, mother," said Sophia in disgust.

"Perhaps it isn't that kind of *Sehnsucht*," suggested the Minister, winking at the secretary.

"I think it is," said the secretary. "Not at all suitable for Sophie."

" Just you wait, Tom," Sophia said.

" It's a Lubitsch film," the secretary continued. " But he's a Jew, so his name isn't mentioned. Like the Lorelei."

" It doesn't sound a nice film," Mrs. Robinson said.

" Oh, mother – a nice film! "

The Minister told David, " If there's anything you feel my daughter shouldn't see, hold your hand up in front of her eyes."

" I'll explain anything you don't understand, if you tell me afterwards, Sophie," the secretary said.

It was all very whimsical and David might have enjoyed, or at least tolerated, it, if the tone of Sophia's answer to the secretary had not struck a chill in him. " Just you wait, Tom " had implied a brother-and-sister intimacy, which was all right if that was what it was. And " Sophie ", as well.

A minute or two later he had another shock. Yesterday's trip was discussed and it turned out that the secretary had been on it, and had bathed with Sophia. David's anxiety was not lessened when it was disclosed, in connection with this swim, that " Tom " had played water-polo for his university.

As soon as they were in the bus he burst out : " You didn't say he was with you yesterday! "

" Why ever should I? " Sophia asked. It was ominous that she took for granted what he was talking about.

" You know why," he said sulkily.

Sophia looked annoyed. She did not answer. When they got out at the Zoo the silence was still on. He was furious at having made a fool of himself. He had a good mind to suggest that they called the film off, but he didn't dare to in case she agreed and went home. However, as they entered the cinema she suddenly squeezed his thumb and he was dizzy with relief for a few seconds. But inside, although she allowed him to hold her hand intermittently, it was not satisfactory. It was as if she were merely remembering her duties as his guest, since he had had to pay five marks for the seats – which he couldn't have afforded, except that it was close to the beginning of the month. But at least the film was splendid, with Miss Dietrich driving a beautiful sports car in Spain.

456

Afterwards Sophia thanked him politely.

"Thank you very much. It was frightfully good."

He might have been her uncle. He decided on a further, more desperate extravagance.

"Let's go over to the Capitol and have some *Schlagsahne*." The whipped cream one could have with coffee, ices and cakes was a weakness of hers.

"No. I think I'd better go back."

"Go back! Now? But why?" he gasped.

"I told you I had a cold coming on. I've got a bit of a headache."

She began to move determinedly towards the bus stop. He didn't believe her. She certainly didn't look as if she had a cold or a headache. In fact she had been more lively at lunch than usual. The picnic yesterday, the swim, "Just you wait, Tom" – these were more likely explanations. Whatever it was she had put up a barrier.

As they crossed Budapesterstrasse he said, "Sophia, for God's sake what's the matter?"

"I've just told you, haven't I? What are you talking about?"

"Oh, my God!"

"I do wish you'd talk sensibly." They reached the pavement.

"What have I done?" he demanded. He was almost in tears. Sophia, who had hurried on ahead, turned and glanced back at him where he had come to a halt. She looked highly exasperated.

"You haven't *done* anything. I tell you, I don't know what you're talking about. I said I had a headache. Well, I *have*. I've also got to be at a dinner party to-night –" She broke off as a bus came up. "Look, I'm catching this, David. Don't you bother to come." As if from a feeling of charity she came back and touched his hand. "Thanks awfully for the film. I enjoyed it, I really did. Don't be so silly."

She hurried away after the bus and was gone. He had been too paralysed to do anything. He stood on the pavement, furious, suspicious, miserable and bewildered. She had been so different in the morning saying she had been "bored" yesterday – it didn't look like that at lunch – and the dinner party doubtless meant that "Tom" would be there, a man who had it over him in every way. More or less a diplomat, a swimming champion, well-dressed and even quite young – it was hopeless, David recognized grimly, if the secretary were interested in Sophia. Full of gloom he walked back towards the Memorial Church island.

The mood of extravagance was still with him, though its purpose was gone, and he went to the Romanisches Café and ordered a coffee with whipped cream – the price was as much as several cheese rolls at the automat, but he didn't care. It was a faint consolation to reflect, as he sat there, "Well, this is what jealousy's like." And he remembered his aunt. He thought bitterly, "Now it's the two of us." It seemed more than ever possible that his life would be like hers. It was a dreary prospect. What, for example, could she have been doing to-day? What had she been doing, for that matter, every day for years? Piano lessons, dusting, cooking – a woman, according to his mother, who ought to have been internationally known. And what had happened to his own fine determination of only a few hours before to be free of love and emotional entanglement? The only fact that emerged was that Sophia had never been so appallingly attractive to him. "God, I'm so damned weak!" he murmured under his breath. He felt a certain dramatic satisfaction at his weakness. And he began to think about his aunt again, with sympathy, as a fellow castaway. Perhaps he ought to go round and see her again. Had she any money at all – would Uncle Rudi send her any? Ought he to go to see him at his office, perhaps, and demand in the name of the family that his aunt should be treated properly?

He spent a moment imagining a stormy but successful interview. Then he relapsed into gloom again. In fact, of course, he would merely look ridiculous. All he could give his aunt was understanding and sympathy. And she wouldn't appreciate how real his understanding was. "Damn being young," he thought angrily.

However, he went to a telephone booth and rang her up.

"*Hier Peters*," she said almost at once.

458

"Hullo. It's me. David."

"Oh, yes, dear." Her tone was flat. He was sure she had been hoping it was Uncle Rudi.

"I – I just rang to see how you were," he said, suddenly awkward. He wanted to convey how deeply he felt for her.

"Perfectly all right, dear. Don't you worry about me. What have you been doing?"

"Nothing. Are you *sure* you're all right?"

"Yes, David, dear."

"Well – well, then, I'll see you at the week-end, then, I expect."

"All right, dear."

As he left the booth he was conscious of the disappointment in her voice. She had not suggested that he came round, but he was sure that she had wanted to – and he had intended suggesting it himself. But he couldn't bring himself to do it. Or was it that he had wanted to be mildly cruel, taking out his own personal troubles on her? "I'm a bastard," he thought gloomily. A sense of guilt was added to his general unhappiness.

The next morning he went to the university, determined to behave towards Sophia with coolness and dignity. She was absent. At lunch-time, unable to resist, he rang up the legation and asked for her. She was in bed with a cold and not available.

He had never had better news. What she had said was true. He must have been out of his mind to doubt her. He walked away from the telephone – he was in the students' club – in a state of exaltation. Almost immediately he played a game of table-tennis against a young S.S. man and had the pleasure of winning easily. He nearly forgot to have lunch. Far from anything having been wrong, she had apparently come out with him in spite of feeling unwell. His ludicrous jealousy vanished.

That evening he went to the swimming-bath in Gartenstrasse, half a mile away, and practised his rather inefficient crawl and mediocre diving, in the hope of putting up a show of some sort when he bathed with her.

In the morning she was still away. The Herr Doktor asked

him if he knew what was wrong and this public suggestion that he was in a position to know filled him with pleasure. At lunch-time he rang the legation again and was put through to her mother.

"She's still in bed," Mrs. Robinson said. "She has a little temperature, nothing much –"

"A temperature!" he exclaimed, as if he had just been told that she had pneumonia.

"It was that swim, you know, and going to the pictures didn't help."

"God, I'm awfully sorry!"

"Well, it can't be helped now," said Mrs. Robinson brusquely, and he felt that she did not like his "God". Some word or other was always becoming a habit with him. It was irritating.

He pretended to be worried, but was delighted. The temperature made her gesture in coming out with him all the more noble. That evening he practised swimming again. He hardly gave a thought to his aunt. In the morning, however – it was Saturday – he remembered that he must ring her up and arrange to go round. She was vaguely on his conscience, but he just wasn't in the mood for her.

He had braced himself to go to the telephone when the Pole asked if he would like to go with him to *Die Fledermaus* in the evening. He had two free tickets from the "Strength through Joy" office. It was a splendid excuse for putting off his aunt, without having to feel guilty about it, and David accepted with gratitude. Then he went happily to the telephone. She answered at once, as if she were waiting by it.

"Aunt Isabel, I'm awfully sorry, I can't come until to-morrow, I'm going to the theatre –"

She sounded disappointed, but, as usual, resigned.

"No, that's all right, dear. What are you going to see?"

"*Fledermaus.*"

"Oh, that's good. The music's charming. Well, until to-morrow – you'll come to lunch? Perhaps we can go to a film –"

"Yes, thanks awfully. Right ho." He added uncomfortably, "Everything all right?"

460

"Oh, yes, dear, thank you."

Then he went swimming. The baths were crowded with Hitler Youth, some of whom were standing in an admiring group round a heavily muscled exhibitionist who demonstrated exercises to them. At the end of the morning he rang the legation, hoping that he would miss Mrs. Robinson.

He was put through to Sophia, and when he heard her "Hullo" he felt unbalanced.

"Hullo! It's me. Are you better? That's wonderful."

"Yes, I'm all right."

"I rang yesterday. I spoke to your mother."

"Yes, she told me."

"You're okay now?" He was already a little nervous, for she sounded very casual.

"Yes, I only had a chill."

"I didn't know how bad you were. God, I was frightfully worried, Sophia, I'm frightfully sorry about the film – I mean, it must have made it worse and you were probably feeling awful."

"Oh, I don't know –"

"I mean, I just want to say I'm frightfully sorry about that afternoon. I was an absolute ass."

"What are you talking about?" Sophia asked, causing him to be panic-stricken.

"Oh, God! Nothing. Well, anyhow, can I come round?"

"Not to-day – I'm only up for an hour or two. I'm supposed to go back to bed."

"To-morrow, then?" he said anxiously.

"Well, all right. We might be going for a drive in the afternoon, if it's fine. Ring up first, though."

He relaxed.

"Right ho! That's wonderful! I'm glad you're all right again, Sophia. Well, I'll ring up in the morning."

"Not till about lunch-time."

"Okay."

"I must go now."

It was about half an hour afterwards, when he was having lunch in the students' club canteen, before he remembered his aunt. "Damn!" he murmured. He was uncomfortable about it, but there was only one solution. As soon as he had finished eating he returned to the telephone.

His excuse was laboured and probably unconvincing. An old invitation he had forgotten about, but now it was still on – he would come round as soon as he could, he would probably be back in the evening –

"Yes, all right, dear. It doesn't matter. I shall be here, anyhow."

When he put down the receiver, he thought, "I really am a bit of a bastard." On the other hand, he reasoned, all her Saturdays and Sundays had been pretty miserable for years, as far as he could see, even when Uncle Rudi was around. It would be ridiculous to mess oneself up – her troubles would have happened, whether he had come to Berlin or not. He returned to his mood of elation and forgot about her.

He spent the afternoon at the hostel working and writing home, until the Pole arrived to start his preparations for the evening. Eau-de-Cologne filled the air. David was not wildly excited about *Die Fledermaus*. The variety show at the Admiralspalast where there was an American who danced on a xylophone would have had more appeal for him. He was still less excited when they reached the theatre – it was the Komische Oper, opposite Friedrichstrasse station – and he found that the Pole's tickets were for standing room behind the circle. The theatre was very warm and the audience humdrum in appearance, as was to be expected if they all came under "Strength through Joy" auspices. David was surprised that the Pole seemed so pleased with everything – when the show started he seemed to be moved to rapture every two or three minutes. He kept whispering, "*Schön, was?*" – "Beautiful, isn't it?" – as did many of the plump women in flouncy dresses who sat in front of them. He applauded vigorously at every opportunity. "Isn't she lovely?" he exclaimed, as an actress approached the footlights. "I'd like to have that one in my arms, wouldn't you?" David was embarrassed, for these unself-conscious reactions kept causing people to turn round. His companion looked delighted. Soon he seemed to lose interest in the stage and started a series of penetrating whispers such as, "That one in front, second row, she has a
462

beautiful neck, don't you think? I find a long neck attractive. I must have a good look when the lights go up. Hey, that's a fat one – on your left – " David was in agony at first, conscious of all the glances and of backs growing rigid in front, but then he began to find it amusing.

In the interval he was fascinated by the ease and speed with which the Pole fell into conversation with two unescorted girls. He might have known them all his life. He produced cigarettes and flicked a lighter with great elegance, talking all the time. David was tongue-tied and full of admiration. The Pole waved his hands, smoothed his sleeves, patted his hair, offered the girls a smell of his handkerchief – their names were Emmi and Greta, they were from Leipzig and on holiday in Berlin. They giggled and nudged each other. They were plump-ish, but, if not pretty, not unattractive either. By the end of the interval David had managed to join in, though he was a little worried that they thought him too young to bother about.

"Not bad?" said the Pole, when they were back. "Shall we meet them afterwards?"

"Naturally."

The Pole winked and gave him a conspirator's nod. David suddenly realized that this might be a momentous evening. Two girls on holiday in Berlin, the Pole clearly knowing all the ropes – what could be more promising? He watched them take their seats on one side of the circle, talking busily. He felt feverish with excitement.

In the second interval the Pole surpassed himself. An arrangement to meet afterwards was made with the greatest of ease. David was astonished how easily it was done. The girls nudged each other and giggled more than ever. He had a satis-factory feeling that they were rather impressed at meeting an Englishman, although they were enchanted by the Pole. The latter bent over their hands at the end of the interval. David bowed. It was as near as he could get to following suit.

Back for the third act the Pole was in an exuberant mood. He clapped and called "Bravo" on the slightest provocation. For his part David's excitement was giving way to nervous-ness, which grew as the finale approached. Suddenly he looked sideways to where the girls were sitting, and to his astonishment saw that they were excusing their way out. He glanced furtively at the Pole.

"I ought to tell him," he thought guiltily.

But the fact was he was rather relieved. It was amusing, also, that they were evidently as scared as he was. His self-respect was uninjured. In no time at all he forgot that he had been scared at all.

The curtain fell, rose, fell, rose – the Pole clapped and called out enthusiastically, attracting attention to the end. Then he turned to David, clapped him on the shoulder and winked again.

"*An die Mensur – los!*" he exclaimed, repeating a phrase used to start students' duels.

"*Los!*" David nodded, unperturbed by his own hypocrisy.

"I can't see them."

"No, nor can I."

"We'll pick them up in the street. I feel feverish, don't you? We shall have some fun with them. You leave it to me."

They joined the crowd going down the stairs. There was no sign in the foyer. The Pole went this way and that, like a dog trying to pick up a scent. They went out into the street and came back again. The Pole was disconsolate.

"Gone! *Disparues!* How frightful!" he exclaimed in a low sad voice. "I don't understand it. They promised!"

So it was Aschingers again, two light beers and some rolls. David pretended to share the gloomy mood.

"Evidently they had cold feet, Stefan."

"Cold feet?"

"It's an English expression," David said, feeling tolerant and on top of the world.

464

CHAPTER NINETEEN

He woke up with the brilliant idea that he would go to hear Niemöller, the anti-Nazi protestant pastor. He had intended going before, for Niemöller had been mentioned with approval by the Minister. This was undoubtedly the morning to go. He would be equipped with some useful lunch-time conversation.

He told Köhler, who was already up and briskly shadow-boxing. The Austrian threw up his hands in good-humoured despair.

"My dear Mr. Englishman, all the churches are nonsense! Talk, talk, talk! Action! That is youth's religion! What name? Niemöller? I've never heard of him."

"He was a U-boat commander, you know."

"U-boats! War! We are finished with war!"

"Even against the Russians? Why do the Hitler Youth learn about camouflage?"

"Ho, ho, ho! Mr. Englishman is full of jokes to-day!"

Some time after Köhler and Habraschka had gone off for their weekly sports day—the Pole, of course, was still asleep—David set off by underground for Dahlem. For Niemöller's church was in the suburb where the Meissners lived—David rather hoped that one of them would see him. He had bought a paper and on the way he was able to read about Marshal Badoglio's triumphant entry into Addis Ababa. "Once more a historical event has fundamentally altered the balance of forces in Europe. That it was impossible to prevent it proves not only the impracticability of the League in its present form, but even more the impossibility of paper decisions, collective boycotts and empty threats halting a people that stands in iron resolution behind its leader in his fight for space and raw materials. The British Government, which is not prepared to consider the justified demand of the German people for the return of its stolen colonies, should take the outcome of the

Abyssinian conflict as a warning—" The train, which had had a Sunday emptiness in the middle of the city, began to fill up at the suburban station before Dahlem. He was surprised when almost everybody got out at the same time as himself, and amazed when he realized that they were all going to the same place as himself.

The church was large and very modern and packed out. He managed to find a place about half-way back. He began to feel excited. The atmosphere was peculiar. The congregation was quite unproletarian and there were several army uniforms about. But for the silence it might have been a matinée audience somewhere. The show was the pastor, a man who had already been under house arrest. It was certain that whenever he preached there would be secret police listening. David glanced around trying to see who looked as if he belonged to the Gestapo. It was thrilling to remember that it was really true, that this wasn't a waxworks exhibition, that the pastor really was in danger. How revolting, David reflected, that he himself had only found the energy to come because of self-interest. But it hadn't occurred to him until now as he sat there. Normally a strong agnostic—he had read Bertrand Russell and several books of the Rationalist Press Association—only pride stopped him from offering a private apology to God. But the softly playing organ, the large and comfortable, up-to-date church, the packed hundreds of people, Germans evidently of a more agreeable kind than he had met, the sense of the magnificence of a man's courage all together stirred him so much that he thought uneasily, " I hope to God I'm not going to get converted or anything," and so, unconsciously, he did pray.

Then there was Niemöller. He appeared suddenly, unobtrusively, getting on with his normal job of conducting a normal Lutheran service. But when he faced them it seemed as if his immensely pale, lined face were carved out of wood. David rather lost his feeling of unease. There was, after all, something slightly theatrical about the performance—it did seem to be a performance—and the Gestapo threat, undeniably real, became somehow less threatening. However, the sermon was a straightforward denunciation of the power of the State.

466

"He's a great man, all right," David thought finally. But he was impatient to get away. Outside was a warm, lovely summer day, one for the Berlin woods and lakes, one for cruising along in the Robinsons' Mercedes. When the service was over it was already a quarter past twelve. About lunch-time, Sophia had said, for ringing up – but he didn't want to leave it too long.

He was relieved to find a telephone booth on the way to the station. He hurried into it and rang up the Legation.

"I think Miss Sophia is not at home, sir," the telephonist said at once.

"Oh, but – she must be – she's expecting me," he exclaimed.

"Wait a minute, please."

He waited tensely. She had said lunch-time; he might be half an hour too early. But when the appalling news came, it was no particular surprise. He could sense it already.

"You wish to speak to Miss Sophia?" He recognized the voice of one of the servants. "She is out for the day, sir. Everyone is out."

"Oh. Er – I suppose there was no message? My name is Proctor."

"I'll go and see, sir."

Another wait, but this time pointless from the start.

"No, sir."

He left the telephone booth, dazed. So that was that. Ditched, ignored, snubbed, trampled on. Perhaps she couldn't help it. But there would have been a message in that case. She had simply forgotten. Or if she hadn't forgotten, hadn't cared. And no doubt the secretary was with them again.

"I hope they eat something that damned well gives them food poisoning," he thought, when he had recovered enough for anger. "It's the end as far as she's concerned. It's the last time I'm going to be treated like this. They can put their bloody legation up their ass."

The sun was hot. It was a perfect day. The underground station was stale and depressing.

The journey back seemed endless. Platz followed Platz, Breitenbach Platz, Rudesheimer Platz, Heidelberger Platz. At

Hohenzollern Platz he remembered that this was where he could get off to go to Aunt Isabel. In the circumstances that was what he should do. In fact he was aware of a certain rough justice in what had happened. But he couldn't bring himself to contemplate it. In any case, why take his depression to add to hers? Nürnberger Platz, Witternberg Platz – half an hour later he was again walking up Friedrichstrasse. He lunched off a cheese roll and coffee at the automat, an act of will, for he nursed a faint hope that there might be a message at the hostel.

Of course, there was none. The hatchway was closed. The Führer's words regarded him impassively from the wall, but he was too depressed to find a solution in them as he had a few days before. The hostel was more or less deserted. In his room there was added to the usual air of stale tobacco the smell of egg – there was a saucer with the remnants of one on the table below the window. He lay on his bed staring up at the dirty-white ceiling. Nor was it only to-day's failure obsessing him, there was last night – he faced the fact now that if he had had any guts at all he would have told the Pole when he saw the girls leaving, so that they could intercept them. Then quite probably it wouldn't have mattered about to-day in the slightest. As it was, there was nothing – nothing last night, nothing to-day, nothing ever. He felt himself to be so worthless that after a time he began a suicide fantasy and considered the wording of a farewell note. "Convinced of the purposelessness of my existence –" He pictured a headline: Student Tragedy in Berlin – 17 years old David Proctor – It was, after all, Werther's end. When he was tired of that, he got up and opened the window – which was kept resolutely closed by the other three – and at once a draught of sweet-smelling air came in, which reminded him of a cricket field. Once he had been a fanatic about cricket. So now he became homesick and felt worse than ever.

It was still only two o'clock. The whole of Sunday after-noon lay relentlessly ahead. He ought, of course, to ring up Aunt Isabel and tell her that as his outing had fallen through he was coming right round. It was the least he could do to hold the old girl's hand – she had sounded pretty disappointed yesterday, and he had to admit that her troubles were a good deal worse than his.

He couldn't do it. "God, I'm a louse," he thought. He dragged himself off the bed and decided instead to take his *Julius Caesar* to the students' club and do some work there.

The club was empty, except for four *skat* players. He settled down to read for the rest of the afternoon. Even the loudspeaker was silent. The only noise was of cards being banged down on the table in the German fashion and the murmur of bidding – *Schneider!*" "*Pik mit zwei!*" "*Mit vier!*" – and the occasional loud-voiced argument. The sun came through the windows, creating a slanting beam of silver-grey dust. Outside, Oranienburgerstrasse was deserted. Everyone was out for the day. David grimly read on, with his aunt all the time at the back of his mind.

At last the club began to wake up and the afternoon was gone. The loudspeaker came on, the canteen opened. People began to come in, but no one he knew. He had a cup of sawdust-tasting *ersatz* coffee. He ought to ring up his aunt. There would be no need now to say anything about his plans not having come off – he had told her yesterday that he would try to go round if he came back early enough. "Why the hell should I bother about her?" he thought impatiently. It annoyed him that she should be on his conscience. But at six o'clock he finally decided to give in. He went to the telephone with the intention of telling Aunt Isabel that he was on his way – and his fingers, directed by a criminal weakness, dialled the number of the legation. For it was possible that the Minister's party was back by now. But his own action shocked him. When the number began to buzz he made an effort and replaced the receiver. He felt a little better for this display of self-respect. But he went back to the canteen without ringing up Aunt Isabel.

He bought another cup of the terrible coffee and sipped it gloomily. He knew that he was avoiding his aunt, partly from fear of another emotional evening, but partly also because of the satisfaction of hurting someone else when he was hurt himself. The result was an empty evening ahead. He could work or go to a film, alone and defeated. He was conscious of being ridiculous and adolescent, but he clung to more dramatic words, loneliness, despair, self-contempt. He kept on feeling guilty about his aunt. What he really wanted was a good excuse for not ringing her up, and if the alternative was an evening by himself he knew he couldn't avoid it.

Then he thought of Mr. Belford. It was the very thing.

CHAPTER TWENTY

"Very well, come along," Mr. Belford said. "You'll have to come to church. No, not the English church, the Russian. It will be a Russian evening. Hurry up."

Far from being welcomed, David had almost had to force the invitation. However, he felt a little better and spent the next half-hour travelling. When he arrived, Mr. Belford opened the door to him, smart and severe in his black Sunday best and holding a folded umbrella.

"Just in time. We were about to go without you."

"I came as quickly as I could –" David stopped short as he became aware that Mr. Belford had a companion, a beetle-browed, tough-looking man of indeterminate age, to whom he was being introduced in French.

"*Sergei, voici le jeune homme dont je t'ai parlé, M. Proctor. David, je veux vous présenter M. Leontovitch.*"

"*Enchanté,*" said Mr. Belford's friend, bowing over David's hand, which he held in a grip of iron.

David blushed and stepped awkwardly one way and then another.

"For your benefit, David, we'll speak French instead of Russian. Sergei doesn't speak English. He is an old and close friend."

"Oh, God, I say, don't bother about me," exclaimed David anxiously; and at the same time he determined not to say a word for the rest of the evening. His French accent was appalling.

In fact, they didn't bother about him. Mr. Belford and his

470

friend chatted speedily while David walked along beside them and above them, tacking from side to side and occasionally apologizing when he bumped. With every minute he felt more ignorant, unnecessary and out of it. It was a relief when they reached the church. The two conversationalists went straight in and he followed.

He was immediately overwhelmed. Outside it was a normal May evening, inside it was like a film about Rasputin, a shadowy darkness lit by candles, icons everywhere. It was crowded. Some people stood in front of an icon, taking turns to kiss the frame. Others stood indeterminately and would suddenly bow and cross themselves rapidly or else, it seemed on individual impulse, collapse briskly on to the stone floor, lie there with arms spread out for a few seconds and then get up as if nothing had happened. A wonderful priest appeared, tall and slim, with a deathly pale face and feverish eyes. He came through flinging incense at the icons. Then people filed past him, kissing his Bible. Interminable sing-song prayers went on and once David counted fifty-three alleluias. The priest went in and out of mysterious doors, manipulating lighting effects. Mr. Belford and Sergei entered into everything with expert enthusiasm. David stood against the wall, fascinated and ill at ease.

It was all still going on when Mr. Belford beckoned to him that it was time to leave.

" Well, did you like it? " he asked in English, when they were outside and David was taking deep breaths of the street's evening air.

" It was marvellous, of course – that priest – "

" He wears a wooden cross, you know, strapped to his back."

" Good lord."

Mr. Belford continued talking in French to Sergei. David began to feel impatient. It was some time before he managed to push in the information in English that he had attended Niemöller's service that morning. Mr. Belford was unmoved.

" Lutherans are so dull, David."

" It was terrifically impressive."

" It wouldn't have been to me. If ever I should stray from

Canterbury, I shall prefer the catechism of Philaret. He, at any rate, was a Romanov."

David resumed a rather sulky silence. Even French and the pretence of including him was dropped when they reached the usual restaurant. Enthusiastic Russian was now spoken. The proprietress was introduced to Sergei, and David was surprised to see that in the light the latter looked rather drab and wore a not very well fitting serge suit. He could certainly eat, however, as well as talk. Half a dozen rolls went down with his *borsch*, and later he ate almost an entire bowl of potatoes. Mr. Belford watched him proudly, and told David, "Dancers always have enormous appetites. Ballet is *the* most exhausting occupation in the world."

David was vaguely shocked.

"A ballet dancer – is that what he is?"

"You impossible boy, haven't you been listening?"

"Well, he doesn't look like one," David said defensively.

"Oh," laughed Mr. Belford, "how would you expect one to *look*?" He turned at once to Sergei, still busy with potatoes, and seemed to be repeating David's comment in Russian.

David was crushed and annoyed. He had been made to look a fool and he now suspected that Mr. Belford was using the evening precisely with that in view, and having a subtle revenge for being thrown over.

"He's a stupid bastard, anyway," he thought. "I was an ass to come. His bloody poetry and his bloody icons. Directly we leave here I shall go back to the hostel."

He reversed his decision almost at once, however, for Mr. Belford became more friendly and mentioned that afterwards they were going to a party given by some Russians. David told himself that the prospect of a new scene made a new situation.

"We'll go as soon as we can persuade Sergei to stop eating," Mr. Belford said fondly.

They had to walk for twenty minutes. They were in a seedy and commercial part of one of the long monotonous streets when Mr. Belford led the way into a courtyard to the entrance of the cheaper block behind. They climbed up four

472

floors, the air smelling vaguely of dirt, anthracite and stale cigars. Several banisters were missing and plaster was coming off the walls. Mr. Belford, a confident guide, walked along a passage and pushed open the door of a flat. Evidently the walls were firmly built, for the noise which at once came out to greet them sounded rather like a public banquet. Inside, David found himself in a small room packed with people. They all sat round a table, some of them in a second row or leaning against the wall. There was a sideboard on which was a most elaborate teapot. Everyone was talking hard, nobody even paused at their entrance except for the hostess, a plump little woman who welcomed Mr. Belford with a mixture of screams and sighs. Sergei kissed hands in various directions. David himself was propelled to a chair at the table vacated for him by someone. A candle was burning in front of an icon on the wall. And everybody talked. He was given a cup of watery tea, and on this, it seemed, they were all drunk. Some were cheerful, others were gloomy, but they all talked. Not all, he realized after a moment. There was a sad-looking young man who appeared to be in tears and two girls who sat wonderfully erect, glancing around with solemn dark eyes and saying nothing at all. Mr. Belford was having a wonderful time pouring out his Russian – he was obviously a favourite. Half the people were speaking French, but when David's nationality became known English also came into use, and the woman beside him exclaimed passionately, " I have spen' such happy days at Bisewater! Yes, it iss true! " David was encouraged, and more so when a glass of vodka was put in front of him. Soon he was being fluent in a mixture of English and his terrible French, and enjoying himself, although now and then he thought guiltily about his aunt.

He had a long conversation with the woman who had been happy in Bayswater. It involved whether or not David believed in God, whether there was a purpose to life or whether, after all, everything was meaningless and futile. Others joined in and were either radiantly pleased with the universe and its management or in the most desperate gloom. The woman beside him kept saying that life was beautiful. In

473

the midst of it he suddenly heard some native English from the sad young man. He was telling one of the silent girls, " All *I* know is that just five minutes before we got into Frankfurt he wanted to borrow my red pullover — " He learnt that some of those present were dancers in a ballet company which was touring Germany and that they were opening in Berlin the night after next at the Schlageter theatre. This explained Sergei. It was rather thrilling to be in a party with such exotic persons — though, like Sergei, none of them appeared so much exotic as knobbly and muscular, and they had a sort of immobile, rubbery look.

" One day, darrling, what iss in you will comm out," said the woman next to him, squeezing his hand hard — which was not too comfortable since she wore half a dozen rings. " You are frustrated at this moment. Z' real you iss to come."

" I know it, you're absolutely right," he said excitedly.

" Life will teach you. Life is z' gr-r-eat teacher, darrling."

" It's experience, I know. That's what I want. Yes, I know."

" Lost for a beautiful body, zere is nothing else in life. We are abandoned to our losts, darrling."

" I absolutely agree with you," David exclaimed. He had had a second vodka and a warm feeling was coming over him. " It's true. I know it's true."

" That pullover took me three months in Brazil," said the sad young man.

" He iss a darrling, that one," said David's friend, with further pressure on his hand. " But it iss good not to be a dancer. They are too self-contained, you understand. If you are a dancer it feels so good just to breathe, you do not need other people. I know thiss, darrling. You need only the ground. All dancers are in lovv with z' ground. A dancer has not a soul."

" Because it's sold? "

" Yes, yes! It has to be sold! You are a brilliant young man," said the woman, staring at him with popping eyes.

Suddenly half a dozen more people crowded into the room, one of them greeted with ecstasy, a small middle-aged man to whom the hostess cried, " *Bon soir, maître!* " A woman with a swan neck rose and curtsied to him between two

474

chairs, which inspired David's companion to sigh dramatically, "What a sight! The old tradition! I have not seen that forr years!" But in spite of the fuss it was at once clear that some bad news had been brought. A telegram was being passed round. The ballet company members showed heavy gloom, despair, anxiety. There was a furious din of exclamatory conversation.

"What is it?"

"I do not know, darrling. Someone has not arrived."

"Knew it would happen," said the sad young man, staring at David with interest.

"What is it?" David asked him.

"It's our pianist. She fell ill in Munich last night, tummy trouble, you know, and didn't come on the train. She was to fly up this evening. *Now*, it seems, she's in hospital."

"What does he say, darrling?"

"They've lost their pianist," said David, becoming terribly excited.

"*Quel malheur!*"

"I've said all along something like this would happen, particularly knowing the lady in question. We'll have to cancel to-morrow. I always knew that Tania would –"

"You want a pianist? *Vous manquez une pianiste?*" David exclaimed. "Listen to me. I know one. Adrian!" No one listened to him. He thumped the table, upsetting his tea. "Listen to me!" He hoped and prayed that the vodka hadn't made him at all drunk. This was a marvellous stroke of luck, an act of God. "Adrian!" he called to Mr. Belford, who at last disengaged himself from Sergei and gave him a severe glance.

"Really, David, you're not behaving at all well. I prefer you in your more modest and retiring mood."

"If they want a pianist, how about my aunt?"

"Your aunt? Frau Peters?" said Mr. Belford, disconcerted.

"She's a marvellous pianist!"

"Yes, of course, I'm sure she is, but, dear child, this is a professional matter –"

"Well, she's a professional."

"Oh, yes, I remember, she teaches. But, David dear, teaching as I, alas, know all too well, is not the same thing as actual performance – do stop banging the table – "

"Teaches! Why, she gave a concert in London and – anyhow, she was brilliant, but she gave it up – but she belongs to the Government music thing, and I know she'd – " He was going to say " jump at the chance ", but corrected himself. " I'm sure she might help, so why not ring up, anyway? " he demanded anxiously. And then seeing Mr. Belford still looking rather sceptical, and even sullen, he felt a rising wave of contempt. He was faced with an alternative course of action, to give in, to accept that he was young and over-affected by two vodkas, or to insist on being heard – to impose his will. Who were these people, anyhow? They couldn't be anything much, or they wouldn't be in this poky little flat. " Ring her up," he repeated, slightly amazed by his determination, but growing more and more excited. Meanwhile the talk went on feverishly amongst the ballet people. Giving Mr. Belford up, David now appealed to Sergei, whose mouth was full of cake, to the sad young man who smiled at him but did not listen, to the woman beside him who smiled and listened but paid no attention – he became furious, a child who had lost his temper amongst emotional grown-ups who did not understand. But the thought of his desolate aunt spurred him on, and so did another thought – of the plaque which read " I however decided – " He therefore kept on interrupting in a voice that grew more and more high-pitched. One must decide, and then with inflexible, fanatical will press one's purpose. It was Herr Hitler's technique, and the Führer himself was slightly responsible for David at last catching the ear of M. Bressilov, the little man who had recently arrived and was the impresario of the ballet company.

" Your aunt iss a pianist, dear boy? She iss good? Where iss she? "

" I'll ring her up! " David said, with a triumphant glance at Mr. Belford.

A few minutes later he was speaking to her, with the impresario standing anxiously at his side.

CHAPTER TWENTY-ONE

He woke up the next morning with a headache, a minor hang-over. In itself this was an occasion of mild pride, but when he thought of all that had happened last night the pride grew almost to bursting point. Really, it showed what could be done! His achievement had been nothing short of enormous. An unbreakable will—his own—had forced itself upon a middle-aged, bald-headed impresario, had apparently saved his company from disaster, had press-ganged a reluctant, middle-aged woman into playing the piano from eleven o'clock until one in the morning and, not least, had made Adrian look extremely small. And it had not been at all easy. It had not only been almost impossible to get anyone to listen to him, but his aunt had shown a maddening lack of enthusiasm. "Oh, no, I couldn't possibly do it," had been her first reaction, which she had maintained solidly, while he and M. Bressilov had pleaded on the telephone—the impresario was in despair—but again he had kept on insisting. For, really, her attitude was fantastic. She had been complaining bitterly about her bad luck only a week before, but she didn't appear to be in the least interested in what seemed to him quite clearly to be a piece of good luck. But he had been diabolically clever! He had pretended to accept her refusal, and had said craftily, "Is it too late for a cup of tea on my way home?" She had said it was not too late, expecting him alone—thus he had been able to use her pathetic and embarrassing desire for his company, for it certainly was late, it was gone half-past ten. Then he had said to M. Bressilov: "If you come with me, I'm sure you can persuade her to play," and the impresario gave a jerky nod, slapped his shoulder and replied, "Yes, yes, I come—there is nothing to lose. Oh, *mon dieu*, I never wish to suffer like this again."

David stared with pleasure at the dirty ceiling above his bed. The throb in his forehead and the discomfort around his eyeballs were both lessened by the contemplation of these peculiarly satisfactory events. The hang-over was in any case part of the price, for he was prepared to admit to himself that the vodka had given his will the courage to express itself. But it had been very amusing to leave the party with the guest of honour – Adrian had looked furious, which was especially funny. M. Bressilov had been most chatty. He wore a wide-brimmed black trilby and a cloak and he carried a stick, and though he had seemed quite at home in the near-slum flat, he was also at home in calling for a taxi outside. It was in the taxi, David now remembered, while M. Bressilov was telling him what a success they had had in Frankfurt, that he had lost his exultation and become very nervous. For it occurred to him that the brilliance of his aunt was something he had all along taken for granted – it was a family tradition. It would be dreadful if, after all, she were not good enough. He felt rather guilty now that these doubts had entered his mind, though last night they had been reasonable enough. But within twenty minutes of their arrival at the Motzstrasse flat, the doubts had all gone for good. M. Bressilov was in ecstasy. For Aunt Isabel, after expressing surprise and even indignation at the sight of the extra guest, had been prevailed upon by M. Bressilov to sit down at the piano. As she sat down she was still saying, " No, I couldn't possibly do it, I haven't played in public, properly, for years – my nephew should not have brought you here – " But soon her fingers were performing their magic and the impresario was sighing his relief.

" You mosst ply for us, you mosst ply for us! " cried M. Bressilov, at midnight, and David had felt a thrill that the claims made for his aunt were justified. For her part, having once started, she was pleased enough to play. David was deeply impressed. She seemed to know every piece of music M. Bressilov mentioned. But though the audition went so well, it was still an uphill battle before she would agree even to attend a rehearsal the next day. M. Bressilov entreated, begged, implored, argued and finally, when she had reluctantly agreed, kissed her hands and embraced David. It was a slight cloud on his triumph, David felt, that Aunt Isabel had displayed no particular enthusiasm or gratitude when she said good night to him; but of course it might be that she was embarrassed at being under an obligation to him. It did not alter the gratifying fact that it was his agency, his insistence, his determination that had done the trick.

"*Heil Hitler*, Herr Proctor," Köhler greeted him amiably from the opposite bed. "Did you enjoy your holy Sunday with the priests? You have prayed hard and sung hymns?"

"Ah, yes," David said, recalling the earlier part of his day with a slight sense of shock. "You ought to go yourself, Köhler—you should learn what you are fighting against. I could hardly get into the church for all the army officers who were crowding there." They were always very sensitive about the army. "Yes, it was magnificent." But the shock he had had was nothing to do with Pastor Niemöller, it was the realization that he had quite forgotten about Sophia. At lunchtime yesterday he had been in despair and yet he could wake up without giving her a thought. "Did you have a successful day of unmilitary sport?" he went on.

"Yes, thank you very much," said Köhler, who accepted the question seriously. "Sport is a wonderful thing, Herr Proctor. The Olympic ideal is really the National Socialist ideal. Comradeship, strength, beauty, sacrifice! We had a lecture about it."

David was in an excellent mood. He felt firmly in charge of his life, to say nothing of other people's lives. And an hour later when he reached the university and found Sophia was not in class, he found himself quite unmoved—although it was true that he had not expected to see her. "Yes, that's all over," he thought. In fact he really couldn't bother to think about Sophia. His aunt was far more interesting.

He decided to miss the second lecture and to go to the rehearsal, for he had made a note last night of where it was to be held. He walked hurriedly down Unter den Linden, down Charlottenstrasse to the Gendarmenmarkt—where the sight of the state theatre reminded him that he really must go and see Gründgens in *Faust* or *Hamlet* or something—and then

479

he went along Jägerstrasse, and found himself finally going upstairs from a café-bar towards the sound of a piano playing. He pushed open a door on the second floor and entered a surprisingly large room, crowded with, as it appeared, lunatics and with his aunt seated at a piano in the corner. He went across to her, passing on the way the sad young man, who was slowly rising from a kneeling position, his hands bent high above his head. She looked surprised when she saw him, and of course went on playing as she said, "Hullo, David, dear, how pale you are — are you awfully tired?"

"Not at all. How are you getting on?"

"You were up so late —" She was interrupted by a sharp double rap on the floor.

"Please, dear, that tempo is too fast," said a voice, and David saw a stocky man in shirt-sleeves, gesturing in despair.

"Oh, I don't think so," said his aunt.

"Please, dear, take it more slowly from twenty-eight."

"But it isn't what the composer —"

"Please, dear, more slowly!"

"Oh, very well," said his aunt, shrugging her shoulders. She began to play again, and the sad young man again rose from his kneeling position. David stood back against the wall, aware that it was unreasonable for him to be paid any attention when they were in the middle of doing something, but nevertheless feeling slightly piqued. But for him, after all, nothing would be happening at all. He was not, in any case, especially sympathetic to the ballet. In the ordinary way he wouldn't dream of going to see it, and everything in the present scene struck him as ridiculous. Adrian's friend Sergei and four girls stood against a bar-rail which ran along the other side of the room, performing bends and stretches. Three girls sat in a little huddled group all sewing away repairing tights and shoe ribbons. Three more girls stood on one leg with the other leg and an arm stretched out. They looked so attractive that David at once felt extraordinarily clumsy, a feeling which was reduced as the piano music became more lively and the sad young man leapt up and down romantically — a splendidly farcical sight, due to the fact that he was wearing ordinary shoes. Everyone except the sewing party seemed to be sweating. He recognized a few faces from last night's party, but felt himself regarded with an unflattering lack of curiosity. Finally there was an interval. The sad young man – his name was Bobby – reeled away panting and clutching a towel. Two girls at once rose from the sewing party and pressed some music on to the pianist. "Ply this, pleace." The combination of their accents and their short ballet skirts once more caused David to feel totally disconnected. His contemptible shyness annoyed him almost as much as the fact of being ignored. As to that, the worst blow of all came when M. Bressilov suddenly appeared, bustling in full of pomp and business, and, glancing at him, first failed to recognize him, and then exclaimed in an off-hand manner, "Aha, the student!" This from a man who had been almost embracing him a few hours before – outside the Fürstenhof Hotel in Potsdamer Platz, where they had parted – seemed monstrous behaviour. He decided to leave. Half-way down the stairs he reflected that he was being extremely childish, for, after all, they *were* busy, but it was too late. It was not really too late, but he informed himself that it was.

Instead of going right away, however, he had a beer in the bar downstairs and, fortified by it, he went up again. His short absence had not been noticed. He went over to the piano where M. Bressilov and the stocky, shirt-sleeved man stood on either side of his aunt. She had stopped playing and an excited conversation was going on concerned with the tempo at which the last piece had to be taken. David stared at his aunt, fascinated. She sounded different, she looked different. She was full of animation.

"But, my darling," M. Bressilov was crying, " it is not what Liszt wanted, it is what Boris wants – "

"*Oui, oui*, and also what zeze poor children can do!" said Boris.

The pianist exclaimed, "As long as you understand that the music is being murdered – "

"*Bon!*" Boris stooped forward and fervently kissed her cheek.

"You make me happy," said M. Bressilov. "Thank God, someone makes me happy."

"I wish to eat," said Boris. "Let us now have twenty minutes for eating."

David had lunch with his aunt downstairs in the café-bar. "It's all quite extraordinary," she told him with restrained excitement – but the excitement was there, he could see. "I don't know that I can possibly go on with it, but of course something's bound to go wrong. It's supposed to open to-morrow. It's a tour that seems to have been fixed up with the Strength through Joy people, so they get a sixty per cent guaranteed audience, and I suppose the rest, if any, is mostly paper. They seem to be quite good, even though it is all on a shoe-string. M. Bressilov is supposed to have been with the Russian ballet, but in what capacity I don't know. I saw the Russian ballet, with your uncle, years ago, when I'd just met him, as a matter of fact. They were at the Alhambra. They don't seem to care about the music, that is what is such a shock – but still I suppose they know what they're doing."

"Quite an amusing crowd to be with, I should think," said David, who could not get over the speed with which the words were tumbling out of her.

"Yes, I agree, they seem charming. I like M. Bressilov, poor man; I wonder he doesn't go crazy looking after them all. He's been all over the world, in fact, I think most of them have. They've had terribly bad luck with their pianists on this trip. It seems they find it awfully difficult to find anyone suitable. They need somebody really good and, of course, concert pianists aren't very interested, especially if they find out what that man Boris, who is the *maître de ballet* – they all have titles – what he wants to do with the music. And you have to be able to play almost anything at first sight, which lots of people who've won prizes at conservatoires can't do. Of course, these people have no idea what they're asking for! They started with two pianists, and one of them deserted in Brussels to get married, and M. Bressilov is suing her, and then they nearly came to a standstill because two pianos are vastly different from one, but anyhow they came on into Germany

482

and it doesn't seem to have mattered – but now, as you know, the other one is down in Munich in bed. I'm expected to do a great deal –"

"I'm sure you'll be wonderful," David said enthusiastically as he got up.

"Oh, must you go, now, dear?"

"Yes, I've got a lecture. I'll come back after it though. You'll still be here?"

"Oh, yes – indefinitely, I should think!"

He couldn't get over it. He went back to the university astonished and gratified. Even the fact that his own part in the matter seemed to have been ignored faded before his excitement.

"The old girl really can do it," he thought, and he was already certain that she was a great pianist, who deserved to be world-famous. A greater pleasure still awaited him when he arrived, Sophia had turned up, looking pale, and was already in her place. She turned towards him with the usual imperious glance and he merely nodded. It was not easy. The desire to prostrate himself in the hope of a kind word was there, but he was firm with himself. The nod was a deliberate indication that he was no longer interested – not interested, even, in an explanation or an apology for yesterday or who was in the party. He thought she looked a little taken aback, and though he hoped this was so, he told himself that he didn't care about that either. His heart thumped. He chatted to the Syrian who sat next to him. He paid no more attention to Sophia. And a delightful, subtle feeling of self-mastery came over him. He was free, he was cured, he had grown out of her.

But when the afternoon lecture was over, his resolution was tested further. He moved at his usual speed towards the door – or forced himself to imitate this normal speed, and of course to move normally on purpose was the most difficult thing in the world. He held his breath all the way out to the landing.

"What's the matter with you?" asked Sophia, who had followed him.

David was forced to breathe.

"I'm not aware that there's anything in particular the matter."

"I heard you rang up yesterday. Sorry we had to go so early."

This was the casual way in which she apologized for behaviour which had nearly driven him to suicide. But it was fortunate, for it stiffened his resistance. She had never looked more attractive. She had the kind of skin which tanned perfectly and it was already becoming faintly golden, so that her lips seemed pale, an effect which stirred him deeply. Moreover, he found it hard not to feel pleased by the fact that she had hurried after him. But her tone enabled him to answer in a reciprocally off-hand way.

"It didn't matter." He remembered in time not to be too abrupt; he did not want to sound as if he cared – he wanted her to get the accurate impression, that he was indifferent.

"You know how it is with everyone shouting at you, I'm afraid I forgot all about it until we were on the way," she said, over her shoulder, as they went downstairs.

"Yes, of course."

"Well, I've said I'm sorry, so there's no need to sound so annoyed."

"Annoyed?" he said. He saw now that she was deliberately trying to humble him. It was clear that she was still under the impression that he would jump through any hoop she held up. "I'm not annoyed at all, in fact I couldn't have come anyway. I had a number of things on – "

He paused. They had reached the courtyard. He was tempted to tell her what had happened, but caution prevented him. Confident as he was in his aunt, there was no reason to overplay his hand. It was still possible that she would be a flop, in which case the less said the better.

"You didn't miss much. What are you doing now?"

"Now? Actually I have got something I must do – "

"Oh, I was wondering if you'd like to come out to Wannsee. I'm going sailing. You could come, too."

"I'm afraid I can't," he said.

"Oh." As if she were determined to hand out a favour,

she went on, "To-morrow evening there's a film *première*, it's a Laurel and Hardy. Would you like to come to that?"

"I'm afraid to-morrow's impossible. Thanks very much all the same."

"You do seem to be busy."

He was conscious of a deep satisfaction.

"Yes — yes, I am, actually. As a matter of fact, I'm rather in a hurry, Sophia. Sorry I can't come."

"What is it you're so mysterious about?"

"I'm not being mysterious about anything as far as I know. I mean, I simply have something to do."

"You're being terribly English all of a sudden, that's all."

"I'm not aware —" His satisfaction was going fast.

"There you go again," she said. "Just because we went off early you have to sulk. You say yourself you couldn't come anyhow."

It was maddening that she did not realize their relationship had changed. He would have given anything to think of a really cutting reply. As it was, he could only maintain a dignified silence which did nothing to enlighten her.

As soon as she had gone, he hurried back to Jägerstrasse. The studio was locked and no sound came from inside. No one could give any information in the café. He rang up the flat, but there was no answer. Now he was able to transfer some of his annoyance to his aunt. Sophia had left no message for him, and nor had she. "Everyone seems to kick me around," he thought. It was unjust and he knew it, but he kept the idea going, determined to be angry with everybody, as he made his way gloomily back to the hostel. It was hot and there was the usual relentlessly blue sky. What would have been pleasanter than to go sailing? That was what he had really wanted to do; he had sacrificed his own pleasure only to find he had been ignored. For there had been what he thought to be a definite arrangement that he would return to the studio. The air in his room was staler than ever. He decided not to open the window. He lay on his bed, opened *Faust*, Part One, and pretended to work. The rest of the afternoon dragged by.

But at six o'clock, when he rang again, his aunt answered. And everything was at once put right.

"Is that you, David, dear? Thank heavens, I was very worried. Did you go back to Jägerstrasse?"

"Yes, I did."

"I had to go to the theatre with M. Bressilov. We waited half an hour for you. Did they tell you?"

"There was no one there."

"Oh, that's terrible" she said angrily. "Had they all gone? Didn't they leave a note? I particularly asked them—"

"It didn't matter," he said, mollified. "How was the *Schlageter*?"

"It's not very attractive, just an old barn really. Do you want to come to supper? I warn you I shall be practising for hours—"

"I'd like to come." And it was only when he had put the receiver down that it occurred to him that he had spoken the truth—it was astonishing, for it was the first time that he had felt any particular desire to go round to the flat.

Next he had a most exciting sensation. On the first kiosk he passed in Friedrichstrasse there was an advertisement for the European Ballet season at the *Schlageter Theatre*. He realized that he had seen it before, unaware of any personal association. Now he felt quite overcome. There the thing was with all the solidity of print and the fact was that he was responsible for it not being cancelled. M. Bressilov and his company became invested with a new importance in his sight, now that he had had proof of their official existence. And he at once became terribly nervous.

But there seemed to be no need. When he arrived at the flat a mild pandemonium was going on. M. Bressilov was there, Adrian's friend Sergei and two girls. All were talking at the tops of their voices, in a mixture of French, Russian and English. David was greeted, and promptly ignored. But now he had no childish feeling that his dignity had been affronted. It was altogether too fascinating that such a lively scene could be taking place in a room which for him had been coincident with dreariness. As for his aunt, her transformation seemed more miraculous every minute. She was not ten, but twenty years younger. She played all the time that she was not talking, and not rushing to the kitchen to bring in more dreadful coffee. "What do you think?" she exclaimed to him as she stood over the stove. "They want me to join them – they're going to Copenhagen, then Sweden and Norway, and then a six weeks' tour in the provinces at home! Can I do it, David? There's the question of labour permits and all that, but I still have my passport, thank God – but it means leaving everything –"

"Then leave everything, for God's sake!" David cried excitedly.

"But I have to think of Rudi –"

"My God! Why?" he exclaimed in amazement. "Think of him –?"

"After all this is his home and I'm his wife – unless he divorces me – a husband can get a divorce since last year, you know, if his wife says unkind things about the Führer – but one mustn't joke about it, I mean it would be a very serious step. You see, I should lose the flat if I go – flats are terribly scarce in Berlin – though I suppose I could keep paying, I couldn't expect Rudi to pay if I'm not here. Yes, I ought to go; I've made such a mess of my life and this is a chance – perhaps a last chance – and I must take it, I'm sure I must take it –"

"Of course you must!"

"He says I must say 'yes'," she said to M. Bressilov, on her way back to the piano.

She was still playing and the others were still talking when he left.

CHAPTER TWENTY-TWO

THE next morning it appeared that Sophia had decided to be more obviously cool towards him. This, he told himself, suited him perfectly. They exchanged quick, rather icy nods and then ignored each other. But he had had time to notice that she was wearing a new, gaily decorated, dark blue cardigan, highly effective against the shining yellow, page-boy hair, and furthermore that she had thrown out the local rules and was wearing lipstick. David told himself that he was indifferent to the development, but at the same time he could not altogether ignore it; what one noticed, one automatically thought about. Was it something that had happened for no particular reason? On the other hand – who had she gone sailing with yesterday? Tom? And there was the slight possibility, of course, that he himself was the cause. He found the mere thought of such a possibility amusing. It was not that she had lost her attraction, but he was conscious even more than he had been yesterday that what he could now regard as a mild infatuation was over. It was a fact that Aunt Isabel was now the person on his mind. He had hardly been able to sleep – anyone might suppose that it was he who was going to play for the ballet. He couldn't wait for this evening, and at the same time he nursed a faint dread that she would not be a success, which went along with his pride and excitement at the fact that he had been responsible for her chance. When one thought of the state she had been in barely ten days ago – indeed the state she had been in for years – he saw clearly the momentous importance of this evening. She had already become a different person. Success to-night could easily mean an entirely new life altogether for her. And what had done it? The quick seizing of an opportunity, determination, will power – it occurred to him that she must certainly have been lacking in some quality or other not to have brought it off before. "My God, it's so easy," he thought, overawed. A further small matter remained unresolved. When he left the flat last night, Mr. Bressilov handed him two tickets for the ballet. Was he, or was he not, to offer one of them to Sophia? He was well aware that he would do so and that it would be a mark of the most contemptible weakness.

When they met at the mid-morning break, politely but without enthusiasm – it was necessary, however, to put up a show before the surrounding Japanese, and both recognized it – David asked how the sailing had gone.

"It was awfully nice," Sophia said.

"I suppose you didn't swim?"

"I'm not allowed to for another week, owing to my chill, you know."

"Yes, still I must say you've recovered pretty quickly."

"Anyhow, the water's still too cold for swimming."

"You should be like me and keep to nice warm indoor baths. Do you know, before thirty-three, they used to have mixed nudist bathing! That must have been fun, mustn't it?" He would not have dreamed of making so gay a remark only a few days ago.

"Great fun," replied Sophia coolly.

"You're looking unusually colourful to-day, if I may say so," he continued.

"Am I? Good."

"Doing anything wonderful this afternoon?" There were no lectures that day after lunch.

"Not exactly wonderful. Riding with Heddi Meissner." She did not add an invitation for him to join them, which amused him.

"The Fräulein would not exactly be flattered by 'not exactly wonderful'," David said, becoming more and more astonished at his power to sustain the light chatter. "Who went with you yesterday that made it awfully nice?"

"A person."

"On the staff?"

"Possibly," Sophia said, and as the bored look came into her eyes he found himself enjoying a subtle game, the pretence of a jealousy he did not feel; it was rather unfair. "Anyhow, I asked you."

"Yes, yes – and to-night, a film *première*."

"Yes, that's right," Sophia said.

"I myself shall be at the ballet."

"Ballet? Do you mean dancing?"

"I always understood that that was what it meant. I suppose they don't have it out in the bush or the veldt or whatever it's called."

"Very funny, everybody laugh. I only did ballet for about five years. Where is it, anyway?"

"The *Schlageter*."

"Oh, yes, I saw it advertised, now I come to think of it –

Q*

489

but why are you going? I shouldn't have thought that was your sort of thing."

"Me? After all my years at the Maryinsky Theatre? My years with Diaghileff? Was I not Albrecht in *Giselle*?" He observed the effect of this mild expertise picked up the night before. She was definitely taken aback. "Besides," he said, playing his ace, "my aunt is the pianist."

"Your aunt!" Sophia said, astonished.

"Yes – I told you about her."

"Not that she was a pianist or anything – I must say, that's rather interesting. Why didn't you tell me yesterday? Is that what all the mystery was about?"

"Well, if it does interest you, I have another ticket," David said carelessly.

"I'm supposed to be going to this film –"

"Yes, of course; it doesn't matter."

"But I'm sure I can get out of it," Sophia said, as they returned to the classroom.

David's feelings were mixed. He tried to ignore the exquisite glow of pleasure which her reaction had caused. He felt like a drunkard who had lost one more battle. The fact was that he had not had the slightest intention of telling her anything, he had intended, on the contrary, not telling her – firstly as a mark of his indifference, and secondly because it was clearly more prudent to make sure of his aunt's success before disclosing what she was doing. He had come into the classroom sure of his control of the situation. And he had promptly crumbled into dust. "I, however, decided –" What a hope – when it came to the point, he hadn't been able to contain himself, everything had come out.

"My God, I'm a maniac," he thought.

At the end of the morning he rang up the flat.

"You've only just caught me," his aunt said. "I've only just this second come in, and I have to be off in five minutes. I was back at the studio this morning while they were all doing their *barre* exercises – how they work, it can't be good for them – then I had to get a new dress, which the company pays for, and this afternoon they're rehearsing on the stage. I'm terribly nervous that I won't stand up to it all. I really

490

don't feel too well, and my chest is troubling me again – it would be just the sort of thing that happens if I were to go down – "

"Oh, my God," said David, horrified.

"It's probably just nerves. I hardly know where I am, David, dear."

"Is there anything I can do? I'm free this afternoon. Shall I come to the theatre? I mean, can I fetch anything for you or something?"

"Nothing, dear. Just keep your fingers crossed."

"I certainly will, but I'm sure everything will be marvellous."

"I only hope I don't let them down, that's all. Come along to the rehearsal if you want to – we'll be there all the afternoon. Just walk in. When it's over I'll have to go home and get some rest. It all seems too good to be true, really. In a way I'm making my début—certainly my Berlin début – it's rather funny, isn't it?"

"Yes, and a European tour just starting – it's terrific!"

"Well, yes, of course, he said that, but I wouldn't like to be too sure – they've had some news from their own pianist to-day, and apparently she's got up – so whether they'll really want two is another matter. Besides, I'm not sure I can really leave Berlin just now – oh, well, anyhow, David, we needn't bother talking about that. Besides, if I don't give a good performance to-night they'll change their minds."

"Don't be such an optimist."

"My dear, I've learnt not to be."

He rang off, conscious of a feeling of exasperation. She so obstinately refused to go up into the clouds. And why should she consider for a second not leaving Berlin? How on earth could you get anywhere if you didn't snap your teeth on to opportunities and keep biting hard? But this reminded him of his own career, and after his usual cheese-roll lunch at the automat, he went on his way back to the hostel, where he found Köhler frowning happily over some maps and lists and posters.

"*Heil Hitler*, Herr Proctor! Look how hard I am working! We have more busy days on Saturday and Sunday – we shall

all be out collecting for the youth hostels. Do you know there were fifty-six new ones built last year, Herr Proctor? That's how the Führer gets things done. It'll be the same this year. The Führer looks after our generation – not like all those old men in black coats you have in England."

"I'm not sure that I care very much about youth hostels, Köhler. I like rich comfortable hotels with no one under forty in sight."

"Aha, you are decadent!" laughed the Austrian gaily. "Here, read the proclamation signed by all the Reich ministers. We have to stick it up everywhere." He held out a small printed poster and read aloud proudly, "To-day in every part of our free and beautiful fatherland there wander happy groups of German youth. Their songs ring out with love for the nation and the Führer. They come from streets and alleys in the towns, they come from factories and schools, all wanting to see and learn about Germany, this Germany made more beautiful by the Führer's deeds. Our main concern – and above all, the Führer's love – is for youth!"

"Jolly good," said David, and then sat on his bed to write to five London editors. To each of them he made the suggestion that the sports journalists they would be sending to Berlin for the Olympic Games would find invaluable the assistance of a German-speaking English student, who could act as guide and interpreter. The idea had occurred to him some days before. If one of them should bite – and why not? – he might find himself a foreign correspondent in next to no time. If he could get his aunt a job he could surely get himself one. This was true, even if he had allowed himself to be a little weak about Sophia. He sealed the envelopes, drunk with self-confidence.

He left Köhler still enraptured with the Reich ministers' message and took the letters with him. He posted them and then took the U-Bahn train to Hallesches Tor, at the far, southern end of Friedrichstrasse. The Schlageter Theatre was five minutes away.

It was not particularly impressive, but, still, it was a Berlin theatre and the poster outside read in large black letters: Ballet Bressilov. No one was about in the foyer, where the decorations consisted of one depressed-looking swastika flag and a large photograph of the Führer over the box office. He could hear the piano going, however, and he went through a swing door straight into the auditorium. It was small and rather tatty but the stage was brilliantly lit. About a dozen girls, some in white ballet skirts and the others in grubby-looking sweaters and trousers, stood in a circle surrounding Sergei and one of the girls who had been at the flat last night. Sergei was balancing her while she revolved on one foot. His aunt was playing a grand piano in the middle of the orchestra pit. Then everyone on the stage began moving about energetically, with much hard breathing and dull thudding of the boards; they all came to rest in poses which they seemed to have difficulty in maintaining. Sergei and the girl sprang into action again, and they were also panting and making noises with their feet which seemed to neutralize their graceful movements. David found the whole thing horrifying. Were people supposed to pay money to watch this? Meanwhile his aunt went on blithely playing away and her endurance seemed to him the only redeeming feature of the scene. He wondered gloomily if there were any way of avoiding bringing Sophia to what must be an evening of fiasco. Why had he had to blurt everything out? Why couldn't he have kept quiet on Sunday night instead of involving his aunt with these people? As he sat there in the back row he felt chilled with anxiety. On the stage the dancers went on rearranging themselves according to some lunatic plan. Ten minutes later they came to a conclusion, and the curtain fell with Sergei and his partner triumphantly statuesque in the middle. Aunt Isabel hit the final chord, and cries of dissatisfaction at once came from several angles. The curtain was raised and lowered again several times while the breathless performers adjusted their positions under the direction of Boris, who was desperate. At the same time an argument began about the lighting, conducted by M. Bressilov, who had been sitting hunched-up in the front row, and a raucous Berlin voice somewhere above. David's panic was increased by the atmosphere of despair and confusion. It seemed that the best thing was to fade away. He crept out again into the foyer and the street.

"I'll have to see it through, I suppose," he thought, and he became slightly more cheerful when he reflected that the Ballet Bressilov had got away with it somehow elsewhere on their tour. But he remained nervous.

Back at the hostel he found a letter waiting. It was from his mother. "I've had a note from Isabel. She says you're very busy and speak like a native and look well. I hope it's all true. I wish you'd persuade her to come over. Which reminds me, talking of sisters, please don't forget that Betty is *your* sister and mind you write to her once this term. I have an idea that she is anxious to show off a letter from abroad. I don't think there's any news here. I had to go to two cocktail parties this morning and I feel a wreck. Oh, but yes, there *is* news, I nearly forgot to tell you my biggest thrill! I broke a hundred! Mrs. Pearson was marking my card and I played marvellously, you would have been quite proud. I needed a five for a ninety-nine, and *holed a chip shot* for a four and ninety-eight! Your father says we must have the ball mounted."

David sighed. Once again he felt slightly ashamed of the fact that his parents had so sheltered an existence.

He went round to the students' club and pretended to work for a couple of hours, that is, he sat at one end of the recreation room with *Faust*, Part One, on his lap, and watched half a dozen young men practising fencing. It was very stuffy. He was glad he was not at school – which had now become a memory of the distant past – but he wished he were playing golf.

He went back to the hostel and prepared himself for the evening with almost as much care as the Pole: clean shirt, polished shoes and slicked-back hair. He considered taking his hat but decided against it. He felt he looked pretty good and Köhler made several admiring sounds, and even brushed some dust off his coat.

"Yes, that is a fine suit, Herr Proctor," he said. "Good cloth."

"English cloth, Köhler."

"Yes, yes," said Köhler affectionately. It was impossible to dislike him.

Half an hour later David was in a bus going down Unter

den Linden towards the Tiergarten. When he arrived at the legation he found Sophia ready and waiting.

"Are you sure you want to come?" he said. "I expect this will be pretty awful. I looked in at the rehearsal this afternoon. It seemed to be frightful."

"Did you?" Sophia was impressed. "Why didn't you tell me? I'd have liked to have come."

"You didn't miss a thing. How was the riding? Fall off your horse?"

"No. What ballet are they doing?"

"I haven't the faintest idea," David said, rather worried by her enthusiasm.

They had coffee and sandwiches in a corner of the large drawing-room – no one was about – and then Sophia disappeared to tell her mother that they were on their way.

"My God, I'm so bored," David thought as he waited. He had noted that she, on the other hand, seemed less bored than ever before.

They had a ten-minute walk to the Potsdamer Platz, where they could take a tram the rest of the way. Sophia held his arm aggressively. It was sad that things always happened when you no longer cared, and slightly pathetic that Sophia obviously thought she was doing him a big favour. In fact he was inclined to think that he hated her.

"I only hope my aunt's feeling all right," he said. "She has chest trouble and she was pretty nervous about it – "

"Tell me about her, David. Why haven't I met her? You never said she did anything."

"She didn't do anything, that is – she hasn't appeared in public for years – "

"How old is she?"

"I don't know, forty something or fifty something, I suppose. She's not supposed to be dancing, fortunately." He gave a crude, nervous chuckle; he wished the whole evening was over. "She's really only substituting for their real pianist. I know she's frightfully good, but she's taken it on at a couple of days' notice, which is rather sporting of her. As a matter of fact – " It was no good, he couldn't resist the temptation. "As a matter of fact I was responsible, more or less. I happened to be at a party on Sunday night, and some of the ballet people were there, and old Bressilov."

He gave a sideways look. She was listening all right. She was really listening and her eyes had taken on a kind of stare.

"Where?" she said finally.

"Oh, just a flat, you know. They're quite amusing, those affairs."

"Well, go on."

"Well, it was simply that I heard about them being stuck and I suggested my aunt. I took old Bressilov back to her flat and she played for him and he fell over her neck so much she agreed to do it. As a matter of fact she's a terrific pianist. I mean, one thing she can do, for example, if you were to bang your hand flat down on the notes, or both hands, and make the hell of a noise, she'd be able to tell you every note you hit – she used to do it when she was a child. She was a child prodigy."

"What was this party? Who did you go with?"

"Never mind." He was amused at the way she was so curious. She was worried stiff that she'd missed something.

"Well, anyway – I'm certainly interested to hear her."

"And, I don't mind telling you, she's had a pretty tough life. She ought to have made a big name, really."

"How about your uncle?" Sophia said. "Is he going to be there?"

"Hell, stop being so inquisitive, my dear girl. As a matter of fact he won't be. As a matter of fact, if you meet my aunt, sort of keep off that subject, will you? As I said, she's had a pretty tough life."

Sophia nodded, impressed.

"And her first husband was killed in the war," he went on, to deepen the effect already achieved. They reached the Potsdamer Platz, which was very crowded and full of traffic, and caught their tram. He was a little ashamed of himself for having been theatrical, but now his feelings became real and he was praying that the evening would turn out all right for his aunt. They hardly spoke for the whole of the journey down the Saarlandstrasse. When they reached the theatre bells were ringing and most of the house was already inside.

496

With the lights on it looked a little more inspiring than it had in the afternoon. David's heart thumped. Inside, the theatre was almost full, and because of this seemed smaller and more intimate – there was a buzz of conversation, as at the beginning or end of a whist drive; this was, in fact, the somewhat undistinguished atmosphere associated with the Strength through Joy movement.

Their seats were in the fifth row. Sophia's appearance amongst Germans, he had noted, always caused some approving looks and sounds, as her blue eyes and blonde hair were so strictly in accordance with the racial ideal; and it was a minor pleasure for him to note also their faint disillusion when English was spoken. It happened as usual, the woman next to her, a plump Frau in a long-sleeved, dreadfully-coloured cotton dress, took one look at her hair and murmured with a sentimental sigh, " *Schön!* " David loathed her, loathed all the other surrounding Germans, and in that moment decided to leave the country and go to France as quickly as possible. Sophia sat smugly reading the programme and he resented her calmness. When he saw the printed line " At the piano – Isabel Rowland " he became quite ill with excitement. The house lights dimmed suddenly and there she was.

As far as he could see she was very pale but composed. She paused briefly in front of the piano. There were one or two hand-claps, but David was too paralysed to add any of his own. He had an impression that the new green dress she wore had changed her appearance, and her face was quite heavily made up. Beside him Sophia said nothing. He held his breath. This was the moment. He had an urgent desire to shut his eyes.

His aunt sat down at the piano, and her head could just be seen in profile below the level of the stage. Conversation in the house died down, but was still going on as she began to play. David was in such a state that he was almost beyond listening, but he was conscious, in wild relief, that it seemed to be all right. A moment later the curtain rose on the first ballet and once again the German woman on Sophia's left was murmuring " *Schön!* " Six Ukrainian peasant girls were floating about the stage. Shortly afterwards two lads of the village sprang in, leaping everywhere with abandon. David glanced sideways to see that Sophia was sitting up and appeared to be enjoying it. He dared to look round. The Strength through Joy audience was showing no signs of restiveness. He relaxed, watched his aunt, fascinated, and finally almost forgot her in watching the stage.

At the end of the ballet the applause was warm.

"Did you like it?" he asked, clapping madly.

"Very good, awfully good," Sophia said.

Almost at once, with the house lights still down, his aunt began her solo interlude, a gay, lyrical piece. David could not bear it. For him it was as if she were performing a delicate conjuring trick which might go wrong at any second. "Oh, God, make her a success, oh, God, make her a success, oh, God, make her a success," he prayed; and the prayer was answered. At the end of it the applause was almost as great as it had been for the ballet. He was so relieved and so happy that there were tears in his eyes. He smiled triumphantly at Sophia, and the woman on her left was saying " Sehr schön ", in approval of the pianist.

"She ought to have taken a bow," said Sophia. "It was lovely. This is fearfully exciting."

But Aunt Isabel was already playing and the curtain was going up again. He no longer loathed the Germans, but felt a warm, comradely feeling for them. The second ballet was very spirited and had no peasants. The company mimed winter sports, with the girls skating and the men ski-ing. It was very well done and highly popular. There was great applause and five or six curtains.

The lights went up for the interval. Full of elation, David guided Sophia towards the crowd moving into the foyer. He felt a light tap on his shoulder and turned.

"Oh, hullo, Adrian."

"I really believe you're avoiding me, David," said Mr. Belford, who was looking very smart. "I've been waving and trying to catch your eye, but it was quite hopeless, and I could only conclude that you were refusing to see me. My dear, what a triumph for Frau Peters! She was divine! She will be the queen of the English community. No one could have guessed. Kindly introduce me to your companion, David."

David did so, very flattered to be addressed in this way – it seemed to confirm his status as a man about the town. Sophia was undoubtedly impressed by his friend.

"Aren't you going round to see her?" asked Mr. Belford, resuming his gay mood after bowing a little like an eighteenth-century courtier.

"Now?" said David, in some confusion.

"Yes, of course. I promised Sergei – who incidentally was *wonderful*, didn't you think? Some of the *point* work of the ladies was not too firm, I thought. But I mustn't be catty. Come along, both of you, if you're coming."

David looked at Sophia, who nodded brightly.

They followed him, through a side door and down some sharply descending steps to the dressing-rooms, which were a network of cubicles beneath the stage. Isabel was in the second one along. The door was open and she was sitting beside a table drinking coffee.

"Hullo, dear."

"You were marvellous," David said incoherently. "My God, you were terrific, it sounded marvellous – this is Sophia. She's in the class with me –"

"How do you do, Miss Rowland," said Sophia.

"Isabel, darrling!" cried M. Bressilov, entering in a state of emotion. "You were splendid – I thank you – the company thank you – I love you, I love you!" He kissed her, and, seeing David, cried, "Aha, the student!" and embraced him, too, stared in amazement at Sophia and rushed away. Aunt Isabel seemed not in the least taken aback.

"Miss Rowland," she said. "That's the first time I've heard it spoken. It sounds so strange – I thought I'd keep to it after all this time, it's like going back and starting all over again. Yes, that's what it is, anyhow. I'm so happy I feel like crying, but I daren't because of my make-up – but I'm starting again. David – I've had such a queer feeling all day, since you telephoned, that things would go well. Yet I was almost prostrate with worry this morning! But they're all so pleased –"

"I should damned well think they are."

"I said to myself, if I really do well to-night, I'll stay with them – Mr. Bressilov has offered me a contract for a year – he said it this afternoon – it's as if my luck's really turned – " She couldn't go on, for more people looked in, girls in white tutus, a man in tights, all concerned with getting a sip of the warm coffee. The prevailing mood was one of agitation, but what fascinated David was the sight of his aunt knowing them all and being known by them, as if she had been in the company for months. She was the square peg suddenly finding herself in the square hole.

On the way back, they had a glimpse of the empty stage from the wings, and David saw complacently that Sophia was quite overwhelmed. There was no doubt about the new respect in her attitude towards him. However dazzling might be her life as a diplomat's daughter she had never been backstage. Nor had he – but nevertheless it seemed as if he were introducing her into the interesting depths of his life.

"See you afterwards, children," said Mr. Belford fondly. He seemed, rather to David's surprise and not altogether to his satisfaction, to be delighted by the presence of Sophia.

A few minutes later the lights went down and his aunt appeared again, this time greeted with applause. Of course, now there was no strain – all was bound to go well. David sat back, and the curtain went up on the ballet which had been in rehearsal in the afternoon. How appalling it had seemed then, and how charming now – it was amazing what difference an audience made. As in the first, there were two ballets in the second half of the show and his aunt played a solo interlude between them – Arenski's *Valse* – which was received even better than before. David and Sophia were both almost breathless with clapping. The final ballet was gay and spirited, more peasant girls and leaping cossacks, and was just the stuff for the Germans. The Bressilov company were greeted rapturously. The ballerinas received bouquets and each took a flower and handed it down to the pianist – this gesture caused great applause.

"Come on," David said exultantly, as soon as it was all over. He was happy for himself and doubly happy for his aunt. No one stopped them from going through the side entrance through the iron door and down the steps – where they were out of sight of anyone and he abruptly pulled

Sophia close, kissed her and was kissed back. He kissed again, in a masterful way. "Do stop," Sophia whispered. "You're smothering — now's not the time for this — " And he stopped, but only because a sound came from the door above them. They continued round the corner to the dressing-room passage with Mr. Belford close behind them. There was a babble of voices along the passage. Agitation had gone from the air and the Ballet Bressilov, exhausted, sweating and panting, now relaxed. The dancers were busy removing their make-up and massaging their limbs with eau-de-Cologne. There was an amiable confusion of visitors where M. Bressilov was holding court, some of the people David remembered from the Sunday night party, a couple of benevolent Nazi officials, one from the Ministry of Propaganda — and in the midst of it all David found his aunt receiving as much praise as if she had been a ballerina.

She clung to him.

"Oh, David, darling, if you knew what this means to me — "

"I'm awfully glad, Aunt Isabel, it was terrific — and some people are going to get a surprise," he said, meaning his uncle. He knew what it meant to her, all right. Looking at her lively, excited face it was almost impossible to believe that this was the lonely, dreary woman of only two weeks ago. "And you can certainly sign the contract now!" he exclaimed, delighted at being able to use such an impresario-like phrase. He felt towards her as if she were a protégée who had made good.

"Yes, I know I'm thinking about that, except that it all seems too wonderful — "

"Don't think about it, sign it," David said, anxiously.

"I know. Has my luck really turned, David? But I've two weeks to think it over — "

"But, Aunt Isabel, what is there to think over? My God, Copenhagen, Stockholm, Oslo, London — "

"Yez, yez!" said M. Bressilov happily. "Lissen to him, darrling, he is a wise young man. You must stay with us. In my opinion it is a matter of fate and destiny that you have been sent to us. Tania will be back to-morrow and I shall have two brrilliant pianists. Yez, darrling, you must stay with us, mustn't she, my young friend? She is not your aunt, she is your sister. Just imagine – it is a miracle – she plays divinely and she has a British passport."

"Then there's David, you see. I mean he's here in Berlin by himself and I'm supposed to be here. I mean what will his parents – "

"Oh, my God!" said David, horrified at this reasoning.

"But he is a big boy," replied M. Bressilov. "That is no problem. You must come. Besides, you are a professional. I bestow upon you the highest possible honour – you are a professional."

"Aunt Isabel, you must!" David exclaimed. He was alarmed and bewildered by the way she was hedging on a matter he thought had been settled.

But his aunt surprised him again by saying gaily, "Yes, I know. I must, I know I must – it's only that it's too wonderful quite to believe – "

But the impresario was not listening. He invited her to join him for drinks at his hotel, he included David and Sophia, and was once more lost in the party – in the narrow space two dozen people were a formidable crowd – David went on listening to the enthusiastic interchange of compliments, with his aunt in the middle, smiling happily, incredulously. Adrian's voice came fluting clearly. "Alas, you are welcomed to a Berlin which is not what it was," he was telling Bobby. Sophia was staring at everyone with the look of an autograph-hunter. "David, I think she's lovely. She has beautiful eyes, hasn't she? And she's not a bit old. I expected someone much older."

"If you knew what I knew," he whispered proudly, "you'd know what a terrific thing this is for her. I'm frightfully pleased, she's had such a stinking time – " The words were effective, if unintentionally patronizing. In fact there was something like a lump in his throat, although when he came to think about it he realized that he didn't know much, and he couldn't really see *why* she had had such a stinking time. If things were suddenly on the mend now, if her luck had turned owing to M. Bressilov, it hadn't been a very hard job to accomplish the turn. Surely there must have been many other chances? It wasn't as if she had lost interest – what she said and the fact that she had kept up her practice proved that. It wasn't as if

502

she hadn't needed money – the piano lessons proved that. Surely there had been other M. Bressilovs over the years, if she had made any attempt to meet them? Of course there had.

But suddenly he felt the pressure of Sophia's hand on his wrist and his wonder became greater. Her hand was withdrawn in a second, she merely wished him to look at someone – there were some odd-looking people about – but in the way she did it there was something half childish, half possessive, some infinitely subtle message. If the world was opening out for his aunt, it was doing so not less for himself. He felt warm with the sheer pressure of living. He began to think of the walk he must take with Sophia back from M. Bressilov's hotel to the Tiergartenstrasse. The evening was a vast success. . . .

CHAPTER TWENTY-THREE

"Yes, I shall sign," she thought, sitting blissfully in the taxi, squeezed next to the little fair-haired girl David had brought. Though overcrowded – "Five of us, cheaper than a tram," David had insisted – the taxi was itself an indication of how her life was altering. It might have been a lifetime since the plump, anxious M. Bressilov had arrived at the flat. But the most amazing thing of all was that after a day of exhausting work and the tension of the evening she was not tired, she felt she could do it all over again – and to-morrow, in fact, she *would* do it all over again, and to-morrow and to-morrow. No, the most amazing thing was to be sitting here, speeding up Saarlandstrasse, going to a party, with David and the girl and Mr. Belford and Sergei, all of them talking twenty to the dozen. The Anhalter station went by on the left. The applause began singing in her ears again. She did not exaggerate it, but it had astonished her – though she knew she had deserved it, she had played well, dear Clement Durrell would not have been wholly disapproving. "Yes, I shall sign –" Then Copenhagen and so on, work, independence, and more money – not an unimportant item – than she had had for years. What luck, what luck! And she would settle in England. A dream was taking shape and she refused to recognize the familiar refrain at the back of her mind, the anxious undertone – it wouldn't happen, it won't happen. For the moment she relied on her nephew, who said with his charming, youthful, innocent arrogance that it must.

They went under the overhead railway and arrived in the gaily-lit-up Potsdamer Platz. They drew up in front of the hotel behind the propaganda man's car in which M. Bressilov and some others had gone.

"Alas, dear Frau Peters," said Mr. Belford, who was bent forward in some discomfort, "I cannot move!"

"Never mind, I'll get out this side," she said, and pushed the door handle, without bothering that all day and most of the night the Potsdamer Platz was a busy place, into which traffic came from five different directions, not only Saarland-strasse, but Potsdamerstrasse, and Leipzigerstrasse and Belle-vuestrasse and Hermann-Goeringstrasse. She squeezed under Mr. Belford and stepped out, still largely thinking of her future. She felt at once a queer sensation, as if all the breath in her body had rushed out. She hardly heard the scream of wheels braking, the panic-stricken, too-late shout.

Unaware of her final misfortune she lay in the road, a life-less bundle at the side of the BMW saloon which had struck her, the centre of a small, growing crowd. Blood spread out beneath her head.

PART THREE

"I shall never get over not seeing her," his mother said. "And it's so awful that it should happen just then – well, I suppose when it happened doesn't matter so much – "

"At least it was after the show," David said. "I mean, she'd had a big moment. She was feeling pretty good for a change."

"Yes. Oh, God, it's such an unnecessary, silly thing."

"It can easily happen."

"And it had to happen to her."

It was not the first but the tenth or fiftieth time at least that they had been over it. Now his mother, who had come to Berlin for the funeral, was on her way home. It was always a pleasure to be with her in public. She was pre-eminently presentable, and a mother could not be more. But the conversation they had had repeated itself endlessly, and he would be relieved when her departure stopped it. For there was nothing to be said about death except that it was death. It was the unarguable fact.

"Yes, precisely," he said. "Just as you say – it had to happen to her. The very words she would have used."

"It still seems unreal to me," his mother said. "You knowing her and talking to her all these months, and me not having seen her for years. What will you do if you see your uncle again?"

"Be frigidly polite. But it's a big city."

"I suppose it's all right for you to be alone here."

"Really – " he protested.

"Well, you know what I mean. This has been a rotten experience for you, darling."

"Anyhow it's only another six weeks, and I'll have finished the course. That'll be enough of this circus for me." Not only a growing boredom with the National Socialists had helped to make up his mind, but the polite and all too speedy replies he had received from London newspaper offices, regretting that their correspondents would find no use for his services – a bitter and private disappointment; moreover it had just been decided that Sophia was to go to Switzerland instead of staying on for her German matriculation. "The best plan is a few months in France, if father's agreeable."

"I quite agree," his mother said, and added irrelevantly, "There was a boy called Talbot – a great friend – he went to France as well – "

"Yes, it's not very original."

"I'm never going to get over the impudence of that man," she said, returning to the subject that was never far away – his uncle's behaviour. The impudence was not that he had returned large as life, shedding crocodile tears, had taken over the flat and attended the funeral – for the police, of course, had contacted him at once. What was unbearable had been the pose of loving husband which he unhesitatingly adopted. His presence ruined the emotional effect of the Church of England service, for David had already done his best to pass on the version of her marriage which Aunt Isabel had given him. His mother was only half convinced, but when Uncle Rudi had given the Hitler salute at the graveside in the Gross-Görschen Cemetery she was from then on prepared to believe anything. It had all been very embarrassing. They had only Isabel's word, in David's keeping. Uncle Rudi himself fully admitted that there had been an estrangement, but he said earnestly, "It was a misunderstanding, a little quarrel. A tiff." They had to go with him to the flat, which had surprised his mother with its drab lack of comfort, as it had David himself a few months before. Uncle Rudi was at his most charming and tactful, he wished them to take whatever memento of Isabel they wished. "Be quite at home, Sarah, please. David, of course, already is," he smiled sadly.

But it had been very hard to find a memento. Except for her clothes, which his mother regarded speechlessly, and the piles of music against the wall by the piano, it seemed as if his aunt had left nothing personal behind. It was hard even to believe that she had ever lived there. Fourteen years of dusting and polishing, of quarrels and boredom and wretchedness, and she had not succeeded in making a recognizable home; it was yet another failure. They went into the bedroom. It was only when he caught a mild scent of lily of the valley from the wardrobe that he could suddenly feel his aunt as she had been, and he realized in astonishment that she had always used this scent; it was as if she were there, and had just come into the room – he felt like a stranger caught intruding, for in all his visits he had never been in there, he had merely looked in at the door. He heard his mother sigh, "Oh, my God –" She had at last found something, a cardboard box, in which were a number of evidently treasured items, dirty, faded scraps of paper, a London bus ticket, two or three old press cuttings from childhood, the stub of a stalls ticket for His Majesty's Theatre, March 18th, 1918, a scribbled message in pencil, barely readable: "Wonderful! G.N.", a birthday greetings card signed carefully in childish writing: "With love from Nicholas Rowland". This was all. They laid them out on the bed and he saw that his mother was crying. Outside Uncle Rudi could be heard talking to someone at the door in harsh, hearty German. "What is it?" his mother asked, and David interpreted that it appeared to be a Nazi collecting some subscription or other for the National Socialist peoples' welfare organization. "*Heil Hitler!*" "*Heileetler!*" the dialogue ended. His mother said, "Let's go, this is too awful – it's no good keeping any of it –" They said good-bye to Uncle Rudi, the unassailable victor. They shook hands – it seemed unavoidable. He wished he could have said something suitably tart to his uncle's face. When they were in the street his mother wept a little.

That, however, was now four days ago. In the meantime they had been sight-seeing, for it was clearly pointless for her not to have a look at Berlin. They had been to Potsdam by steamer. They had been up the Radio tower and the Rathaus tower, and they had seen the nearly-completed Olympic stadium. They had lunched at the legation. Now they sat in the vestibule of the Eden Hotel and waited for her cases to come down.

"He still has a certain charm, I admit," she went on. "But of course the fact is she was mad to marry him. We all tried to talk sense to her, your father, me, Mr. Durrell who was her teacher – then, again, it seemed romantic. If only I'd known how badly off she was I could have sent her things, I could have come over and visited her – I keep feeling so guilty about it – but she always gave the impression that she was comfortably off, perfectly happy. Why in God's name didn't she leave him? She was in love with him, I suppose, poor dear."

" I don't think it was that, mother, at all. I think she knew it would turn out badly and that's *why* she married him," he said.

His mother regarded him fondly, but with the inattentive look that was apt to come into the eyes of either of his parents when he said something serious. Then she glanced beyond him.

" I think I see the cases. We must drink up the coffee and be off."

" What I mean is – " he paused. He was not quite sure what he did mean, and yet somehow he was conscious of a feeling of discovery. " What I mean is – that night she told me everything – there was something queer – I've been thinking about it a lot – there was something complacent about her, I don't mean she wasn't unhappy but she was sort of proud of *being* unhappy. And then when old Bressilov was trying to sign her up – she wanted to do it, she was crazy to do it – she would keep on making objections, like having to stay in Berlin because I was here – she was wanting something to spoil it, even though she wanted to do it – "

" Yes, dear. Do drink your coffee. You're talking perfect nonsense and I don't really think it's quite nice."

" I'm sure I'm right," he said eagerly. The idea grew on him. " You influence things somehow. I don't believe you have all that bad luck if you're really determined – "

" Dying like that isn't very good luck, darling."

She thought him insensitive, but he knew it was love which found him the words to describe the death of his aunt.

" It was her triumph," he said.